CW00750534

SOUTHERN BASTARDS

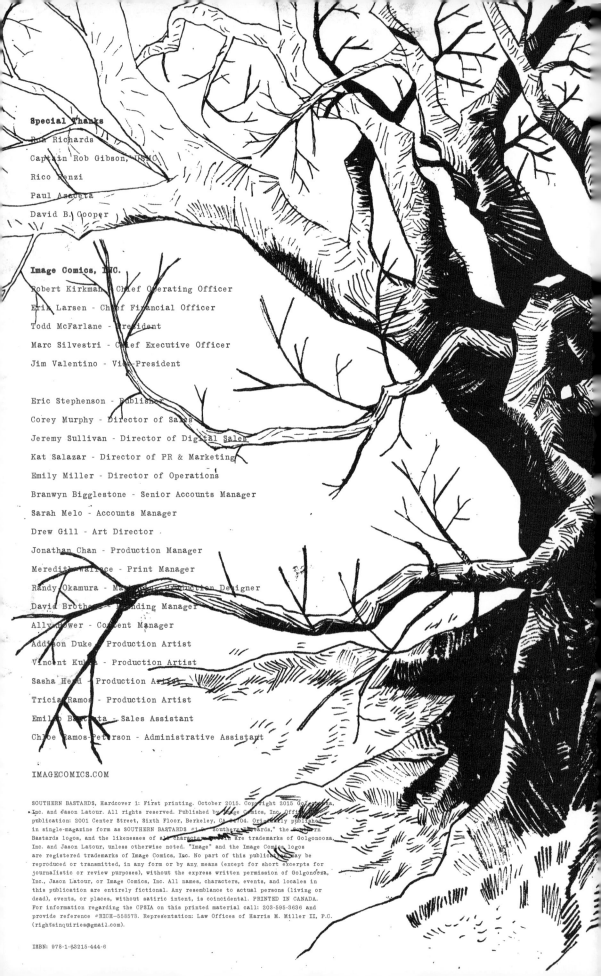

Special Thanks

Rob Richards

Captain Rob Gibson, USMC

Rico Renzi

Paul Azaceta

David B. Cooper

Image Comics, INC.

Robert Kirkman - Chief Operating Officer

Erik Larsen - Chief Financial Officer

Todd McFarlane - President

Marc Silvestri - Chief Executive Officer

Jim Valentino - Vice-President

Eric Stephenson - Publisher

Corey Murphy - Director of Sales

Jeremy Sullivan - Director of Digital Sales

Kat Salazar - Director of PR & Marketing

Emily Miller - Director of Operations

Branwyn Bigglestone - Senior Accounts Manager

Sarah Melo - Accounts Manager

Drew Gill - Art Director

Jonathan Chan - Production Manager

Meredith Wallace - Print Manager

Randy Okamura - Marketing Production Designer

David Brothers - Branding Manager

Ally Power - Content Manager

Addison Duke - Production Artist

Vincent Kukua - Production Artist

Sasha Head - Production Artist

Tricia Ramos - Production Artist

Emilio Bautista - Sales Assistant

Chloe Ramos-Peterson - Administrative Assistant

IMAGECOMICS.COM

SOUTHERN BASTARDS, Hardcover 1: First printing. October 2015. Copyright 2015 Golgonooza,
Inc. and Jason Latour. All rights reserved. Published by Image Comics, Inc. Office of
publication: 2001 Center Street, Sixth Floor, Berkeley, CA 94704. Originally published
in single-magazine form as SOUTHERN BASTARDS #1-8. "Southern Bastards," the Southern
Bastards logos, and the likenesses of all characters herein are trademarks of Golgonooza,
Inc. and Jason Latour, unless otherwise noted. "Image" and the Image Comics logos
are registered trademarks of Image Comics, Inc. No part of this publication may be
reproduced or transmitted, in any form or by any means (except for short excerpts for
journalistic or review purposes), without the express written permission of Golgonooza,
Inc., Jason Latour, or Image Comics, Inc. All names, characters, events, and locales in
this publication are entirely fictional. Any resemblance to actual persons (living or
dead), events, or places, without satiric intent, is coincidental. PRINTED IN CANADA.
For information regarding the CPSIA on this printed material call: 203-595-3636 and
provide reference #RICH-558573. Representation: Law Offices of Harris M. Miller II, P.C.
(rightsinquiries@gmail.com).

ISBN: 978-1-63215-444-6

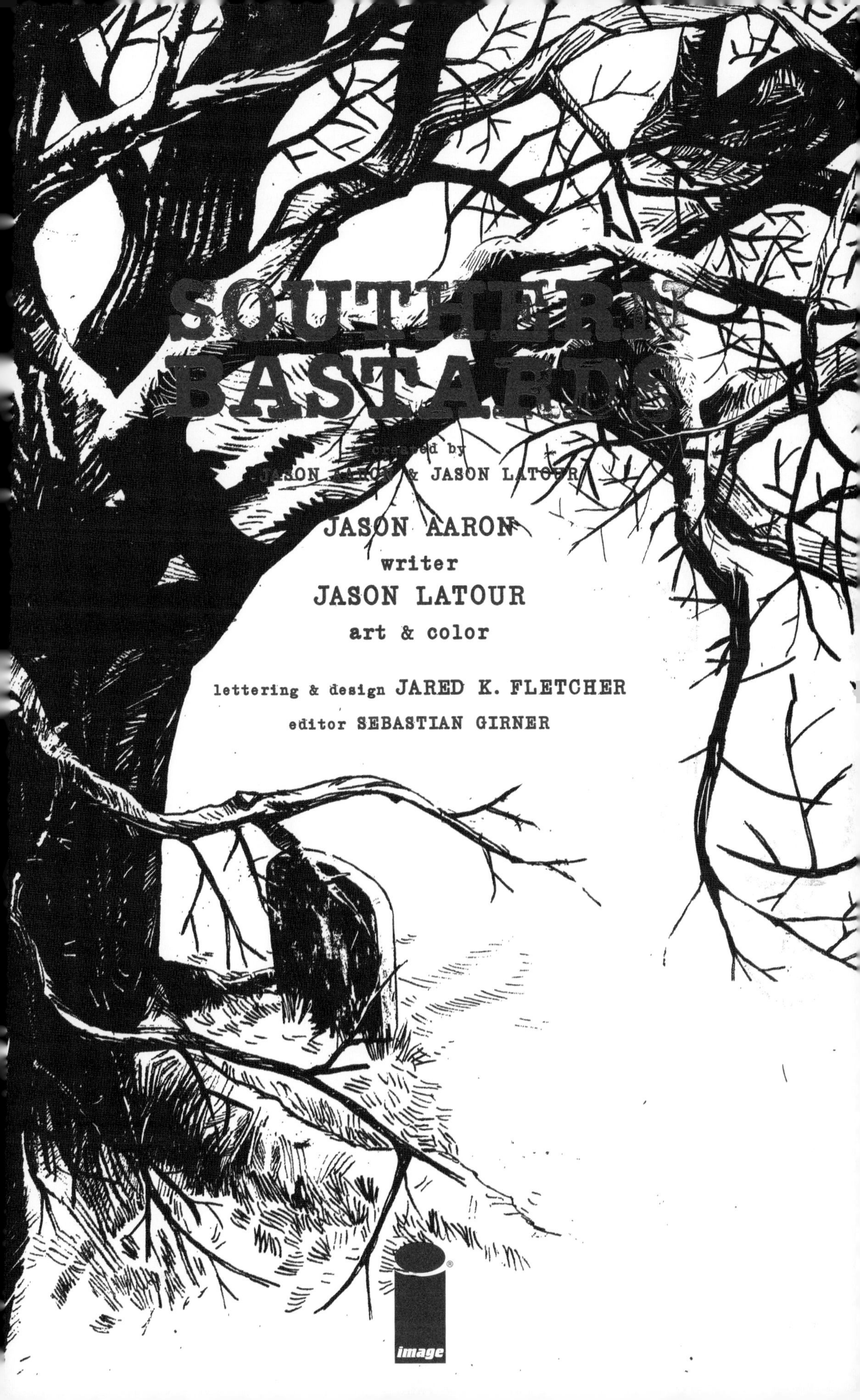

SOUTHERN BASTARDS

created by
JASON AARON & JASON LATOUR

JASON AARON
writer

JASON LATOUR
art & color

lettering & design JARED K. FLETCHER

editor SEBASTIAN GIRNER

image

I love The South.

The South also scares the living shit out of me.

I was born in Alabama. In a dry county, in a town called Jasper, birthplace of the guy who played "Goober" on the Andy Griffith Show and the 400 pound fighter they call "Butterbean." My grandfather was a Baptist preacher and a coal miner. My great-grandfather died of rabies. My great-great-grandfather once stabbed a man to death in an argument over some sheep. I was raised on "Hee-Haw," the Crimson Tide, pork rinds and Jesus. I've memorized songs by all three generations of Hanks. I still get choked up whenever I hear Bear Bryant's voice. I've stood in William Faulkner's house.

I love being from The South.

But I don't live there anymore. And I don't plan on ever moving back.

The South is more peaceful than any other place I've ever been. But more primal too. More timeless. But more haunted. More spiritual. More hateful. More beautiful. More scarred.

And that's what this series is about. About a place you can love and hate and miss and fear all at the same time. I've always considered myself a Southern writer, and I think you can see that in a lot of the stuff I've done over the years. In the characters of SCALPED. In the way I wrote WOLVERINE for Marvel. Hell, even in my THOR GOD OF THUNDER.

But with this series, I finally get to go full country. So expect lots of BBQ. And football. And rednecks and senseless violence. And maybe even a laugh or two. Thanks for dropping by. Hope you'll stick around for a spell. We've got lots of bastards we'd like to introduce you to.

--Jason Aaron

I was born and raised in a Carolinas border town called Charlotte. A place that was about as far "North" as I ever really knew growing up. See, back then places like New York were for superheroes. If we had any of those I was never given any cause to look up and see them.

When I got older I finally worked up the courage to travel some. For a while I moved deeper into The South's syrupy bloodstream--first to Atlanta and then to Florida, where I spent equal time avoiding the weirdness and the sunshine. I criss-crossed the country until eventually I found myself walking around Brooklyn in the snow-- Listening to country music--Getting angry. Angry for letting The South beat me. For letting them run me off. For letting them steal my home from me.

So I wrote LOOSE ENDS. I got a great job writing and drawing all those superheroes I used to dream about being. I moved back home and stared The South in her face. It ain't always easy, but I'm probably happier than I've ever been. Today I can and often do laugh about all the drama and stress this place has caused me. A lot of its absurdity is even endearing.

And yet, somehow...deep down...I'm still angry as hell.

So this book is for them. The assholes you might think Southerners are. The rednecks we're afraid we might really be. This book is designed to bury them sons of bitches. To spit on their graves. Because I fucking hate those bastards with every part of me.

Because I love The South with all I've got.

--Jason Latour

Here Was a Man

Chapter One

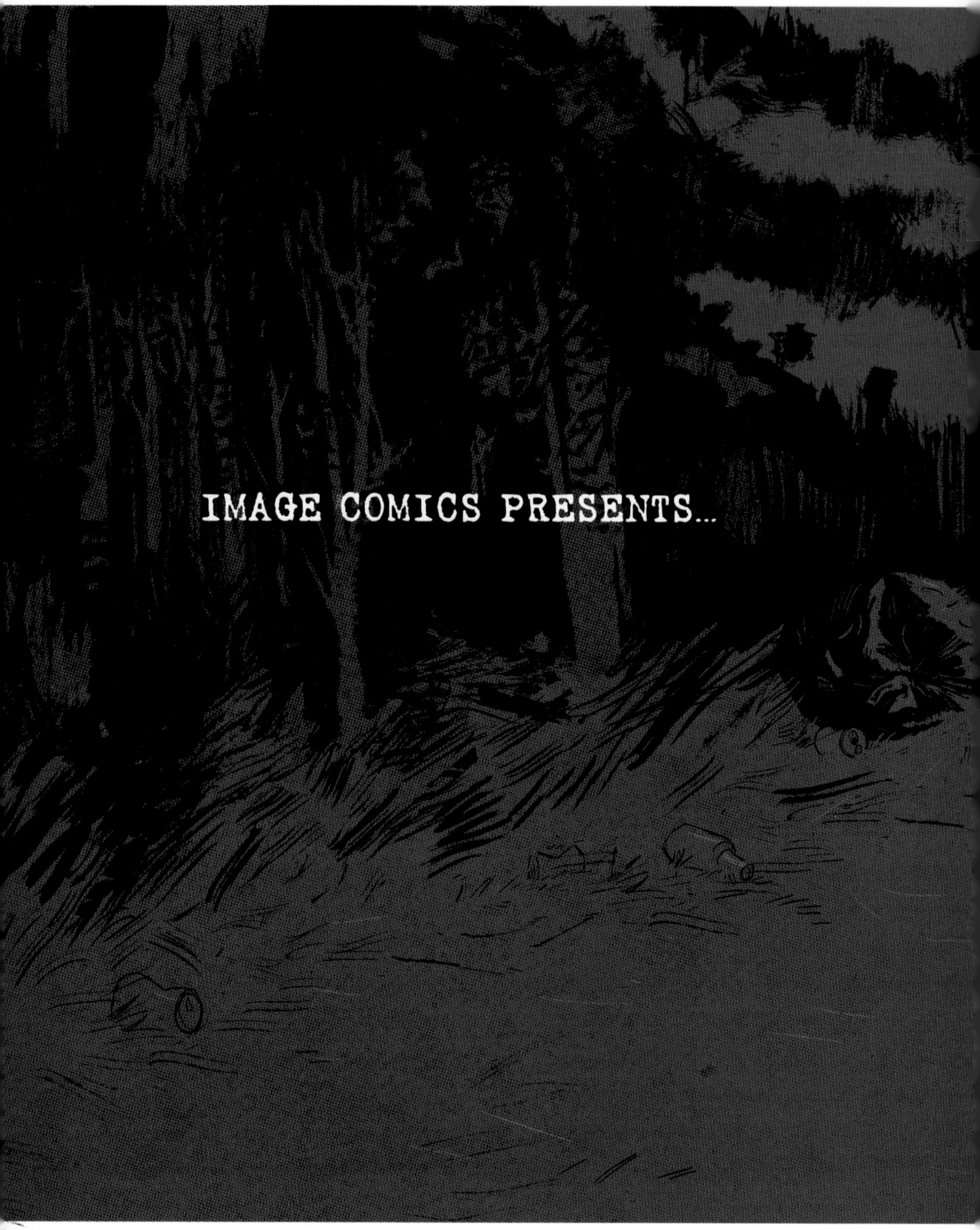
IMAGE COMICS PRESENTS...

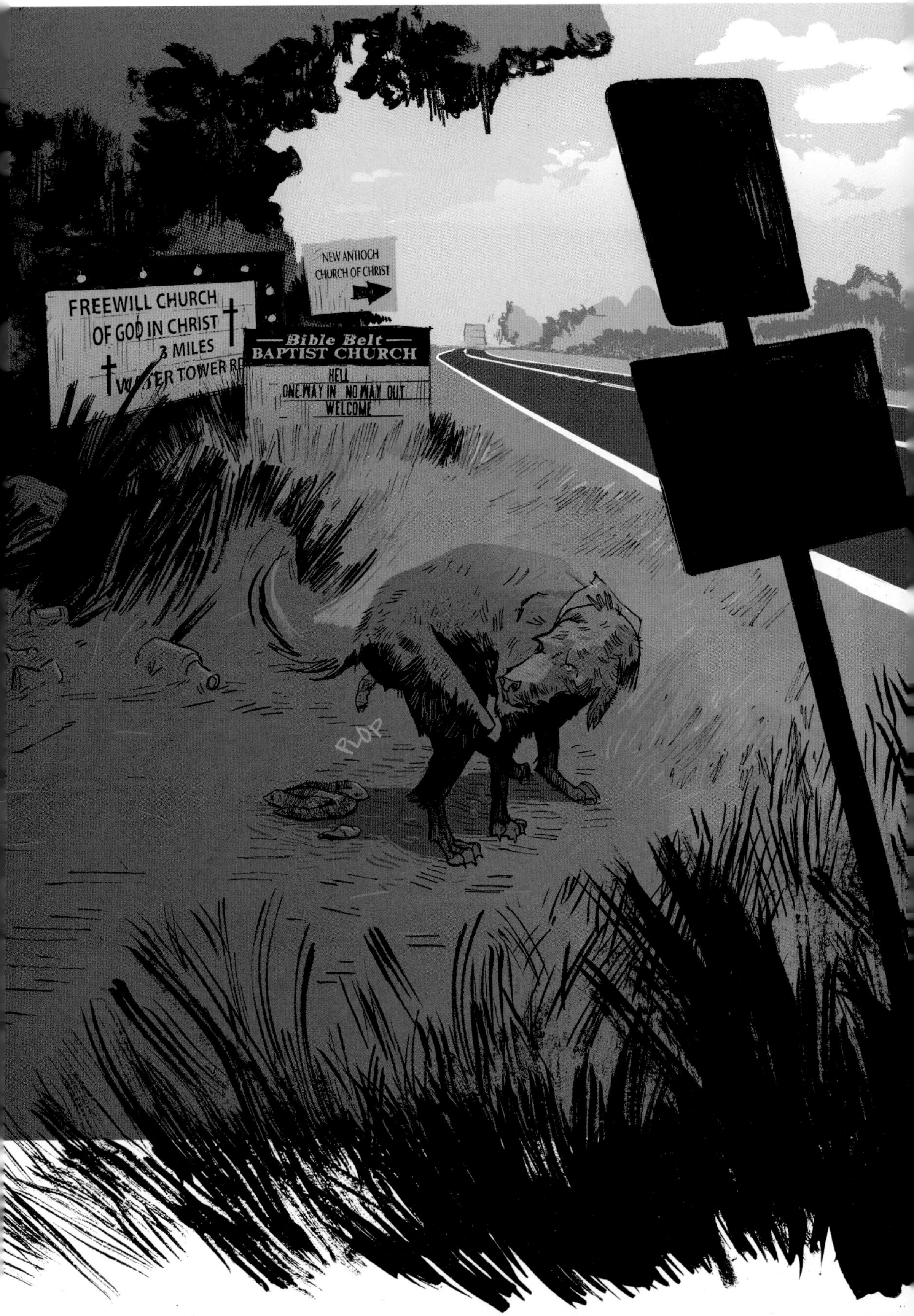

FREEWILL CHURCH
OF GOD IN CHRIST
3 MILES
TOWER
NEW ANTIOCH
CHURCH OF CHRIST
Bible Belt
BAPTIST CHURCH
HELL
ONE WAY IN NO WAY OUT
WELCOME
PLOP

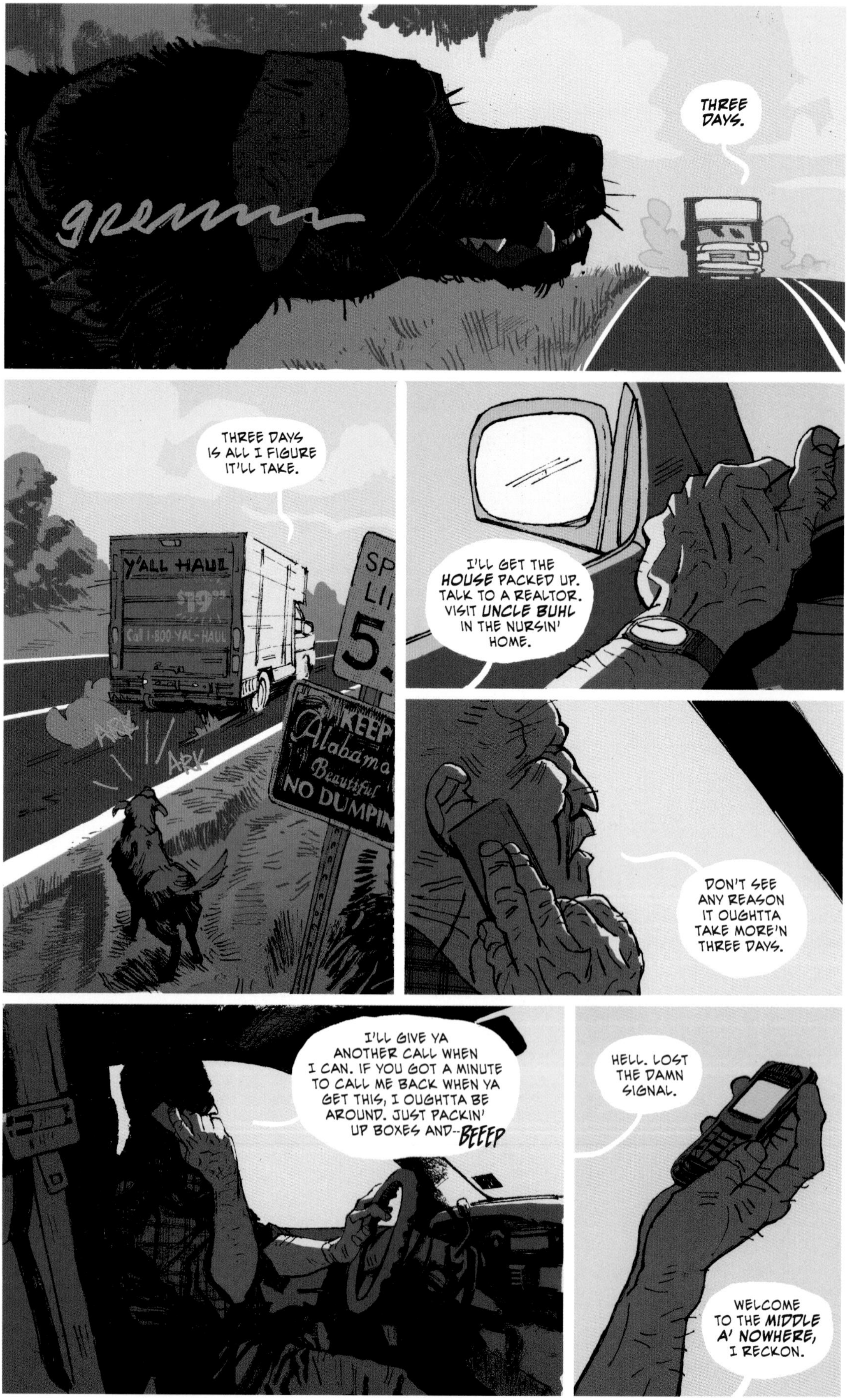
grrrrrr
THREE DAYS.
THREE DAYS IS ALL I FIGURE IT'LL TAKE.
Y'ALL HAUL
Call 1-800-YAL-HAUL
ARK
ARK
KEEP Alabama Beautiful NO DUMPIN
I'LL GET THE HOUSE PACKED UP. TALK TO A REALTOR. VISIT UNCLE BUHL IN THE NURSIN' HOME.
DON'T SEE ANY REASON IT OUGHTTA TAKE MORE'N THREE DAYS.
I'LL GIVE YA ANOTHER CALL WHEN I CAN. IF YOU GOT A MINUTE TO CALL ME BACK WHEN YA GET THIS, I OUGHTTA BE AROUND. JUST PACKIN' UP BOXES AND--BEEEP
HELL. LOST THE DAMN SIGNAL.
WELCOME TO THE MIDDLE A' NOWHERE, I RECKON.

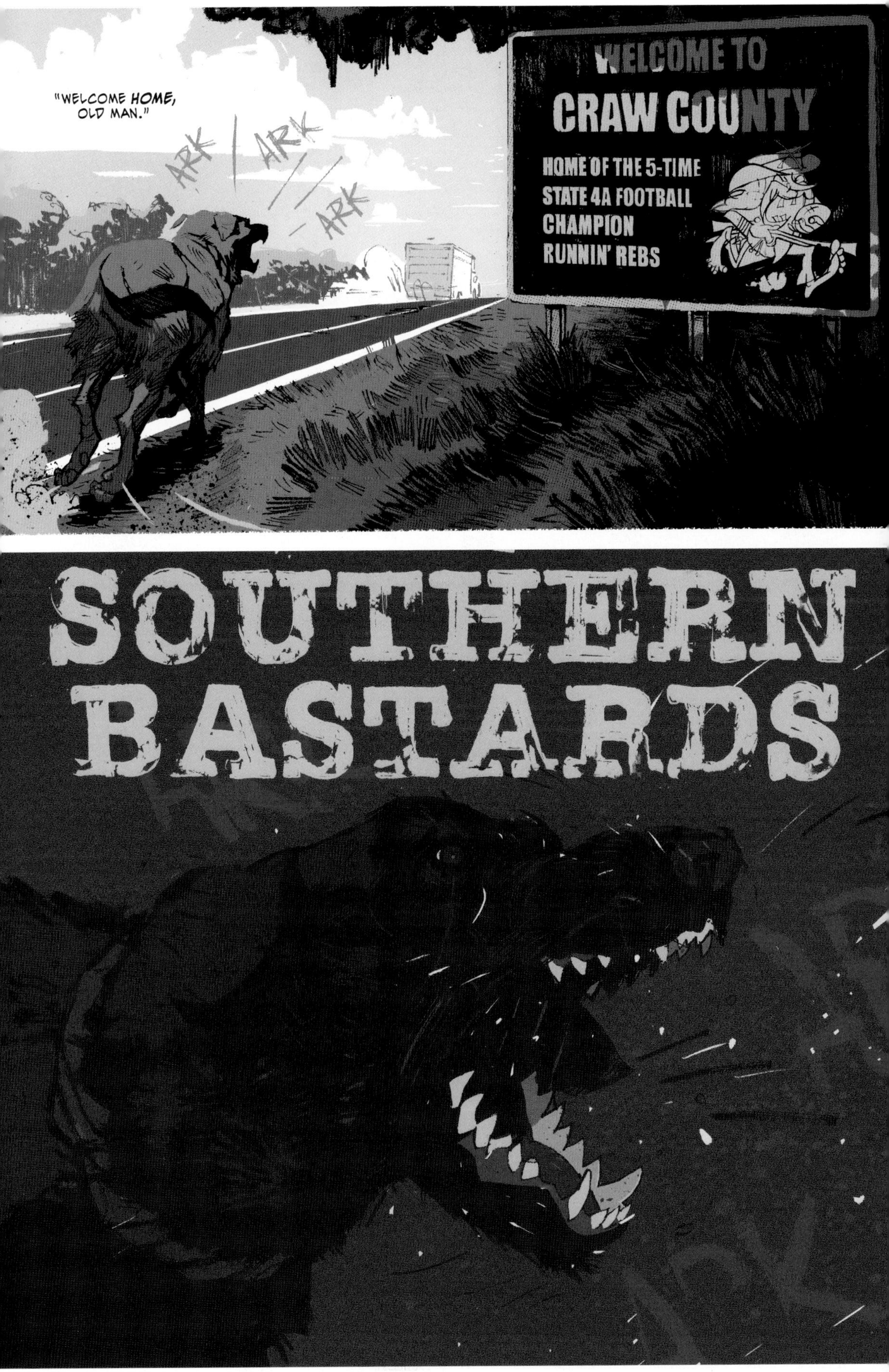
"WELCOME HOME, OLD MAN."
ARK
ARK
ARK
WELCOME TO
CRAW COUNTY
HOME OF THE 5-TIME
STATE 4A FOOTBALL
CHAMPION
RUNNIN' REBS
SOUTHERN
BASTARDS

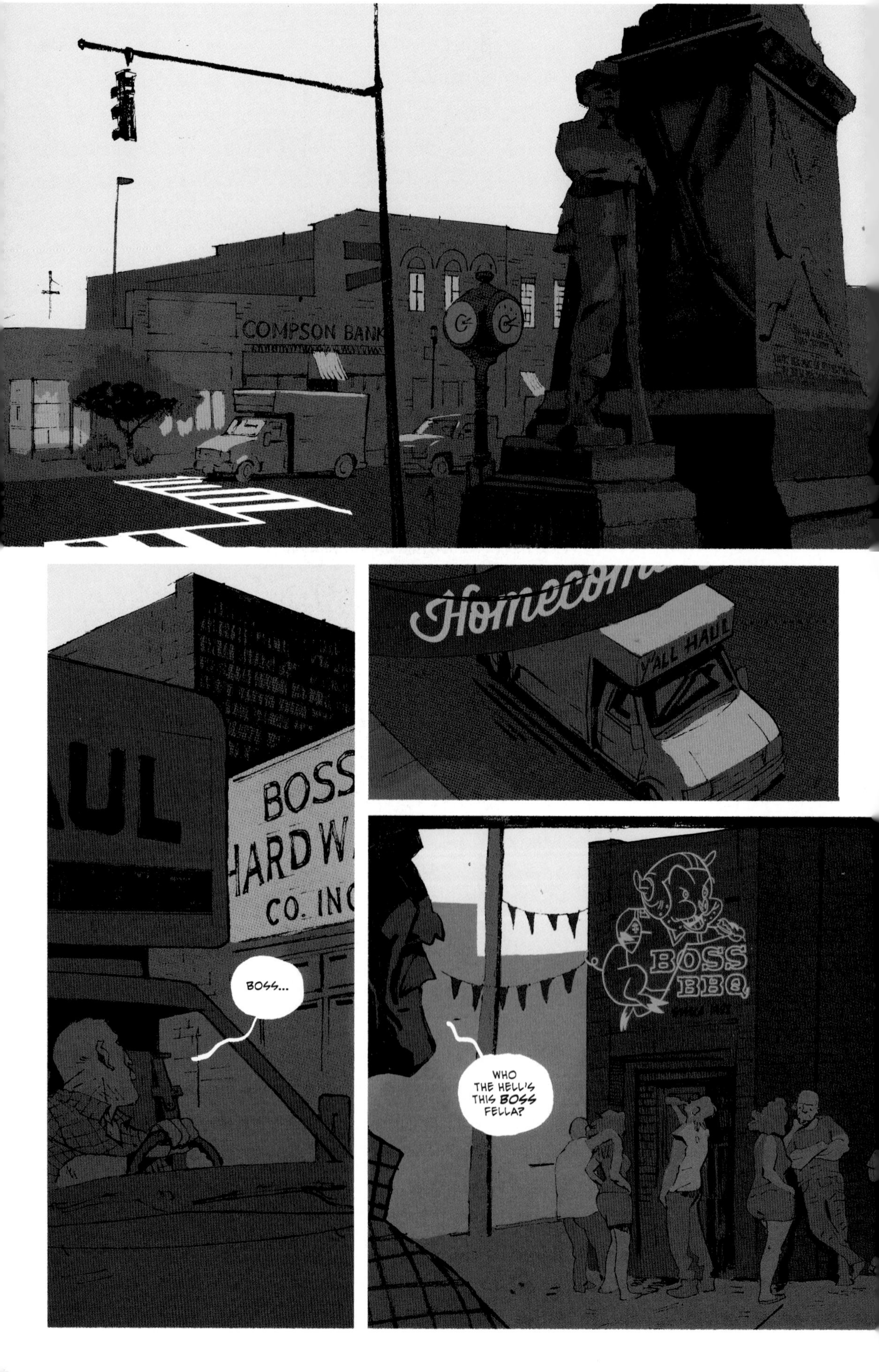
COMPSON BANK
AUL
BOSS
HARDW
CO. INC
BOSS...
Homecom
Y'ALL HAUL
BOSS
BBQ
WHO THE HELL'S THIS **BOSS** FELLA?

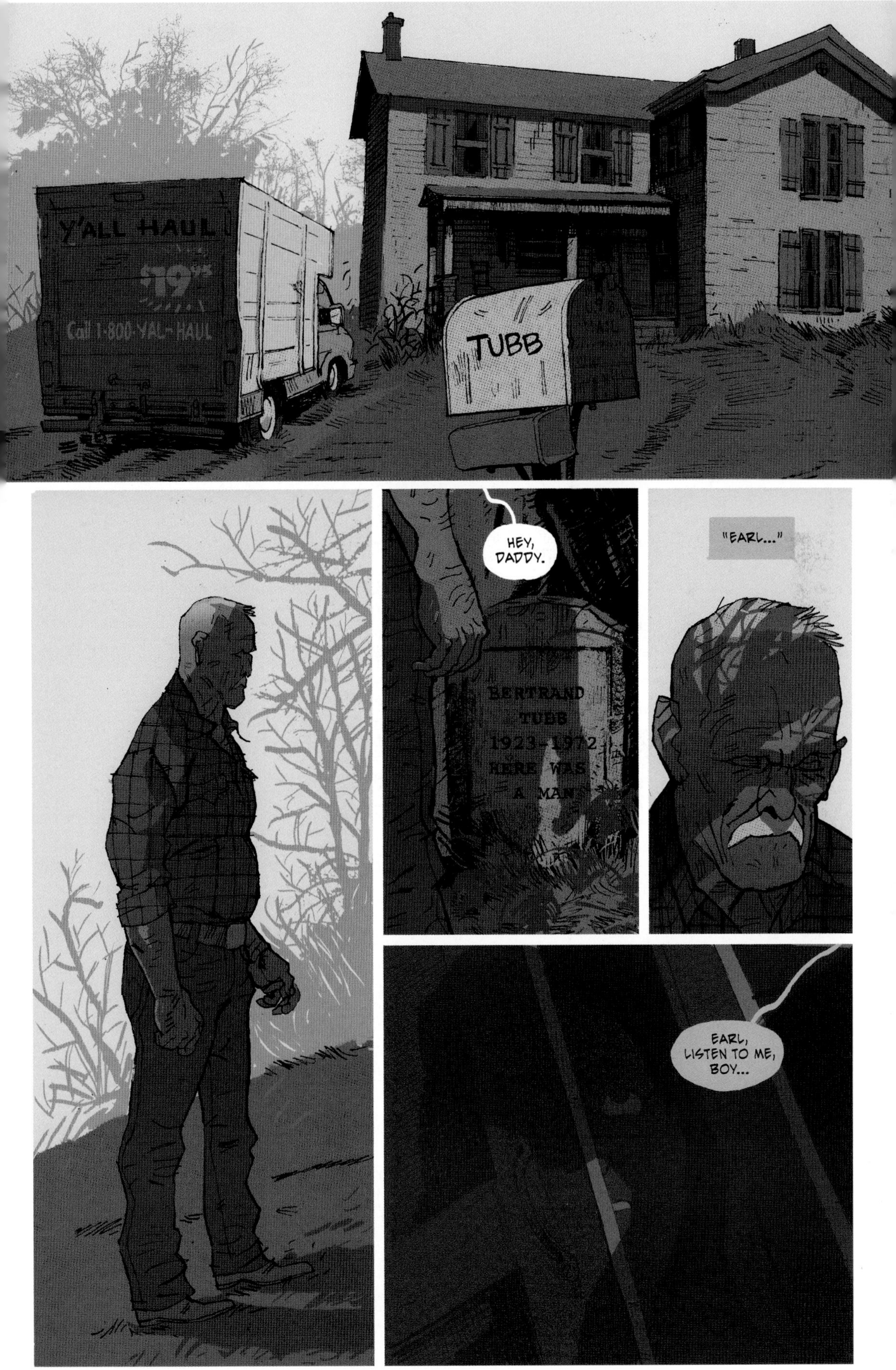
Y'ALL HAUL
$19.95
Call 1-800-YAL-HAUL
TUBB
HEY, DADDY.
BERTRAND TUBB 1923-1972 HERE WAS A MAN
"EARL..."
EARL, LISTEN TO ME, BOY...

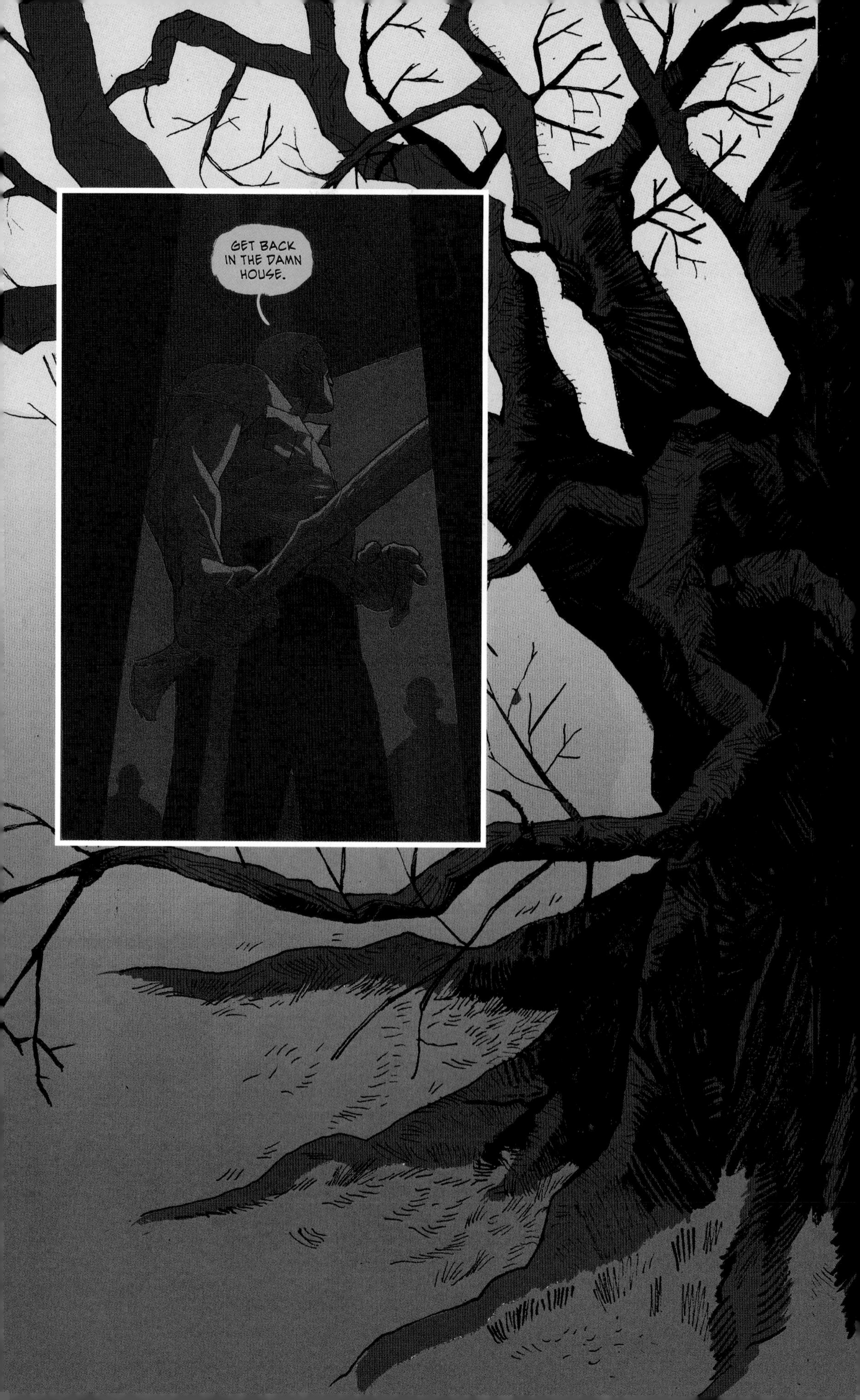
GET BACK IN THE DAMN HOUSE.

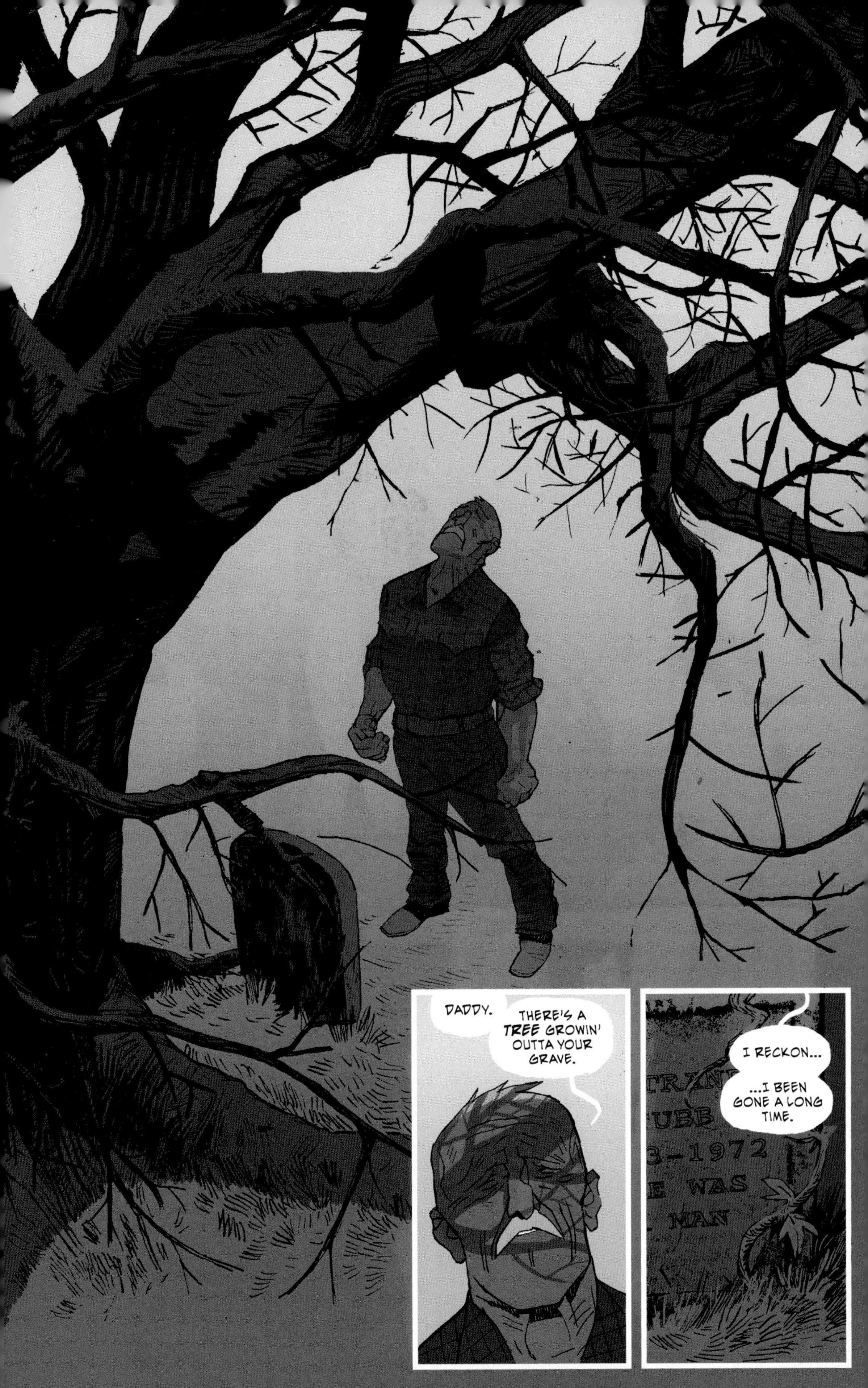
DADDY.
THERE'S A TREE GROWIN' OUTTA YOUR GRAVE.
I RECKON...
...I BEEN GONE A LONG TIME.

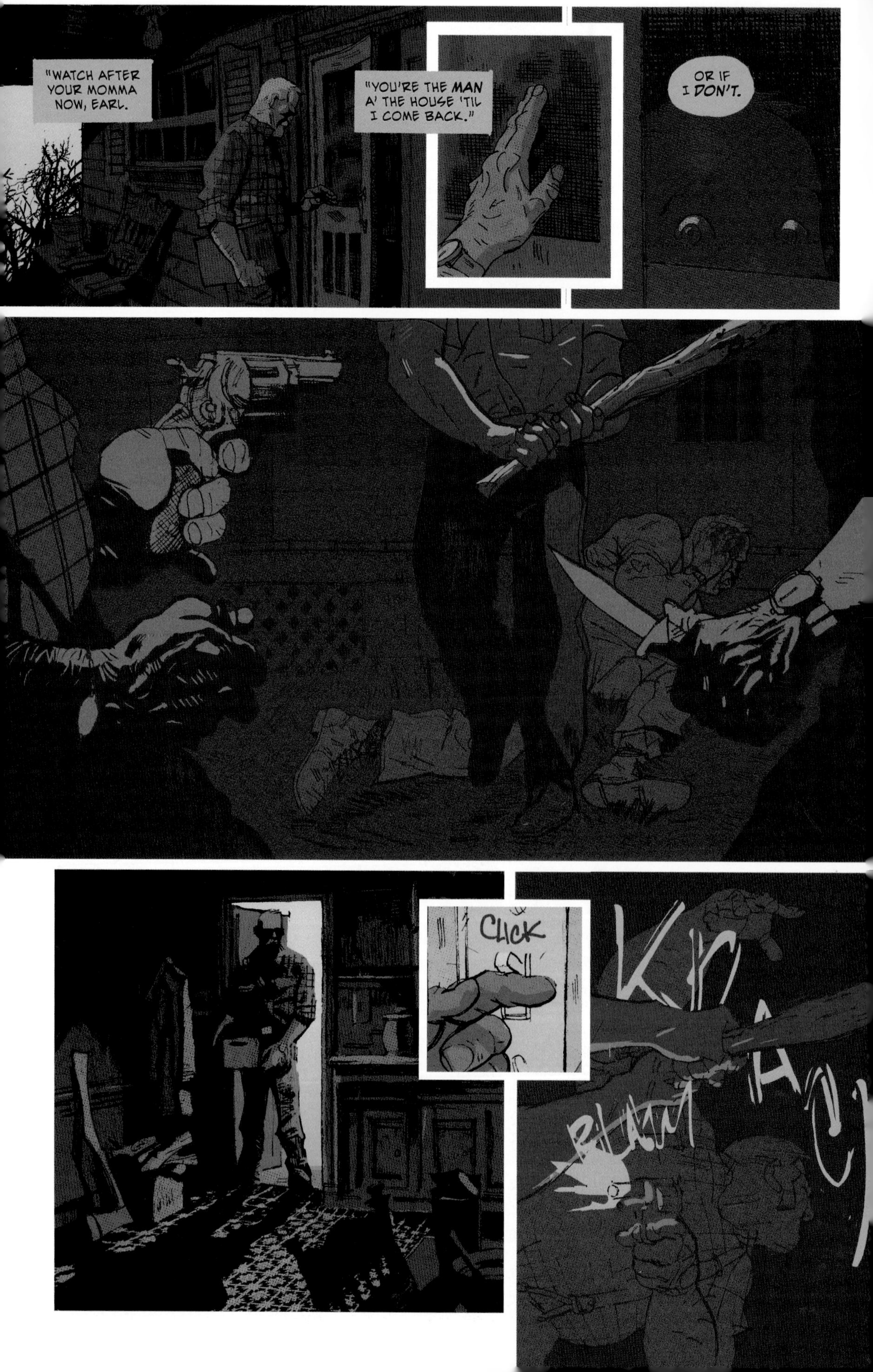
"WATCH AFTER YOUR MOMMA NOW, EARL.
"YOU'RE THE MAN A' THE HOUSE 'TIL I COME BACK."
OR IF I DON'T.
CLICK

SHERIFF SHOT

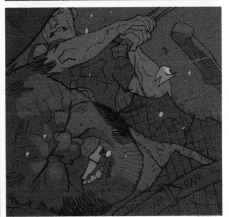

BACK TO WALL TUBB
TOOK LAW IN OWN HANDS

his one-man battle against
owerful syndicate of crooks
riff Bertrand Tubb of Craw
Alabama, was said to have
en the law into his own hands
a number of occasions. And
of the law-abiding citizens
he community said he was
y justified in doing so.

THE STICK THAT
SAVED CRAW COUNTY

OW ONE ALABAMA SHERIFF T

ATTACKED AT HOME
SHERIFF TUBB VOWS
NOT TO QUIT

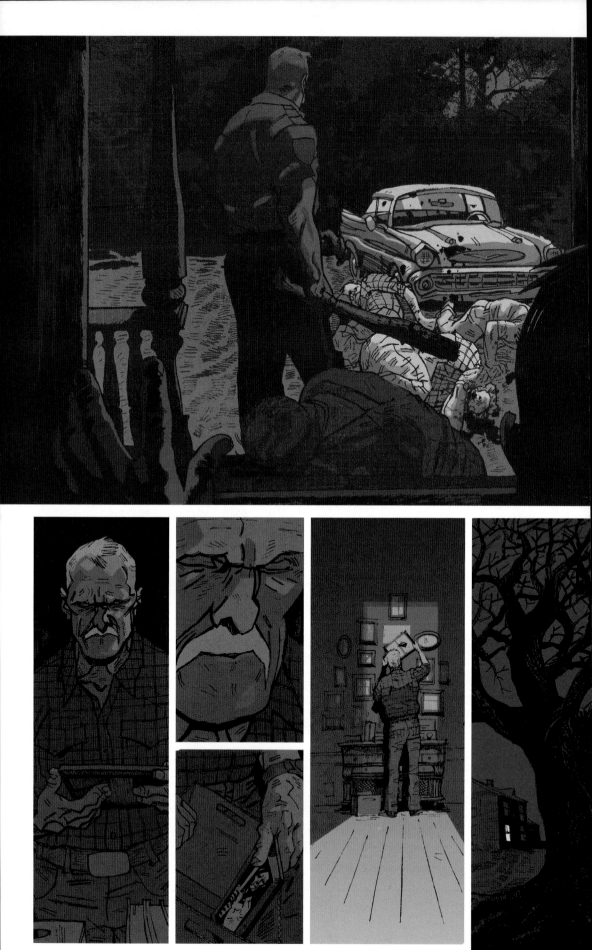

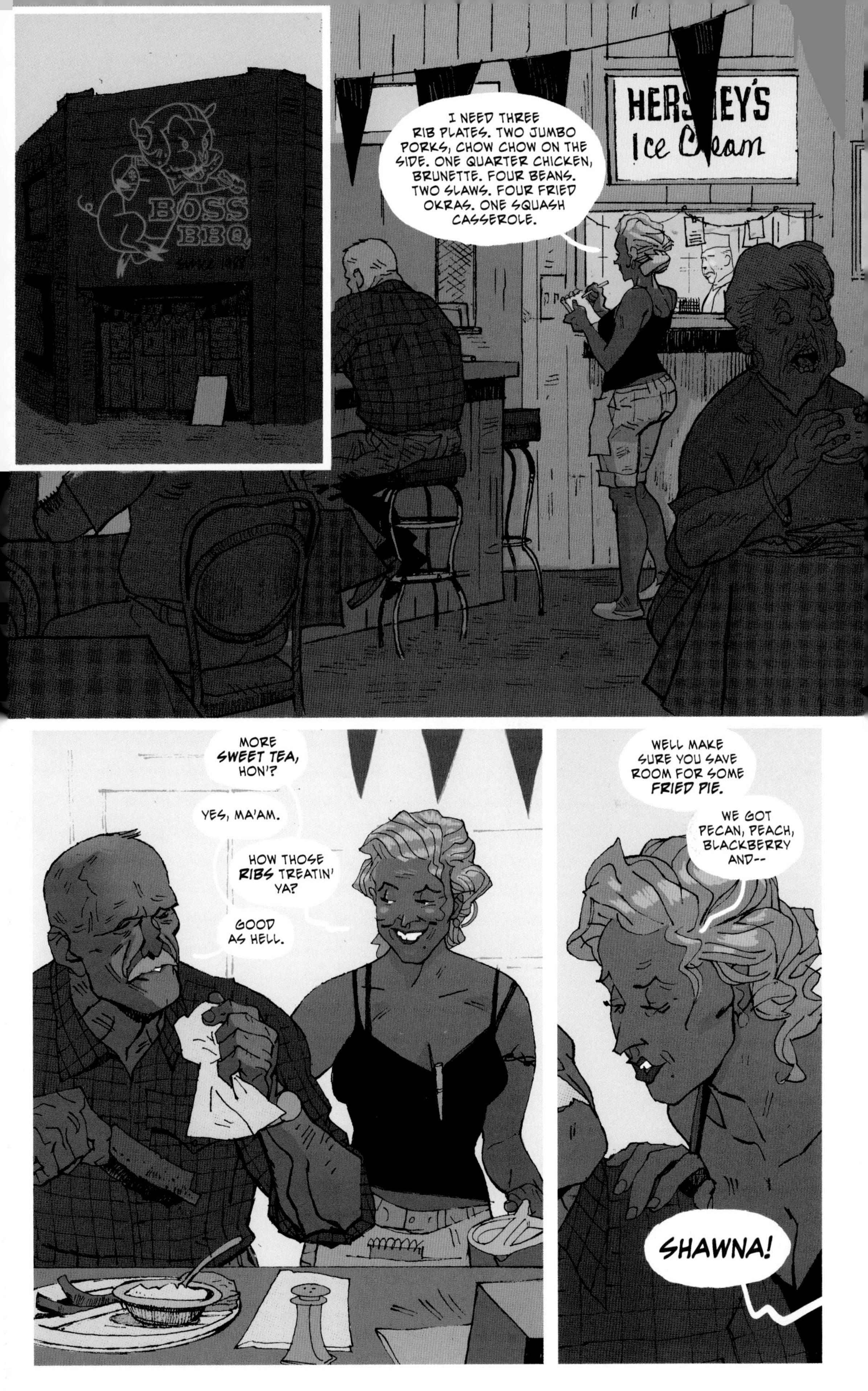
BOSS BBQ
I NEED THREE RIB PLATES. TWO JUMBO PORKS, CHOW CHOW ON THE SIDE. ONE QUARTER CHICKEN, BRUNETTE. FOUR BEANS. TWO SLAWS. FOUR FRIED OKRAS. ONE SQUASH CASSEROLE.
MORE SWEET TEA, HON'?
YES, MA'AM.
HOW THOSE RIBS TREATIN' YA?
GOOD AS HELL.
WELL MAKE SURE YOU SAVE ROOM FOR SOME FRIED PIE.
WE GOT PECAN, PEACH, BLACKBERRY AND--
SHAWNA!

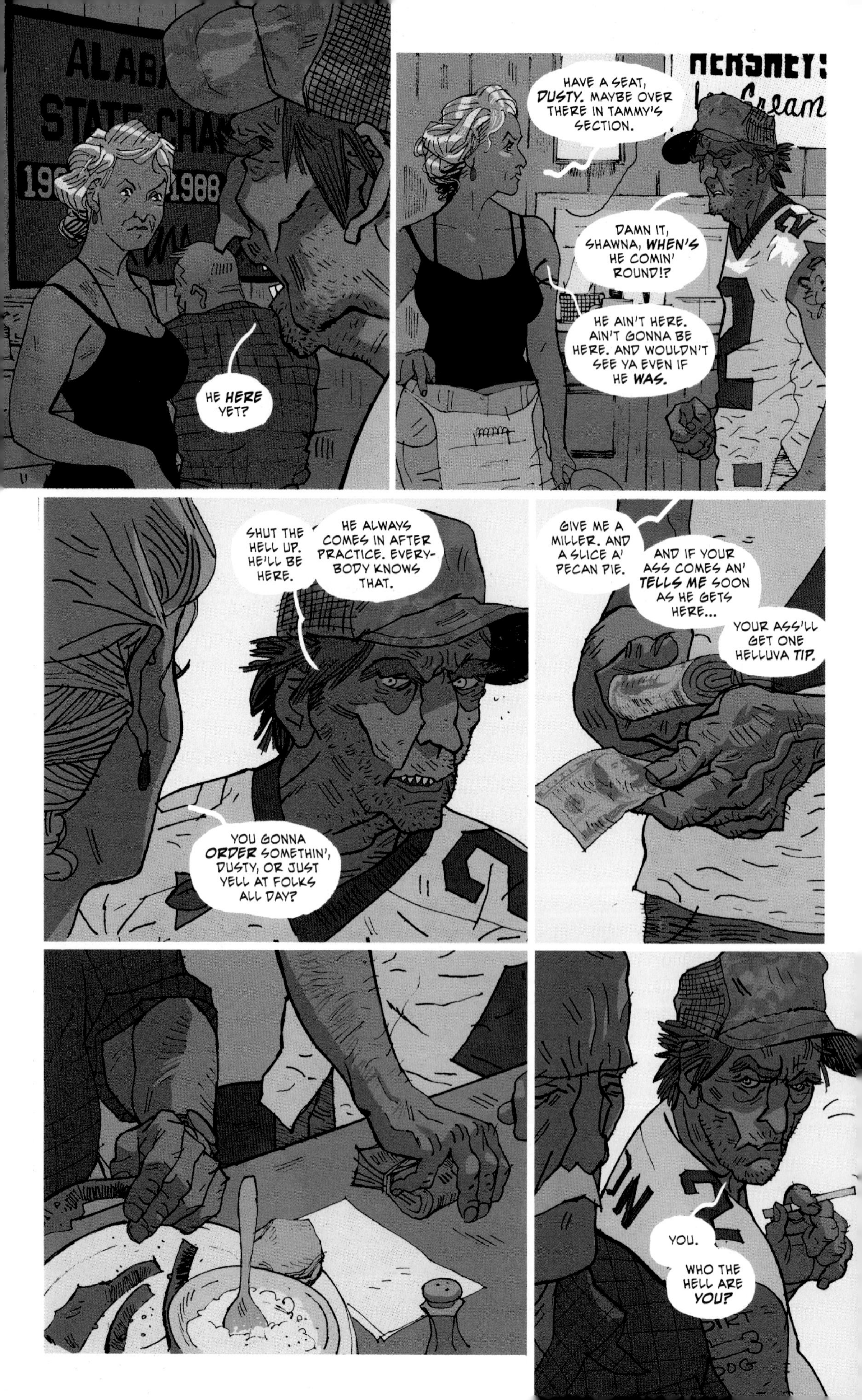

ALABA
STATE CHAM
19
1988
HE HERE YET?
HERSHEY'S
Ice Cream
HAVE A SEAT, DUSTY. MAYBE OVER THERE IN TAMMY'S SECTION.
DAMN IT, SHAWNA, WHEN'S HE COMIN' ROUND!?
HE AIN'T HERE. AIN'T GONNA BE HERE. AND WOULDN'T SEE YA EVEN IF HE WAS.
SHUT THE HELL UP. HE'LL BE HERE.
HE ALWAYS COMES IN AFTER PRACTICE. EVERYBODY KNOWS THAT.
YOU GONNA ORDER SOMETHIN', DUSTY, OR JUST YELL AT FOLKS ALL DAY?
GIVE ME A MILLER. AND A SLICE A' PECAN PIE.
AND IF YOUR ASS COMES AN' TELLS ME SOON AS HE GETS HERE...
YOUR ASS'LL GET ONE HELLUVA TIP.
YOU.
WHO THE HELL ARE YOU?

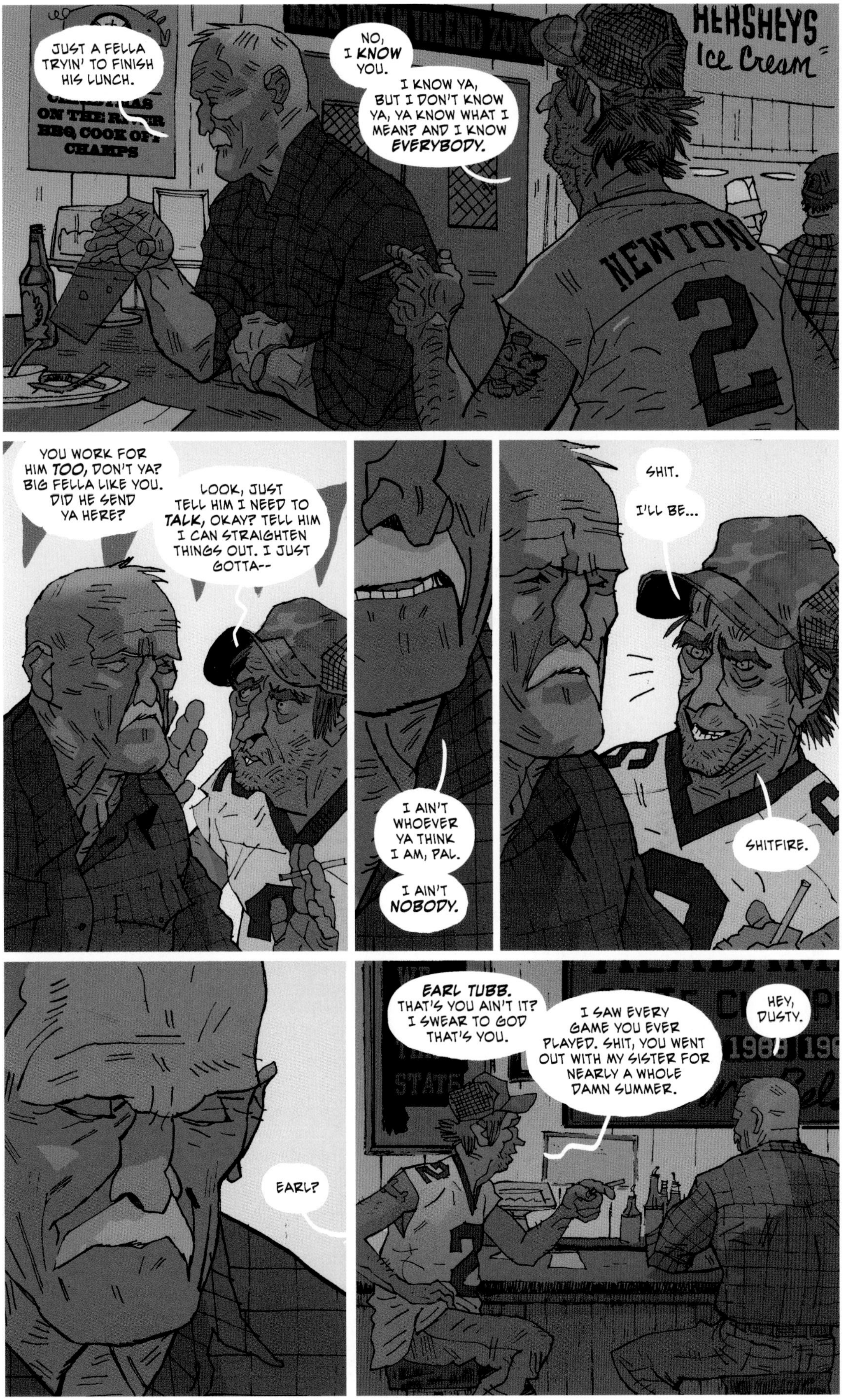
HERSHEYS Ice Cream
CHRISTMAS ON THE RIVER BBQ COOK OFF CHAMPS
JUST A FELLA TRYIN' TO FINISH HIS LUNCH.
NO, I KNOW YOU.
I KNOW YA, BUT I DON'T KNOW YA, YA KNOW WHAT I MEAN? AND I KNOW EVERYBODY.
NEWTON 2
YOU WORK FOR HIM TOO, DON'T YA? BIG FELLA LIKE YOU. DID HE SEND YA HERE?
LOOK, JUST TELL HIM I NEED TO TALK, OKAY? TELL HIM I CAN STRAIGHTEN THINGS OUT. I JUST GOTTA--
I AIN'T WHOEVER YA THINK I AM, PAL.
I AIN'T NOBODY.
SHIT.
I'LL BE...
SHITFIRE.
EARL?
EARL TUBB. THAT'S YOU AIN'T IT? I SWEAR TO GOD THAT'S YOU.
I SAW EVERY GAME YOU EVER PLAYED. SHIT, YOU WENT OUT WITH MY SISTER FOR NEARLY A WHOLE DAMN SUMMER.
HEY, DUSTY.

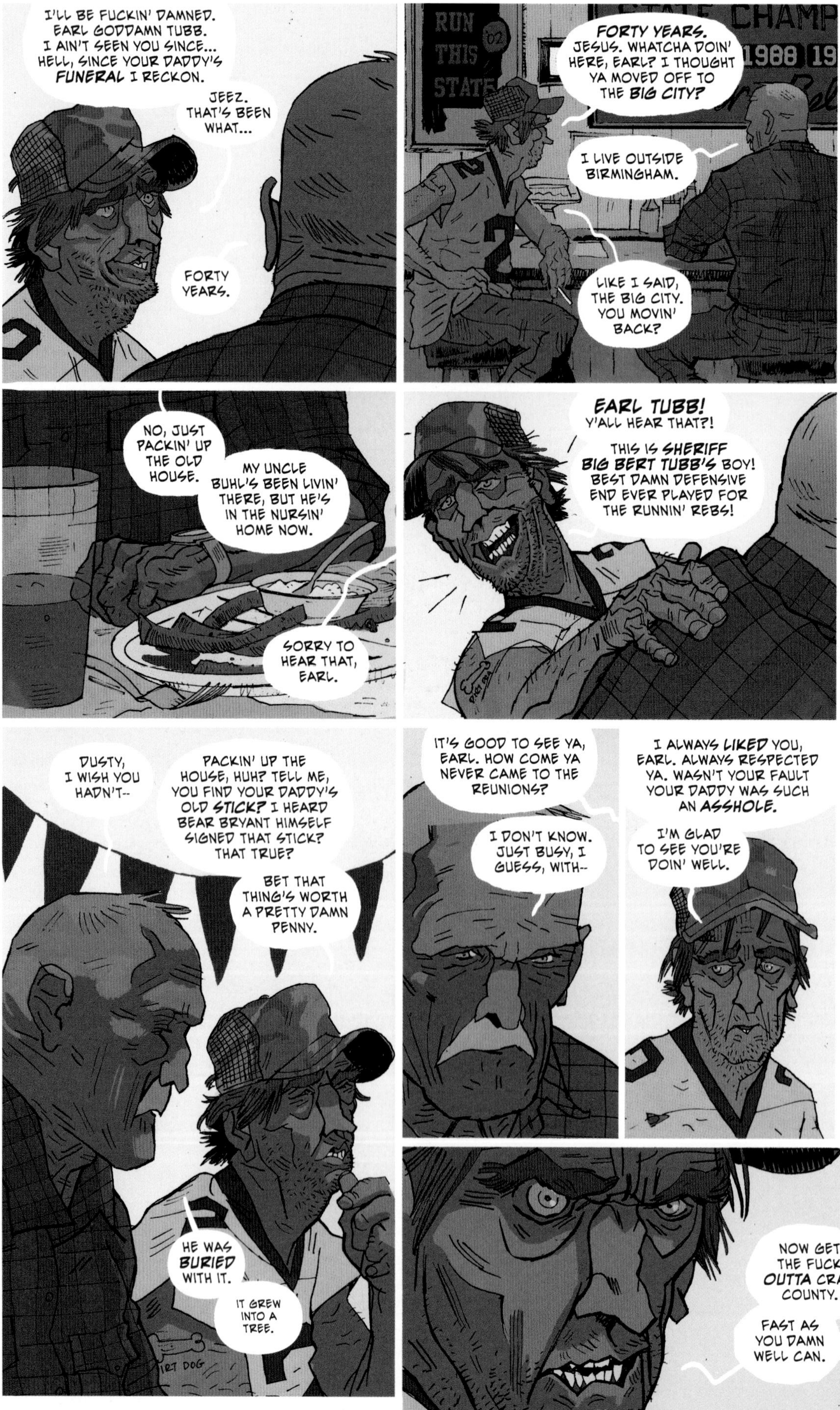

I'LL BE FUCKIN' DAMNED. EARL GODDAMN TUBB. I AIN'T SEEN YOU SINCE... HELL, SINCE YOUR DADDY'S FUNERAL I RECKON.
JEEZ. THAT'S BEEN WHAT...
FORTY YEARS.
RUN THIS STATE
STATE CHAMP
1988
FORTY YEARS. JESUS. WHATCHA DOIN' HERE, EARL? I THOUGHT YA MOVED OFF TO THE BIG CITY?
I LIVE OUTSIDE BIRMINGHAM.
LIKE I SAID, THE BIG CITY. YOU MOVIN' BACK?
NO, JUST PACKIN' UP THE OLD HOUSE.
MY UNCLE BUHL'S BEEN LIVIN' THERE, BUT HE'S IN THE NURSIN' HOME NOW.
SORRY TO HEAR THAT, EARL.
EARL TUBB! Y'ALL HEAR THAT?!
THIS IS SHERIFF BIG BERT TUBB'S BOY! BEST DAMN DEFENSIVE END EVER PLAYED FOR THE RUNNIN' REBS!
DUSTY, I WISH YOU HADN'T--
PACKIN' UP THE HOUSE, HUH? TELL ME, YOU FIND YOUR DADDY'S OLD STICK? I HEARD BEAR BRYANT HIMSELF SIGNED THAT STICK? THAT TRUE?
BET THAT THING'S WORTH A PRETTY DAMN PENNY.
HE WAS BURIED WITH IT.
IT GREW INTO A TREE.
IT'S GOOD TO SEE YA, EARL. HOW COME YA NEVER CAME TO THE REUNIONS?
I DON'T KNOW. JUST BUSY, I GUESS, WITH--
I ALWAYS LIKED YOU, EARL. ALWAYS RESPECTED YA. WASN'T YOUR FAULT YOUR DADDY WAS SUCH AN ASSHOLE.
I'M GLAD TO SEE YOU'RE DOIN' WELL.
NOW GET THE FUCK OUTTA CRAW COUNTY.
FAST AS YOU DAMN WELL CAN.

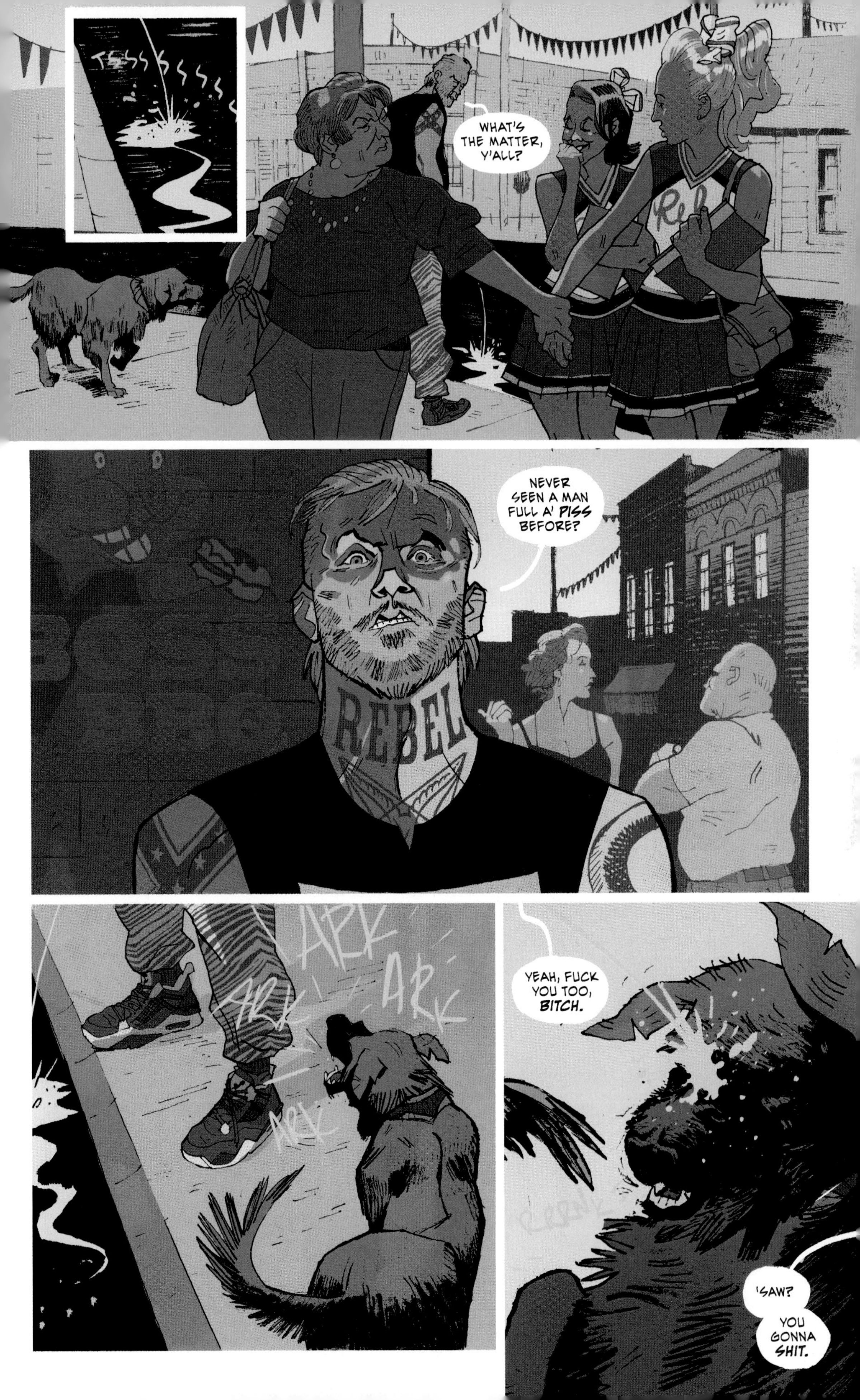
TSSSSSSS
WHAT'S THE MATTER, Y'ALL?
NEVER SEEN A MAN FULL A' PISS BEFORE?
REBEL
ARK
ARK
ARK
ARK
YEAH, FUCK YOU TOO, BITCH.
RRRNK
'SAW?
YOU GONNA SHIT.

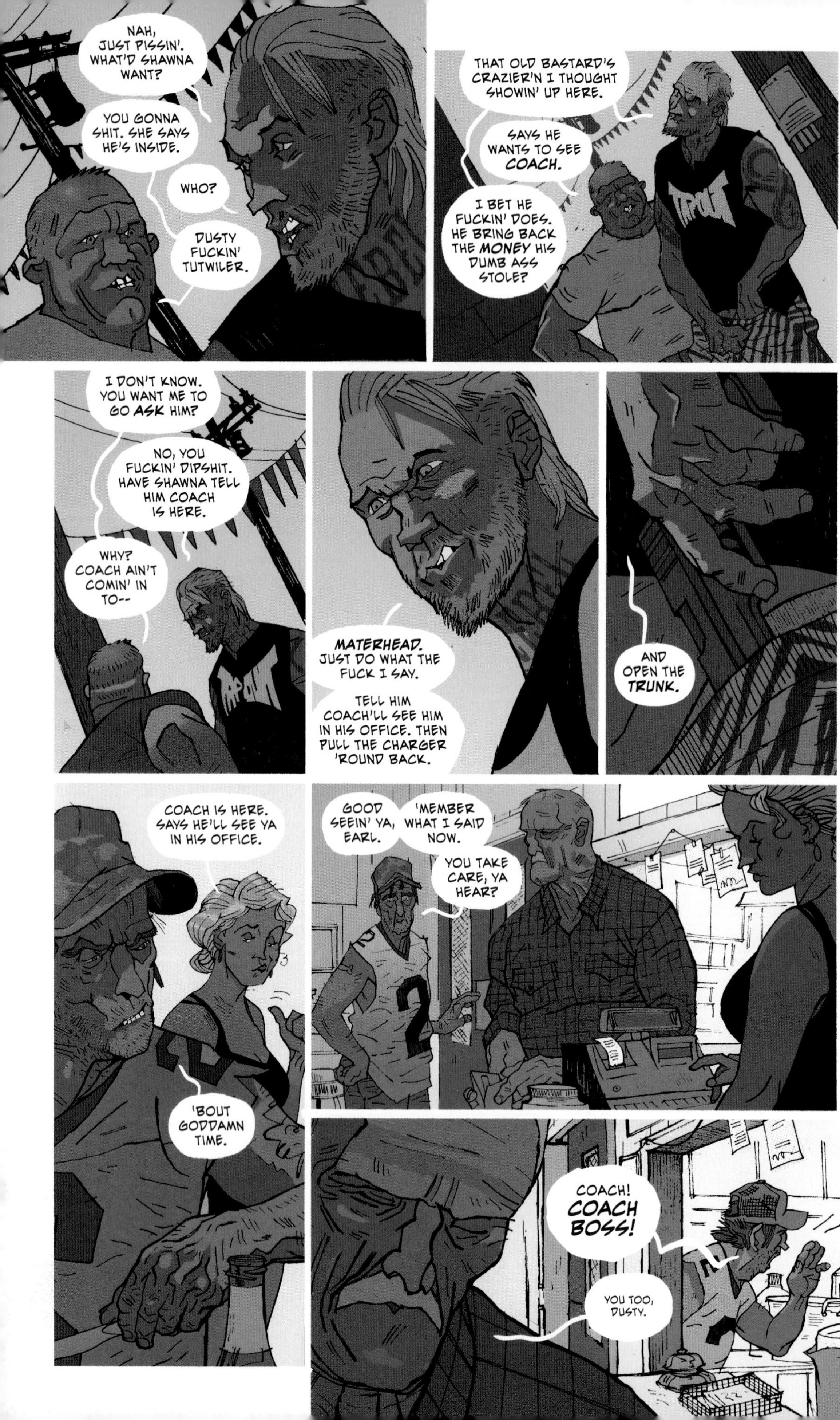
NAH, JUST PISSIN'. WHAT'D SHAWNA WANT?
YOU GONNA SHIT. SHE SAYS HE'S INSIDE.
WHO?
DUSTY FUCKIN' TUTWILER.
THAT OLD BASTARD'S CRAZIER'N I THOUGHT SHOWIN' UP HERE.
SAYS HE WANTS TO SEE COACH.
I BET HE FUCKIN' DOES. HE BRING BACK THE MONEY HIS DUMB ASS STOLE?
I DON'T KNOW. YOU WANT ME TO GO ASK HIM?
NO, YOU FUCKIN' DIPSHIT. HAVE SHAWNA TELL HIM COACH IS HERE.
WHY? COACH AIN'T COMIN' IN TO--
MATERHEAD. JUST DO WHAT THE FUCK I SAY.
TELL HIM COACH'LL SEE HIM IN HIS OFFICE. THEN PULL THE CHARGER 'ROUND BACK.
AND OPEN THE TRUNK.
COACH IS HERE. SAYS HE'LL SEE YA IN HIS OFFICE.
'BOUT GODDAMN TIME.
GOOD SEEIN' YA, EARL.
'MEMBER WHAT I SAID NOW.
YOU TAKE CARE, YA HEAR?
COACH! COACH BOSS!
YOU TOO, DUSTY.

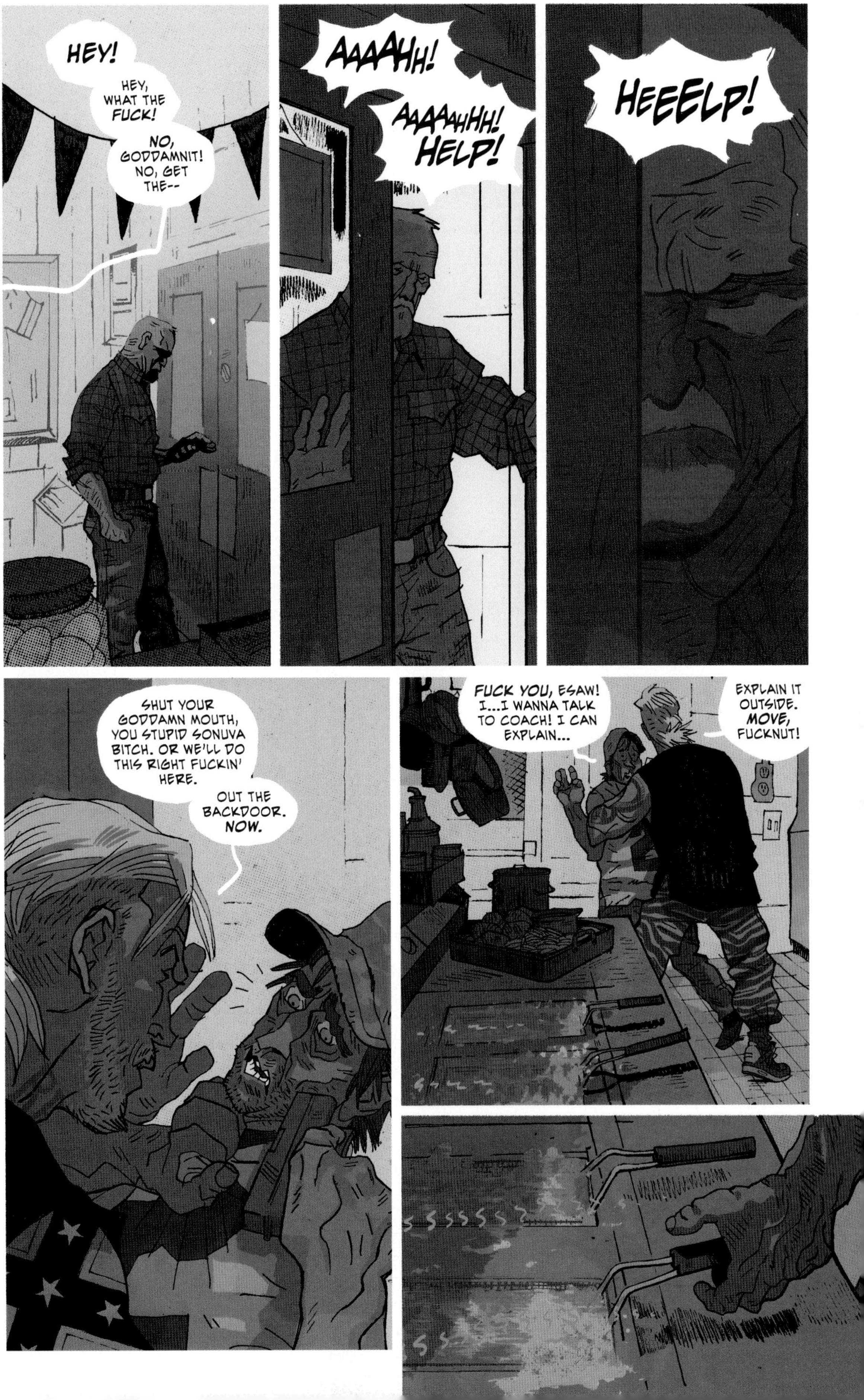
HEY!
HEY, WHAT THE FUCK!
NO, GODDAMNIT! NO, GET THE--
AAAAHH!
AAAAAHHH! HELP!
HEEEELP!
SHUT YOUR GODDAMN MOUTH, YOU STUPID SONUVA BITCH. OR WE'LL DO THIS RIGHT FUCKIN' HERE.
OUT THE BACKDOOR. NOW.
FUCK YOU, ESAW! I...I WANNA TALK TO COACH! I CAN EXPLAIN...
EXPLAIN IT OUTSIDE. MOVE, FUCKNUT!

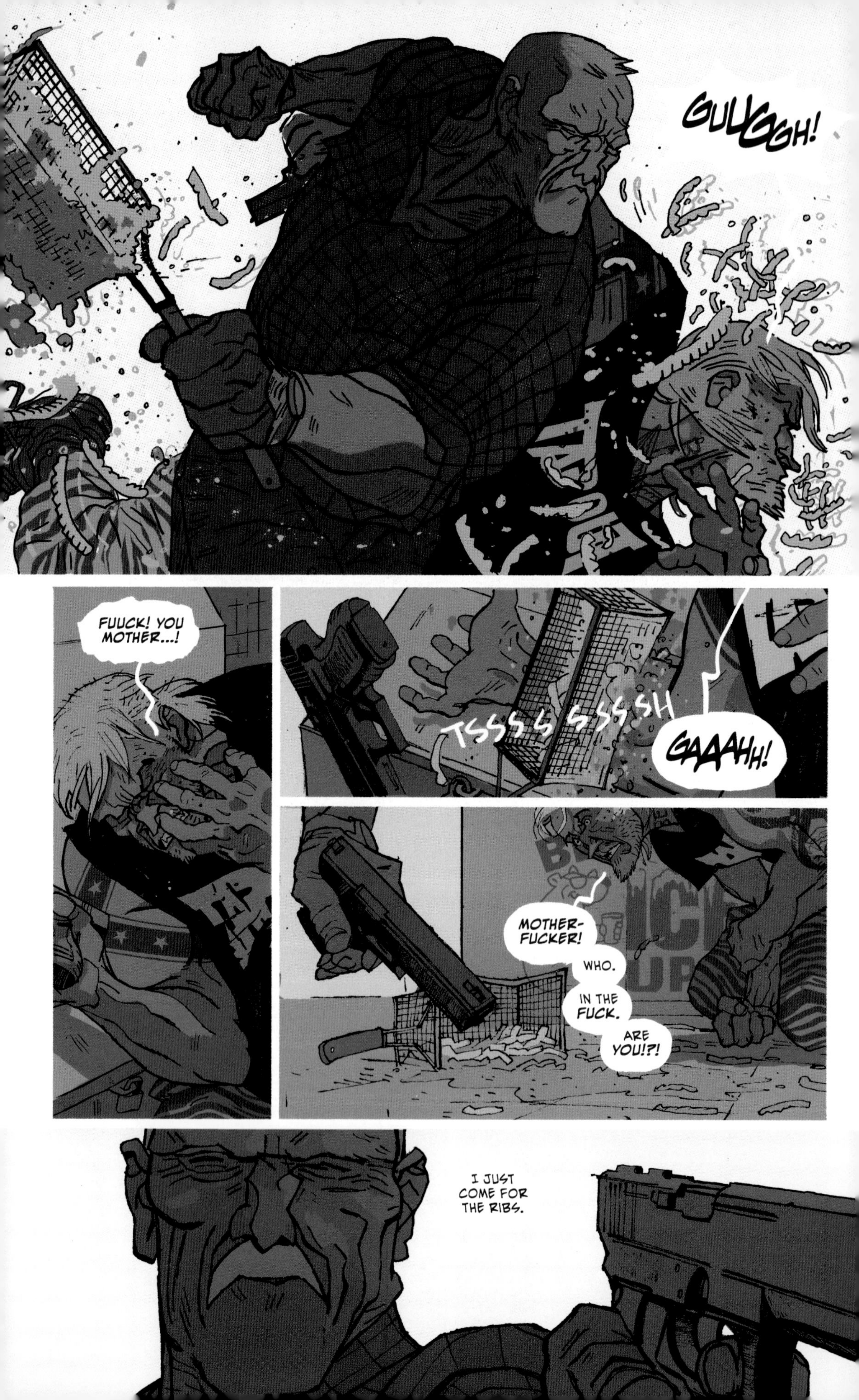
GULLGGH!
FUUCK! YOU MOTHER...!
TSSSS SSSSH
GAAAHH!
MOTHER-FUCKER!
WHO.
IN THE FUCK.
ARE YOU!?!
I JUST COME FOR THE RIBS.

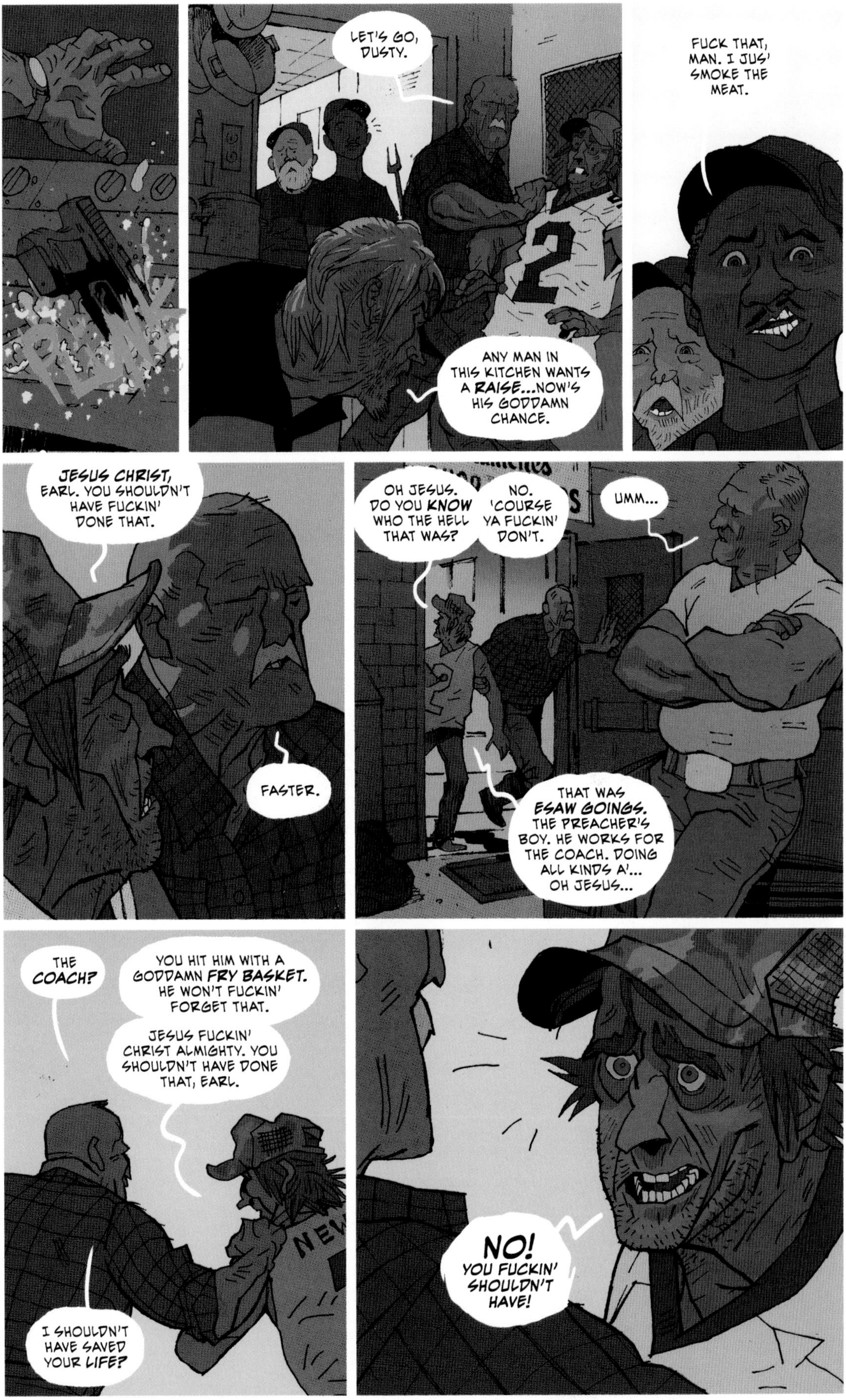

LET'S GO, DUSTY.
ANY MAN IN THIS KITCHEN WANTS A RAISE...NOW'S HIS GODDAMN CHANCE.
FUCK THAT, MAN. I JUS' SMOKE THE MEAT.
JESUS CHRIST, EARL. YOU SHOULDN'T HAVE FUCKIN' DONE THAT.
FASTER.
OH JESUS. DO YOU KNOW WHO THE HELL THAT WAS?
NO. 'COURSE YA FUCKIN' DON'T.
UMM...
THAT WAS ESAW GOINGS. THE PREACHER'S BOY. HE WORKS FOR THE COACH. DOING ALL KINDS A'... OH JESUS...
THE COACH?
YOU HIT HIM WITH A GODDAMN FRY BASKET. HE WON'T FUCKIN' FORGET THAT.
JESUS FUCKIN' CHRIST ALMIGHTY. YOU SHOULDN'T HAVE DONE THAT, EARL.
I SHOULDN'T HAVE SAVED YOUR LIFE?
NO! YOU FUCKIN' SHOULDN'T HAVE!

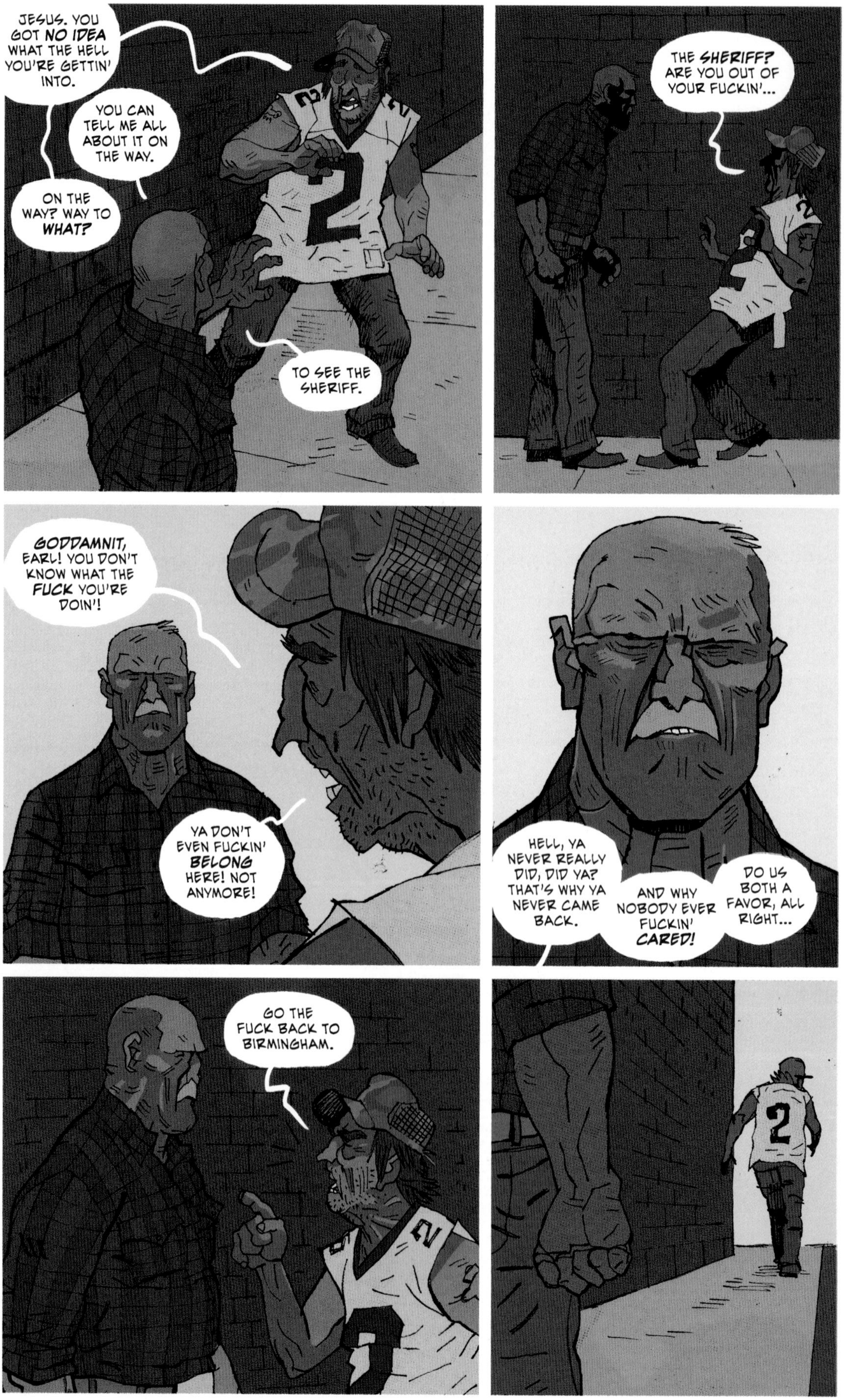
JESUS. YOU GOT NO IDEA WHAT THE HELL YOU'RE GETTIN' INTO.
YOU CAN TELL ME ALL ABOUT IT ON THE WAY.
ON THE WAY? WAY TO WHAT?
TO SEE THE SHERIFF.
THE SHERIFF? ARE YOU OUT OF YOUR FUCKIN'...
GODDAMNIT, EARL! YOU DON'T KNOW WHAT THE FUCK YOU'RE DOIN'!
YA DON'T EVEN FUCKIN' BELONG HERE! NOT ANYMORE!
HELL, YA NEVER REALLY DID, DID YA? THAT'S WHY YA NEVER CAME BACK.
AND WHY NOBODY EVER FUCKIN' CARED!
DO US BOTH A FAVOR, ALL RIGHT...
GO THE FUCK BACK TO BIRMINGHAM.

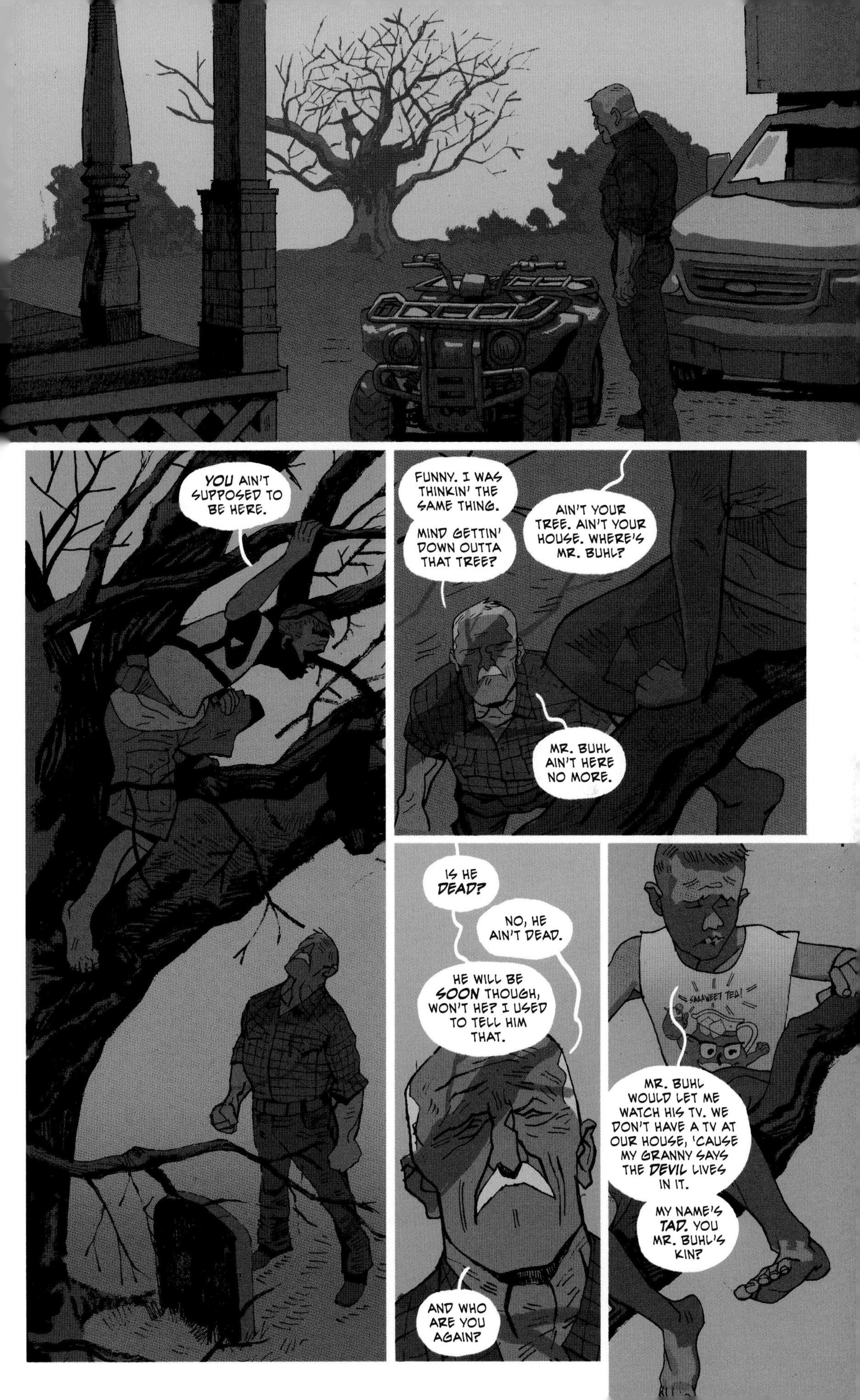
YOU AIN'T SUPPOSED TO BE HERE.
FUNNY. I WAS THINKIN' THE SAME THING.
MIND GETTIN' DOWN OUTTA THAT TREE?
AIN'T YOUR TREE. AIN'T YOUR HOUSE. WHERE'S MR. BUHL?
MR. BUHL AIN'T HERE NO MORE.
IS HE DEAD?
NO, HE AIN'T DEAD.
HE WILL BE SOON THOUGH, WON'T HE? I USED TO TELL HIM THAT.
AND WHO ARE YOU AGAIN?
SAAAWEET TEA!
MR. BUHL WOULD LET ME WATCH HIS TV. WE DON'T HAVE A TV AT OUR HOUSE, 'CAUSE MY GRANNY SAYS THE DEVIL LIVES IN IT.
MY NAME'S TAD. YOU MR. BUHL'S KIN?

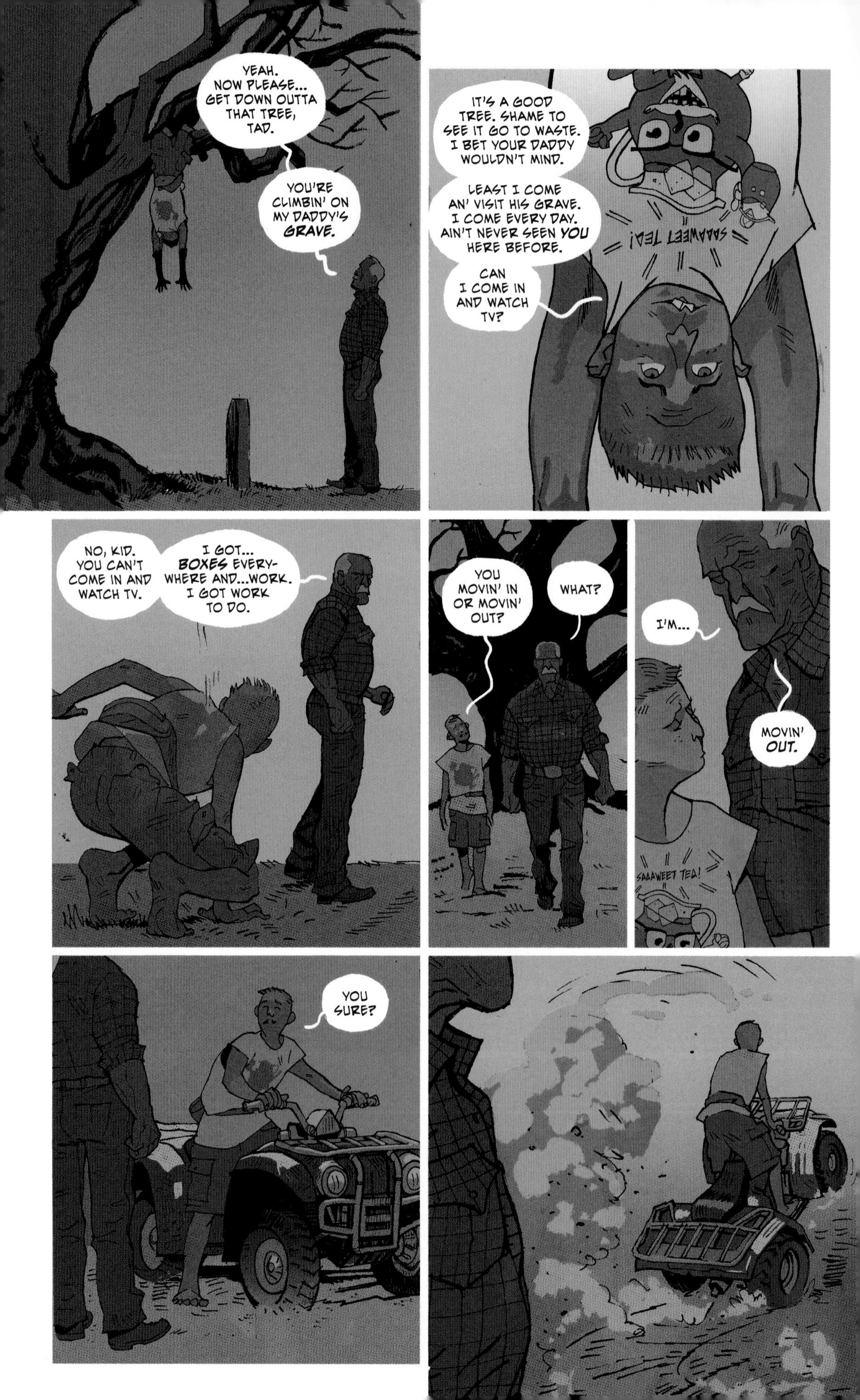
YEAH. NOW PLEASE... GET DOWN OUTTA THAT TREE, TAD.
YOU'RE CLIMBIN' ON MY DADDY'S GRAVE.
IT'S A GOOD TREE. SHAME TO SEE IT GO TO WASTE. I BET YOUR DADDY WOULDN'T MIND.
LEAST I COME AN' VISIT HIS GRAVE. I COME EVERY DAY. AIN'T NEVER SEEN YOU HERE BEFORE.
CAN I COME IN AND WATCH TV?
SAAAWEET TEA!
NO, KID. YOU CAN'T COME IN AND WATCH TV.
I GOT... BOXES EVERY-WHERE AND...WORK. I GOT WORK TO DO.
YOU MOVIN' IN OR MOVIN' OUT?
WHAT?
I'M...
MOVIN' OUT.
SAAAWEET TEA!
YOU SURE?

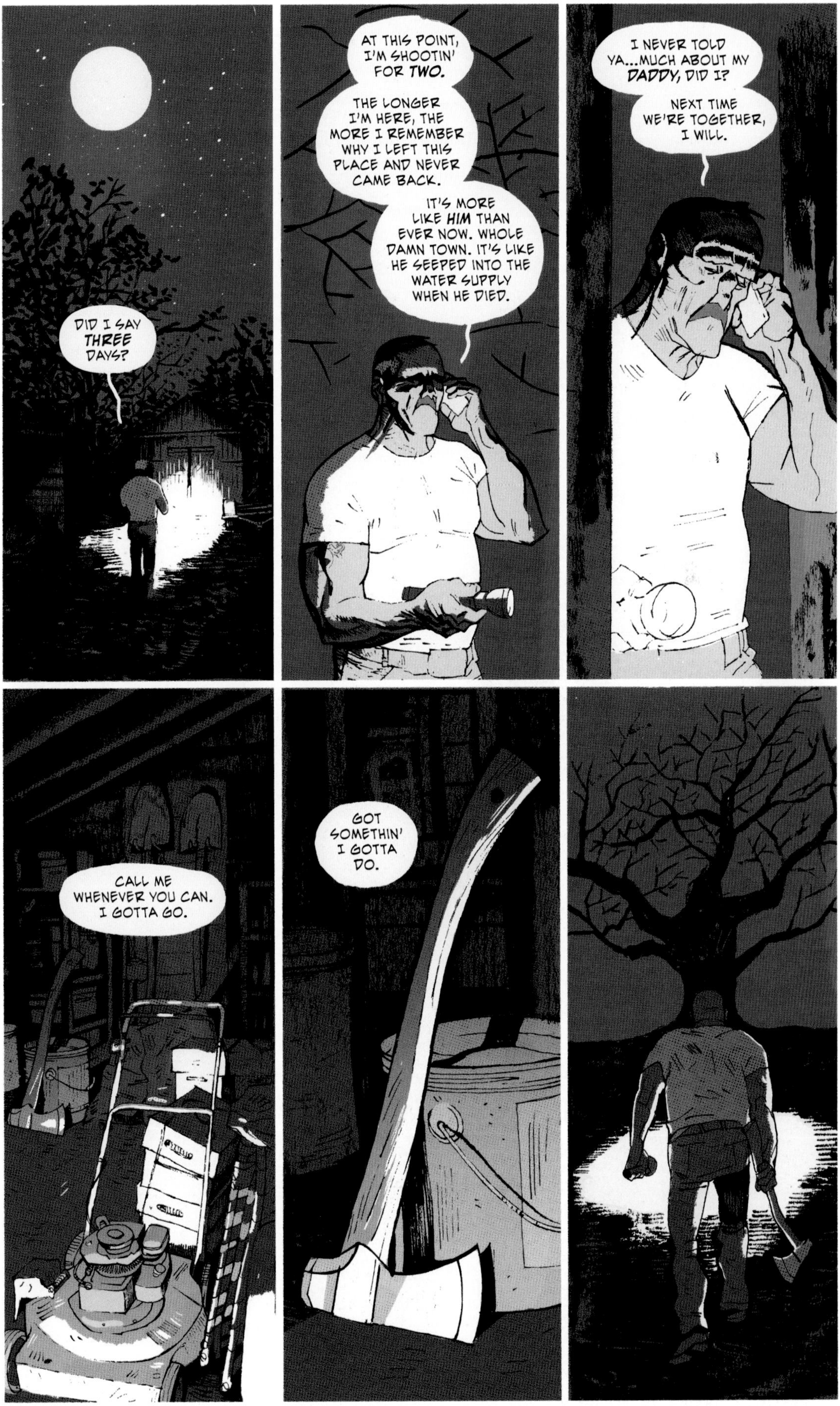
DID I SAY THREE DAYS?
AT THIS POINT, I'M SHOOTIN' FOR TWO.
THE LONGER I'M HERE, THE MORE I REMEMBER WHY I LEFT THIS PLACE AND NEVER CAME BACK.
IT'S MORE LIKE HIM THAN EVER NOW. WHOLE DAMN TOWN. IT'S LIKE HE SEEPED INTO THE WATER SUPPLY WHEN HE DIED.
I NEVER TOLD YA...MUCH ABOUT MY DADDY, DID I?
NEXT TIME WE'RE TOGETHER, I WILL.
CALL ME WHENEVER YOU CAN. I GOTTA GO.
GOT SOMETHIN' I GOTTA DO.

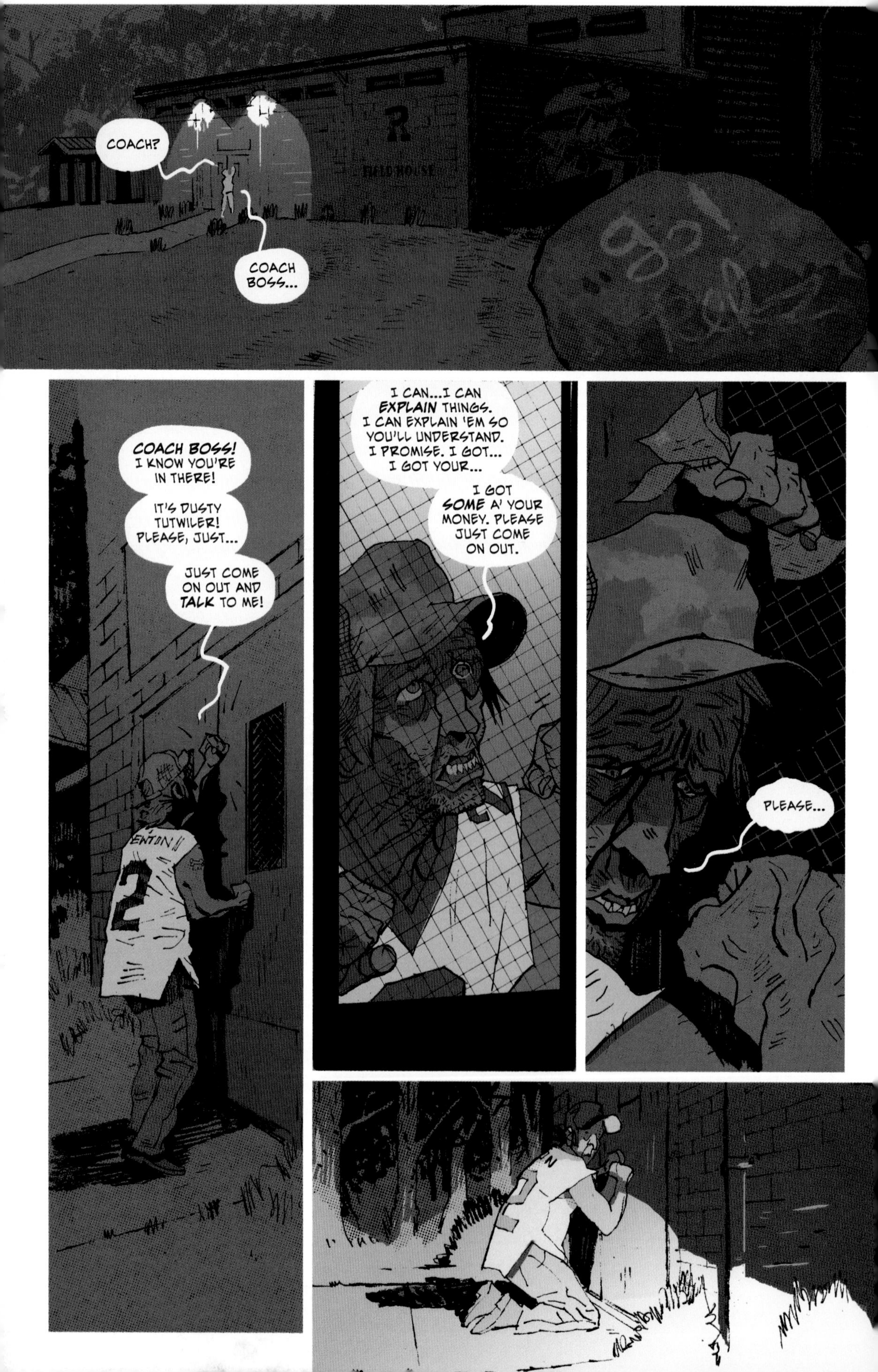
COACH?
COACH BOSS...
FIELD HOUSE
COACH BOSS! I KNOW YOU'RE IN THERE!
IT'S DUSTY TUTWILER! PLEASE, JUST...
JUST COME ON OUT AND TALK TO ME!
I CAN...I CAN EXPLAIN THINGS. I CAN EXPLAIN 'EM SO YOU'LL UNDERSTAND. I PROMISE. I GOT... I GOT YOUR...
I GOT SOME A' YOUR MONEY. PLEASE JUST COME ON OUT.
PLEASE...

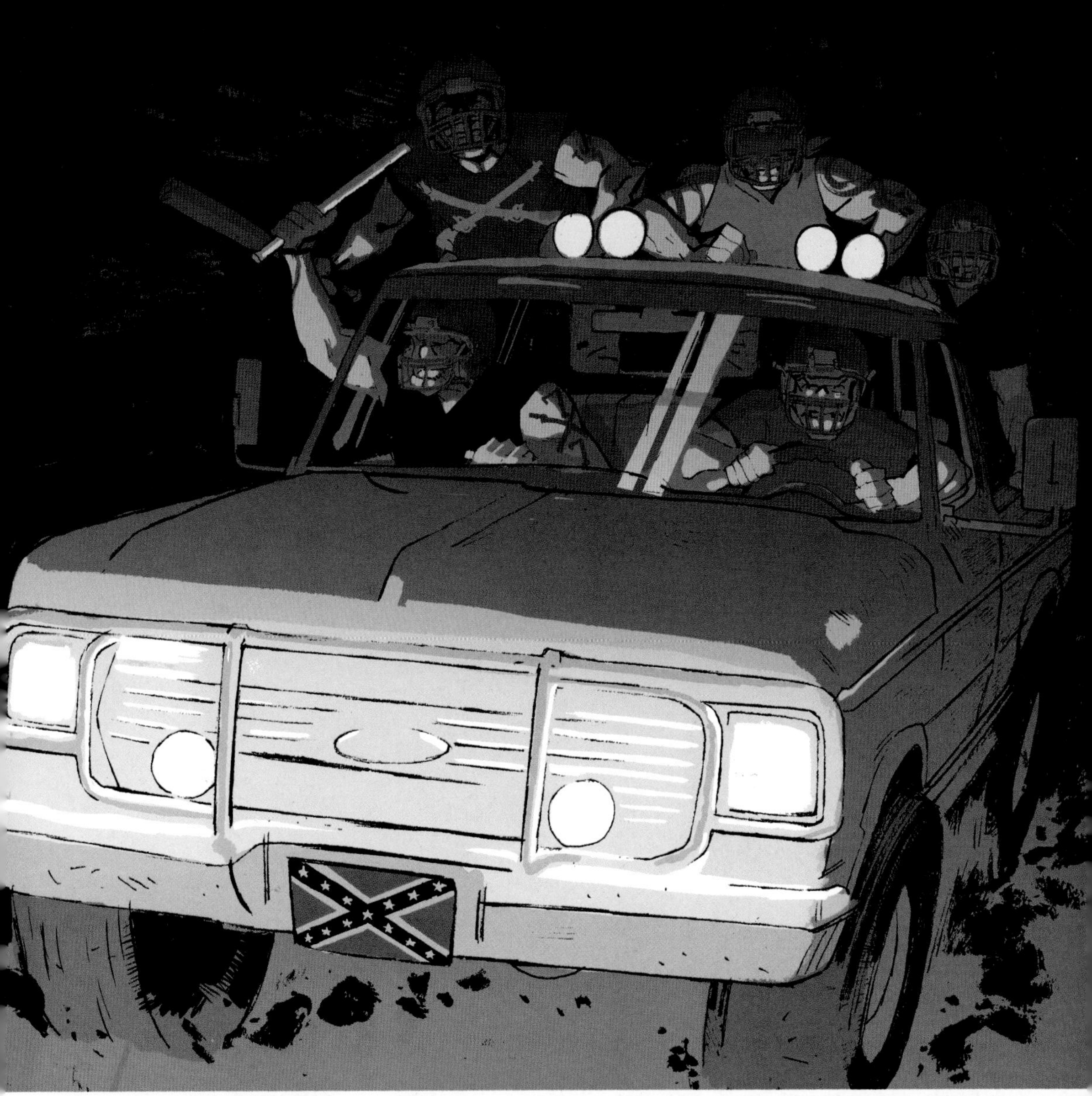

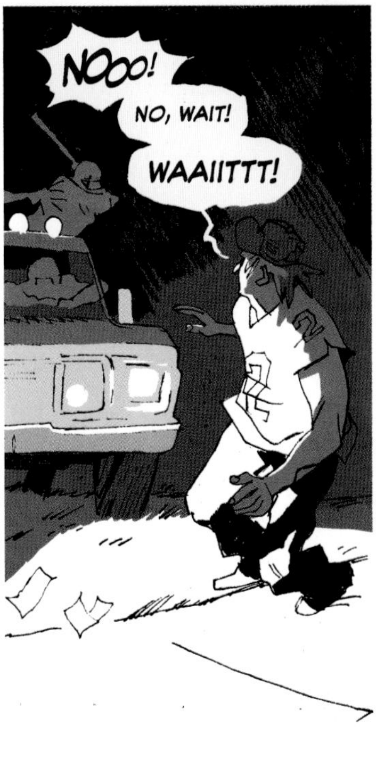
NOOO!
NO, WAIT!
WAAIITTT!

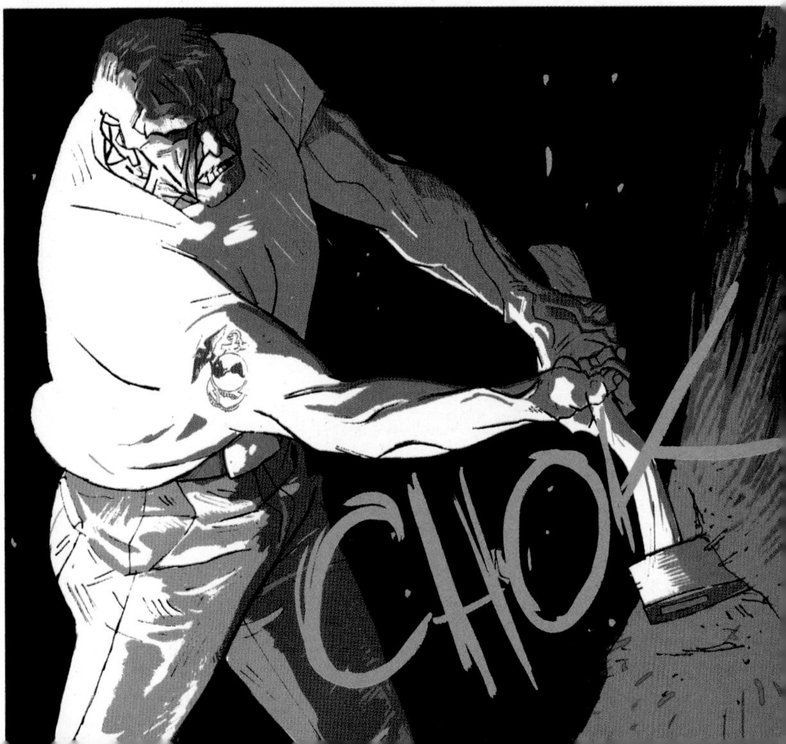
CHOK

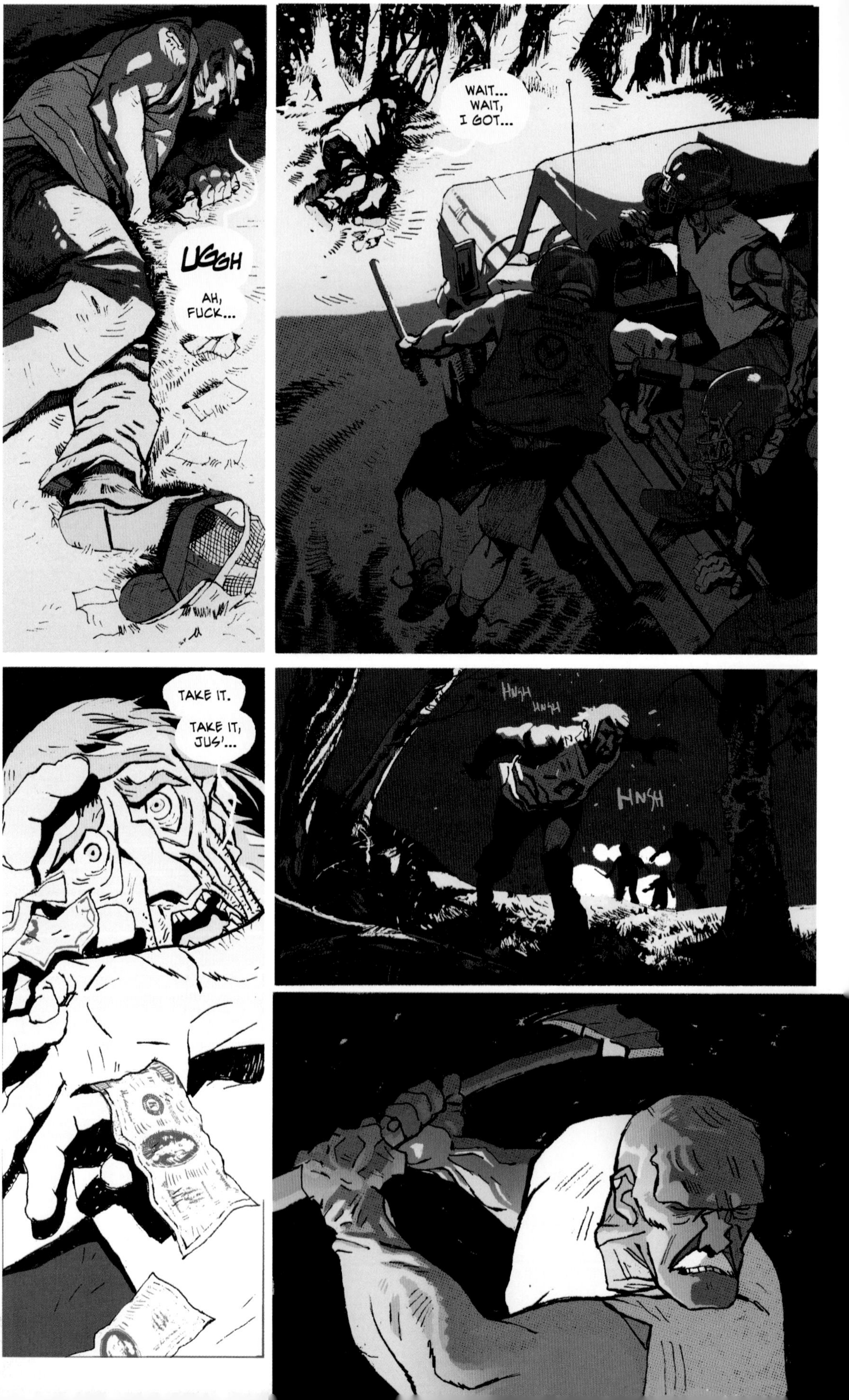
UGGH
AH, FUCK...
WAIT... WAIT, I GOT...
TAKE IT.
TAKE IT, JUS'...
HNSH
HNSH
HNSH

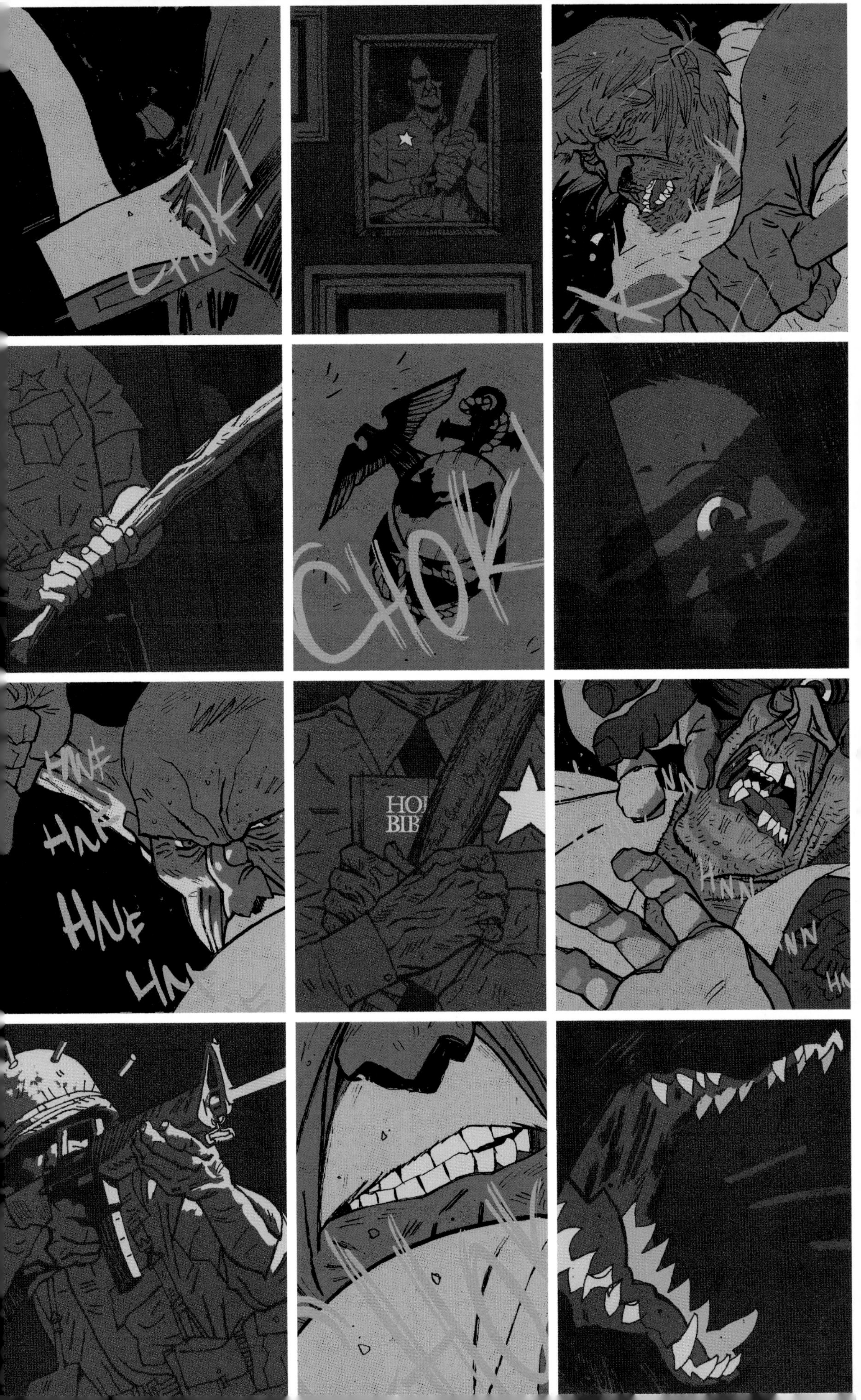
CHOK!
CHOK!
HNF
HNF
HNF
HNN

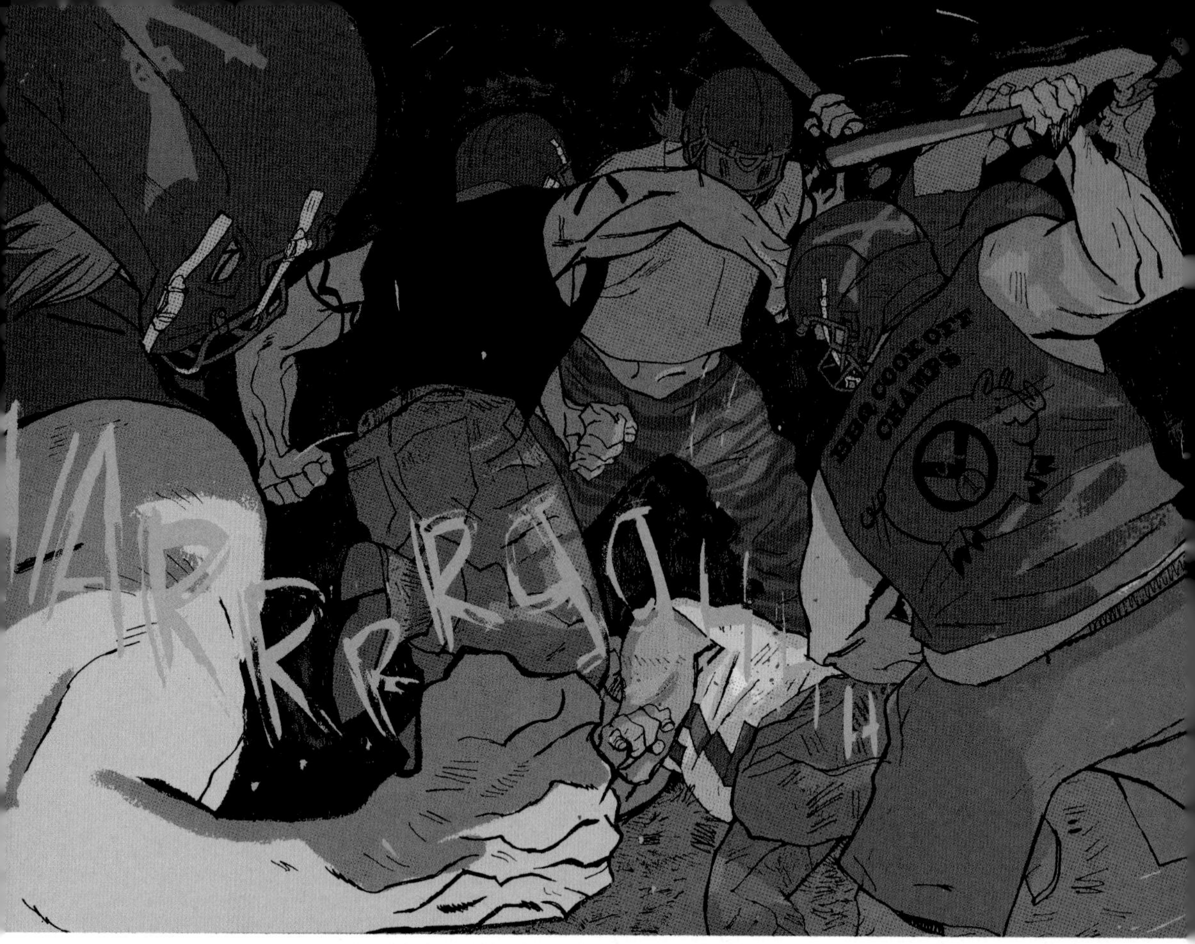
BBQ COOK OFF CHAMPS

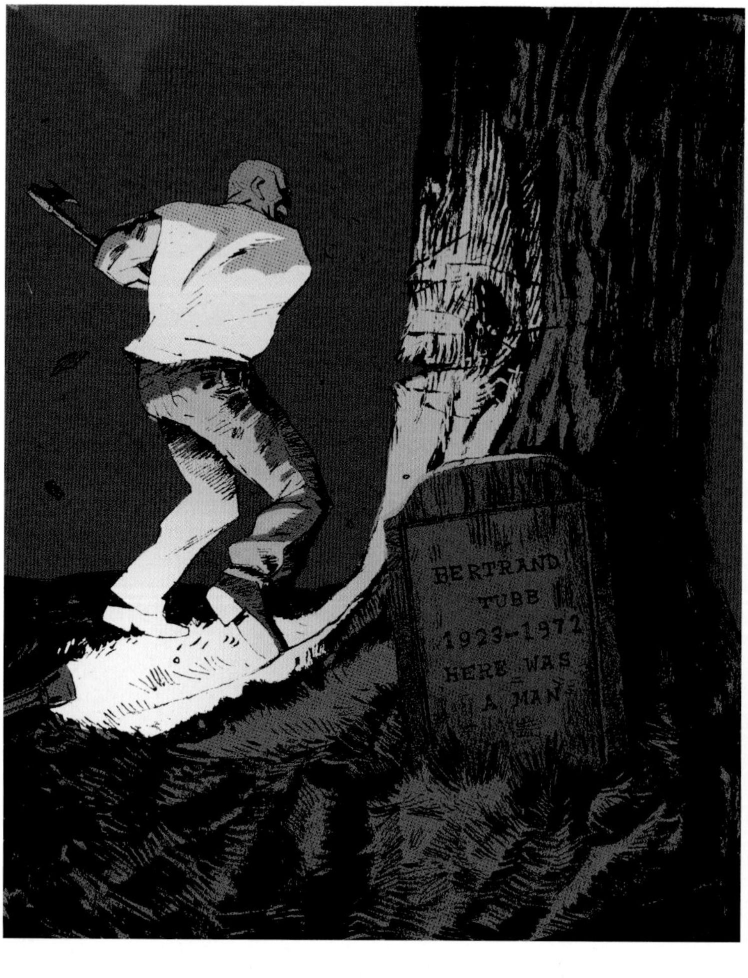
BERTRAND
TUBB
1923-1972
HERE WAS
A MAN

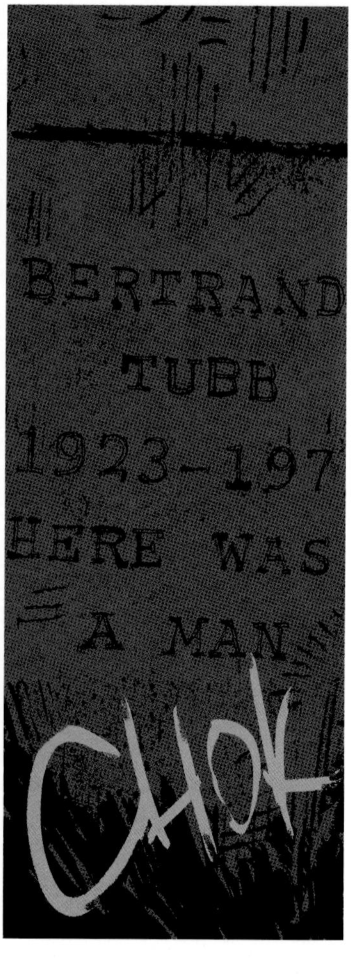
BERTRAND
TUBB
1923-197
HERE WAS
A MAN
CHOK

Here Was a Man

Chapter Two

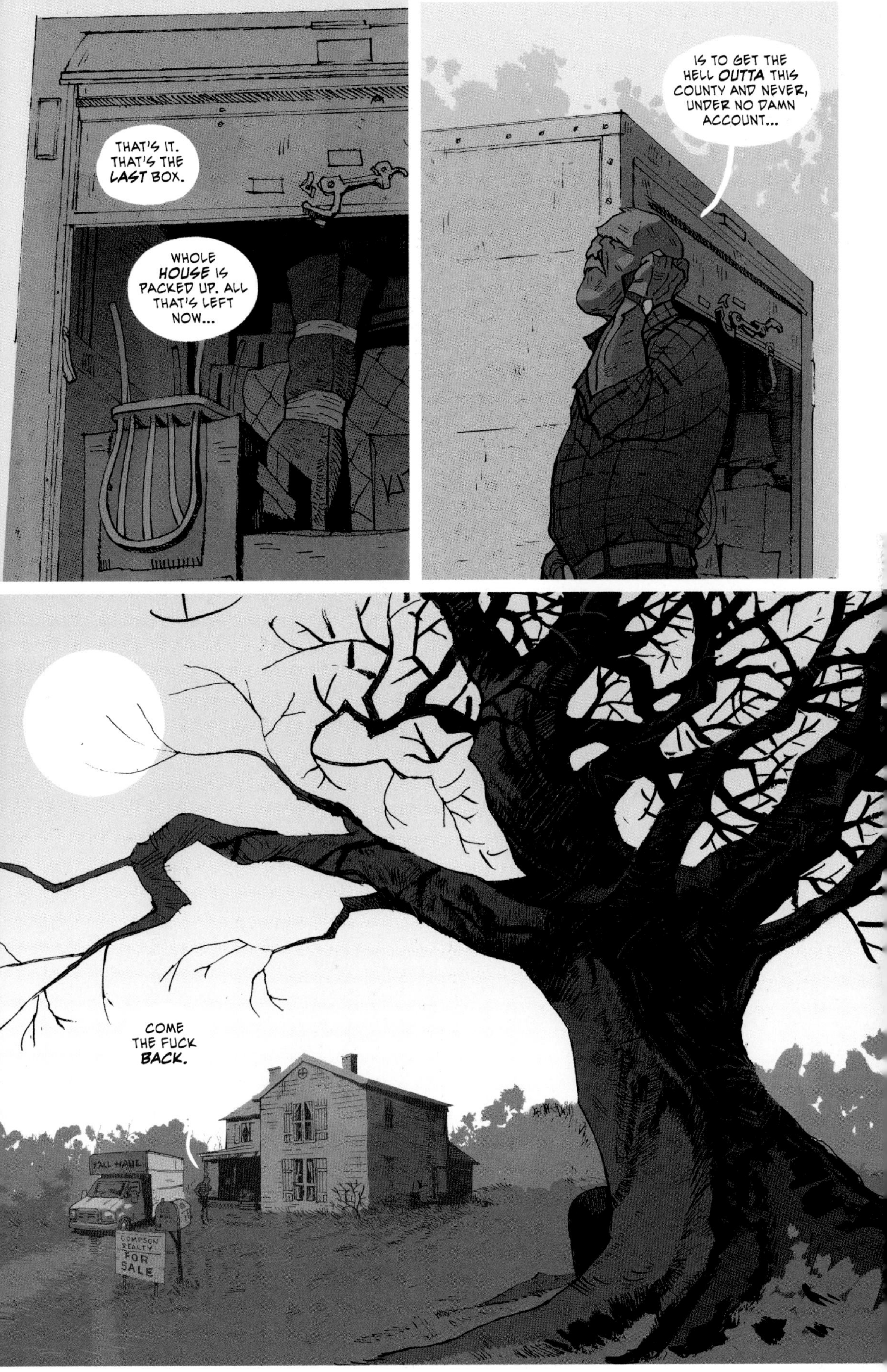
THAT'S IT. THAT'S THE *LAST* BOX.
WHOLE *HOUSE* IS PACKED UP. ALL THAT'S LEFT NOW...
IS TO GET THE HELL *OUTTA* THIS COUNTY AND NEVER, UNDER NO DAMN ACCOUNT...
COME THE FUCK **BACK.**
Y'ALL HAUL
COMPSON REALTY
FOR SALE

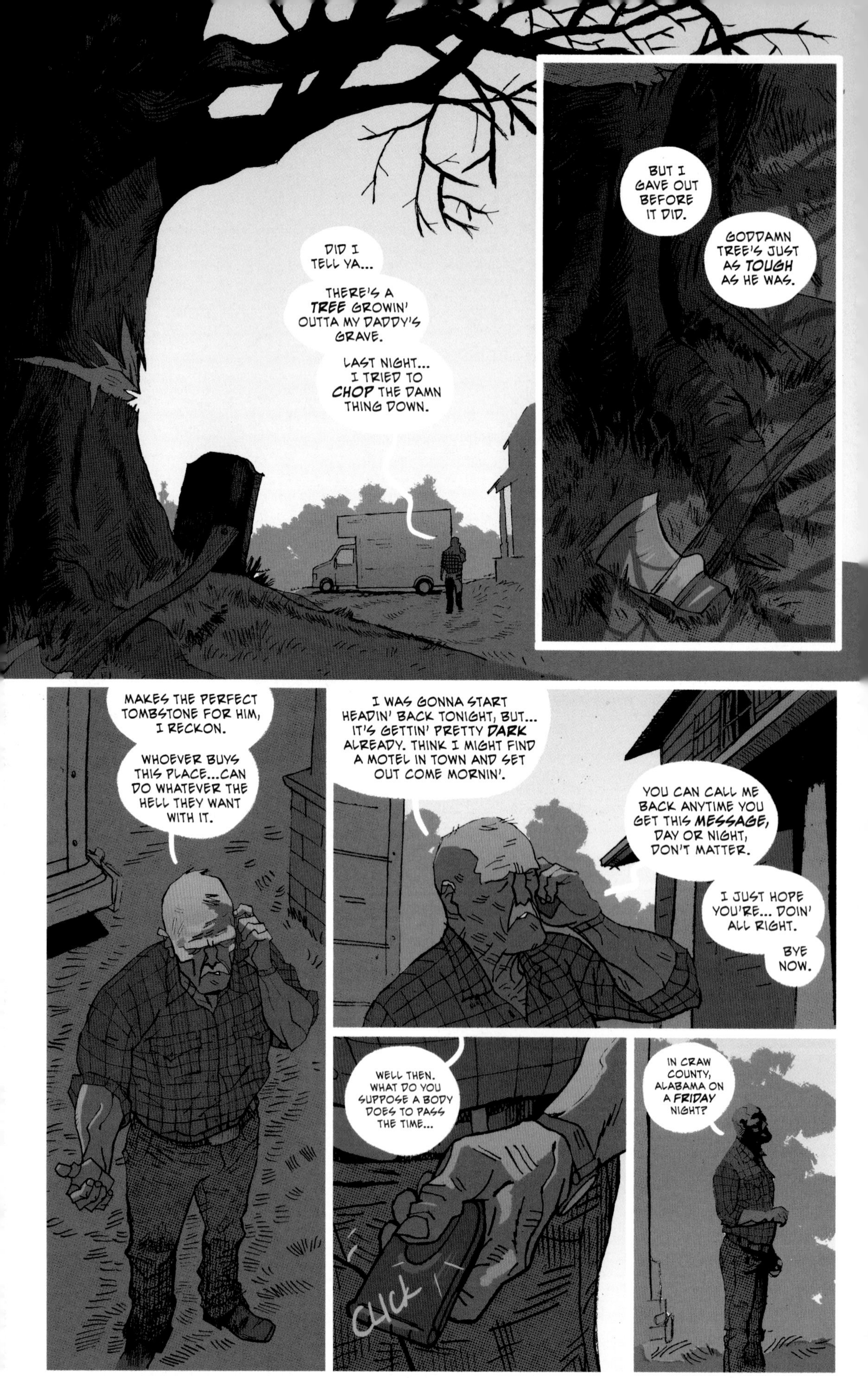
DID I TELL YA...
THERE'S A TREE GROWIN' OUTTA MY DADDY'S GRAVE.
LAST NIGHT... I TRIED TO CHOP THE DAMN THING DOWN.
BUT I GAVE OUT BEFORE IT DID.
GODDAMN TREE'S JUST AS TOUGH AS HE WAS.
MAKES THE PERFECT TOMBSTONE FOR HIM, I RECKON.
WHOEVER BUYS THIS PLACE...CAN DO WHATEVER THE HELL THEY WANT WITH IT.
I WAS GONNA START HEADIN' BACK TONIGHT, BUT... IT'S GETTIN' PRETTY DARK ALREADY. THINK I MIGHT FIND A MOTEL IN TOWN AND SET OUT COME MORNIN'.
YOU CAN CALL ME BACK ANYTIME YOU GET THIS MESSAGE, DAY OR NIGHT, DON'T MATTER.
I JUST HOPE YOU'RE... DOIN' ALL RIGHT.
BYE NOW.
WELL THEN. WHAT DO YOU SUPPOSE A BODY DOES TO PASS THE TIME...
CLICK
IN CRAW COUNTY, ALABAMA ON A FRIDAY NIGHT?

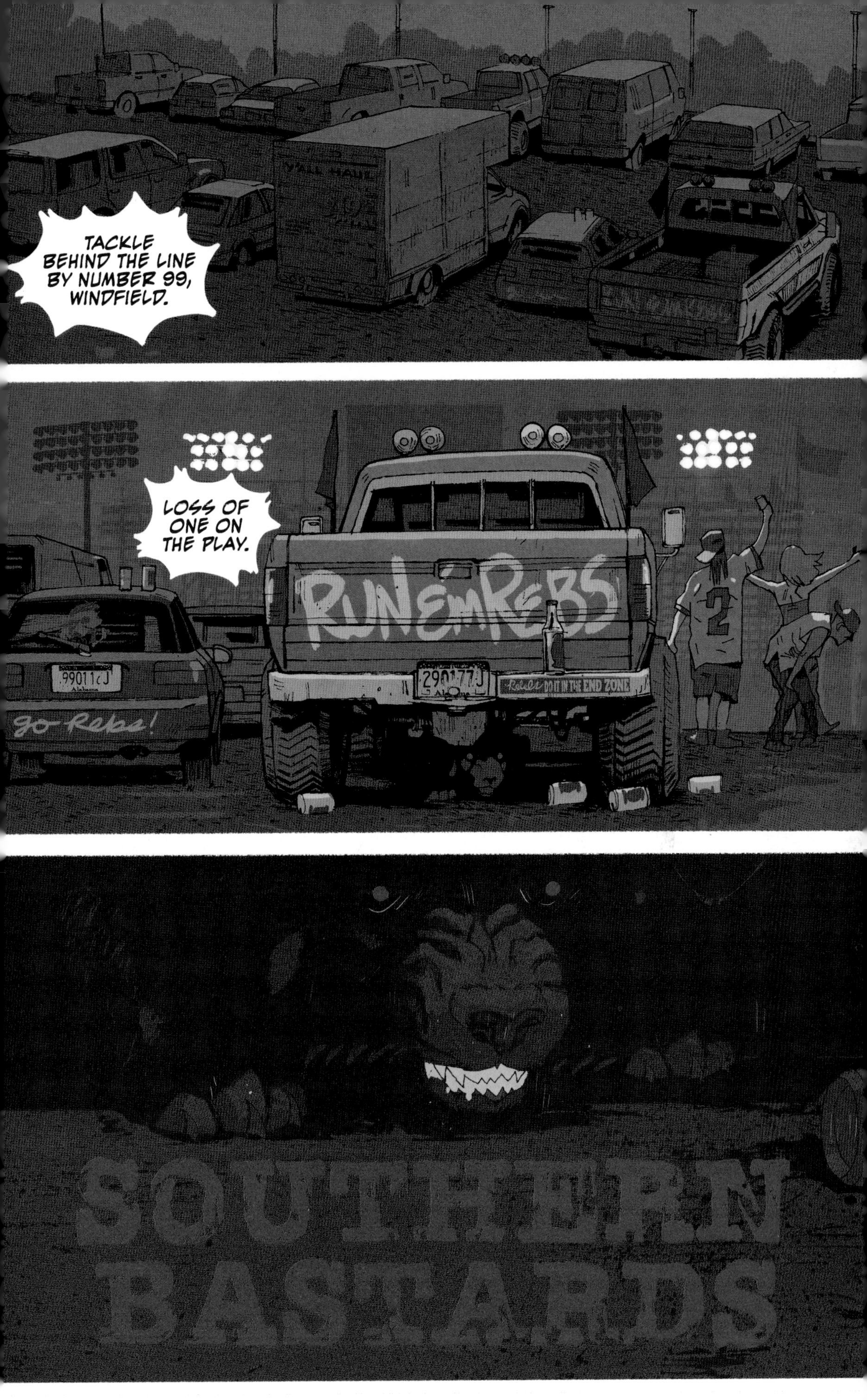
Y'ALL HAUL
TACKLE BEHIND THE LINE BY NUMBER 99, WINDFIELD.
LOSS OF ONE ON THE PLAY.
RUNEMREBS
go Rebs!
Rebs DO IT IN THE END ZONE
SOUTHERN BASTARDS

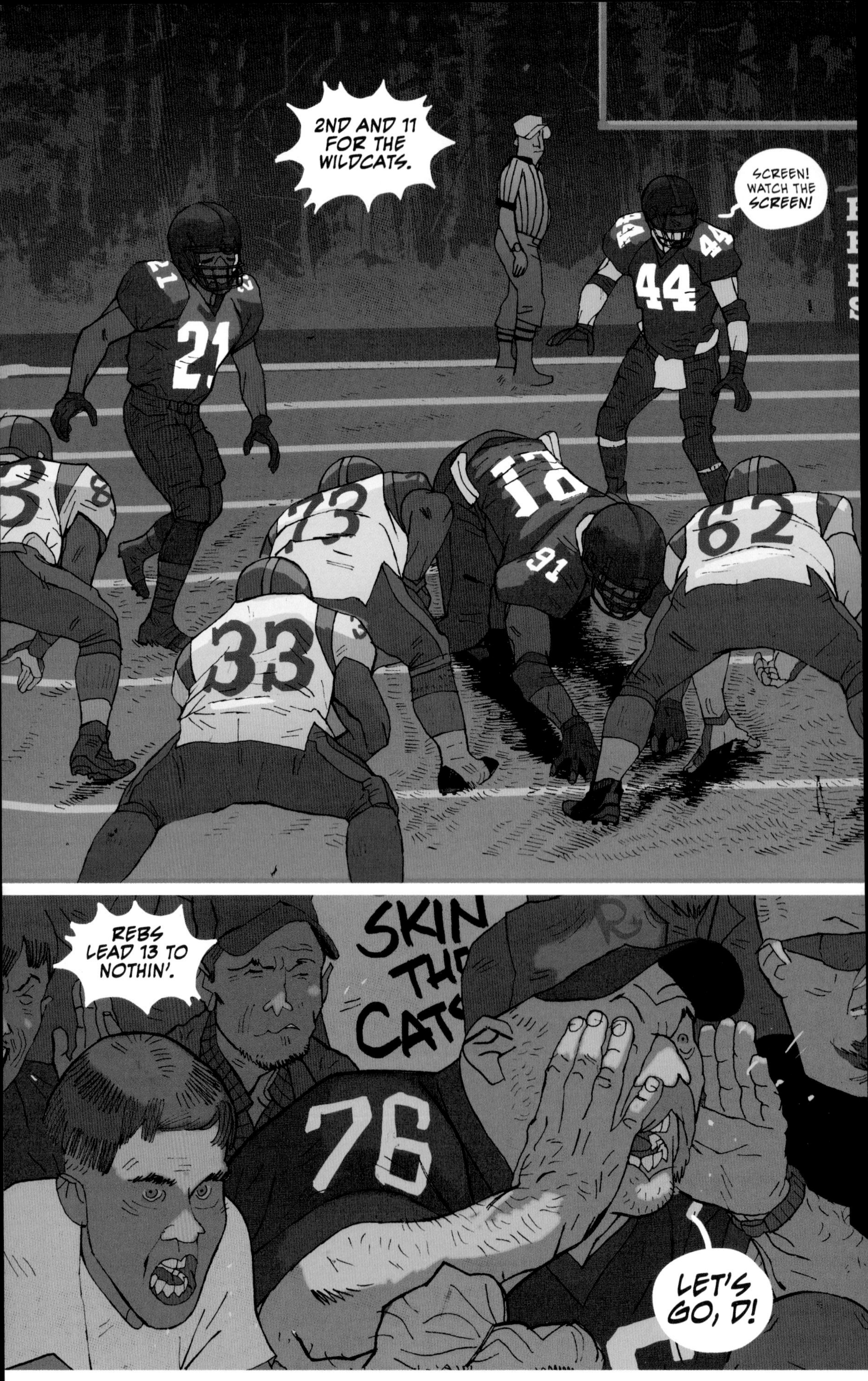
2ND AND 11 FOR THE WILDCATS.
SCREEN! WATCH THE SCREEN!
REBS LEAD 13 TO NOTHIN'.
SKIN
LET'S GO, D!

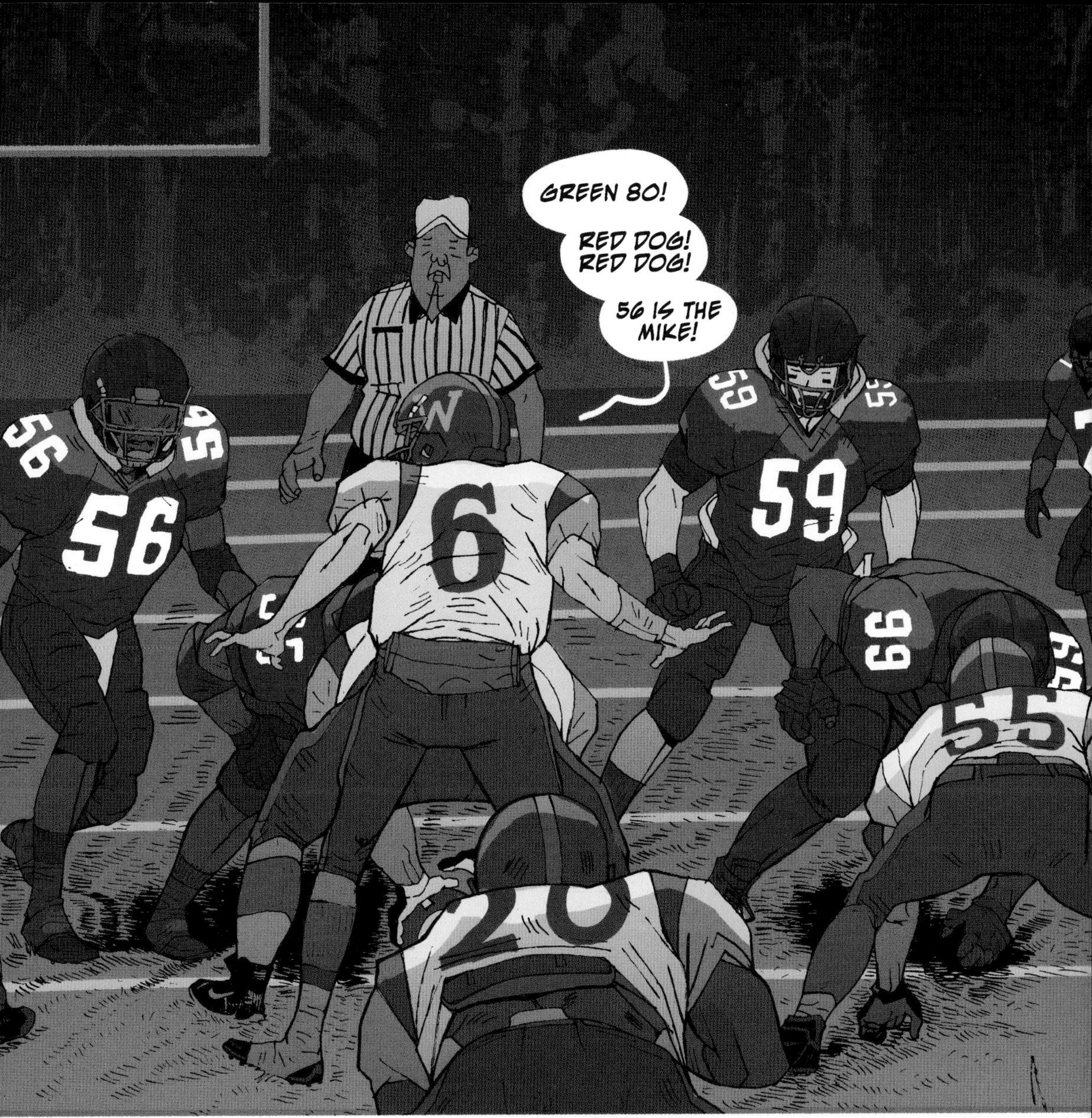
GREEN 80!
RED DOG! RED DOG!
56 IS THE MIKE!

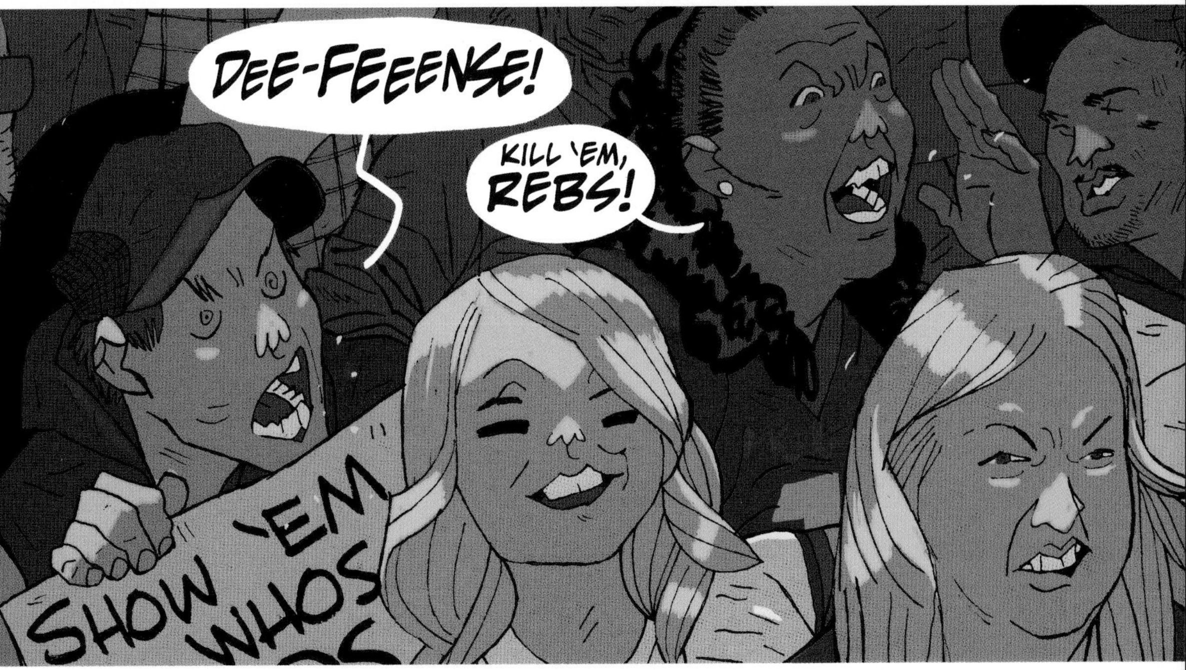
DEE-FEEENSE!
KILL 'EM, REBS!
SHOW 'EM WHOS

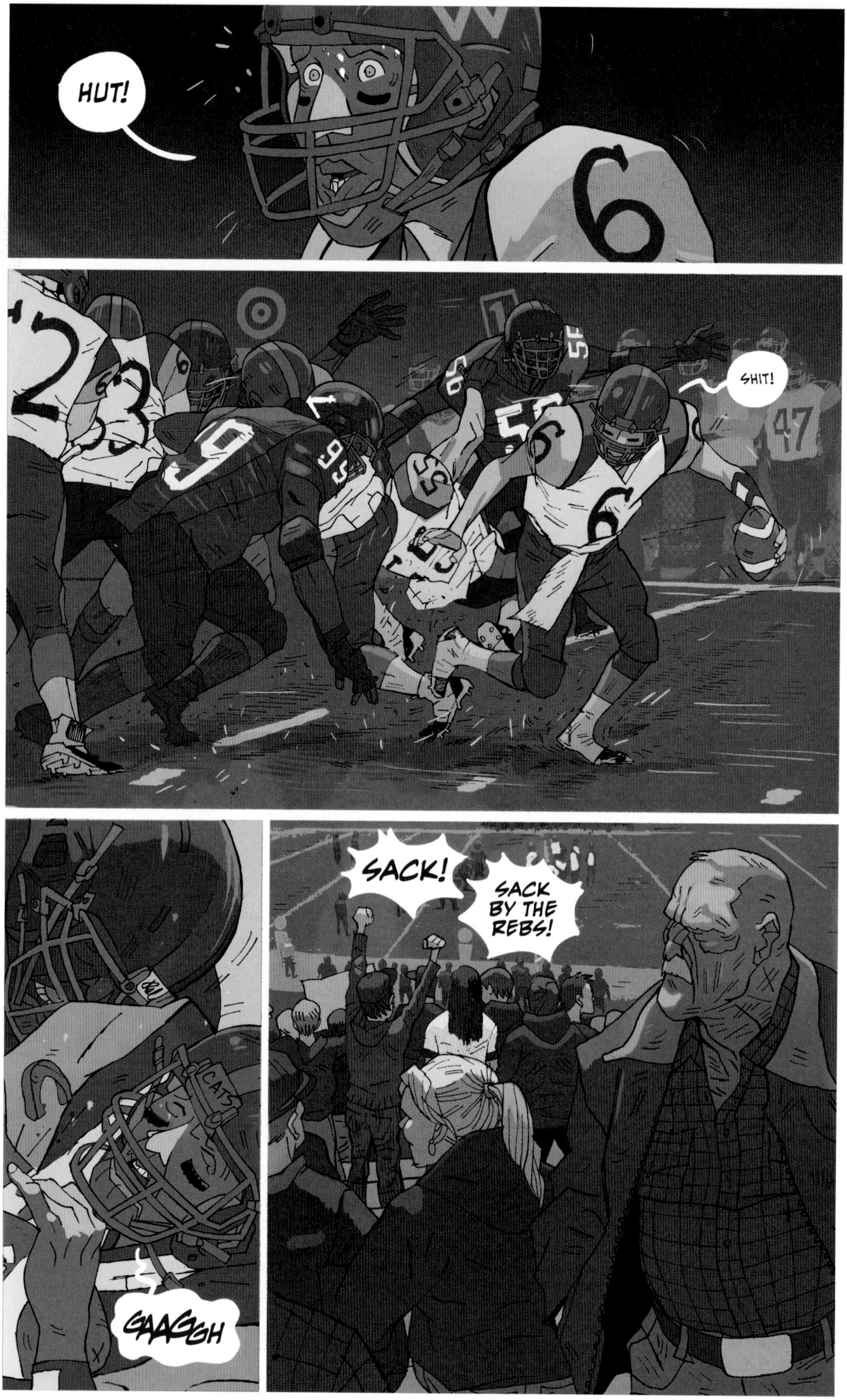
HUT!
SHIT!
GAAGGH
SACK!
SACK BY THE REBS!

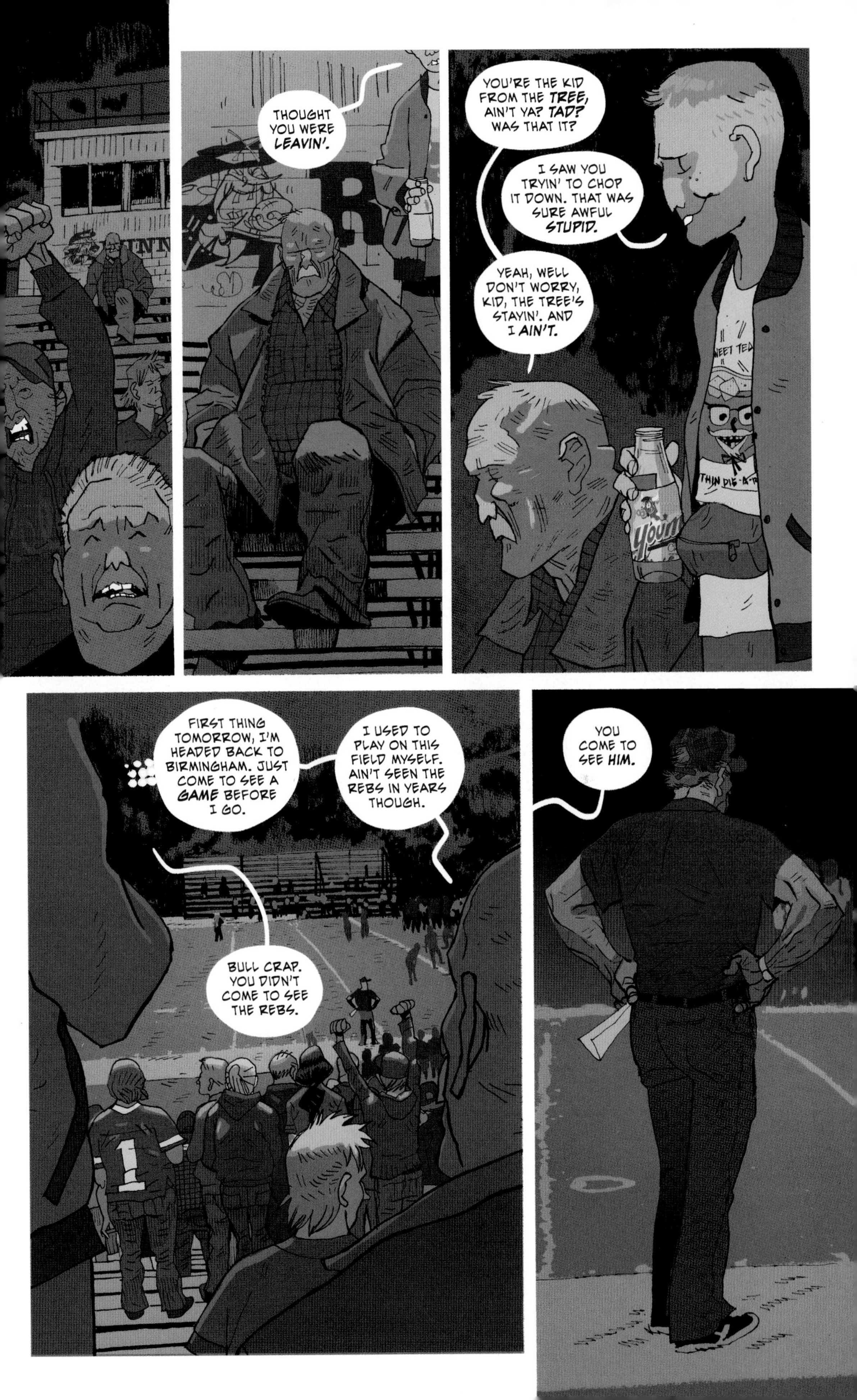
THOUGHT YOU WERE LEAVIN'.
YOU'RE THE KID FROM THE TREE, AIN'T YA? TAD? WAS THAT IT?
I SAW YOU TRYIN' TO CHOP IT DOWN. THAT WAS SURE AWFUL STUPID.
YEAH, WELL DON'T WORRY, KID, THE TREE'S STAYIN'. AND I AIN'T.
FIRST THING TOMORROW, I'M HEADED BACK TO BIRMINGHAM. JUST COME TO SEE A GAME BEFORE I GO.
I USED TO PLAY ON THIS FIELD MYSELF. AIN'T SEEN THE REBS IN YEARS THOUGH.
BULL CRAP. YOU DIDN'T COME TO SEE THE REBS.
YOU COME TO SEE HIM.

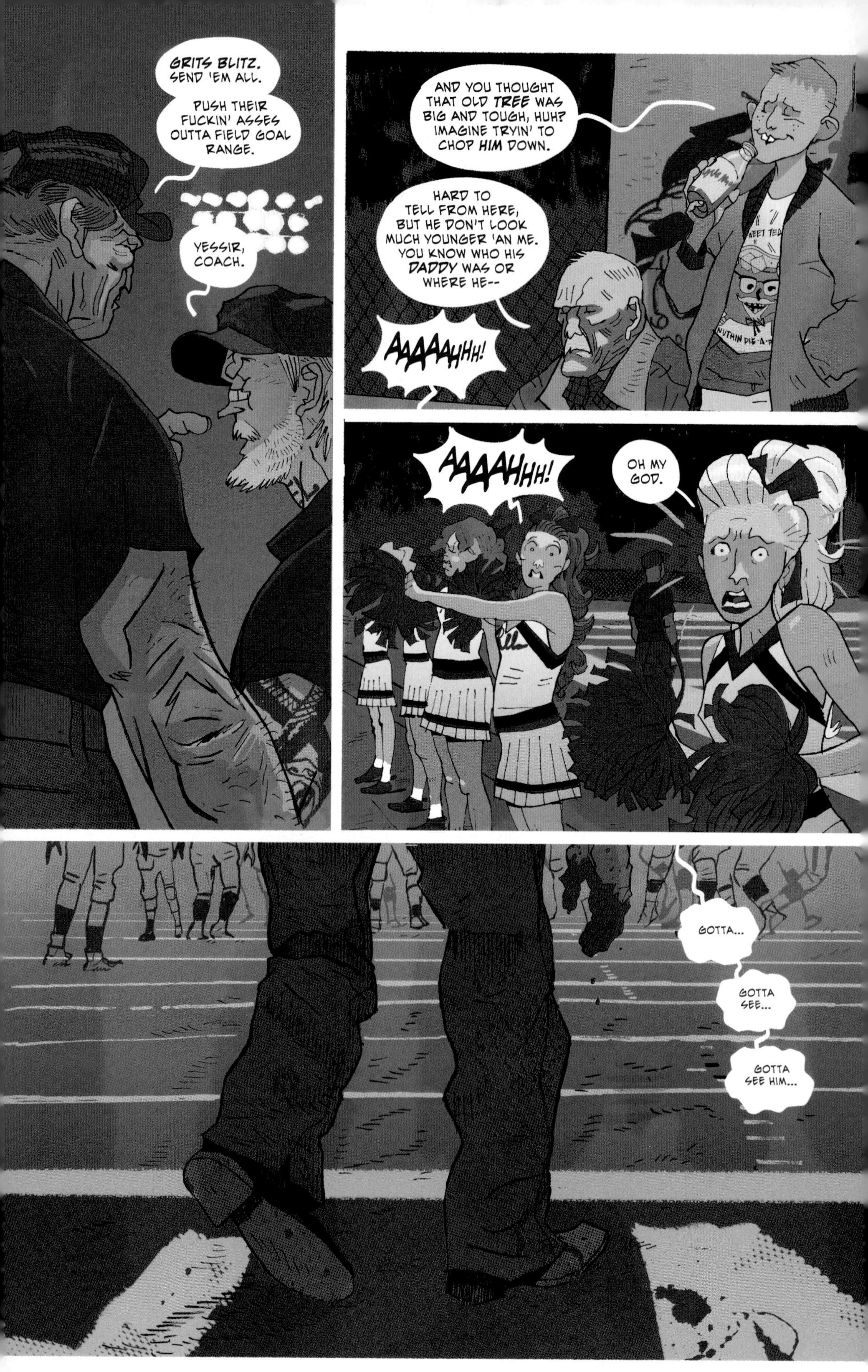
GRITS BLITZ. SEND 'EM ALL.
PUSH THEIR FUCKIN' ASSES OUTTA FIELD GOAL RANGE.
YESSIR, COACH.
AND YOU THOUGHT THAT OLD TREE WAS BIG AND TOUGH, HUH? IMAGINE TRYIN' TO CHOP HIM DOWN.
HARD TO TELL FROM HERE, BUT HE DON'T LOOK MUCH YOUNGER 'AN ME. YOU KNOW WHO HIS DADDY WAS OR WHERE HE--
AAAAAHHH!
AAAAHHH!
OH MY GOD.
GOTTA...
GOTTA SEE...
GOTTA SEE HIM...

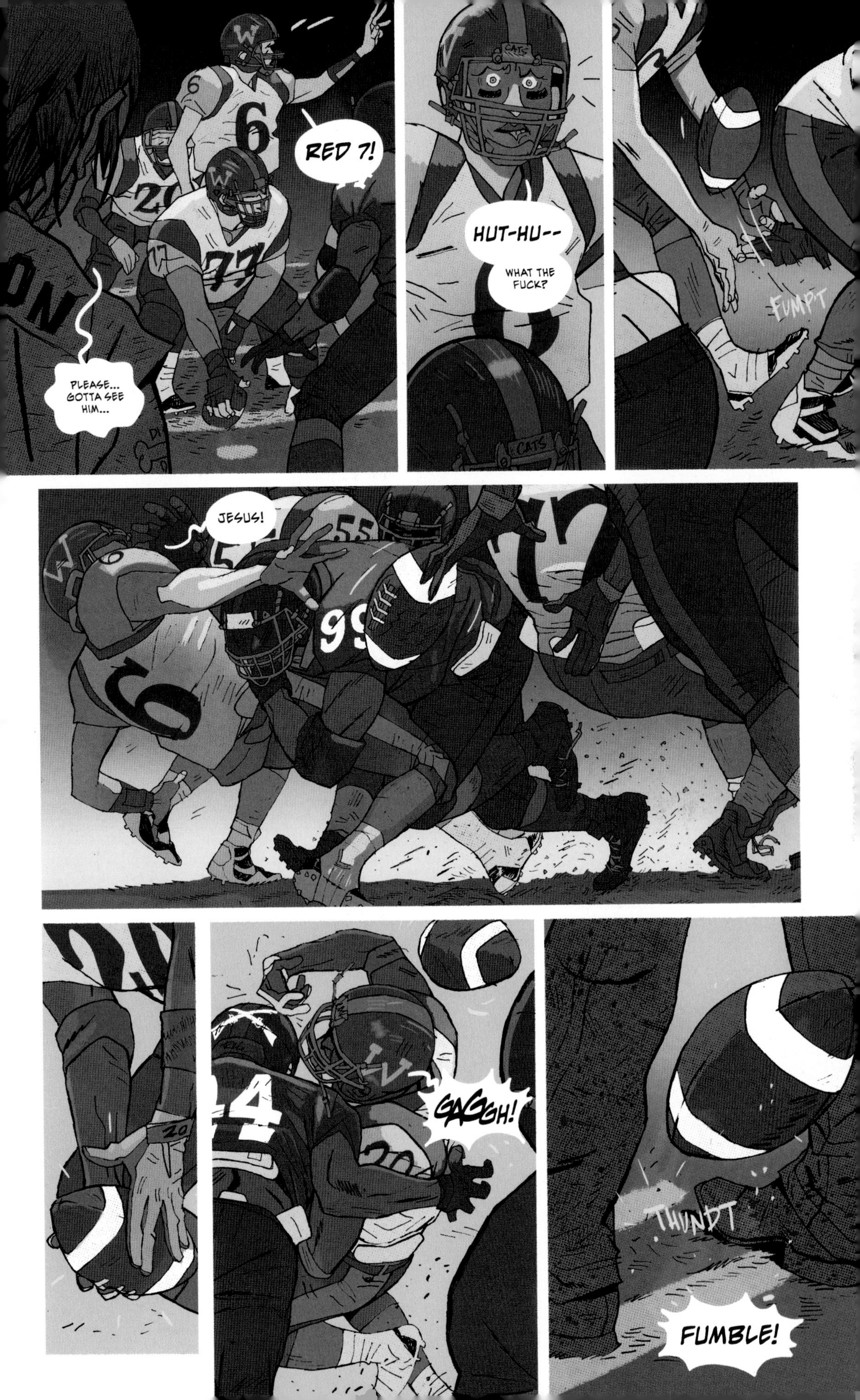
RED 7!
PLEASE... GOTTA SEE HIM...
HUT-HU--
WHAT THE FUCK?
FUMPT
JESUS!
GAGGH!
THUNDT
FUMBLE!

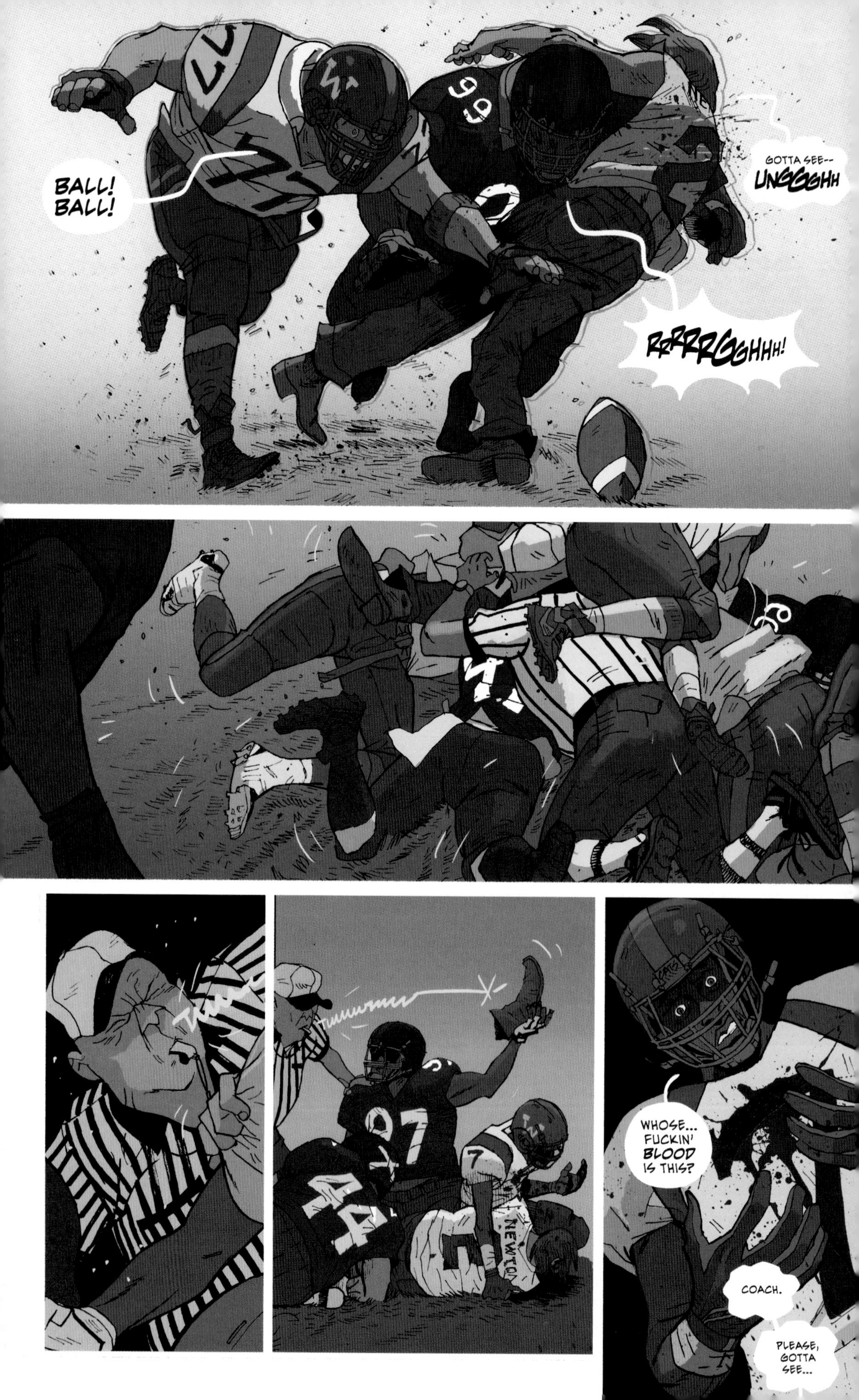
BALL! BALL!
GOTTA SEE-- UNGGGHH
RRRRRGGHHH!
WHOSE... FUCKIN' BLOOD IS THIS?
COACH.
PLEASE, GOTTA SEE...

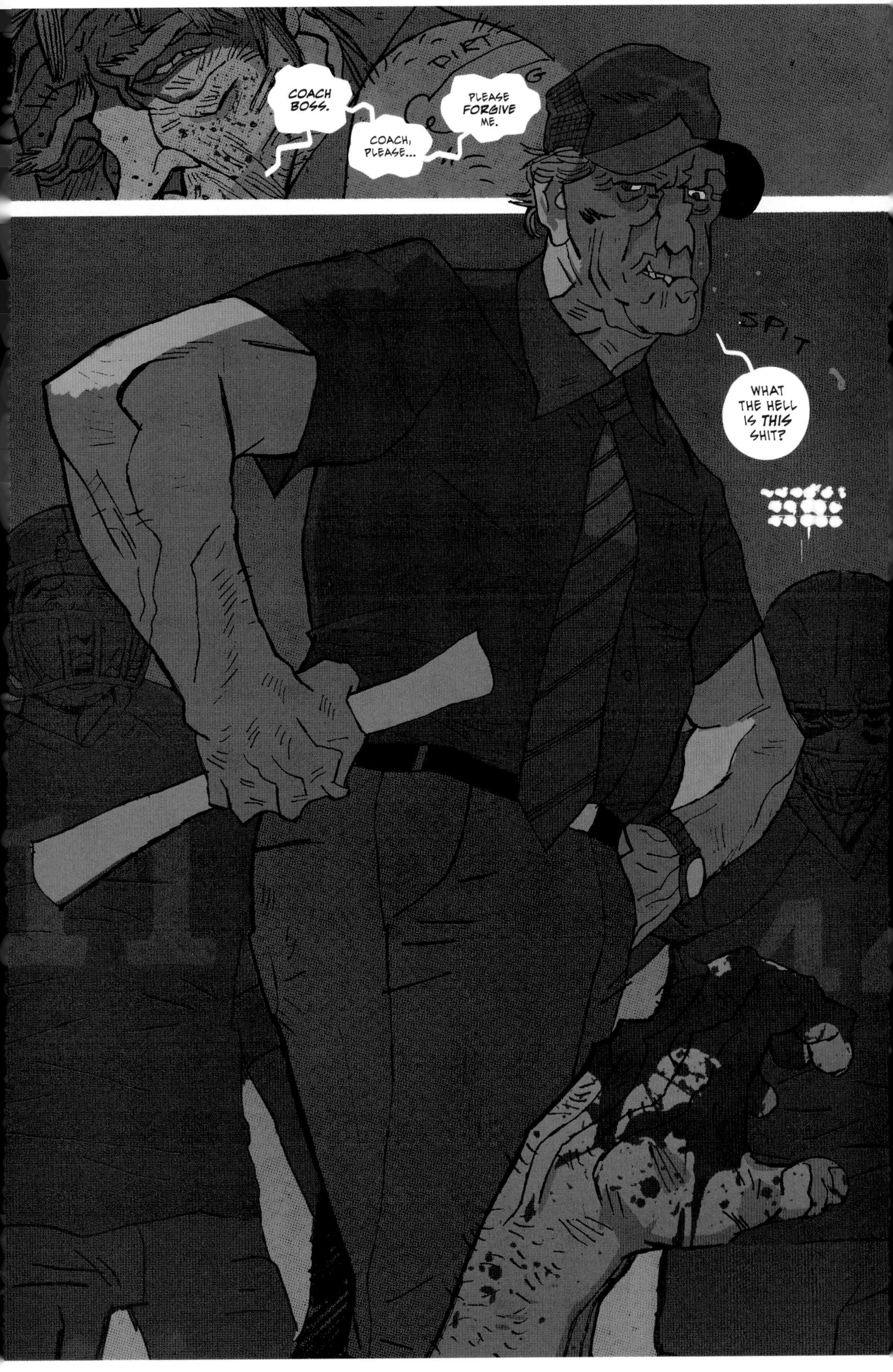
COACH BOSS.
COACH, PLEASE...
PLEASE FORGIVE ME.
SPIT
WHAT THE HELL IS THIS SHIT?

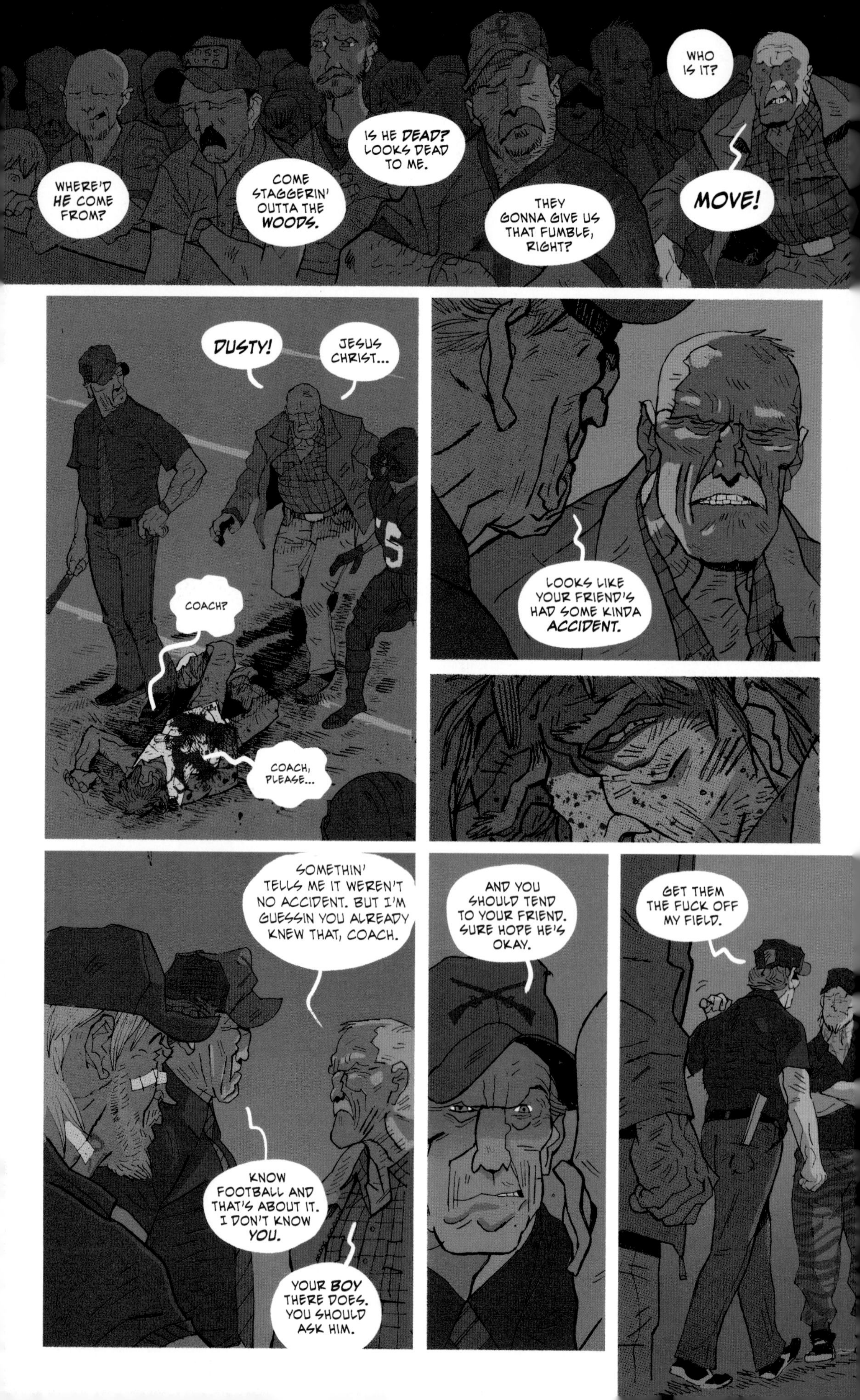
WHERE'D HE COME FROM?
COME STAGGERIN' OUTTA THE WOODS.
IS HE DEAD? LOOKS DEAD TO ME.
THEY GONNA GIVE US THAT FUMBLE, RIGHT?
WHO IS IT?
MOVE!
DUSTY!
JESUS CHRIST...
COACH?
COACH, PLEASE...
LOOKS LIKE YOUR FRIEND'S HAD SOME KINDA ACCIDENT.
SOMETHIN' TELLS ME IT WEREN'T NO ACCIDENT. BUT I'M GUESSIN YOU ALREADY KNEW THAT, COACH.
KNOW FOOTBALL AND THAT'S ABOUT IT. I DON'T KNOW YOU.
YOUR BOY THERE DOES. YOU SHOULD ASK HIM.
AND YOU SHOULD TEND TO YOUR FRIEND. SURE HOPE HE'S OKAY.
GET THEM THE FUCK OFF MY FIELD.

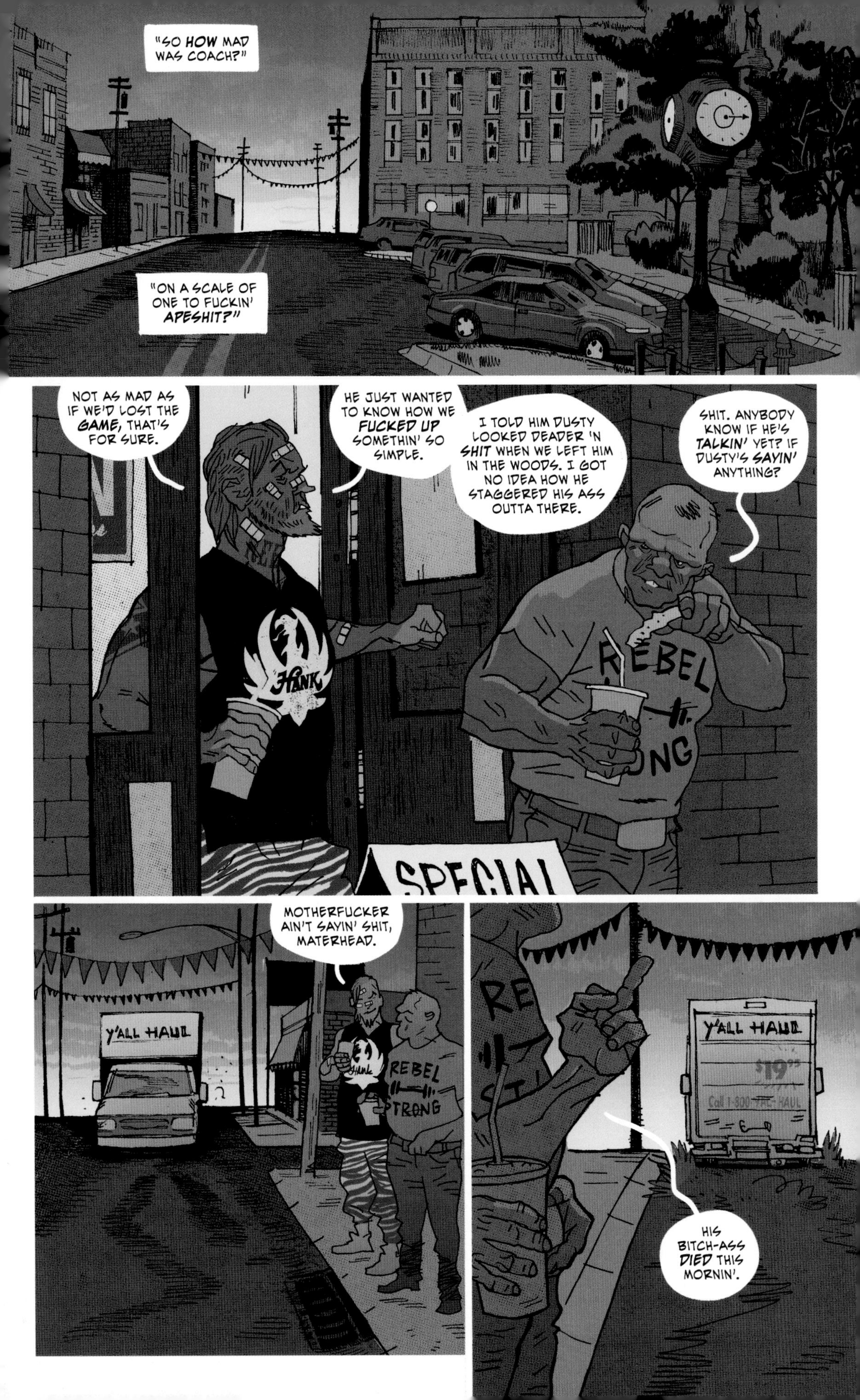
"SO HOW MAD WAS COACH?"
"ON A SCALE OF ONE TO FUCKIN' APESHIT?"
NOT AS MAD AS IF WE'D LOST THE GAME, THAT'S FOR SURE.
HE JUST WANTED TO KNOW HOW WE FUCKED UP SOMETHIN' SO SIMPLE.
I TOLD HIM DUSTY LOOKED DEADER 'N SHIT WHEN WE LEFT HIM IN THE WOODS. I GOT NO IDEA HOW HE STAGGERED HIS ASS OUTTA THERE.
SHIT. ANYBODY KNOW IF HE'S TALKIN' YET? IF DUSTY'S SAYIN' ANYTHING?
HANK
REBEL STRONG
SPECIAL
MOTHERFUCKER AIN'T SAYIN' SHIT, MATERHEAD.
Y'ALL HAUL
Y'ALL HAUL
$19.95
HIS BITCH-ASS DIED THIS MORNIN'.

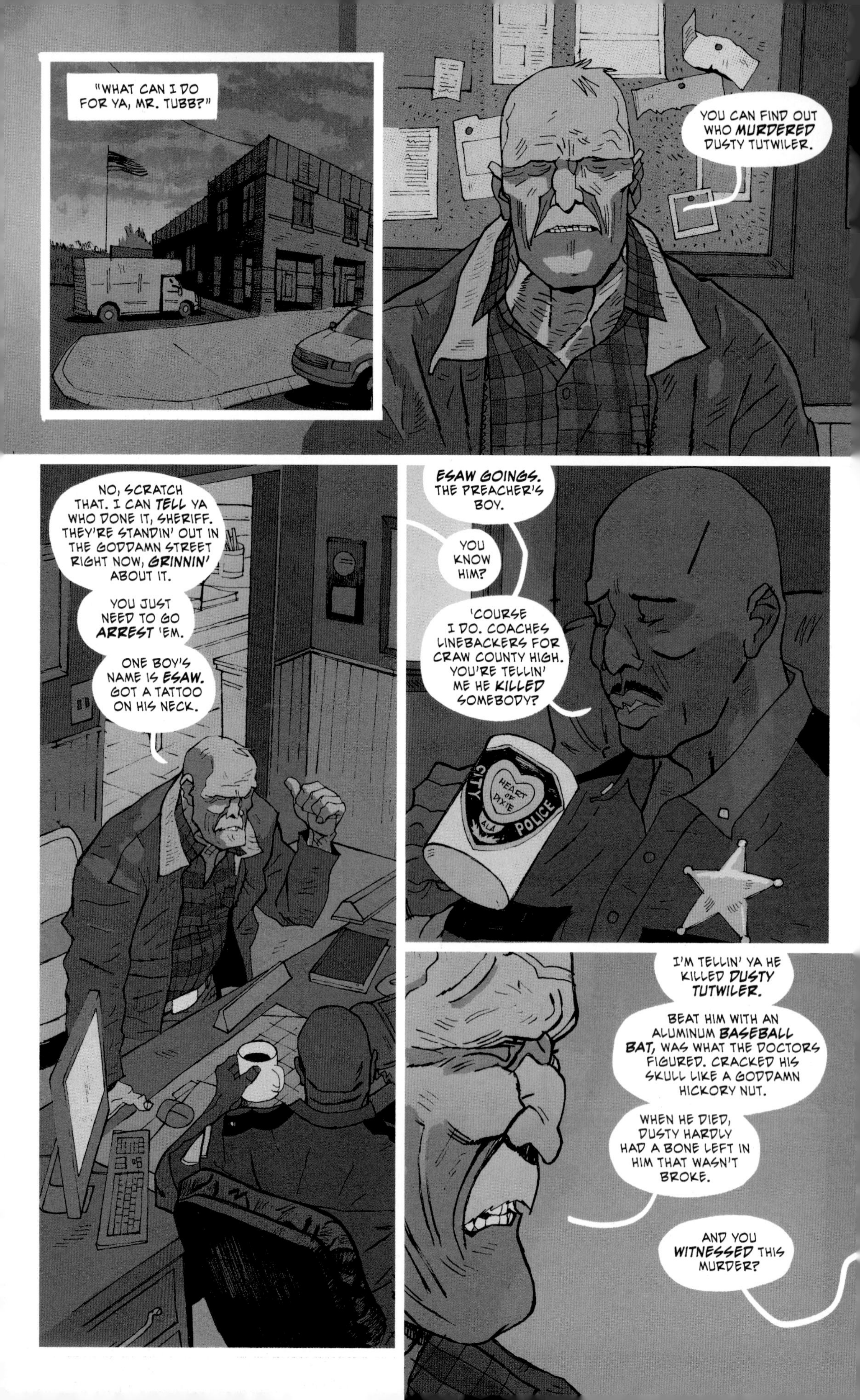
"WHAT CAN I DO FOR YA, MR. TUBB?"
YOU CAN FIND OUT WHO MURDERED DUSTY TUTWILER.
NO, SCRATCH THAT. I CAN TELL YA WHO DONE IT, SHERIFF. THEY'RE STANDIN' OUT IN THE GODDAMN STREET RIGHT NOW, GRINNIN' ABOUT IT.
YOU JUST NEED TO GO ARREST 'EM.
ONE BOY'S NAME IS ESAW. GOT A TATTOO ON HIS NECK.
ESAW GOINGS. THE PREACHER'S BOY.
YOU KNOW HIM?
'COURSE I DO. COACHES LINEBACKERS FOR CRAW COUNTY HIGH. YOU'RE TELLIN' ME HE KILLED SOMEBODY?
CITY
HEART OF DIXIE
ALA
POLICE
I'M TELLIN' YA HE KILLED DUSTY TUTWILER.
BEAT HIM WITH AN ALUMINUM BASEBALL BAT, WAS WHAT THE DOCTORS FIGURED. CRACKED HIS SKULL LIKE A GODDAMN HICKORY NUT.
WHEN HE DIED, DUSTY HARDLY HAD A BONE LEFT IN HIM THAT WASN'T BROKE.
AND YOU WITNESSED THIS MURDER?

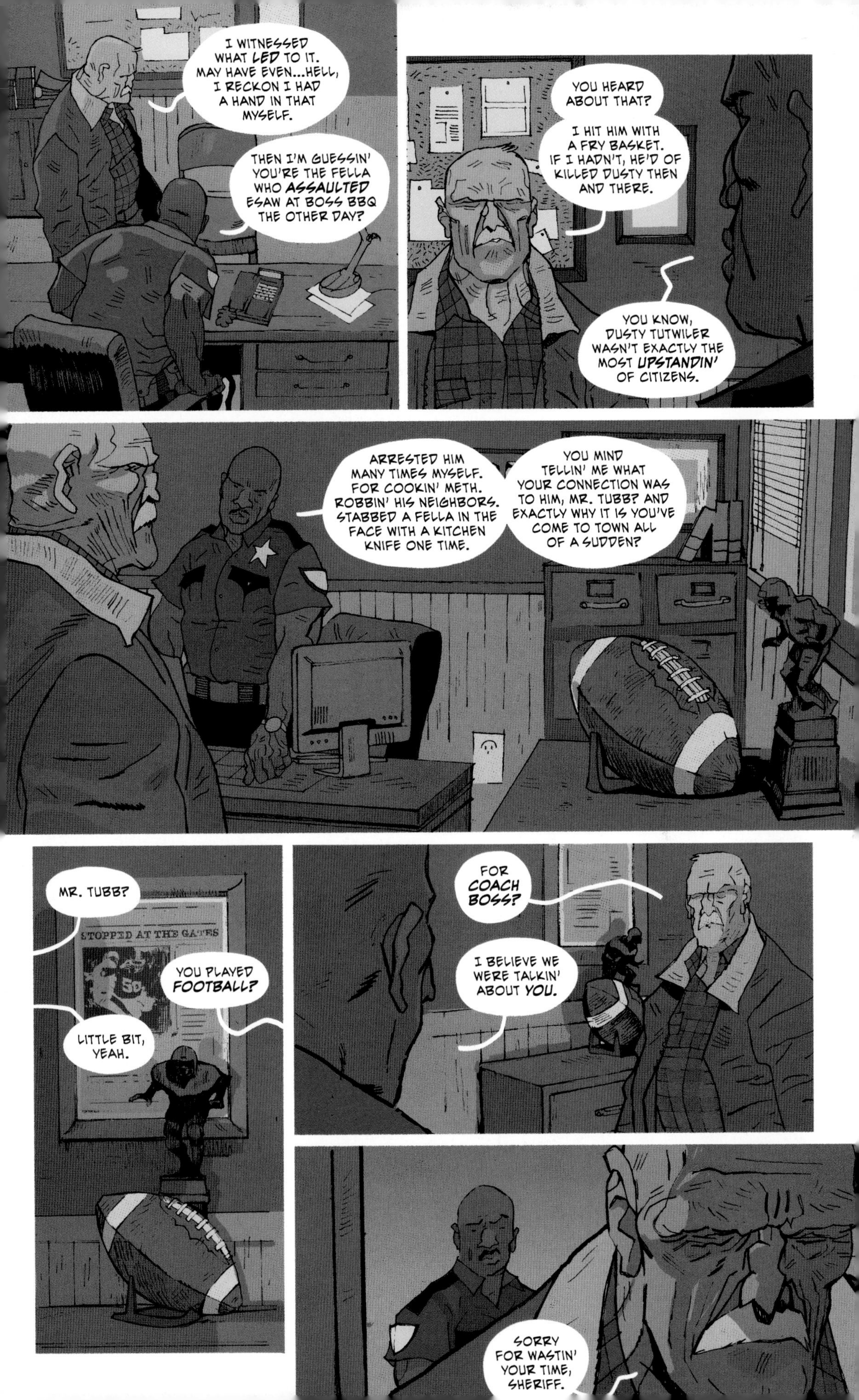
I WITNESSED WHAT LED TO IT. MAY HAVE EVEN...HELL, I RECKON I HAD A HAND IN THAT MYSELF.
THEN I'M GUESSIN' YOU'RE THE FELLA WHO ASSAULTED ESAW AT BOSS BBQ THE OTHER DAY?
YOU HEARD ABOUT THAT?
I HIT HIM WITH A FRY BASKET. IF I HADN'T, HE'D OF KILLED DUSTY THEN AND THERE.
YOU KNOW, DUSTY TUTWILER WASN'T EXACTLY THE MOST UPSTANDIN' OF CITIZENS.
ARRESTED HIM MANY TIMES MYSELF. FOR COOKIN' METH. ROBBIN' HIS NEIGHBORS. STABBED A FELLA IN THE FACE WITH A KITCHEN KNIFE ONE TIME.
YOU MIND TELLIN' ME WHAT YOUR CONNECTION WAS TO HIM, MR. TUBB? AND EXACTLY WHY IT IS YOU'VE COME TO TOWN ALL OF A SUDDEN?
MR. TUBB?
STOPPED AT THE GATES
YOU PLAYED FOOTBALL?
LITTLE BIT, YEAH.
FOR COACH BOSS?
I BELIEVE WE WERE TALKIN' ABOUT YOU.
SORRY FOR WASTIN' YOUR TIME, SHERIFF.

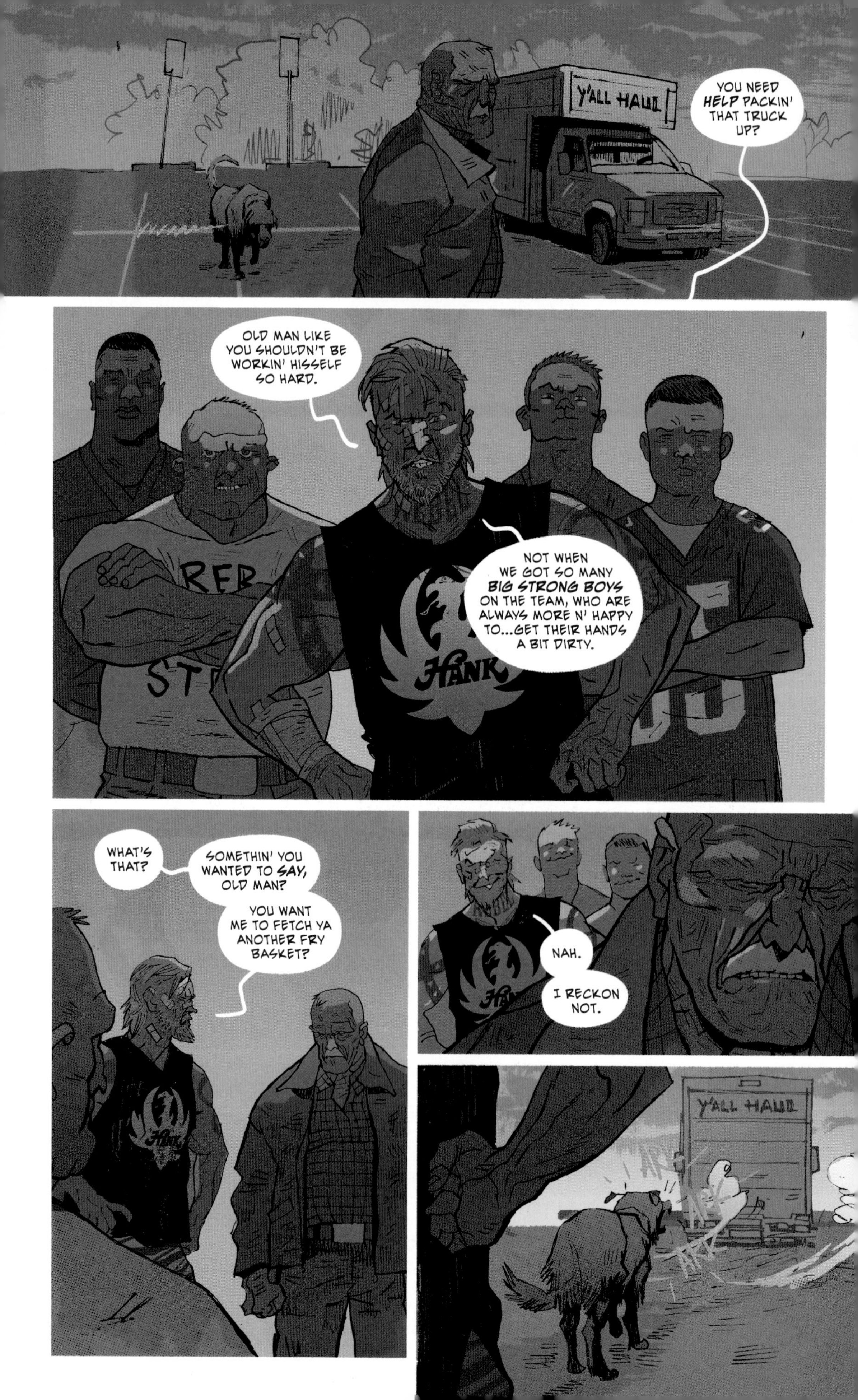
Y'ALL HAUL
YOU NEED HELP PACKIN' THAT TRUCK UP?
OLD MAN LIKE YOU SHOULDN'T BE WORKIN' HISSELF SO HARD.
NOT WHEN WE GOT SO MANY BIG STRONG BOYS ON THE TEAM, WHO ARE ALWAYS MORE N' HAPPY TO...GET THEIR HANDS A BIT DIRTY.
HANK
WHAT'S THAT?
SOMETHIN' YOU WANTED TO SAY, OLD MAN?
YOU WANT ME TO FETCH YA ANOTHER FRY BASKET?
NAH.
I RECKON NOT.
Y'ALL HAUL
ARF
ARF
ARF

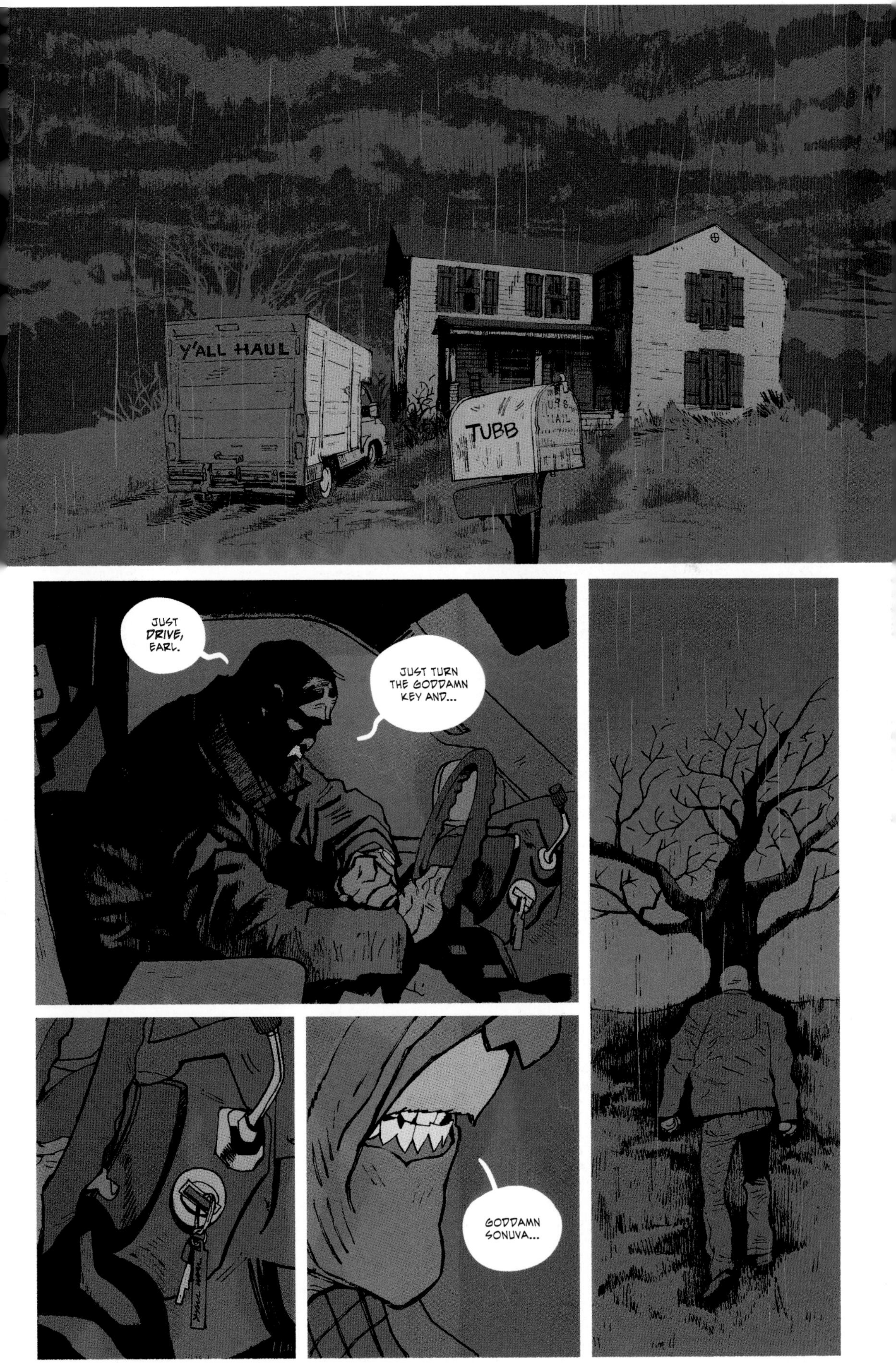
Y'ALL HAUL
TUBB
U.S. MAIL
JUST DRIVE, EARL.
JUST TURN THE GODDAMN KEY AND...
GODDAMN SONUVA...

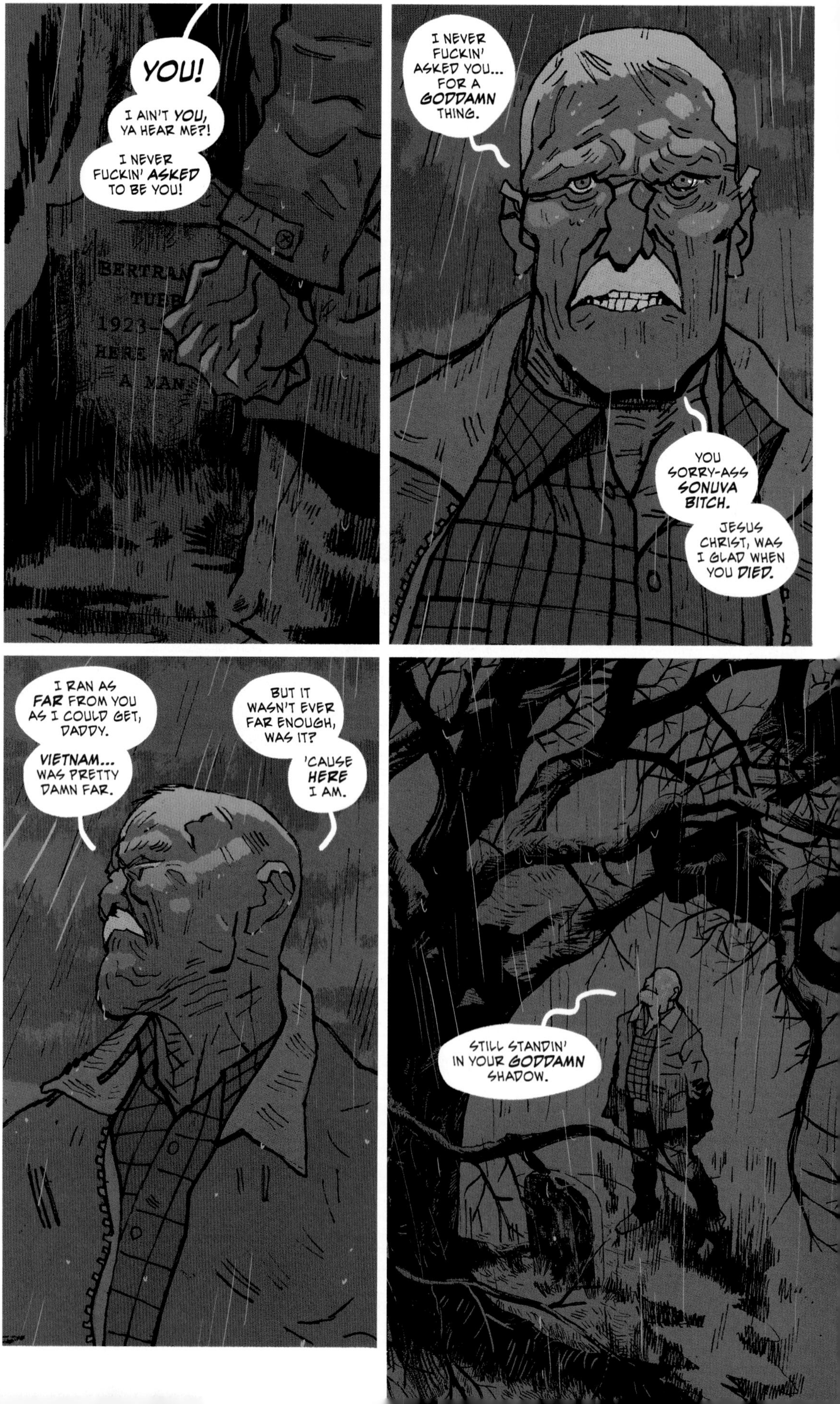
YOU!
I AIN'T YOU, YA HEAR ME?!
I NEVER FUCKIN' ASKED TO BE YOU!
I NEVER FUCKIN' ASKED YOU... FOR A GODDAMN THING.
YOU SORRY-ASS SONUVA BITCH.
JESUS CHRIST, WAS I GLAD WHEN YOU DIED.
I RAN AS FAR FROM YOU AS I COULD GET, DADDY.
VIETNAM... WAS PRETTY DAMN FAR.
BUT IT WASN'T EVER FAR ENOUGH, WAS IT?
'CAUSE HERE I AM.
STILL STANDIN' IN YOUR GODDAMN SHADOW.

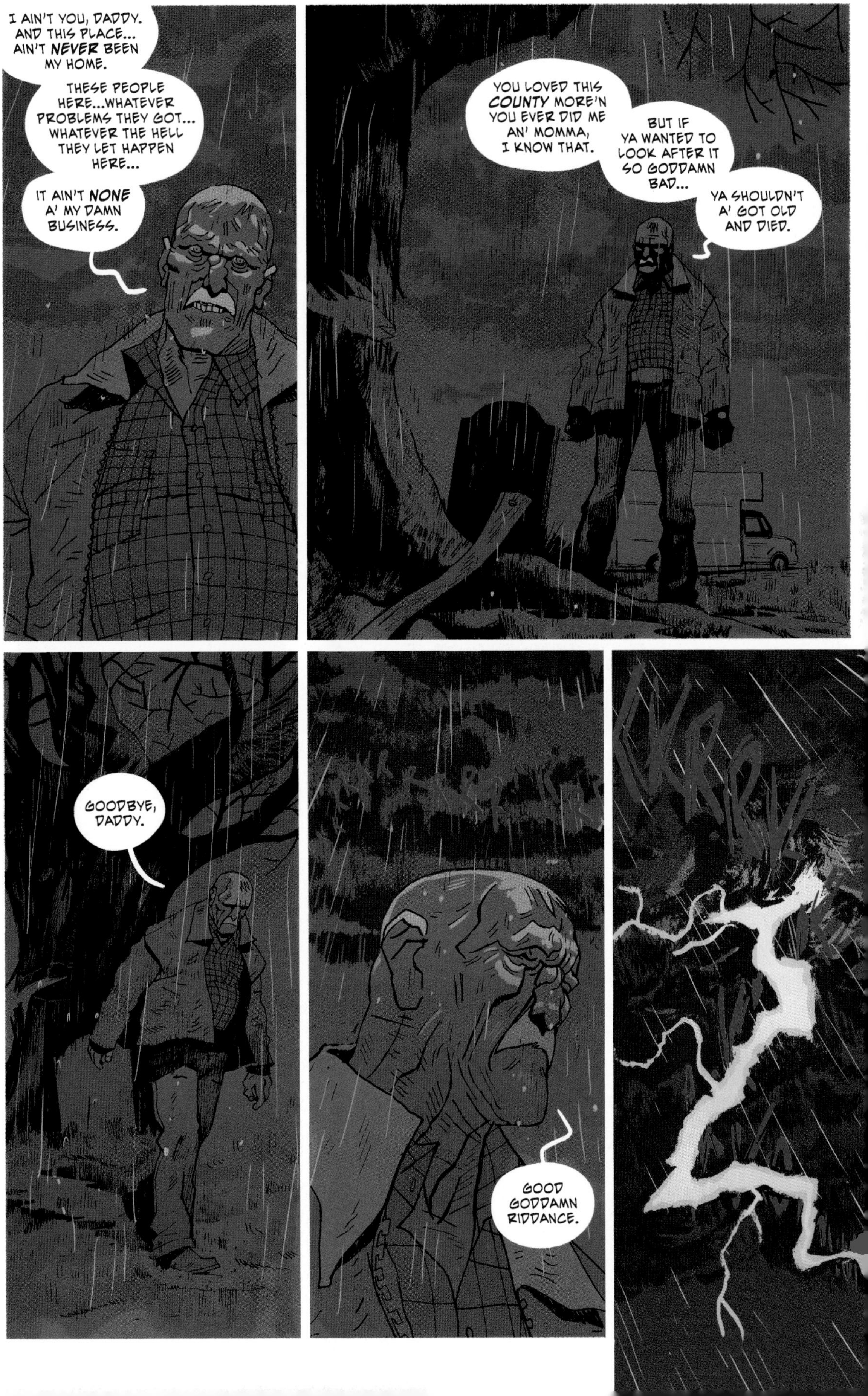
I AIN'T YOU, DADDY. AND THIS PLACE... AIN'T NEVER BEEN MY HOME.
THESE PEOPLE HERE...WHATEVER PROBLEMS THEY GOT... WHATEVER THE HELL THEY LET HAPPEN HERE...
IT AIN'T NONE A' MY DAMN BUSINESS.
YOU LOVED THIS COUNTY MORE'N YOU EVER DID ME AN' MOMMA, I KNOW THAT.
BUT IF YA WANTED TO LOOK AFTER IT SO GODDAMN BAD...
YA SHOULDN'T A' GOT OLD AND DIED.
GOODBYE, DADDY.
GOOD GODDAMN RIDDANCE.

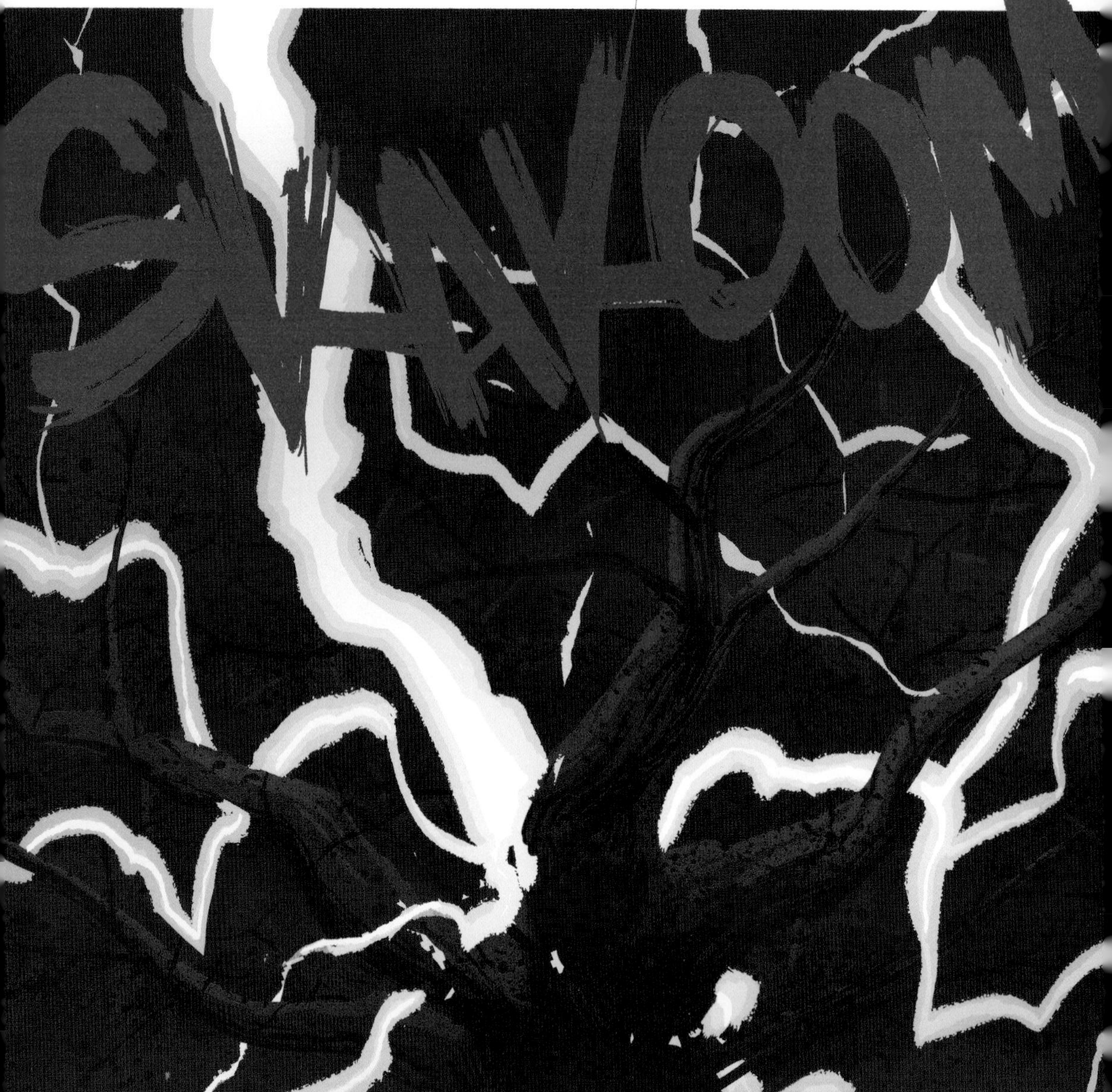
SHAVOOM

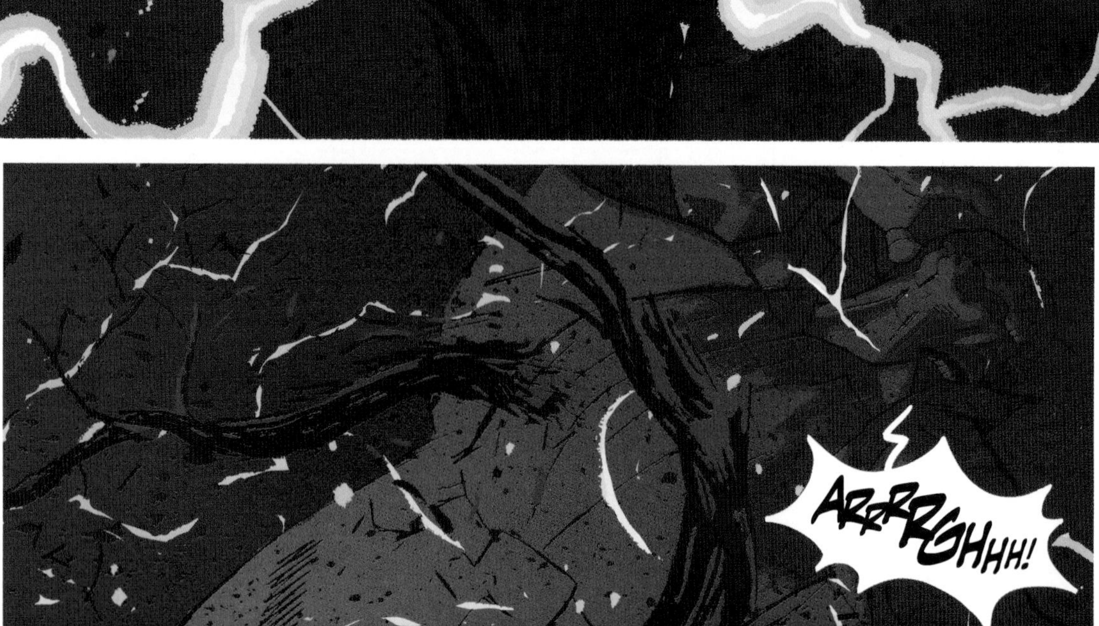
ARRRRGHHH!

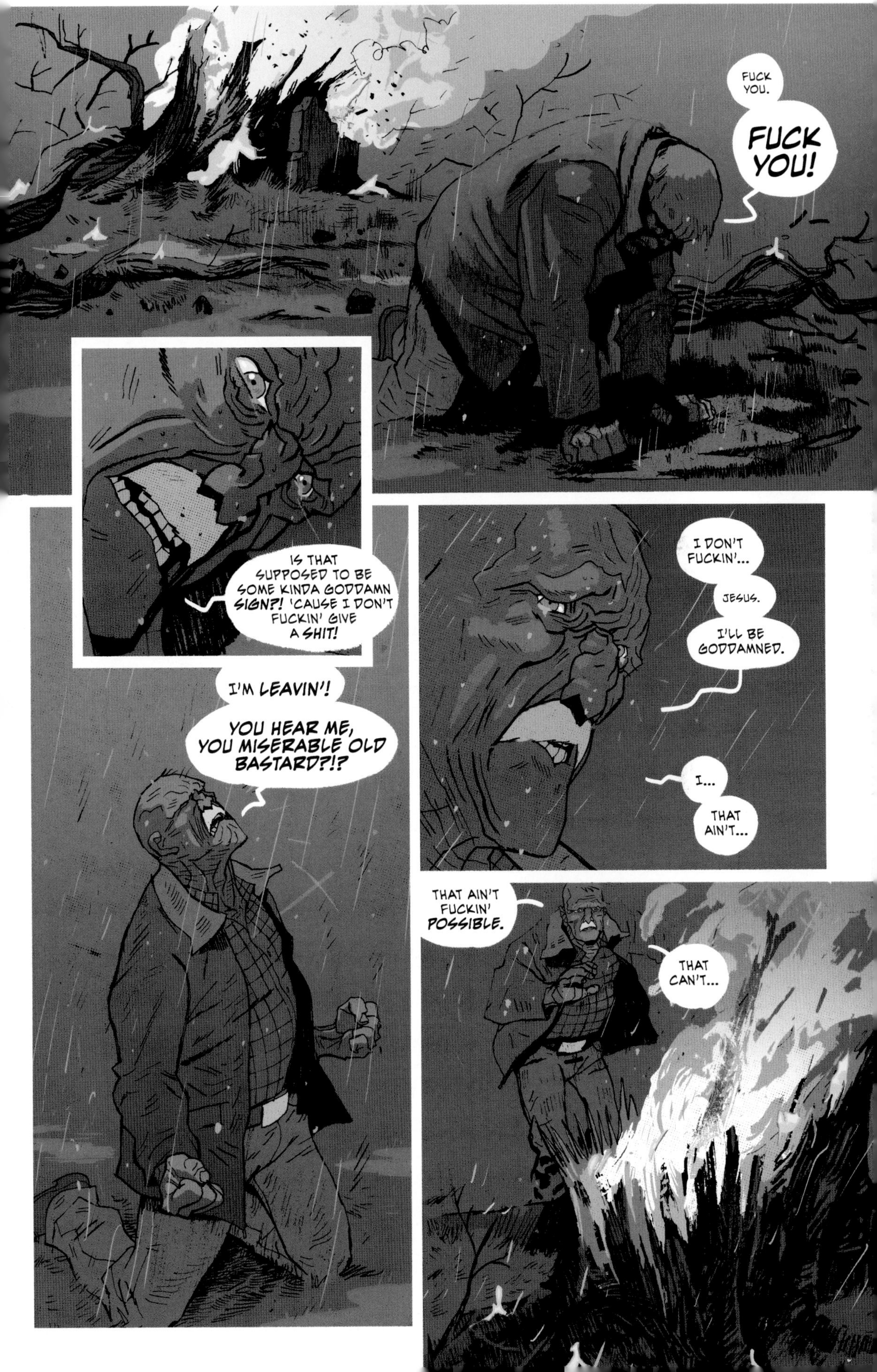
FUCK YOU.
FUCK YOU!
IS THAT SUPPOSED TO BE SOME KINDA GODDAMN SIGN?! 'CAUSE I DON'T FUCKIN' GIVE A SHIT!
I'M LEAVIN'!
YOU HEAR ME, YOU MISERABLE OLD BASTARD?!?
I DON'T FUCKIN'...
JESUS.
I'LL BE GODDAMNED.
I...
THAT AIN'T...
THAT AIN'T FUCKIN' POSSIBLE.
THAT CAN'T...

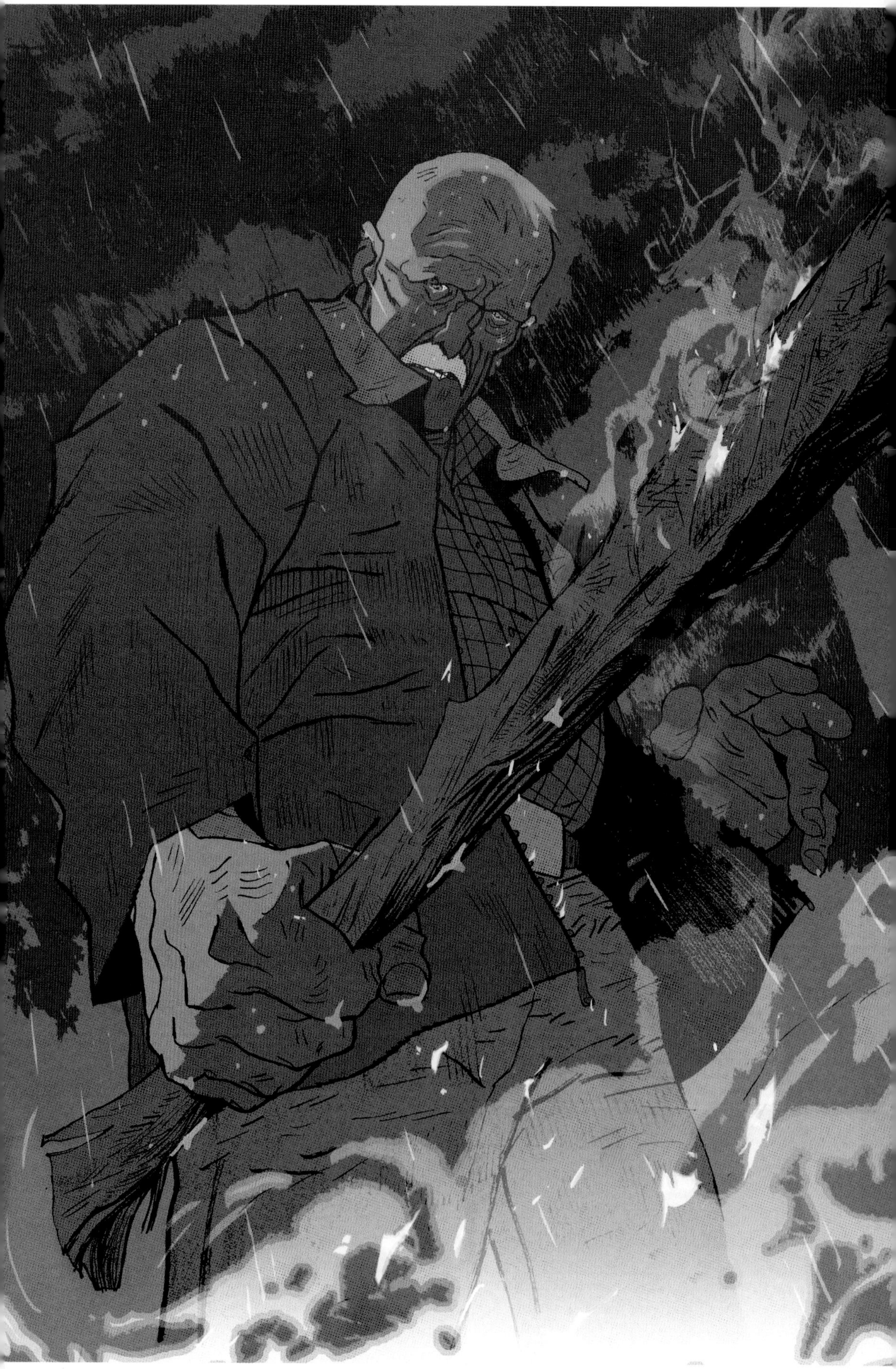

Here Was a Man

Chapter Three

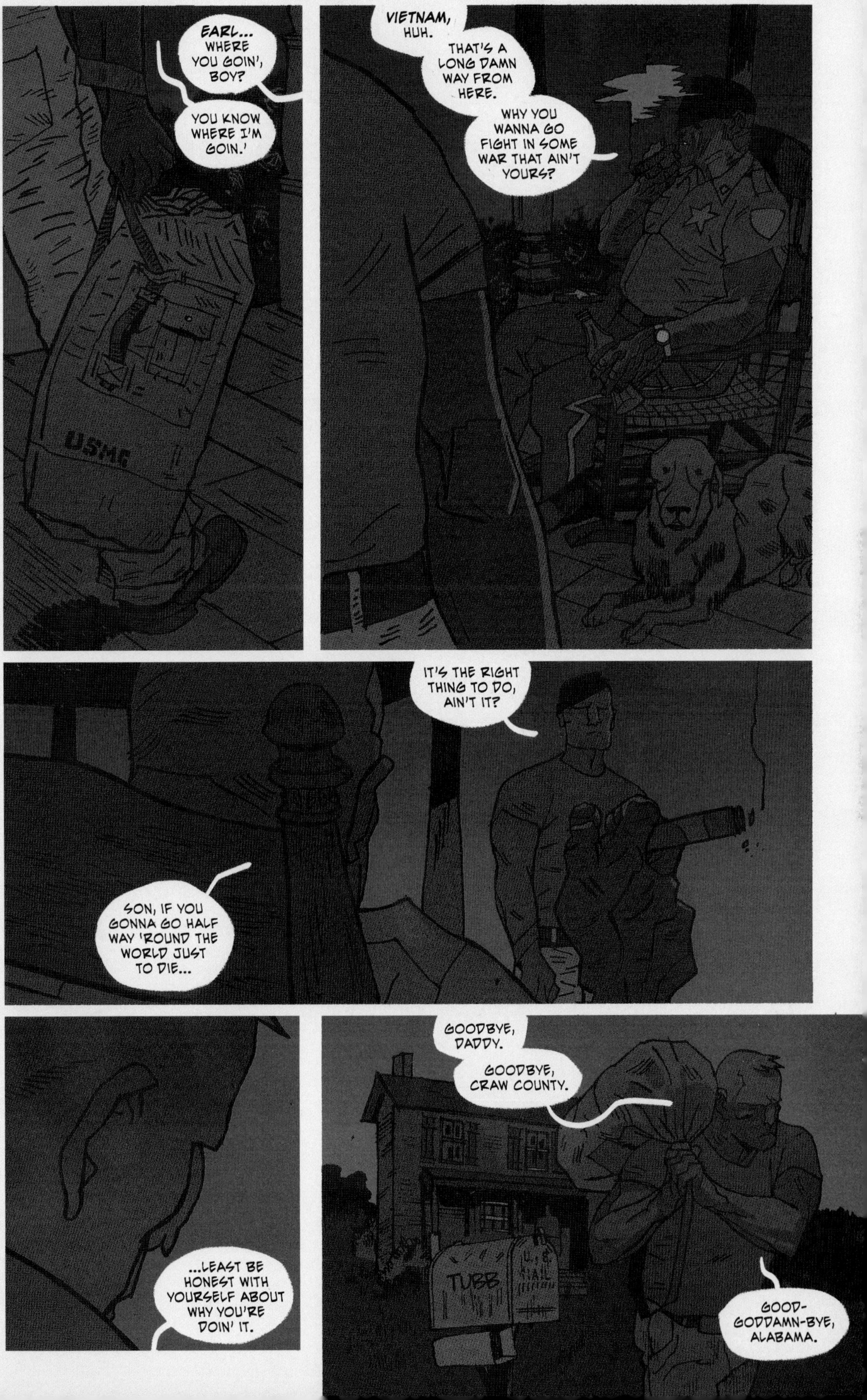
EARL... WHERE YOU GOIN', BOY?
YOU KNOW WHERE I'M GOIN.'
USMC
VIETNAM, HUH.
THAT'S A LONG DAMN WAY FROM HERE.
WHY YOU WANNA GO FIGHT IN SOME WAR THAT AIN'T YOURS?
IT'S THE RIGHT THING TO DO, AIN'T IT?
SON, IF YOU GONNA GO HALF WAY 'ROUND THE WORLD JUST TO DIE...
...LEAST BE HONEST WITH YOURSELF ABOUT WHY YOU'RE DOIN' IT.
GOODBYE, DADDY.
GOODBYE, CRAW COUNTY.
TUBB
GOOD-GODDAMN-BYE, ALABAMA.

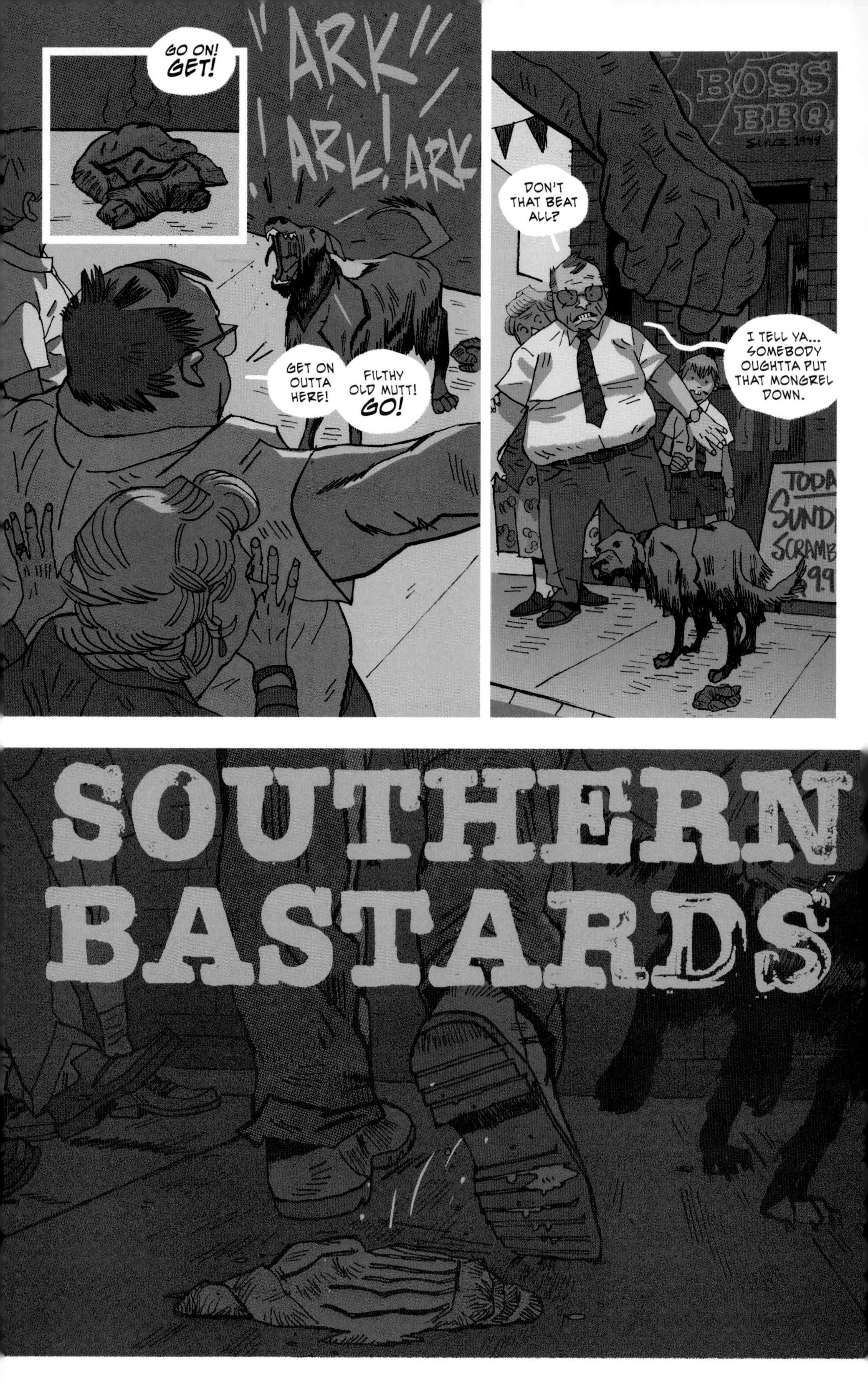
GO ON! GET!
ARK! ARK! ARK
GET ON OUTTA HERE!
FILTHY OLD MUTT! GO!
BOSS BBQ
DON'T THAT BEAT ALL?
I TELL YA... SOMEBODY OUGHTTA PUT THAT MONGREL DOWN.
SOUTHERN BASTARDS

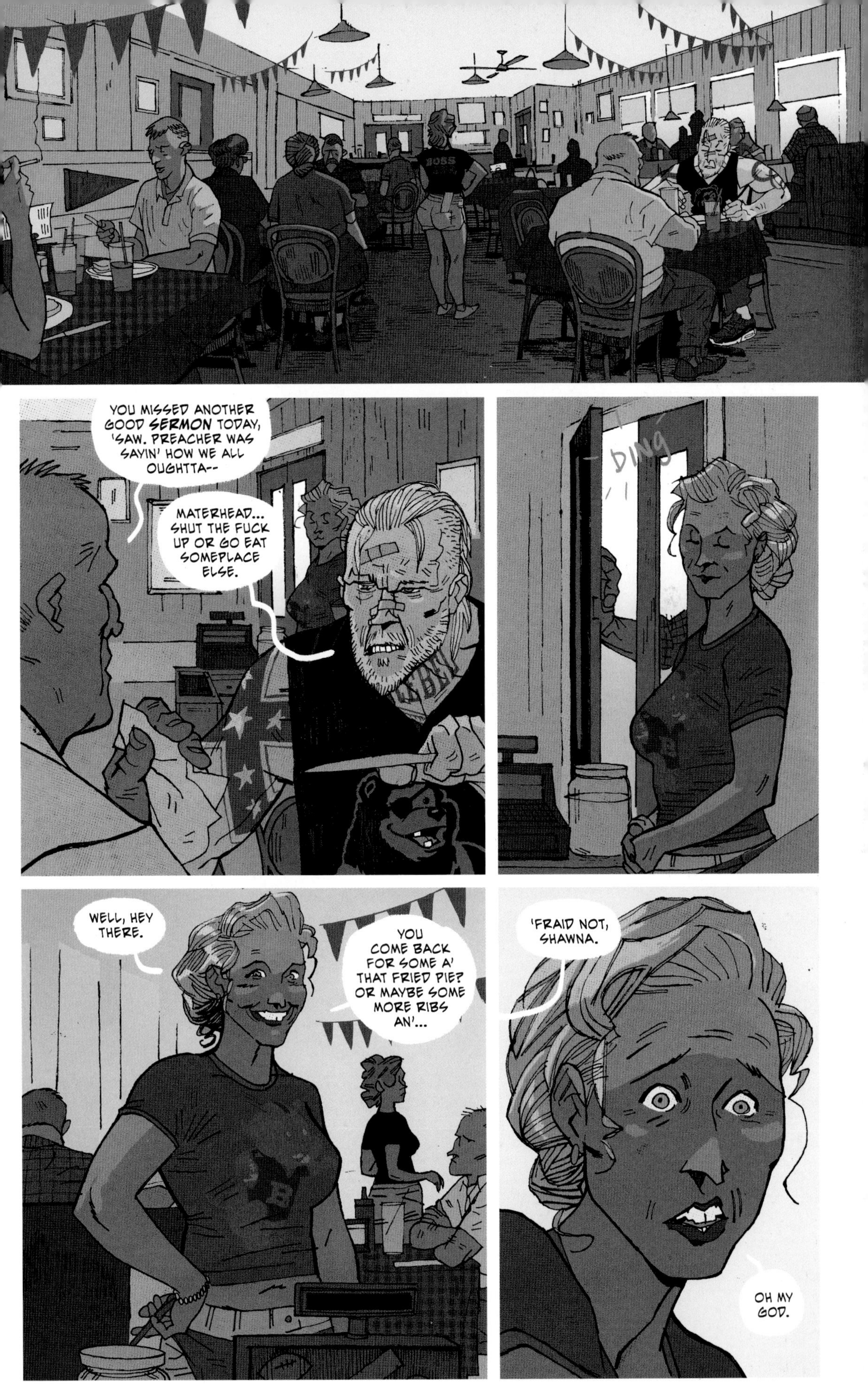

YOU MISSED ANOTHER GOOD SERMON TODAY, 'SAW. PREACHER WAS SAYIN' HOW WE ALL OUGHTTA--
MATERHEAD... SHUT THE FUCK UP OR GO EAT SOMEPLACE ELSE.
DING
WELL, HEY THERE.
YOU COME BACK FOR SOME A' THAT FRIED PIE? OR MAYBE SOME MORE RIBS AN'...
'FRAID NOT, SHAWNA.
OH MY GOD.

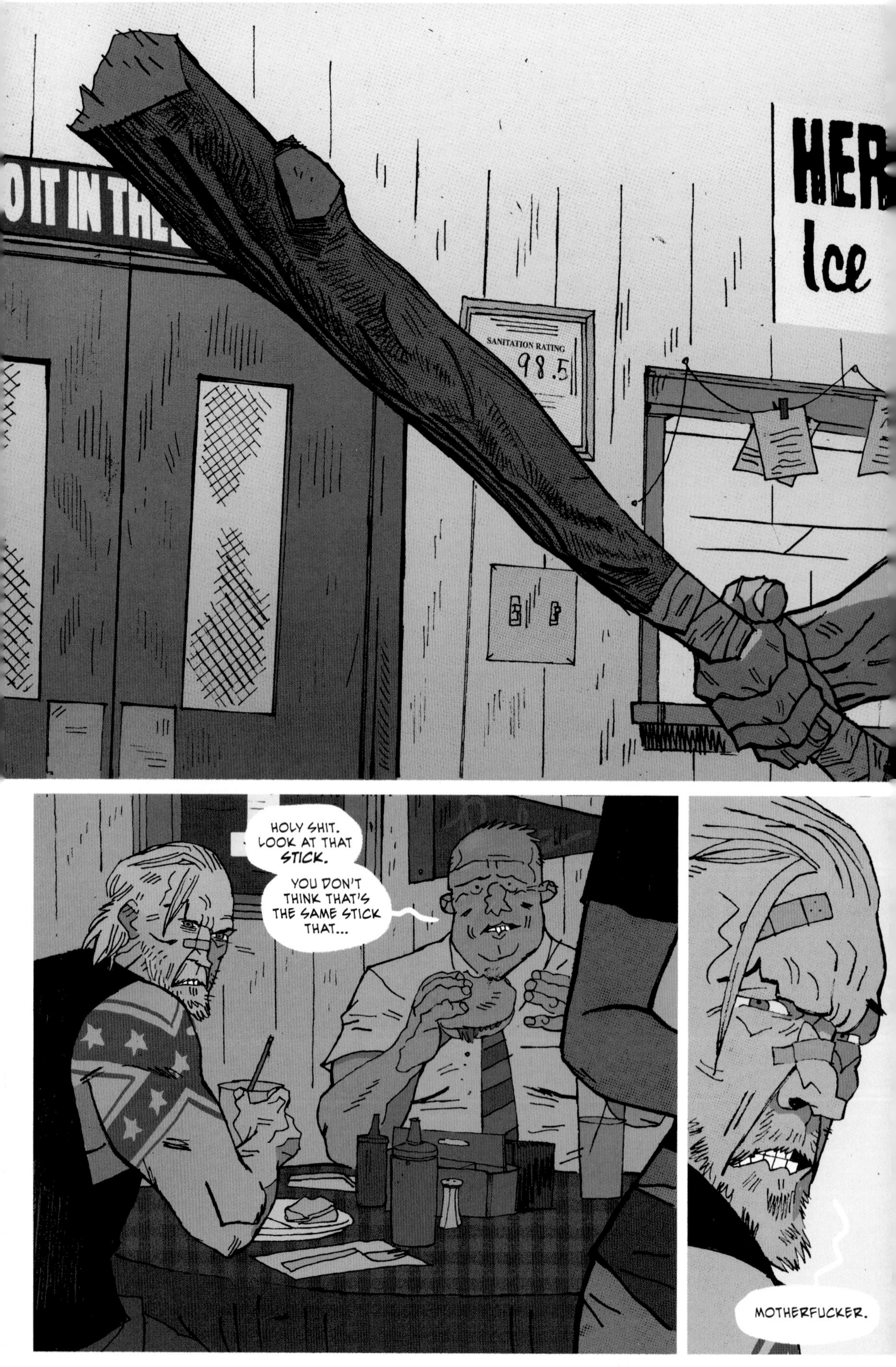
O IT IN THE
SANITATION RATING
98.5
HER
Ice
HOLY SHIT. LOOK AT THAT STICK.
YOU DON'T THINK THAT'S THE SAME STICK THAT...
MOTHERFUCKER.

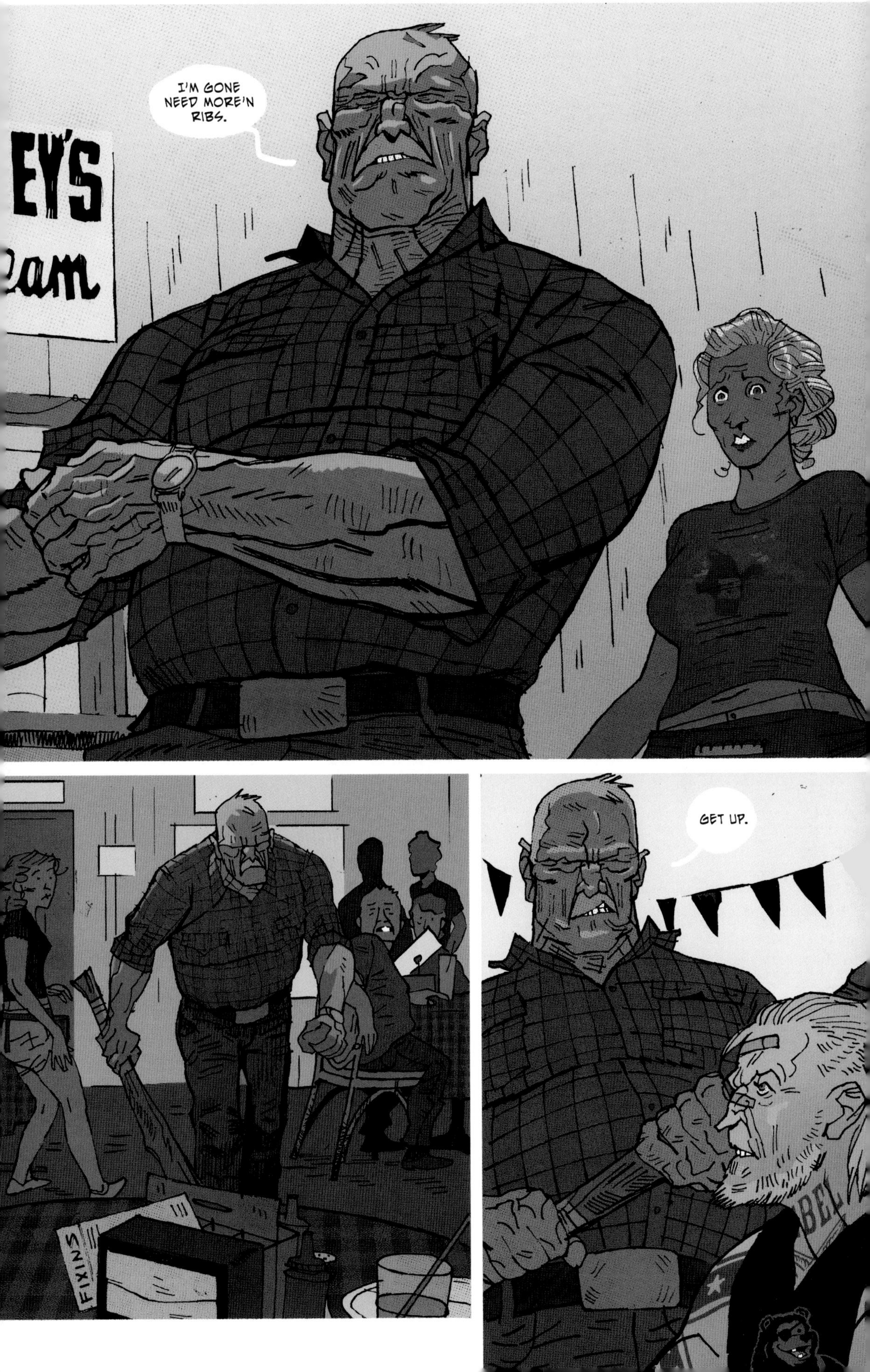
I'M GONE NEED MORE'N RIBS.
FIXINS
GET UP.

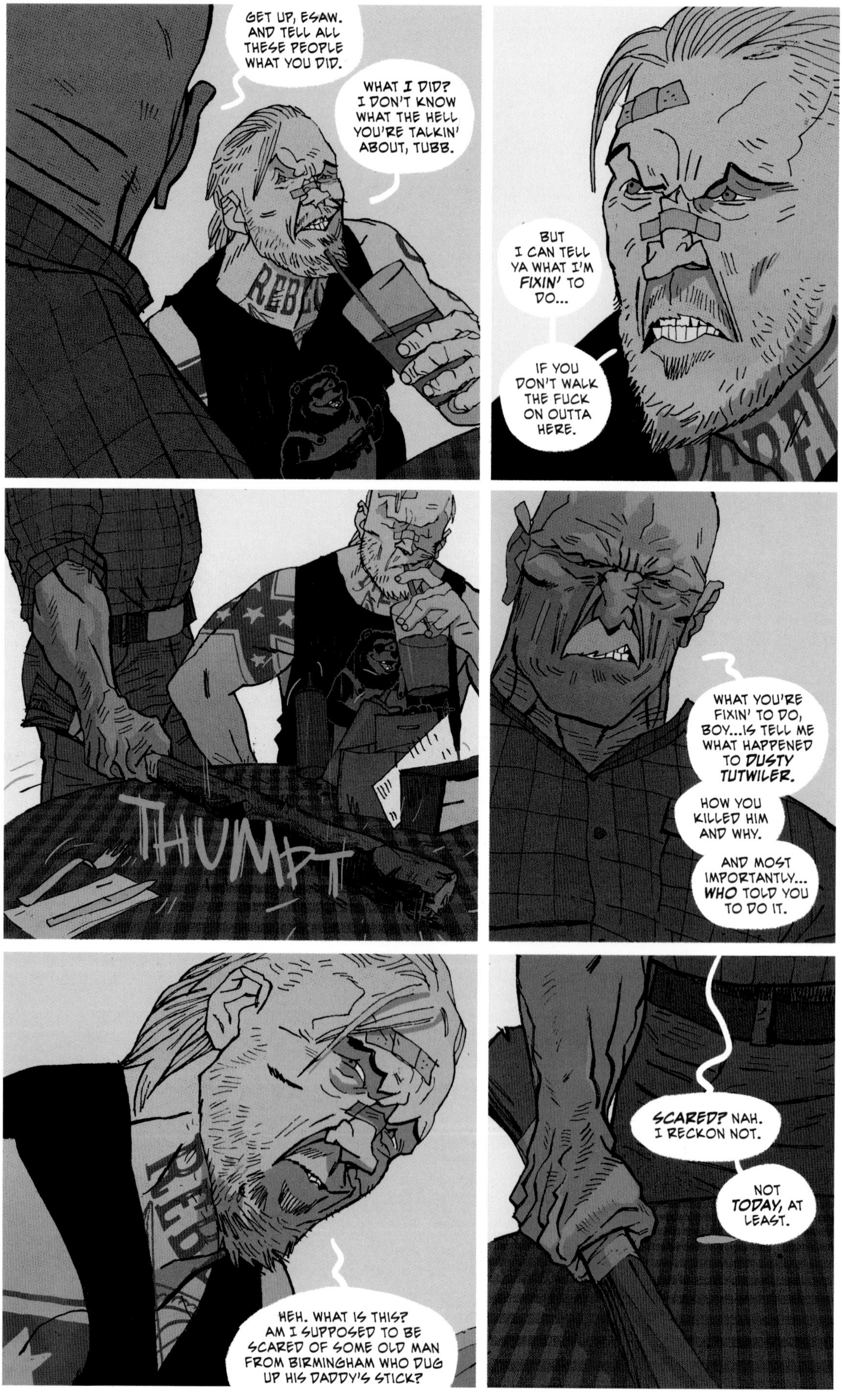
GET UP, ESAW. AND TELL ALL THESE PEOPLE WHAT YOU DID.
WHAT I DID? I DON'T KNOW WHAT THE HELL YOU'RE TALKIN' ABOUT, TUBB.
BUT I CAN TELL YA WHAT I'M FIXIN' TO DO...
IF YOU DON'T WALK THE FUCK ON OUTTA HERE.
THUMPT
WHAT YOU'RE FIXIN' TO DO, BOY...IS TELL ME WHAT HAPPENED TO DUSTY TUTWILER.
HOW YOU KILLED HIM AND WHY.
AND MOST IMPORTANTLY... WHO TOLD YOU TO DO IT.
HEH. WHAT IS THIS? AM I SUPPOSED TO BE SCARED OF SOME OLD MAN FROM BIRMINGHAM WHO DUG UP HIS DADDY'S STICK?
SCARED? NAH. I RECKON NOT.
NOT TODAY, AT LEAST.

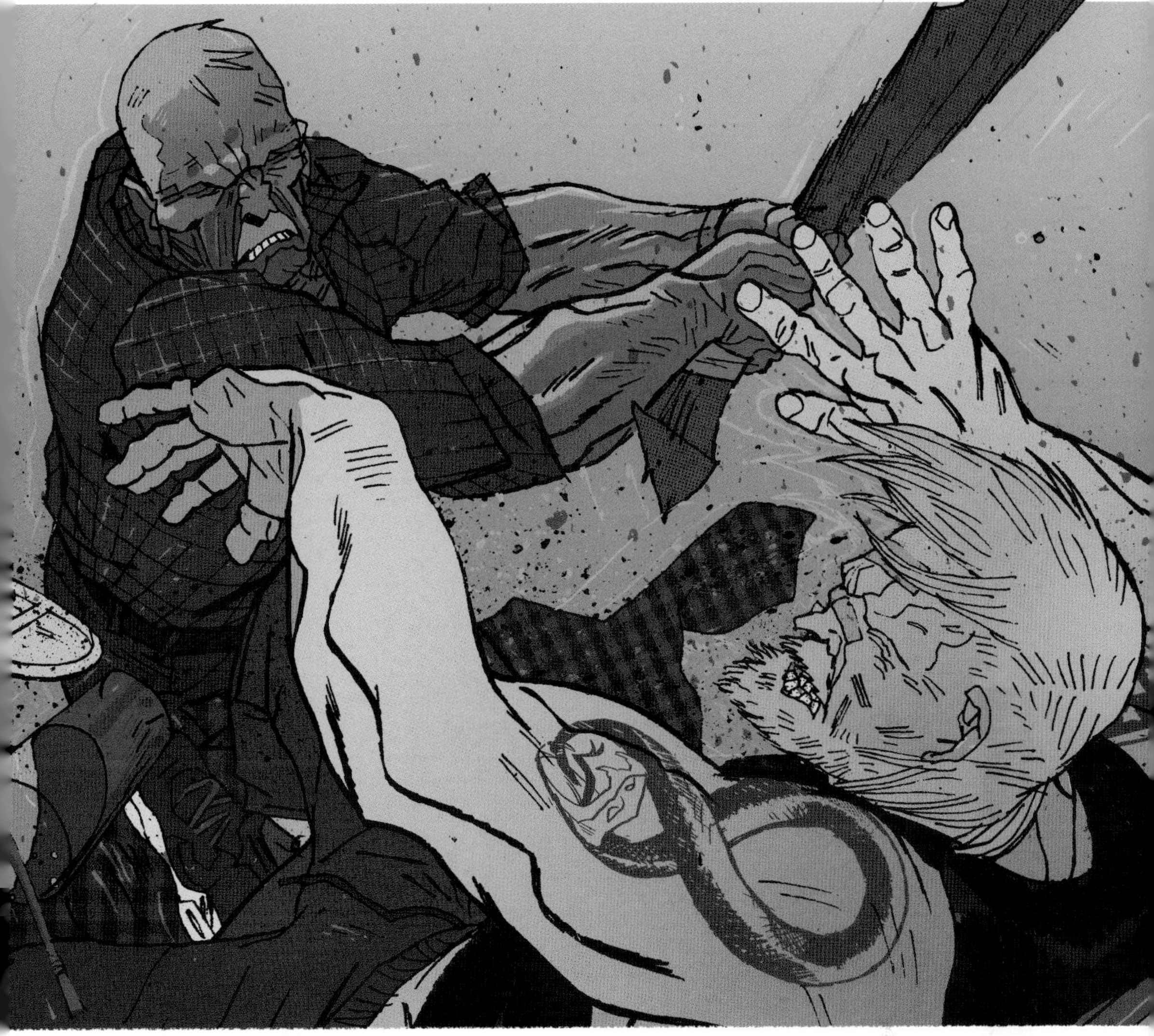

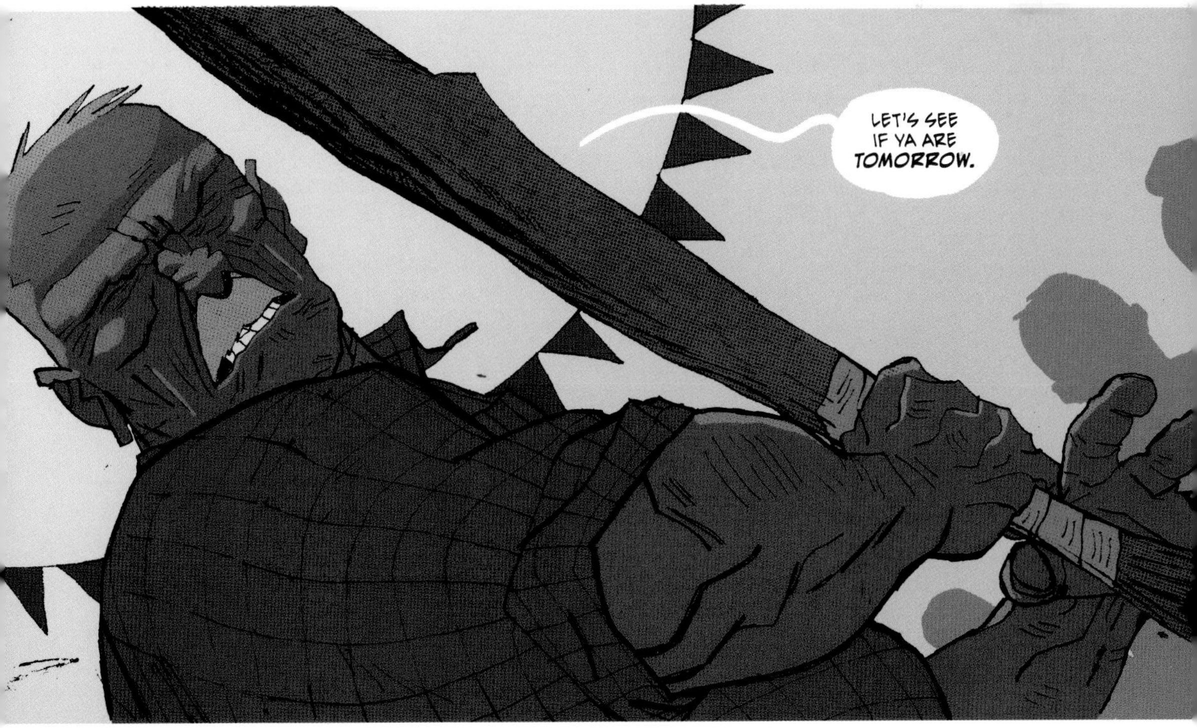
LET'S SEE IF YA ARE TOMORROW.

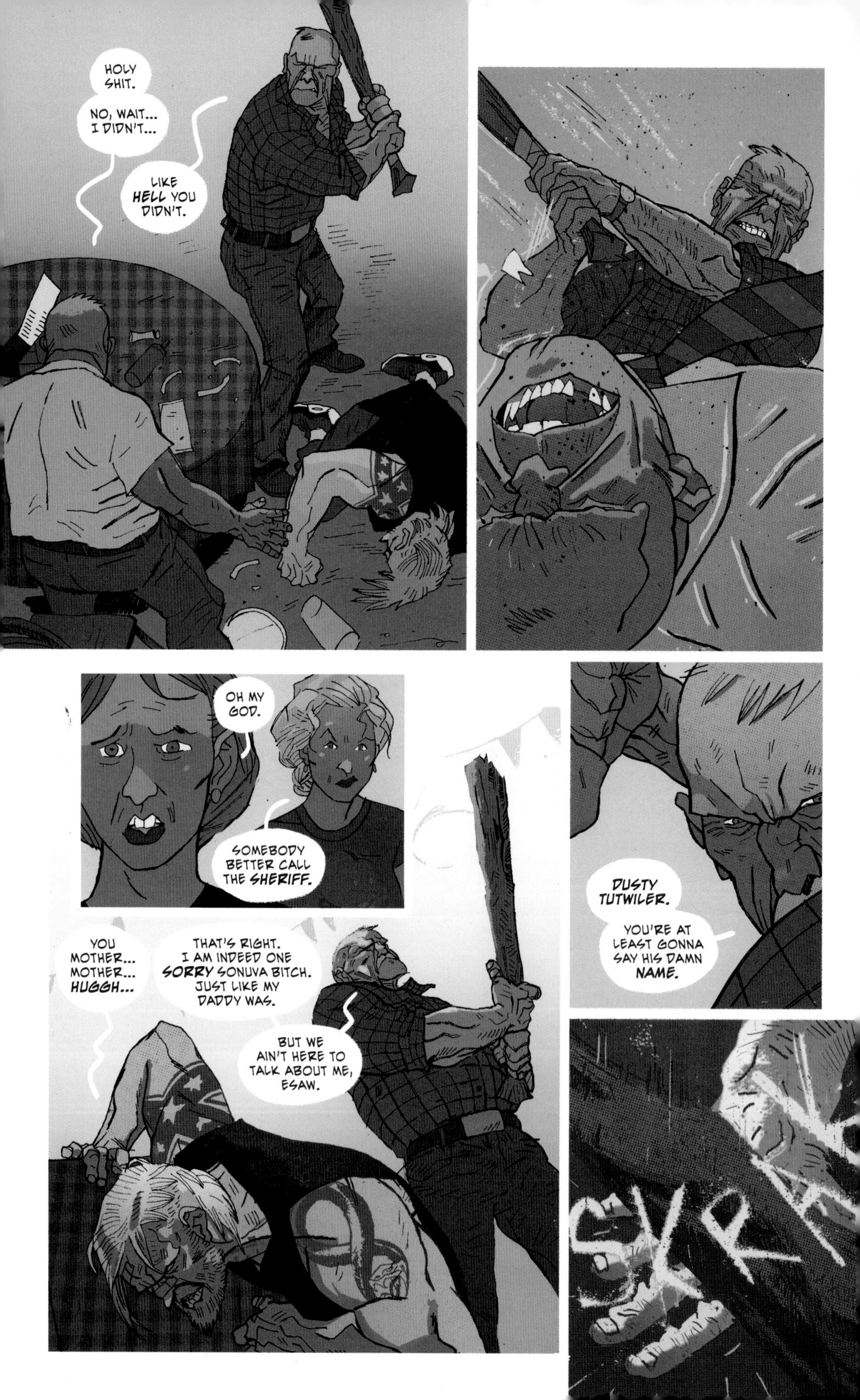
HOLY SHIT.
NO, WAIT... I DIDN'T...
LIKE HELL YOU DIDN'T.
OH MY GOD.
SOMEBODY BETTER CALL THE SHERIFF.
DUSTY TUTWILER.
YOU'RE AT LEAST GONNA SAY HIS DAMN NAME.
YOU MOTHER... MOTHER... HUGGH...
THAT'S RIGHT. I AM INDEED ONE SORRY SONUVA BITCH. JUST LIKE MY DADDY WAS.
BUT WE AIN'T HERE TO TALK ABOUT ME, ESAW.

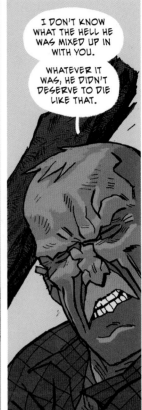

I DON'T KNOW WHAT THE HELL HE WAS MIXED UP IN WITH YOU.

WHATEVER IT WAS, HE DIDN'T DESERVE TO DIE LIKE THAT.

A *DOG* DON'T DESERVE TO DIE LIKE THAT.

SOMEBODY'S GONNA ANSWER FOR WHAT HAPPENED TO DUSTY.

FOR WHAT'S HAPPENED TO THIS WHOLE DAMN COUNTY.

YOU...

YOU'RE DEAD.

NAH. FOR THE FIRST TIME IN FOREVER...

I DON'T THINK I AM.

KNOW WHAT, SHAWNA?

I THINK I *WILL* HAVE SOME A' THEM RIBS.

AND I'LL BE BACK FOR SOME MORE TOMORROW.

AND EVERY DAY AFTER THAT, UNTIL I GET SOME ANSWERS.

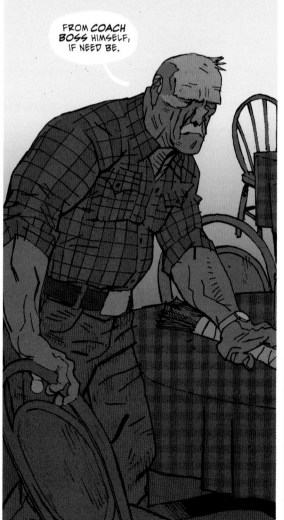

FROM *COACH BOSS* HIMSELF, IF NEED BE.

ANYBODY ELSE WHO AIN'T HAPPY WITH THE WAY THIS COUNTY IS BEIN' RUN OR THE FOLKS WHO FIGURE THEY'RE RUNNIN' IT...

WELL, LIKE I SAID, I'LL BE HERE TOMORROW.

WHY DON'T Y'ALL COME *JOIN* ME?

SUNDAY SCRAMBLE

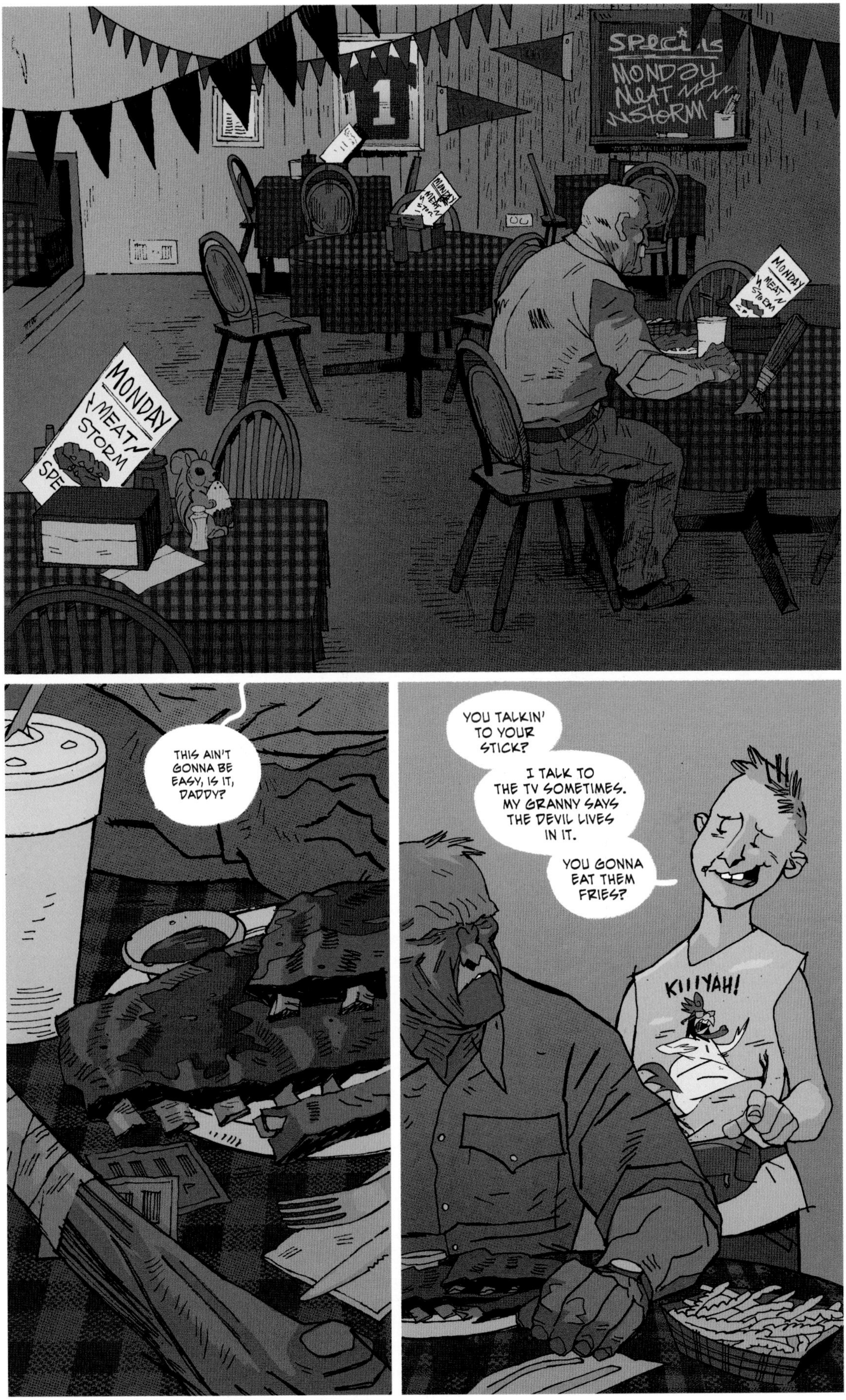
SPECIALS
MONDAY
MEAT
STORM
MONDAY
MEAT
STORM
MONDAY
MEAT
STORM
SPE
THIS AIN'T GONNA BE EASY, IS IT, DADDY?
YOU TALKIN' TO YOUR STICK?
I TALK TO THE TV SOMETIMES. MY GRANNY SAYS THE DEVIL LIVES IN IT.
YOU GONNA EAT THEM FRIES?
KIIYAH!

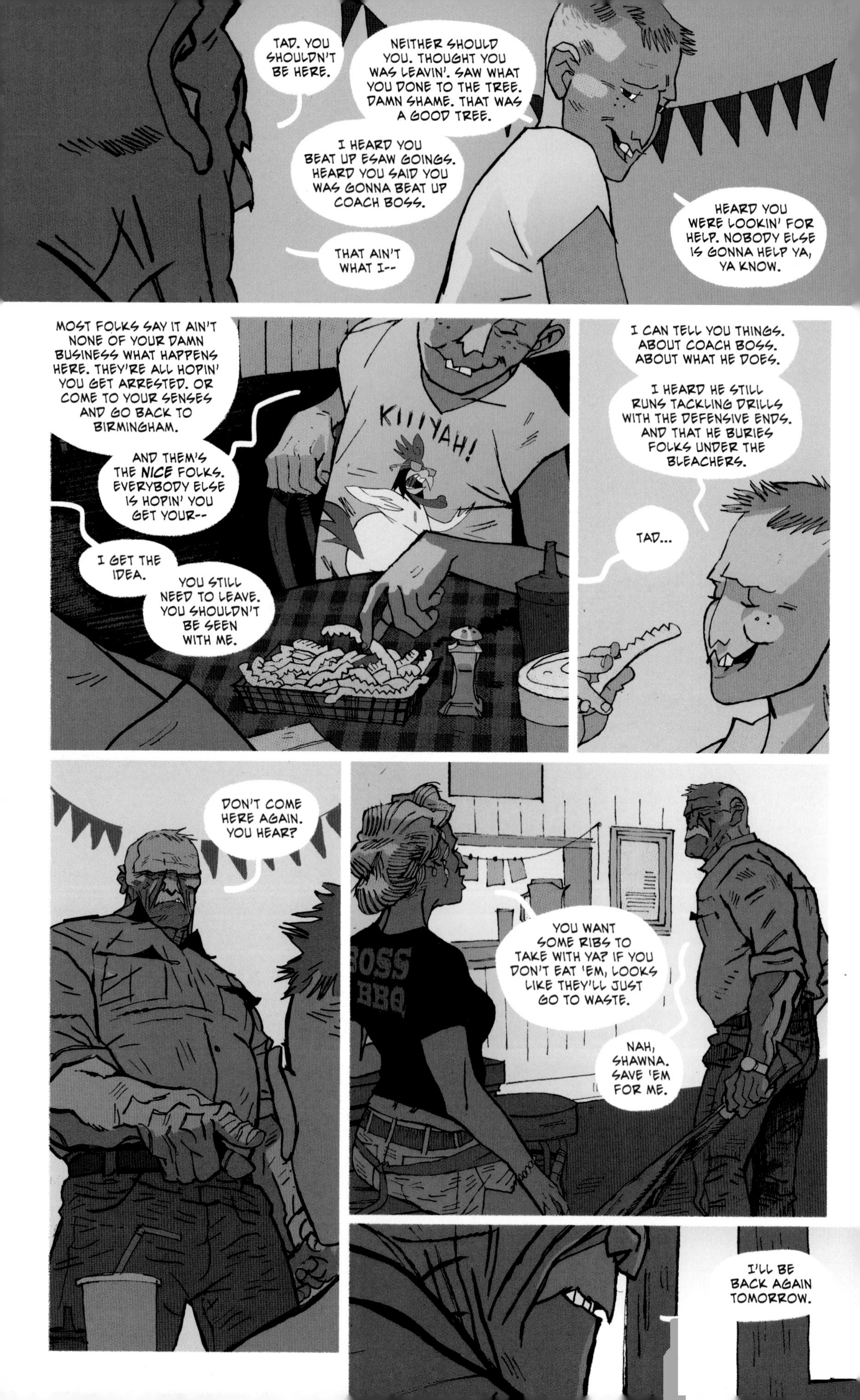
TAD. YOU SHOULDN'T BE HERE.
NEITHER SHOULD YOU. THOUGHT YOU WAS LEAVIN'. SAW WHAT YOU DONE TO THE TREE. DAMN SHAME. THAT WAS A GOOD TREE.
I HEARD YOU BEAT UP ESAW GOINGS. HEARD YOU SAID YOU WAS GONNA BEAT UP COACH BOSS.
THAT AIN'T WHAT I--
HEARD YOU WERE LOOKIN' FOR HELP. NOBODY ELSE IS GONNA HELP YA, YA KNOW.
MOST FOLKS SAY IT AIN'T NONE OF YOUR DAMN BUSINESS WHAT HAPPENS HERE. THEY'RE ALL HOPIN' YOU GET ARRESTED. OR COME TO YOUR SENSES AND GO BACK TO BIRMINGHAM.
KIIIYAH!
AND THEM'S THE NICE FOLKS. EVERYBODY ELSE IS HOPIN' YOU GET YOUR--
I GET THE IDEA.
YOU STILL NEED TO LEAVE. YOU SHOULDN'T BE SEEN WITH ME.
I CAN TELL YOU THINGS. ABOUT COACH BOSS. ABOUT WHAT HE DOES.
I HEARD HE STILL RUNS TACKLING DRILLS WITH THE DEFENSIVE ENDS. AND THAT HE BURIES FOLKS UNDER THE BLEACHERS.
TAD...
DON'T COME HERE AGAIN. YOU HEAR?
BOSS BBQ
YOU WANT SOME RIBS TO TAKE WITH YA? IF YOU DON'T EAT 'EM, LOOKS LIKE THEY'LL JUST GO TO WASTE.
NAH, SHAWNA. SAVE 'EM FOR ME.
I'LL BE BACK AGAIN TOMORROW.

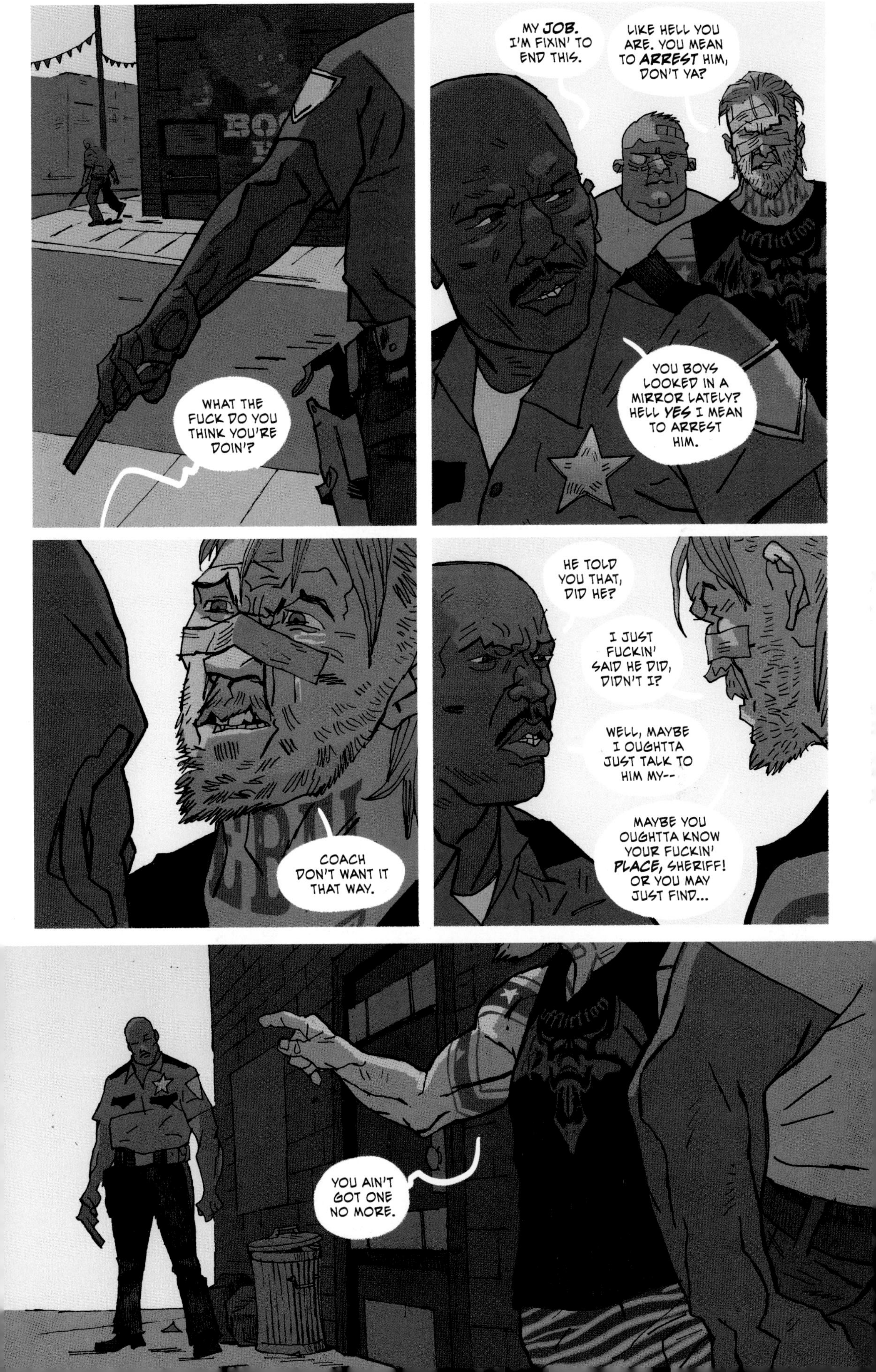
WHAT THE FUCK DO YOU THINK YOU'RE DOIN'?
MY JOB. I'M FIXIN' TO END THIS.
LIKE HELL YOU ARE. YOU MEAN TO ARREST HIM, DON'T YA?
YOU BOYS LOOKED IN A MIRROR LATELY? HELL YES I MEAN TO ARREST HIM.
COACH DON'T WANT IT THAT WAY.
HE TOLD YOU THAT, DID HE?
I JUST FUCKIN' SAID HE DID, DIDN'T I?
WELL, MAYBE I OUGHTTA JUST TALK TO HIM MY--
MAYBE YOU OUGHTTA KNOW YOUR FUCKIN' PLACE, SHERIFF! OR YOU MAY JUST FIND...
YOU AIN'T GOT ONE NO MORE.

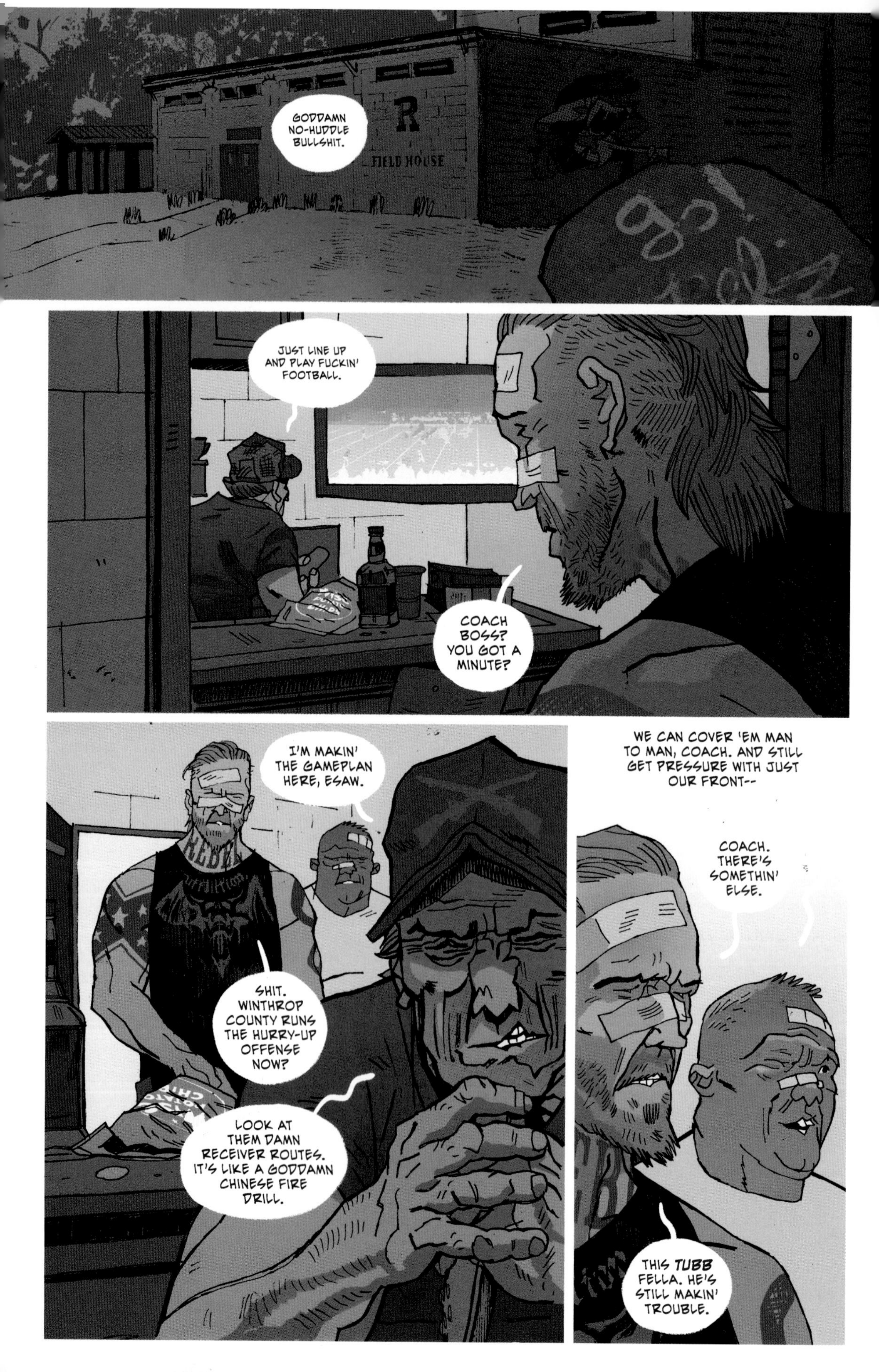
GODDAMN NO-HUDDLE BULLSHIT.
R
FIELD HOUSE
JUST LINE UP AND PLAY FUCKIN' FOOTBALL.
COACH BOSS? YOU GOT A MINUTE?
I'M MAKIN' THE GAMEPLAN HERE, ESAW.
SHIT. WINTHROP COUNTY RUNS THE HURRY-UP OFFENSE NOW?
LOOK AT THEM DAMN RECEIVER ROUTES. IT'S LIKE A GODDAMN CHINESE FIRE DRILL.
WE CAN COVER 'EM MAN TO MAN, COACH. AND STILL GET PRESSURE WITH JUST OUR FRONT--
COACH. THERE'S SOMETHIN' ELSE.
THIS *TUBB* FELLA. HE'S STILL MAKIN' TROUBLE.

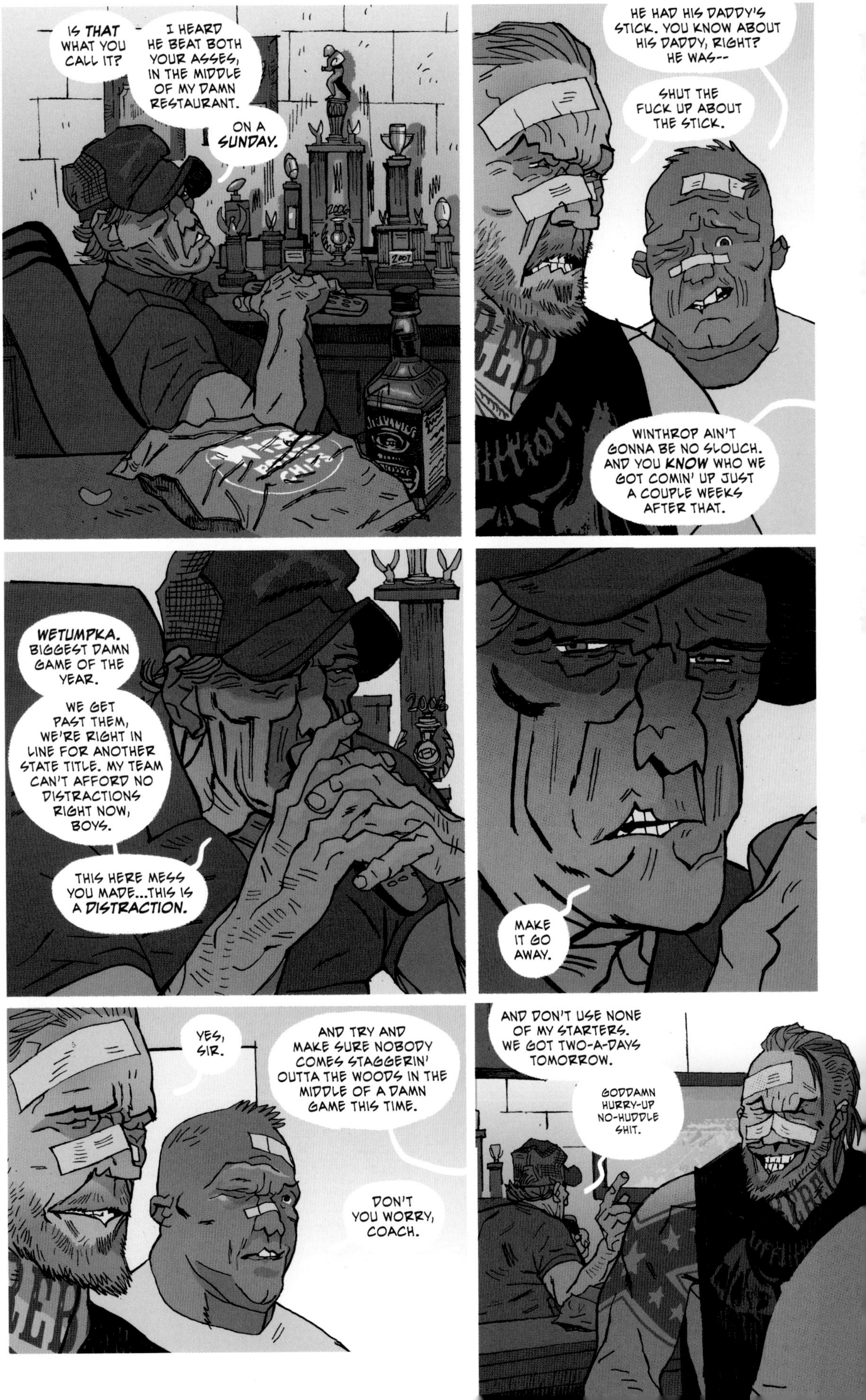
IS THAT WHAT YOU CALL IT?
I HEARD HE BEAT BOTH YOUR ASSES, IN THE MIDDLE OF MY DAMN RESTAURANT.
ON A SUNDAY.
HE HAD HIS DADDY'S STICK. YOU KNOW ABOUT HIS DADDY, RIGHT? HE WAS--
SHUT THE FUCK UP ABOUT THE STICK.
WINTHROP AIN'T GONNA BE NO SLOUCH. AND YOU KNOW WHO WE GOT COMIN' UP JUST A COUPLE WEEKS AFTER THAT.
WETUMPKA. BIGGEST DAMN GAME OF THE YEAR.
WE GET PAST THEM, WE'RE RIGHT IN LINE FOR ANOTHER STATE TITLE. MY TEAM CAN'T AFFORD NO DISTRACTIONS RIGHT NOW, BOYS.
THIS HERE MESS YOU MADE...THIS IS A DISTRACTION.
MAKE IT GO AWAY.
YES, SIR.
AND TRY AND MAKE SURE NOBODY COMES STAGGERIN' OUTTA THE WOODS IN THE MIDDLE OF A DAMN GAME THIS TIME.
DON'T YOU WORRY, COACH.
AND DON'T USE NONE OF MY STARTERS. WE GOT TWO-A-DAYS TOMORROW.
GODDAMN HURRY-UP NO-HUDDLE SHIT.

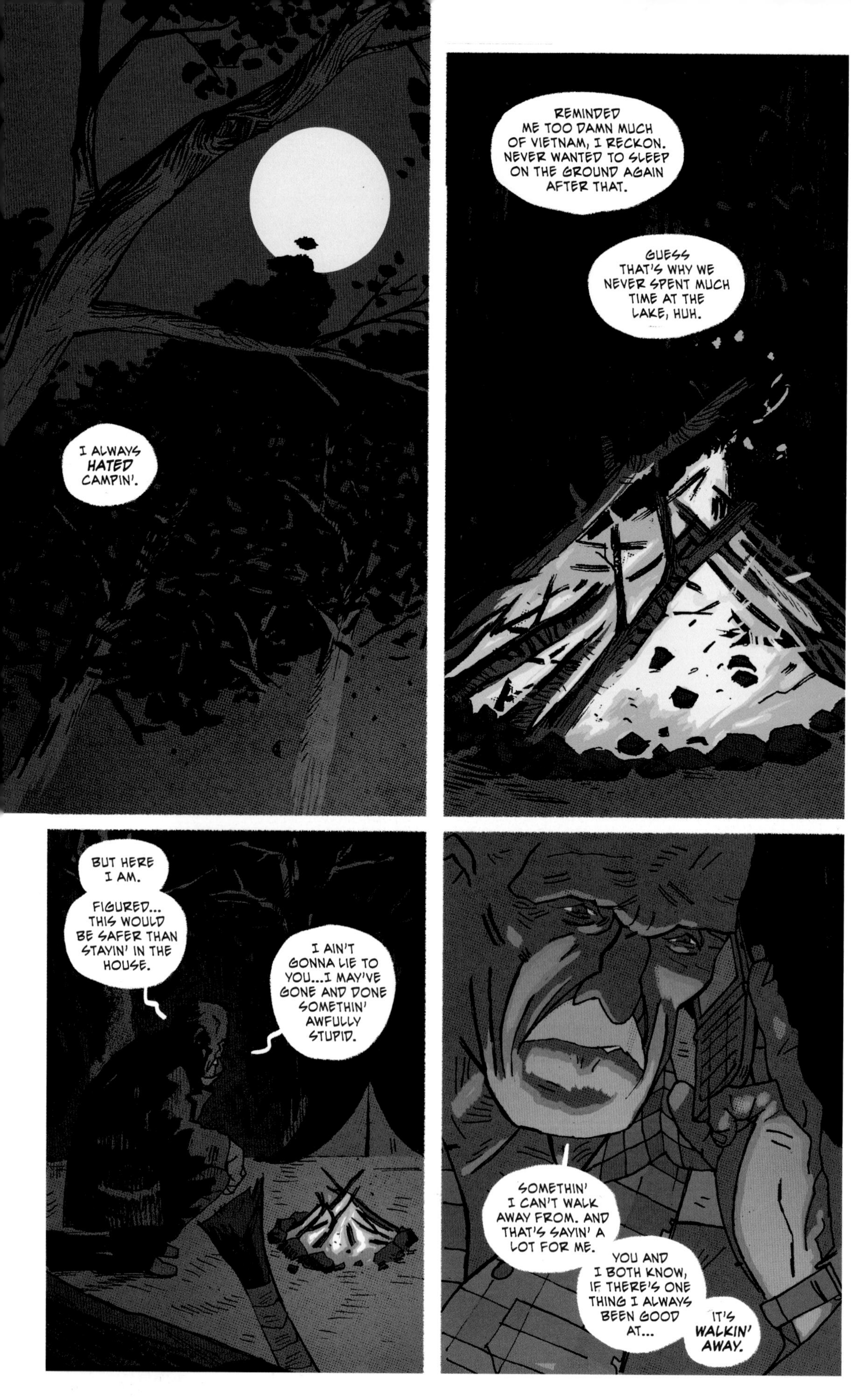
I ALWAYS HATED CAMPIN'.
REMINDED ME TOO DAMN MUCH OF VIETNAM, I RECKON. NEVER WANTED TO SLEEP ON THE GROUND AGAIN AFTER THAT.
GUESS THAT'S WHY WE NEVER SPENT MUCH TIME AT THE LAKE, HUH.
BUT HERE I AM.
FIGURED... THIS WOULD BE SAFER THAN STAYIN' IN THE HOUSE.
I AIN'T GONNA LIE TO YOU...I MAY'VE GONE AND DONE SOMETHIN' AWFULLY STUPID.
SOMETHIN' I CAN'T WALK AWAY FROM. AND THAT'S SAYIN' A LOT FOR ME.
YOU AND I BOTH KNOW, IF THERE'S ONE THING I ALWAYS BEEN GOOD AT...
IT'S WALKIN' AWAY.

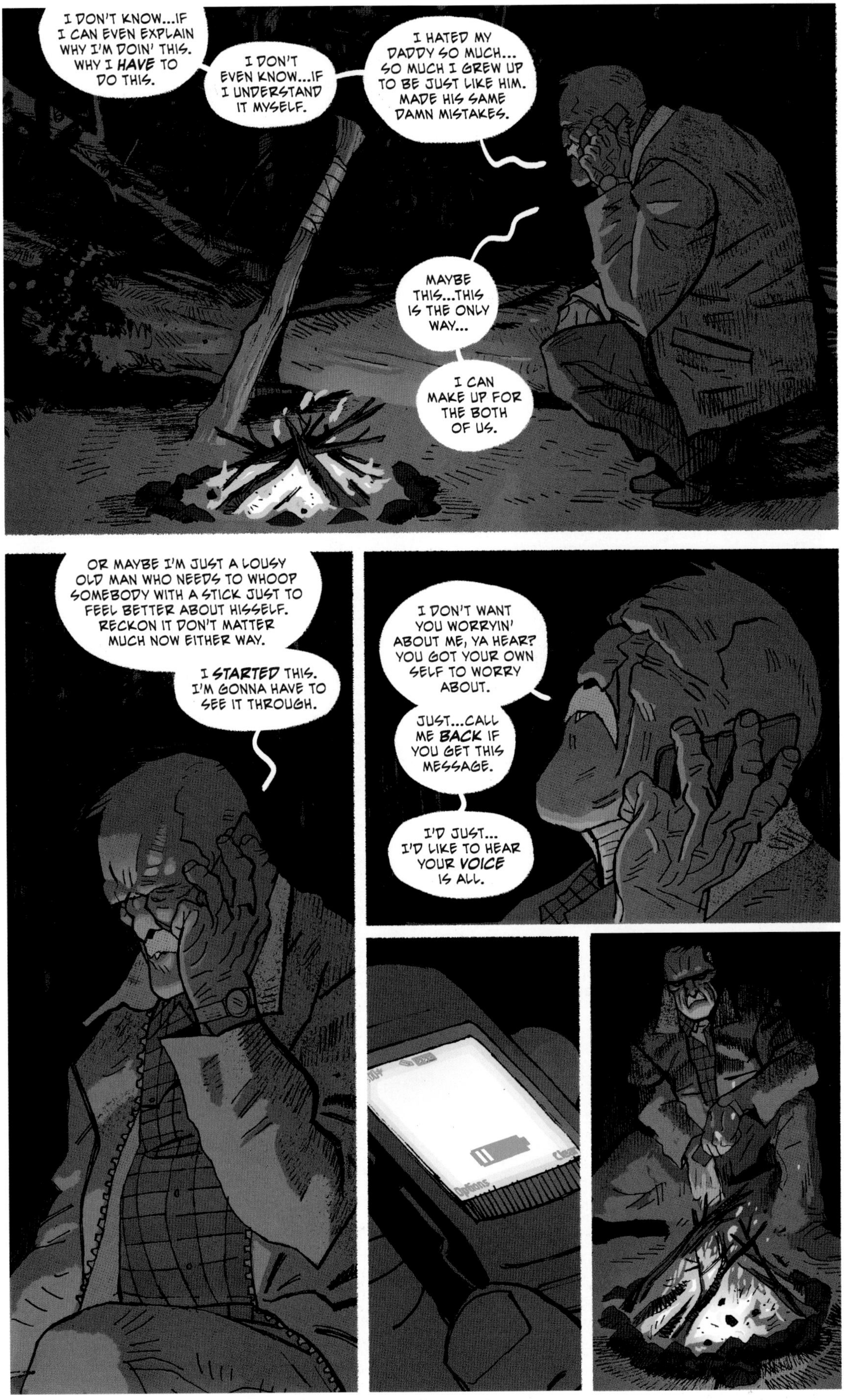
I DON'T KNOW...IF I CAN EVEN EXPLAIN WHY I'M DOIN' THIS. WHY I **HAVE** TO DO THIS.
I DON'T EVEN KNOW...IF I UNDERSTAND IT MYSELF.
I HATED MY DADDY SO MUCH... SO MUCH I GREW UP TO BE JUST LIKE HIM. MADE HIS SAME DAMN MISTAKES.
MAYBE THIS...THIS IS THE ONLY WAY...
I CAN MAKE UP FOR THE BOTH OF US.
OR MAYBE I'M JUST A LOUSY OLD MAN WHO NEEDS TO WHOOP SOMEBODY WITH A STICK JUST TO FEEL BETTER ABOUT HISSELF. RECKON IT DON'T MATTER MUCH NOW EITHER WAY.
I **STARTED** THIS. I'M GONNA HAVE TO SEE IT THROUGH.
I DON'T WANT YOU WORRYIN' ABOUT ME, YA HEAR? YOU GOT YOUR OWN SELF TO WORRY ABOUT.
JUST...CALL ME **BACK** IF YOU GET THIS MESSAGE.
I'D JUST... I'D LIKE TO HEAR YOUR **VOICE** IS ALL.

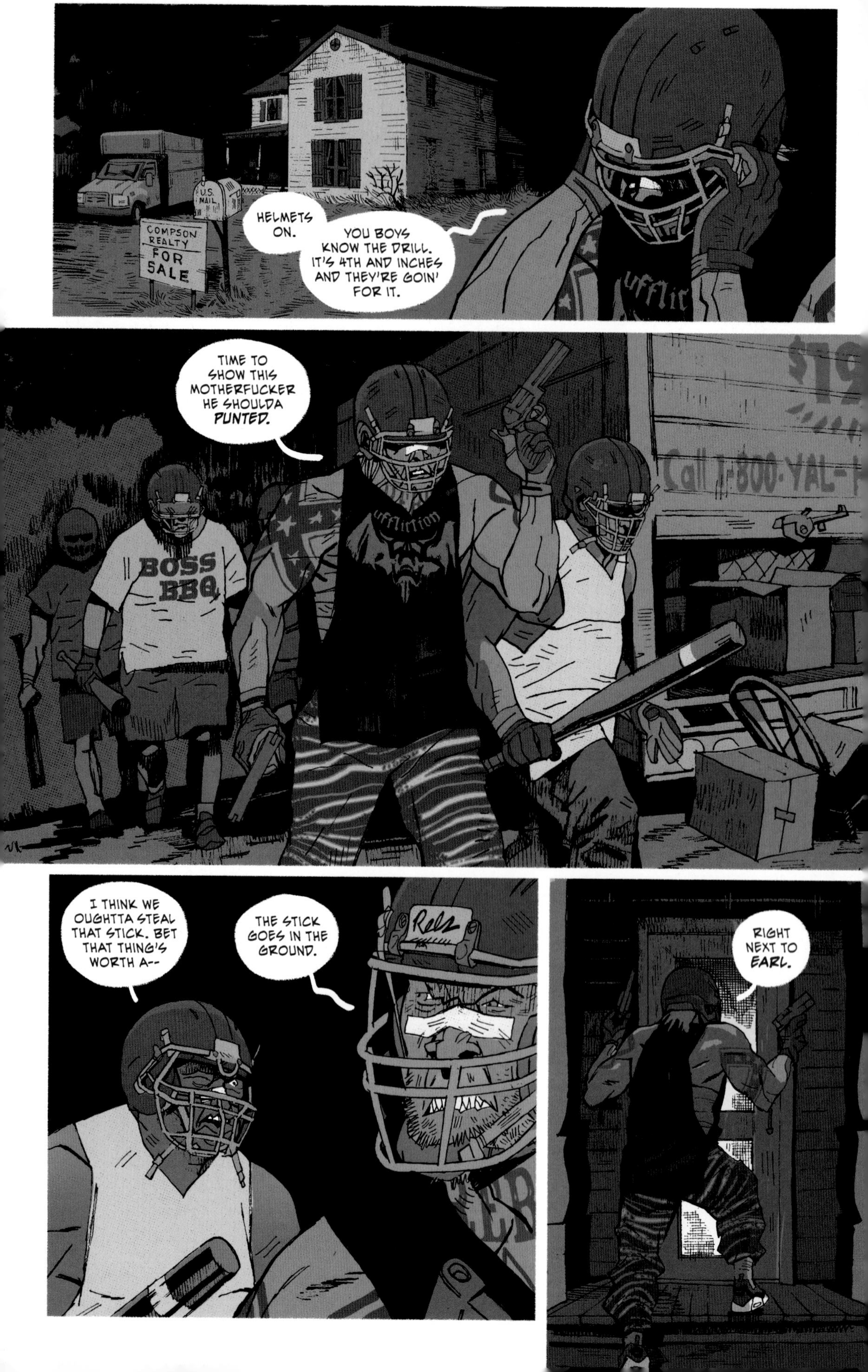
U.S. MAIL
COMPSON REALTY
FOR SALE
HELMETS ON.
YOU BOYS KNOW THE DRILL. IT'S 4TH AND INCHES AND THEY'RE GOIN' FOR IT.
TIME TO SHOW THIS MOTHERFUCKER HE SHOULDA *PUNTED.*
BOSS BBQ
Call 1-800-YAL-
I THINK WE OUGHTTA STEAL THAT STICK. BET THAT THING'S WORTH A--
THE STICK GOES IN THE GROUND.
RIGHT NEXT TO *EARL.*

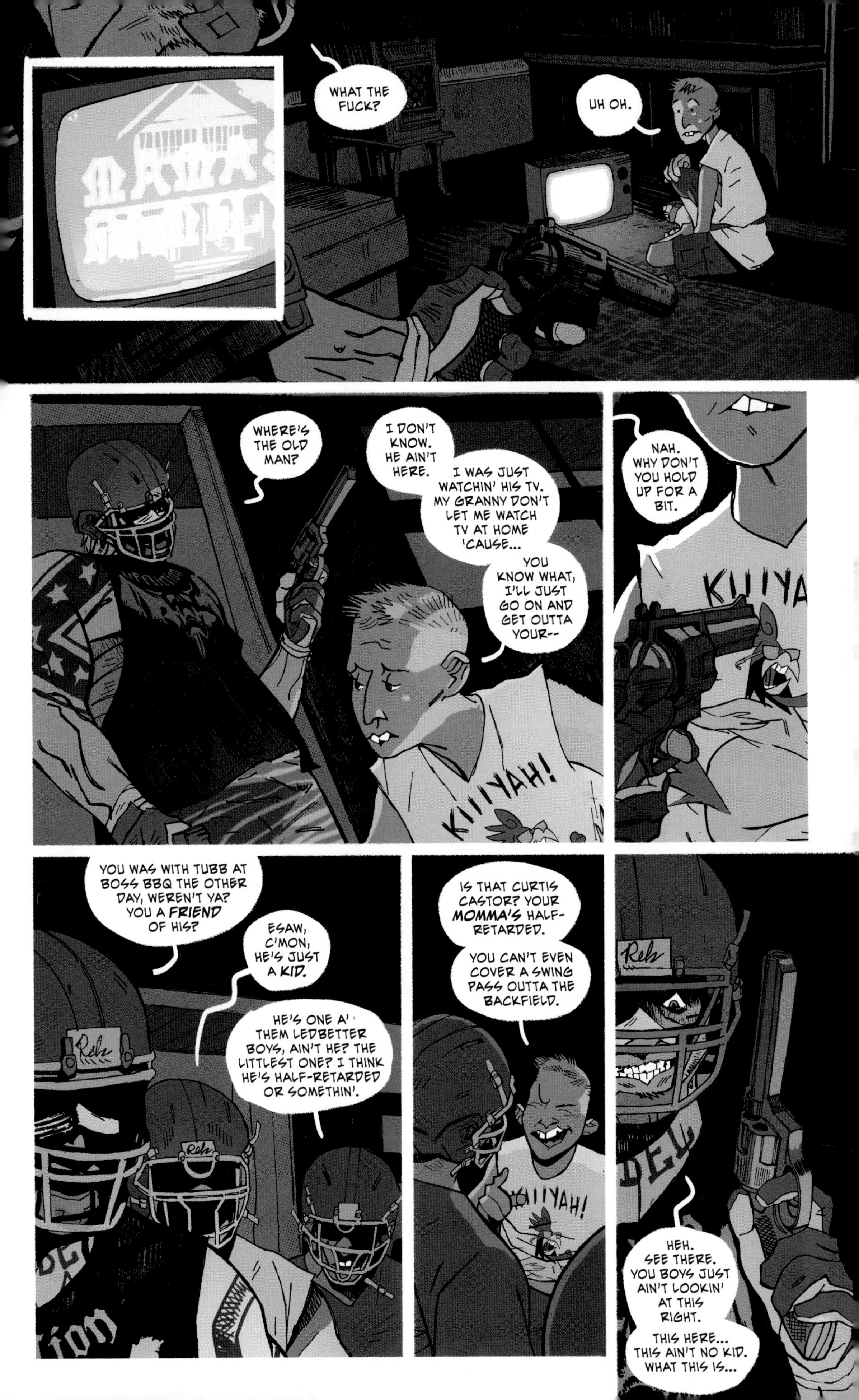
WHAT THE FUCK?
UH OH.
WHERE'S THE OLD MAN?
I DON'T KNOW. HE AIN'T HERE.
I WAS JUST WATCHIN' HIS TV. MY GRANNY DON'T LET ME WATCH TV AT HOME 'CAUSE...
YOU KNOW WHAT, I'LL JUST GO ON AND GET OUTTA YOUR--
KIIIYAH!
NAH. WHY DON'T YOU HOLD UP FOR A BIT.
KIIIYA
YOU WAS WITH TUBB AT BOSS BBQ THE OTHER DAY, WEREN'T YA? YOU A **FRIEND** OF HIS?
ESAW, C'MON, HE'S JUST A **KID**.
HE'S ONE A' THEM LEDBETTER BOYS, AIN'T HE? THE LITTLEST ONE? I THINK HE'S HALF-RETARDED OR SOMETHIN'.
IS THAT CURTIS CASTOR? YOUR **MOMMA'S** HALF-RETARDED.
YOU CAN'T EVEN COVER A SWING PASS OUTTA THE BACKFIELD.
KIIIYAH!
HEH. SEE THERE. YOU BOYS JUST AIN'T LOOKIN' AT THIS RIGHT.
THIS HERE... THIS AIN'T NO KID. WHAT THIS IS...

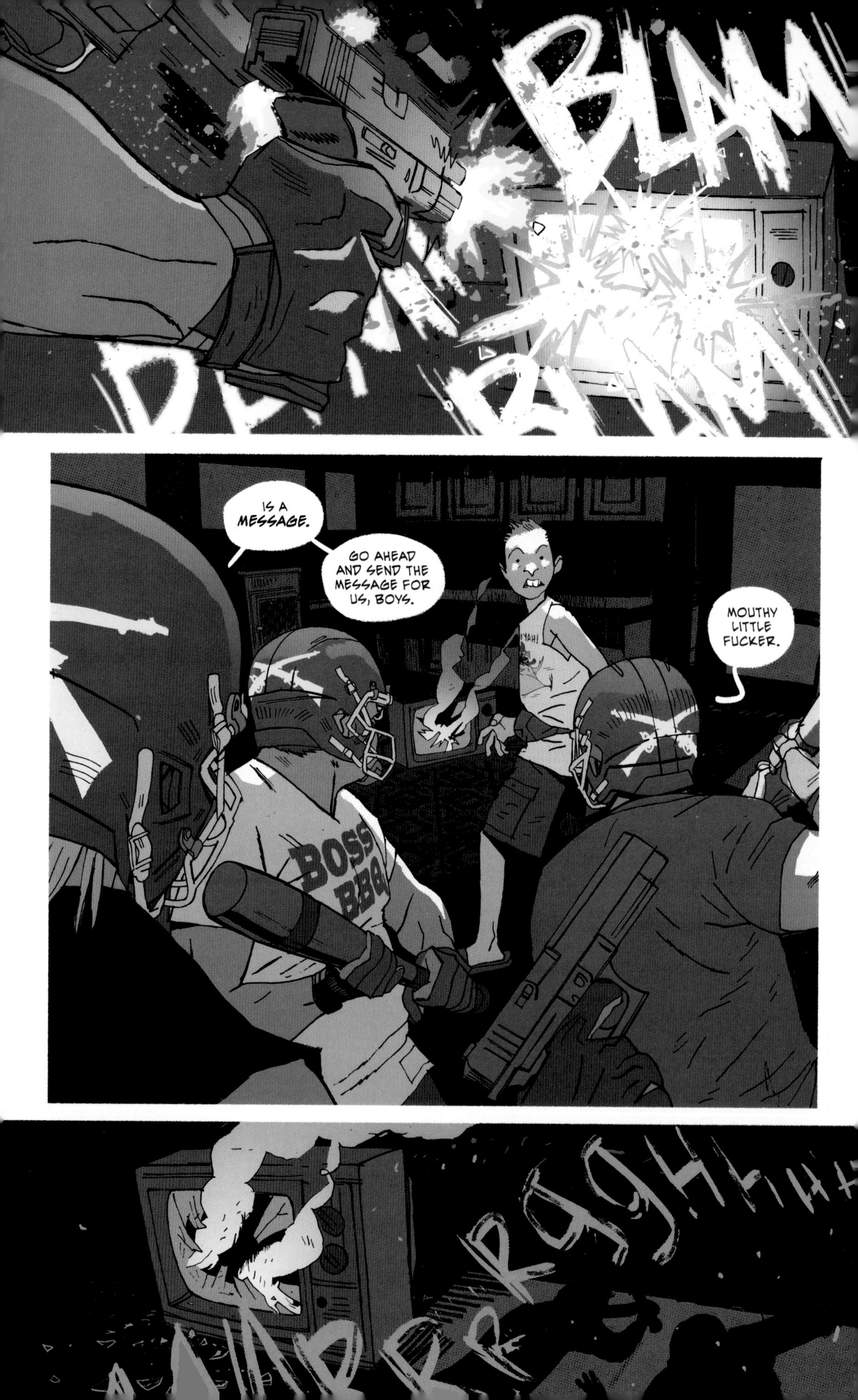
BLAM
IS A MESSAGE.
GO AHEAD AND SEND THE MESSAGE FOR US, BOYS.
MOUTHY LITTLE FUCKER.
BOSS BBQ

Here Was a Man

Chapter Four

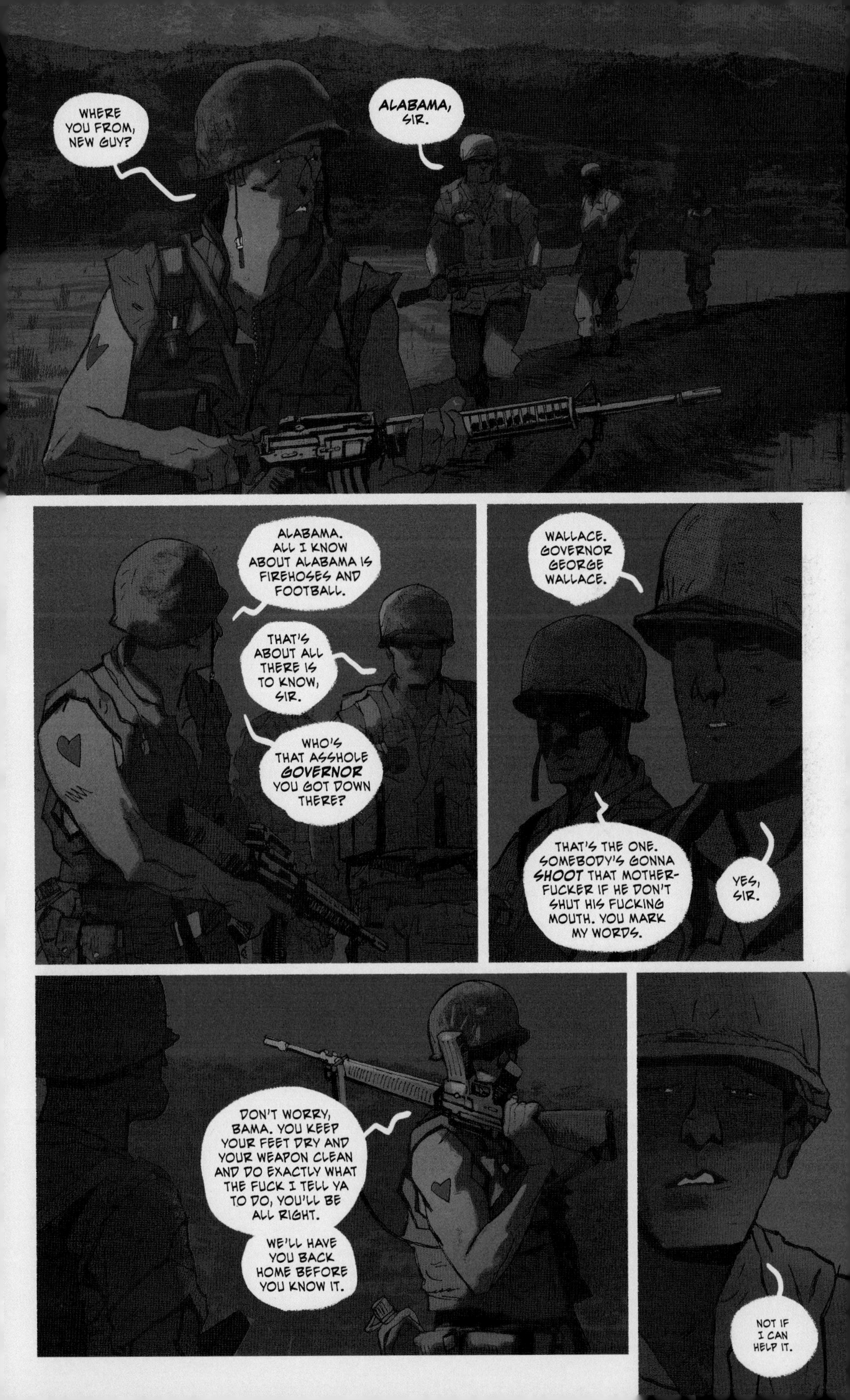
WHERE YOU FROM, NEW GUY?
ALABAMA, SIR.
ALABAMA. ALL I KNOW ABOUT ALABAMA IS FIREHOSES AND FOOTBALL.
THAT'S ABOUT ALL THERE IS TO KNOW, SIR.
WHO'S THAT ASSHOLE GOVERNOR YOU GOT DOWN THERE?
WALLACE. GOVERNOR GEORGE WALLACE.
THAT'S THE ONE. SOMEBODY'S GONNA SHOOT THAT MOTHER-FUCKER IF HE DON'T SHUT HIS FUCKING MOUTH. YOU MARK MY WORDS.
YES, SIR.
DON'T WORRY, BAMA. YOU KEEP YOUR FEET DRY AND YOUR WEAPON CLEAN AND DO EXACTLY WHAT THE FUCK I TELL YA TO DO, YOU'LL BE ALL RIGHT.
WE'LL HAVE YOU BACK HOME BEFORE YOU KNOW IT.
NOT IF I CAN HELP IT.

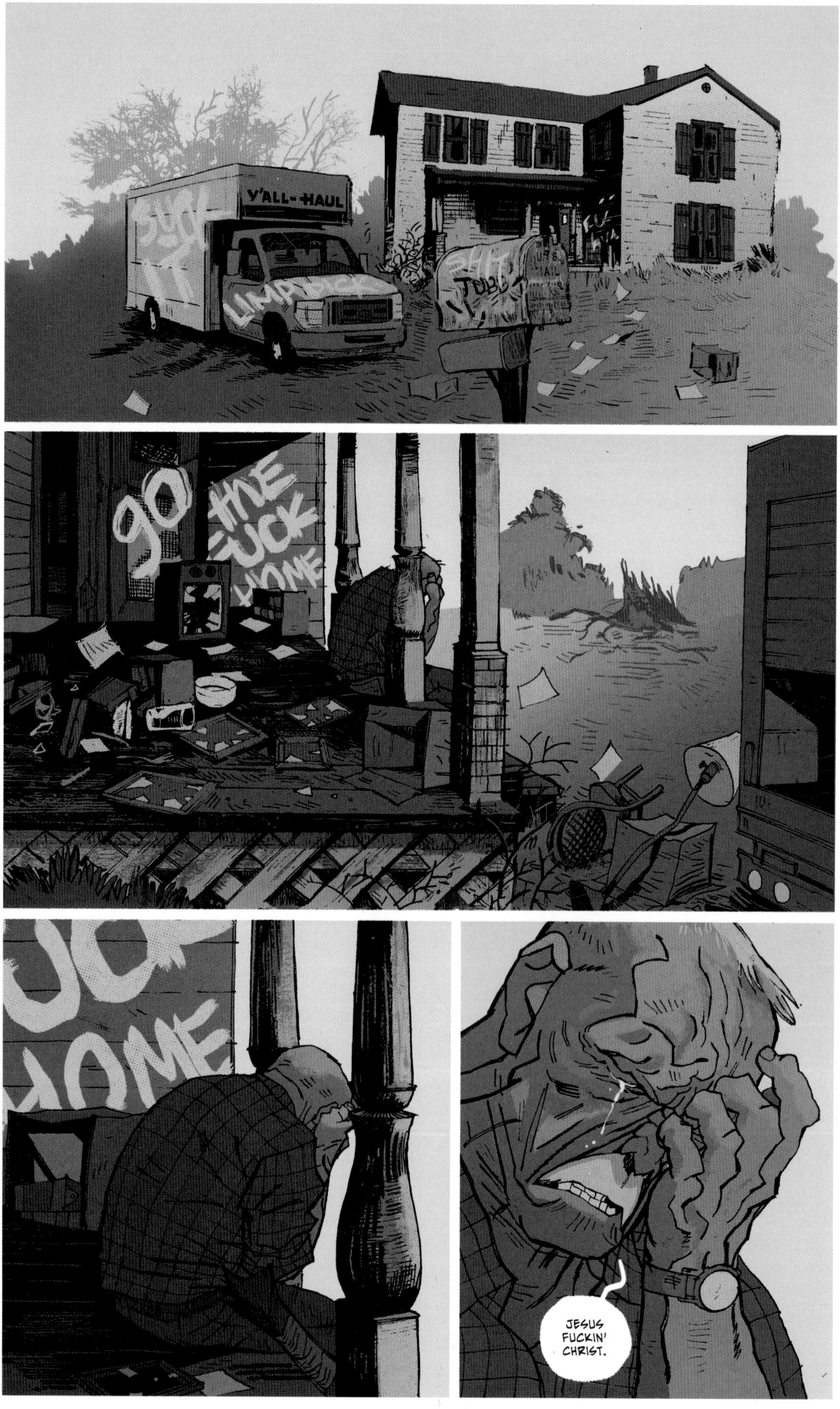
Y'ALL-HAUL
JESUS FUCKIN' CHRIST.

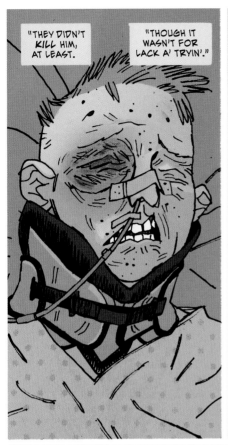

"THEY DIDN'T *KILL* HIM, AT LEAST.

"THOUGH IT WASN'T FOR LACK A' TRYIN'."

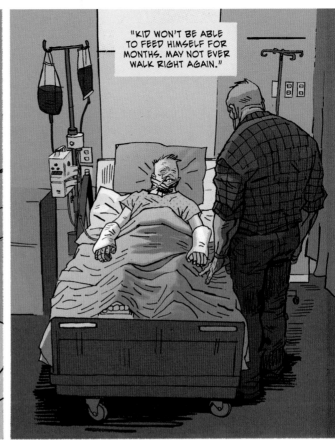

"KID WON'T BE ABLE TO FEED HIMSELF FOR MONTHS. MAY NOT EVER WALK RIGHT AGAIN."

"CERTAINLY WON'T BE CLIMBIN' NO MORE TREES."

"THIS HAS ALL GONE WAY TOO FAR. I SHOULDA LEFT WHEN I HAD THE CHANCE. SHOULDA PACKED UP AND BEEN GONE.

"SHOULDA..."

BUT I DIDN'T.

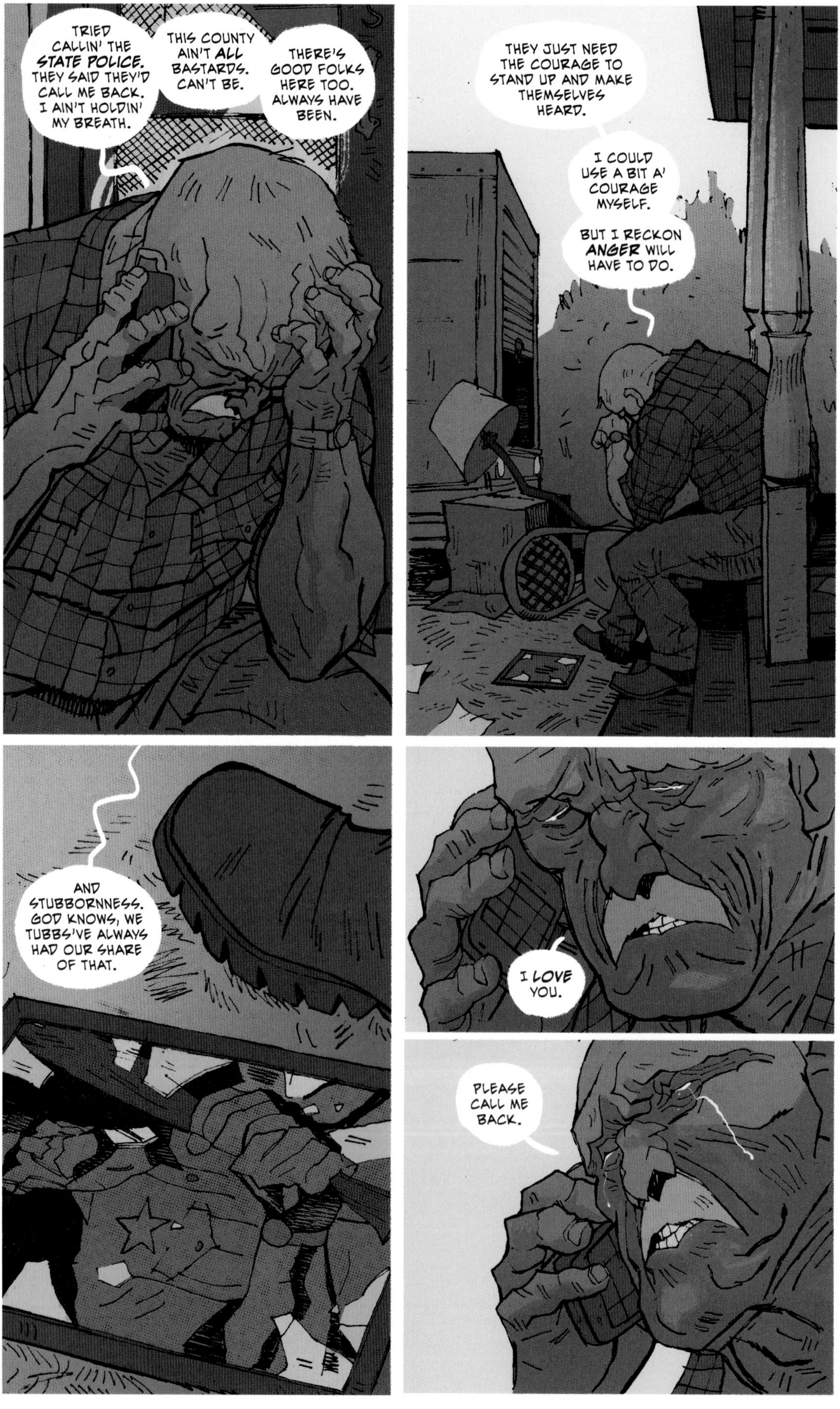
TRIED CALLIN' THE STATE POLICE. THEY SAID THEY'D CALL ME BACK. I AIN'T HOLDIN' MY BREATH.
THIS COUNTY AIN'T ALL BASTARDS. CAN'T BE.
THERE'S GOOD FOLKS HERE TOO. ALWAYS HAVE BEEN.
THEY JUST NEED THE COURAGE TO STAND UP AND MAKE THEMSELVES HEARD.
I COULD USE A BIT A' COURAGE MYSELF.
BUT I RECKON ANGER WILL HAVE TO DO.
AND STUBBORNNESS. GOD KNOWS, WE TUBBS'VE ALWAYS HAD OUR SHARE OF THAT.
I LOVE YOU.
PLEASE CALL ME BACK.

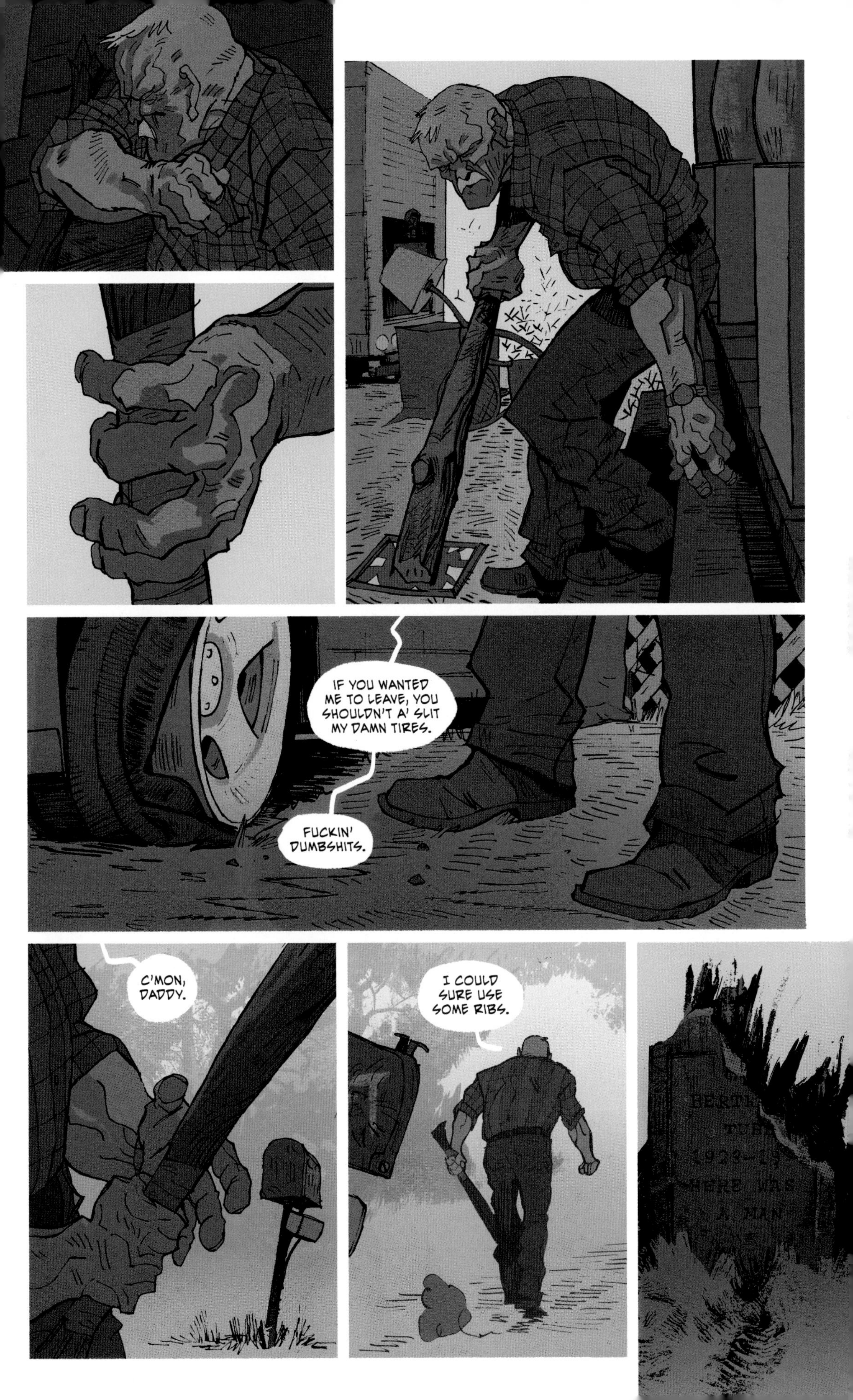
IF YOU WANTED ME TO LEAVE, YOU SHOULDN'T A' SLIT MY DAMN TIRES.
FUCKIN' DUMBSHITS.
C'MON, DADDY.
I COULD SURE USE SOME RIBS.

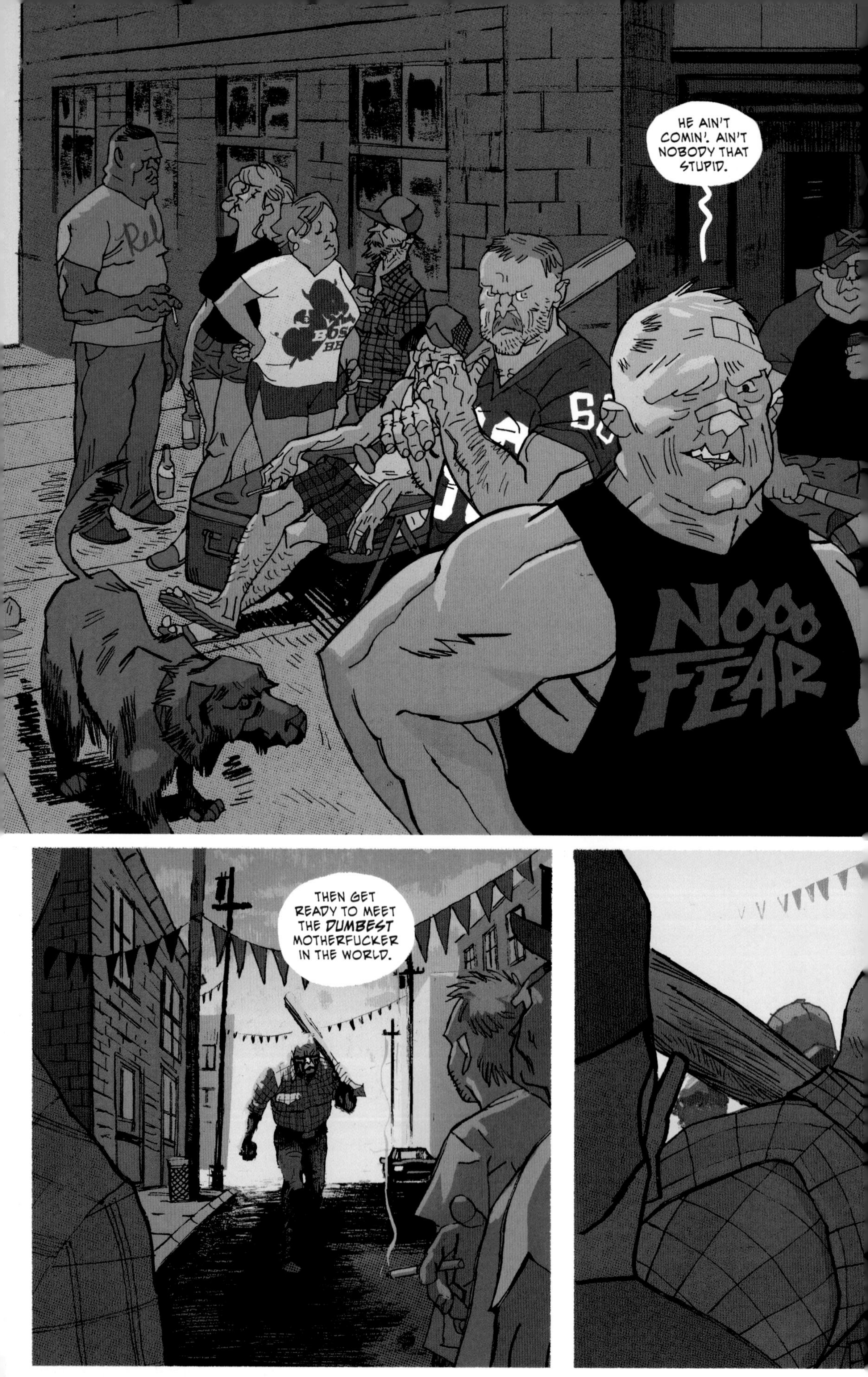
HE AIN'T COMIN'. AIN'T NOBODY THAT STUPID.
THEN GET READY TO MEET THE *DUMBEST* MOTHERFUCKER IN THE WORLD.

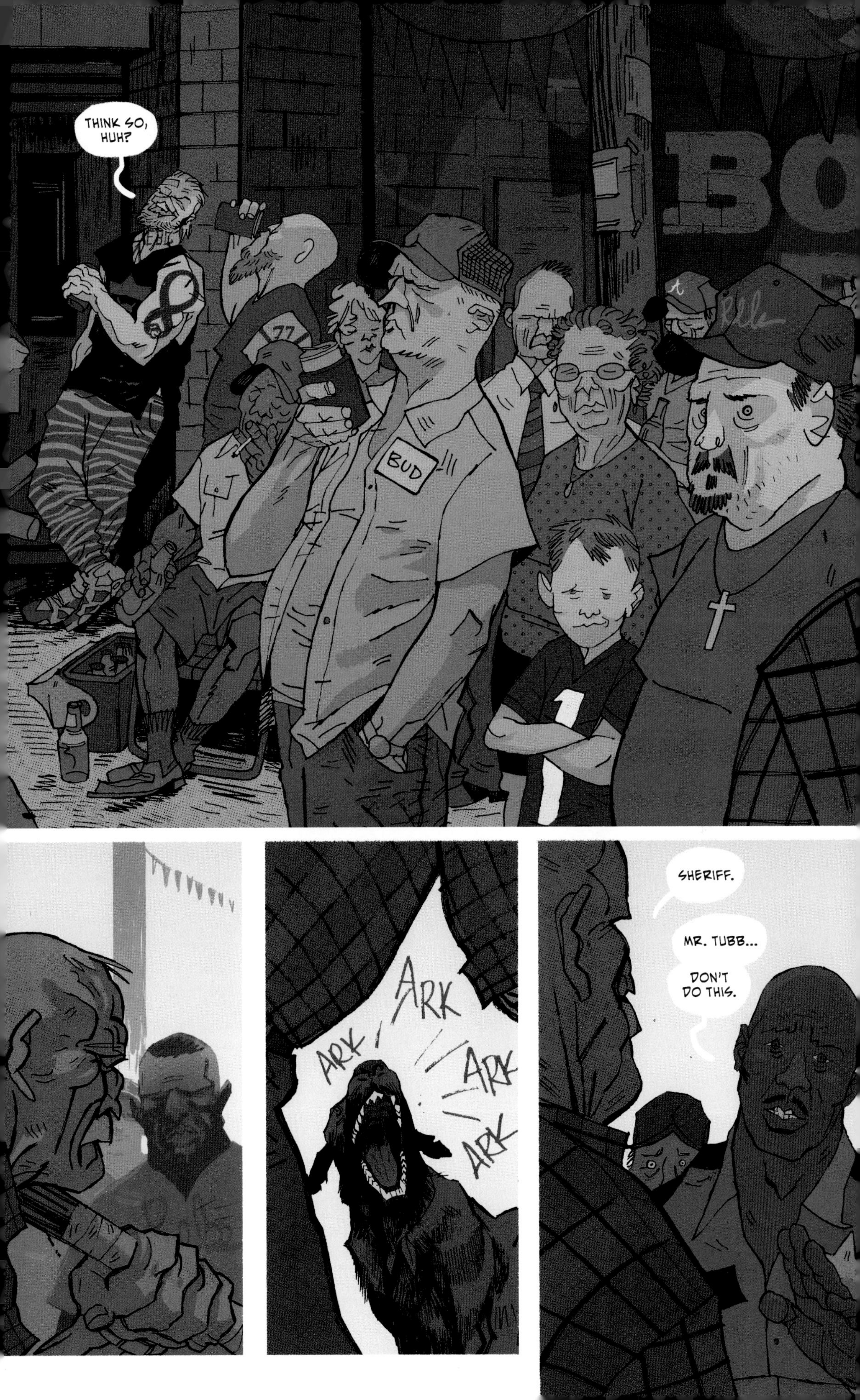
THINK SO, HUH?
BUD
ARK
ARK
ARK
ARK
SHERIFF.
MR. TUBB...
DON'T DO THIS.

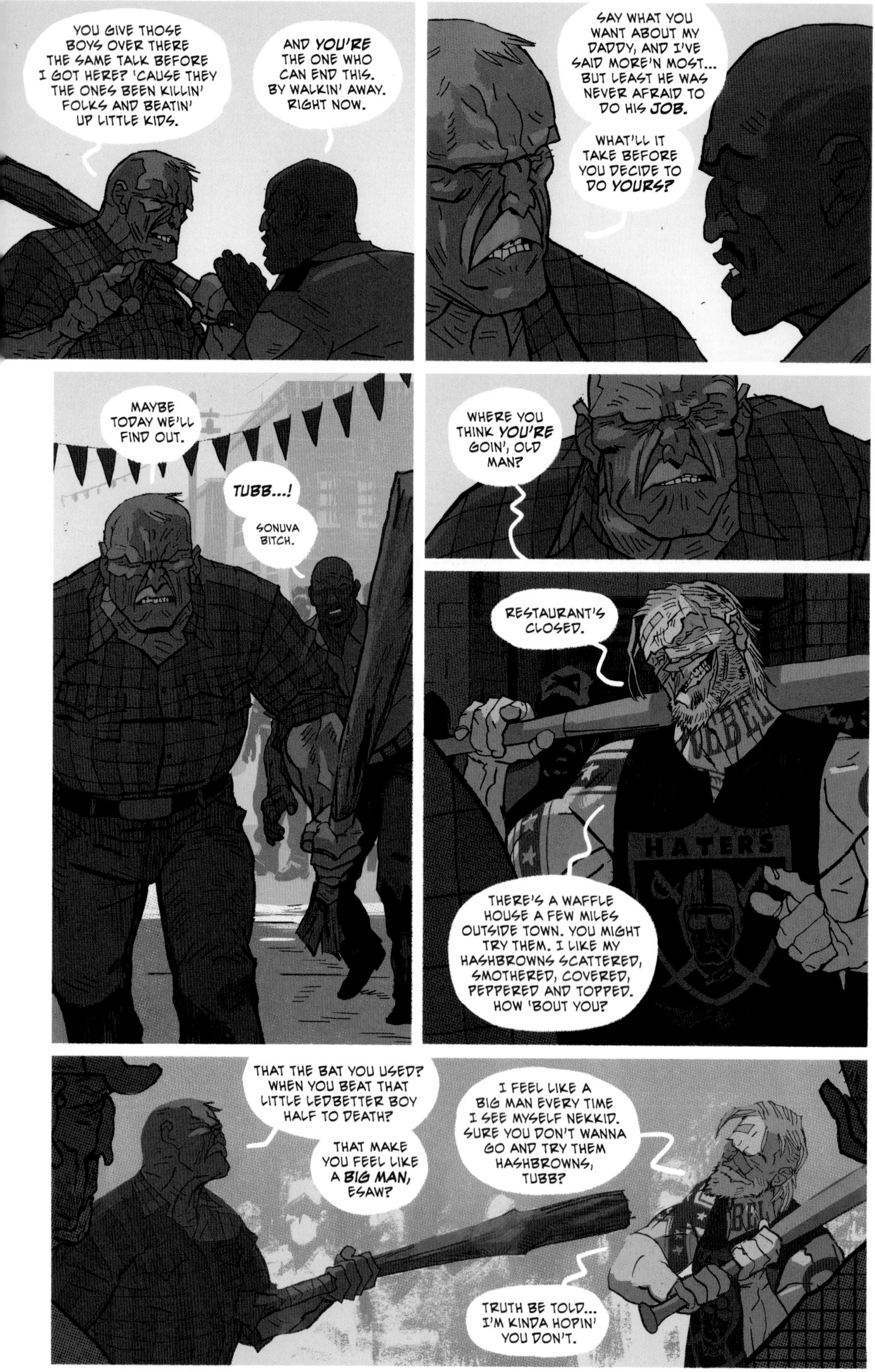
YOU GIVE THOSE BOYS OVER THERE THE SAME TALK BEFORE I GOT HERE? 'CAUSE THEY THE ONES BEEN KILLIN' FOLKS AND BEATIN' UP LITTLE KIDS.
AND YOU'RE THE ONE WHO CAN END THIS. BY WALKIN' AWAY. RIGHT NOW.
SAY WHAT YOU WANT ABOUT MY DADDY, AND I'VE SAID MORE'N MOST... BUT LEAST HE WAS NEVER AFRAID TO DO HIS JOB.
WHAT'LL IT TAKE BEFORE YOU DECIDE TO DO YOURS?
MAYBE TODAY WE'LL FIND OUT.
TUBB...!
SONUVA BITCH.
WHERE YOU THINK YOU'RE GOIN', OLD MAN?
RESTAURANT'S CLOSED.
HATERS
THERE'S A WAFFLE HOUSE A FEW MILES OUTSIDE TOWN. YOU MIGHT TRY THEM. I LIKE MY HASHBROWNS SCATTERED, SMOTHERED, COVERED, PEPPERED AND TOPPED. HOW 'BOUT YOU?
THAT THE BAT YOU USED? WHEN YOU BEAT THAT LITTLE LEDBETTER BOY HALF TO DEATH?
THAT MAKE YOU FEEL LIKE A BIG MAN, ESAW?
I FEEL LIKE A BIG MAN EVERY TIME I SEE MYSELF NEKKID. SURE YOU DON'T WANNA GO AND TRY THEM HASHBROWNS, TUBB?
TRUTH BE TOLD... I'M KINDA HOPIN' YOU DON'T.

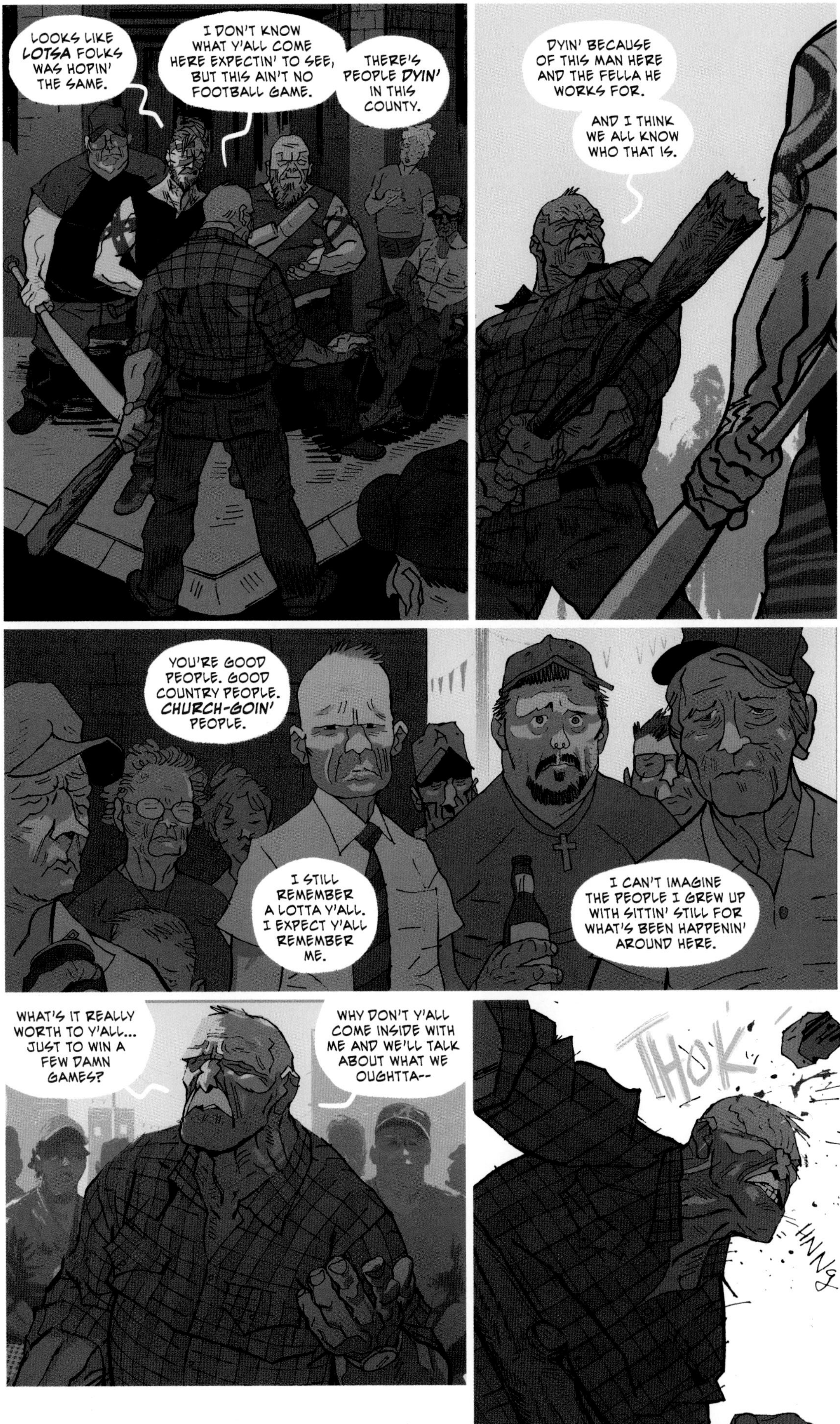
LOOKS LIKE LOTSA FOLKS WAS HOPIN' THE SAME.
I DON'T KNOW WHAT Y'ALL COME HERE EXPECTIN' TO SEE, BUT THIS AIN'T NO FOOTBALL GAME.
THERE'S PEOPLE DYIN' IN THIS COUNTY.
DYIN' BECAUSE OF THIS MAN HERE AND THE FELLA HE WORKS FOR.
AND I THINK WE ALL KNOW WHO THAT IS.
YOU'RE GOOD PEOPLE. GOOD COUNTRY PEOPLE. CHURCH-GOIN' PEOPLE.
I STILL REMEMBER A LOTTA Y'ALL. I EXPECT Y'ALL REMEMBER ME.
I CAN'T IMAGINE THE PEOPLE I GREW UP WITH SITTIN' STILL FOR WHAT'S BEEN HAPPENIN' AROUND HERE.
WHAT'S IT REALLY WORTH TO Y'ALL... JUST TO WIN A FEW DAMN GAMES?
WHY DON'T Y'ALL COME INSIDE WITH ME AND WE'LL TALK ABOUT WHAT WE OUGHTTA--
THOK
HNNg

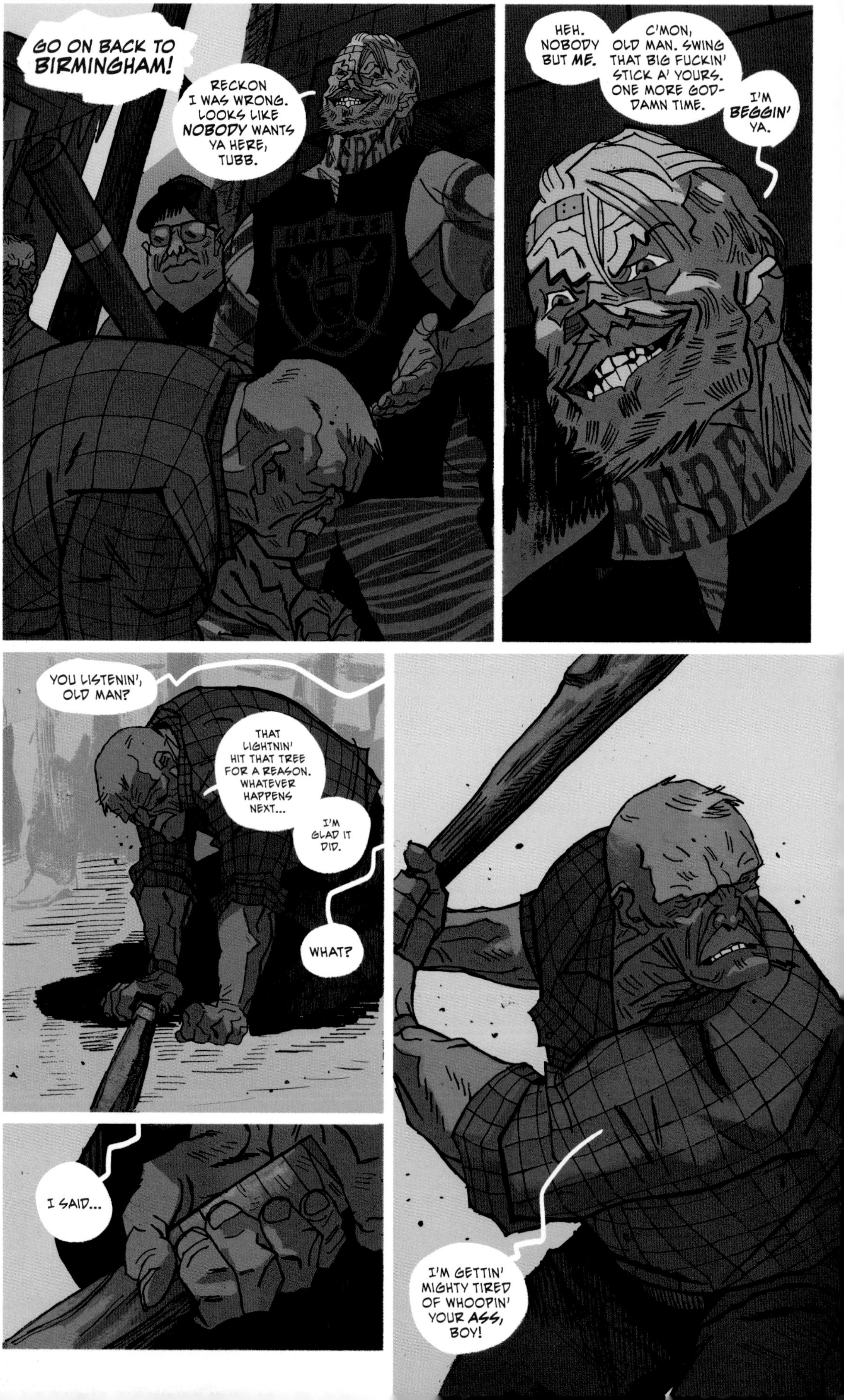
GO ON BACK TO BIRMINGHAM!
RECKON I WAS WRONG. LOOKS LIKE NOBODY WANTS YA HERE, TUBB.
HEH. NOBODY BUT ME.
C'MON, OLD MAN. SWING THAT BIG FUCKIN' STICK A' YOURS. ONE MORE GOD-DAMN TIME.
I'M BEGGIN' YA.
YOU LISTENIN', OLD MAN?
THAT LIGHTNIN' HIT THAT TREE FOR A REASON. WHATEVER HAPPENS NEXT...
I'M GLAD IT DID.
WHAT?
I SAID...
I'M GETTIN' MIGHTY TIRED OF WHOOPIN' YOUR ASS, BOY!

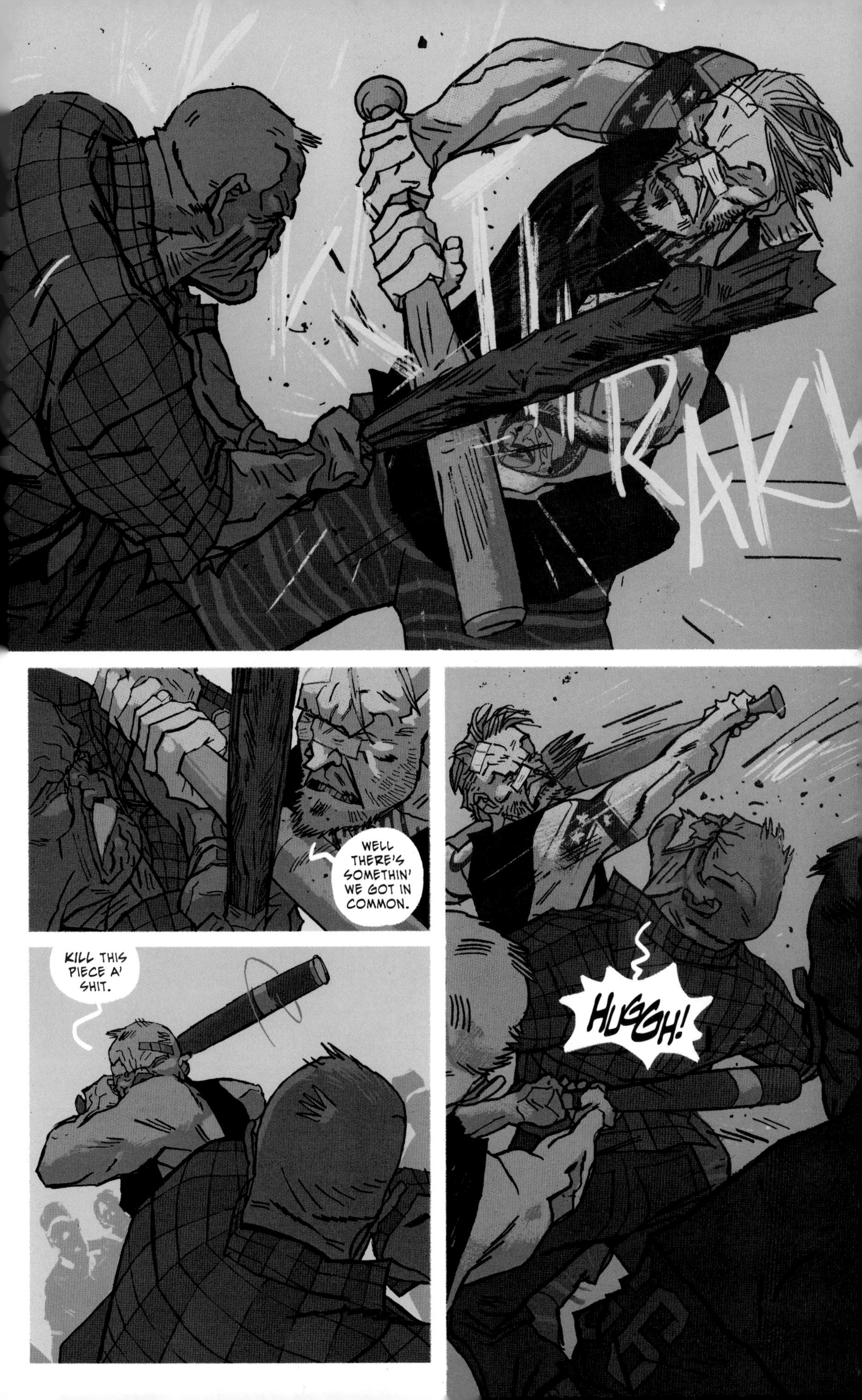
KRAK
WELL THERE'S SOMETHIN' WE GOT IN COMMON.
KILL THIS PIECE A' SHIT.
HUGGH!

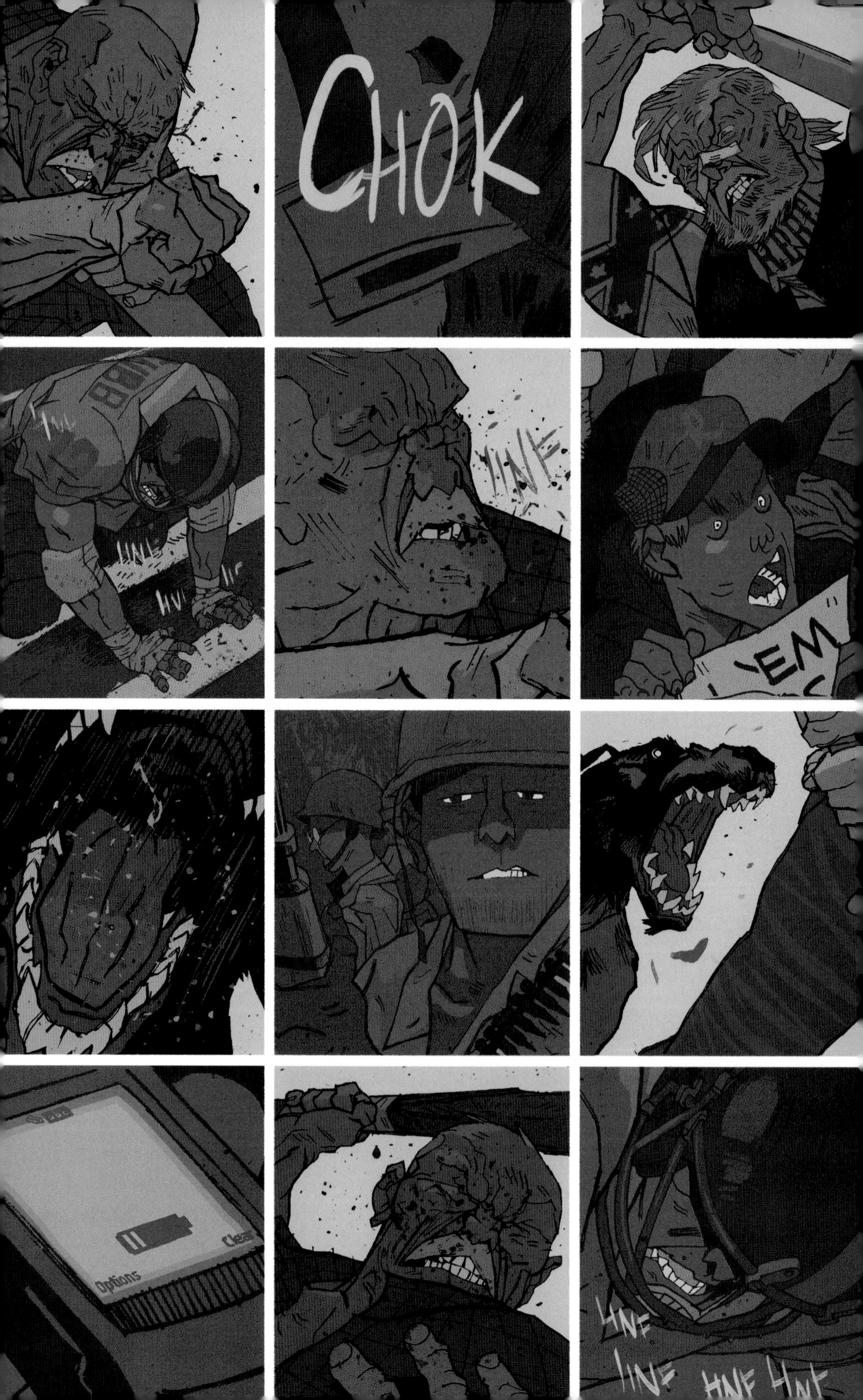
CHOK
HNF
EM
Options
Clear
HNF
HNF
HNF HNF

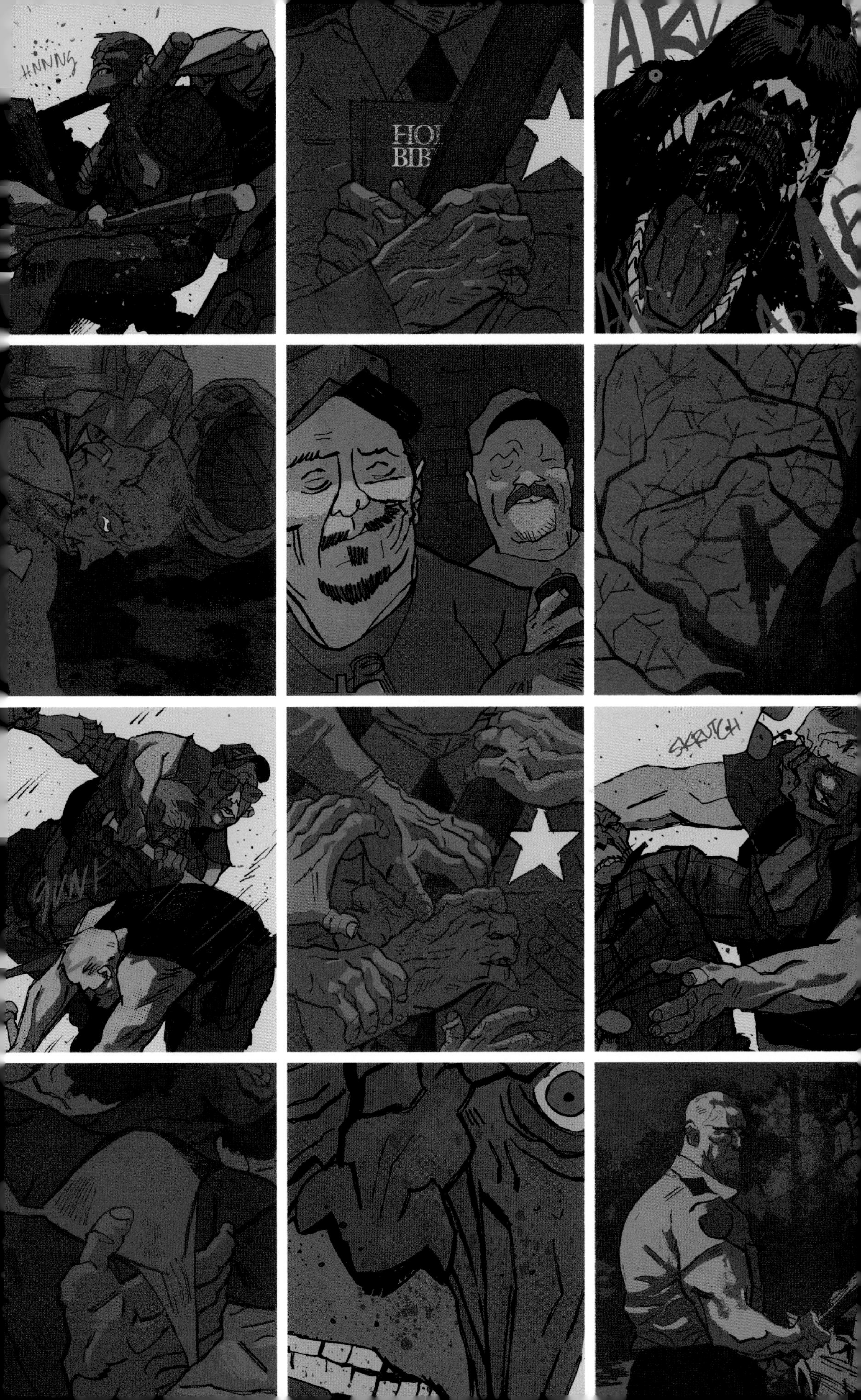
HNNNG
HOL
BIB
SKRUTCH

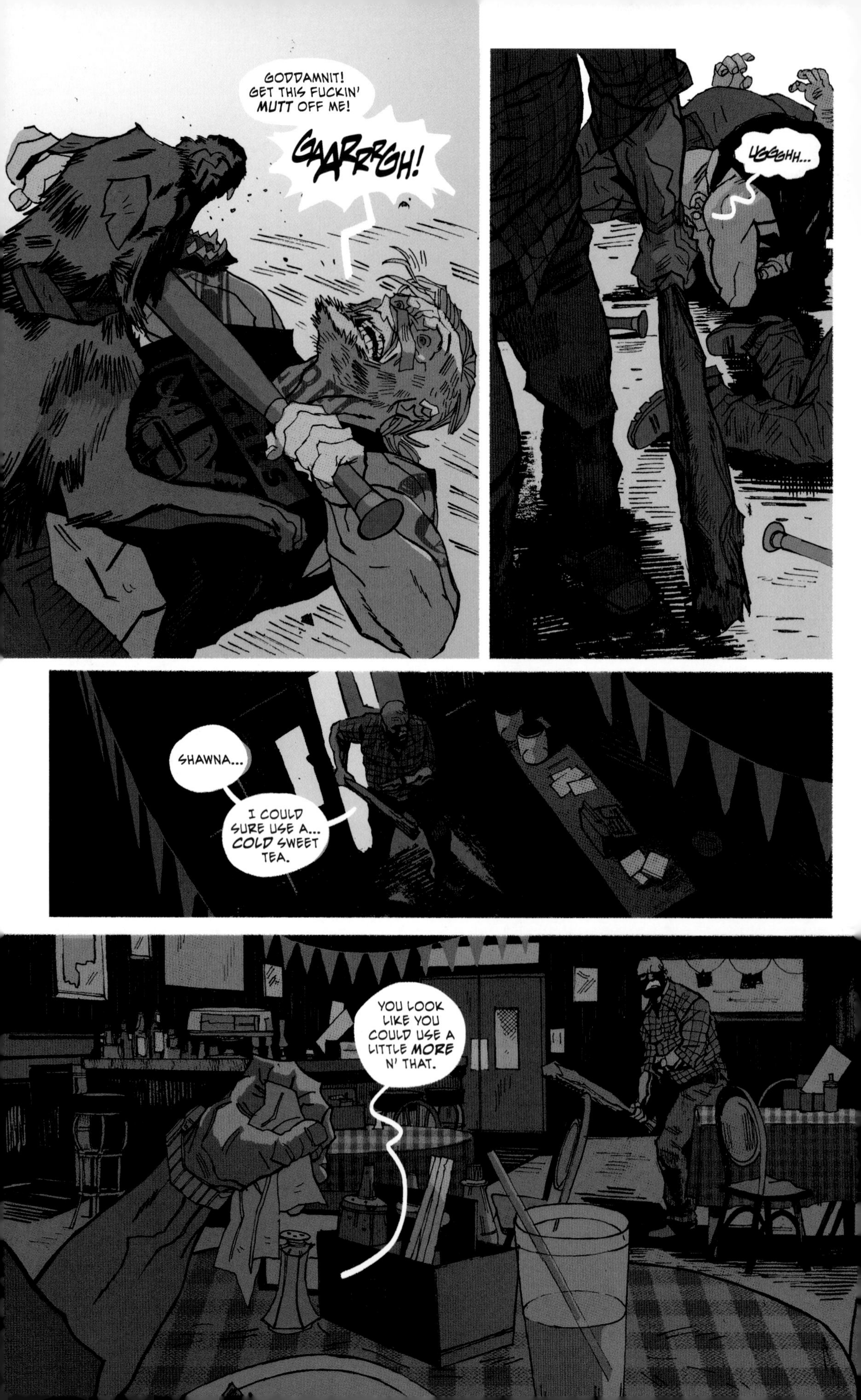
GODDAMNIT! GET THIS FUCKIN' **MUTT** OFF ME!
GAARRRGH!
UGGGHH...
SHAWNA...
I COULD SURE USE A... **COLD** SWEET TEA.
YOU LOOK LIKE YOU COULD USE A LITTLE **MORE** N' THAT.

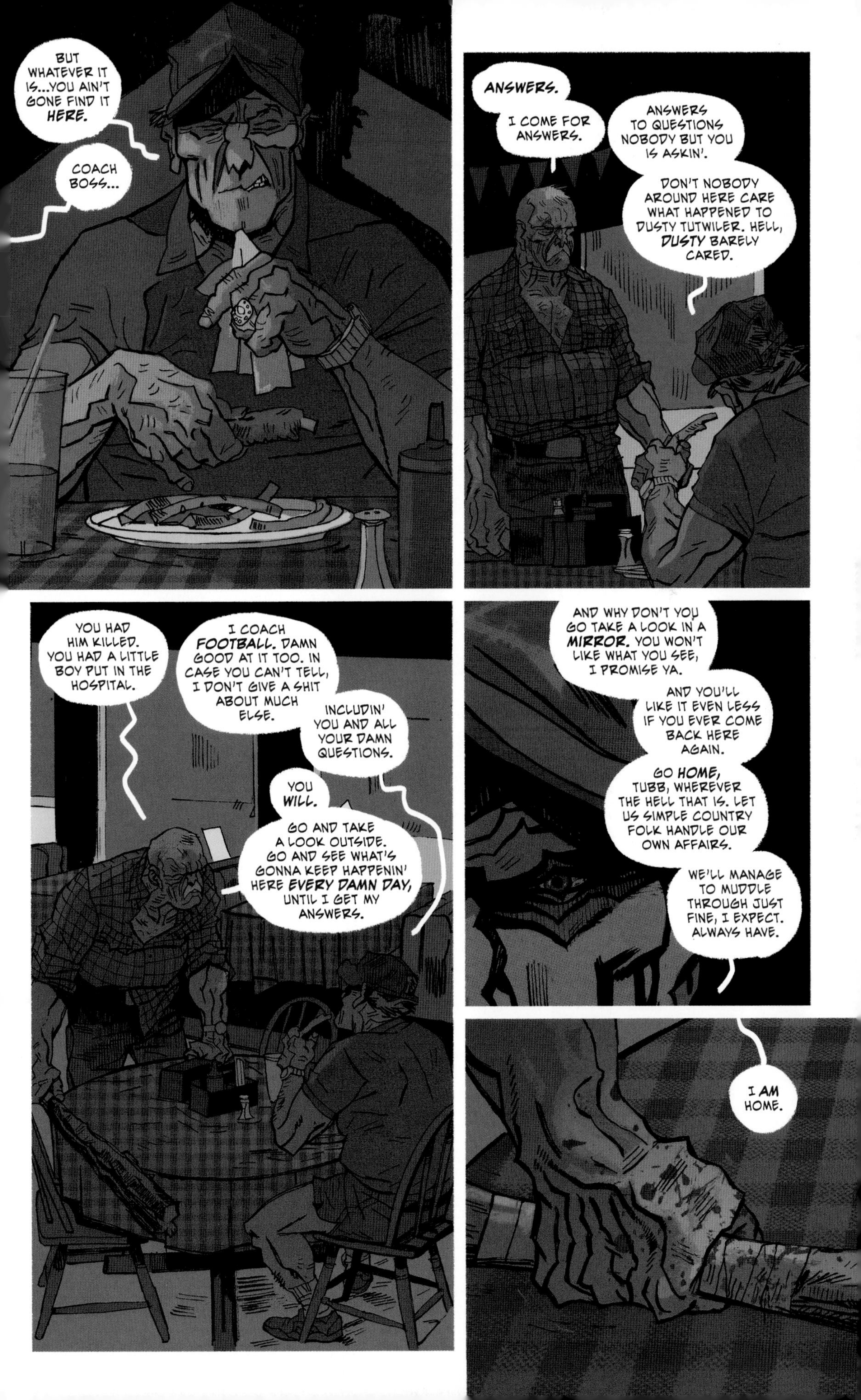
BUT WHATEVER IT IS...YOU AIN'T GONE FIND IT **HERE.**
COACH BOSS...
ANSWERS.
I COME FOR ANSWERS.
ANSWERS TO QUESTIONS NOBODY BUT YOU IS ASKIN'.
DON'T NOBODY AROUND HERE CARE WHAT HAPPENED TO DUSTY TUTWILER. HELL, **DUSTY** BARELY CARED.
YOU HAD HIM KILLED. YOU HAD A LITTLE BOY PUT IN THE HOSPITAL.
I COACH **FOOTBALL.** DAMN GOOD AT IT TOO. IN CASE YOU CAN'T TELL, I DON'T GIVE A SHIT ABOUT MUCH ELSE.
INCLUDIN' YOU AND ALL YOUR DAMN QUESTIONS.
YOU **WILL.**
GO AND TAKE A LOOK OUTSIDE. GO AND SEE WHAT'S GONNA KEEP HAPPENIN' HERE **EVERY DAMN DAY,** UNTIL I GET MY ANSWERS.
AND WHY DON'T YOU GO TAKE A LOOK IN A **MIRROR.** YOU WON'T LIKE WHAT YOU SEE, I PROMISE YA.
AND YOU'LL LIKE IT EVEN LESS IF YOU EVER COME BACK HERE AGAIN.
GO **HOME,** TUBB, WHEREVER THE HELL THAT IS. LET US SIMPLE COUNTRY FOLK HANDLE OUR OWN AFFAIRS.
WE'LL MANAGE TO MUDDLE THROUGH JUST FINE, I EXPECT. ALWAYS HAVE.
I **AM** HOME.

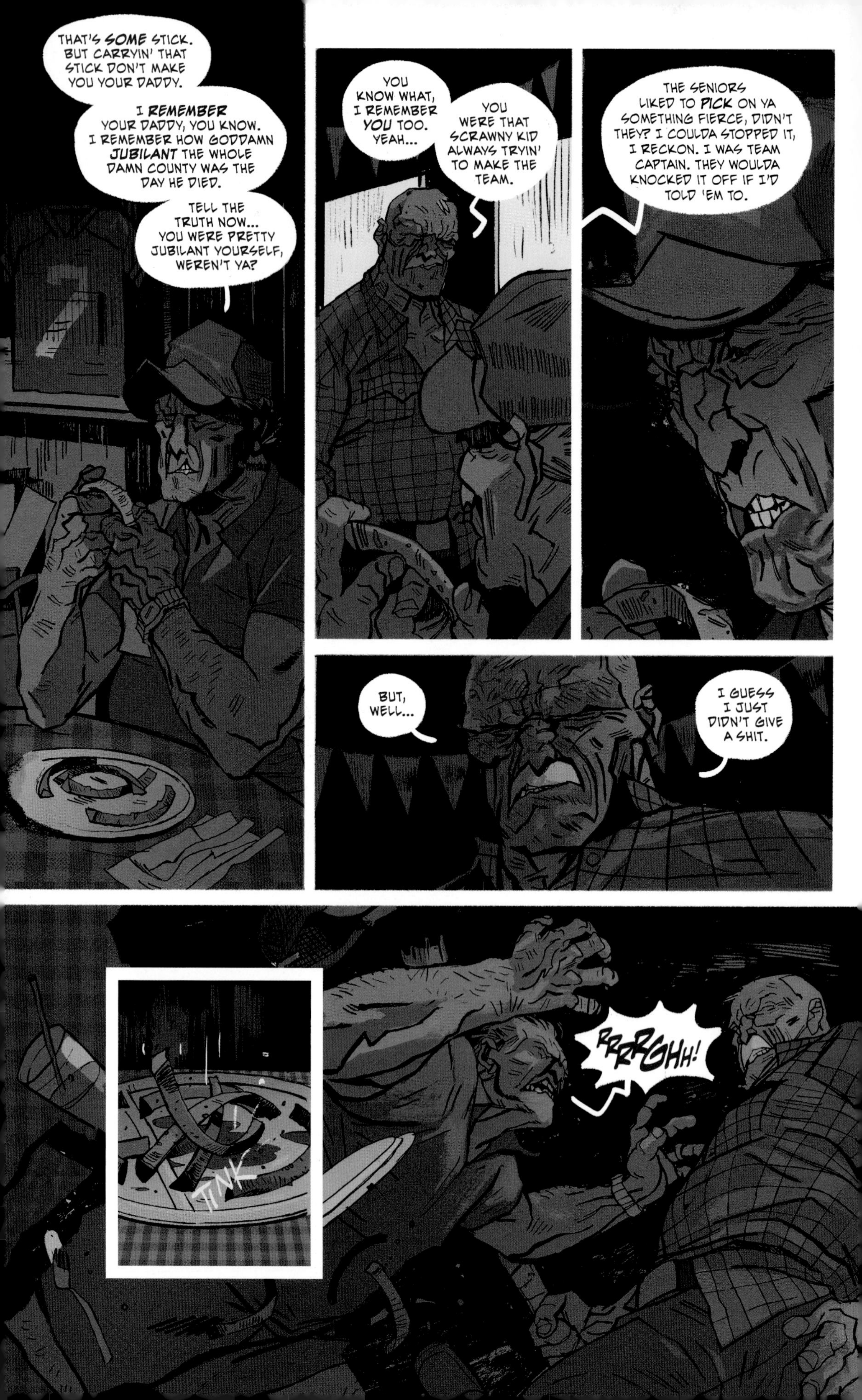

THAT'S SOME STICK. BUT CARRYIN' THAT STICK DON'T MAKE YOU YOUR DADDY.
I REMEMBER YOUR DADDY, YOU KNOW. I REMEMBER HOW GODDAMN JUBILANT THE WHOLE DAMN COUNTY WAS THE DAY HE DIED.
TELL THE TRUTH NOW... YOU WERE PRETTY JUBILANT YOURSELF, WEREN'T YA?
YOU KNOW WHAT, I REMEMBER YOU TOO. YEAH...
YOU WERE THAT SCRAWNY KID ALWAYS TRYIN' TO MAKE THE TEAM.
THE SENIORS LIKED TO PICK ON YA SOMETHING FIERCE, DIDN'T THEY? I COULDA STOPPED IT, I RECKON. I WAS TEAM CAPTAIN. THEY WOULDA KNOCKED IT OFF IF I'D TOLD 'EM TO.
BUT, WELL...
I GUESS I JUST DIDN'T GIVE A SHIT.
TINK
RRRRGHH!

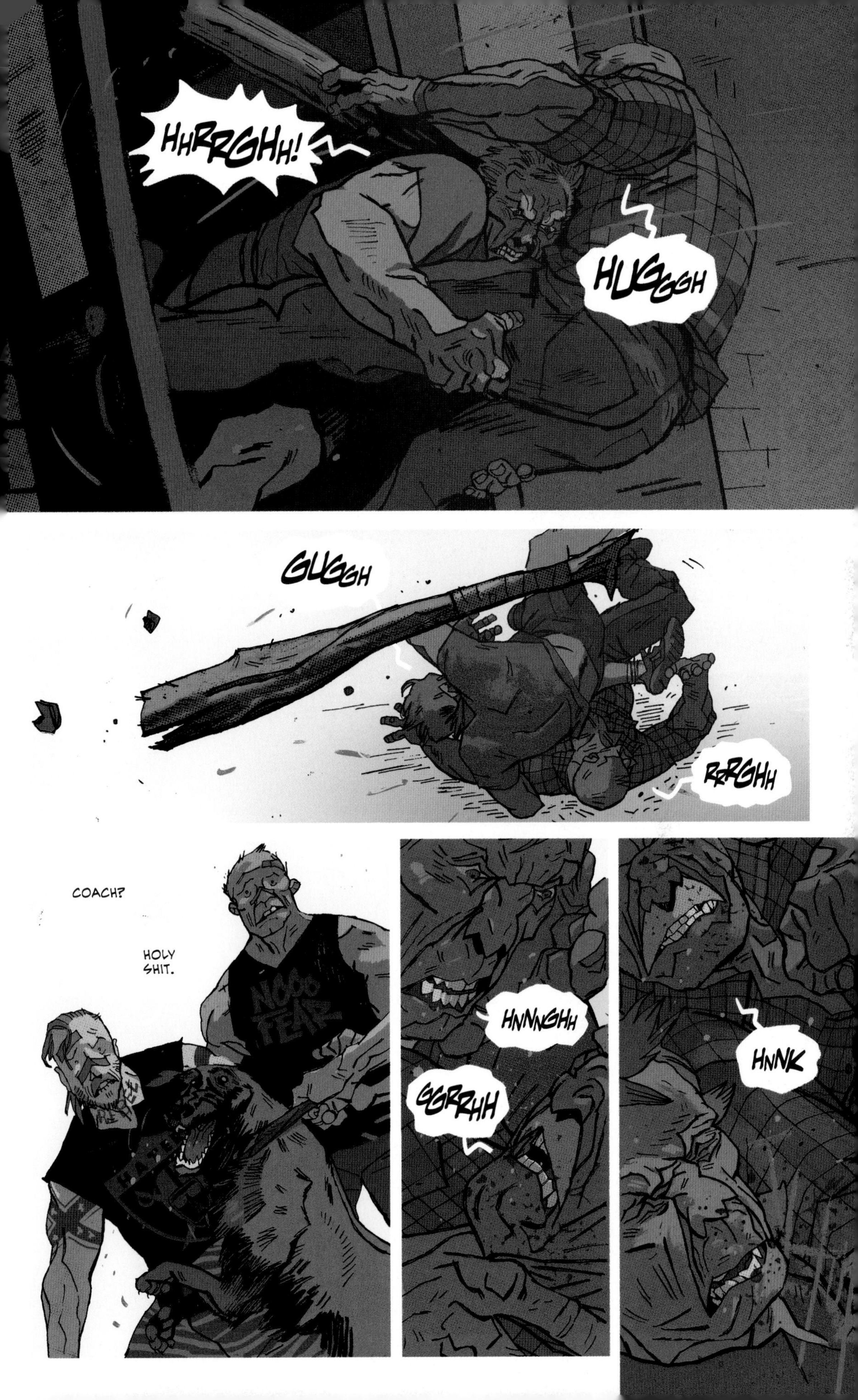
HHRRGHH!
HUGGGH
GUGGGH
RRRGHH
COACH?
HOLY SHIT.
HNNNGHH
GGRRHH
HNNK

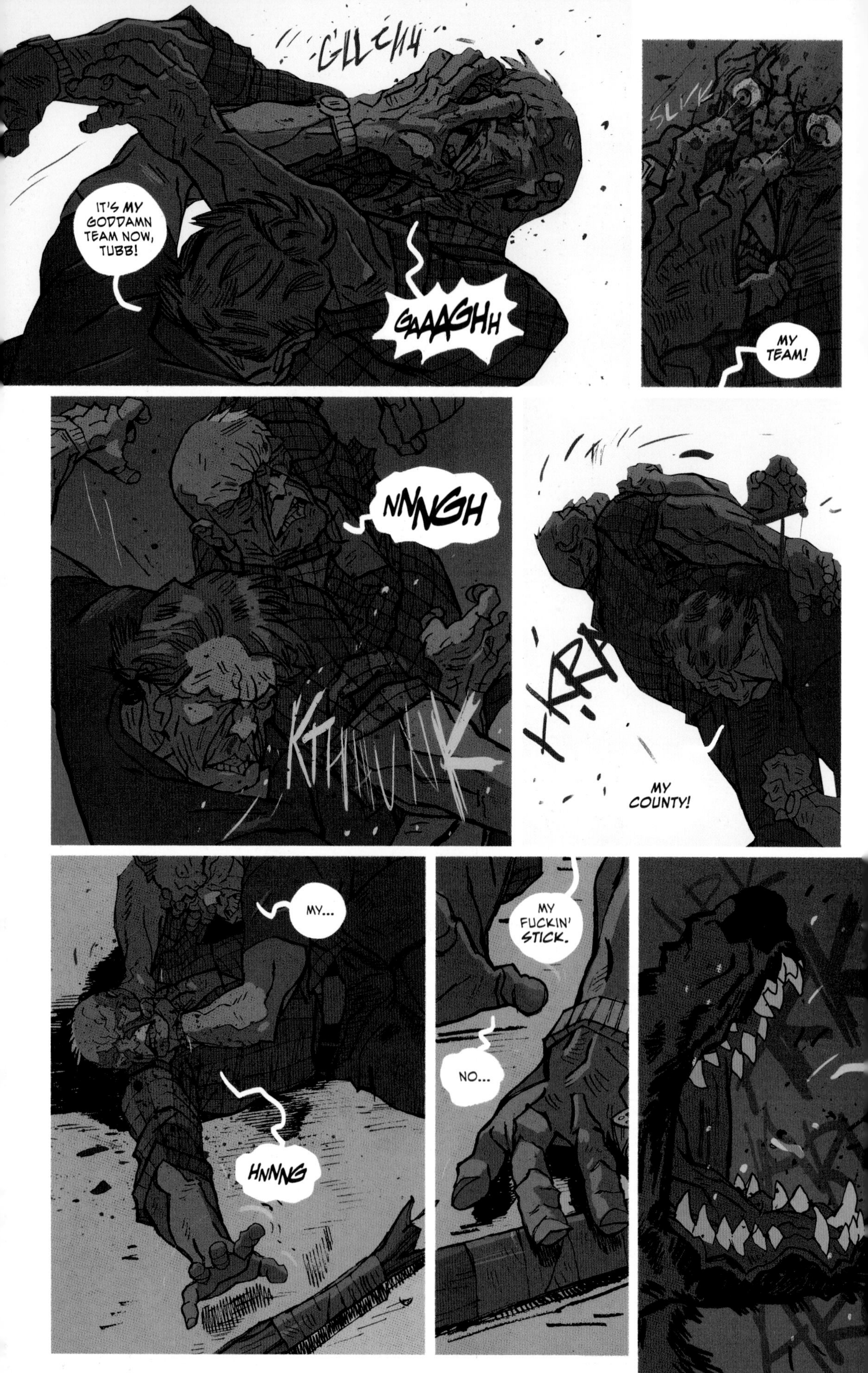
GLLCHH
IT'S MY GODDAMN TEAM NOW, TUBB!
GAAAGHH
SLICK
MY TEAM!
NNNGH
KTHUNK
KRR
MY COUNTY!
MY...
HNNNG
MY FUCKIN' STICK.
NO...

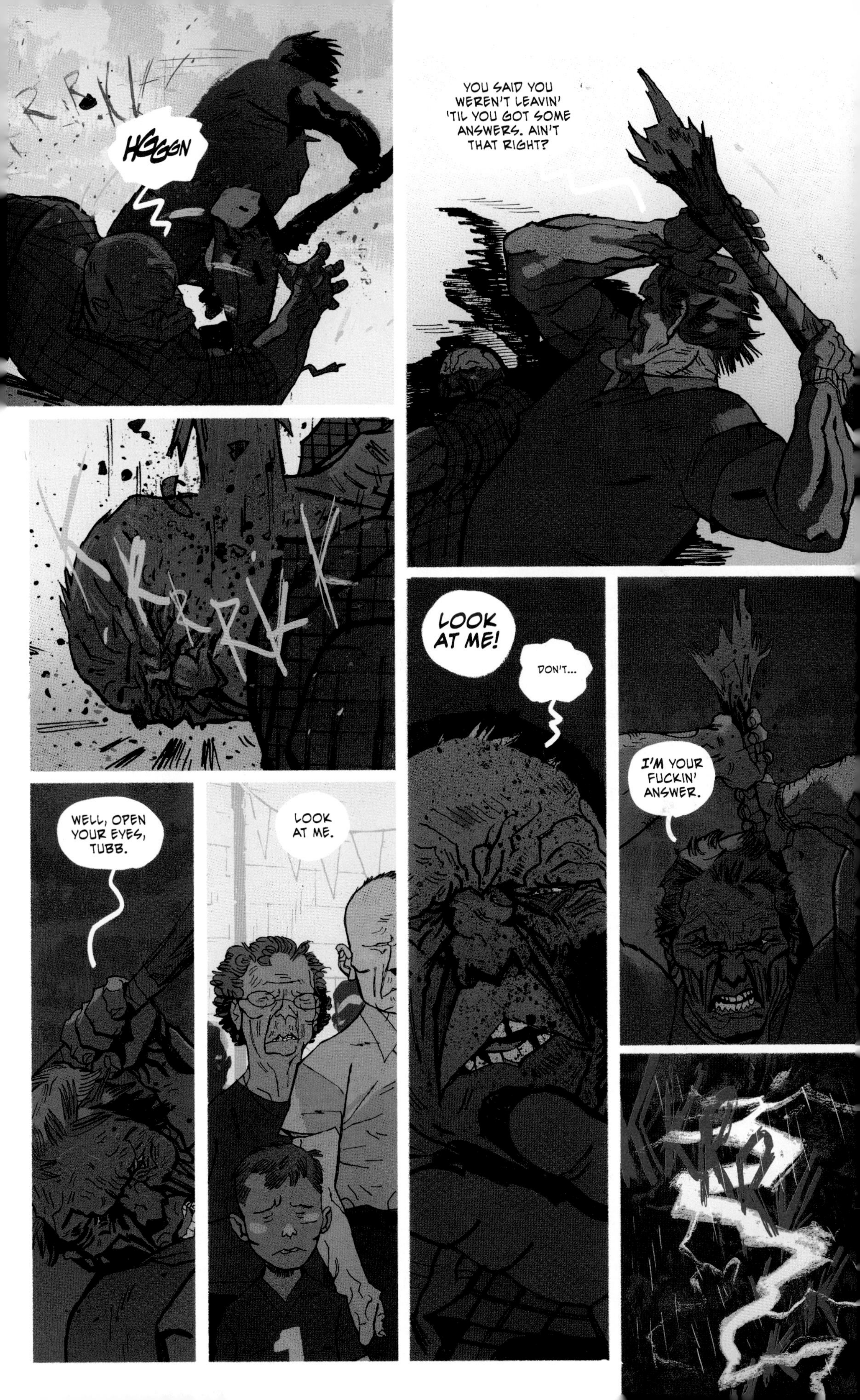
HGGGN
YOU SAID YOU WEREN'T LEAVIN' 'TIL YOU GOT SOME ANSWERS. AIN'T THAT RIGHT?
WELL, OPEN YOUR EYES, TUBB.
LOOK AT ME.
LOOK AT ME!
DON'T...
I'M YOUR FUCKIN' ANSWER.

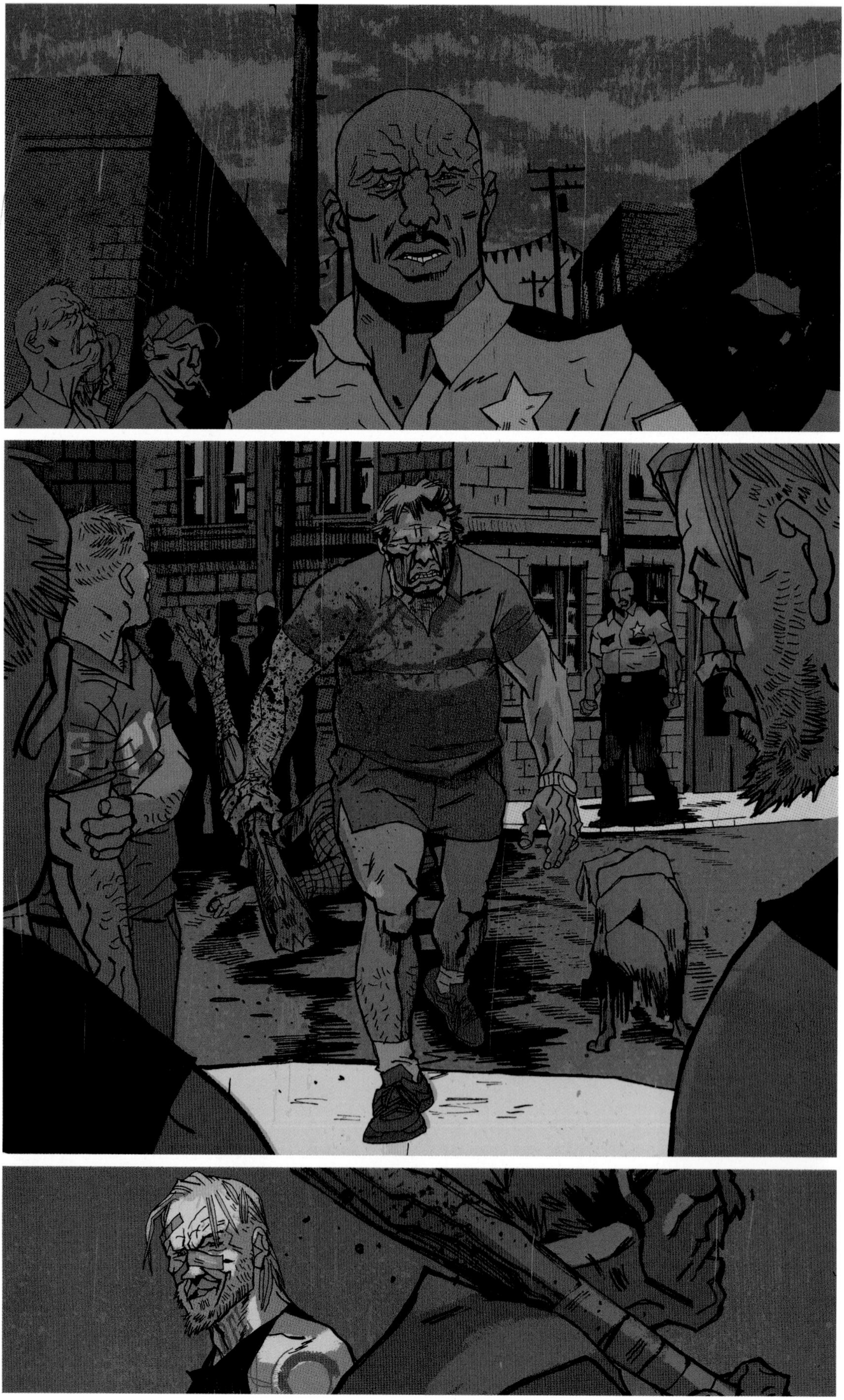

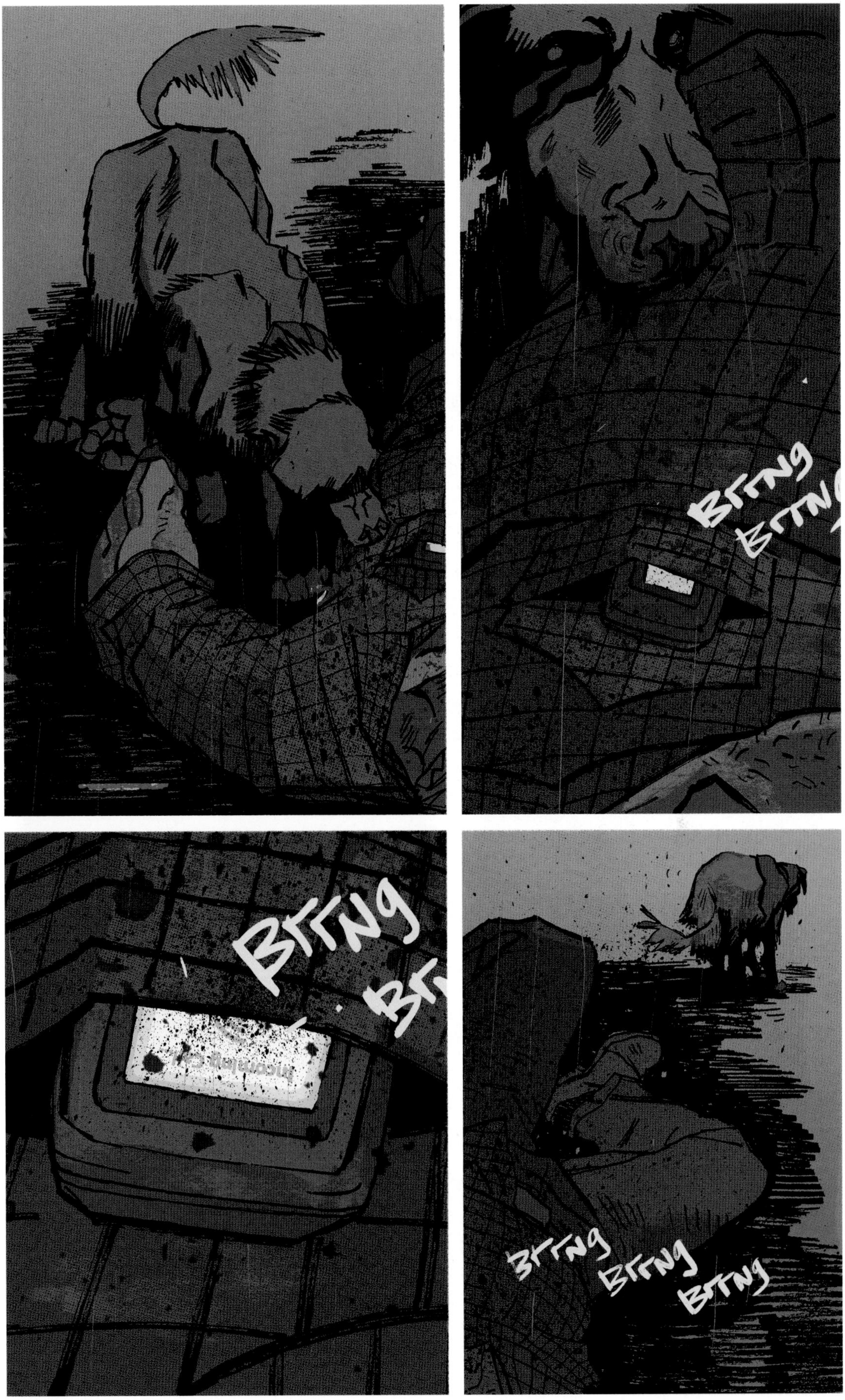
Brrng
Brrng
Brrng
Brrng
Brrng
Brrng

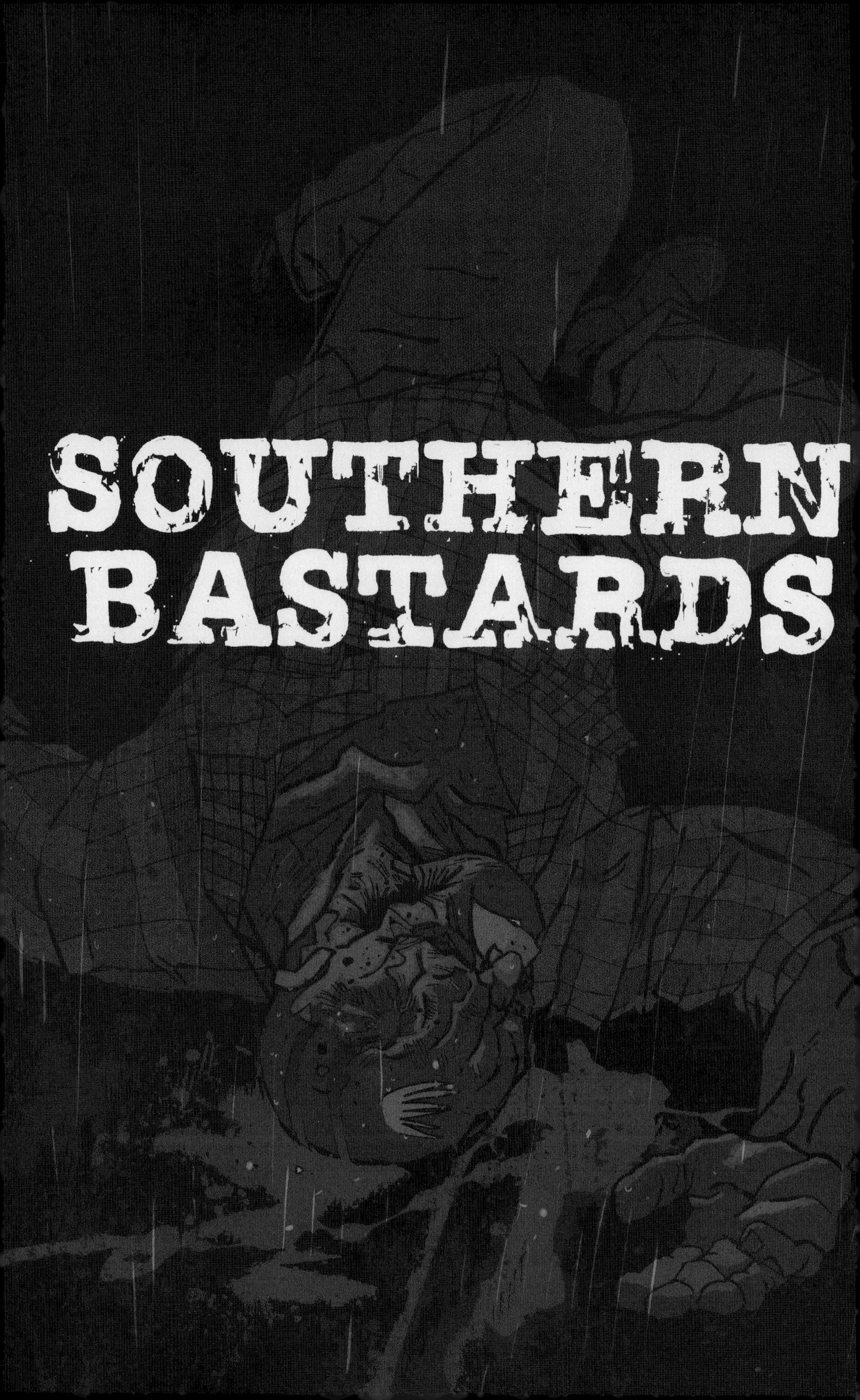
SOUTHERN
BASTARDS

"HERE WAS A MAN"

epilogue

BRRNG
BRRNG
THIS IS EARL. LEAVE A MESSAGE.
BEEEEP
HEY.
IT'S ME.

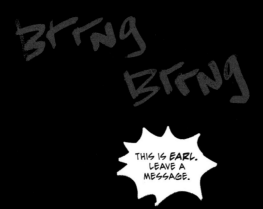

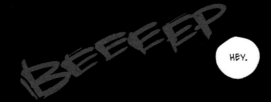

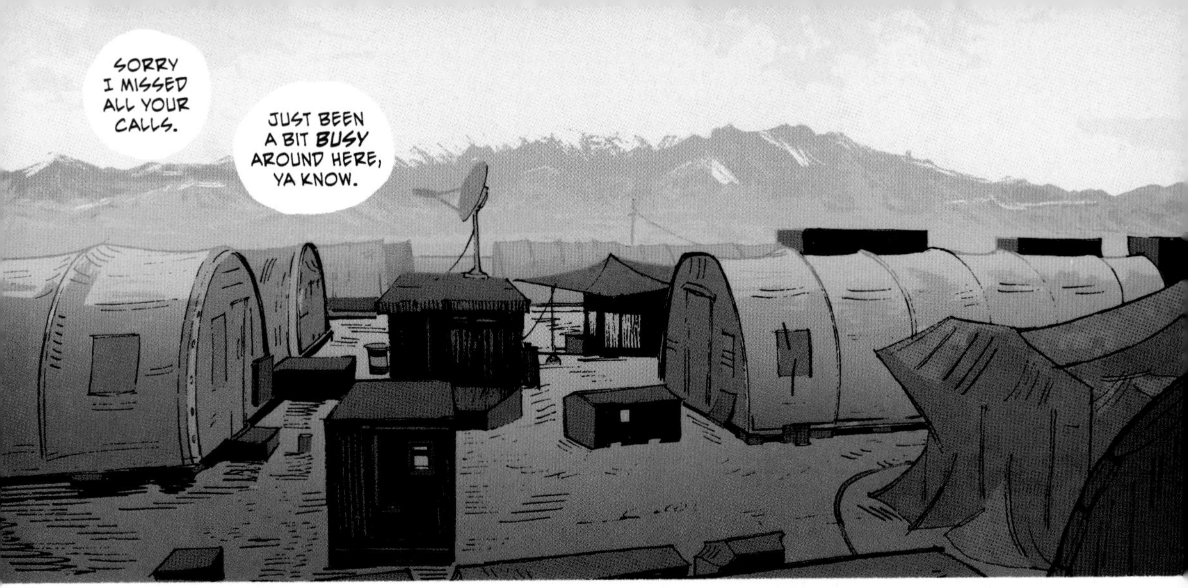
SORRY I MISSED ALL YOUR CALLS.
JUST BEEN A BIT BUSY AROUND HERE, YA KNOW.

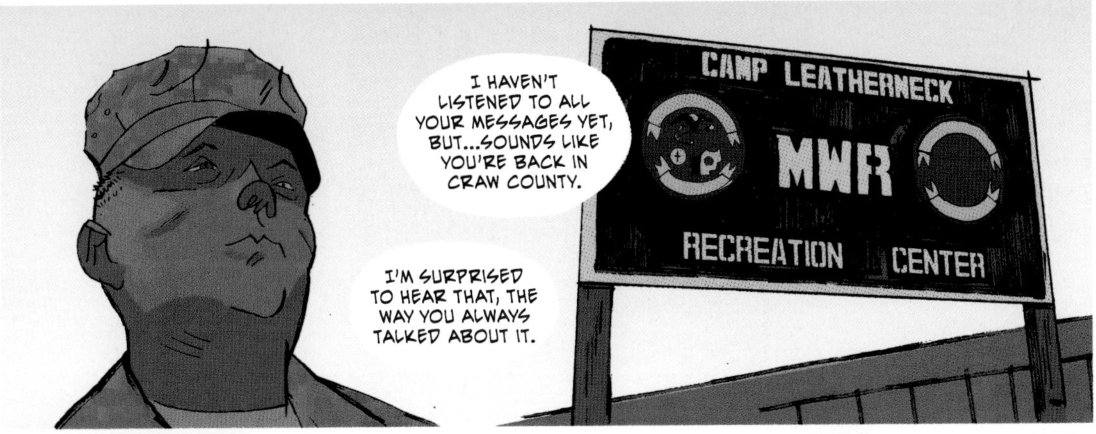
CAMP LEATHERNECK
MWR
RECREATION CENTER
I HAVEN'T LISTENED TO ALL YOUR MESSAGES YET, BUT...SOUNDS LIKE YOU'RE BACK IN CRAW COUNTY.
I'M SURPRISED TO HEAR THAT, THE WAY YOU ALWAYS TALKED ABOUT IT.

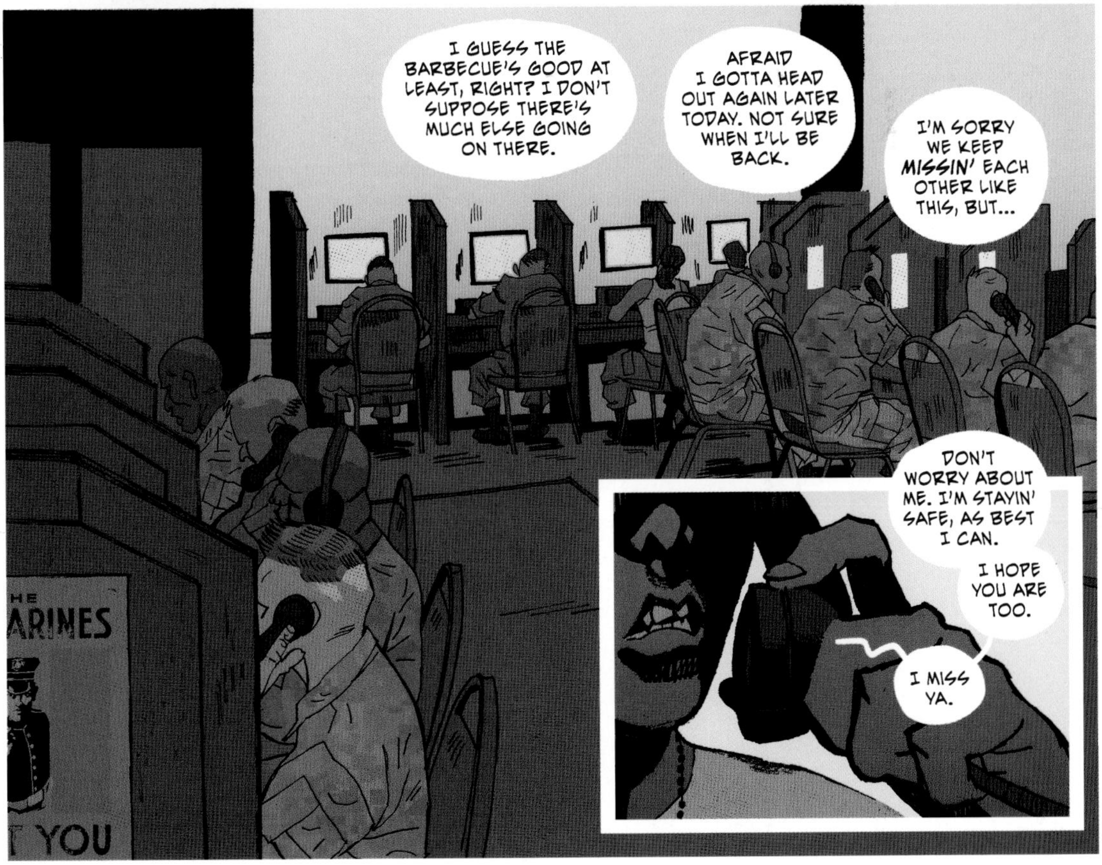
I GUESS THE BARBECUE'S GOOD AT LEAST, RIGHT? I DON'T SUPPOSE THERE'S MUCH ELSE GOING ON THERE.
AFRAID I GOTTA HEAD OUT AGAIN LATER TODAY. NOT SURE WHEN I'LL BE BACK.
I'M SORRY WE KEEP MISSIN' EACH OTHER LIKE THIS, BUT...
DON'T WORRY ABOUT ME. I'M STAYIN' SAFE, AS BEST I CAN.
I HOPE YOU ARE TOO.
I MISS YA.

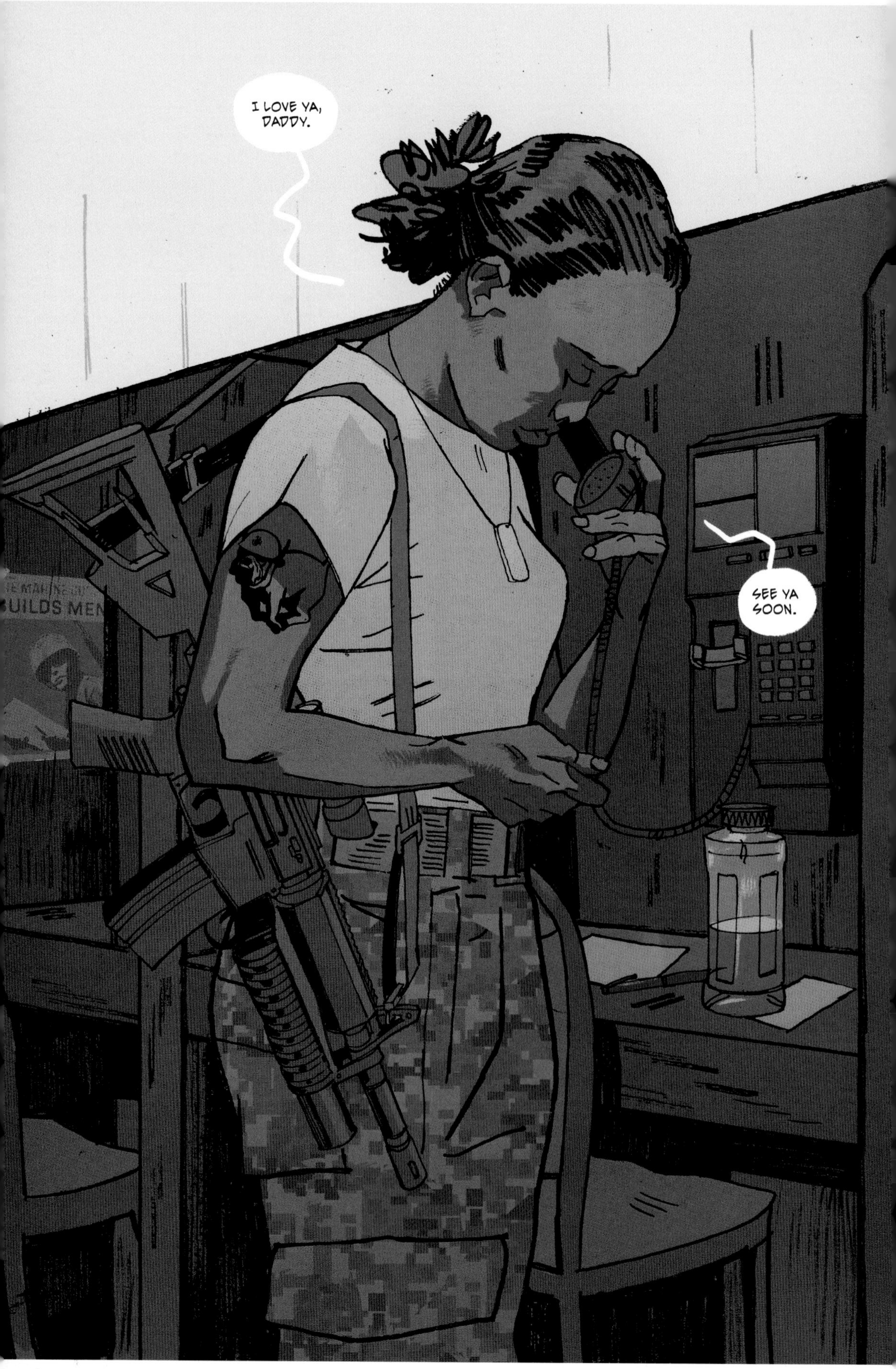
I LOVE YA, DADDY.
SEE YA SOON.

Gridiron

Chapter One

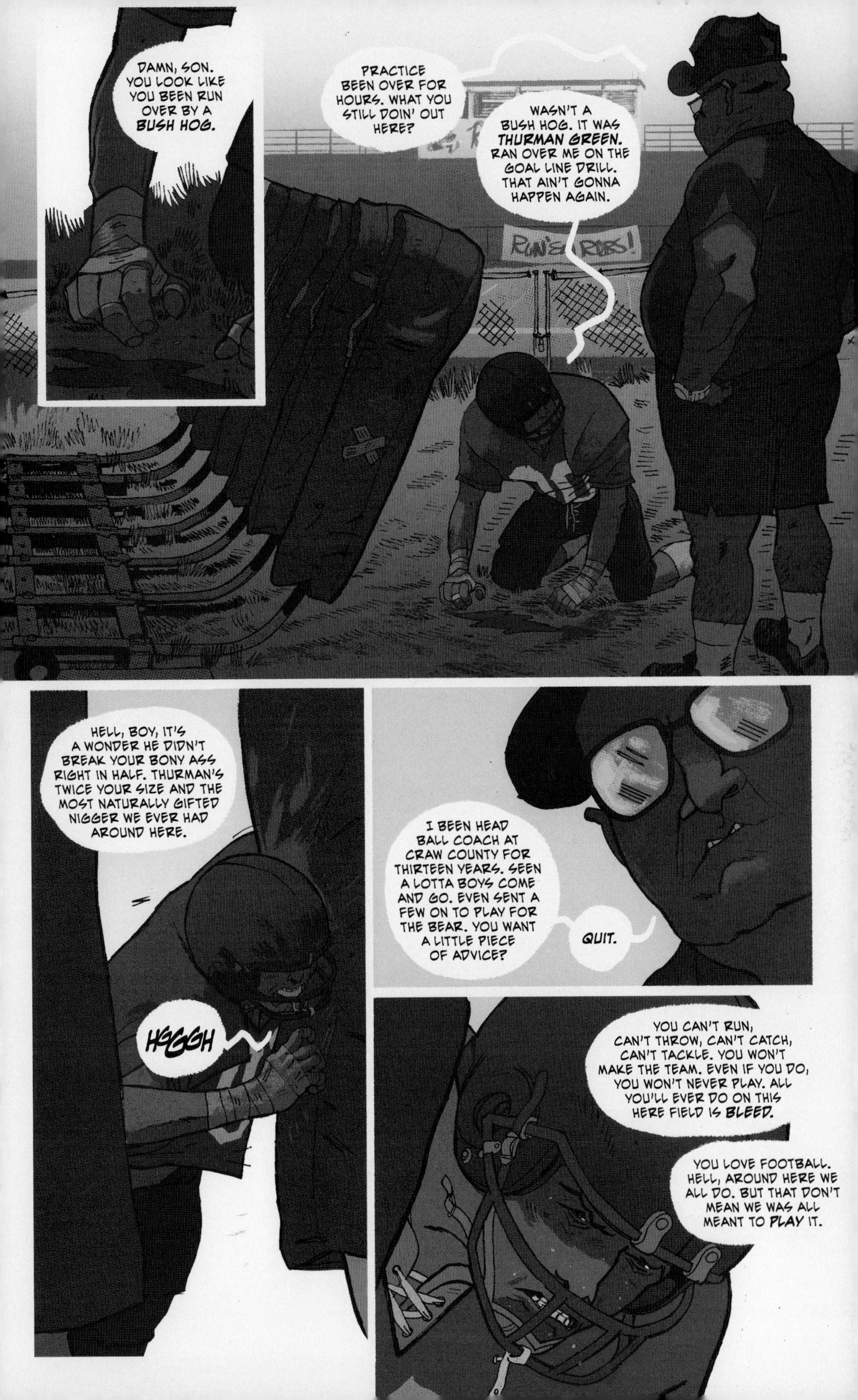
DAMN, SON. YOU LOOK LIKE YOU BEEN RUN OVER BY A **BUSH HOG.**
PRACTICE BEEN OVER FOR HOURS. WHAT YOU STILL DOIN' OUT HERE?
WASN'T A BUSH HOG. IT WAS **THURMAN GREEN.** RAN OVER ME ON THE GOAL LINE DRILL. THAT AIN'T GONNA HAPPEN AGAIN.
HELL, BOY, IT'S A WONDER HE DIDN'T BREAK YOUR BONY ASS RIGHT IN HALF. THURMAN'S TWICE YOUR SIZE AND THE MOST NATURALLY GIFTED NIGGER WE EVER HAD AROUND HERE.
HGGGH
I BEEN HEAD BALL COACH AT CRAW COUNTY FOR THIRTEEN YEARS. SEEN A LOTTA BOYS COME AND GO. EVEN SENT A FEW ON TO PLAY FOR THE BEAR. YOU WANT A LITTLE PIECE OF ADVICE?
QUIT.
YOU CAN'T RUN, CAN'T THROW, CAN'T CATCH, CAN'T TACKLE. YOU WON'T MAKE THE TEAM. EVEN IF YOU DO, YOU WON'T NEVER PLAY. ALL YOU'LL EVER DO ON THIS HERE FIELD IS **BLEED.**
YOU LOVE FOOTBALL. HELL, AROUND HERE WE ALL DO. BUT THAT DON'T MEAN WE WAS ALL MEANT TO **PLAY** IT.

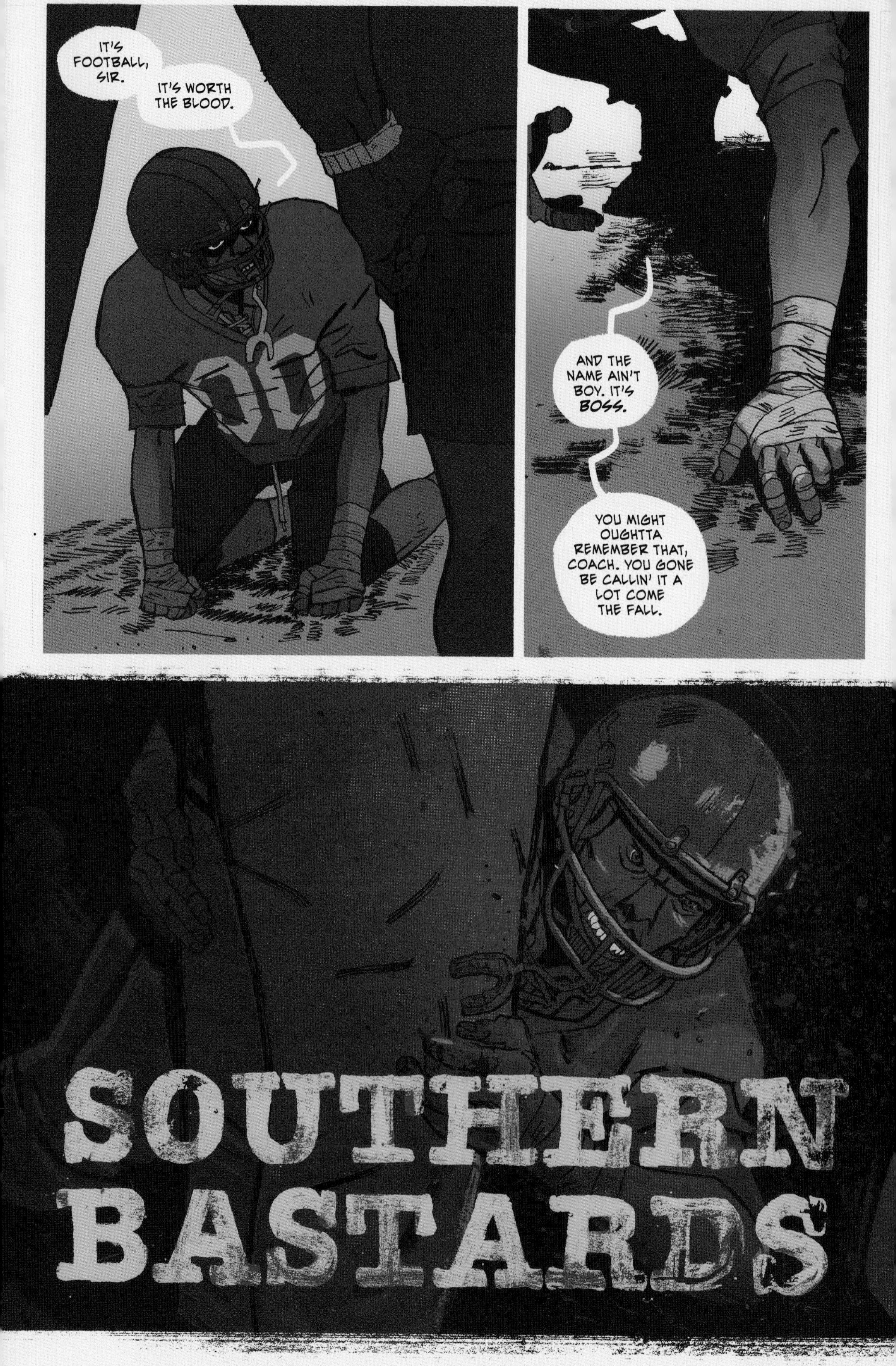
IT'S FOOTBALL, SIR.
IT'S WORTH THE BLOOD.
AND THE NAME AIN'T BOY. IT'S *BOSS*.
YOU MIGHT OUGHTTA REMEMBER THAT, COACH. YOU GONE BE CALLIN' IT A LOT COME THE FALL.
SOUTHERN BASTARDS

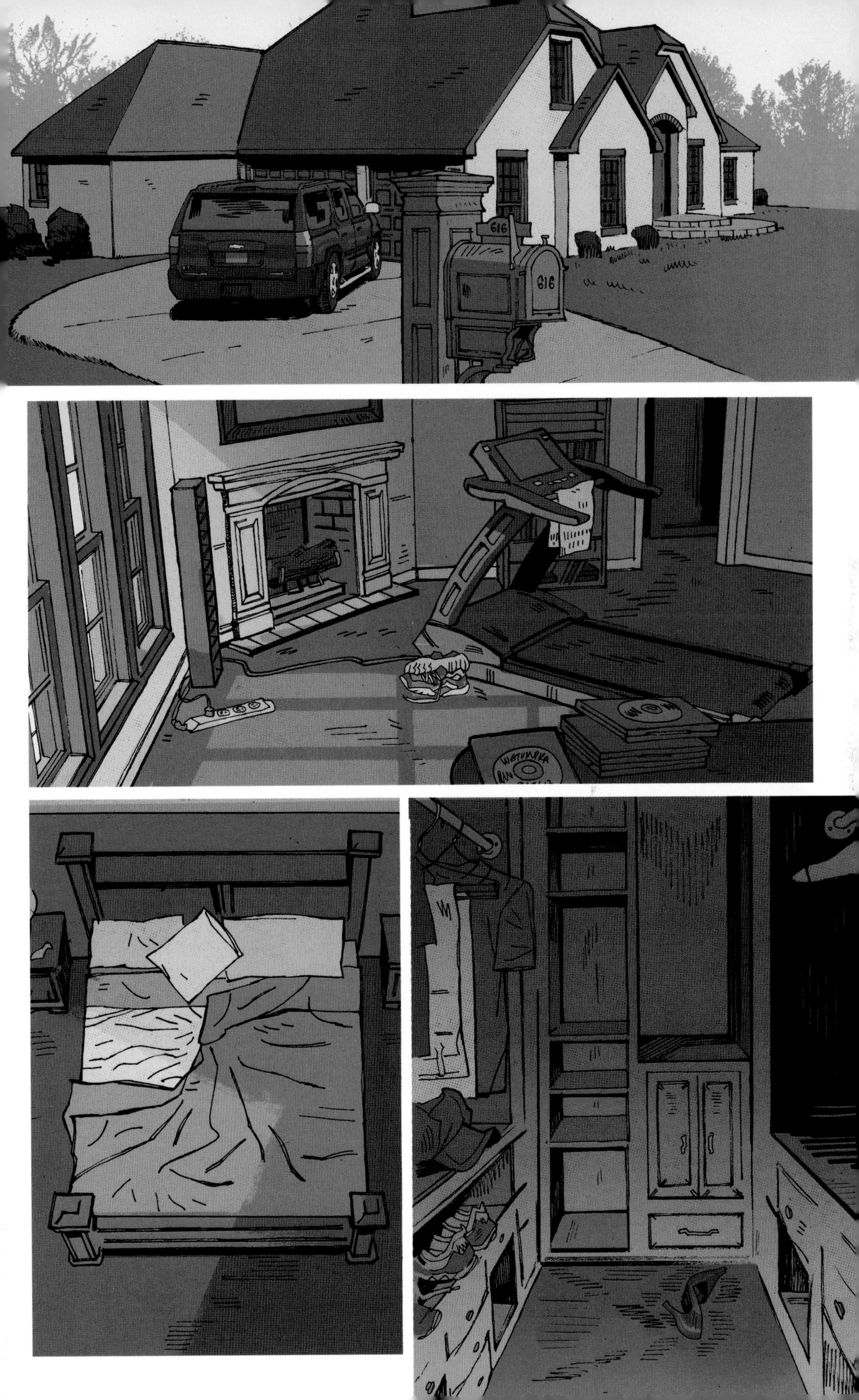
616
616
WETUMPKA

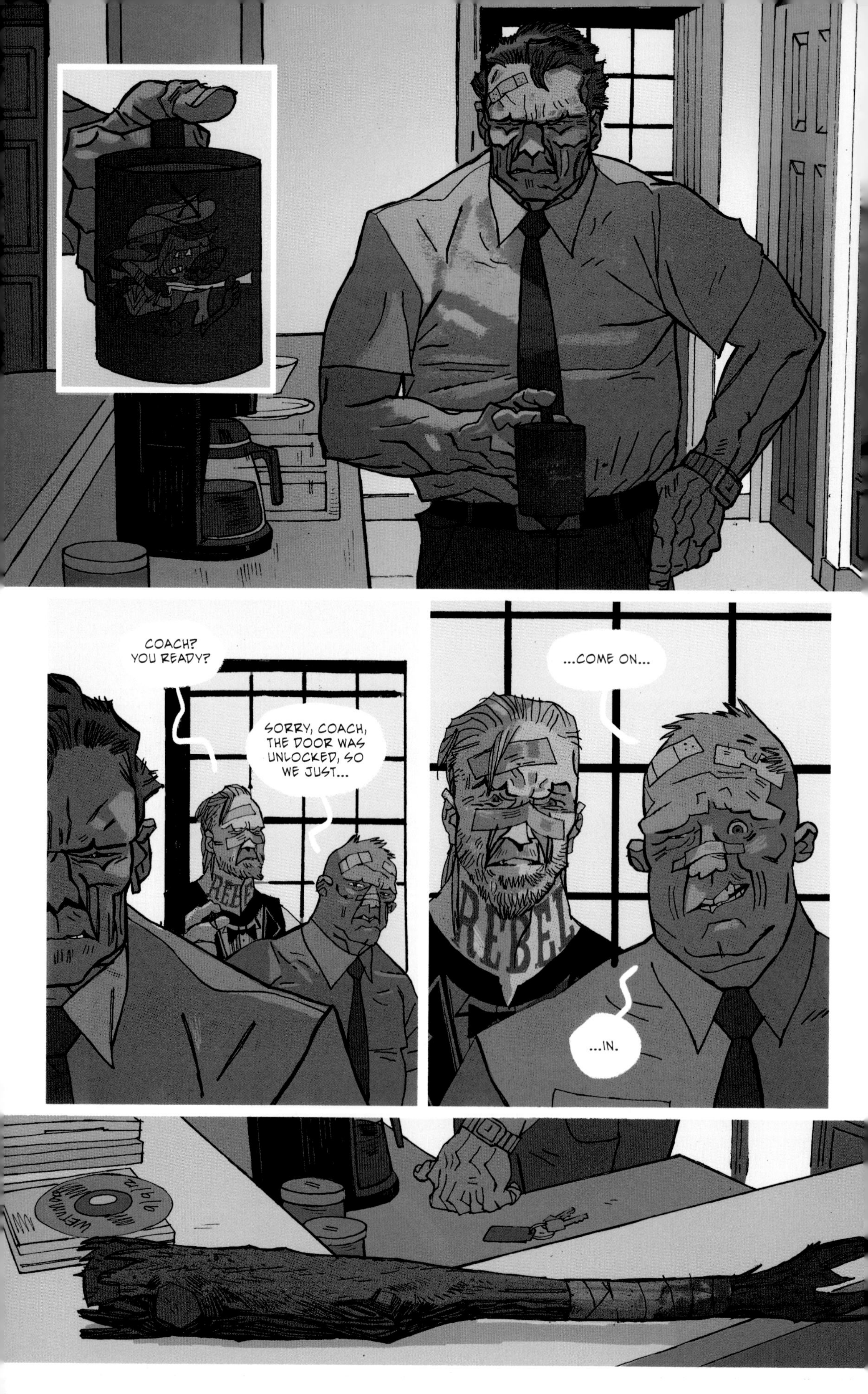
COACH? YOU READY?
SORRY, COACH, THE DOOR WAS UNLOCKED, SO WE JUST...
...COME ON...
...IN.
REBEL
9/9/12

HOLY SHIT. HE AIN'T EVEN CLEANED THE *BLOOD* OFF.

COACH...I REALLY DON'T THINK YOU OUGHTTA HAVE THAT STICK AROUND. NOT AFTER...

...WHAT YOU *DONE* WITH IT.

COACH?

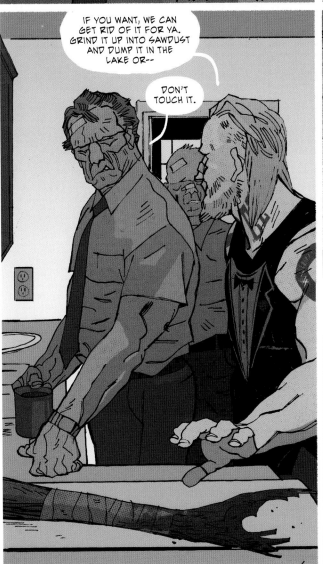

IF YOU WANT, WE CAN GET RID OF IT FOR YA. GRIND IT UP INTO SAWDUST AND DUMP IT IN THE LAKE OR--

DON'T TOUCH IT.

LET'S GO.

COACH, YOU... YOU SURE THIS THING TODAY IS A GOOD IDEA?

I MEAN, ME AND ESAW, WE BEEN TALKIN,' AND WE THINK...MAYBE IT AIN'T. WE THINK YOU SHOULDN'T GO, NOT TO THIS, NOT AFTER--

JESUS CHRIST, I'LL GO BY MY GODDAMN SELF IF I GOT TO.

YOU BOYS ACT LIKE YOU NEVER BEEN TO A *FUNERAL* BEFORE.

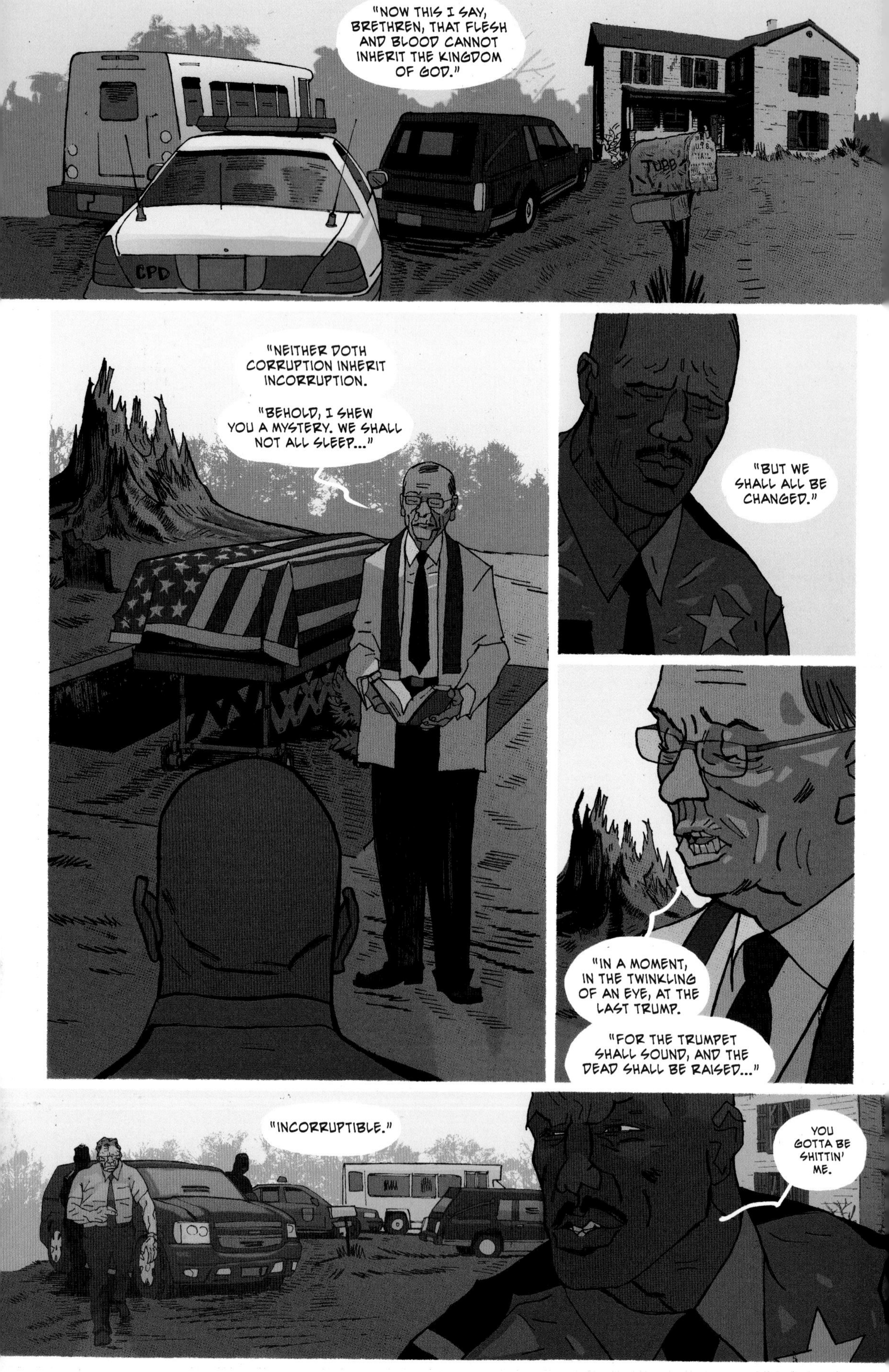
"NOW THIS I SAY, BRETHREN, THAT FLESH AND BLOOD CANNOT INHERIT THE KINGDOM OF GOD."
CPD
"NEITHER DOTH CORRUPTION INHERIT INCORRUPTION.
"BEHOLD, I SHEW YOU A MYSTERY. WE SHALL NOT ALL SLEEP..."
"BUT WE SHALL ALL BE CHANGED."
"IN A MOMENT, IN THE TWINKLING OF AN EYE, AT THE LAST TRUMP.
"FOR THE TRUMPET SHALL SOUND, AND THE DEAD SHALL BE RAISED..."
"INCORRUPTIBLE."
YOU GOTTA BE SHITTIN' ME.

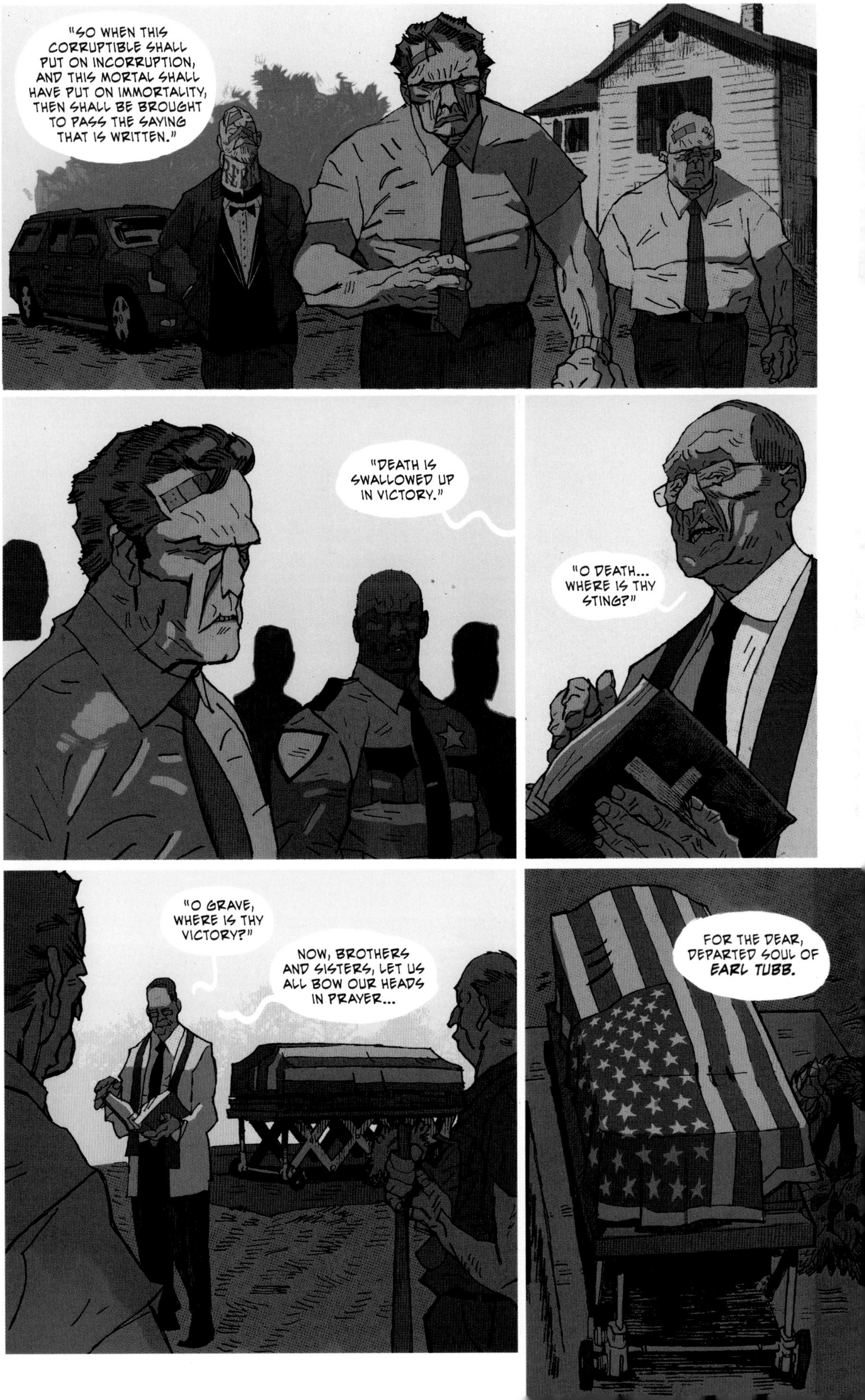
"SO WHEN THIS CORRUPTIBLE SHALL PUT ON INCORRUPTION, AND THIS MORTAL SHALL HAVE PUT ON IMMORTALITY, THEN SHALL BE BROUGHT TO PASS THE SAYING THAT IS WRITTEN."
"DEATH IS SWALLOWED UP IN VICTORY."
"O DEATH... WHERE IS THY STING?"
"O GRAVE, WHERE IS THY VICTORY?"
NOW, BROTHERS AND SISTERS, LET US ALL BOW OUR HEADS IN PRAYER...
FOR THE DEAR, DEPARTED SOUL OF EARL TUBB.

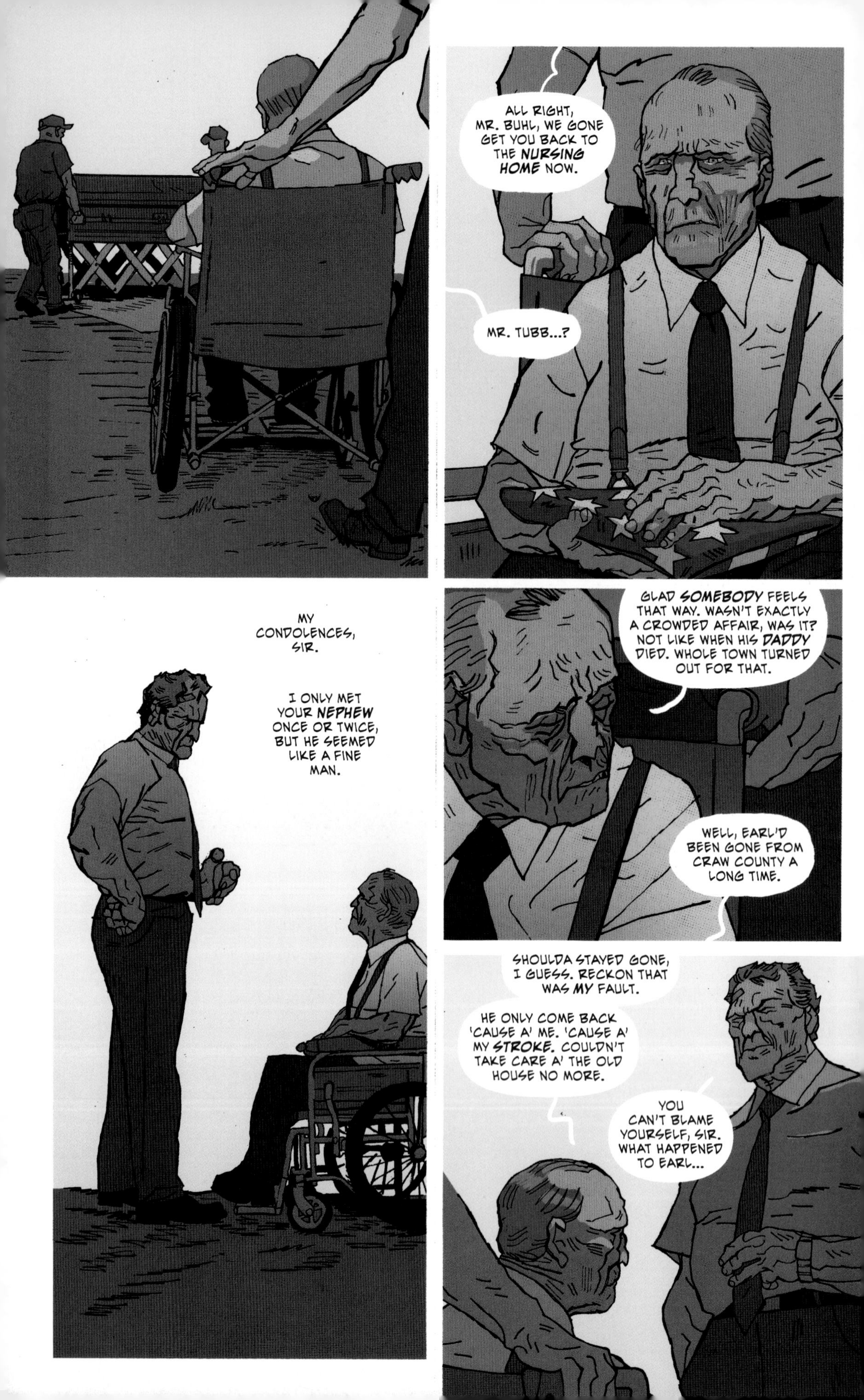
ALL RIGHT, MR. BUHL, WE GONE GET YOU BACK TO THE NURSING HOME NOW.
MR. TUBB...?
MY CONDOLENCES, SIR.
I ONLY MET YOUR NEPHEW ONCE OR TWICE, BUT HE SEEMED LIKE A FINE MAN.
GLAD SOMEBODY FEELS THAT WAY. WASN'T EXACTLY A CROWDED AFFAIR, WAS IT? NOT LIKE WHEN HIS DADDY DIED. WHOLE TOWN TURNED OUT FOR THAT.
WELL, EARL'D BEEN GONE FROM CRAW COUNTY A LONG TIME.
SHOULDA STAYED GONE, I GUESS. RECKON THAT WAS MY FAULT.
HE ONLY COME BACK 'CAUSE A' ME. 'CAUSE A' MY STROKE. COULDN'T TAKE CARE A' THE OLD HOUSE NO MORE.
YOU CAN'T BLAME YOURSELF, SIR. WHAT HAPPENED TO EARL...

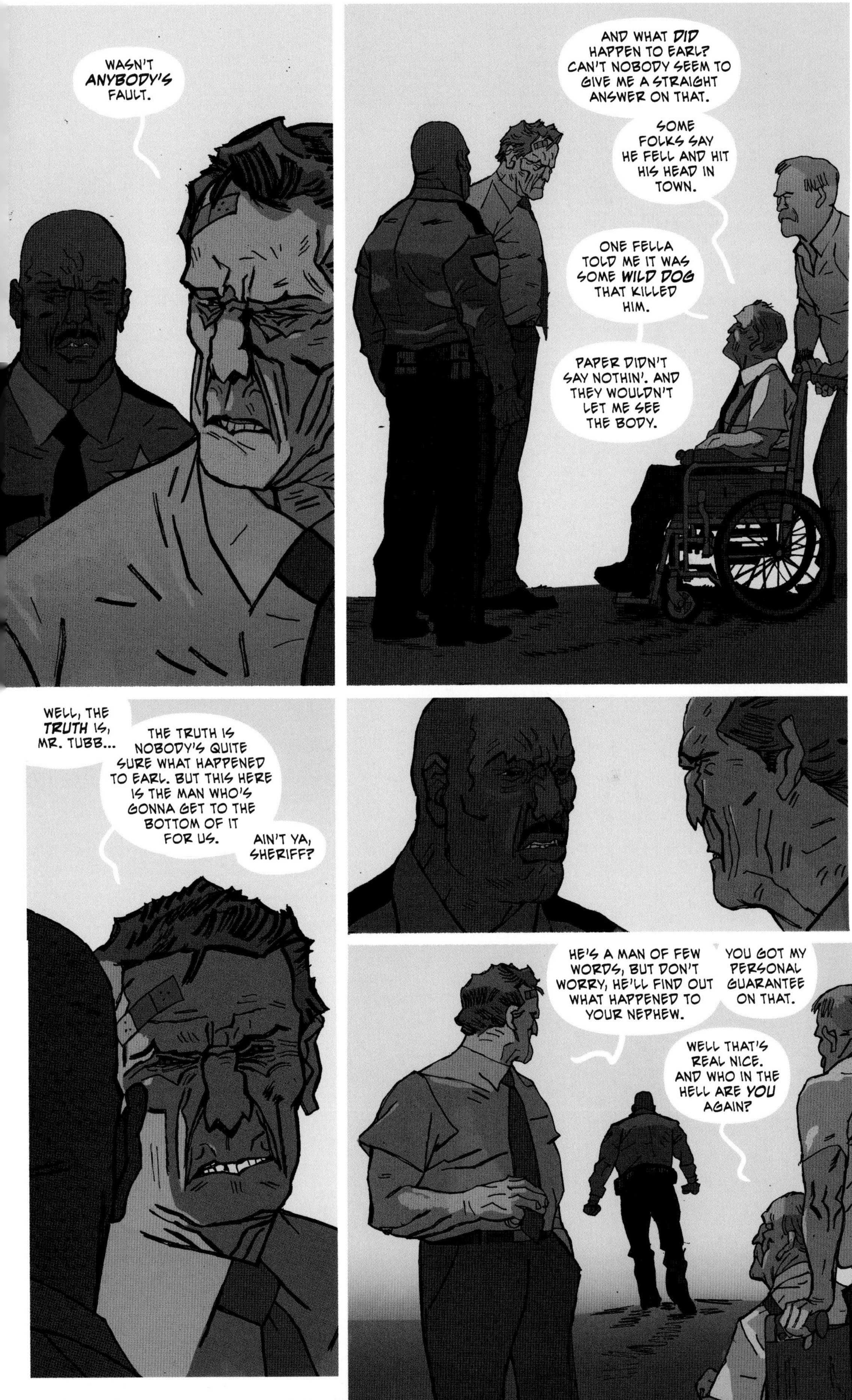
WASN'T ANYBODY'S FAULT.
AND WHAT DID HAPPEN TO EARL? CAN'T NOBODY SEEM TO GIVE ME A STRAIGHT ANSWER ON THAT.
SOME FOLKS SAY HE FELL AND HIT HIS HEAD IN TOWN.
ONE FELLA TOLD ME IT WAS SOME WILD DOG THAT KILLED HIM.
PAPER DIDN'T SAY NOTHIN'. AND THEY WOULDN'T LET ME SEE THE BODY.
WELL, THE TRUTH IS, MR. TUBB...
THE TRUTH IS NOBODY'S QUITE SURE WHAT HAPPENED TO EARL. BUT THIS HERE IS THE MAN WHO'S GONNA GET TO THE BOTTOM OF IT FOR US.
AIN'T YA, SHERIFF?
HE'S A MAN OF FEW WORDS, BUT DON'T WORRY, HE'LL FIND OUT WHAT HAPPENED TO YOUR NEPHEW.
YOU GOT MY PERSONAL GUARANTEE ON THAT.
WELL THAT'S REAL NICE. AND WHO IN THE HELL ARE YOU AGAIN?

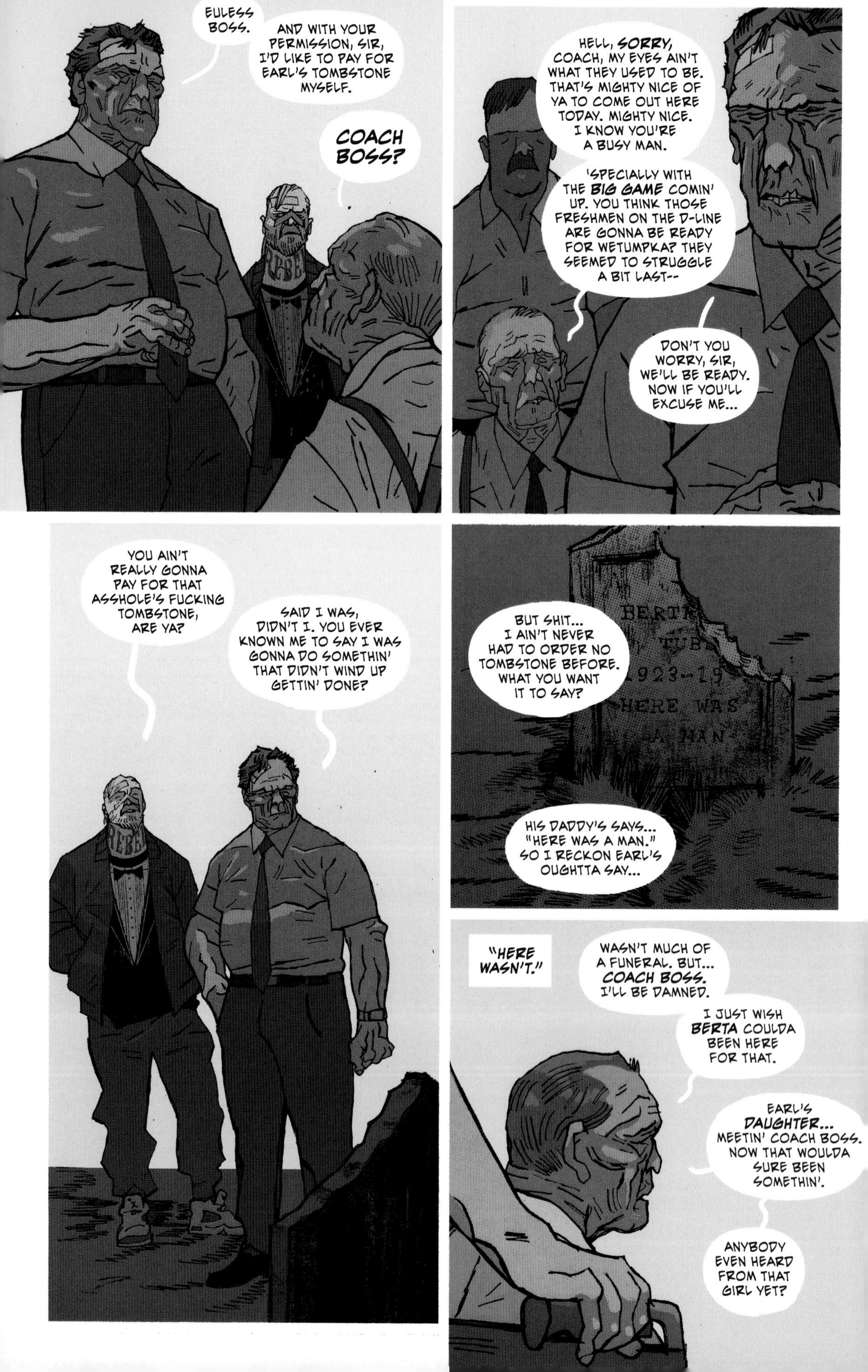
EULESS BOSS.
AND WITH YOUR PERMISSION, SIR, I'D LIKE TO PAY FOR EARL'S TOMBSTONE MYSELF.
COACH BOSS?
HELL, SORRY, COACH, MY EYES AIN'T WHAT THEY USED TO BE. THAT'S MIGHTY NICE OF YA TO COME OUT HERE TODAY. MIGHTY NICE. I KNOW YOU'RE A BUSY MAN.
'SPECIALLY WITH THE BIG GAME COMIN' UP. YOU THINK THOSE FRESHMEN ON THE D-LINE ARE GONNA BE READY FOR WETUMPKA? THEY SEEMED TO STRUGGLE A BIT LAST--
DON'T YOU WORRY, SIR, WE'LL BE READY. NOW IF YOU'LL EXCUSE ME...
YOU AIN'T REALLY GONNA PAY FOR THAT ASSHOLE'S FUCKING TOMBSTONE, ARE YA?
SAID I WAS, DIDN'T I. YOU EVER KNOWN ME TO SAY I WAS GONNA DO SOMETHIN' THAT DIDN'T WIND UP GETTIN' DONE?
BUT SHIT... I AIN'T NEVER HAD TO ORDER NO TOMBSTONE BEFORE. WHAT YOU WANT IT TO SAY?
HIS DADDY'S SAYS... "HERE WAS A MAN." SO I RECKON EARL'S OUGHTTA SAY...
"HERE WASN'T."
WASN'T MUCH OF A FUNERAL. BUT... COACH BOSS. I'LL BE DAMNED.
I JUST WISH BERTA COULDA BEEN HERE FOR THAT.
EARL'S DAUGHTER... MEETIN' COACH BOSS. NOW THAT WOULDA SURE BEEN SOMETHIN'.
ANYBODY EVEN HEARD FROM THAT GIRL YET?

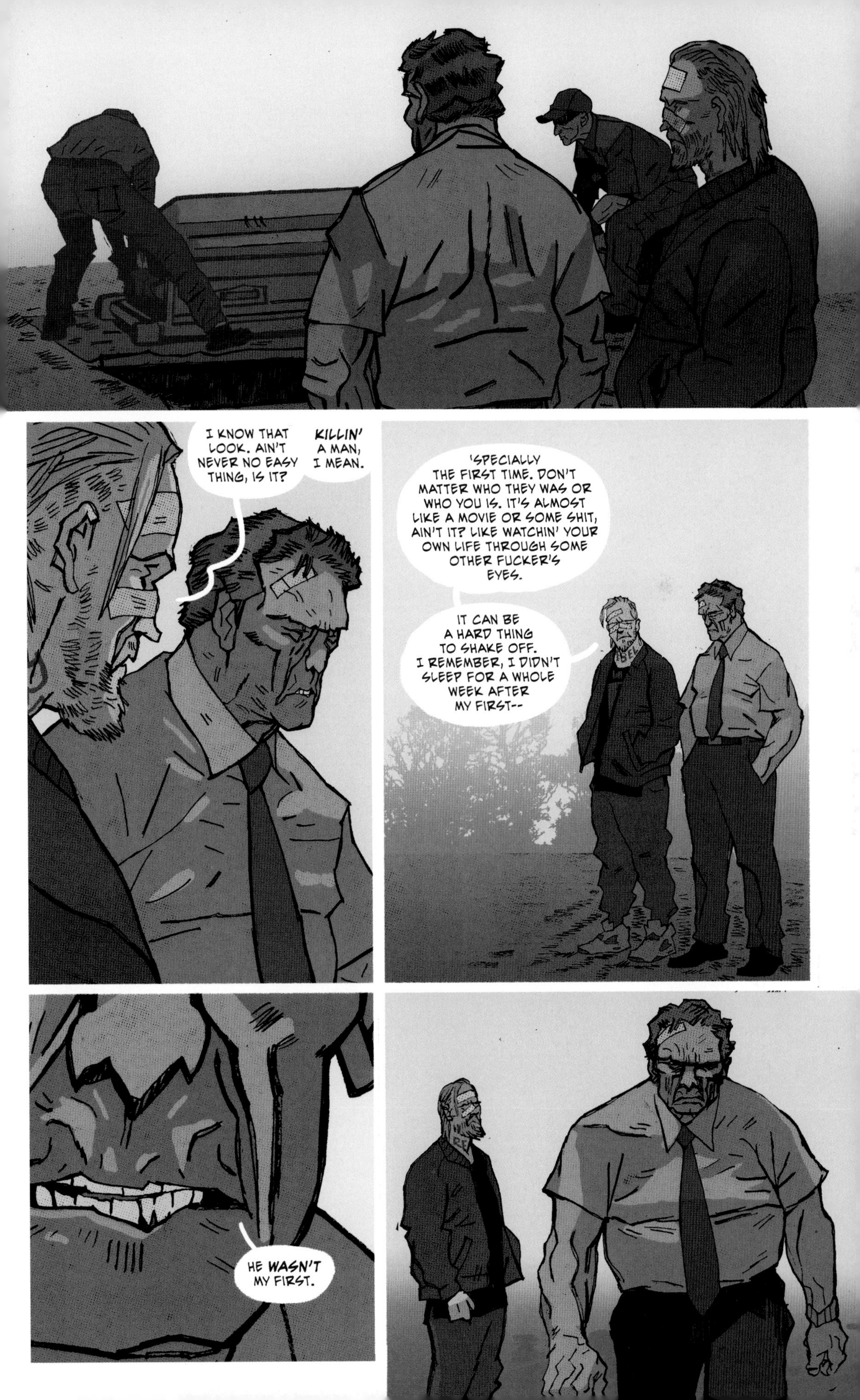
I KNOW THAT LOOK. AIN'T NEVER NO EASY THING, IS IT?
KILLIN' A MAN, I MEAN.
'SPECIALLY THE FIRST TIME. DON'T MATTER WHO THEY WAS OR WHO YOU IS. IT'S ALMOST LIKE A MOVIE OR SOME SHIT, AIN'T IT? LIKE WATCHIN' YOUR OWN LIFE THROUGH SOME OTHER FUCKER'S EYES.
IT CAN BE A HARD THING TO SHAKE OFF. I REMEMBER, I DIDN'T SLEEP FOR A WHOLE WEEK AFTER MY FIRST--
HE WASN'T MY FIRST.

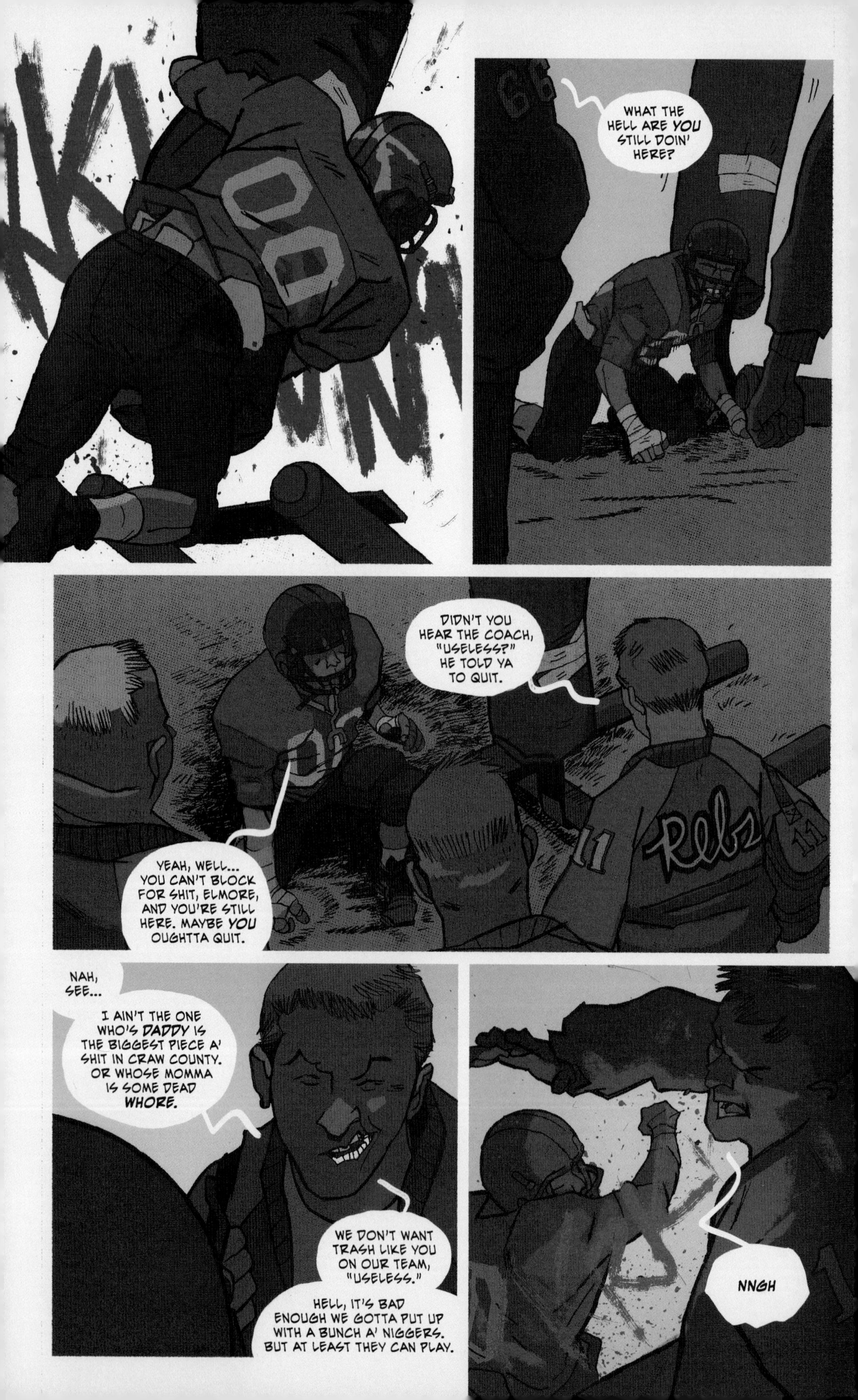
WHAT THE HELL ARE YOU STILL DOIN' HERE?
DIDN'T YOU HEAR THE COACH, "USELESS?" HE TOLD YA TO QUIT.
YEAH, WELL... YOU CAN'T BLOCK FOR SHIT, ELMORE, AND YOU'RE STILL HERE. MAYBE YOU OUGHTTA QUIT.
NAH, SEE...
I AIN'T THE ONE WHO'S DADDY IS THE BIGGEST PIECE A' SHIT IN CRAW COUNTY. OR WHOSE MOMMA IS SOME DEAD WHORE.
WE DON'T WANT TRASH LIKE YOU ON OUR TEAM, "USELESS."
HELL, IT'S BAD ENOUGH WE GOTTA PUT UP WITH A BUNCH A' NIGGERS. BUT AT LEAST THEY CAN PLAY.
NNGH

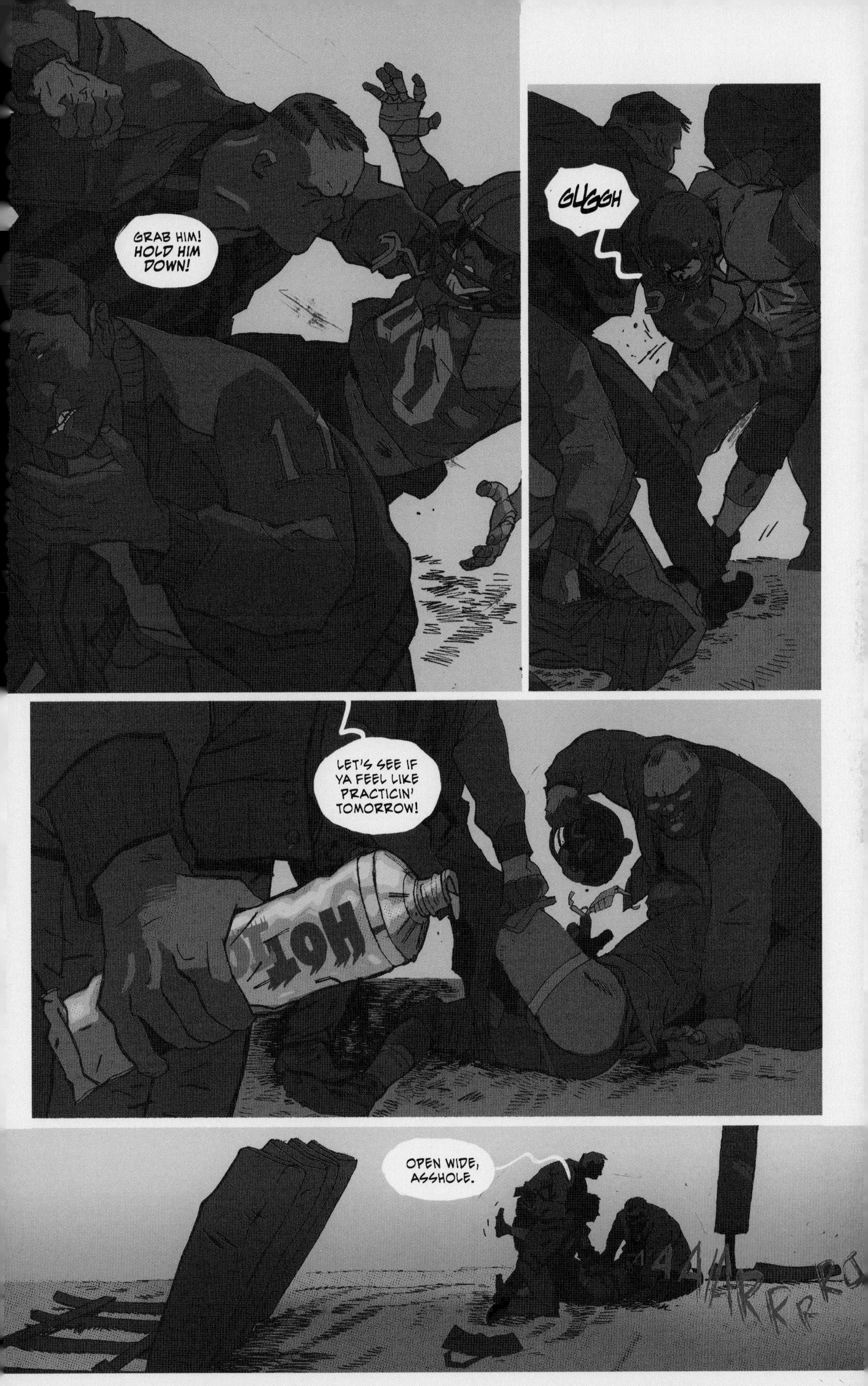
GRAB HIM! HOLD HIM DOWN!
GUGGH
LET'S SEE IF YA FEEL LIKE PRACTICIN' TOMORROW!
OPEN WIDE, ASSHOLE.

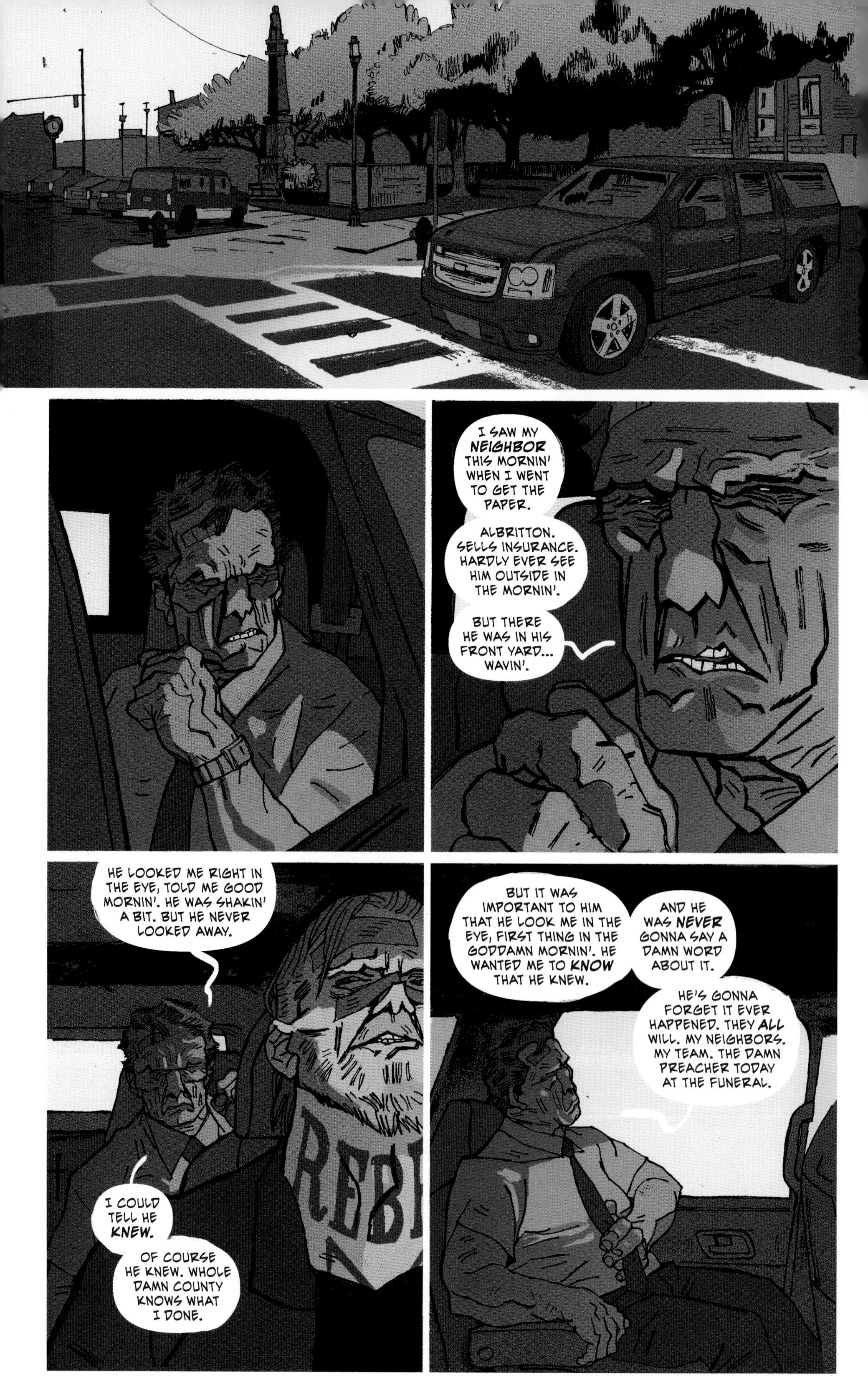

I SAW MY NEIGHBOR THIS MORNIN' WHEN I WENT TO GET THE PAPER.
ALBRITTON. SELLS INSURANCE. HARDLY EVER SEE HIM OUTSIDE IN THE MORNIN'.
BUT THERE HE WAS IN HIS FRONT YARD... WAVIN'.
HE LOOKED ME RIGHT IN THE EYE, TOLD ME GOOD MORNIN'. HE WAS SHAKIN' A BIT. BUT HE NEVER LOOKED AWAY.
REB
I COULD TELL HE KNEW.
OF COURSE HE KNEW. WHOLE DAMN COUNTY KNOWS WHAT I DONE.
BUT IT WAS IMPORTANT TO HIM THAT HE LOOK ME IN THE EYE, FIRST THING IN THE GODDAMN MORNIN'. HE WANTED ME TO KNOW THAT HE KNEW.
AND HE WAS NEVER GONNA SAY A DAMN WORD ABOUT IT.
HE'S GONNA FORGET IT EVER HAPPENED. THEY ALL WILL. MY NEIGHBORS. MY TEAM. THE DAMN PREACHER TODAY AT THE FUNERAL.

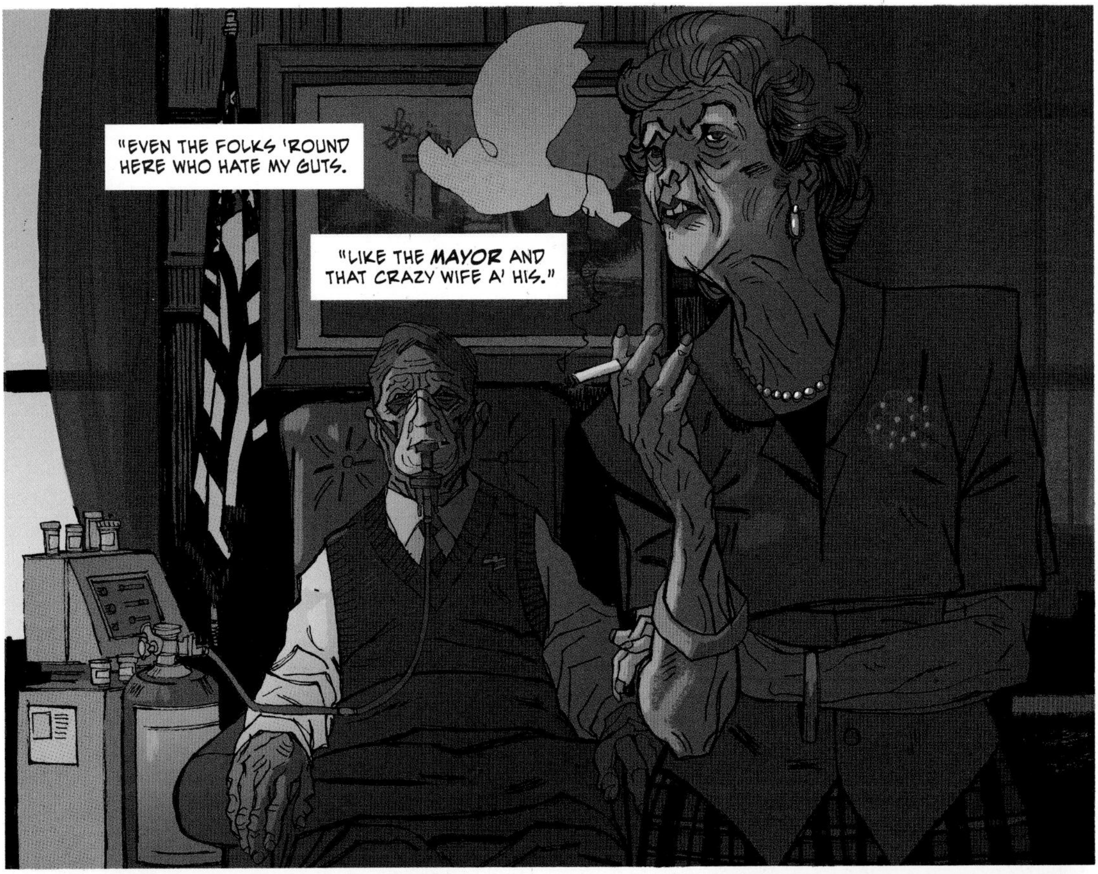
"EVEN THE FOLKS 'ROUND HERE WHO HATE MY GUTS.
"LIKE THE MAYOR AND THAT CRAZY WIFE A' HIS."

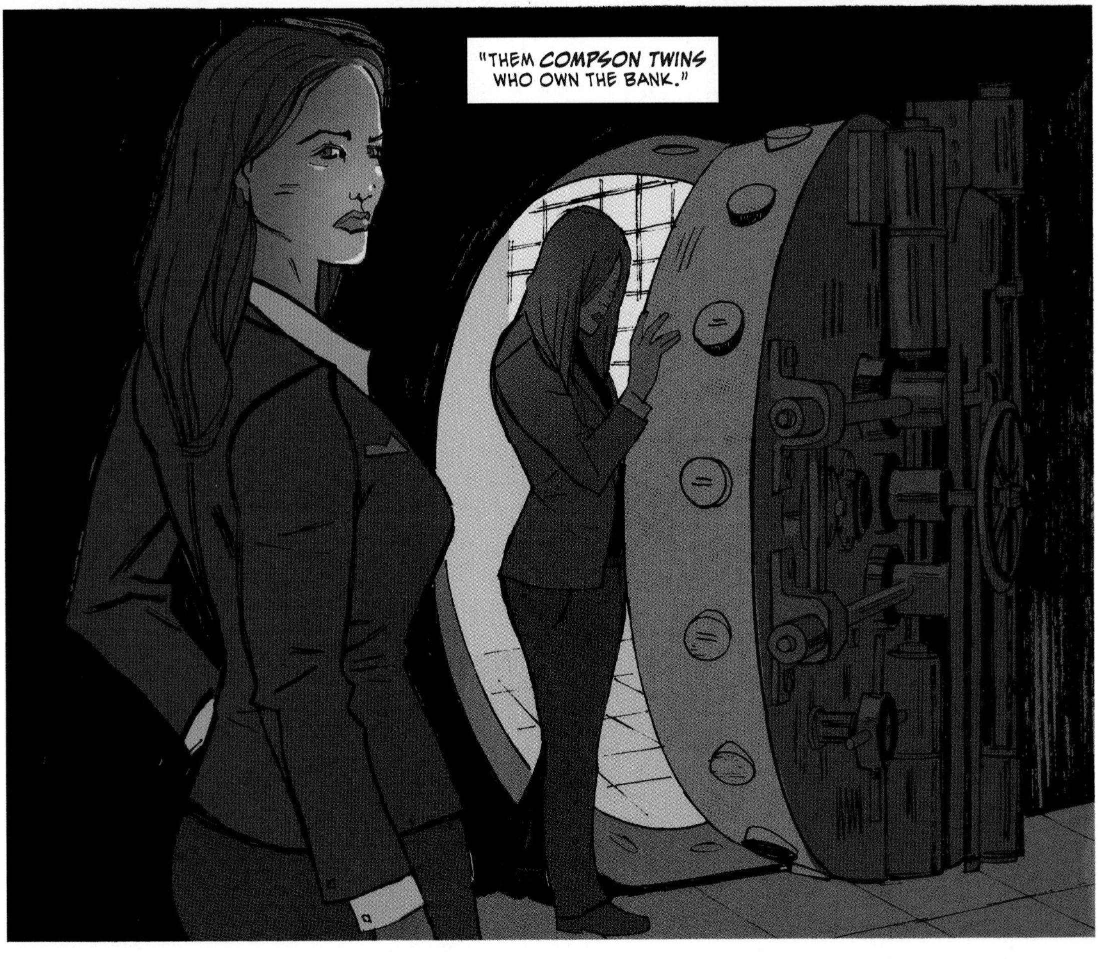
"THEM COMPSON TWINS WHO OWN THE BANK."

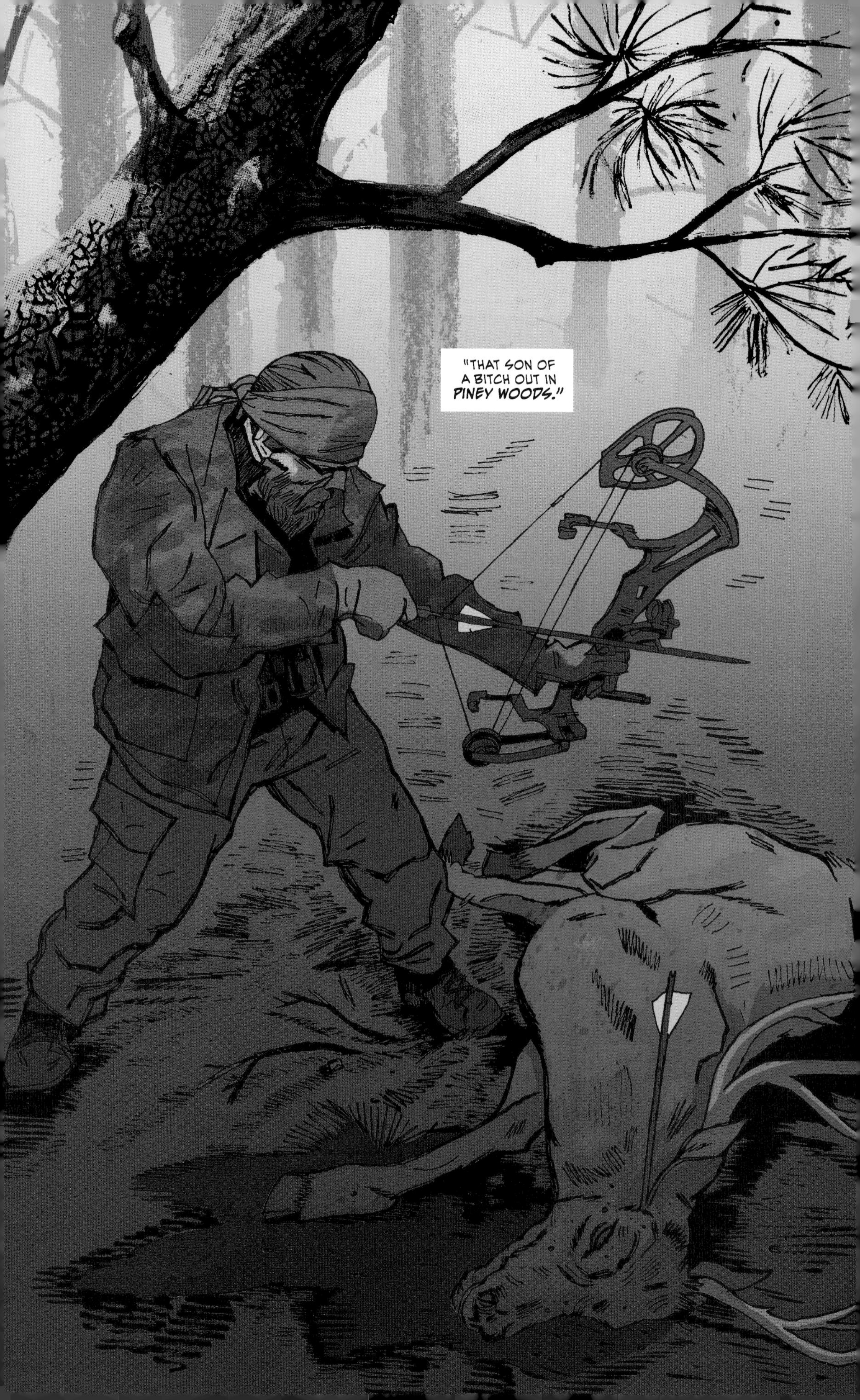
"THAT SON OF A BITCH OUT IN PINEY WOODS."

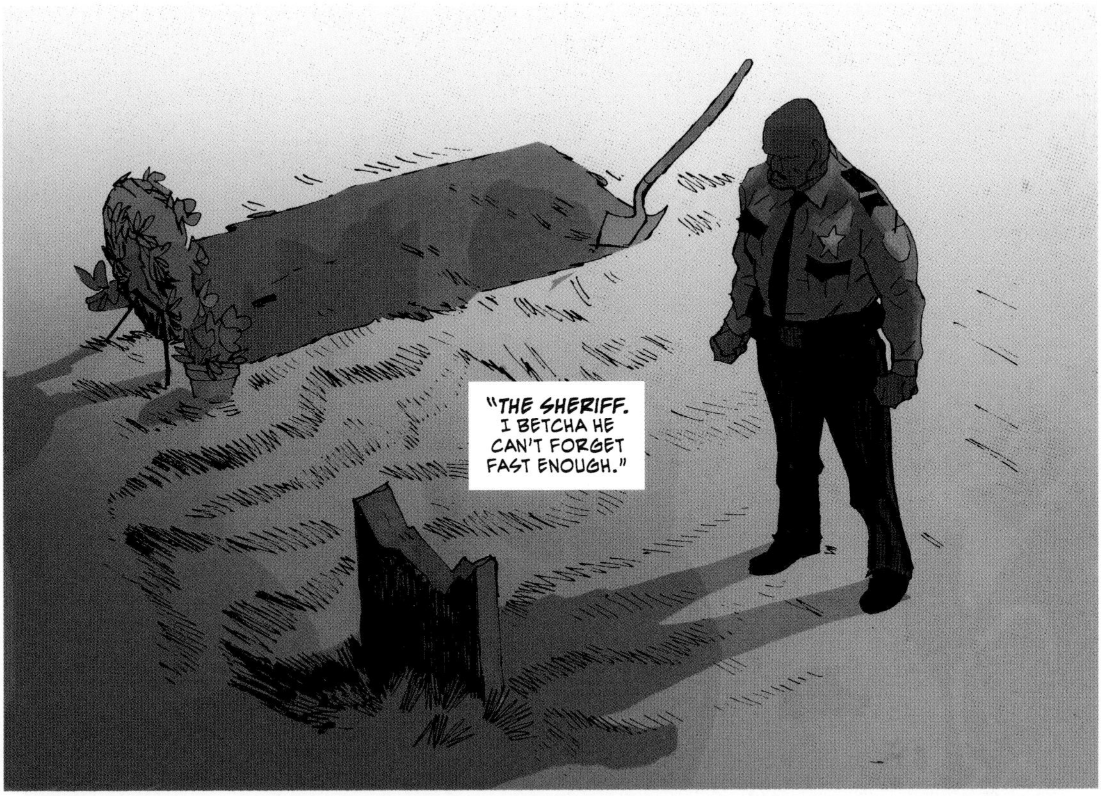
"THE SHERIFF.
I BETCHA HE
CAN'T FORGET
FAST ENOUGH."

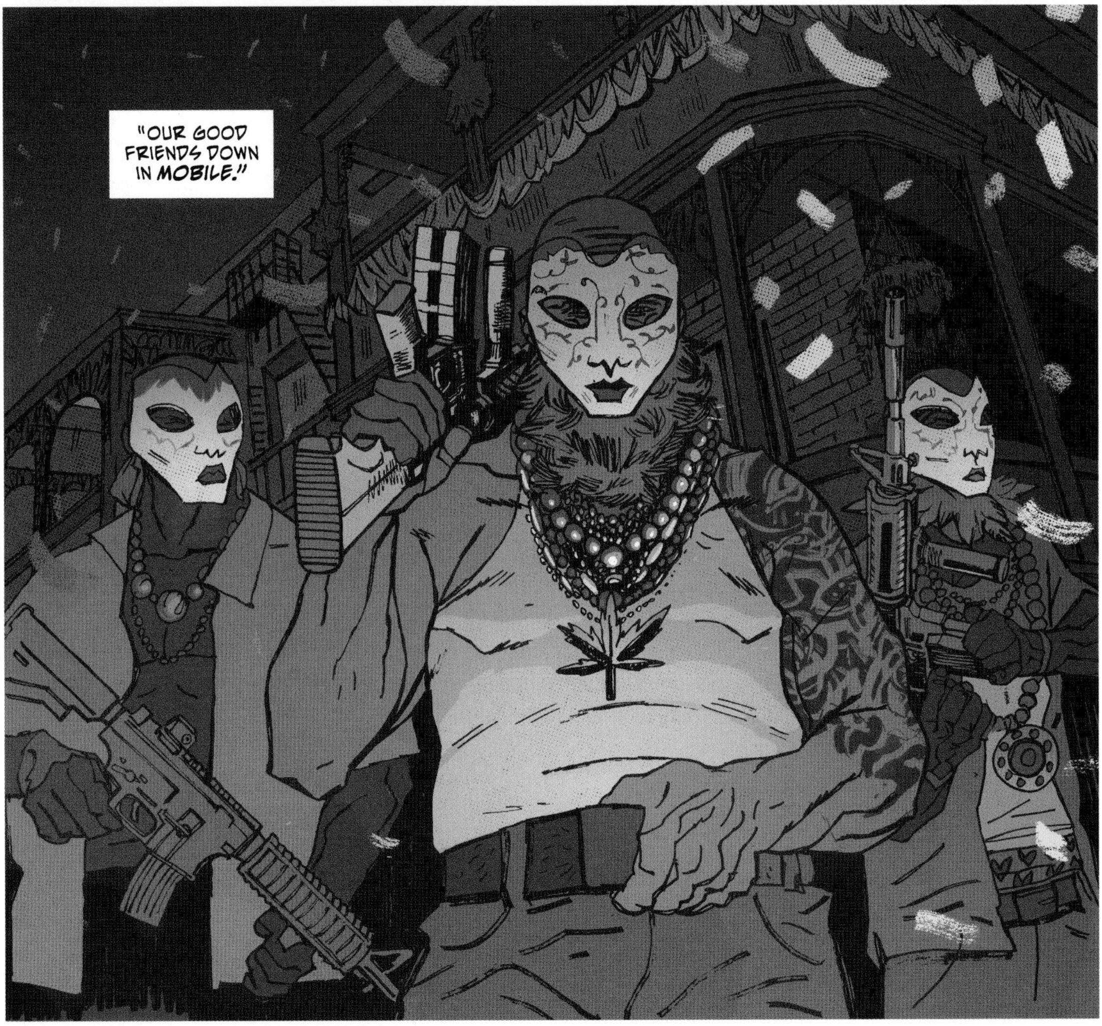
"OUR GOOD
FRIENDS DOWN
IN MOBILE."

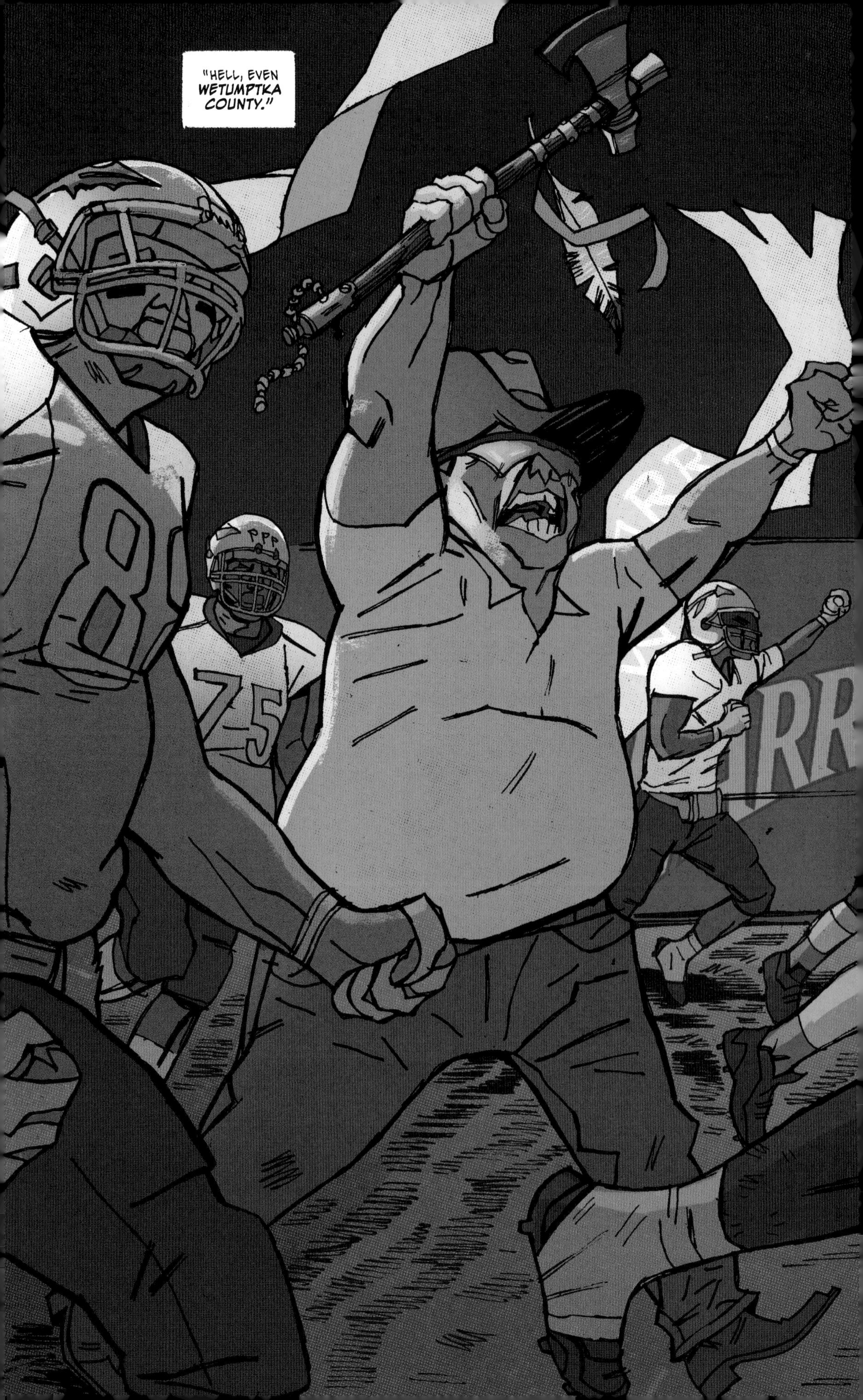
"HELL, EVEN WETUMPTKA COUNTY."

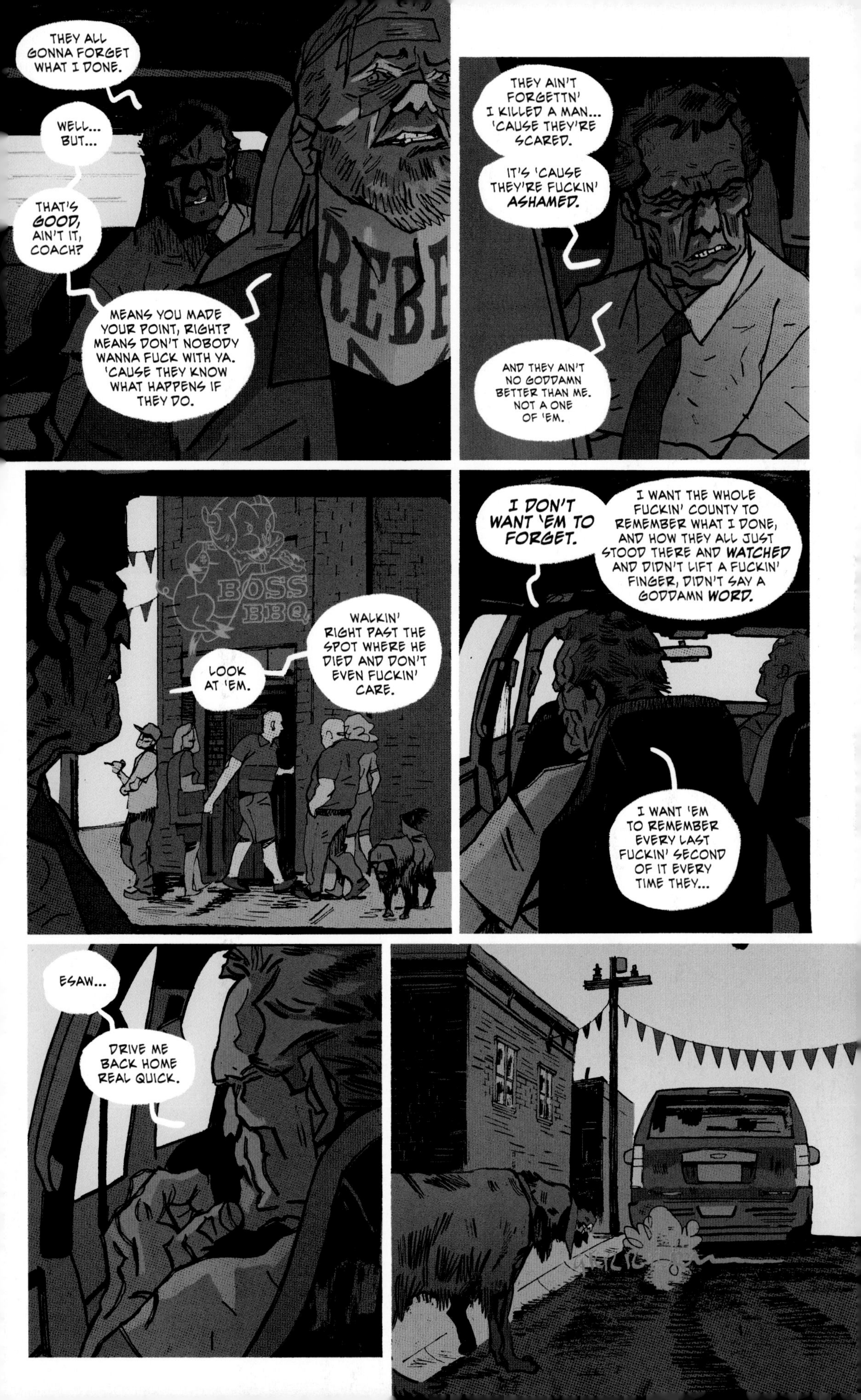
THEY ALL GONNA FORGET WHAT I DONE.
WELL... BUT...
THAT'S GOOD, AIN'T IT, COACH?
MEANS YOU MADE YOUR POINT, RIGHT? MEANS DON'T NOBODY WANNA FUCK WITH YA. 'CAUSE THEY KNOW WHAT HAPPENS IF THEY DO.
THEY AIN'T FORGETTN' I KILLED A MAN... 'CAUSE THEY'RE SCARED.
IT'S 'CAUSE THEY'RE FUCKIN' ASHAMED.
AND THEY AIN'T NO GODDAMN BETTER THAN ME. NOT A ONE OF 'EM.
BOSS BBQ
LOOK AT 'EM.
WALKIN' RIGHT PAST THE SPOT WHERE HE DIED AND DON'T EVEN FUCKIN' CARE.
I DON'T WANT 'EM TO FORGET.
I WANT THE WHOLE FUCKIN' COUNTY TO REMEMBER WHAT I DONE, AND HOW THEY ALL JUST STOOD THERE AND WATCHED AND DIDN'T LIFT A FUCKIN' FINGER, DIDN'T SAY A GODDAMN WORD.
I WANT 'EM TO REMEMBER EVERY LAST FUCKIN' SECOND OF IT EVERY TIME THEY...
ESAW...
DRIVE ME BACK HOME REAL QUICK.

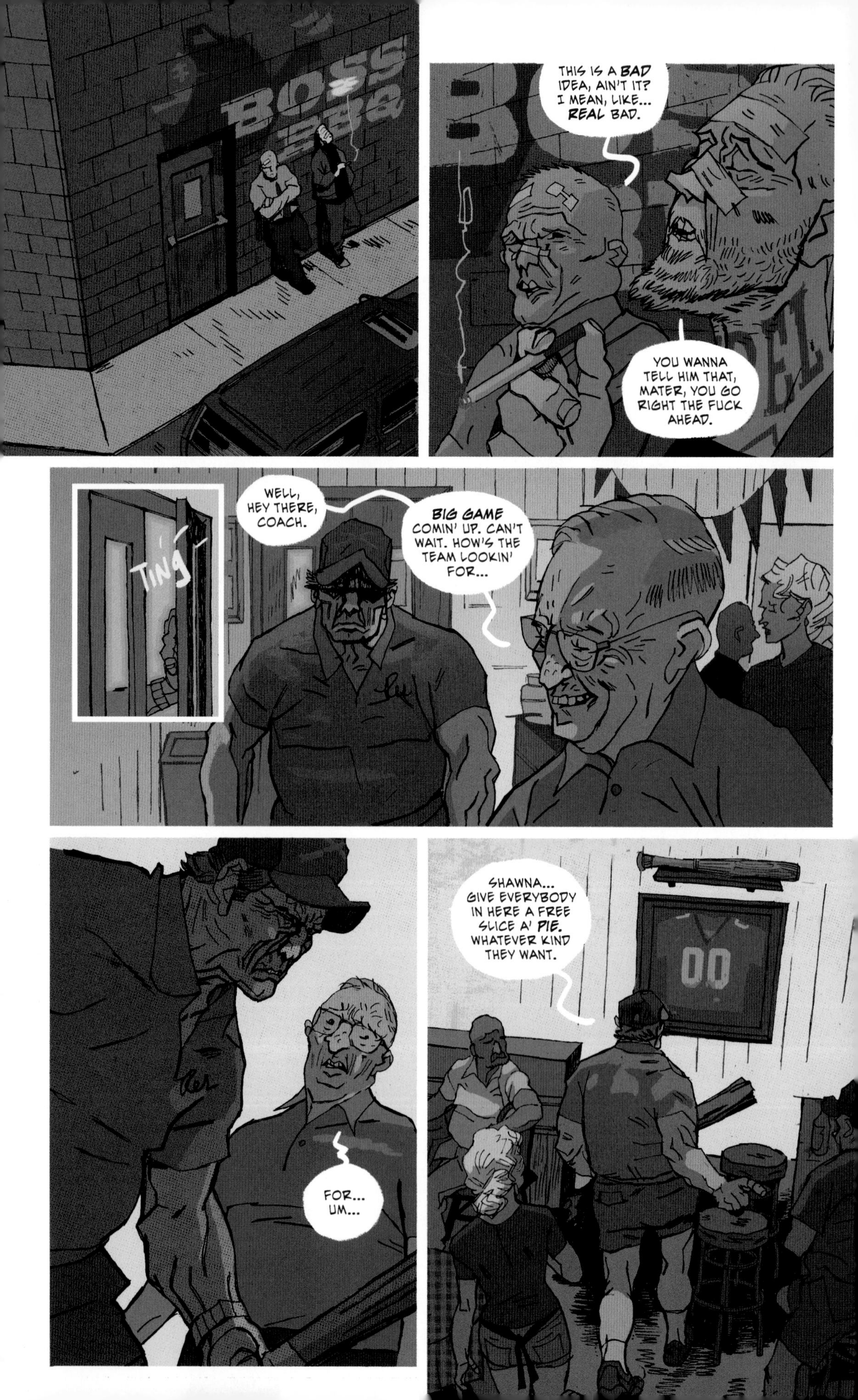
BOSS BBQ
THIS IS A BAD IDEA, AIN'T IT? I MEAN, LIKE... REAL BAD.
YOU WANNA TELL HIM THAT, MATER, YOU GO RIGHT THE FUCK AHEAD.
TING
WELL, HEY THERE, COACH.
BIG GAME COMIN' UP. CAN'T WAIT. HOW'S THE TEAM LOOKIN' FOR...
FOR... UM...
SHAWNA... GIVE EVERYBODY IN HERE A FREE SLICE A' PIE. WHATEVER KIND THEY WANT.
00

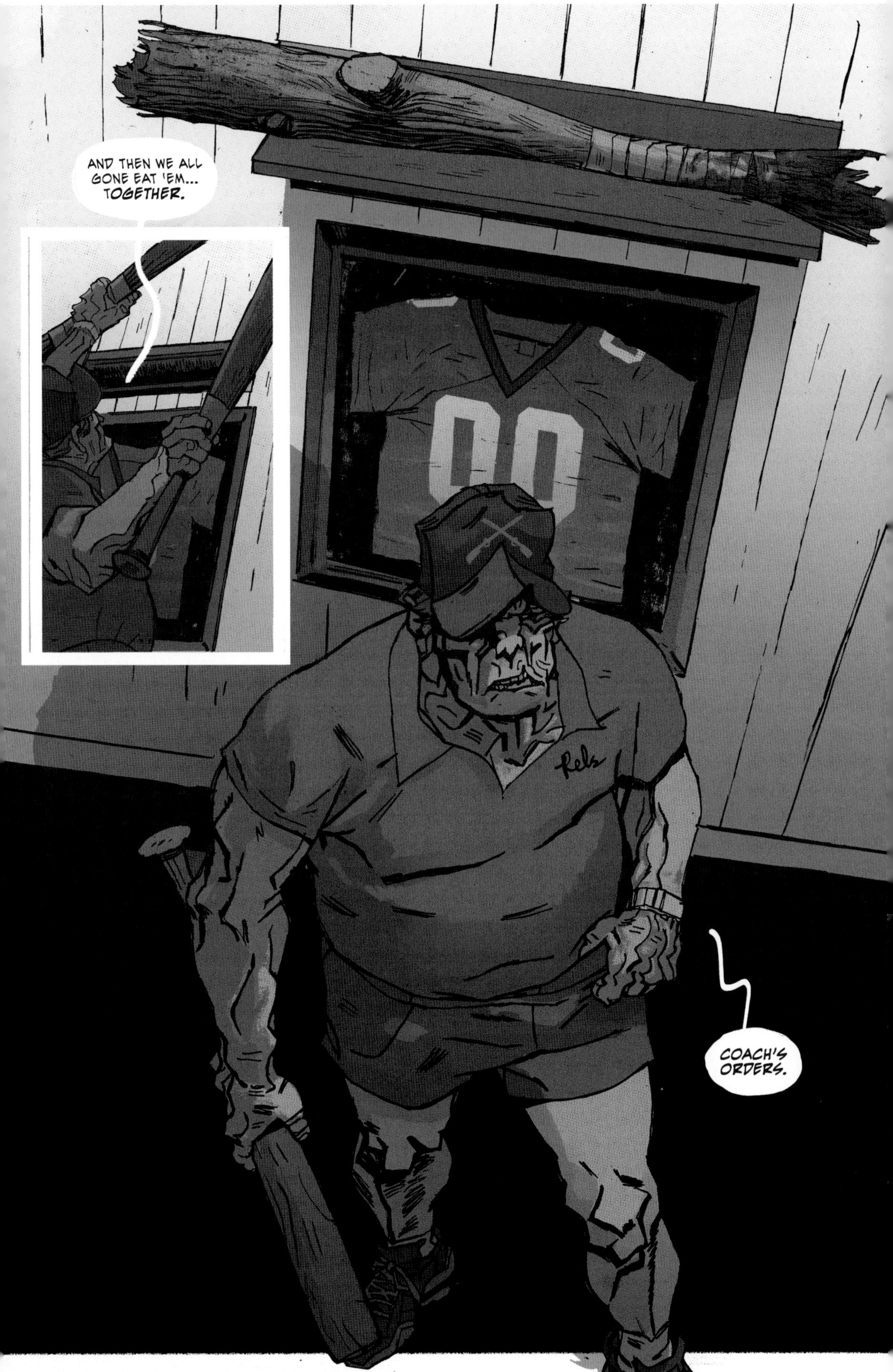
AND THEN WE ALL GONE EAT 'EM... TOGETHER.
COACH'S ORDERS.

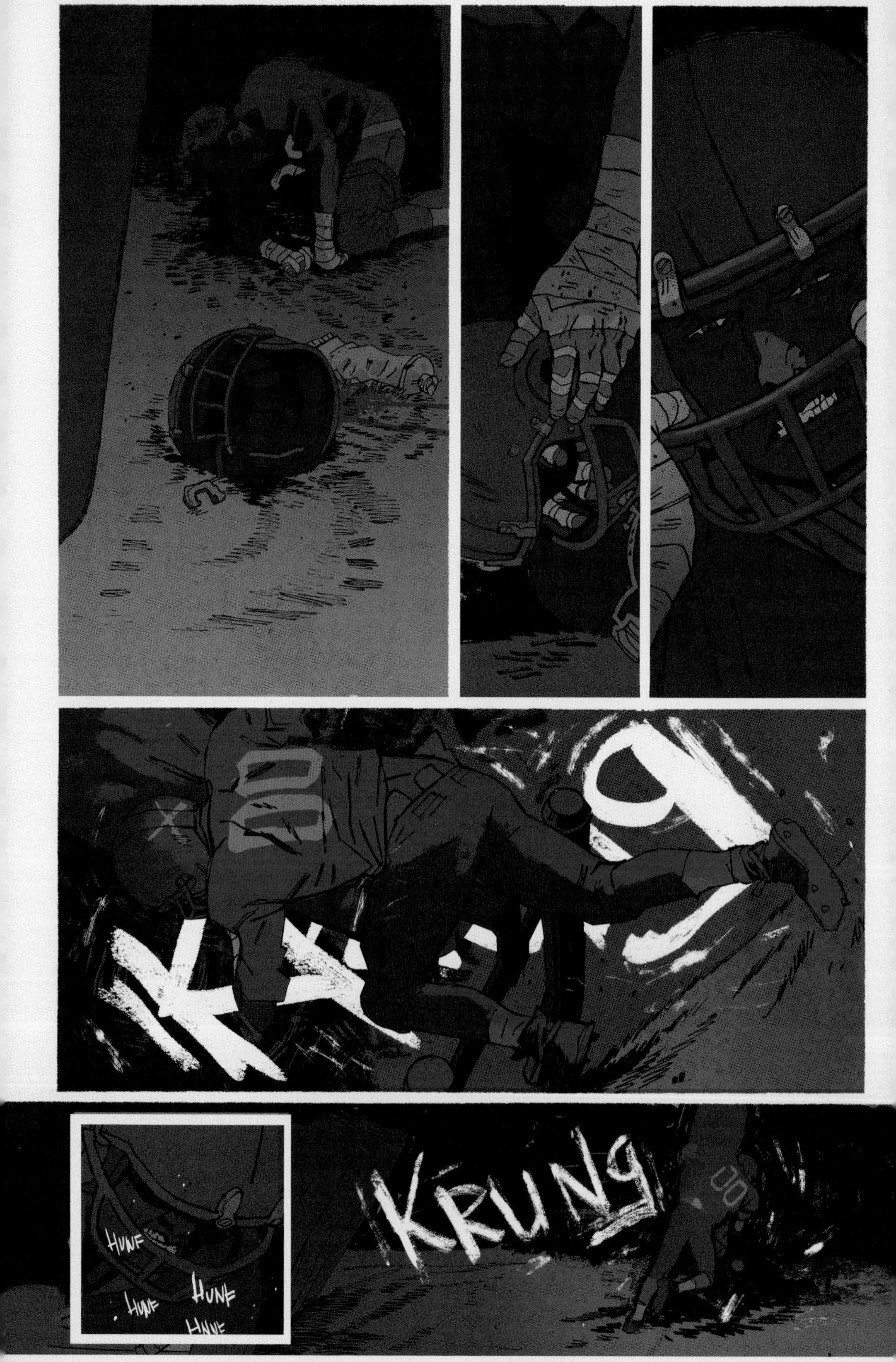
HUNF
HUNF
HUNF
KRUNG

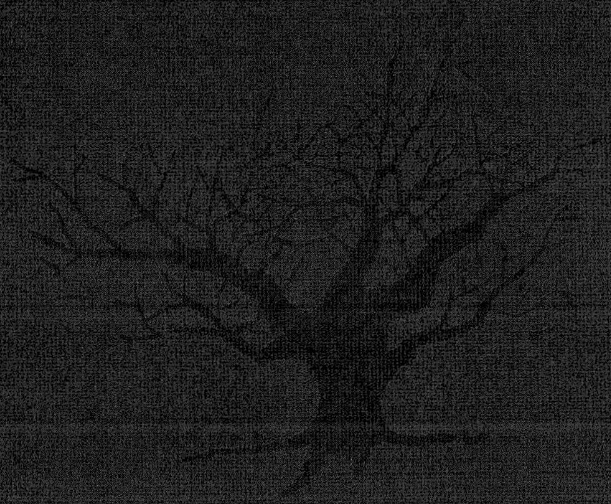

Gridiron

Chapter Two

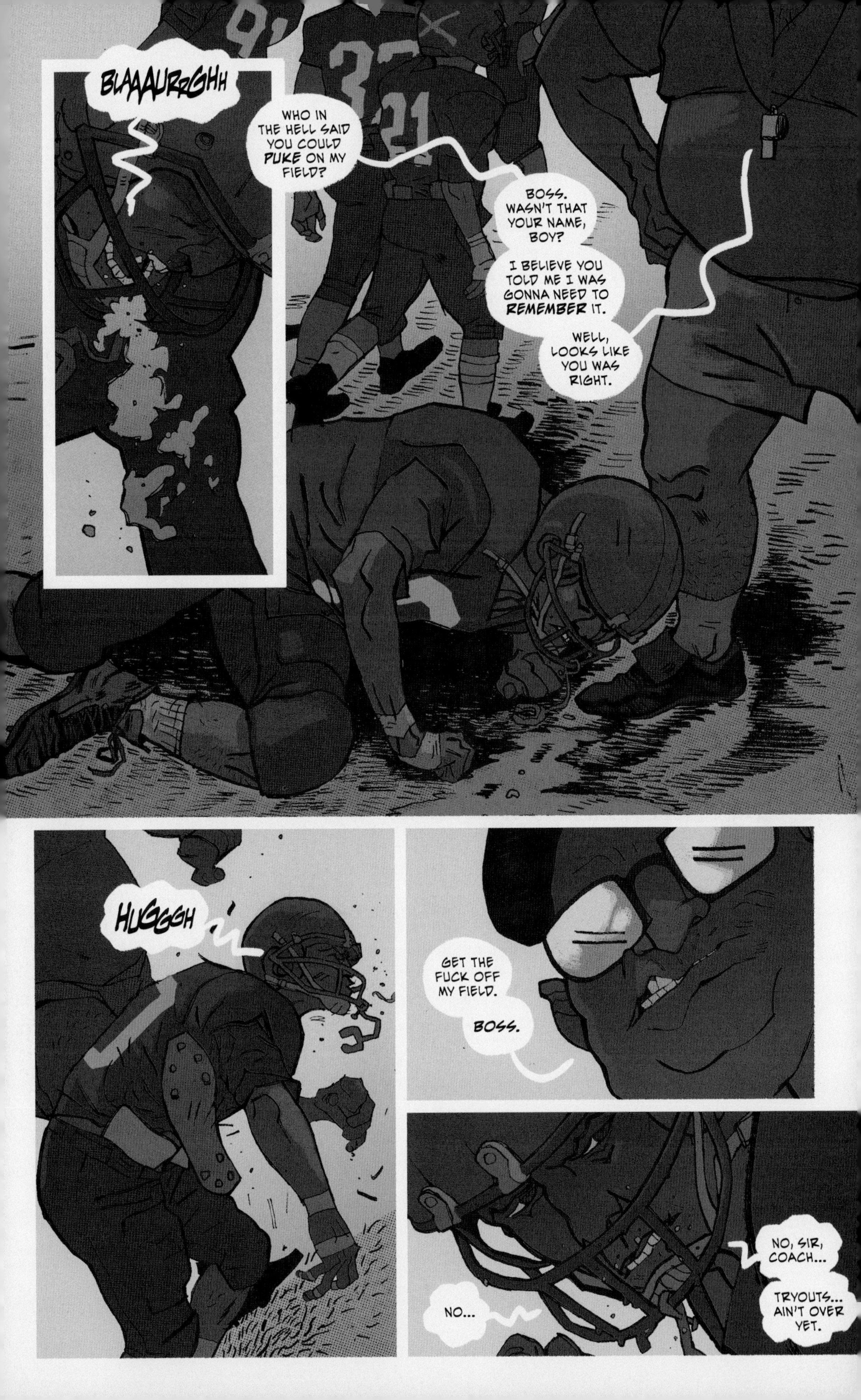
BLAAAURRGHH
WHO IN THE HELL SAID YOU COULD PUKE ON MY FIELD?
BOSS. WASN'T THAT YOUR NAME, BOY?
I BELIEVE YOU TOLD ME I WAS GONNA NEED TO REMEMBER IT.
WELL, LOOKS LIKE YOU WAS RIGHT.
HUGGGH
GET THE FUCK OFF MY FIELD.
BOSS.
NO, SIR, COACH...
TRYOUTS... AIN'T OVER YET.
NO...

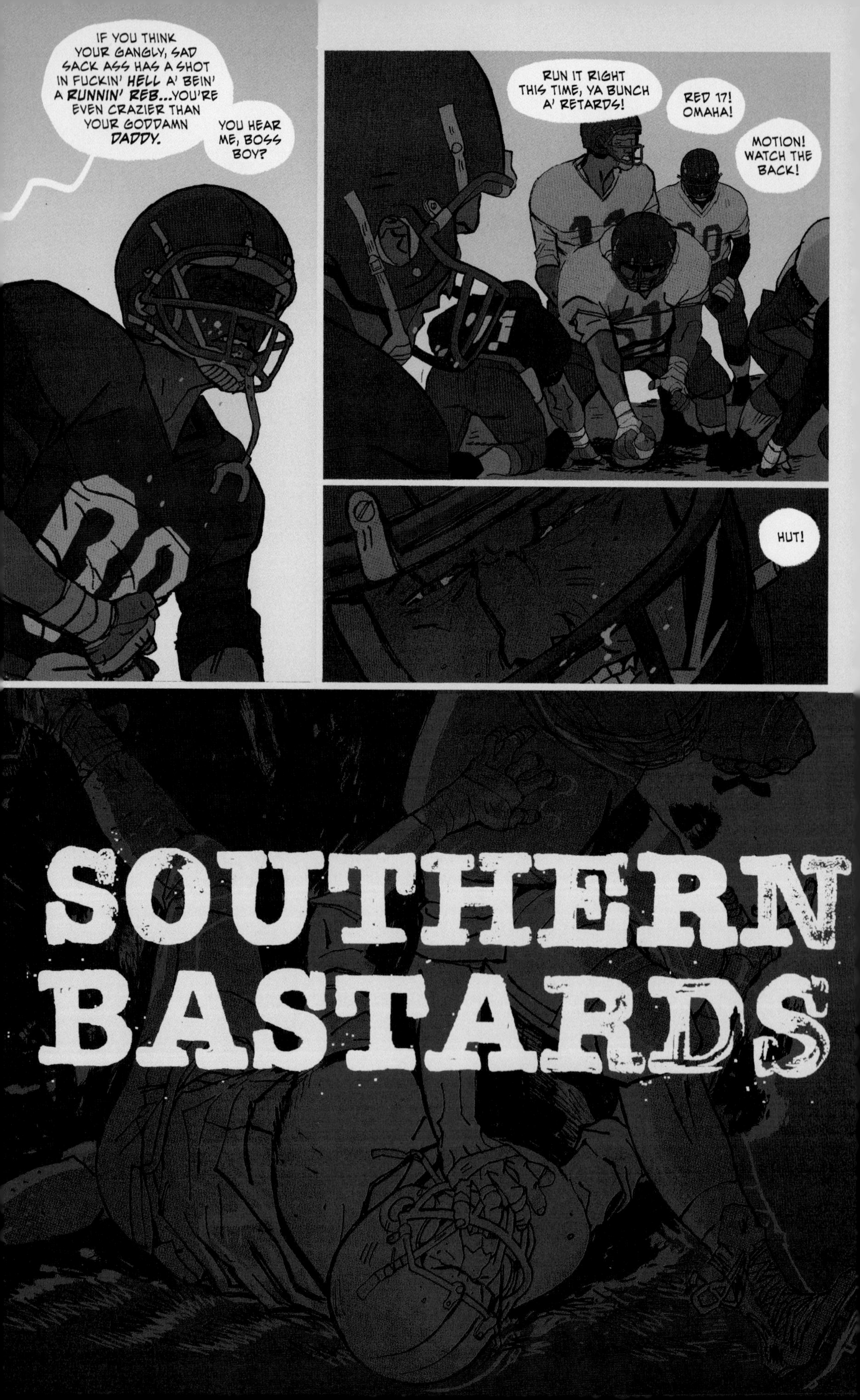
IF YOU THINK YOUR GANGLY, SAD SACK ASS HAS A SHOT IN FUCKIN' HELL A' BEIN' A RUNNIN' REB...YOU'RE EVEN CRAZIER THAN YOUR GODDAMN DADDY.
YOU HEAR ME, BOSS BOY?
RUN IT RIGHT THIS TIME, YA BUNCH A' RETARDS!
RED 17! OMAHA!
MOTION! WATCH THE BACK!
HUT!
SOUTHERN BASTARDS

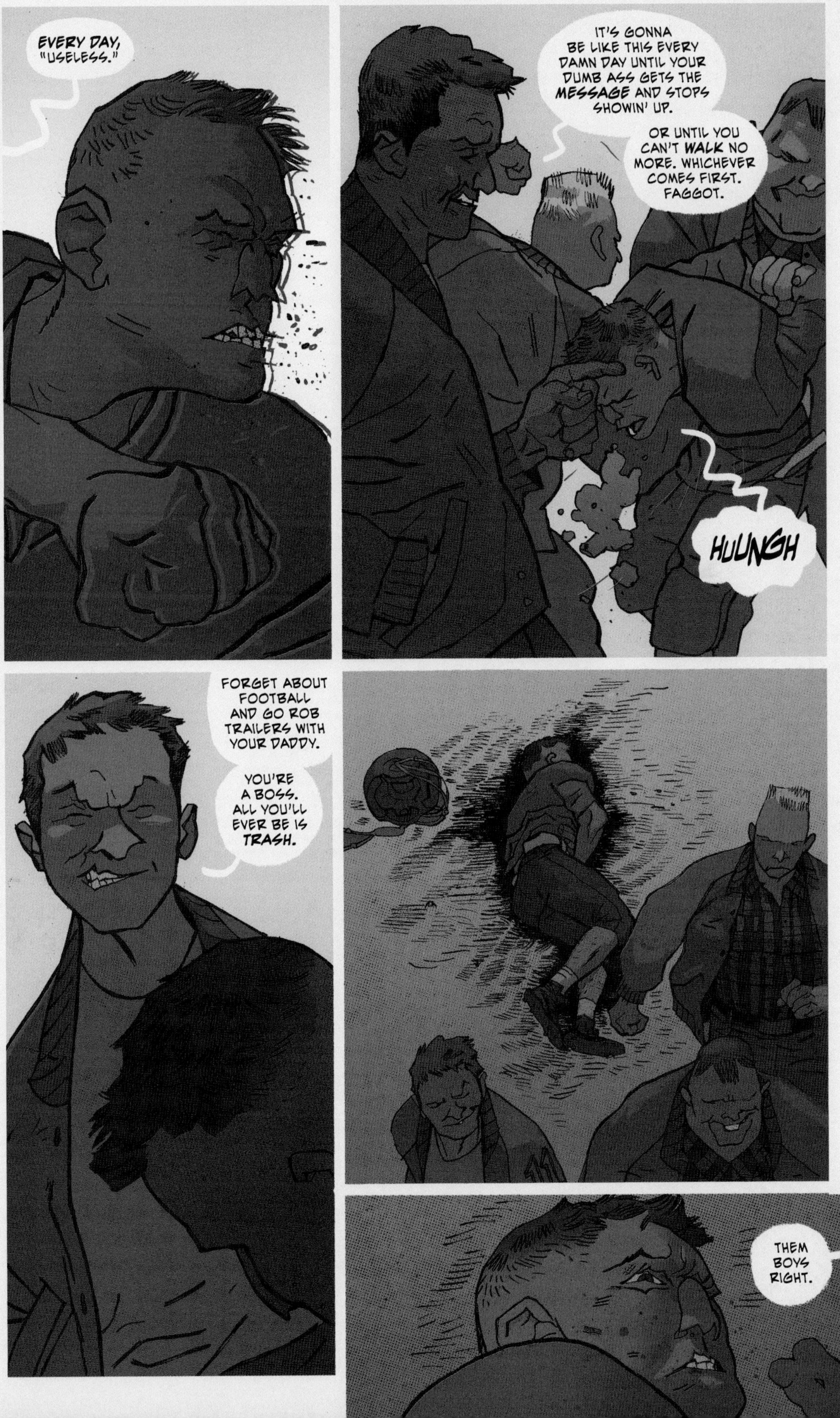
EVERY DAY, "USELESS."
IT'S GONNA BE LIKE THIS EVERY DAMN DAY UNTIL YOUR DUMB ASS GETS THE MESSAGE AND STOPS SHOWIN' UP.
OR UNTIL YOU CAN'T WALK NO MORE. WHICHEVER COMES FIRST. FAGGOT.
HUUNGH
FORGET ABOUT FOOTBALL AND GO ROB TRAILERS WITH YOUR DADDY.
YOU'RE A BOSS. ALL YOU'LL EVER BE IS TRASH.
THEM BOYS RIGHT.

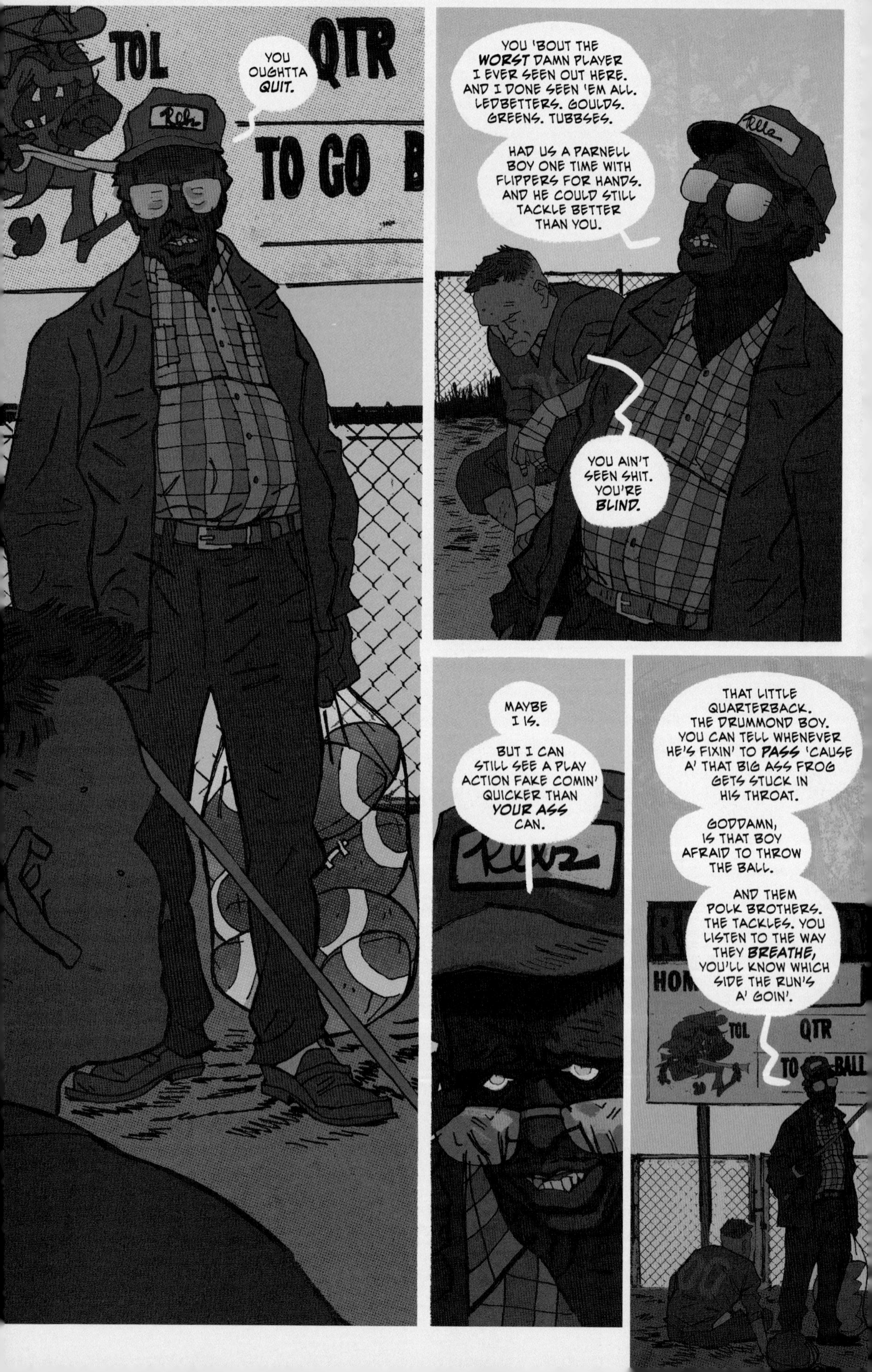
TOL QTR
TO GO B
YOU OUGHTTA QUIT.
YOU 'BOUT THE WORST DAMN PLAYER I EVER SEEN OUT HERE. AND I DONE SEEN 'EM ALL. LEDBETTERS. GOULDS. GREENS. TUBBSES.
HAD US A PARNELL BOY ONE TIME WITH FLIPPERS FOR HANDS. AND HE COULD STILL TACKLE BETTER THAN YOU.
YOU AIN'T SEEN SHIT. YOU'RE BLIND.
MAYBE I IS.
BUT I CAN STILL SEE A PLAY ACTION FAKE COMIN' QUICKER THAN YOUR ASS CAN.
THAT LITTLE QUARTERBACK. THE DRUMMOND BOY. YOU CAN TELL WHENEVER HE'S FIXIN' TO PASS 'CAUSE A' THAT BIG ASS FROG GETS STUCK IN HIS THROAT.
GODDAMN, IS THAT BOY AFRAID TO THROW THE BALL.
AND THEM POLK BROTHERS. THE TACKLES. YOU LISTEN TO THE WAY THEY BREATHE, YOU'LL KNOW WHICH SIDE THE RUN'S A' GOIN'.
HOM
TOL QTR
TO BALL

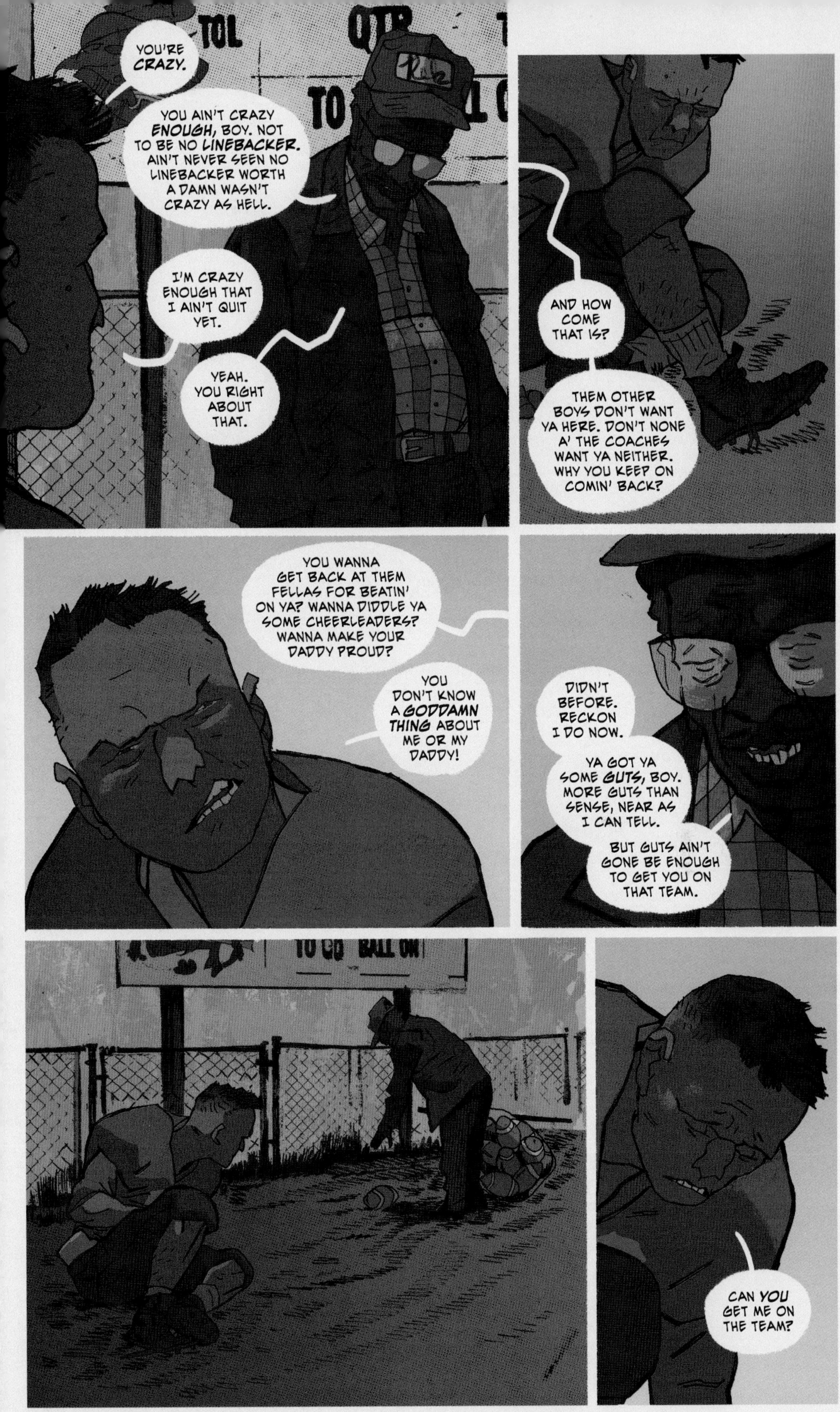
TOL QTR
TO ALL O
YOU'RE CRAZY.
YOU AIN'T CRAZY ENOUGH, BOY. NOT TO BE NO LINEBACKER. AIN'T NEVER SEEN NO LINEBACKER WORTH A DAMN WASN'T CRAZY AS HELL.
I'M CRAZY ENOUGH THAT I AIN'T QUIT YET.
YEAH. YOU RIGHT ABOUT THAT.
AND HOW COME THAT IS?
THEM OTHER BOYS DON'T WANT YA HERE. DON'T NONE A' THE COACHES WANT YA NEITHER. WHY YOU KEEP ON COMIN' BACK?
YOU WANNA GET BACK AT THEM FELLAS FOR BEATIN' ON YA? WANNA DIDDLE YA SOME CHEERLEADERS? WANNA MAKE YOUR DADDY PROUD?
YOU DON'T KNOW A GODDAMN THING ABOUT ME OR MY DADDY!
DIDN'T BEFORE. RECKON I DO NOW.
YA GOT YA SOME GUTS, BOY. MORE GUTS THAN SENSE, NEAR AS I CAN TELL.
BUT GUTS AIN'T GONE BE ENOUGH TO GET YOU ON THAT TEAM.
TO GO BALL ON
CAN YOU GET ME ON THE TEAM?

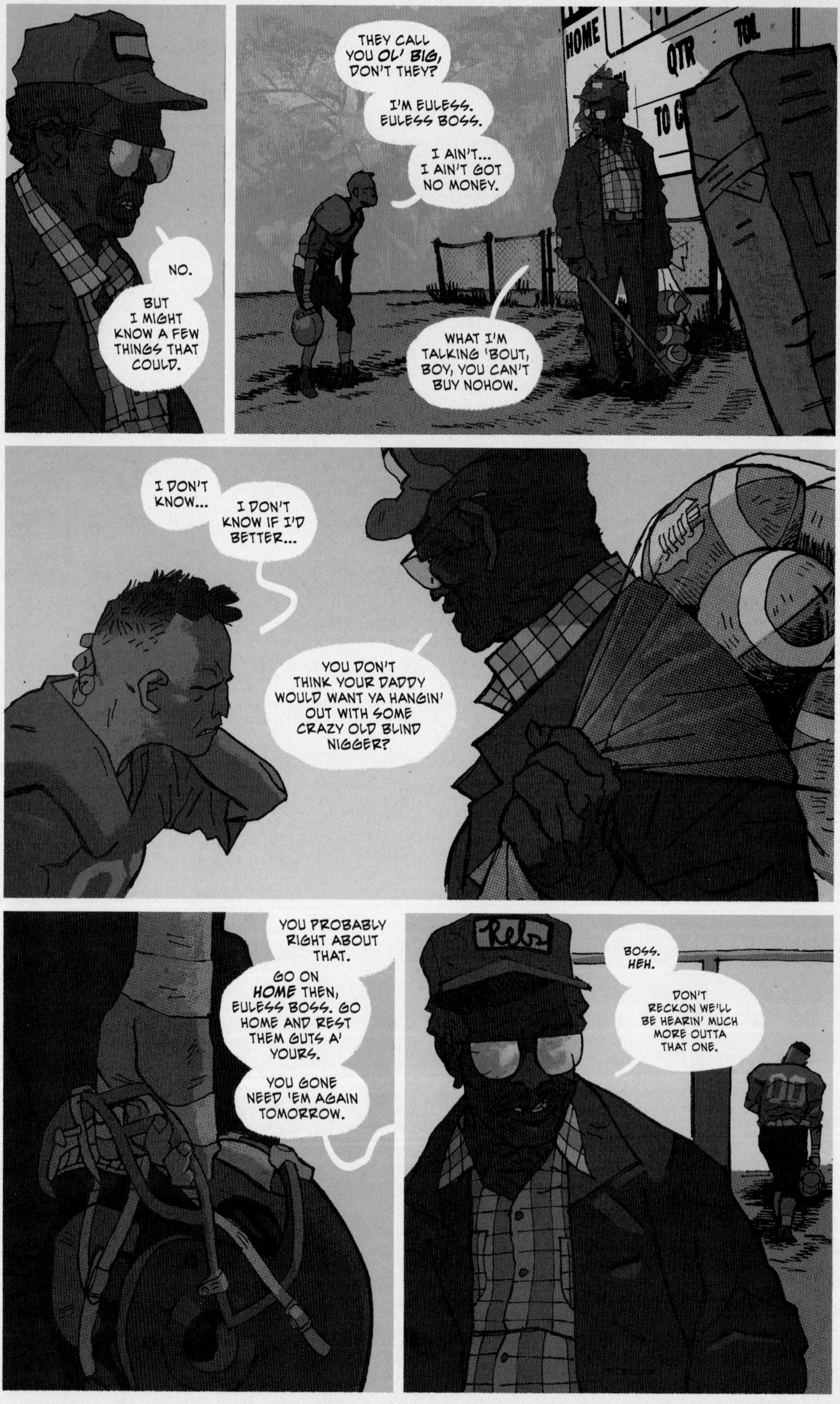

NO.
BUT I MIGHT KNOW A FEW THINGS THAT COULD.
THEY CALL YOU OL' BIG, DON'T THEY?
I'M EULESS. EULESS BOSS.
I AIN'T... I AIN'T GOT NO MONEY.
HOME
QTR
TOL
TO G
WHAT I'M TALKING 'BOUT, BOY, YOU CAN'T BUY NOHOW.
I DON'T KNOW...
I DON'T KNOW IF I'D BETTER...
YOU DON'T THINK YOUR DADDY WOULD WANT YA HANGIN' OUT WITH SOME CRAZY OLD BLIND NIGGER?
YOU PROBABLY RIGHT ABOUT THAT.
GO ON HOME THEN, EULESS BOSS. GO HOME AND REST THEM GUTS A' YOURS.
YOU GONE NEED 'EM AGAIN TOMORROW.
Rebs
BOSS. HEH.
DON'T RECKON WE'LL BE HEARIN' MUCH MORE OUTTA THAT ONE.
00

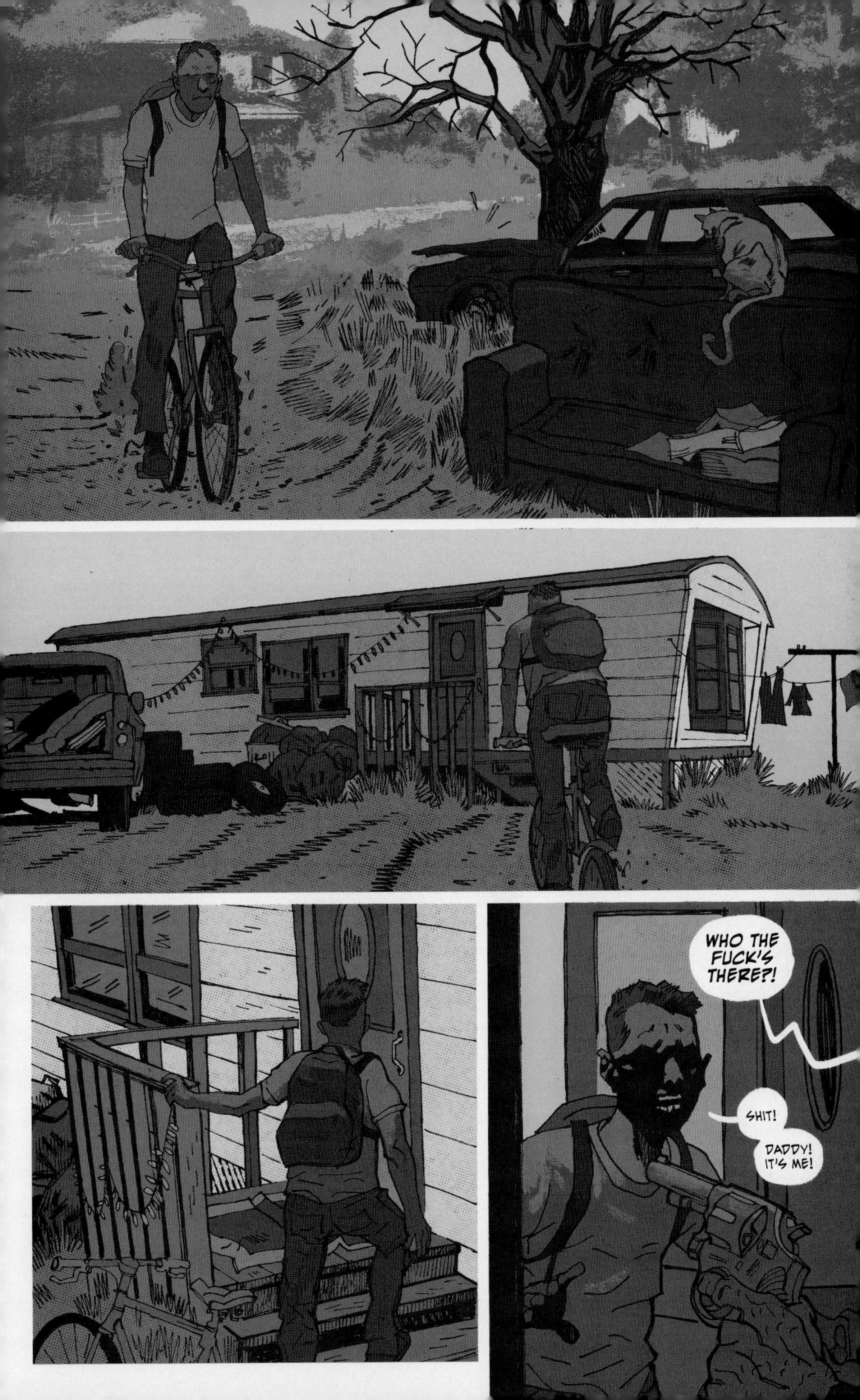
WHO THE FUCK'S THERE?!
SHIT!
DADDY! IT'S ME!

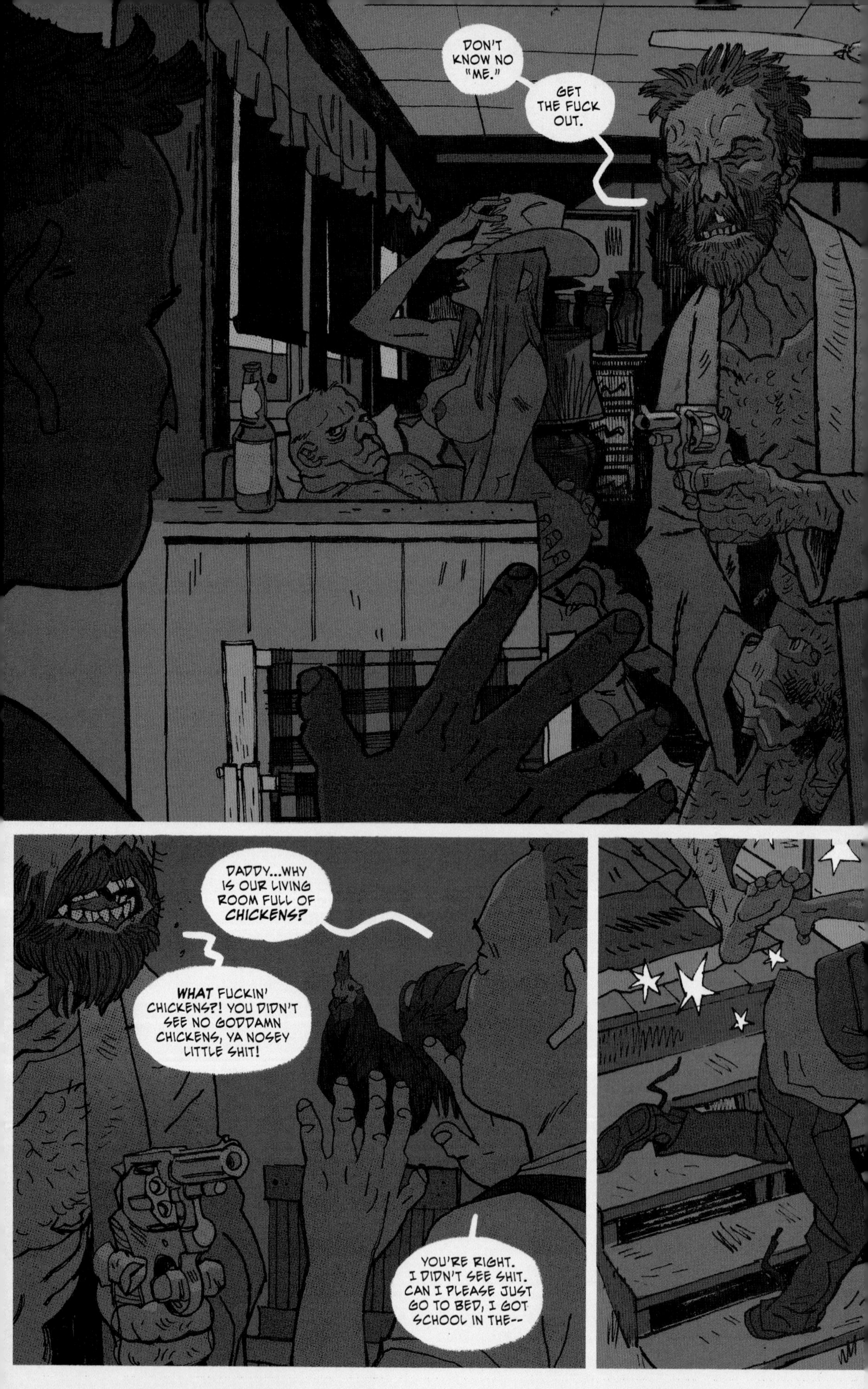
DON'T KNOW NO "ME."
GET THE FUCK OUT.
DADDY...WHY IS OUR LIVING ROOM FULL OF CHICKENS?
WHAT FUCKIN' CHICKENS?! YOU DIDN'T SEE NO GODDAMN CHICKENS, YA NOSEY LITTLE SHIT!
YOU'RE RIGHT. I DIDN'T SEE SHIT. CAN I PLEASE JUST GO TO BED, I GOT SCHOOL IN THE--

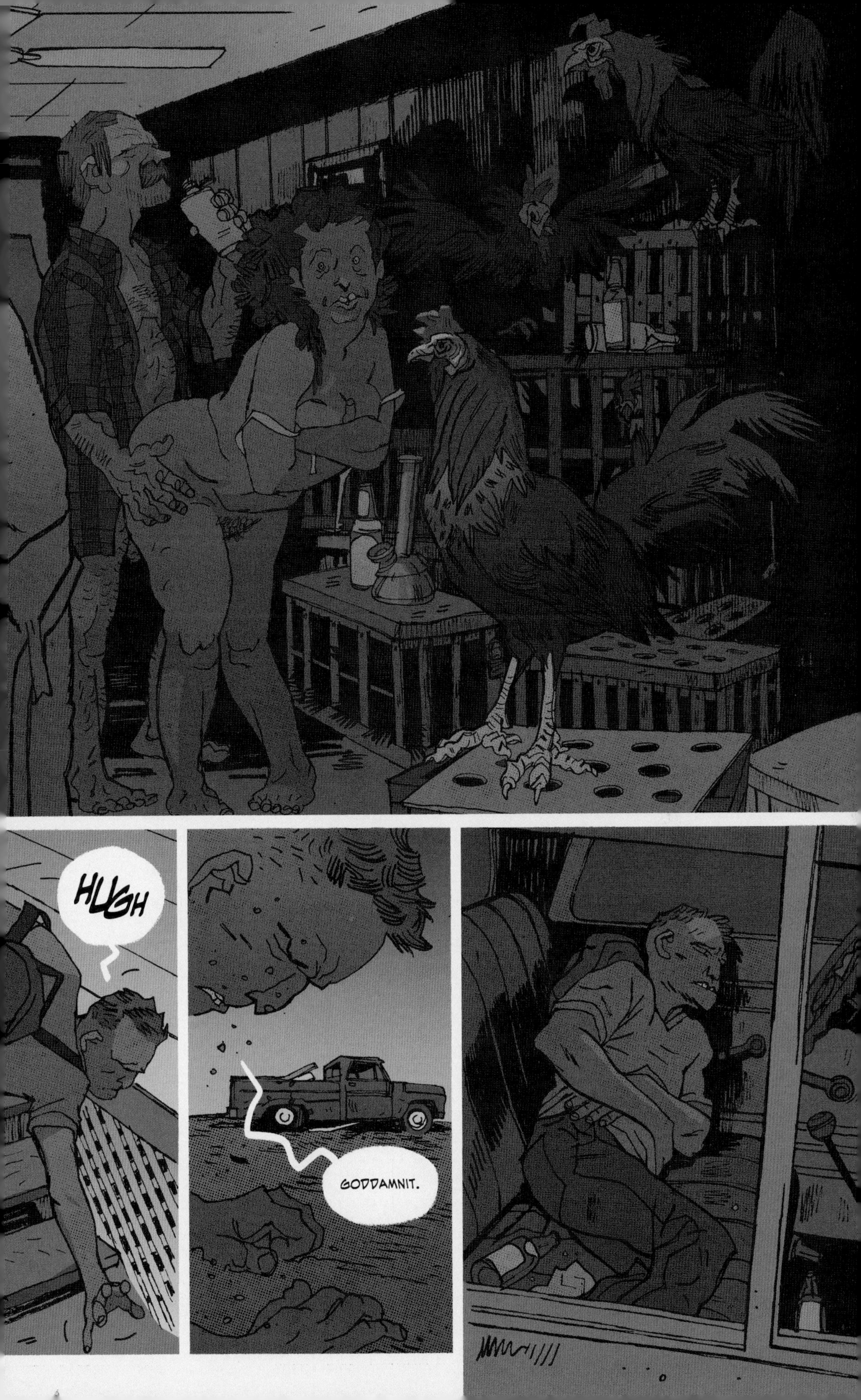
HUGH
GODDAMNIT.

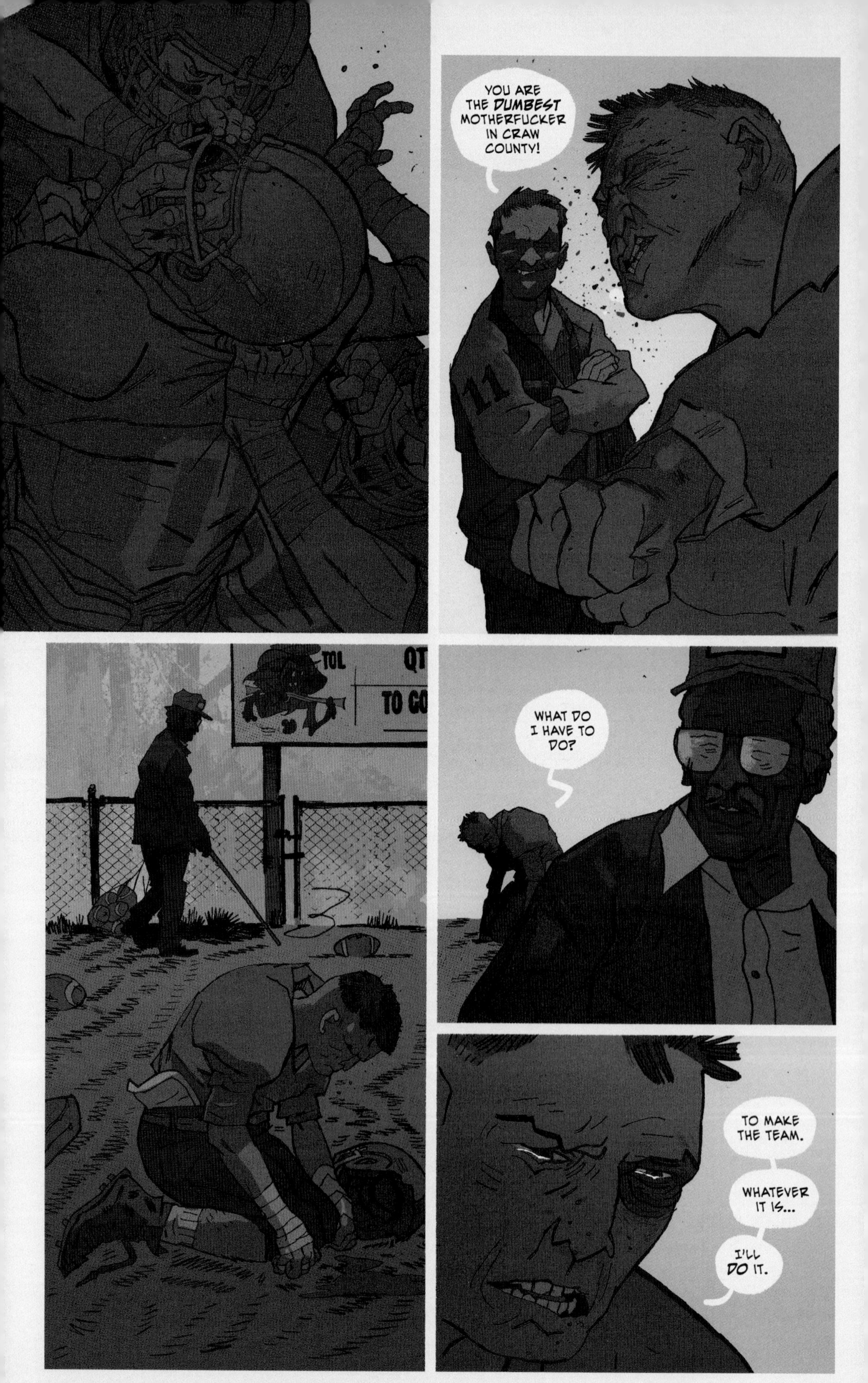
YOU ARE THE DUMBEST MOTHERFUCKER IN CRAW COUNTY!
TOL
QT
TO GO
WHAT DO I HAVE TO DO?
TO MAKE THE TEAM.
WHATEVER IT IS...
I'LL DO IT.

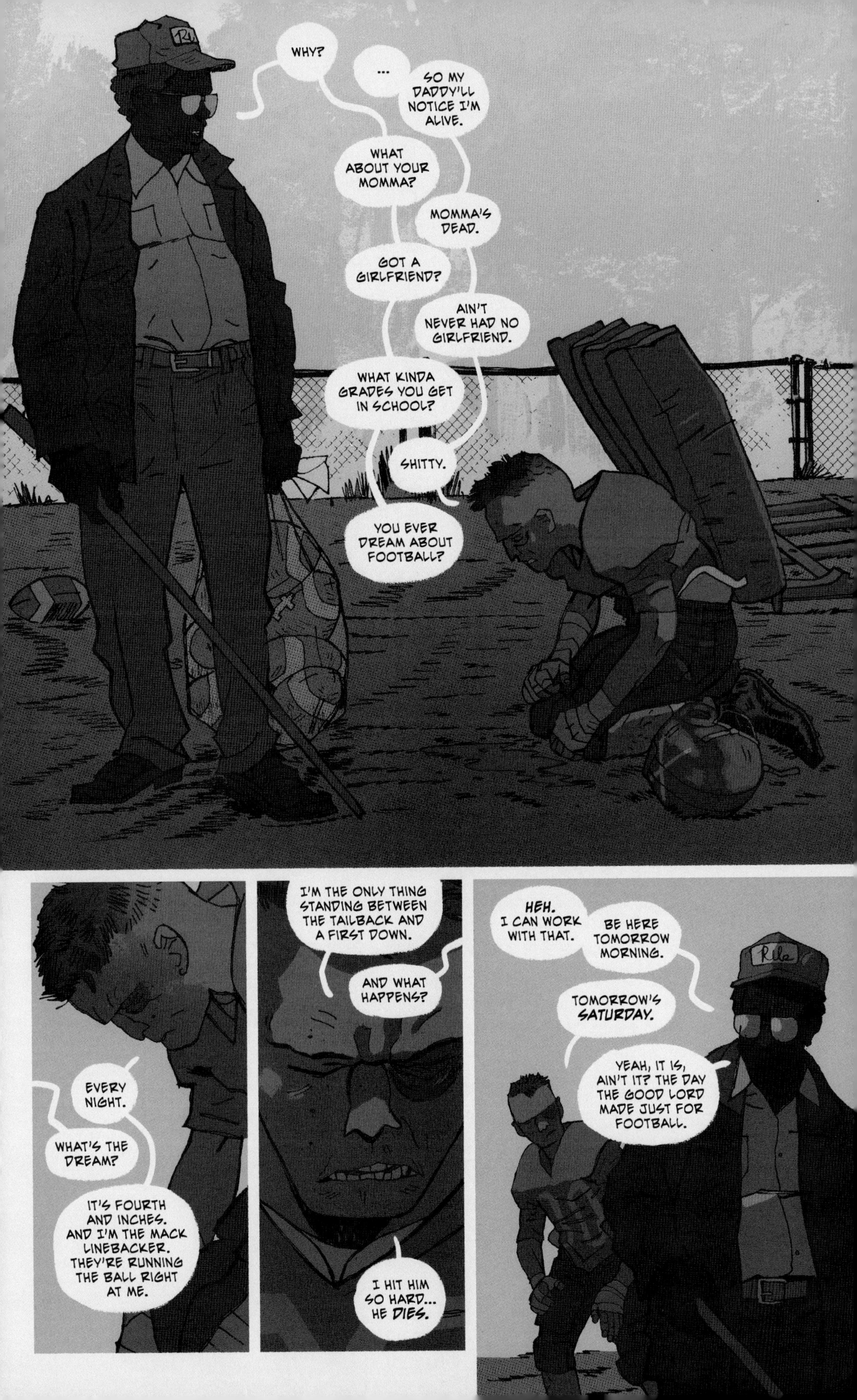
WHY?
...
SO MY DADDY'LL NOTICE I'M ALIVE.
WHAT ABOUT YOUR MOMMA?
MOMMA'S DEAD.
GOT A GIRLFRIEND?
AIN'T NEVER HAD NO GIRLFRIEND.
WHAT KINDA GRADES YOU GET IN SCHOOL?
SHITTY.
YOU EVER DREAM ABOUT FOOTBALL?
EVERY NIGHT.
WHAT'S THE DREAM?
IT'S FOURTH AND INCHES. AND I'M THE MACK LINEBACKER. THEY'RE RUNNING THE BALL RIGHT AT ME.
I'M THE ONLY THING STANDING BETWEEN THE TAILBACK AND A FIRST DOWN.
AND WHAT HAPPENS?
I HIT HIM SO HARD... HE DIES.
HEH. I CAN WORK WITH THAT.
BE HERE TOMORROW MORNING.
TOMORROW'S SATURDAY.
YEAH, IT IS, AIN'T IT? THE DAY THE GOOD LORD MADE JUST FOR FOOTBALL.

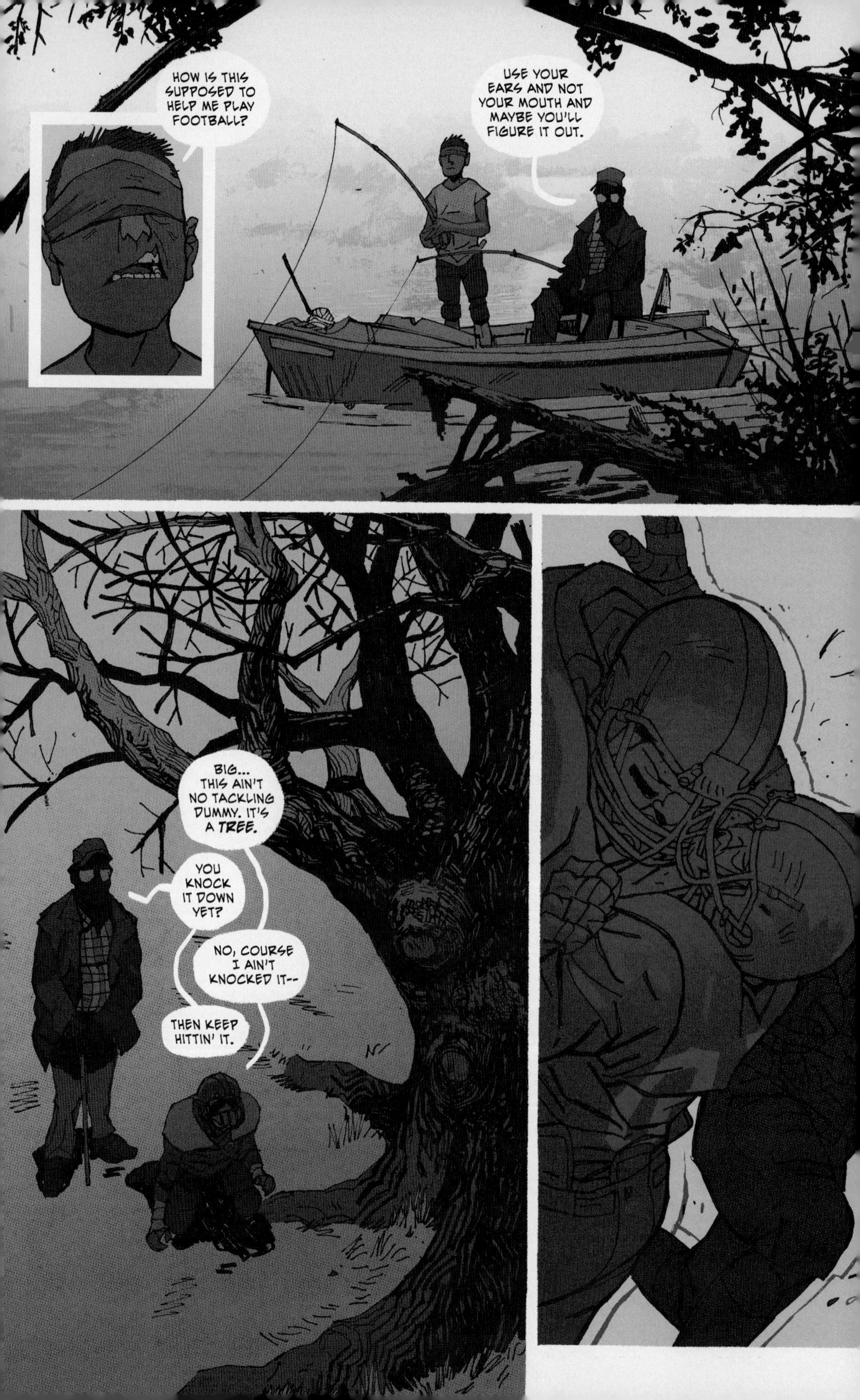
HOW IS THIS SUPPOSED TO HELP ME PLAY FOOTBALL?
USE YOUR EARS AND NOT YOUR MOUTH AND MAYBE YOU'LL FIGURE IT OUT.
BIG... THIS AIN'T NO TACKLING DUMMY. IT'S A TREE.
YOU KNOCK IT DOWN YET?
NO, COURSE I AIN'T KNOCKED IT--
THEN KEEP HITTIN' IT.

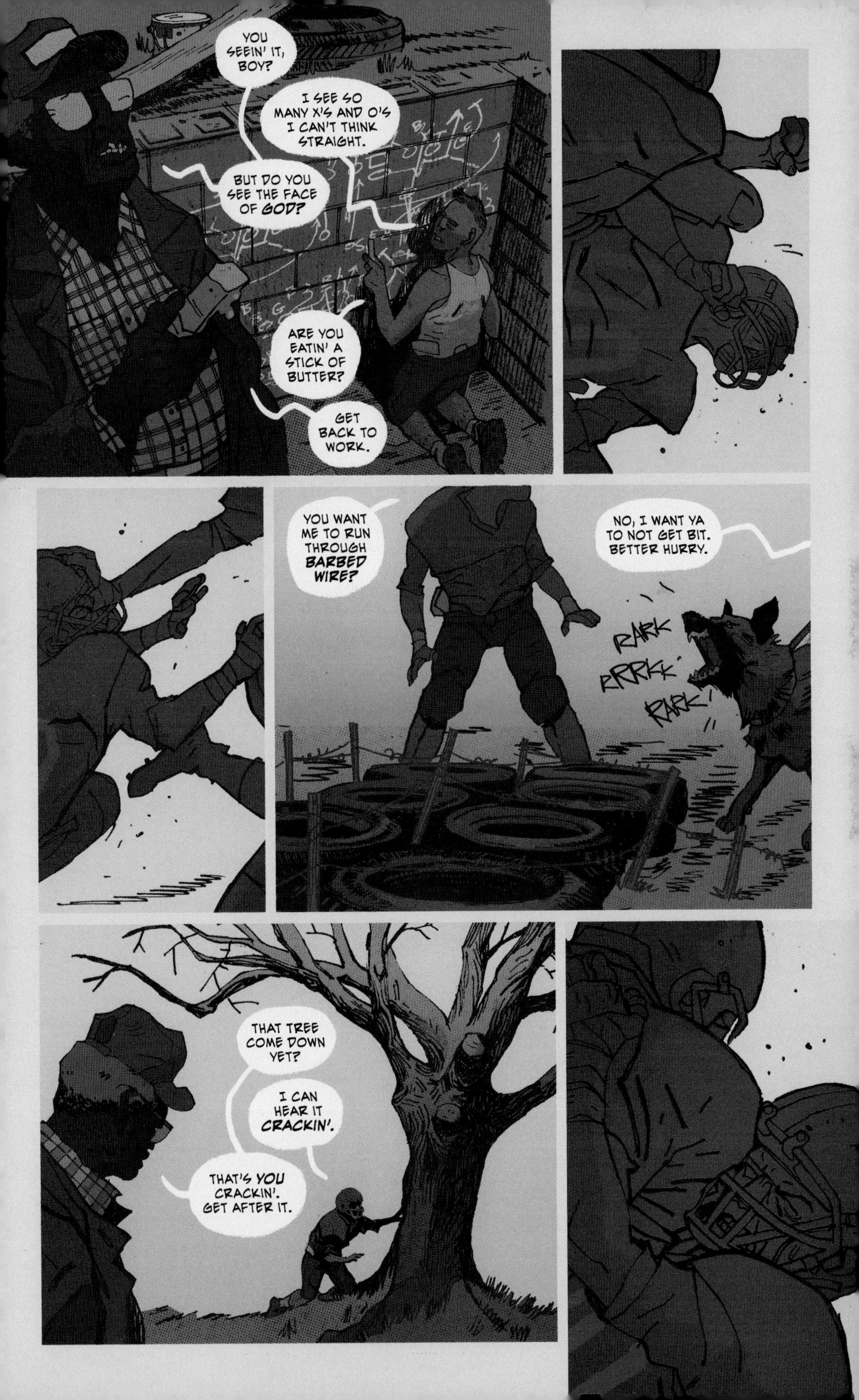
YOU SEEIN' IT, BOY?
I SEE SO MANY X'S AND O'S I CAN'T THINK STRAIGHT.
BUT DO YOU SEE THE FACE OF GOD?
ARE YOU EATIN' A STICK OF BUTTER?
GET BACK TO WORK.
YOU WANT ME TO RUN THROUGH BARBED WIRE?
NO, I WANT YA TO NOT GET BIT. BETTER HURRY.
RARK
RRRKK
RARK
THAT TREE COME DOWN YET?
I CAN HEAR IT CRACKIN'.
THAT'S YOU CRACKIN'. GET AFTER IT.

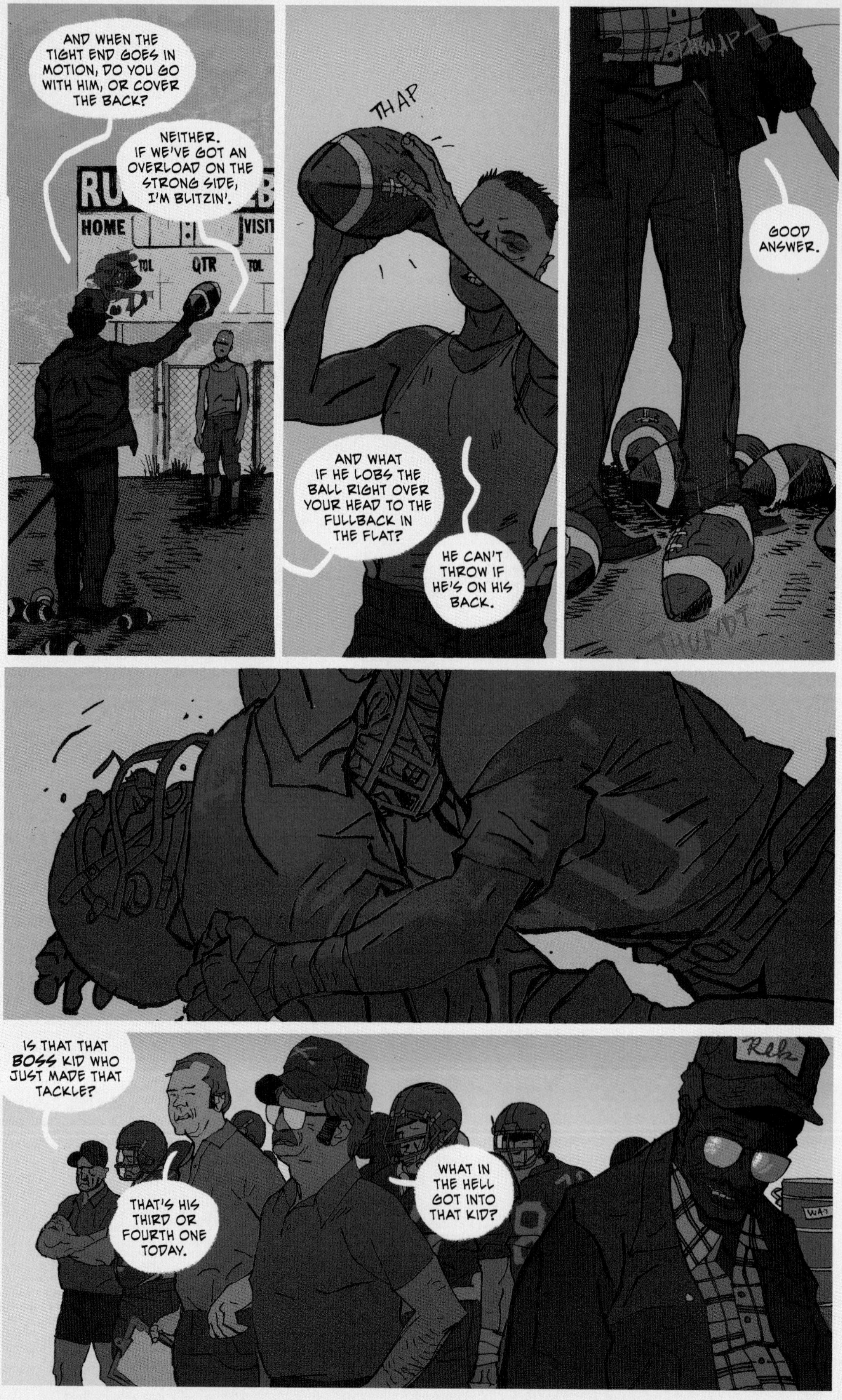
AND WHEN THE TIGHT END GOES IN MOTION, DO YOU GO WITH HIM, OR COVER THE BACK?
NEITHER. IF WE'VE GOT AN OVERLOAD ON THE STRONG SIDE, I'M BLITZIN'.
HOME
VISIT
TOL
QTR
TOL
THAP
AND WHAT IF HE LOBS THE BALL RIGHT OVER YOUR HEAD TO THE FULLBACK IN THE FLAT?
HE CAN'T THROW IF HE'S ON HIS BACK.
GOOD ANSWER.
THUNDT
IS THAT THAT BOSS KID WHO JUST MADE THAT TACKLE?
THAT'S HIS THIRD OR FOURTH ONE TODAY.
WHAT IN THE HELL GOT INTO THAT KID?

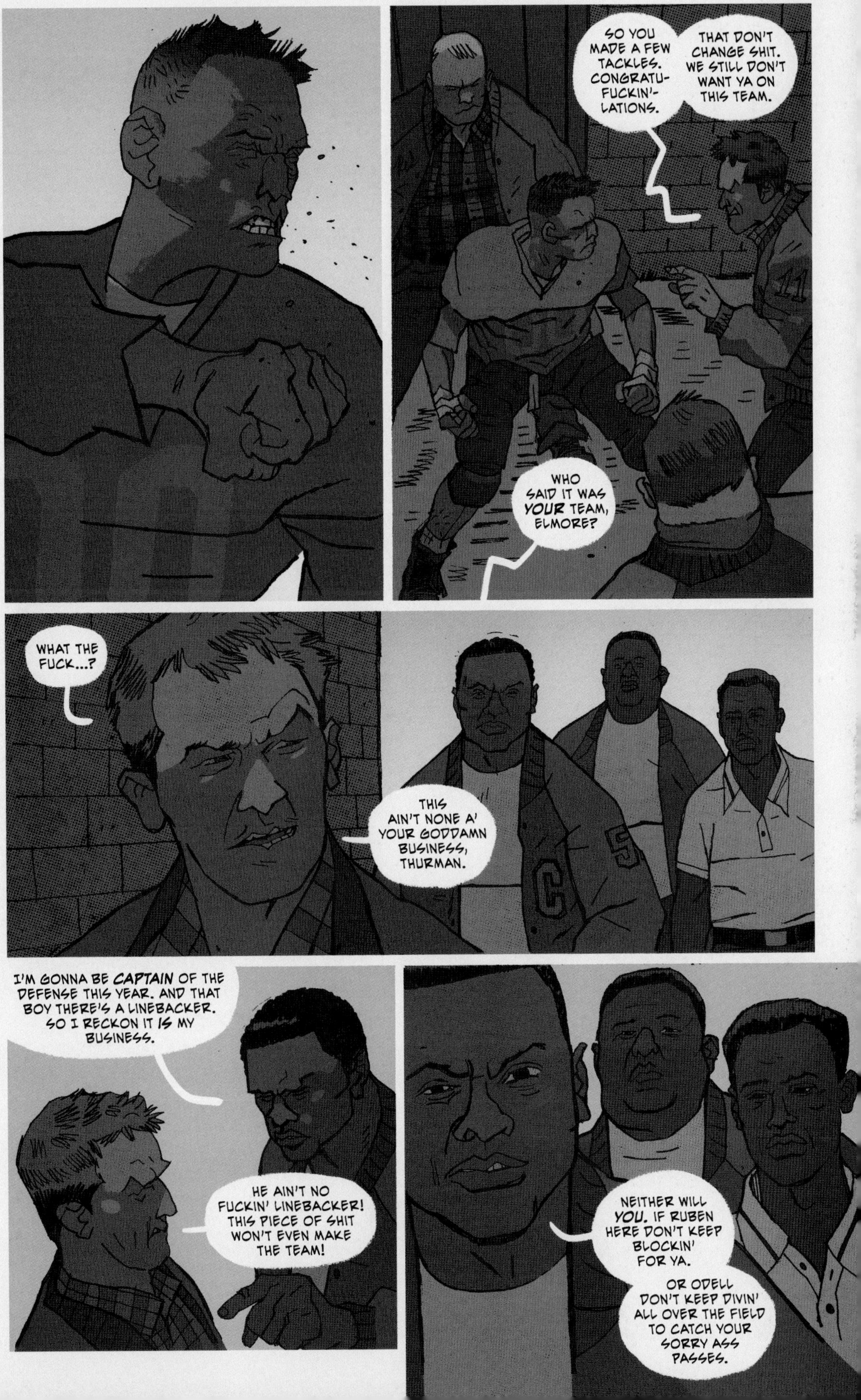
SO YOU MADE A FEW TACKLES. CONGRATU-FUCKIN'-LATIONS.
THAT DON'T CHANGE SHIT. WE STILL DON'T WANT YA ON THIS TEAM.
WHO SAID IT WAS YOUR TEAM, ELMORE?
WHAT THE FUCK...?
THIS AIN'T NONE A' YOUR GODDAMN BUSINESS, THURMAN.
I'M GONNA BE CAPTAIN OF THE DEFENSE THIS YEAR. AND THAT BOY THERE'S A LINEBACKER. SO I RECKON IT IS MY BUSINESS.
HE AIN'T NO FUCKIN' LINEBACKER! THIS PIECE OF SHIT WON'T EVEN MAKE THE TEAM!
NEITHER WILL YOU. IF RUBEN HERE DON'T KEEP BLOCKIN' FOR YA.
OR ODELL DON'T KEEP DIVIN' ALL OVER THE FIELD TO CATCH YOUR SORRY ASS PASSES.

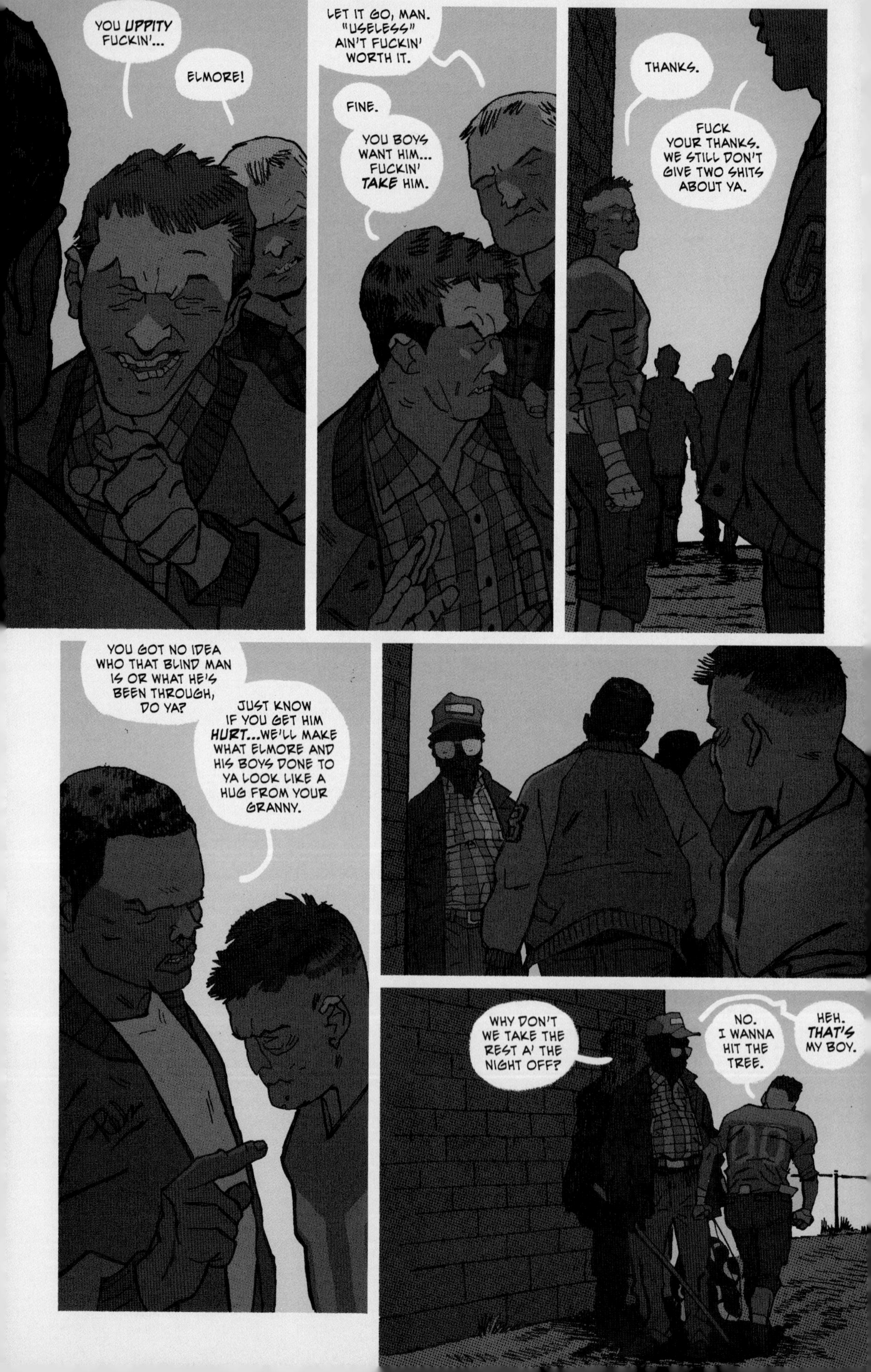
YOU *UPPITY* FUCKIN'...
ELMORE!
LET IT GO, MAN. "USELESS" AIN'T FUCKIN' WORTH IT.
FINE.
YOU BOYS WANT HIM... FUCKIN' *TAKE* HIM.
THANKS.
FUCK YOUR THANKS. WE STILL DON'T GIVE TWO SHITS ABOUT YA.
YOU GOT NO IDEA WHO THAT BLIND MAN IS OR WHAT HE'S BEEN THROUGH, DO YA?
JUST KNOW IF YOU GET HIM *HURT*...WE'LL MAKE WHAT ELMORE AND HIS BOYS DONE TO YA LOOK LIKE A HUG FROM YOUR GRANNY.
WHY DON'T WE TAKE THE REST A' THE NIGHT OFF?
NO. I WANNA HIT THE TREE.
HEH. *THAT'S* MY BOY.

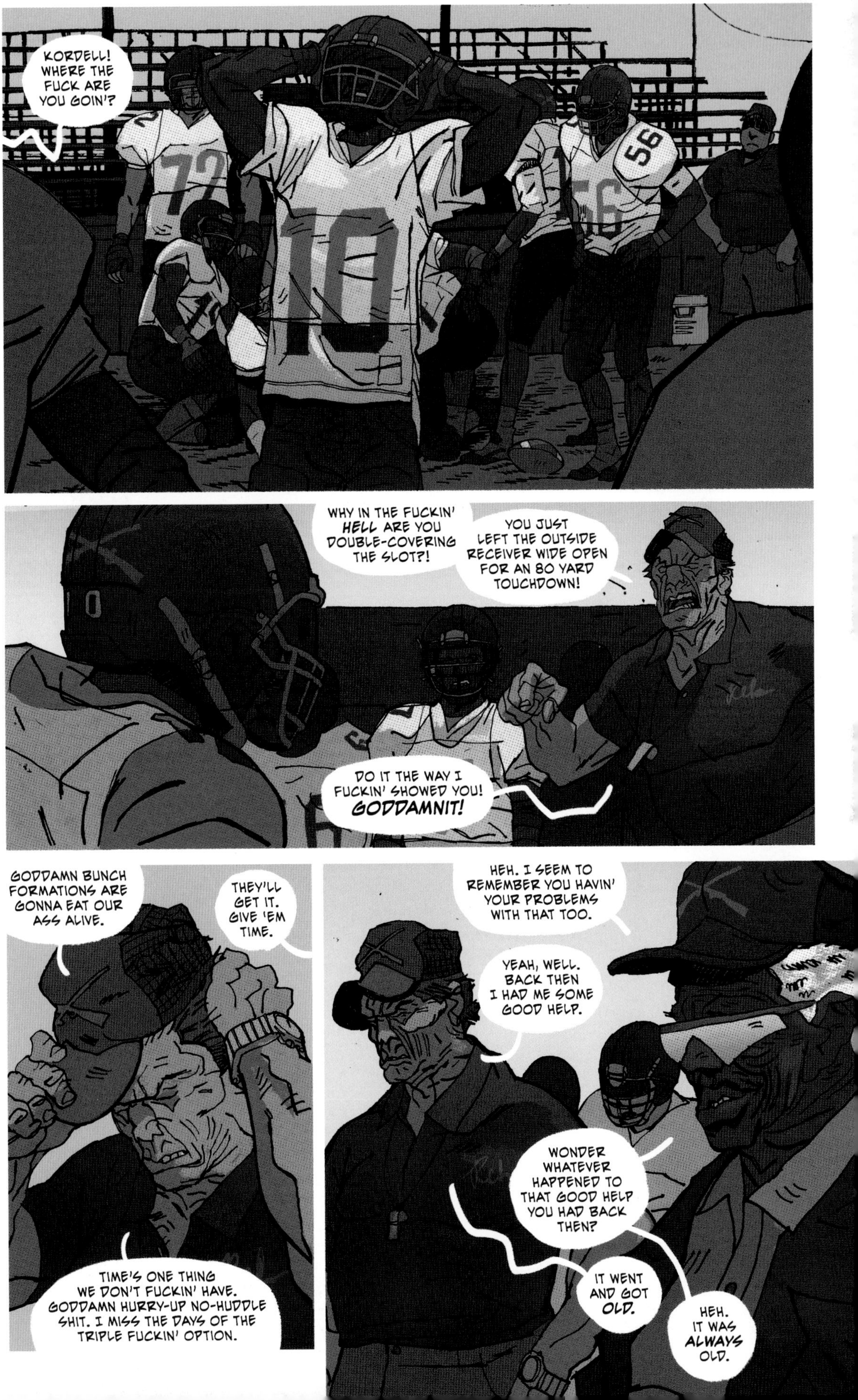
KORDELL! WHERE THE FUCK ARE YOU GOIN'?
WHY IN THE FUCKIN' HELL ARE YOU DOUBLE-COVERING THE SLOT?!
YOU JUST LEFT THE OUTSIDE RECEIVER WIDE OPEN FOR AN 80 YARD TOUCHDOWN!
DO IT THE WAY I FUCKIN' SHOWED YOU! GODDAMNIT!
GODDAMN BUNCH FORMATIONS ARE GONNA EAT OUR ASS ALIVE.
THEY'LL GET IT. GIVE 'EM TIME.
TIME'S ONE THING WE DON'T FUCKIN' HAVE. GODDAMN HURRY-UP NO-HUDDLE SHIT. I MISS THE DAYS OF THE TRIPLE FUCKIN' OPTION.
HEH. I SEEM TO REMEMBER YOU HAVIN' YOUR PROBLEMS WITH THAT TOO.
YEAH, WELL. BACK THEN I HAD ME SOME GOOD HELP.
WONDER WHATEVER HAPPENED TO THAT GOOD HELP YOU HAD BACK THEN?
IT WENT AND GOT OLD.
HEH. IT WAS ALWAYS OLD.

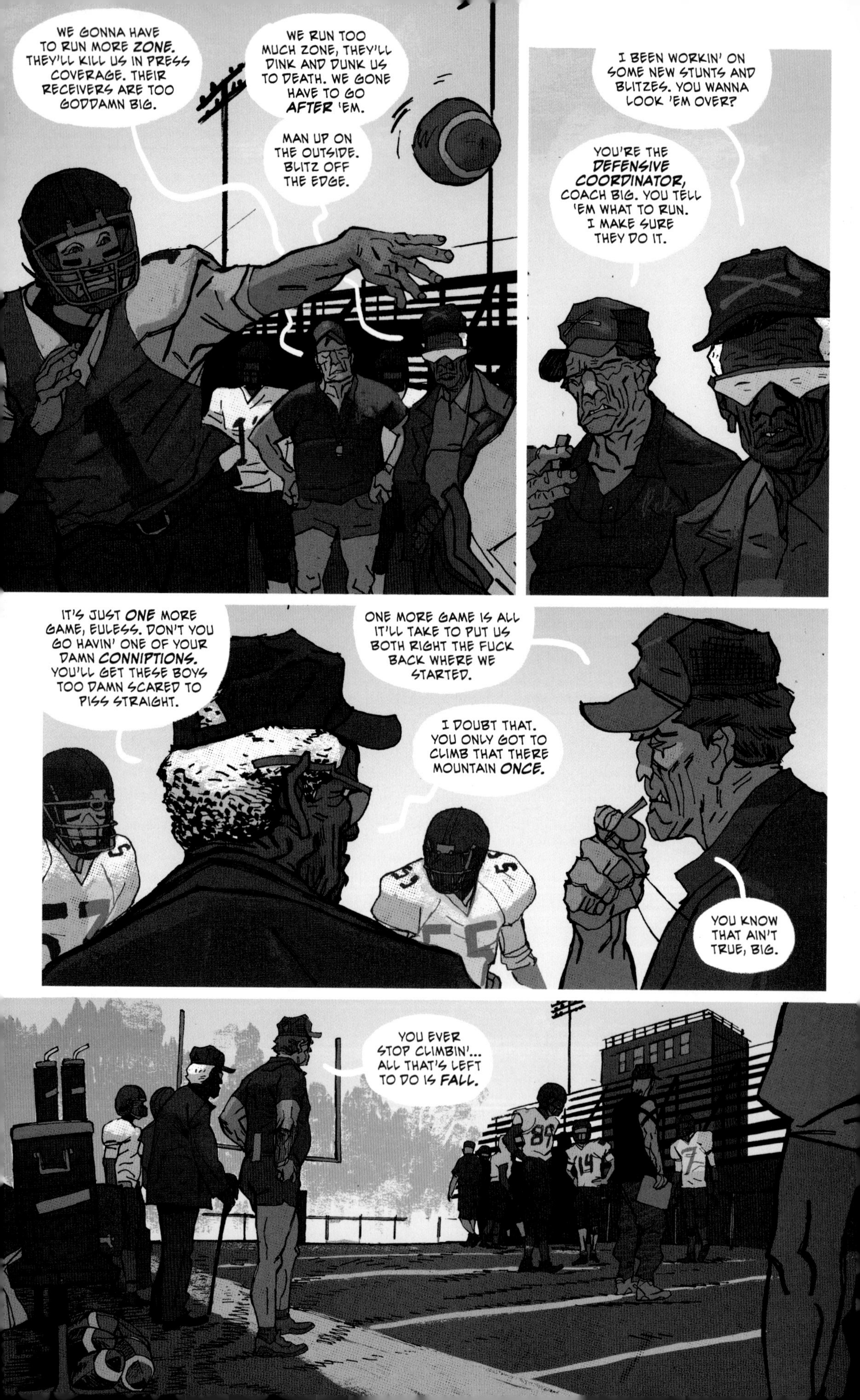
WE GONNA HAVE TO RUN MORE ZONE. THEY'LL KILL US IN PRESS COVERAGE. THEIR RECEIVERS ARE TOO GODDAMN BIG.
WE RUN TOO MUCH ZONE, THEY'LL DINK AND DUNK US TO DEATH. WE GONE HAVE TO GO AFTER 'EM.
MAN UP ON THE OUTSIDE. BLITZ OFF THE EDGE.
I BEEN WORKIN' ON SOME NEW STUNTS AND BLITZES. YOU WANNA LOOK 'EM OVER?
YOU'RE THE DEFENSIVE COORDINATOR, COACH BIG. YOU TELL 'EM WHAT TO RUN. I MAKE SURE THEY DO IT.
IT'S JUST ONE MORE GAME, EULESS. DON'T YOU GO HAVIN' ONE OF YOUR DAMN CONNIPTIONS. YOU'LL GET THESE BOYS TOO DAMN SCARED TO PISS STRAIGHT.
ONE MORE GAME IS ALL IT'LL TAKE TO PUT US BOTH RIGHT THE FUCK BACK WHERE WE STARTED.
I DOUBT THAT. YOU ONLY GOT TO CLIMB THAT THERE MOUNTAIN ONCE.
YOU KNOW THAT AIN'T TRUE, BIG.
YOU EVER STOP CLIMBIN'... ALL THAT'S LEFT TO DO IS FALL.

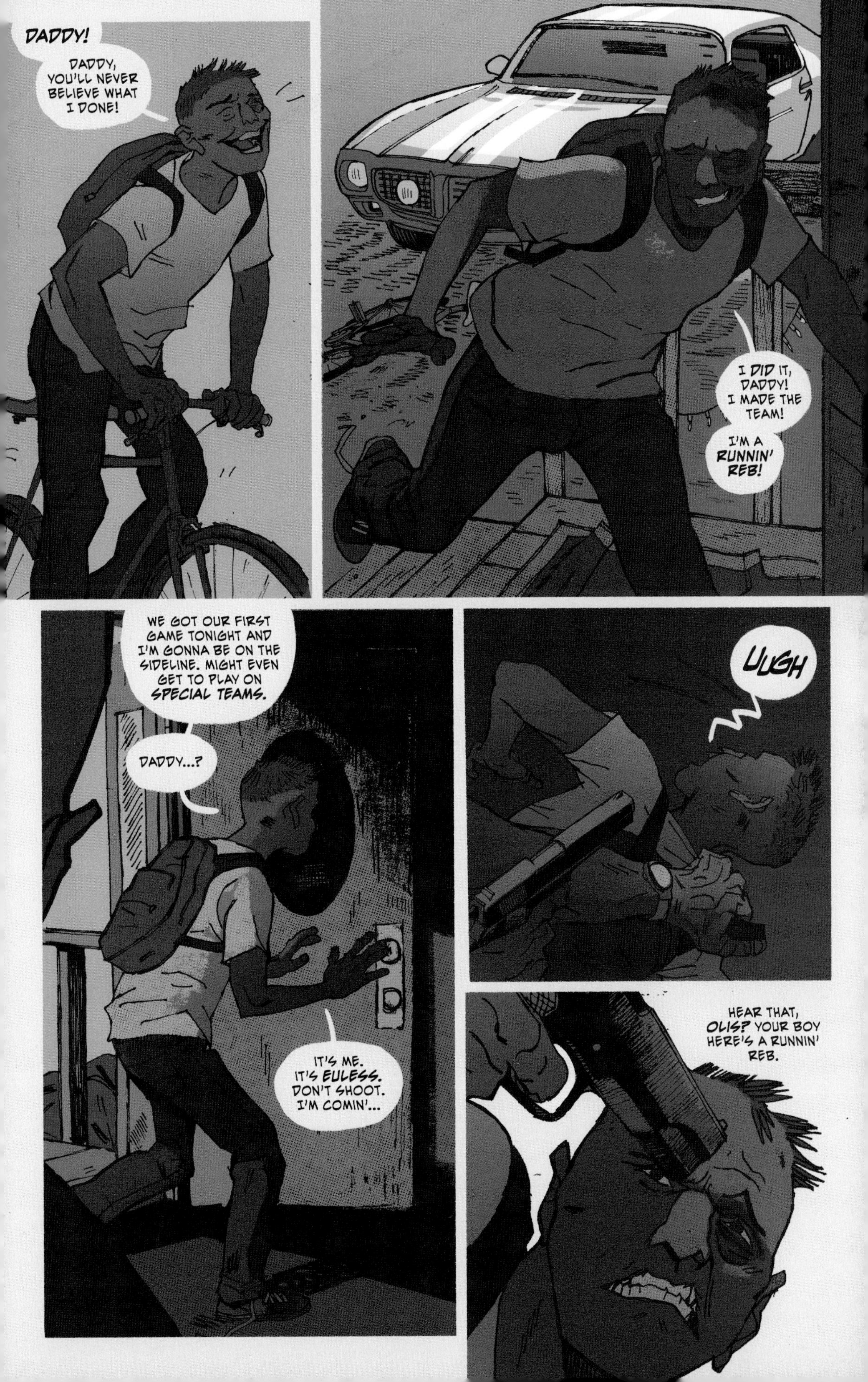
DADDY!
DADDY, YOU'LL NEVER BELIEVE WHAT I DONE!
I DID IT, DADDY! I MADE THE TEAM!
I'M A RUNNIN' REB!
WE GOT OUR FIRST GAME TONIGHT AND I'M GONNA BE ON THE SIDELINE. MIGHT EVEN GET TO PLAY ON SPECIAL TEAMS.
DADDY...?
IT'S ME. IT'S EULESS. DON'T SHOOT. I'M COMIN'...
UUGH
HEAR THAT, OLIS? YOUR BOY HERE'S A RUNNIN' REB.

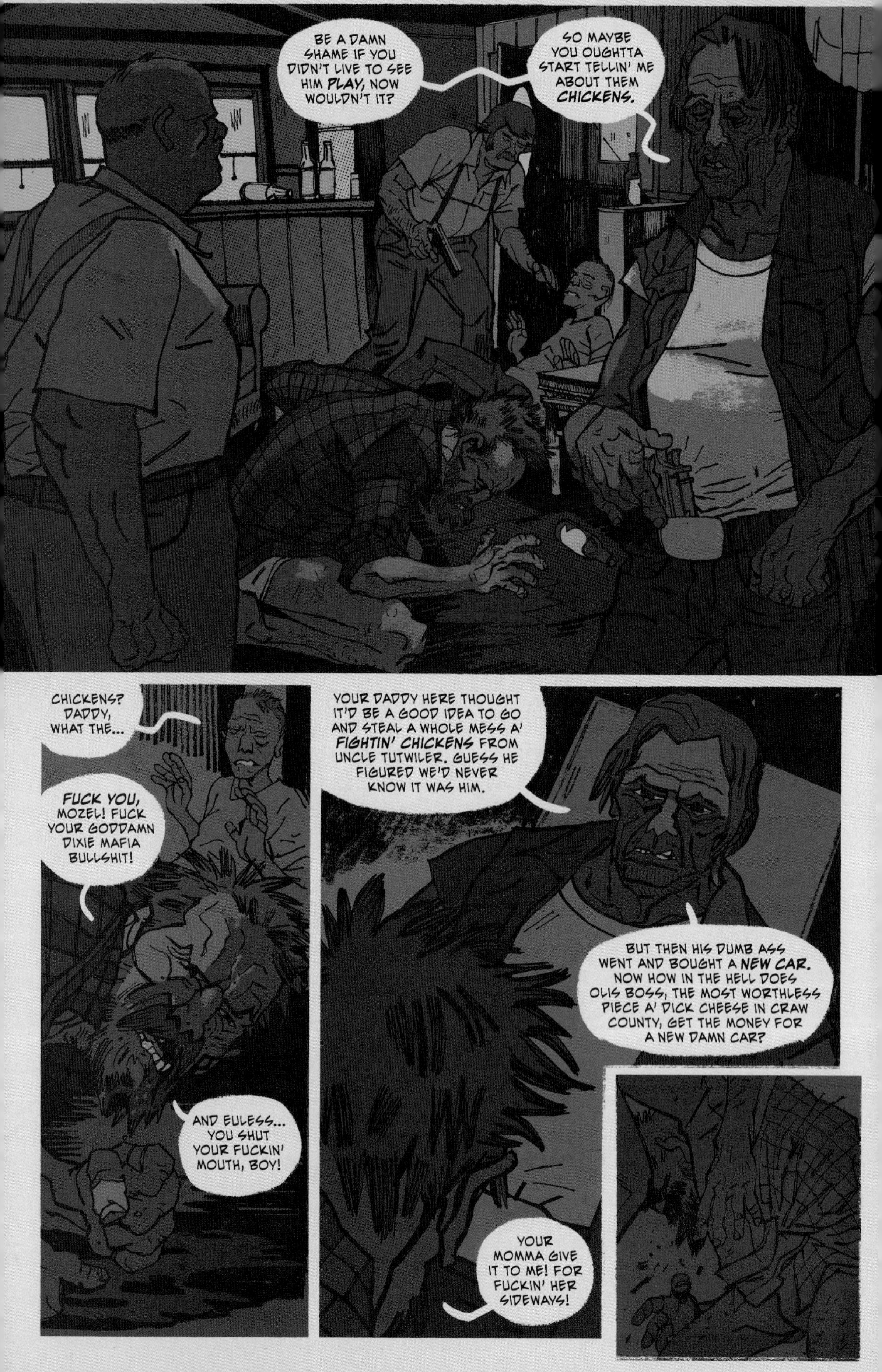
BE A DAMN SHAME IF YOU DIDN'T LIVE TO SEE HIM PLAY, NOW WOULDN'T IT?
SO MAYBE YOU OUGHTTA START TELLIN' ME ABOUT THEM CHICKENS.
CHICKENS? DADDY, WHAT THE...
FUCK YOU, MOZEL! FUCK YOUR GODDAMN DIXIE MAFIA BULLSHIT!
AND EULESS... YOU SHUT YOUR FUCKIN' MOUTH, BOY!
YOUR DADDY HERE THOUGHT IT'D BE A GOOD IDEA TO GO AND STEAL A WHOLE MESS A' FIGHTIN' CHICKENS FROM UNCLE TUTWILER. GUESS HE FIGURED WE'D NEVER KNOW IT WAS HIM.
BUT THEN HIS DUMB ASS WENT AND BOUGHT A NEW CAR. NOW HOW IN THE HELL DOES OLIS BOSS, THE MOST WORTHLESS PIECE A' DICK CHEESE IN CRAW COUNTY, GET THE MONEY FOR A NEW DAMN CAR?
YOUR MOMMA GIVE IT TO ME! FOR FUCKIN' HER SIDEWAYS!

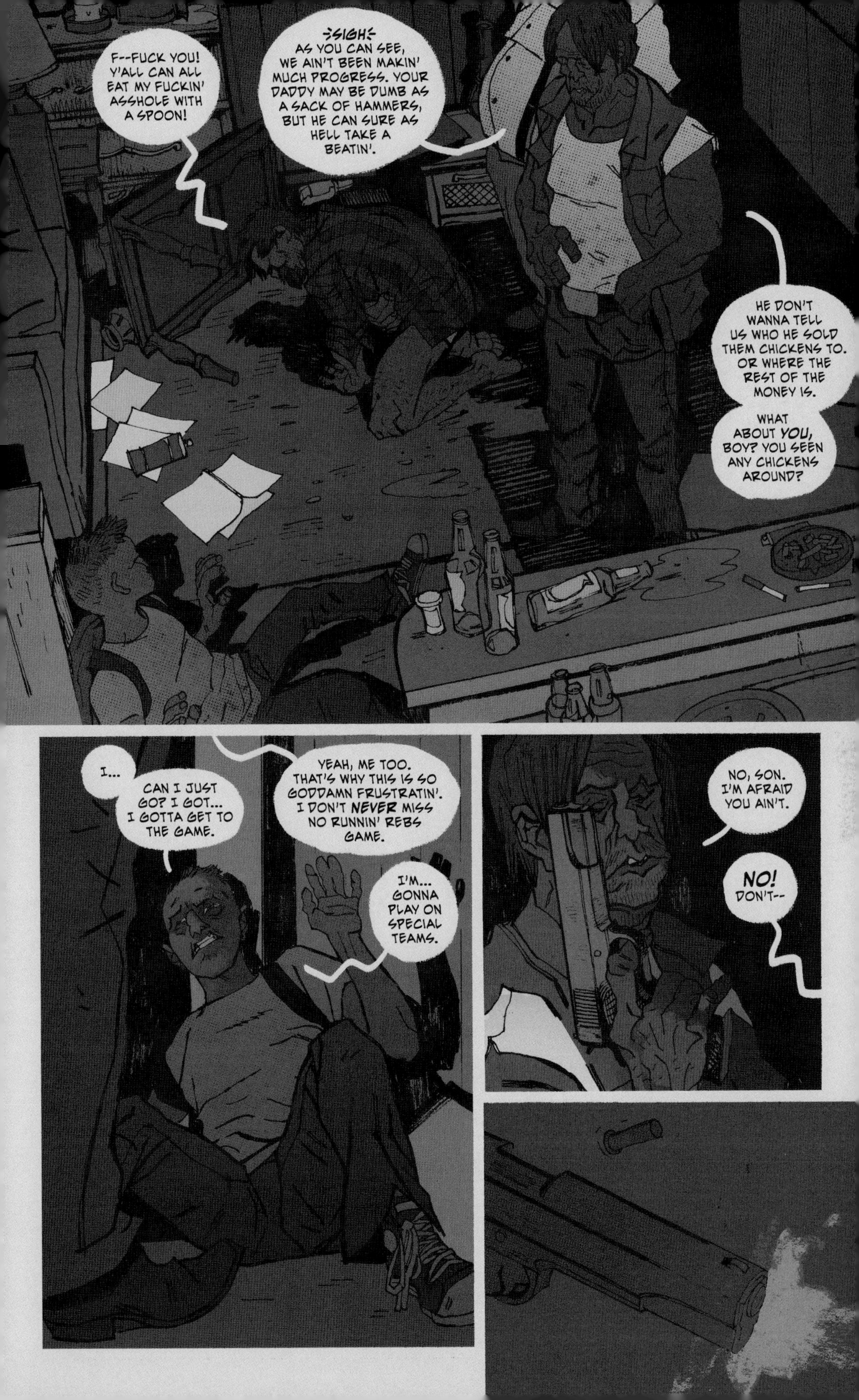
F--FUCK YOU! Y'ALL CAN ALL EAT MY FUCKIN' ASSHOLE WITH A SPOON!
SIGH AS YOU CAN SEE, WE AIN'T BEEN MAKIN' MUCH PROGRESS. YOUR DADDY MAY BE DUMB AS A SACK OF HAMMERS, BUT HE CAN SURE AS HELL TAKE A BEATIN'.
HE DON'T WANNA TELL US WHO HE SOLD THEM CHICKENS TO. OR WHERE THE REST OF THE MONEY IS.
WHAT ABOUT *YOU*, BOY? YOU SEEN ANY CHICKENS AROUND?
I...
CAN I JUST GO? I GOT... I GOTTA GET TO THE GAME.
YEAH, ME TOO. THAT'S WHY THIS IS SO GODDAMN FRUSTRATIN'. I DON'T **NEVER** MISS NO RUNNIN' REBS GAME.
I'M... GONNA PLAY ON SPECIAL TEAMS.
NO, SON. I'M AFRAID YOU AIN'T.
NO! DON'T--

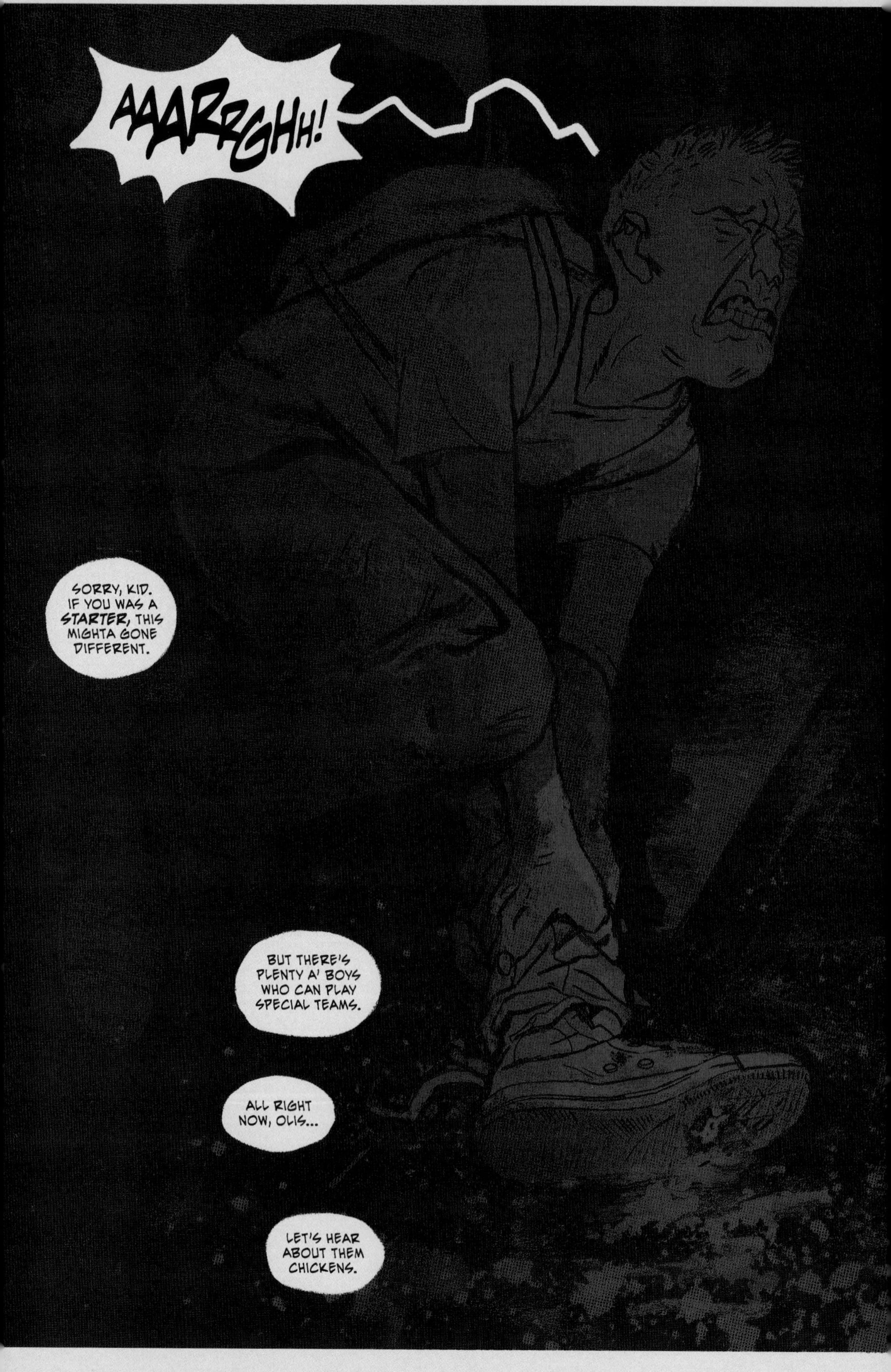
AAARRGHH!
SORRY, KID. IF YOU WAS A STARTER, THIS MIGHTA GONE DIFFERENT.
BUT THERE'S PLENTY A' BOYS WHO CAN PLAY SPECIAL TEAMS.
ALL RIGHT NOW, OLIS...
LET'S HEAR ABOUT THEM CHICKENS.

Gridiron

Chapter Three

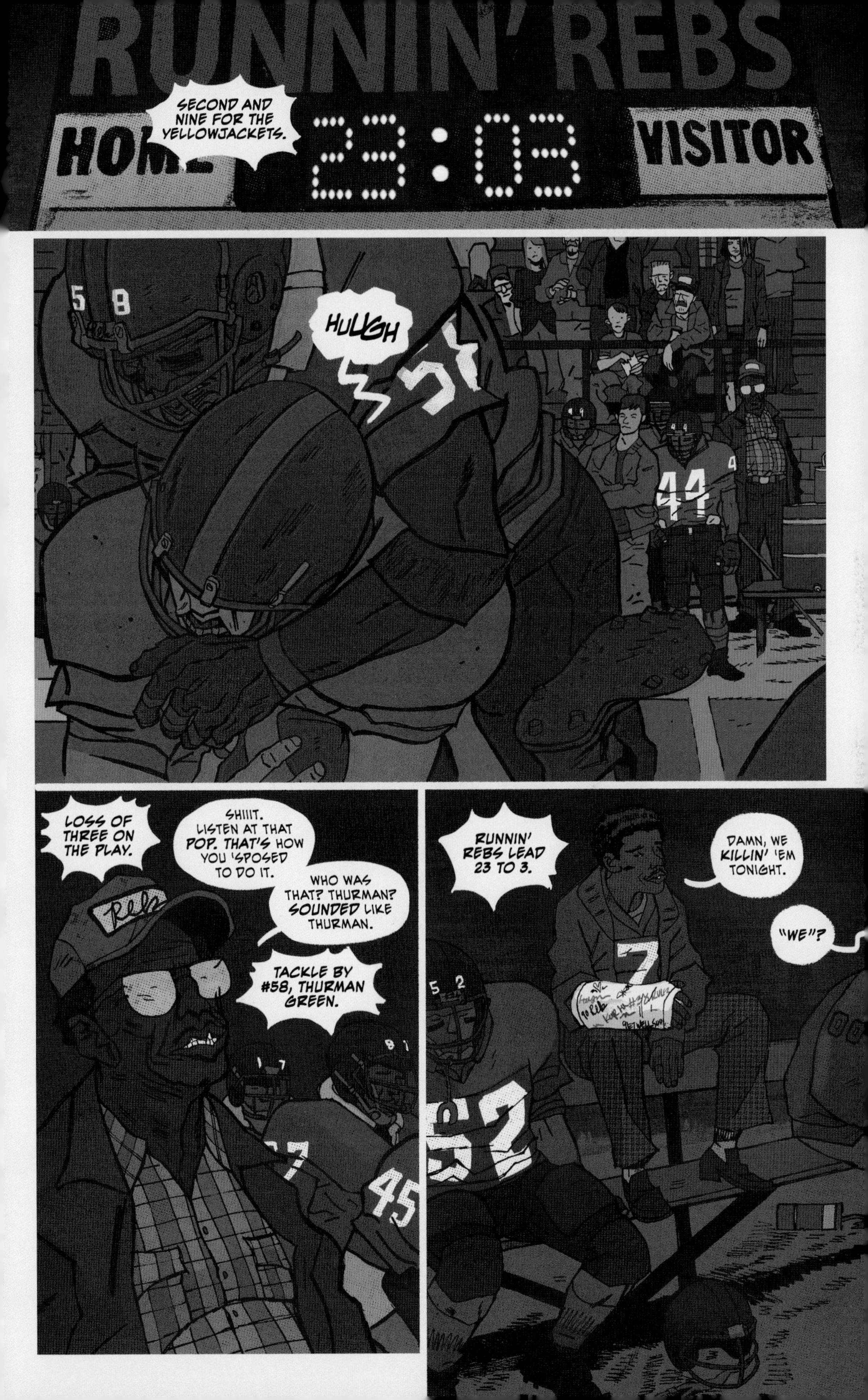
RUNNIN' REBS
SECOND AND NINE FOR THE YELLOWJACKETS.
HOME
23:03
VISITOR
HULUGH
LOSS OF THREE ON THE PLAY.
SHIIIT. LISTEN AT THAT POP. THAT'S HOW YOU 'SPOSED TO DO IT.
WHO WAS THAT? THURMAN? SOUNDED LIKE THURMAN.
TACKLE BY #58, THURMAN GREEN.
RUNNIN' REBS LEAD 23 TO 3.
DAMN, WE KILLIN' 'EM TONIGHT.
"WE"?

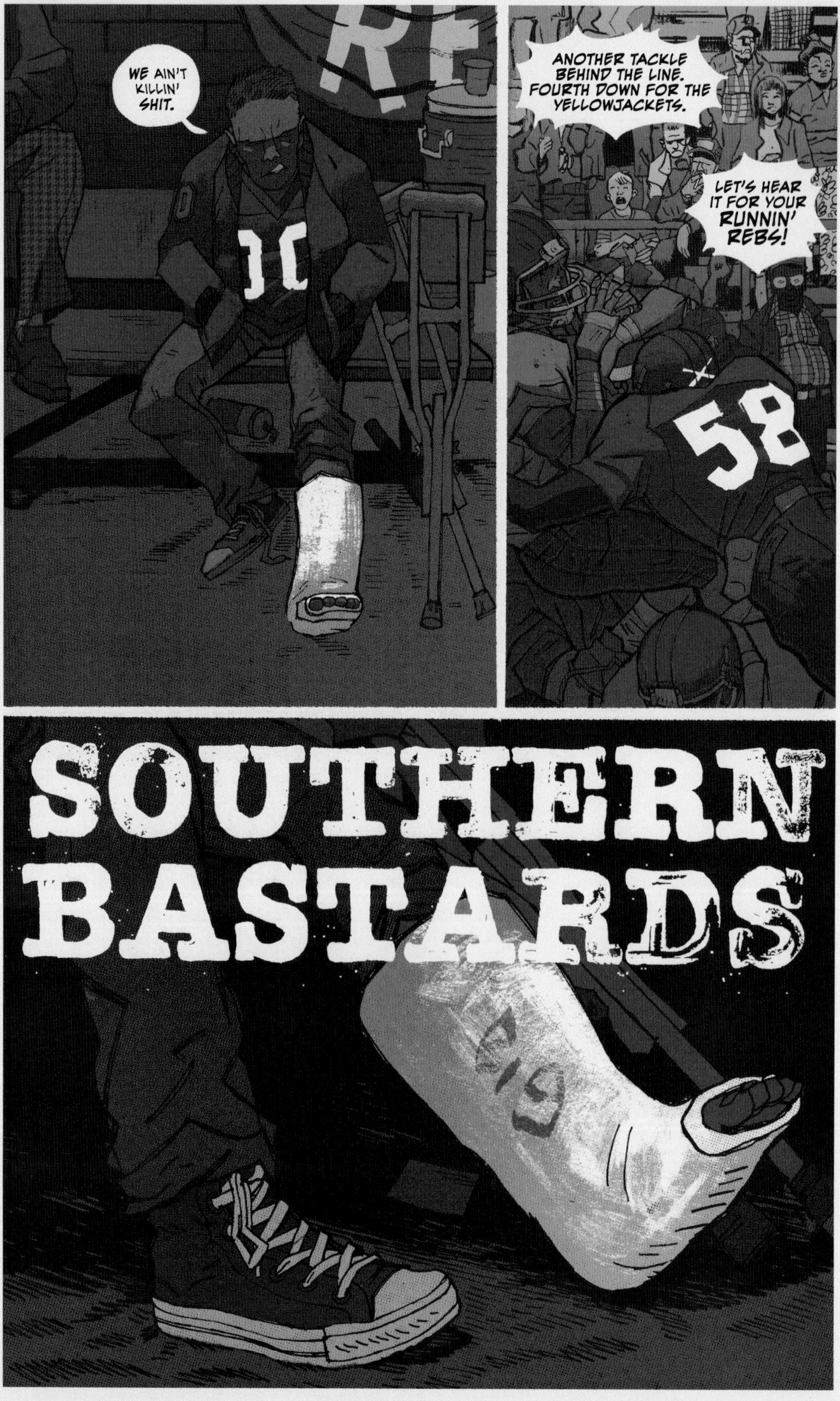
WE AIN'T KILLIN' SHIT.
ANOTHER TACKLE BEHIND THE LINE. FOURTH DOWN FOR THE YELLOWJACKETS.
LET'S HEAR IT FOR YOUR RUNNIN' REBS!
SOUTHERN BASTARDS

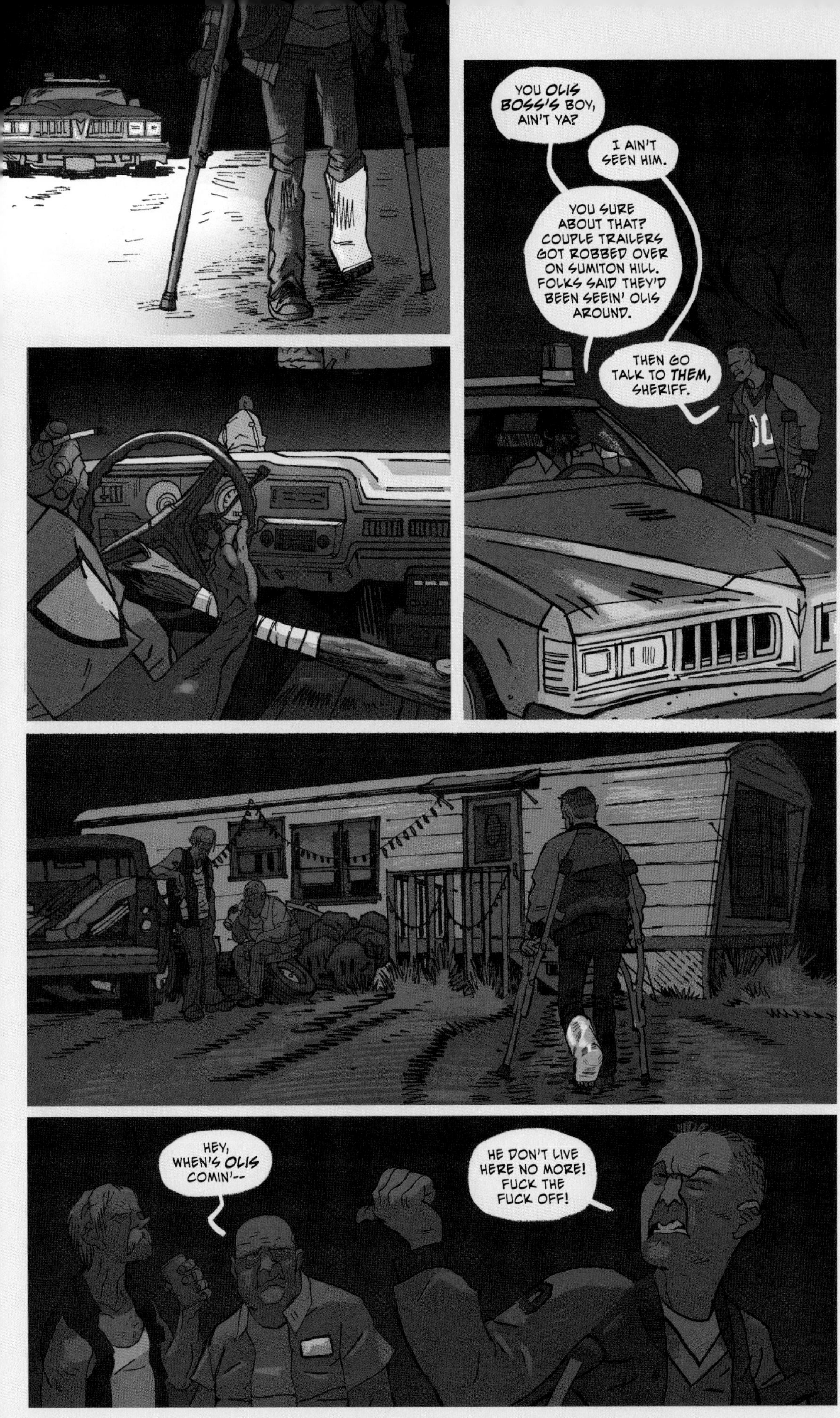
YOU OLIS BOSS'S BOY, AIN'T YA?
I AIN'T SEEN HIM.
YOU SURE ABOUT THAT? COUPLE TRAILERS GOT ROBBED OVER ON SUMITON HILL. FOLKS SAID THEY'D BEEN SEEIN' OLIS AROUND.
THEN GO TALK TO THEM, SHERIFF.
HEY, WHEN'S OLIS COMIN'--
HE DON'T LIVE HERE NO MORE! FUCK THE FUCK OFF!

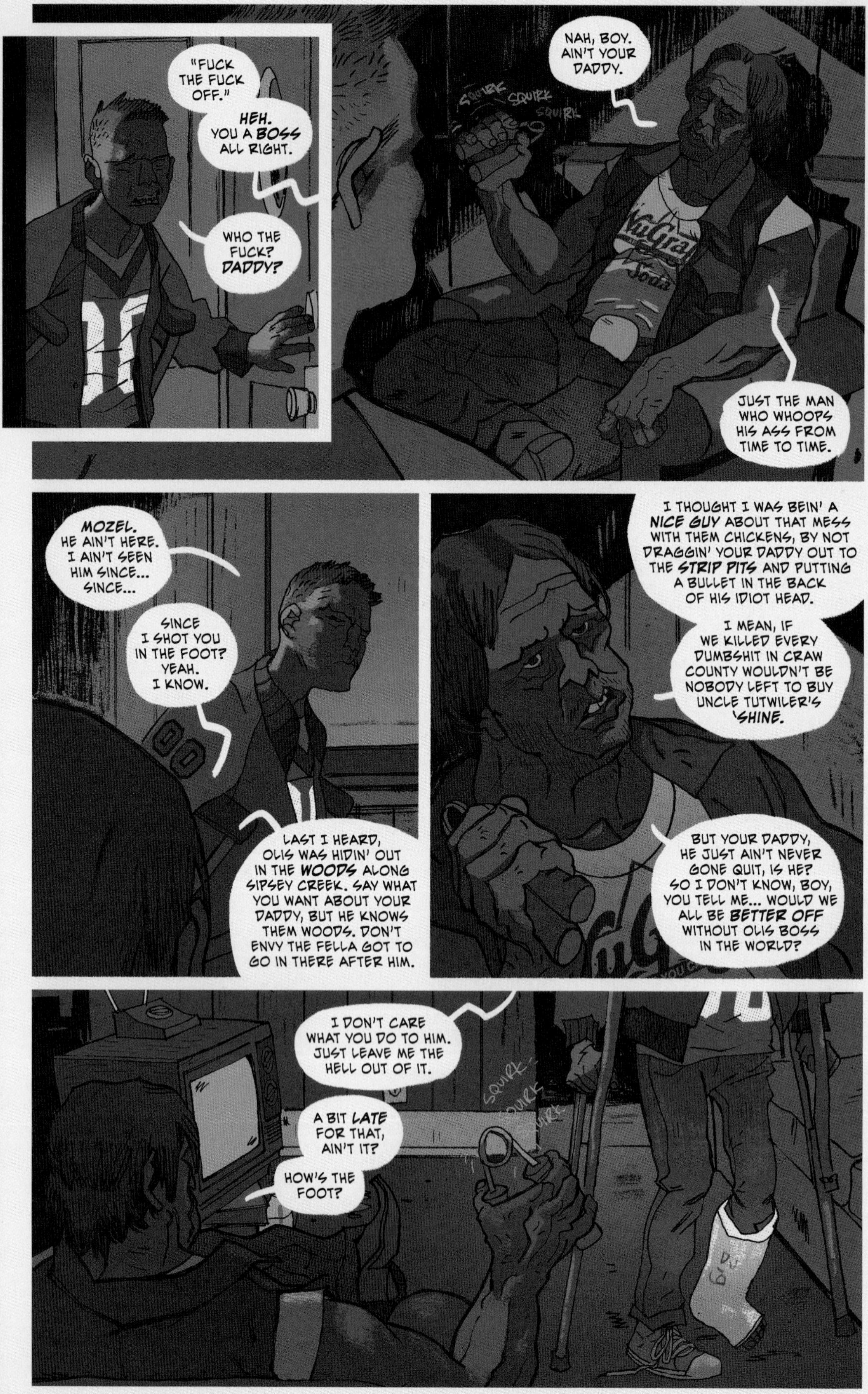
"FUCK THE FUCK OFF."
HEH. YOU A BOSS ALL RIGHT.
WHO THE FUCK? DADDY?
NAH, BOY. AIN'T YOUR DADDY.
SQUIRK SQUIRK SQUIRK
JUST THE MAN WHO WHOOPS HIS ASS FROM TIME TO TIME.
MOZEL. HE AIN'T HERE. I AIN'T SEEN HIM SINCE... SINCE...
SINCE I SHOT YOU IN THE FOOT? YEAH. I KNOW.
LAST I HEARD, OLIS WAS HIDIN' OUT IN THE WOODS ALONG SIPSEY CREEK. SAY WHAT YOU WANT ABOUT YOUR DADDY, BUT HE KNOWS THEM WOODS. DON'T ENVY THE FELLA GOT TO GO IN THERE AFTER HIM.
I THOUGHT I WAS BEIN' A NICE GUY ABOUT THAT MESS WITH THEM CHICKENS, BY NOT DRAGGIN' YOUR DADDY OUT TO THE STRIP PITS AND PUTTING A BULLET IN THE BACK OF HIS IDIOT HEAD.
I MEAN, IF WE KILLED EVERY DUMBSHIT IN CRAW COUNTY WOULDN'T BE NOBODY LEFT TO BUY UNCLE TUTWILER'S 'SHINE.
BUT YOUR DADDY, HE JUST AIN'T NEVER GONE QUIT, IS HE? SO I DON'T KNOW, BOY, YOU TELL ME... WOULD WE ALL BE BETTER OFF WITHOUT OLIS BOSS IN THE WORLD?
I DON'T CARE WHAT YOU DO TO HIM. JUST LEAVE ME THE HELL OUT OF IT.
SQUIRK SQUIRK SQUIRK
A BIT LATE FOR THAT, AIN'T IT?
HOW'S THE FOOT?

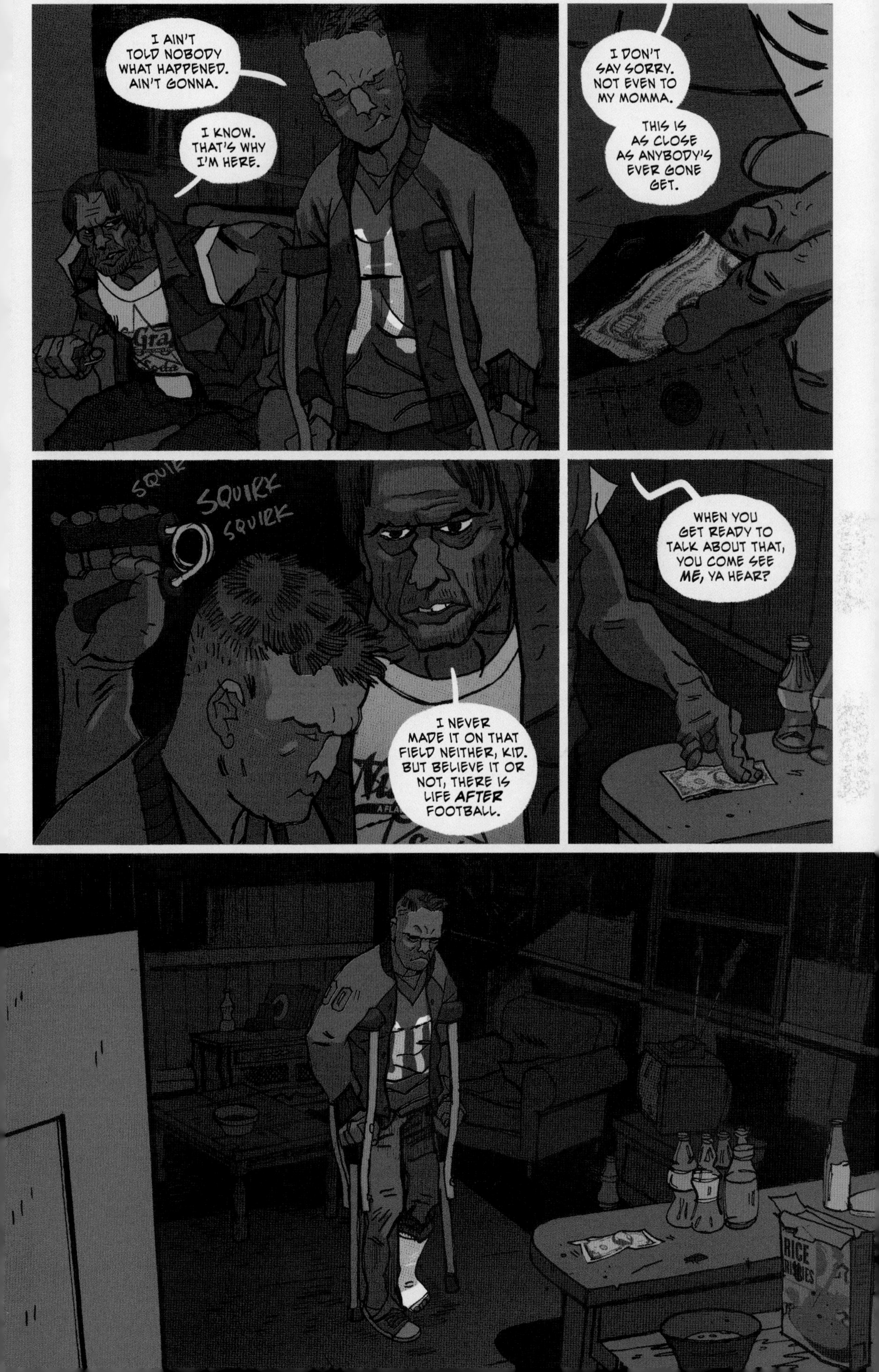
I AIN'T TOLD NOBODY WHAT HAPPENED. AIN'T GONNA.
I KNOW. THAT'S WHY I'M HERE.
I DON'T SAY SORRY. NOT EVEN TO MY MOMMA.
THIS IS AS CLOSE AS ANYBODY'S EVER GONE GET.
SQUIRK
SQUIRK
SQUIRK
I NEVER MADE IT ON THAT FIELD NEITHER, KID. BUT BELIEVE IT OR NOT, THERE IS LIFE AFTER FOOTBALL.
WHEN YOU GET READY TO TALK ABOUT THAT, YOU COME SEE ME, YA HEAR?
RICE

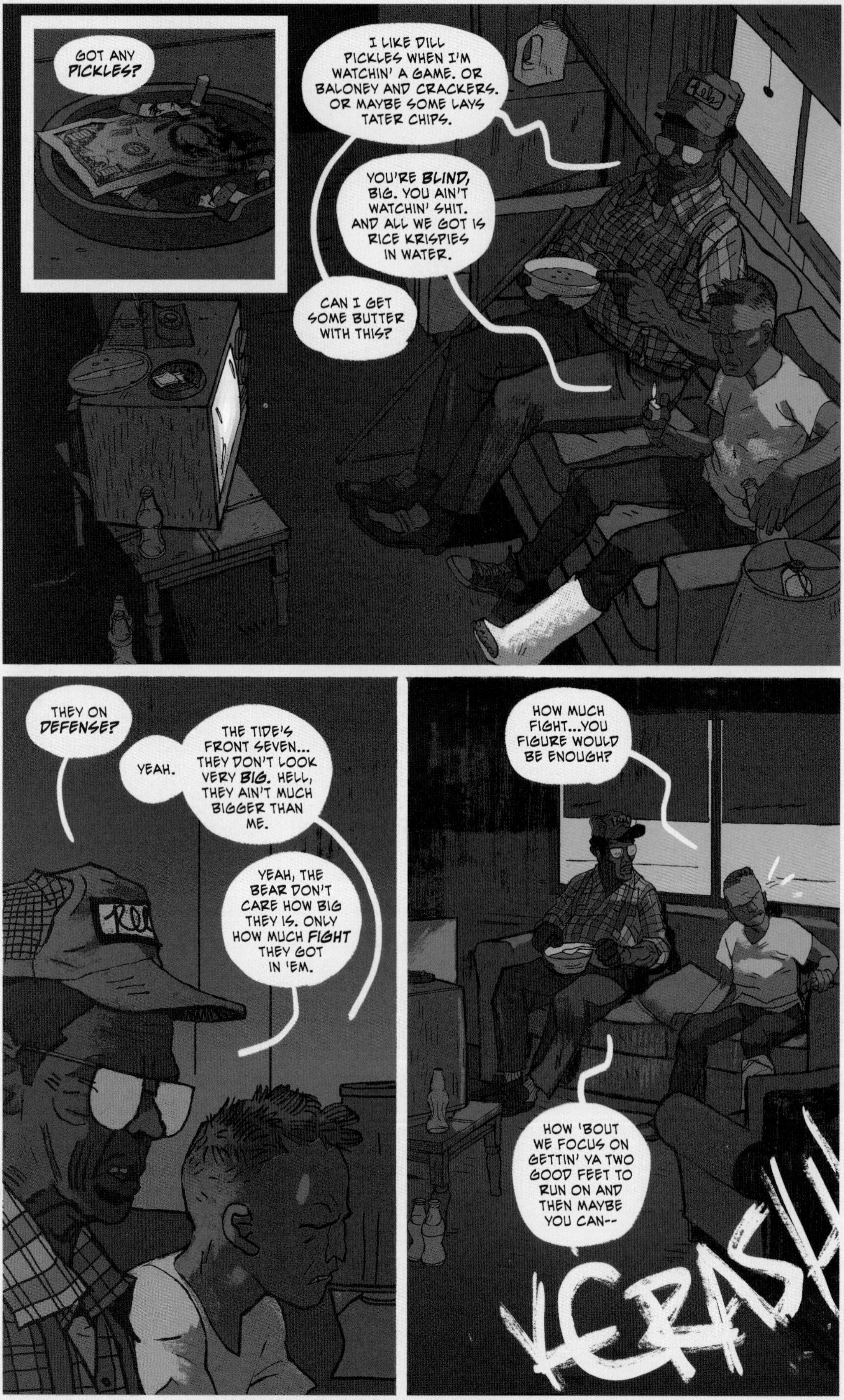
GOT ANY PICKLES?
I LIKE DILL PICKLES WHEN I'M WATCHIN' A GAME. OR BALONEY AND CRACKERS. OR MAYBE SOME LAYS TATER CHIPS.
YOU'RE BLIND, BIG. YOU AIN'T WATCHIN' SHIT. AND ALL WE GOT IS RICE KRISPIES IN WATER.
CAN I GET SOME BUTTER WITH THIS?
THEY ON DEFENSE?
YEAH.
THE TIDE'S FRONT SEVEN... THEY DON'T LOOK VERY BIG. HELL, THEY AIN'T MUCH BIGGER THAN ME.
YEAH, THE BEAR DON'T CARE HOW BIG THEY IS. ONLY HOW MUCH FIGHT THEY GOT IN 'EM.
HOW MUCH FIGHT...YOU FIGURE WOULD BE ENOUGH?
HOW 'BOUT WE FOCUS ON GETTIN' YA TWO GOOD FEET TO RUN ON AND THEN MAYBE YOU CAN--
KCRASH

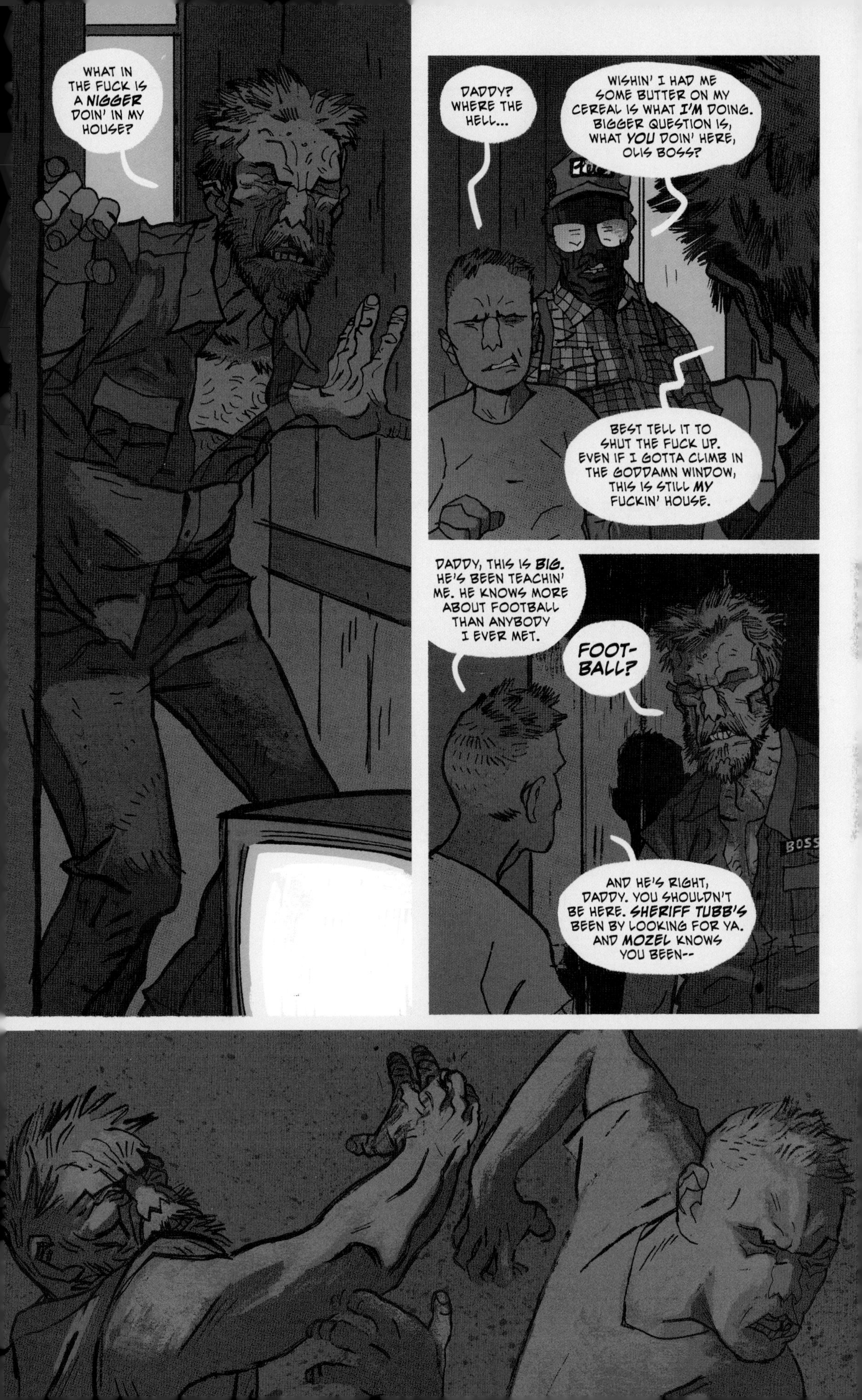
WHAT IN THE FUCK IS A NIGGER DOIN' IN MY HOUSE?
DADDY? WHERE THE HELL...
WISHIN' I HAD ME SOME BUTTER ON MY CEREAL IS WHAT I'M DOING. BIGGER QUESTION IS, WHAT YOU DOIN' HERE, OLIS BOSS?
BEST TELL IT TO SHUT THE FUCK UP. EVEN IF I GOTTA CLIMB IN THE GODDAMN WINDOW, THIS IS STILL MY FUCKIN' HOUSE.
DADDY, THIS IS BIG. HE'S BEEN TEACHIN' ME. HE KNOWS MORE ABOUT FOOTBALL THAN ANYBODY I EVER MET.
FOOT-BALL?
BOSS
AND HE'S RIGHT, DADDY. YOU SHOULDN'T BE HERE. SHERIFF TUBB'S BEEN BY LOOKING FOR YA. AND MOZEL KNOWS YOU BEEN--

GO ON! OUT THE FUCK ON OUT, BOY! AND TAKE YOUR NEW NIGGER DADDY WITH YA! OR I SWEAR TO CHRIST I'LL...

GAAAGH

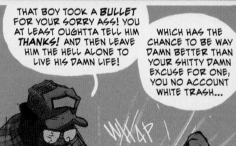

THAT BOY TOOK A *BULLET* FOR YOUR SORRY ASS! YOU AT LEAST OUGHTTA TELL HIM *THANKS!* AND THEN LEAVE HIM THE HELL ALONE TO LIVE HIS DAMN LIFE!

WHICH HAS THE CHANCE TO BE WAY DAMN BETTER THAN YOUR SHITTY DAMN EXCUSE FOR ONE, YOU NO ACCOUNT WHITE TRASH...

WHAP
WHAP

HUUGGH

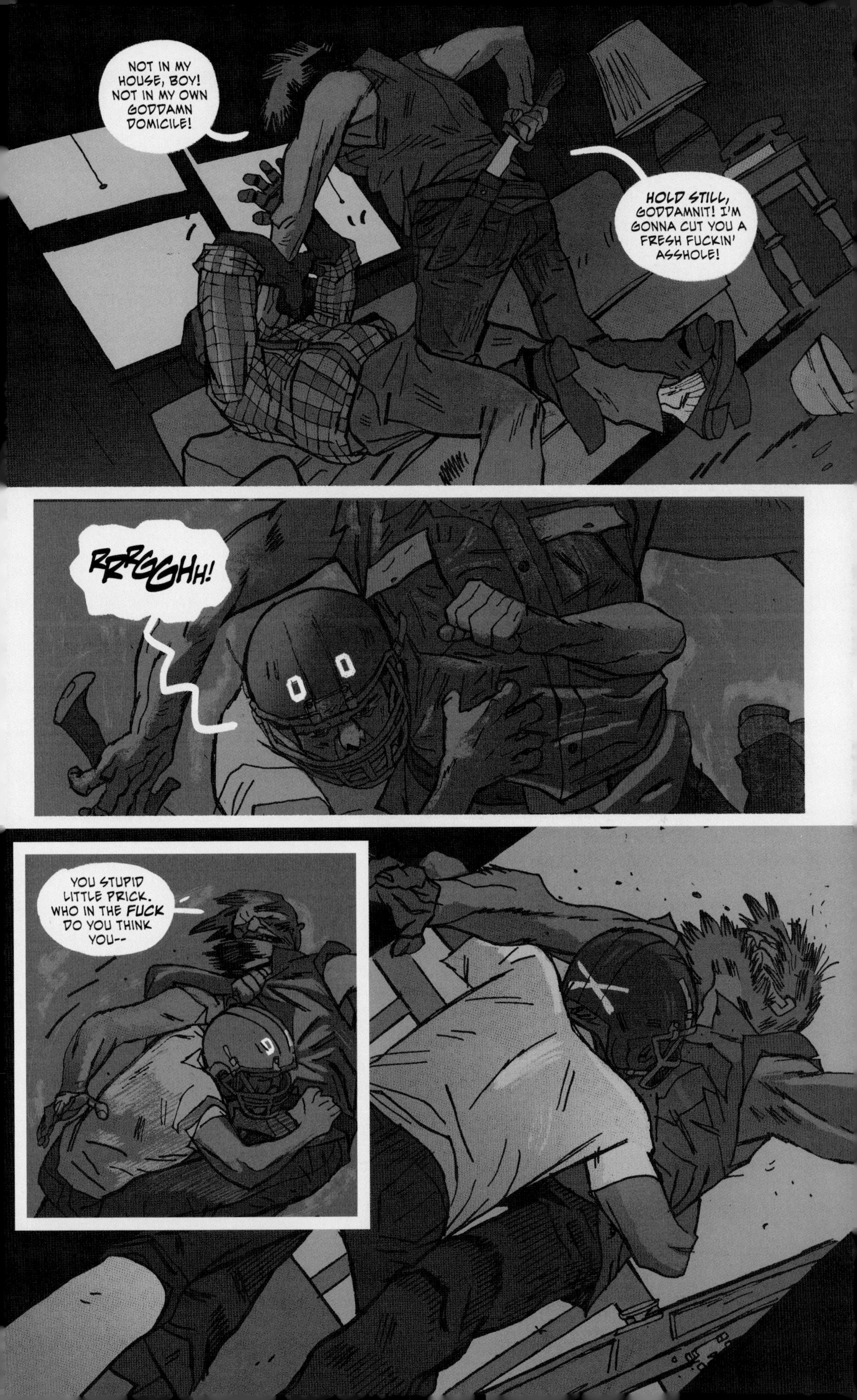
NOT IN MY HOUSE, BOY! NOT IN MY OWN GODDAMN DOMICILE!
HOLD STILL, GODDAMNIT! I'M GONNA CUT YOU A FRESH FUCKIN' ASSHOLE!
RRRGGHH!
YOU STUPID LITTLE PRICK. WHO IN THE FUCK DO YOU THINK YOU--

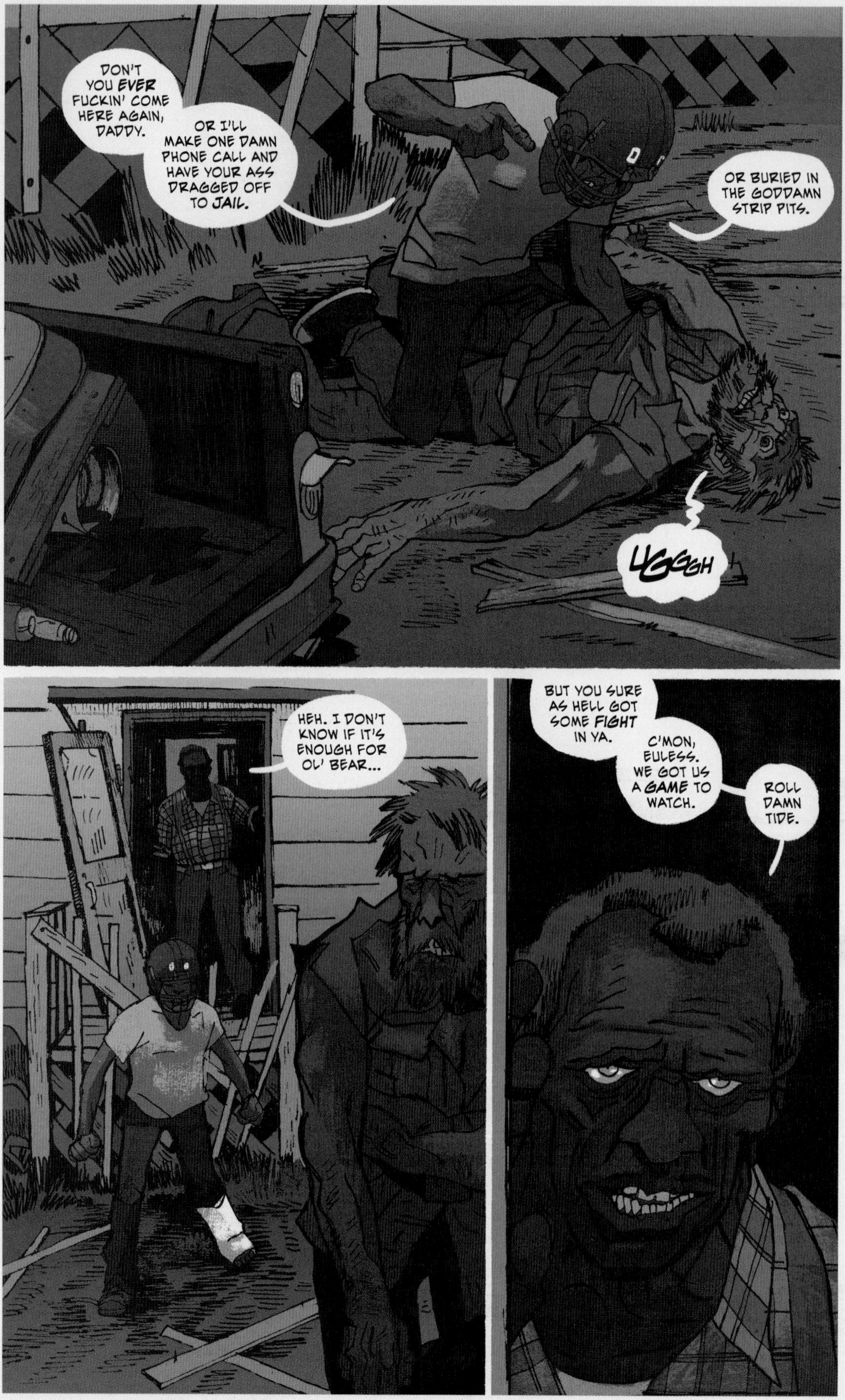

DON'T YOU EVER FUCKIN' COME HERE AGAIN, DADDY.
OR I'LL MAKE ONE DAMN PHONE CALL AND HAVE YOUR ASS DRAGGED OFF TO JAIL.
OR BURIED IN THE GODDAMN STRIP PITS.
UGGGH
HEH. I DON'T KNOW IF IT'S ENOUGH FOR OL' BEAR...
BUT YOU SURE AS HELL GOT SOME FIGHT IN YA.
C'MON, EULESS. WE GOT US A GAME TO WATCH.
ROLL DAMN TIDE.

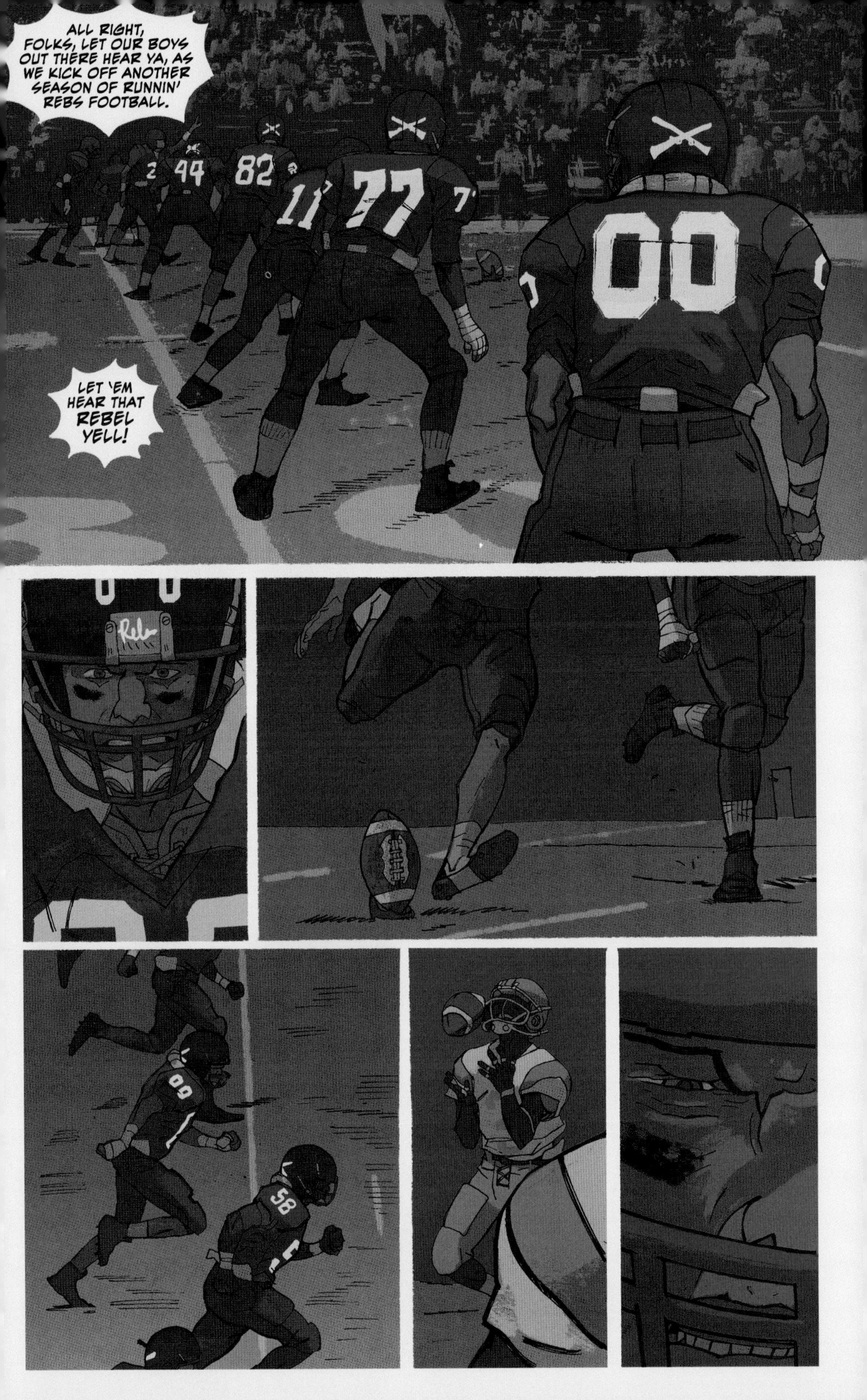
ALL RIGHT, FOLKS, LET OUR BOYS OUT THERE HEAR YA, AS WE KICK OFF ANOTHER SEASON OF RUNNIN' REBS FOOTBALL.
LET 'EM HEAR THAT REBEL YELL!

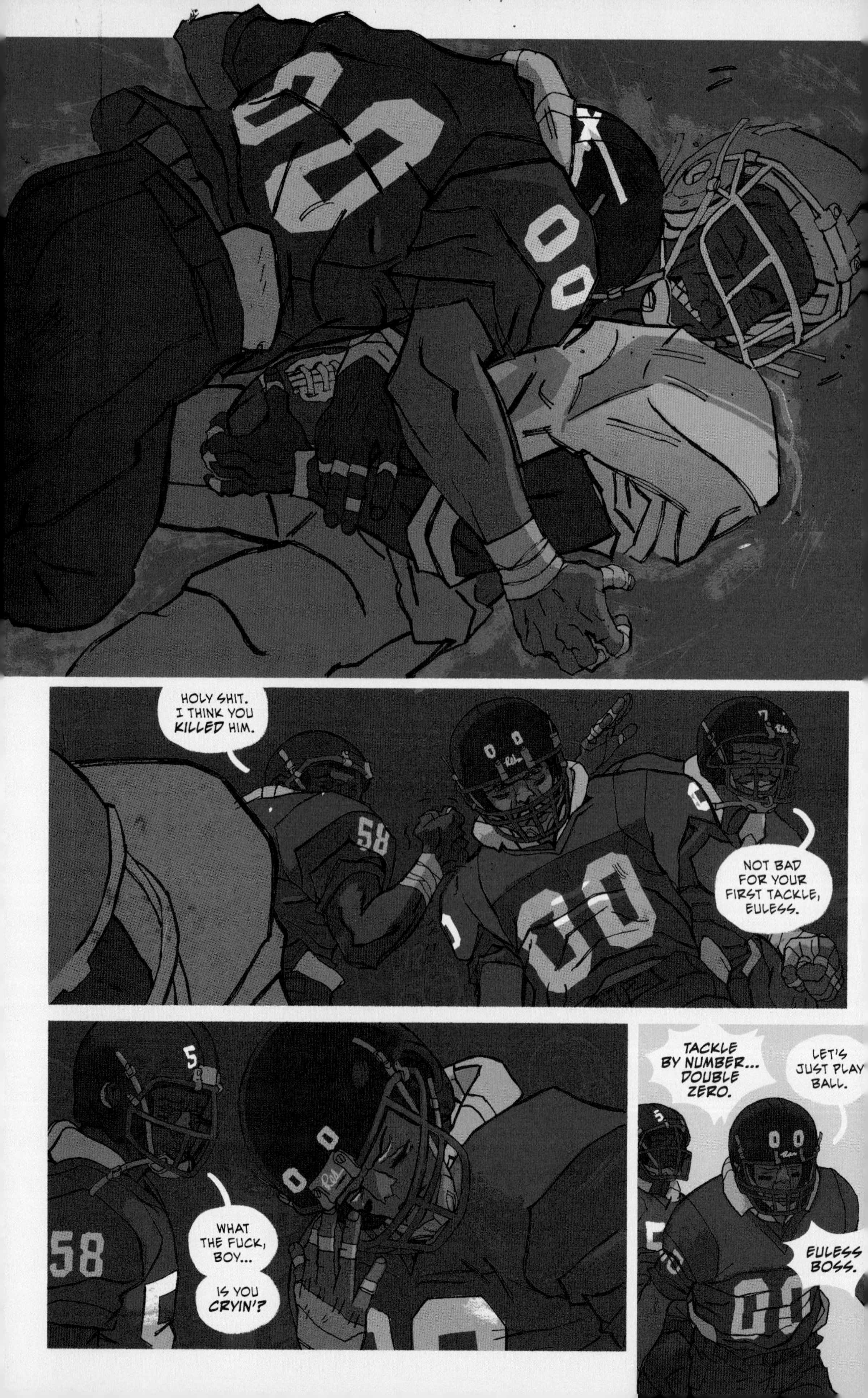
HOLY SHIT. I THINK YOU KILLED HIM.
NOT BAD FOR YOUR FIRST TACKLE, EULESS.
WHAT THE FUCK, BOY...
IS YOU CRYIN'?
TACKLE BY NUMBER... DOUBLE ZERO.
LET'S JUST PLAY BALL.
EULESS BOSS.

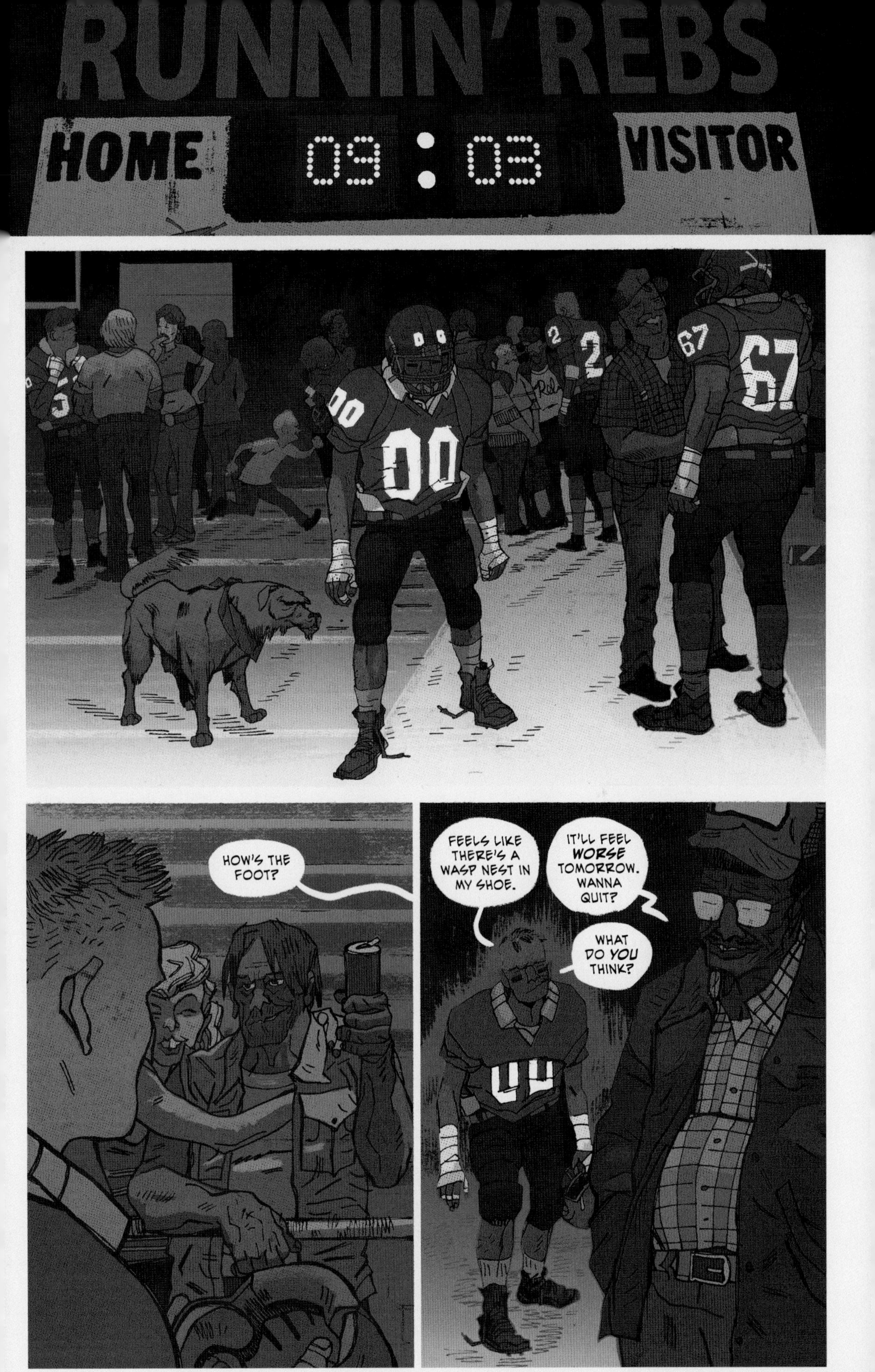
RUNNIN' REBS
HOME
09 : 03
VISITOR
HOW'S THE FOOT?
FEELS LIKE THERE'S A WASP NEST IN MY SHOE.
IT'LL FEEL *WORSE* TOMORROW. WANNA QUIT?
WHAT DO *YOU* THINK?

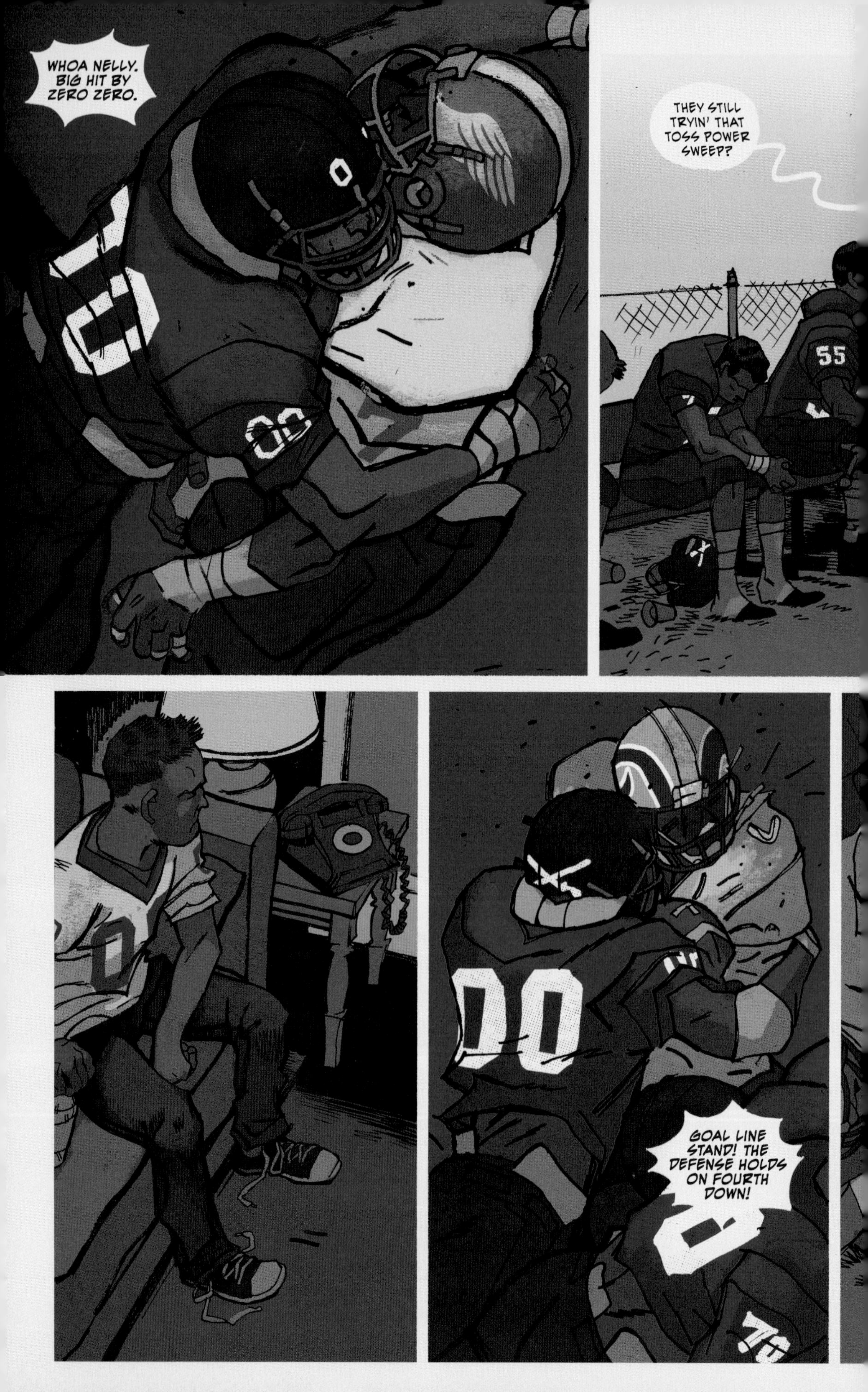
WHOA NELLY. BIG HIT BY ZERO ZERO.
THEY STILL TRYIN' THAT TOSS POWER SWEEP?
GOAL LINE STAND! THE DEFENSE HOLDS ON FOURTH DOWN!

YEAH. JUST LIKE YOU SAID.

KEEP AFTER 'EM THEN. SHOW 'EM THEY SHOULDA PASSED.

PICKED OFF! INTERCEPTION BY DOUBLE O!

FUMBLE! WHO'S GONNA COME UP WITH IT?

NOW LET'S OPEN OUR HISTORY BOOKS TO PAGE...

WILL SOMEBODY WAKE UP EULESS?

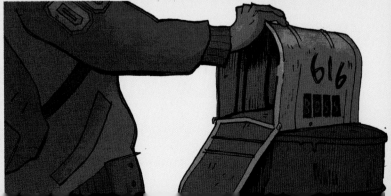

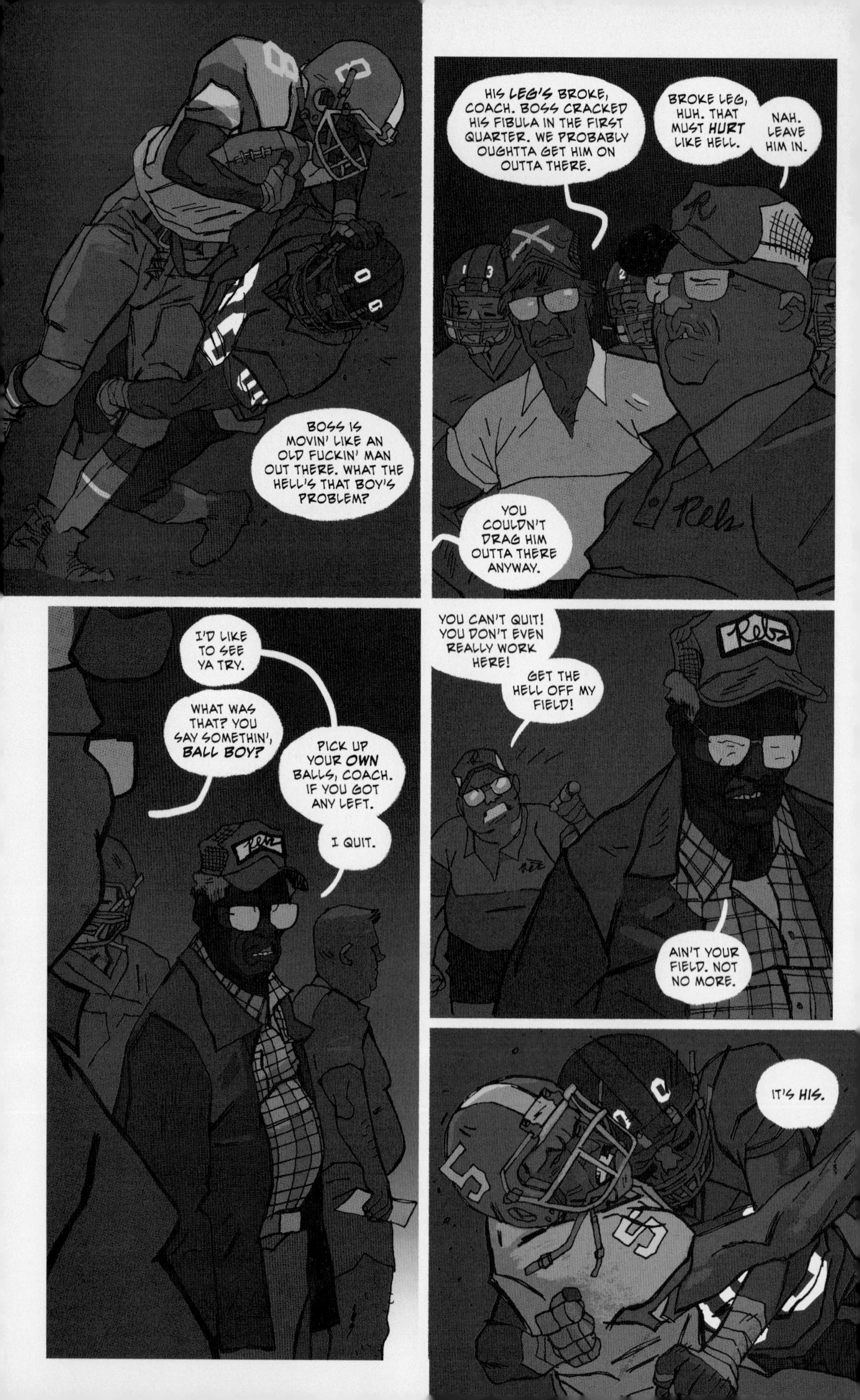
BOSS IS MOVIN' LIKE AN OLD FUCKIN' MAN OUT THERE. WHAT THE HELL'S THAT BOY'S PROBLEM?
HIS LEG'S BROKE, COACH. BOSS CRACKED HIS FIBULA IN THE FIRST QUARTER. WE PROBABLY OUGHTTA GET HIM ON OUTTA THERE.
BROKE LEG, HUH. THAT MUST HURT LIKE HELL.
NAH. LEAVE HIM IN.
YOU COULDN'T DRAG HIM OUTTA THERE ANYWAY.
I'D LIKE TO SEE YA TRY.
WHAT WAS THAT? YOU SAY SOMETHIN', BALL BOY?
PICK UP YOUR OWN BALLS, COACH. IF YOU GOT ANY LEFT.
I QUIT.
YOU CAN'T QUIT! YOU DON'T EVEN REALLY WORK HERE!
GET THE HELL OFF MY FIELD!
AIN'T YOUR FIELD. NOT NO MORE.
IT'S HIS.

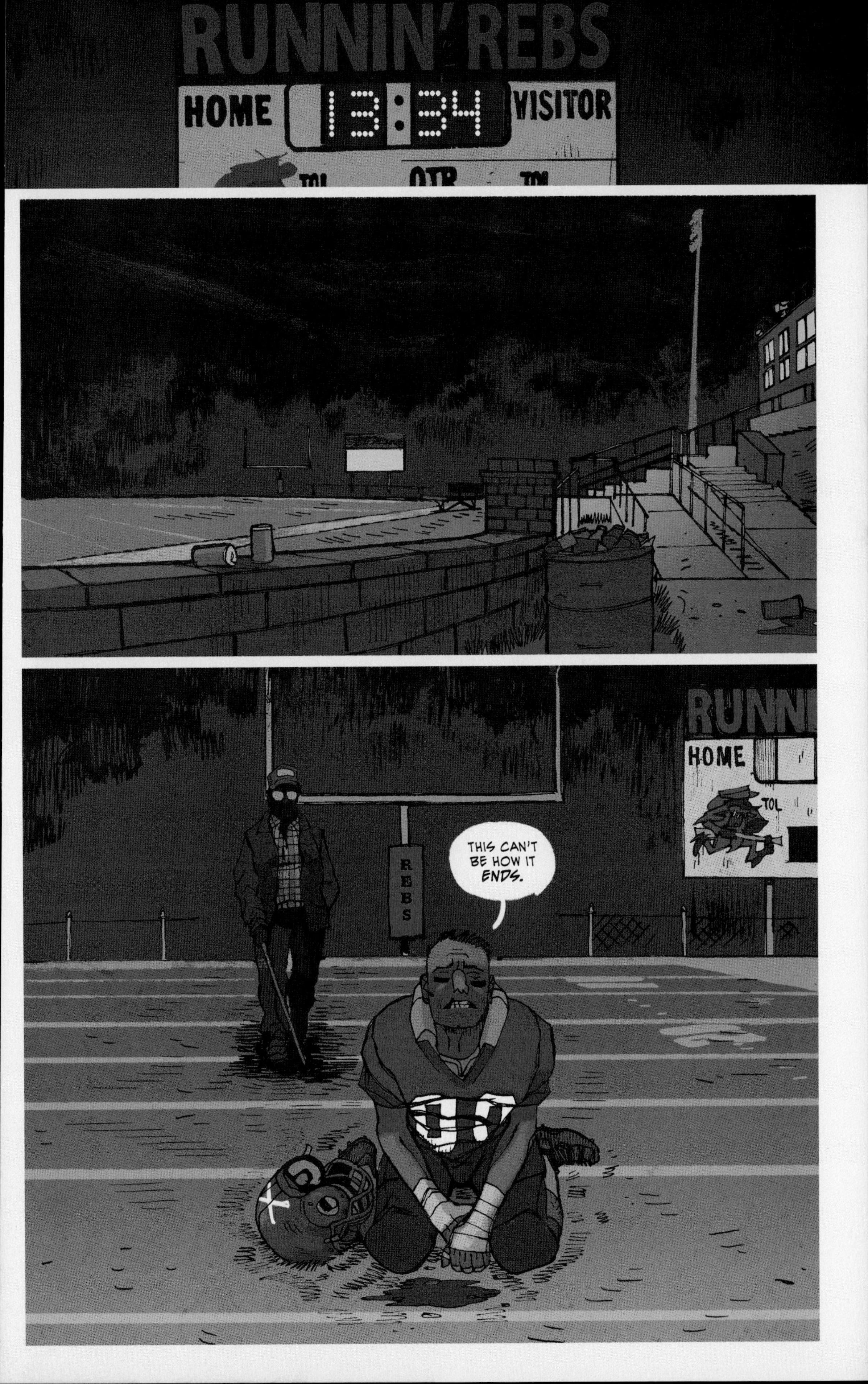
RUNNIN' REBS
HOME
13:34
VISITOR
QTR
TOL
REBS
THIS CAN'T BE HOW IT ENDS.

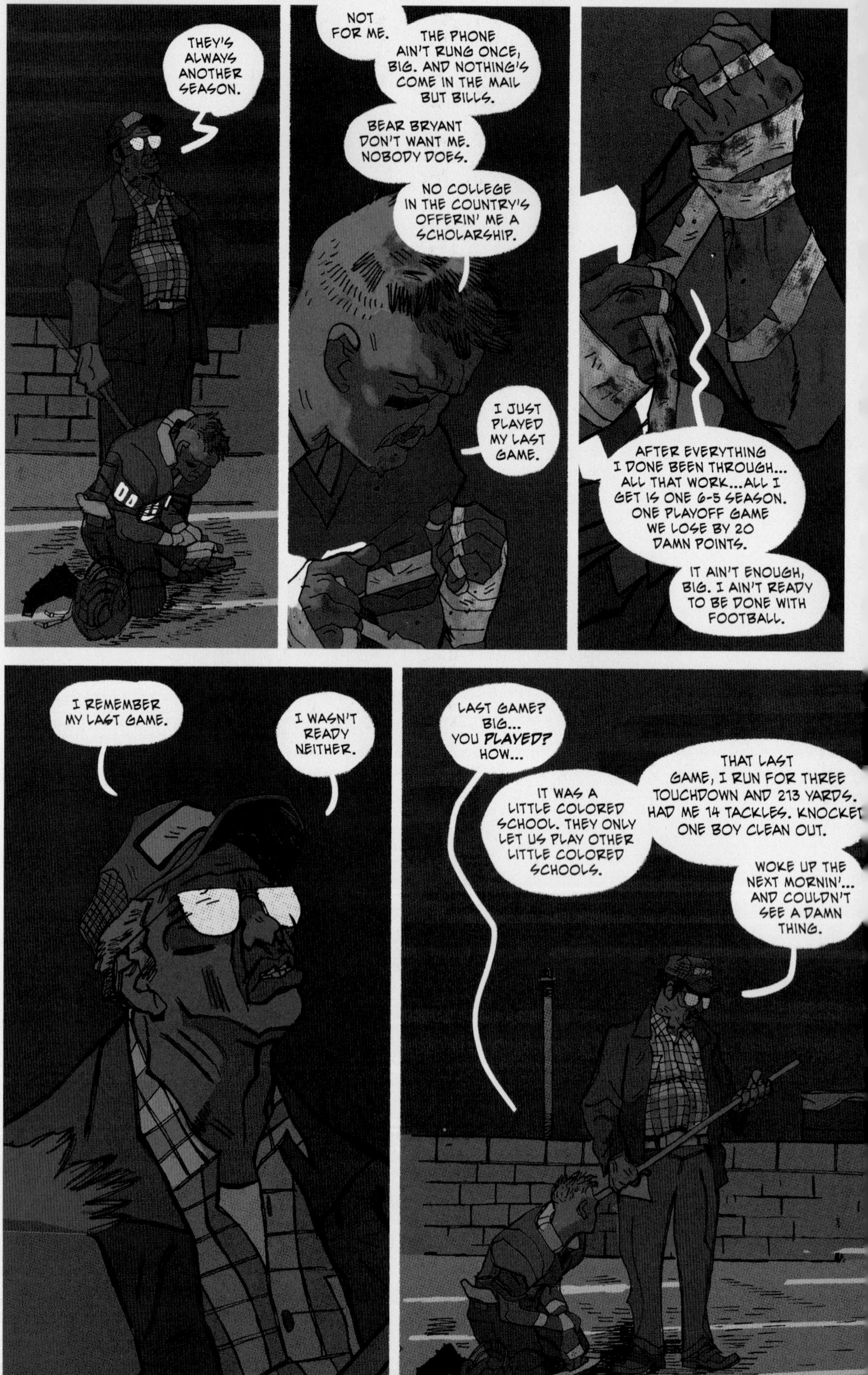
THEY'S ALWAYS ANOTHER SEASON.
NOT FOR ME.
THE PHONE AIN'T RUNG ONCE, BIG. AND NOTHING'S COME IN THE MAIL BUT BILLS.
BEAR BRYANT DON'T WANT ME. NOBODY DOES.
NO COLLEGE IN THE COUNTRY'S OFFERIN' ME A SCHOLARSHIP.
I JUST PLAYED MY LAST GAME.
AFTER EVERYTHING I DONE BEEN THROUGH... ALL THAT WORK...ALL I GET IS ONE 6-5 SEASON. ONE PLAYOFF GAME WE LOSE BY 20 DAMN POINTS.
IT AIN'T ENOUGH, BIG. I AIN'T READY TO BE DONE WITH FOOTBALL.
I REMEMBER MY LAST GAME.
I WASN'T READY NEITHER.
LAST GAME? BIG... YOU PLAYED? HOW...
IT WAS A LITTLE COLORED SCHOOL. THEY ONLY LET US PLAY OTHER LITTLE COLORED SCHOOLS.
THAT LAST GAME, I RUN FOR THREE TOUCHDOWN AND 213 YARDS. HAD ME 14 TACKLES. KNOCKED ONE BOY CLEAN OUT.
WOKE UP THE NEXT MORNIN'... AND COULDN'T SEE A DAMN THING.

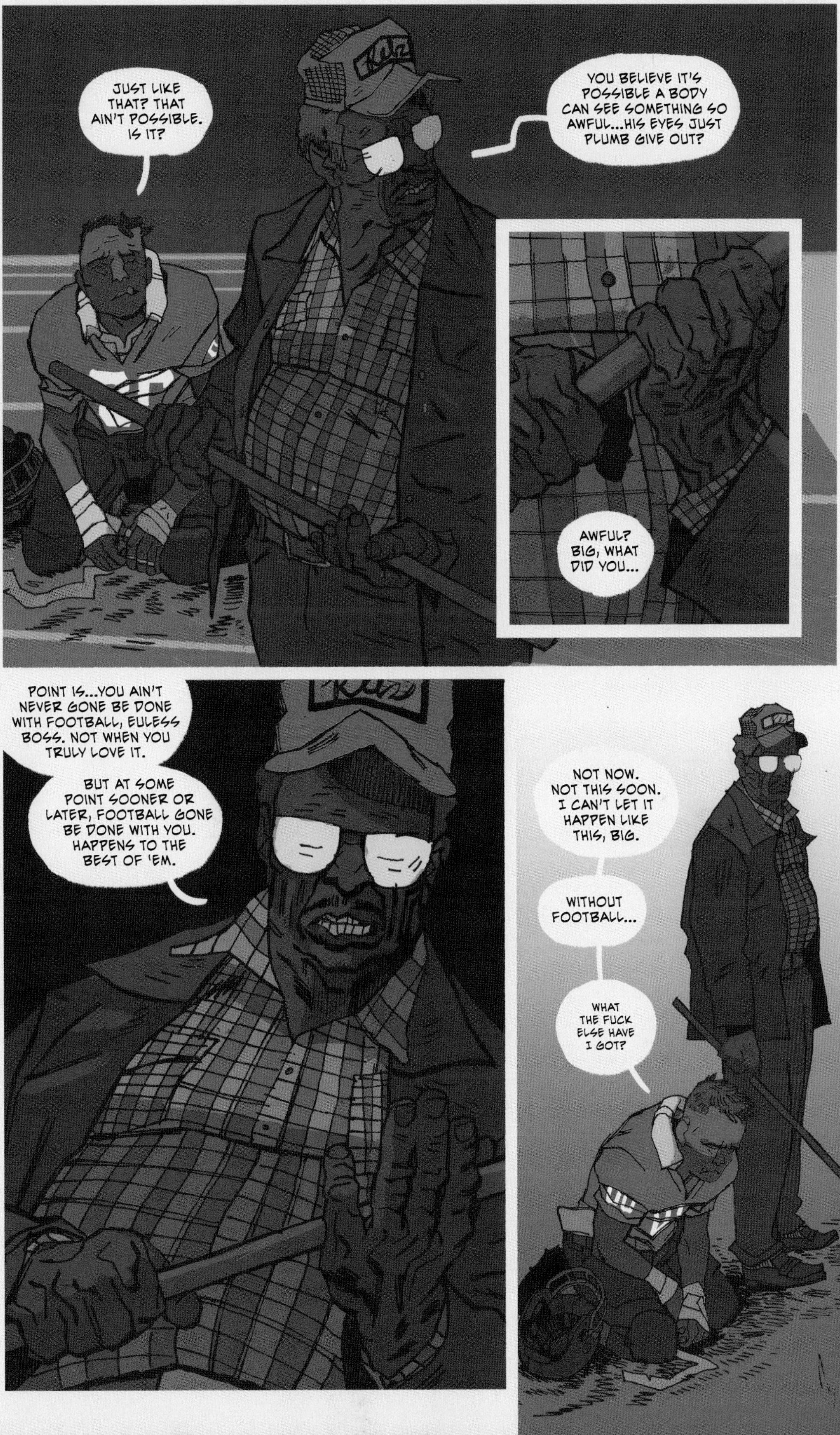
JUST LIKE THAT? THAT AIN'T POSSIBLE. IS IT?
YOU BELIEVE IT'S POSSIBLE A BODY CAN SEE SOMETHING SO AWFUL...HIS EYES JUST PLUMB GIVE OUT?
AWFUL? BIG, WHAT DID YOU...
POINT IS...YOU AIN'T NEVER GONE BE DONE WITH FOOTBALL, EULESS BOSS. NOT WHEN YOU TRULY LOVE IT.
BUT AT SOME POINT SOONER OR LATER, FOOTBALL GONE BE DONE WITH YOU. HAPPENS TO THE BEST OF 'EM.
NOT NOW. NOT THIS SOON. I CAN'T LET IT HAPPEN LIKE THIS, BIG.
WITHOUT FOOTBALL...
WHAT THE FUCK ELSE HAVE I GOT?

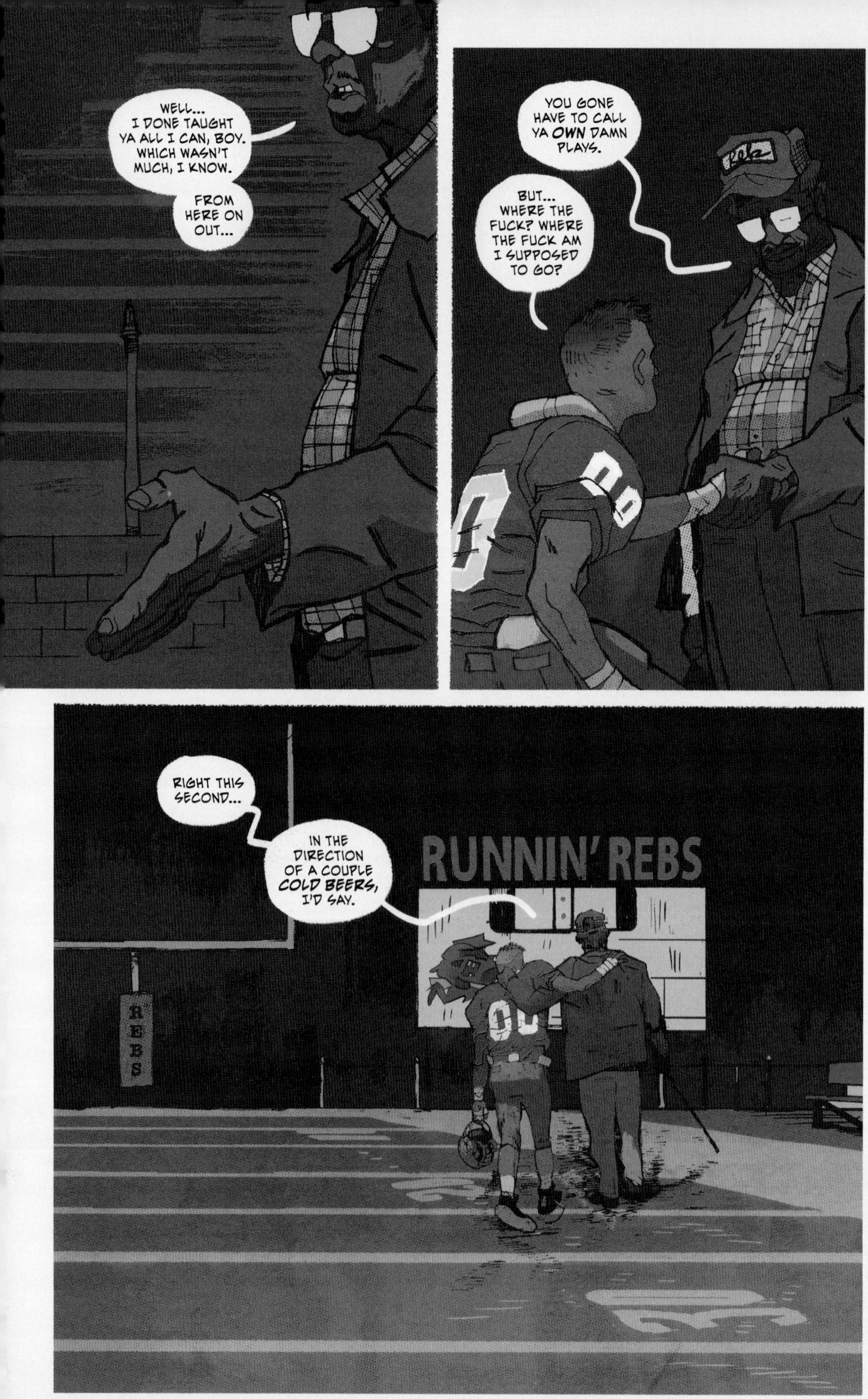
WELL... I DONE TAUGHT YA ALL I CAN, BOY. WHICH WASN'T MUCH, I KNOW.
FROM HERE ON OUT...
YOU GONE HAVE TO CALL YA OWN DAMN PLAYS.
BUT... WHERE THE FUCK? WHERE THE FUCK AM I SUPPOSED TO GO?
RIGHT THIS SECOND...
IN THE DIRECTION OF A COUPLE COLD BEERS, I'D SAY.
RUNNIN' REBS
REBS

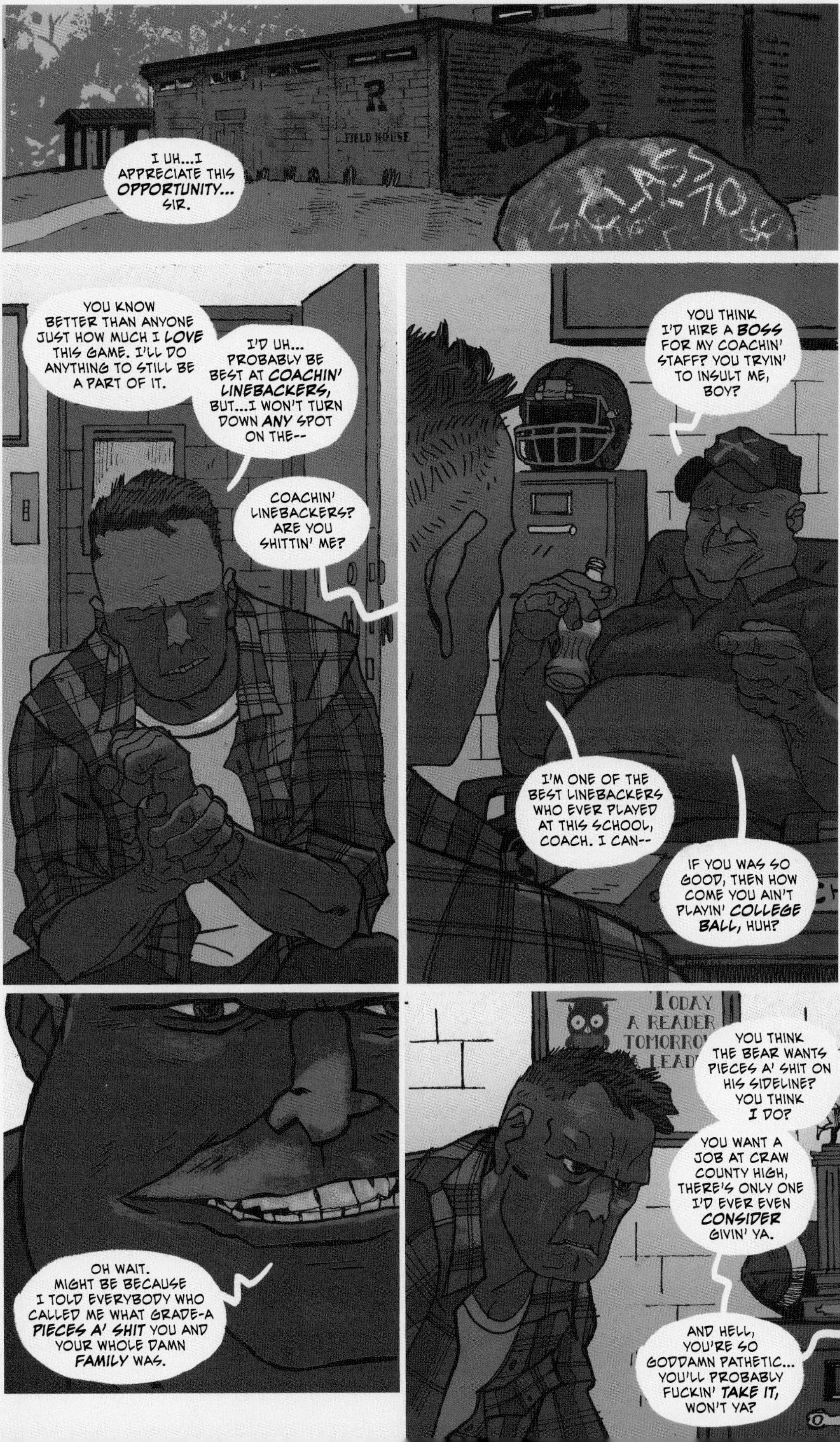
FIELD HOUSE
I UH...I APPRECIATE THIS OPPORTUNITY... SIR.
YOU KNOW BETTER THAN ANYONE JUST HOW MUCH I LOVE THIS GAME. I'LL DO ANYTHING TO STILL BE A PART OF IT.
I'D UH... PROBABLY BE BEST AT COACHIN' LINEBACKERS, BUT...I WON'T TURN DOWN ANY SPOT ON THE--
COACHIN' LINEBACKERS? ARE YOU SHITTIN' ME?
YOU THINK I'D HIRE A BOSS FOR MY COACHIN' STAFF? YOU TRYIN' TO INSULT ME, BOY?
I'M ONE OF THE BEST LINEBACKERS WHO EVER PLAYED AT THIS SCHOOL, COACH. I CAN--
IF YOU WAS SO GOOD, THEN HOW COME YOU AIN'T PLAYIN' COLLEGE BALL, HUH?
OH WAIT. MIGHT BE BECAUSE I TOLD EVERYBODY WHO CALLED ME WHAT GRADE-A PIECES A' SHIT YOU AND YOUR WHOLE DAMN FAMILY WAS.
YOU THINK THE BEAR WANTS PIECES A' SHIT ON HIS SIDELINE? YOU THINK I DO?
YOU WANT A JOB AT CRAW COUNTY HIGH, THERE'S ONLY ONE I'D EVER EVEN CONSIDER GIVIN' YA.
AND HELL, YOU'RE SO GODDAMN PATHETIC... YOU'LL PROBABLY FUCKIN' TAKE IT, WON'T YA?

"YOU CAN START RIGHT NOW.
"GRAB A SACK AND GET TO WORK...
"BALL BOY."
REBS
HOME

Gridiron

Chapter Four

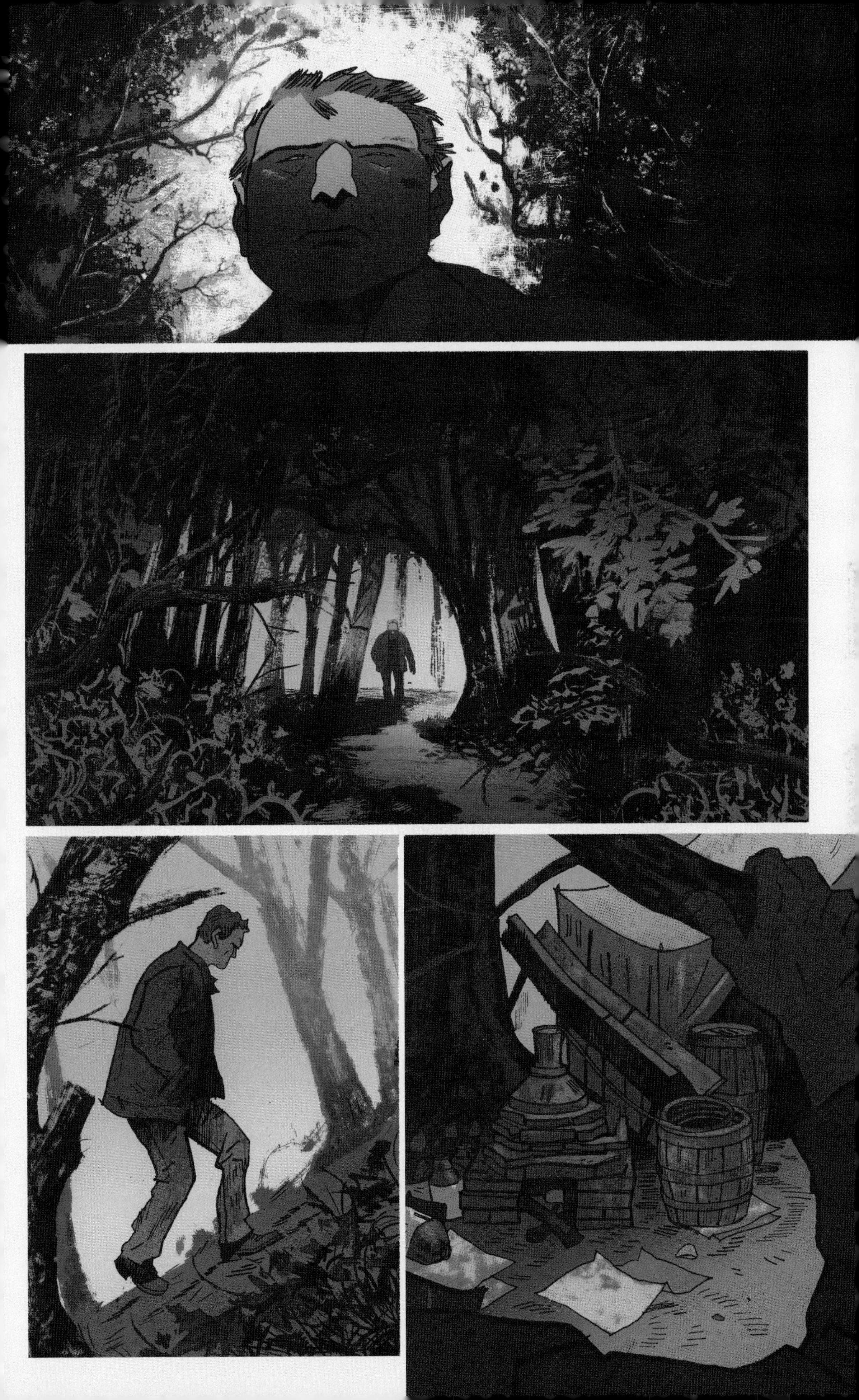

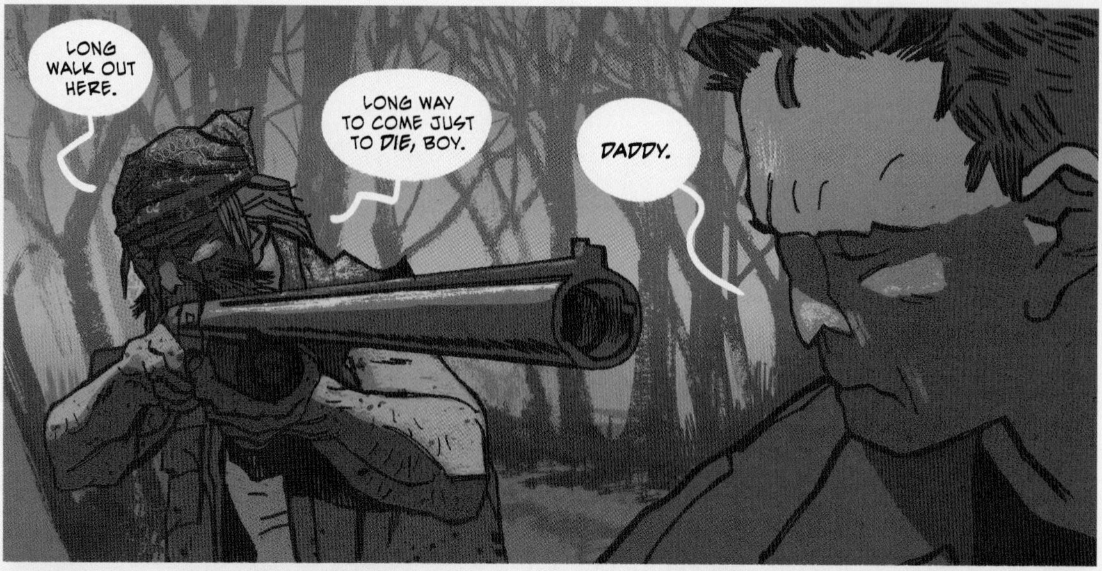
LONG WALK OUT HERE.
LONG WAY TO COME JUST TO DIE, BOY.
DADDY.

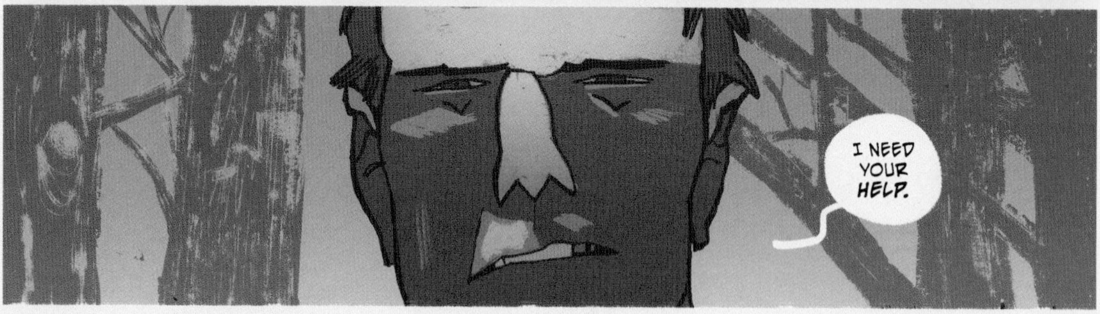
I NEED YOUR HELP.

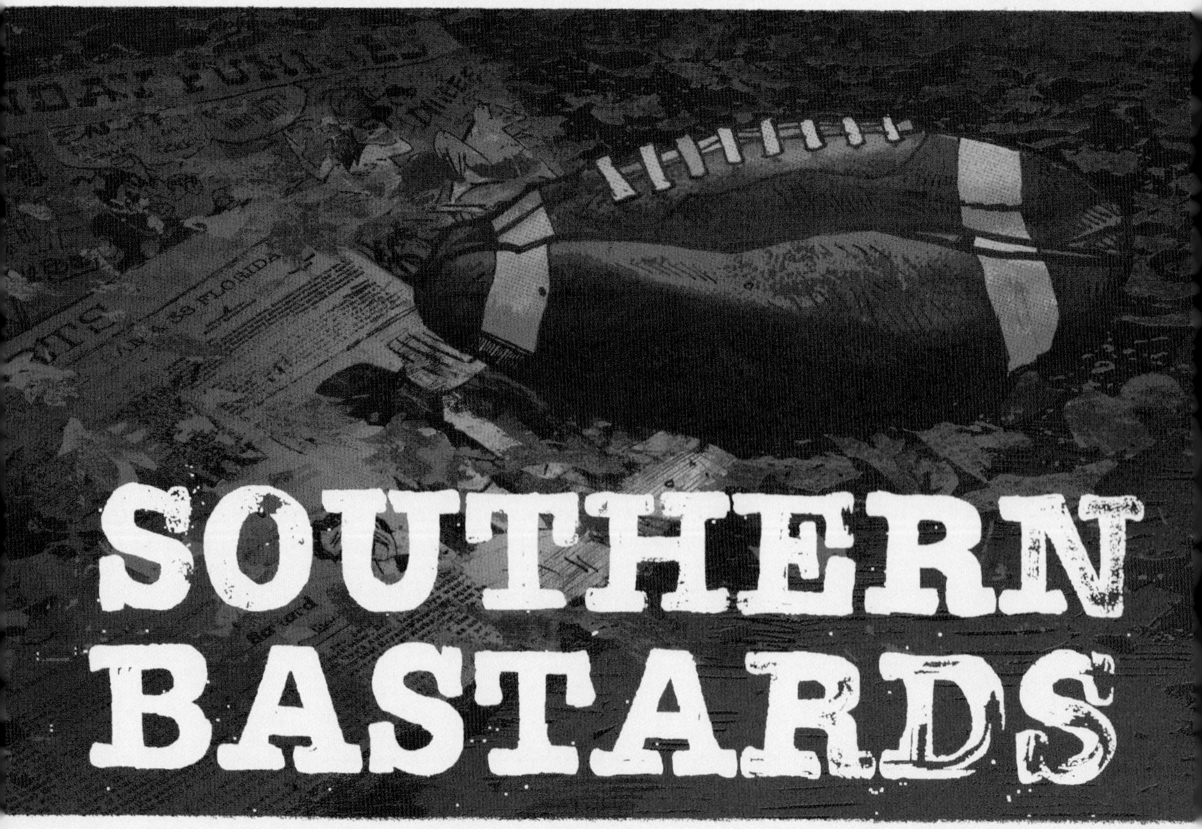
SOUTHERN BASTARDS

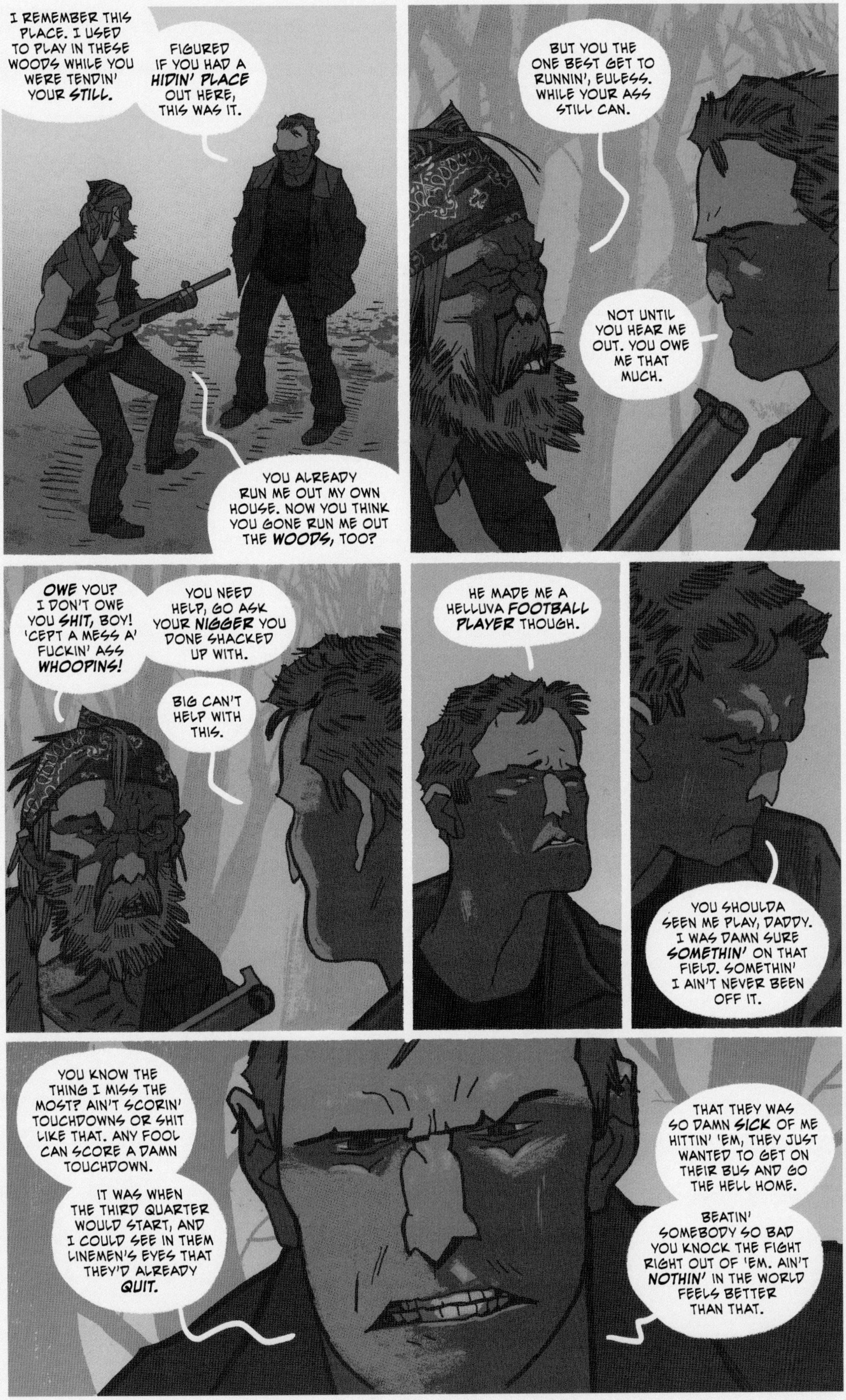
I REMEMBER THIS PLACE. I USED TO PLAY IN THESE WOODS WHILE YOU WERE TENDIN' YOUR STILL.
FIGURED IF YOU HAD A HIDIN' PLACE OUT HERE, THIS WAS IT.
YOU ALREADY RUN ME OUT MY OWN HOUSE. NOW YOU THINK YOU GONE RUN ME OUT THE WOODS, TOO?
BUT YOU THE ONE BEST GET TO RUNNIN', EULESS. WHILE YOUR ASS STILL CAN.
NOT UNTIL YOU HEAR ME OUT. YOU OWE ME THAT MUCH.
OWE YOU? I DON'T OWE YOU SHIT, BOY! 'CEPT A MESS A' FUCKIN' ASS WHOOPINS!
YOU NEED HELP, GO ASK YOUR NIGGER YOU DONE SHACKED UP WITH.
BIG CAN'T HELP WITH THIS.
HE MADE ME A HELLUVA FOOTBALL PLAYER THOUGH.
YOU SHOULDA SEEN ME PLAY, DADDY. I WAS DAMN SURE SOMETHIN' ON THAT FIELD. SOMETHIN' I AIN'T NEVER BEEN OFF IT.
YOU KNOW THE THING I MISS THE MOST? AIN'T SCORIN' TOUCHDOWNS OR SHIT LIKE THAT. ANY FOOL CAN SCORE A DAMN TOUCHDOWN.
IT WAS WHEN THE THIRD QUARTER WOULD START, AND I COULD SEE IN THEM LINEMEN'S EYES THAT THEY'D ALREADY QUIT.
THAT THEY WAS SO DAMN SICK OF ME HITTIN' 'EM, THEY JUST WANTED TO GET ON THEIR BUS AND GO THE HELL HOME.
BEATIN' SOMEBODY SO BAD YOU KNOCK THE FIGHT RIGHT OUT OF 'EM. AIN'T NOTHIN' IN THE WORLD FEELS BETTER THAN THAT.

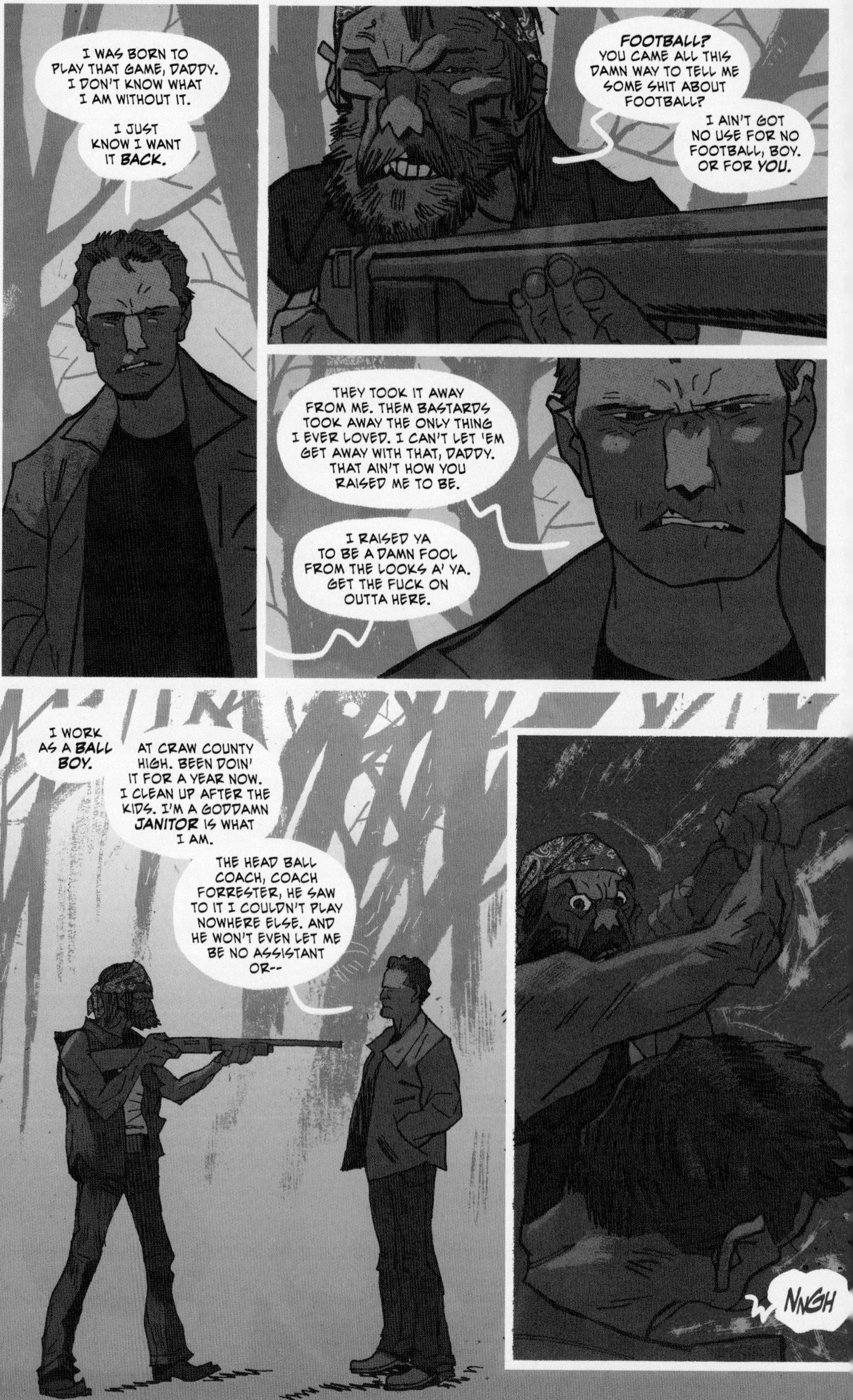
I WAS BORN TO PLAY THAT GAME, DADDY. I DON'T KNOW WHAT I AM WITHOUT IT.
I JUST KNOW I WANT IT BACK.
FOOTBALL? YOU CAME ALL THIS DAMN WAY TO TELL ME SOME SHIT ABOUT FOOTBALL?
I AIN'T GOT NO USE FOR NO FOOTBALL, BOY. OR FOR YOU.
THEY TOOK IT AWAY FROM ME. THEM BASTARDS TOOK AWAY THE ONLY THING I EVER LOVED. I CAN'T LET 'EM GET AWAY WITH THAT, DADDY. THAT AIN'T HOW YOU RAISED ME TO BE.
I RAISED YA TO BE A DAMN FOOL FROM THE LOOKS A' YA. GET THE FUCK ON OUTTA HERE.
I WORK AS A BALL BOY.
AT CRAW COUNTY HIGH. BEEN DOIN' IT FOR A YEAR NOW. I CLEAN UP AFTER THE KIDS. I'M A GODDAMN JANITOR IS WHAT I AM.
THE HEAD BALL COACH, COACH FORRESTER, HE SAW TO IT I COULDN'T PLAY NOWHERE ELSE. AND HE WON'T EVEN LET ME BE NO ASSISTANT OR--
NNGH

YOU THINK I WON'T **KILL** YOU JUST 'CAUSE YOU MY OWN BLOOD?

I **AM** YOUR BLOOD. AND IT'S 'CAUSE A' THAT BLOOD THAT I'M HERE.

IT'S **YOUR** DAMN FAULT I LOST EVERYTHING.

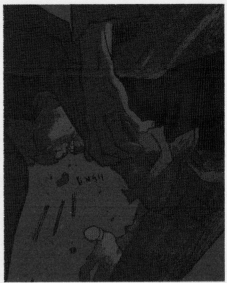

I COULDN'T PLAY COLLEGE BALL 'CAUSE OF YOU. WOULDN'T NO SCHOOLS TAKE ME, ONCE THEY HEARD ABOUT MY DADDY THE BOOTLEGGER. THE THIEF.

THE BIGGEST PIECE A' SHIT IN CRAW COUNTY.

THAT'S WHAT YOU **ARE**, AIN'T IT, DADDY?

THAT'S WHY YOU'RE HIDIN' OUT HERE IN THE WOODS. WHY MOZEL AND HIS MEN ARE OUT HUNTIN' YA AGAIN.

NNGH

YOU'RE WHY I LOST THE THING I LOVE, DADDY.

AND YOU'RE THE ONLY MAN ALIVE WHO CAN HELP ME GET IT BACK.

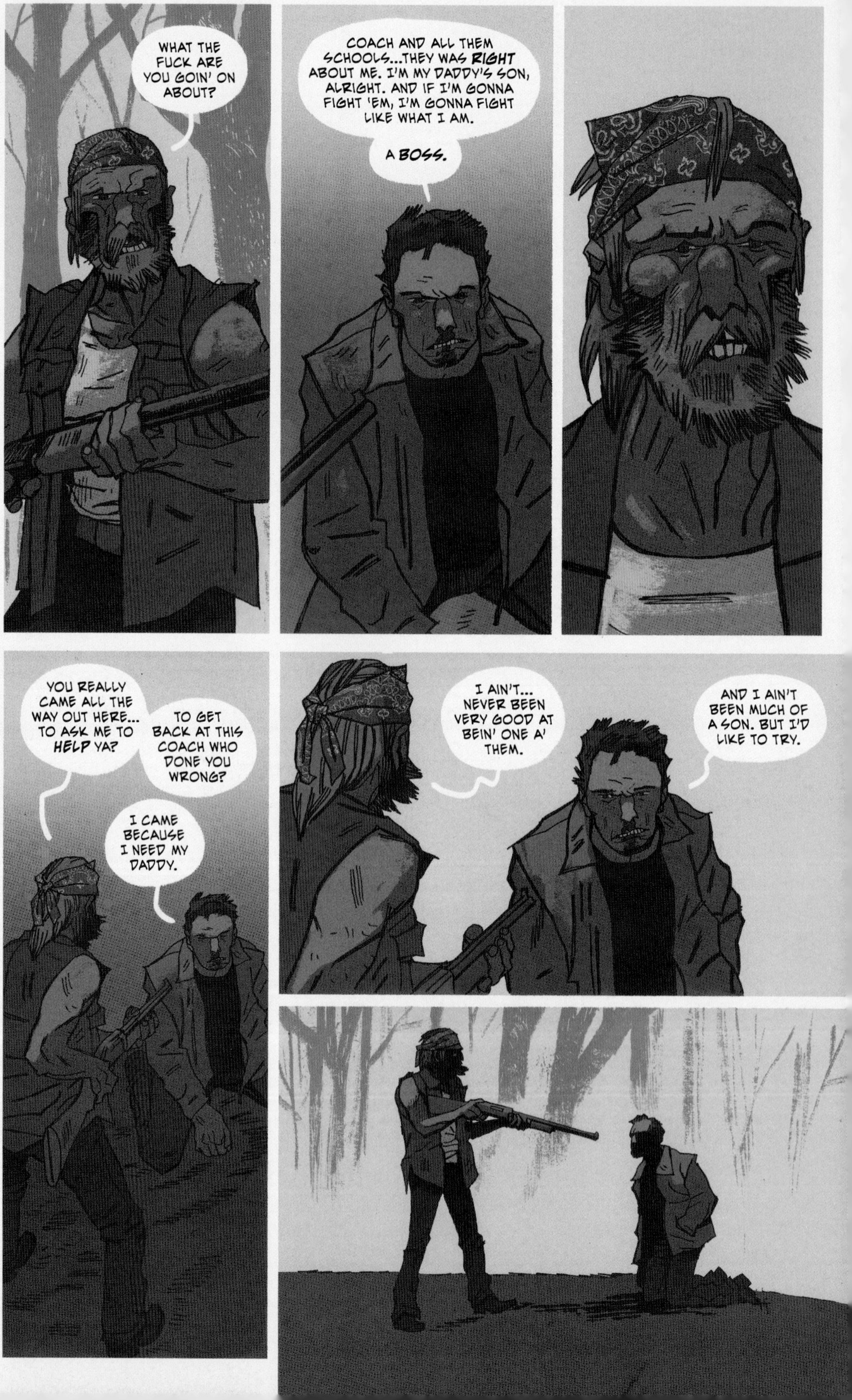
WHAT THE FUCK ARE YOU GOIN' ON ABOUT?
COACH AND ALL THEM SCHOOLS...THEY WAS RIGHT ABOUT ME. I'M MY DADDY'S SON, ALRIGHT. AND IF I'M GONNA FIGHT 'EM, I'M GONNA FIGHT LIKE WHAT I AM.
A BOSS.
YOU REALLY CAME ALL THE WAY OUT HERE... TO ASK ME TO HELP YA?
TO GET BACK AT THIS COACH WHO DONE YOU WRONG?
I CAME BECAUSE I NEED MY DADDY.
I AIN'T... NEVER BEEN VERY GOOD AT BEIN' ONE A' THEM.
AND I AIN'T BEEN MUCH OF A SON. BUT I'D LIKE TO TRY.

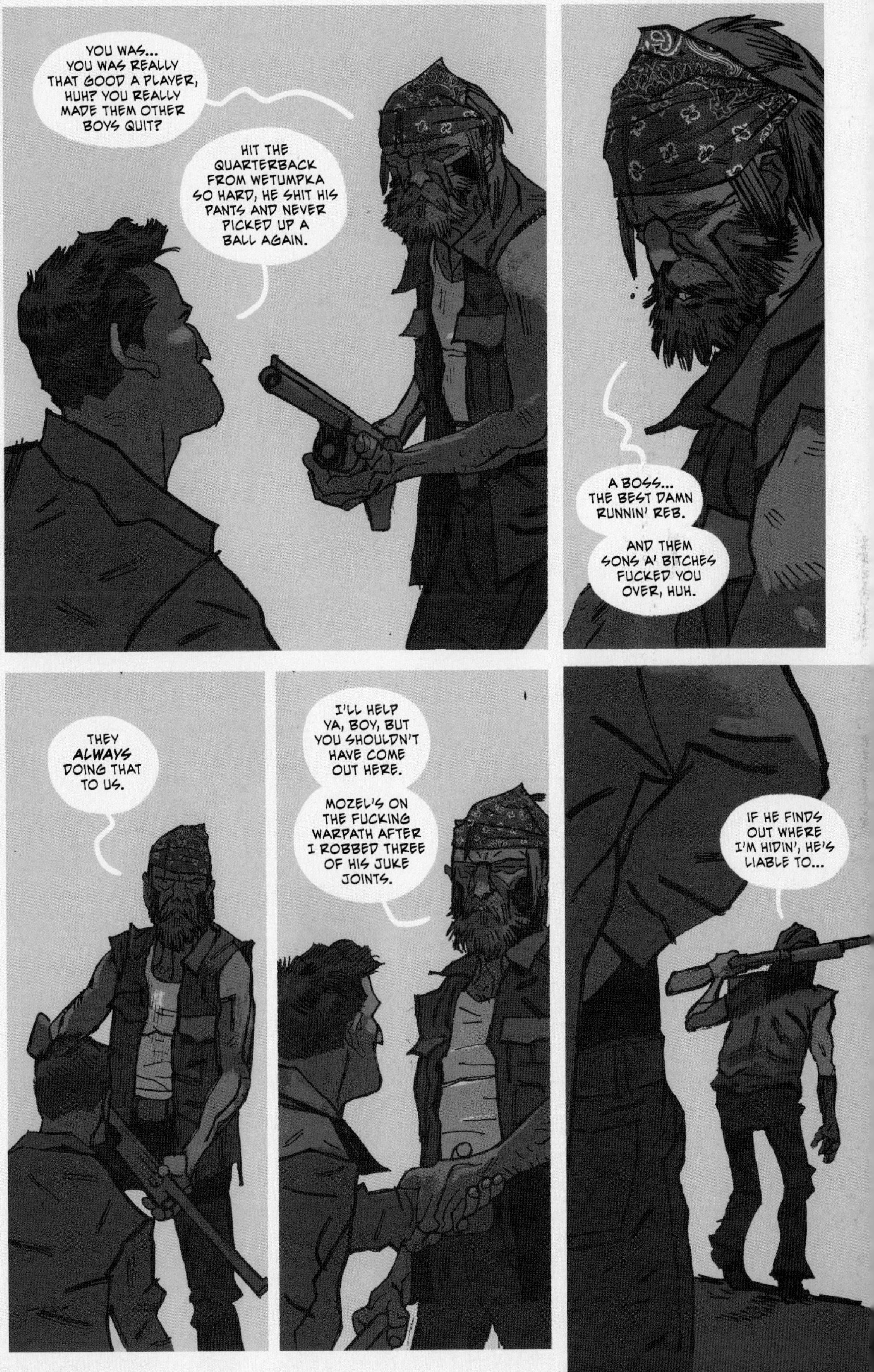
YOU WAS... YOU WAS REALLY THAT GOOD A PLAYER, HUH? YOU REALLY MADE THEM OTHER BOYS QUIT?
HIT THE QUARTERBACK FROM WETUMPKA SO HARD, HE SHIT HIS PANTS AND NEVER PICKED UP A BALL AGAIN.
A BOSS... THE BEST DAMN RUNNIN' REB.
AND THEM SONS A' BITCHES FUCKED YOU OVER, HUH.
THEY **ALWAYS** DOING THAT TO US.
I'LL HELP YA, BOY, BUT YOU SHOULDN'T HAVE COME OUT HERE.
MOZEL'S ON THE FUCKING WARPATH AFTER I ROBBED THREE OF HIS JUKE JOINTS.
IF HE FINDS OUT WHERE I'M HIDIN', HE'S LIABLE TO...

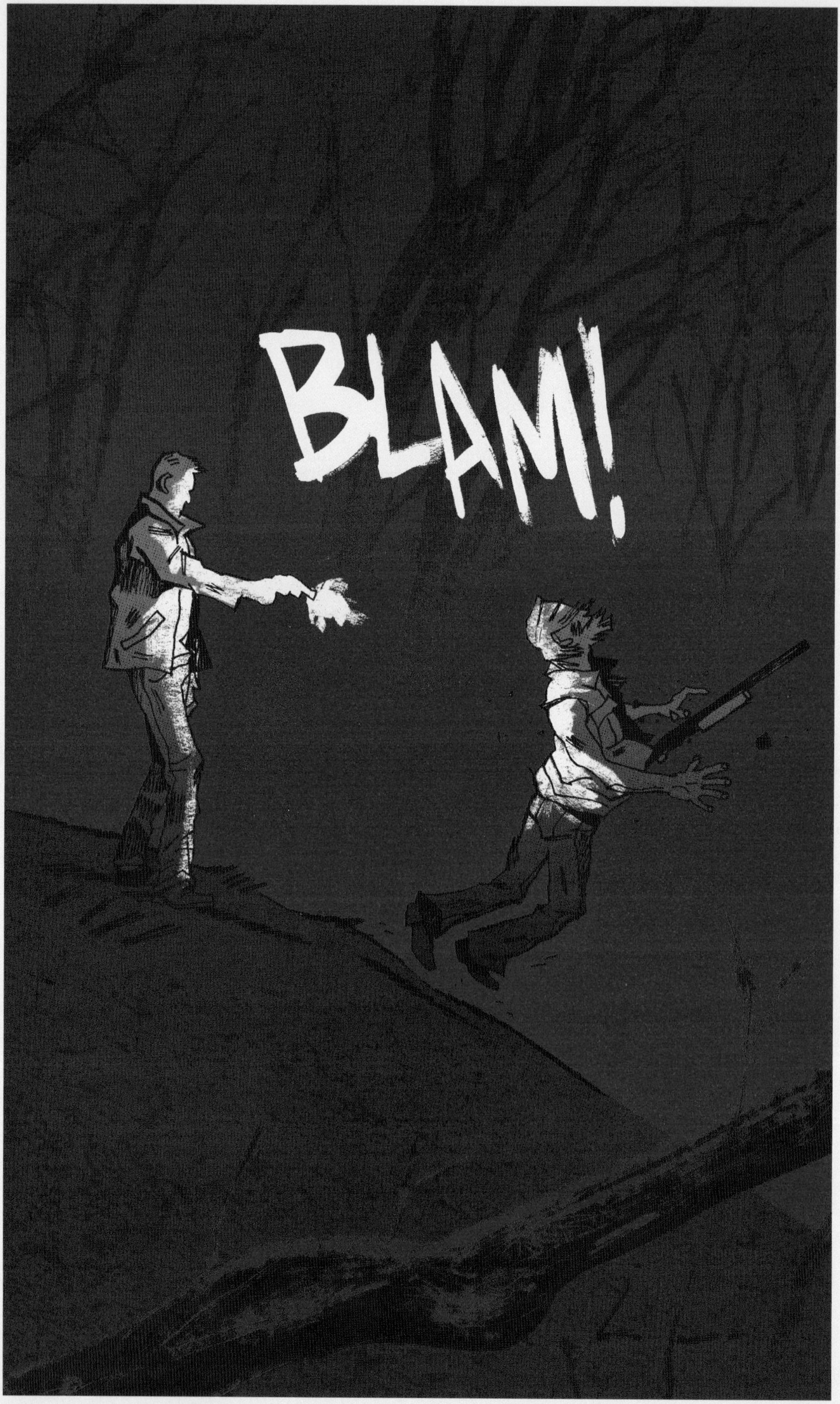
BLAM!

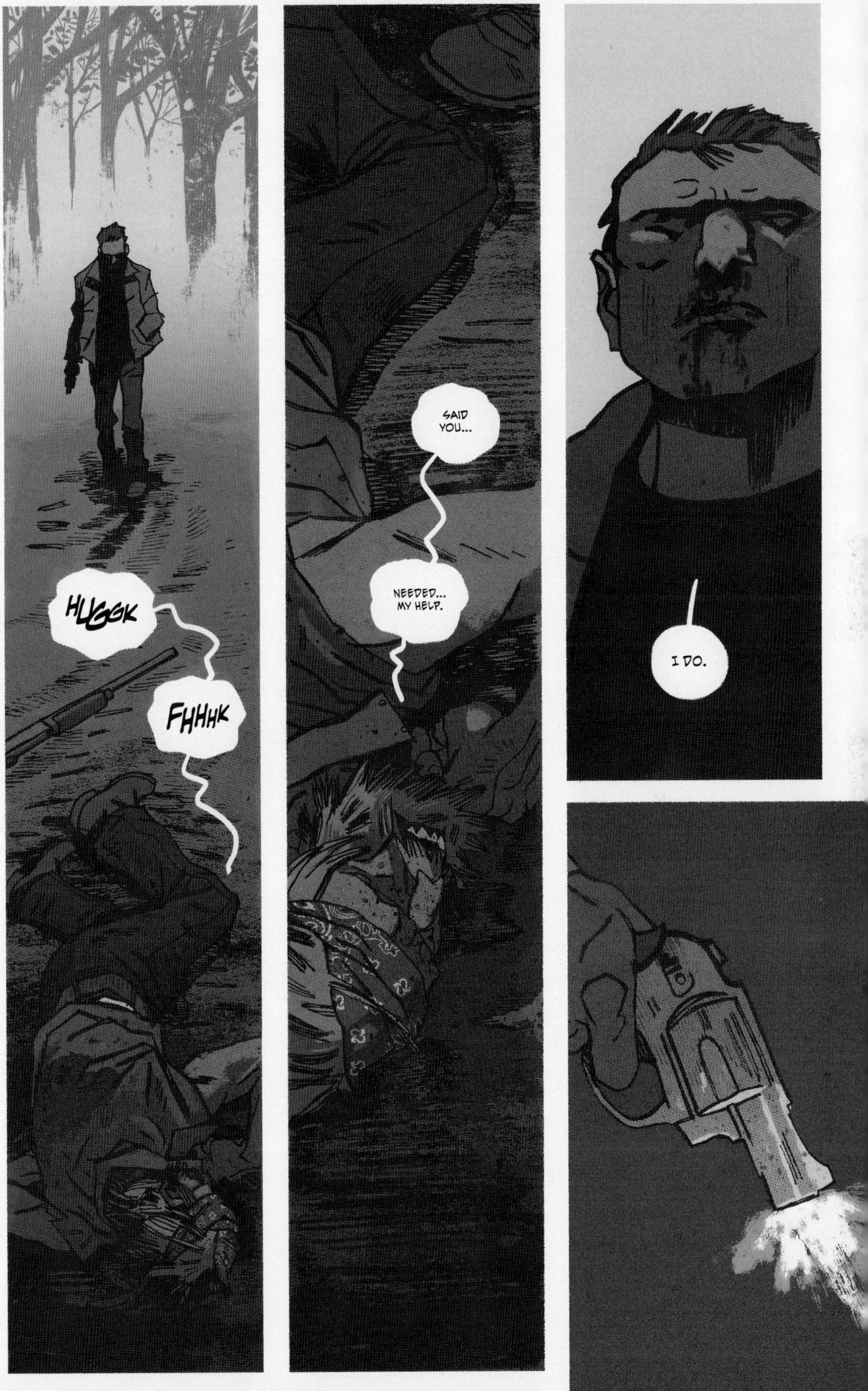
HUGGK
FHHHK
SAID YOU...
NEEDED... MY HELP.
I DO.

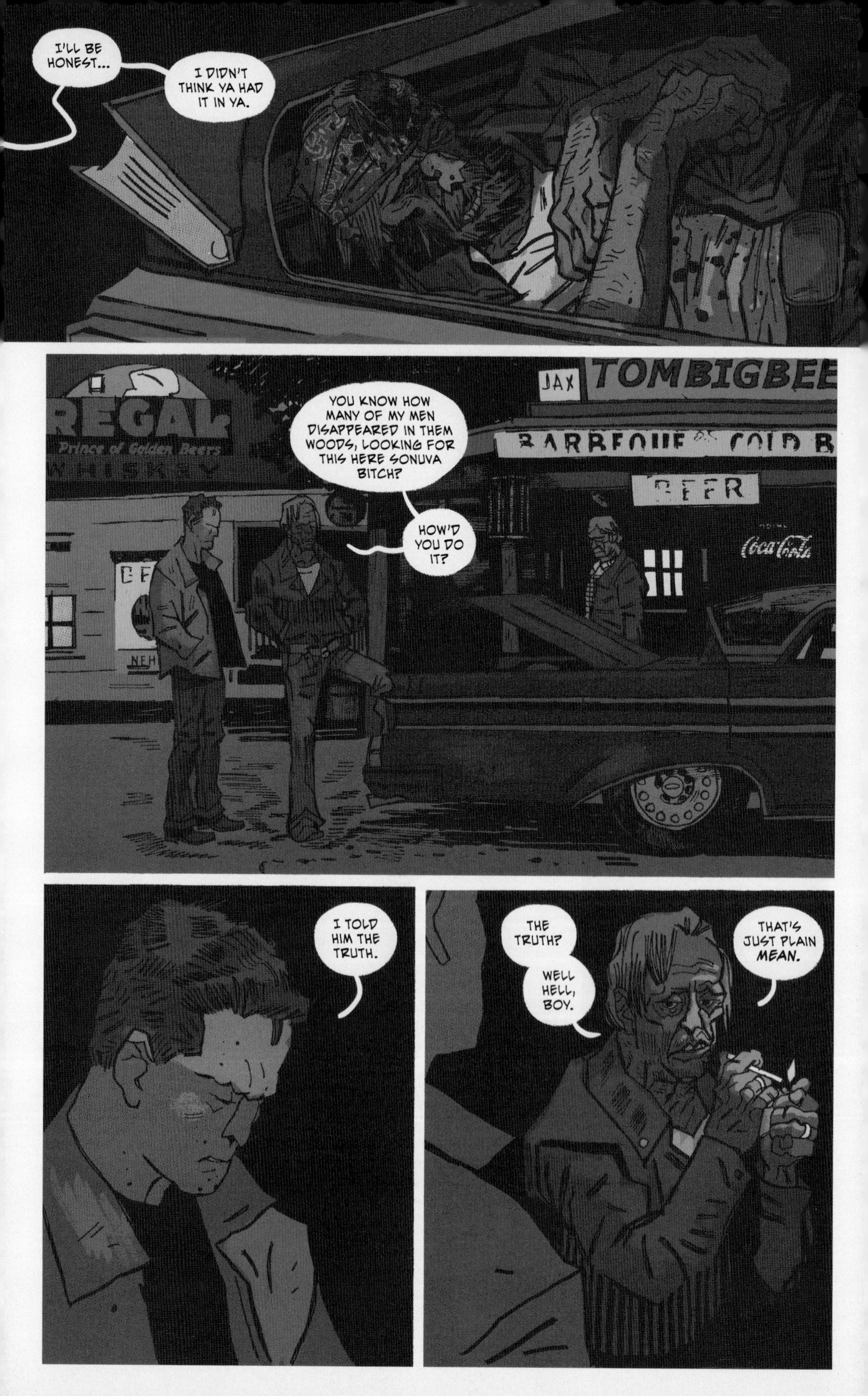
I'LL BE HONEST...
I DIDN'T THINK YA HAD IT IN YA.
REGAL
Prince of Golden Beers
JAX
TOMBIGBEE
YOU KNOW HOW MANY OF MY MEN DISAPPEARED IN THEM WOODS, LOOKING FOR THIS HERE SONUVA BITCH?
HOW'D YOU DO IT?
Coca-Cola
I TOLD HIM THE TRUTH.
THE TRUTH?
WELL HELL, BOY.
THAT'S JUST PLAIN **MEAN.**

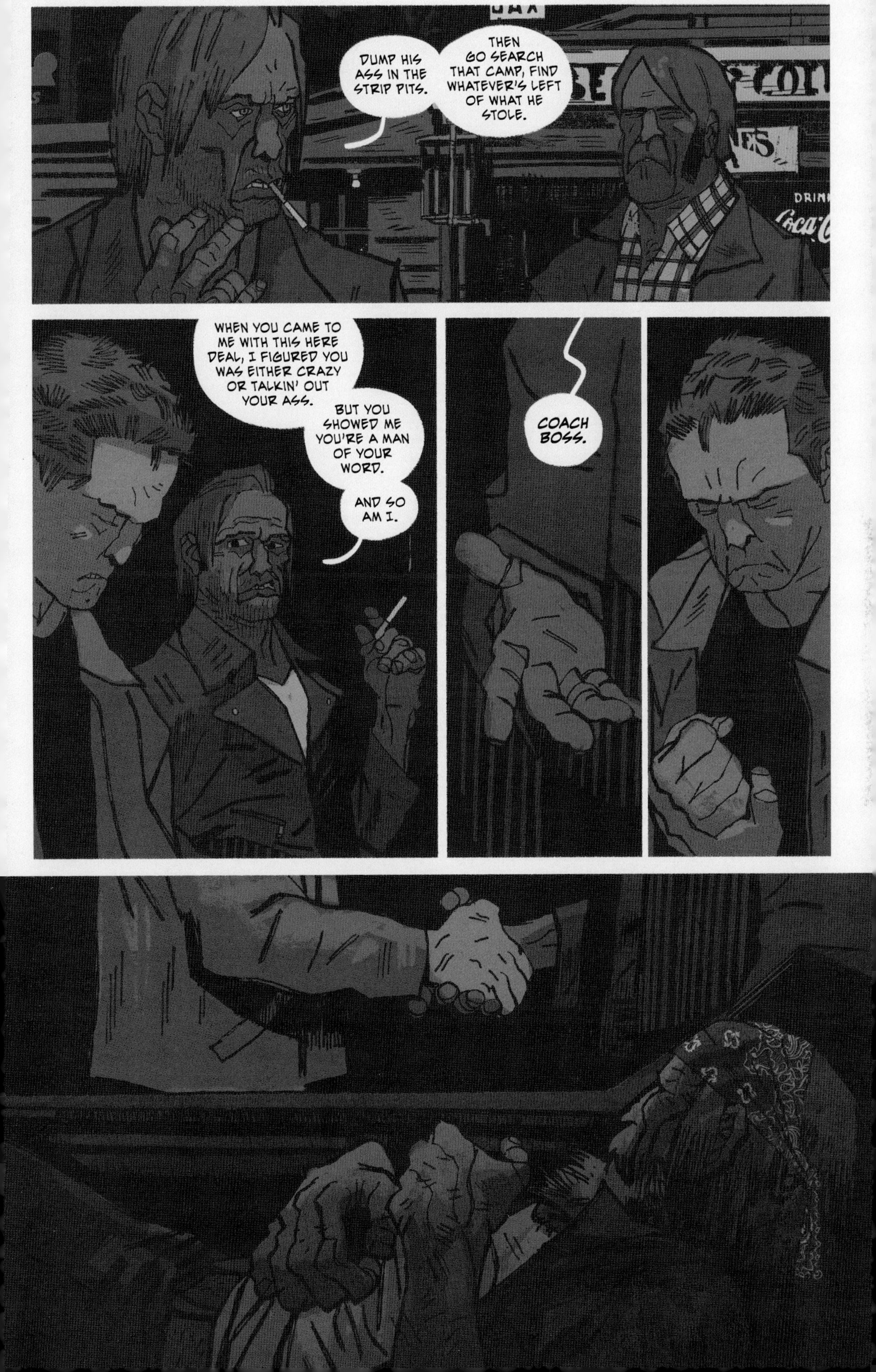
DUMP HIS ASS IN THE STRIP PITS.
THEN GO SEARCH THAT CAMP, FIND WHATEVER'S LEFT OF WHAT HE STOLE.
DRINK
Coca-Cola
WHEN YOU CAME TO ME WITH THIS HERE DEAL, I FIGURED YOU WAS EITHER CRAZY OR TALKIN' OUT YOUR ASS.
BUT YOU SHOWED ME YOU'RE A MAN OF YOUR WORD.
AND SO AM I.
COACH BOSS.

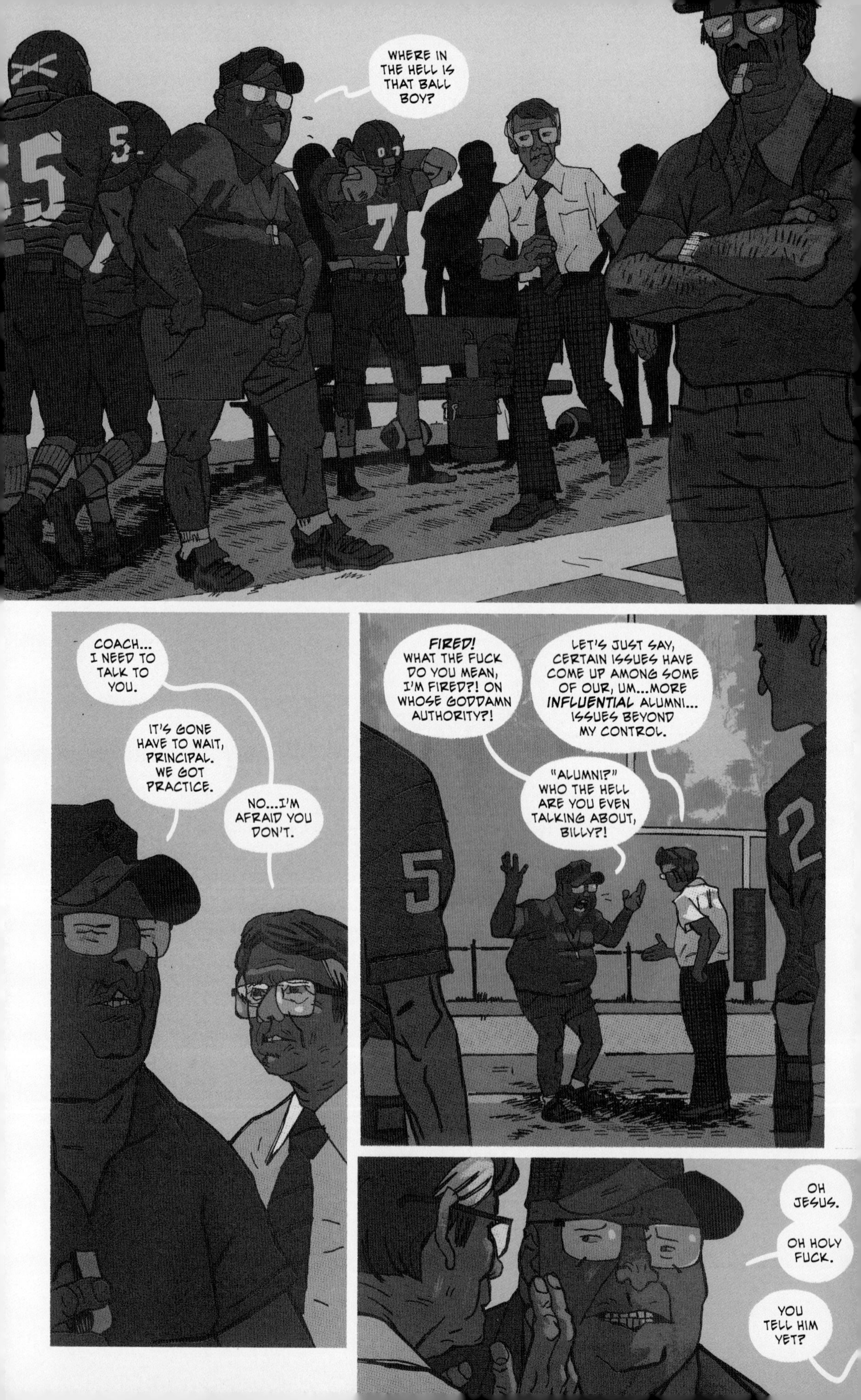
WHERE IN THE HELL IS THAT BALL BOY?
COACH... I NEED TO TALK TO YOU.
IT'S GONE HAVE TO WAIT, PRINCIPAL. WE GOT PRACTICE.
NO...I'M AFRAID YOU DON'T.
FIRED! WHAT THE FUCK DO YOU MEAN, I'M FIRED?! ON WHOSE GODDAMN AUTHORITY?!
LET'S JUST SAY, CERTAIN ISSUES HAVE COME UP AMONG SOME OF OUR, UM...MORE INFLUENTIAL ALUMNI... ISSUES BEYOND MY CONTROL.
"ALUMNI?" WHO THE HELL ARE YOU EVEN TALKING ABOUT, BILLY?!
OH JESUS.
OH HOLY FUCK.
YOU TELL HIM YET?

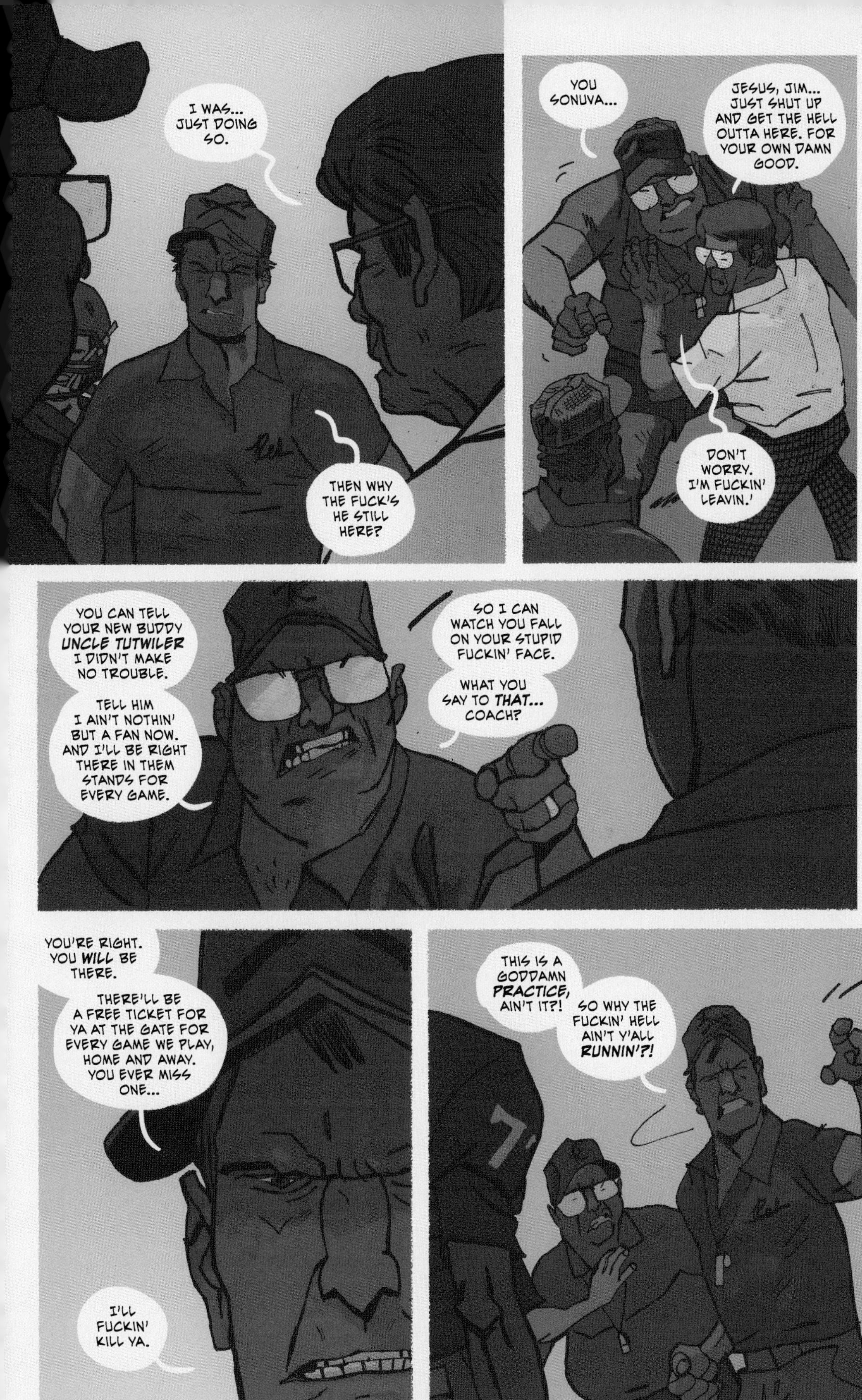
I WAS... JUST DOING SO.
THEN WHY THE FUCK'S HE STILL HERE?
YOU SONUVA...
JESUS, JIM... JUST SHUT UP AND GET THE HELL OUTTA HERE. FOR YOUR OWN DAMN GOOD.
DON'T WORRY. I'M FUCKIN' LEAVIN.'
YOU CAN TELL YOUR NEW BUDDY UNCLE TUTWILER I DIDN'T MAKE NO TROUBLE.
TELL HIM I AIN'T NOTHIN' BUT A FAN NOW. AND I'LL BE RIGHT THERE IN THEM STANDS FOR EVERY GAME.
SO I CAN WATCH YOU FALL ON YOUR STUPID FUCKIN' FACE.
WHAT YOU SAY TO THAT... COACH?
YOU'RE RIGHT. YOU WILL BE THERE.
THERE'LL BE A FREE TICKET FOR YA AT THE GATE FOR EVERY GAME WE PLAY, HOME AND AWAY. YOU EVER MISS ONE...
I'LL FUCKIN' KILL YA.
THIS IS A GODDAMN PRACTICE, AIN'T IT?!
SO WHY THE FUCKIN' HELL AIN'T Y'ALL RUNNIN'?!

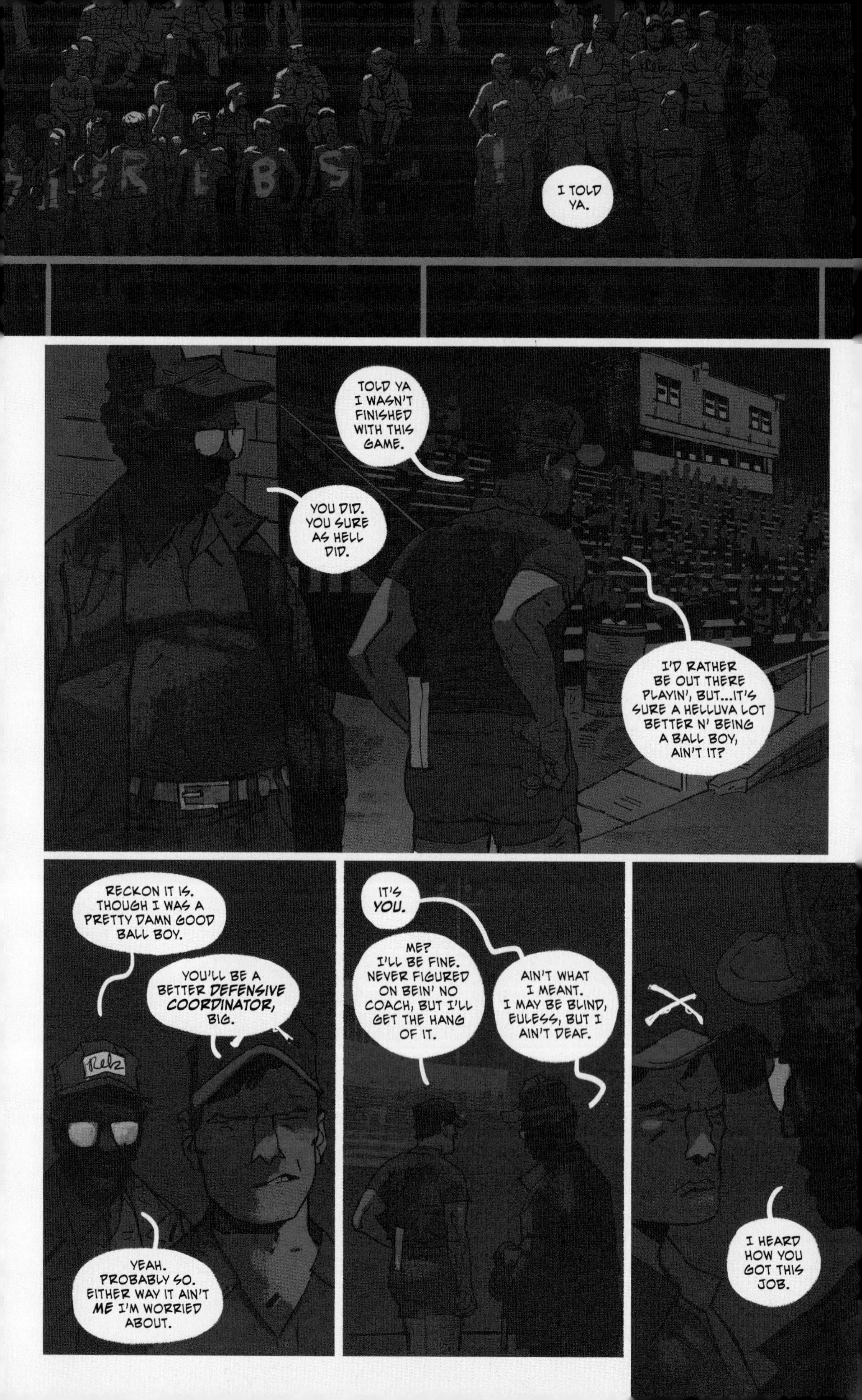
I TOLD YA.
TOLD YA I WASN'T FINISHED WITH THIS GAME.
YOU DID. YOU SURE AS HELL DID.
I'D RATHER BE OUT THERE PLAYIN', BUT...IT'S SURE A HELLUVA LOT BETTER N' BEING A BALL BOY, AIN'T IT?
RECKON IT IS. THOUGH I WAS A PRETTY DAMN GOOD BALL BOY.
YOU'LL BE A BETTER DEFENSIVE COORDINATOR, BIG.
YEAH. PROBABLY SO. EITHER WAY IT AIN'T ME I'M WORRIED ABOUT.
IT'S YOU.
ME? I'LL BE FINE. NEVER FIGURED ON BEIN' NO COACH, BUT I'LL GET THE HANG OF IT.
AIN'T WHAT I MEANT. I MAY BE BLIND, EULESS, BUT I AIN'T DEAF.
I HEARD HOW YOU GOT THIS JOB.

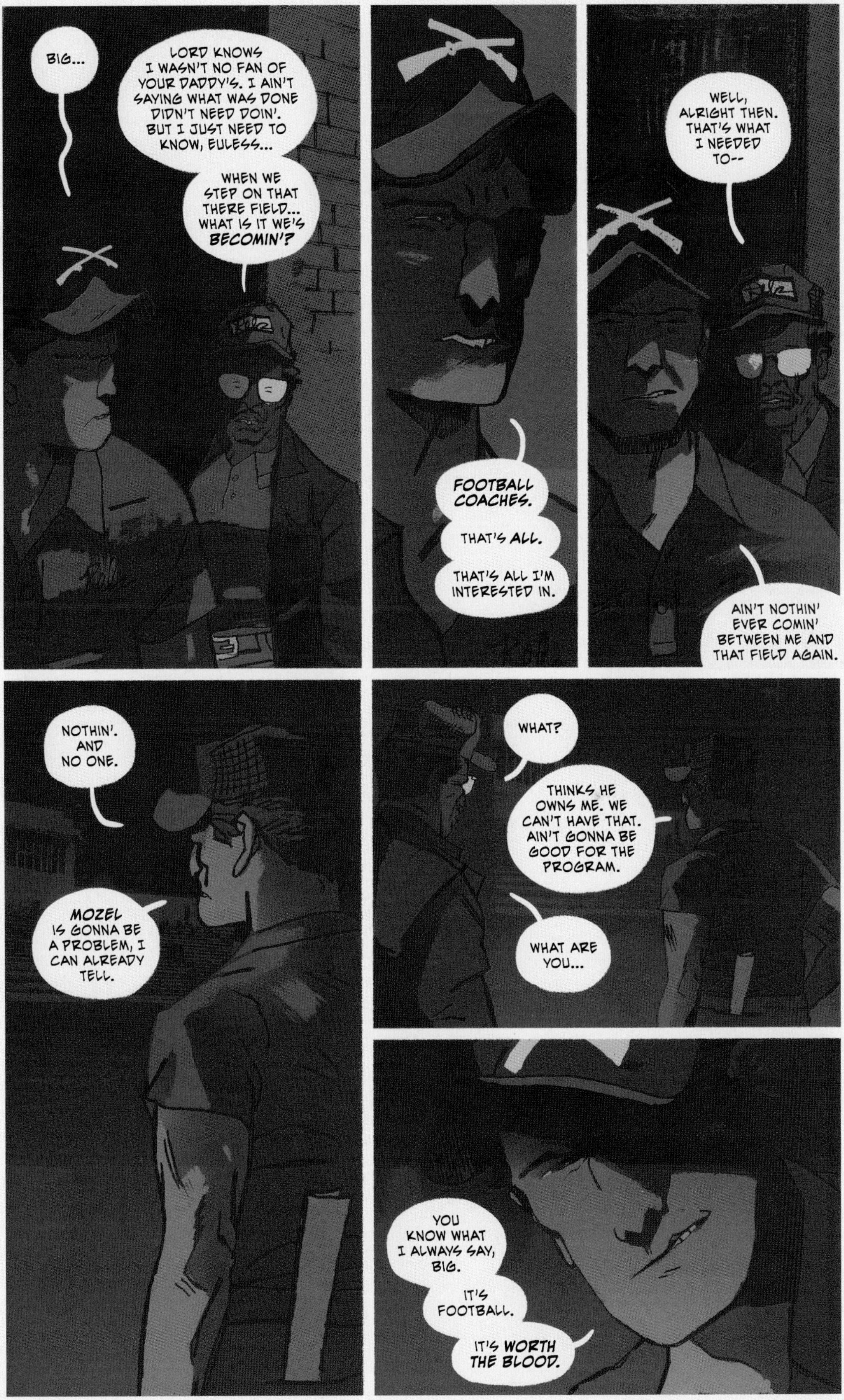
BIG...
LORD KNOWS I WASN'T NO FAN OF YOUR DADDY'S. I AIN'T SAYING WHAT WAS DONE DIDN'T NEED DOIN'. BUT I JUST NEED TO KNOW, EULESS...
WHEN WE STEP ON THAT THERE FIELD... WHAT IS IT WE'S BECOMIN'?
FOOTBALL COACHES.
THAT'S ALL.
THAT'S ALL I'M INTERESTED IN.
WELL, ALRIGHT THEN. THAT'S WHAT I NEEDED TO--
AIN'T NOTHIN' EVER COMIN' BETWEEN ME AND THAT FIELD AGAIN.
NOTHIN'. AND NO ONE.
MOZEL IS GONNA BE A PROBLEM, I CAN ALREADY TELL.
WHAT?
THINKS HE OWNS ME. WE CAN'T HAVE THAT. AIN'T GONNA BE GOOD FOR THE PROGRAM.
WHAT ARE YOU...
YOU KNOW WHAT I ALWAYS SAY, BIG.
IT'S FOOTBALL.
IT'S WORTH THE BLOOD.

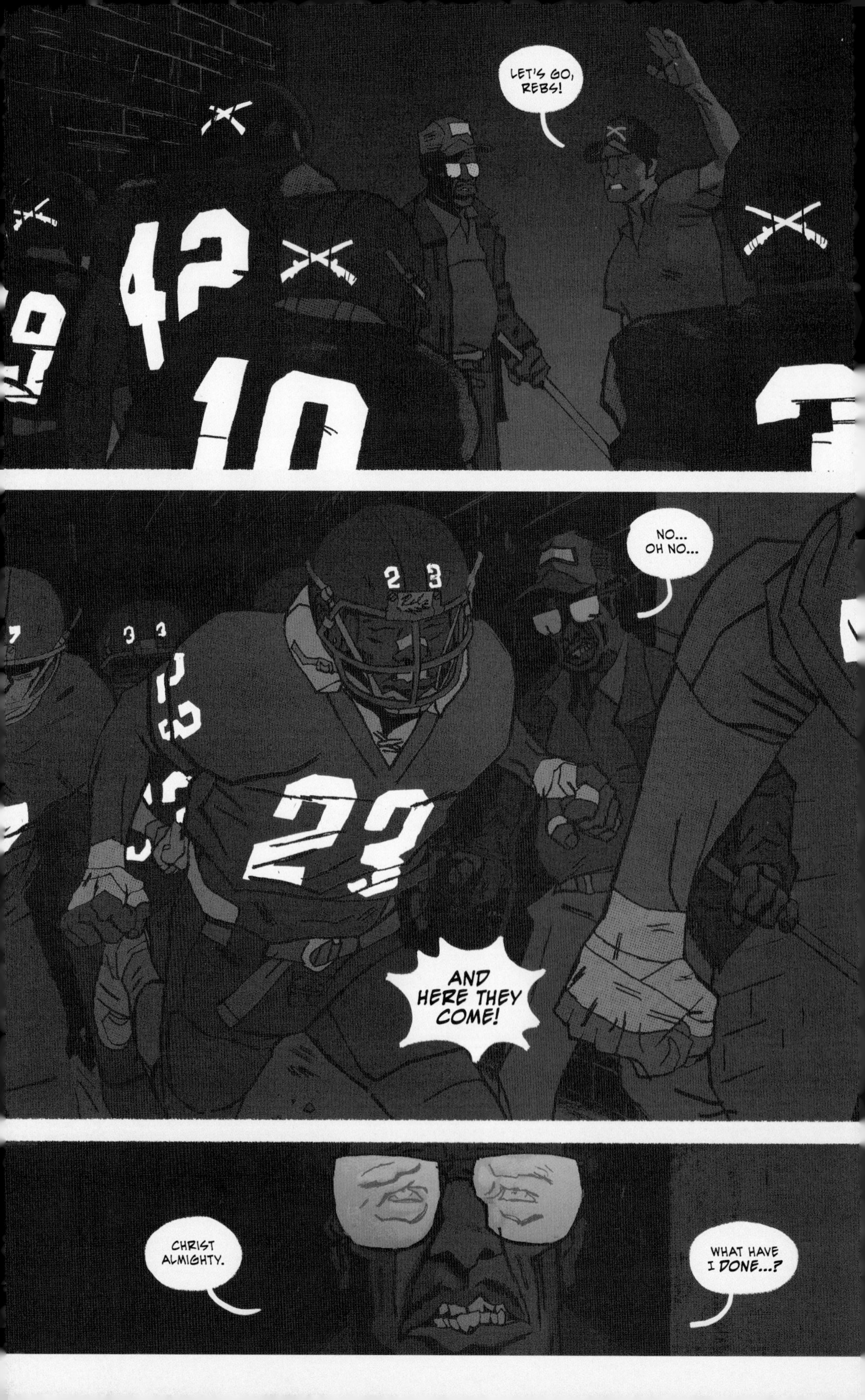
LET'S GO, REBS!
NO... OH NO...
AND HERE THEY COME!
CHRIST ALMIGHTY.
WHAT HAVE I DONE...?

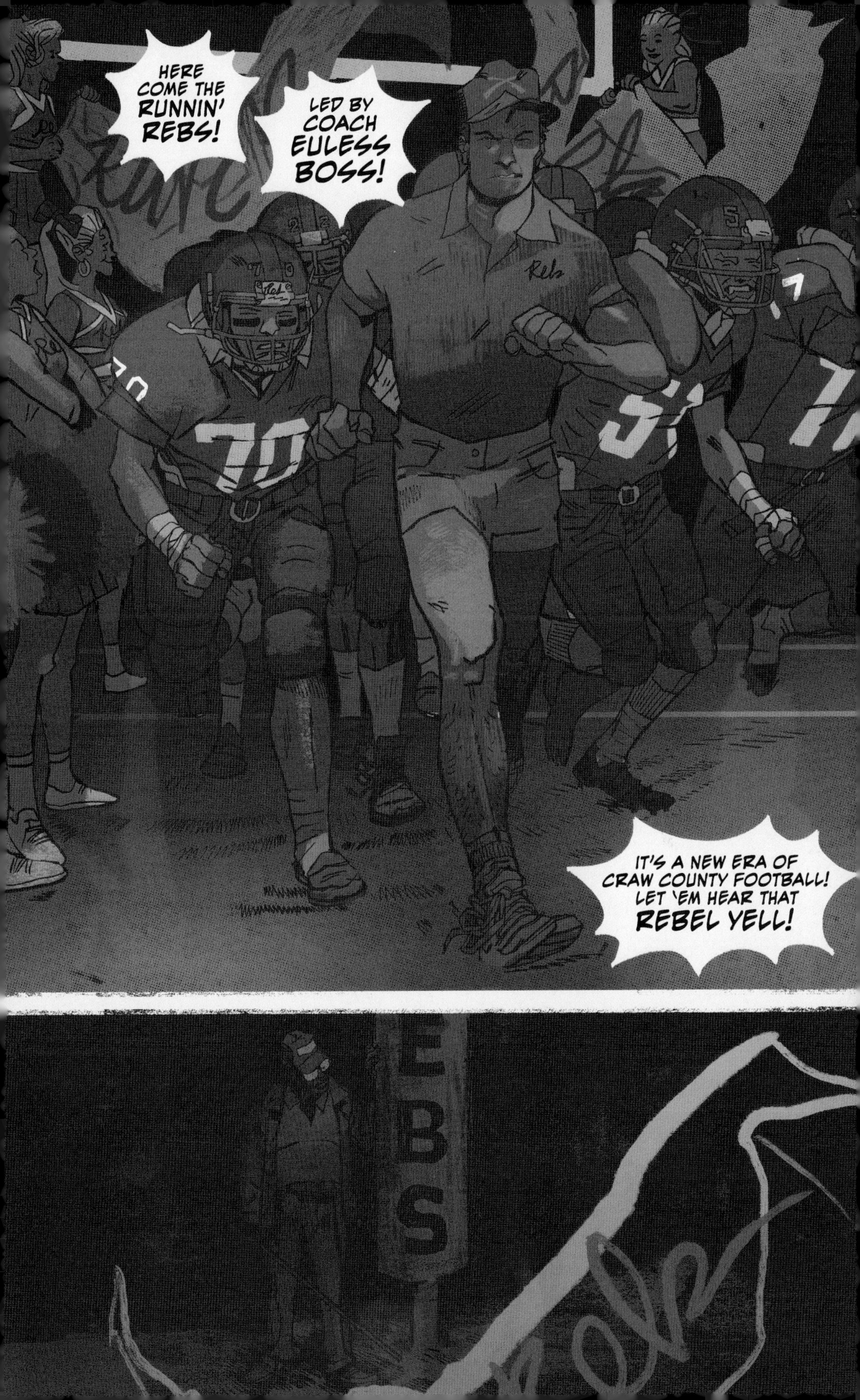
HERE COME THE RUNNIN' REBS!
LED BY COACH EULESS BOSS!
IT'S A NEW ERA OF CRAW COUNTY FOOTBALL! LET 'EM HEAR THAT REBEL YELL!
EBS

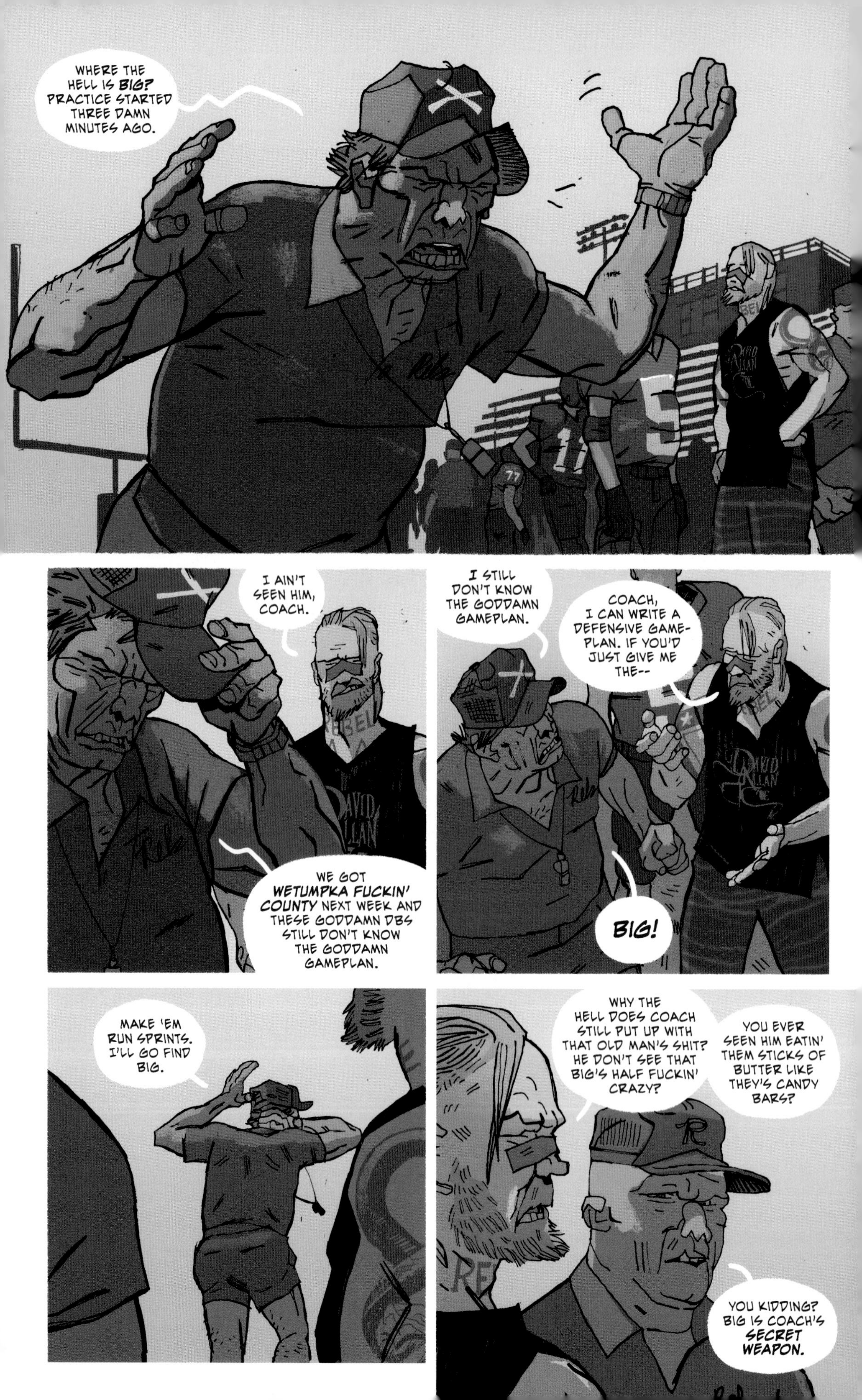
WHERE THE HELL IS **BIG?** PRACTICE STARTED THREE DAMN MINUTES AGO.
I AIN'T SEEN HIM, COACH.
WE GOT ***WETUMPKA FUCKIN' COUNTY*** NEXT WEEK AND THESE GODDAMN DBS STILL DON'T KNOW THE GODDAMN GAMEPLAN.
I STILL DON'T KNOW THE GODDAMN GAMEPLAN.
COACH, I CAN WRITE A DEFENSIVE GAME-PLAN. IF YOU'D JUST GIVE ME THE--
BIG!
MAKE 'EM RUN SPRINTS. I'LL GO FIND BIG.
WHY THE HELL DOES COACH STILL PUT UP WITH THAT OLD MAN'S SHIT? HE DON'T SEE THAT BIG'S HALF FUCKIN' CRAZY?
YOU EVER SEEN HIM EATIN' THEM STICKS OF BUTTER LIKE THEY'S CANDY BARS?
YOU KIDDING? BIG IS COACH'S **SECRET WEAPON.**

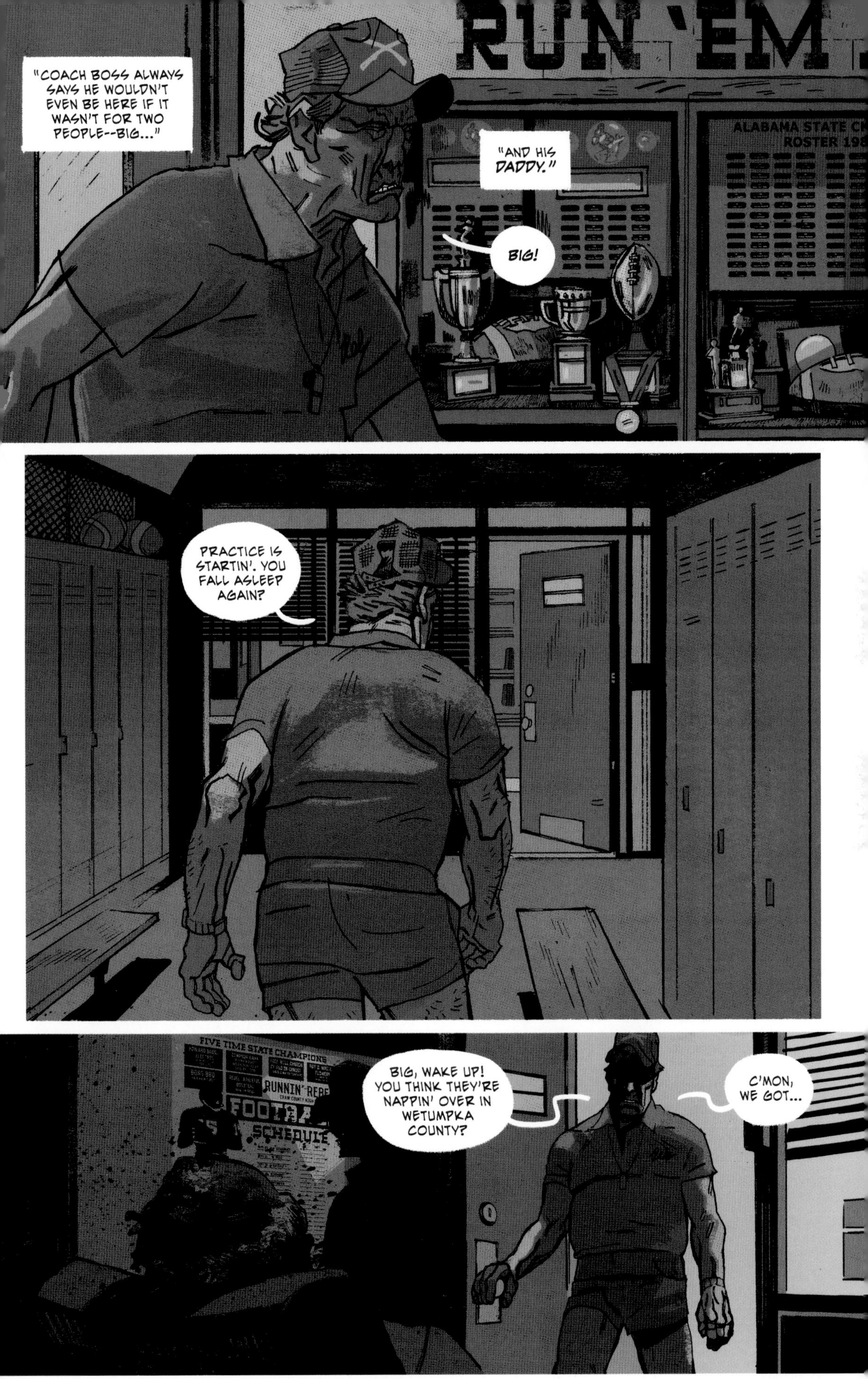
RUN 'EM
"COACH BOSS ALWAYS SAYS HE WOULDN'T EVEN BE HERE IF IT WASN'T FOR TWO PEOPLE--BIG..."
"AND HIS DADDY."
BIG!
PRACTICE IS STARTIN'. YOU FALL ASLEEP AGAIN?
FIVE TIME STATE CHAMPIONS
SCHEDULE
BIG, WAKE UP! YOU THINK THEY'RE NAPPIN' OVER IN WETUMPKA COUNTY?
C'MON, WE GOT...

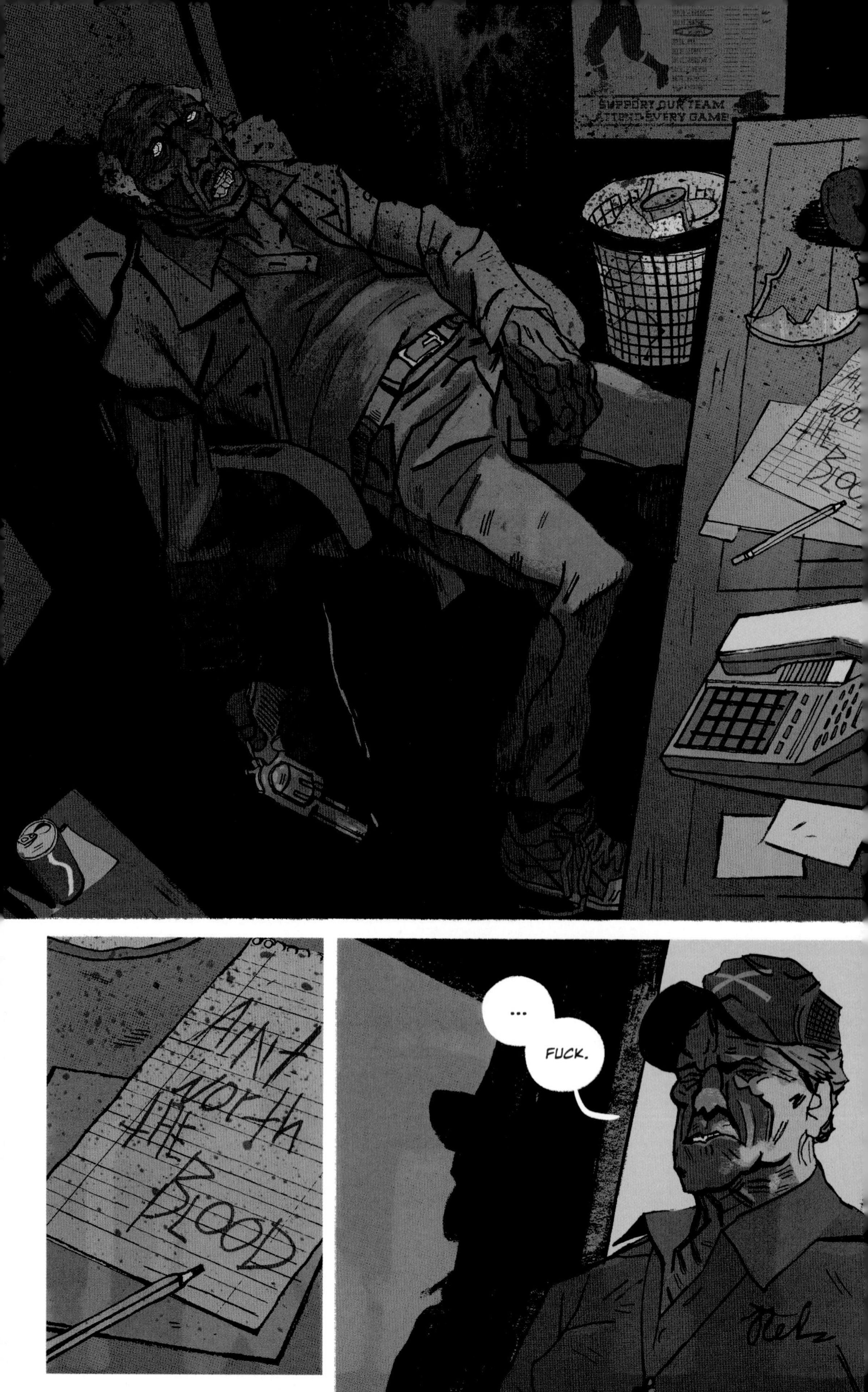
SUPPORT OUR TEAM
ATTEND EVERY GAME
AIN'T WORTH THE BLOOD
...
FUCK.

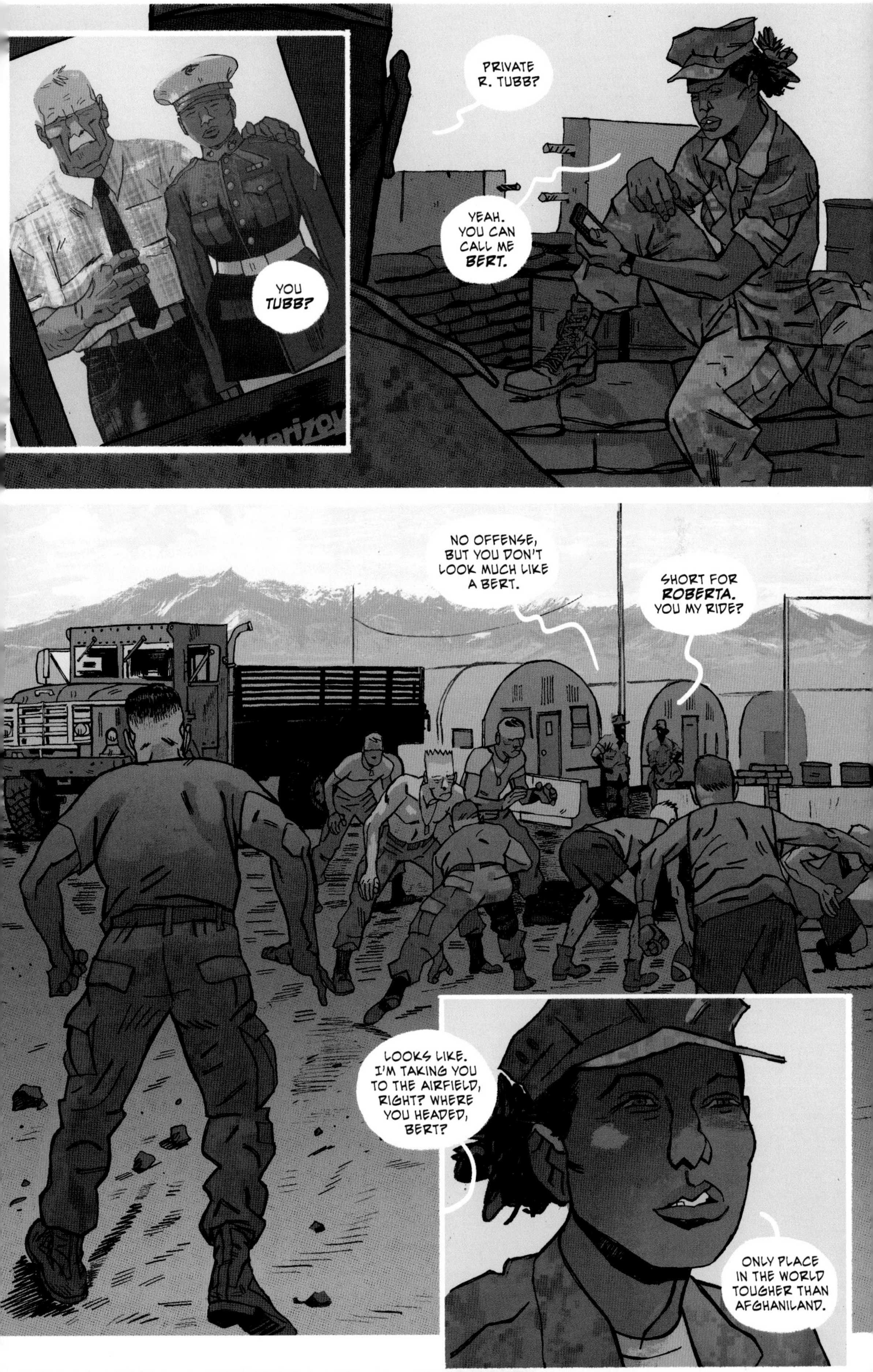
PRIVATE R. TUBB?
YOU TUBB?
YEAH. YOU CAN CALL ME BERT.
NO OFFENSE, BUT YOU DON'T LOOK MUCH LIKE A BERT.
SHORT FOR ROBERTA. YOU MY RIDE?
LOOKS LIKE. I'M TAKING YOU TO THE AIRFIELD, RIGHT? WHERE YOU HEADED, BERT?
ONLY PLACE IN THE WORLD TOUGHER THAN AFGHANILAND.

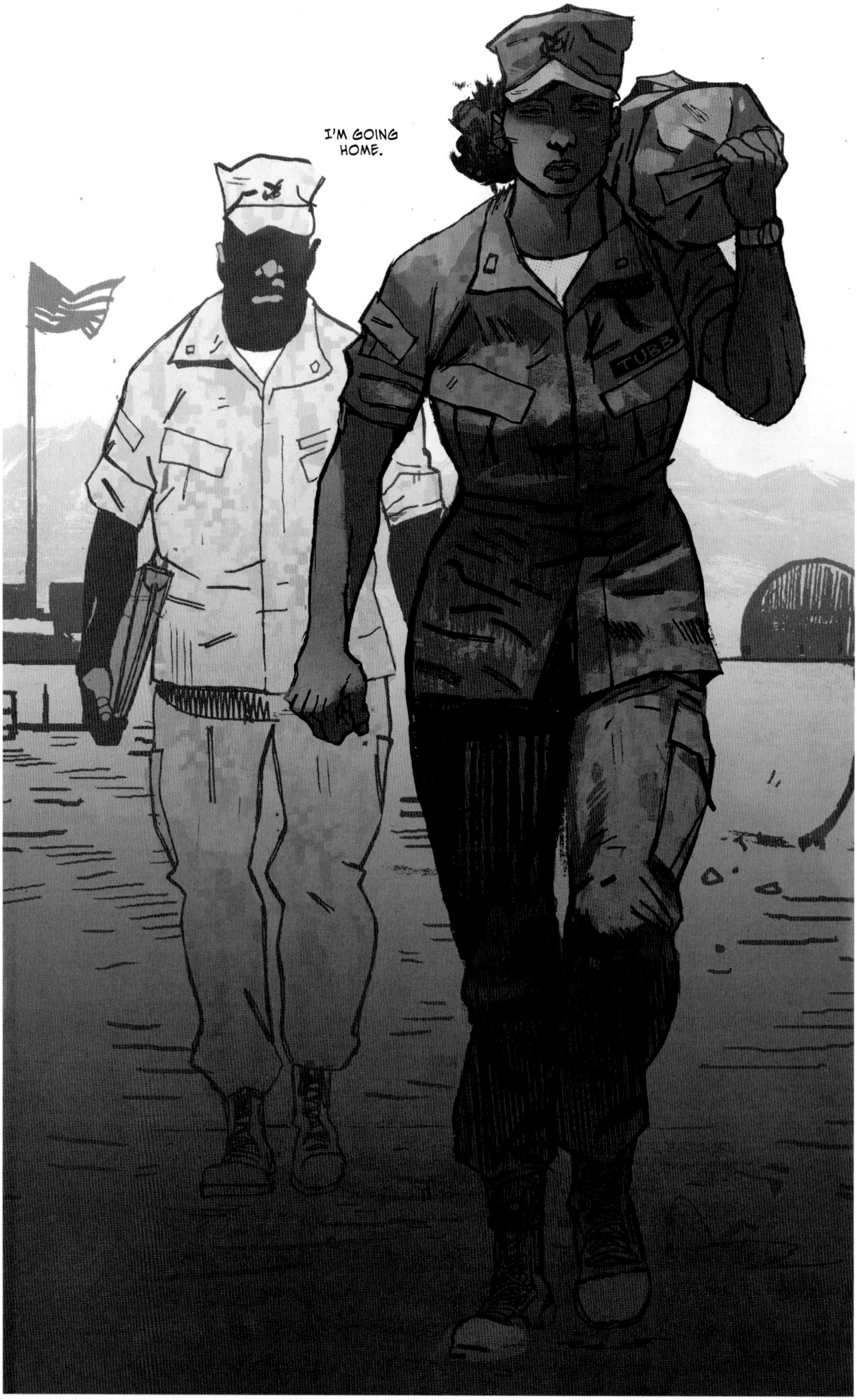
I'M GOING HOME.
TUBB

JASON AARON writes comic books. Like the crime series SCALPED for DC/Vertigo and books like GHOST RIDER, WOLVERINE, INCREDIBLE HULK, PUNISHER MAX, and WOLVERINE AND THE X-MEN for Marvel.

His most recent projects include the Southern hitman series MEN OF WRATH at Icon, as well as STAR WARS and THOR at Marvel.

He was born in Alabama, but currently resides in Kansas City.

Jason enjoys many things, but shaving is not one of them.

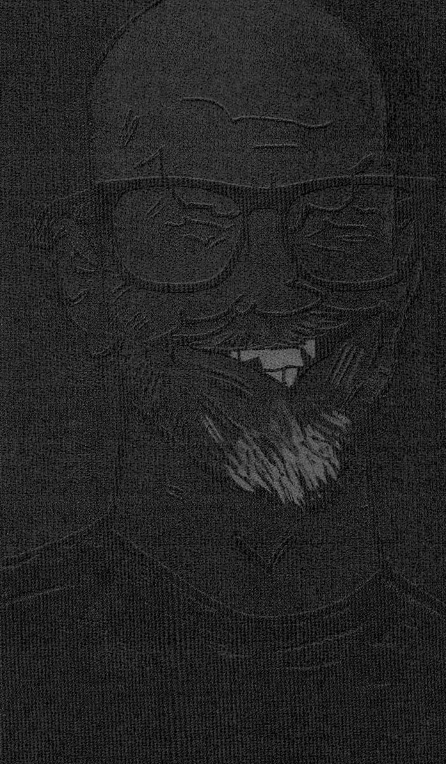

JASON LATOUR is a comic book artist and writer.

His art can be seen in Quentin Tarantino's DJANGO UNCHAINED, Mike Mignola's B.P.R.D., SLEDGEHAMMER 44, Marvel's WOLVERINE, and SCALPED for DC/Vertigo.

As a writer he's penned the creator-owned Southern Crime Romance: LOOSE ENDS, Marvel's WINTER SOLDIER, WOLVERINE AND THE X-MEN (vol. 2), and GWEN STACY: SPIDER-WOMAN.

Charlotte, NC is where he learned to draw(1).

SOUTHERN BASTARDS

Cover Gallery

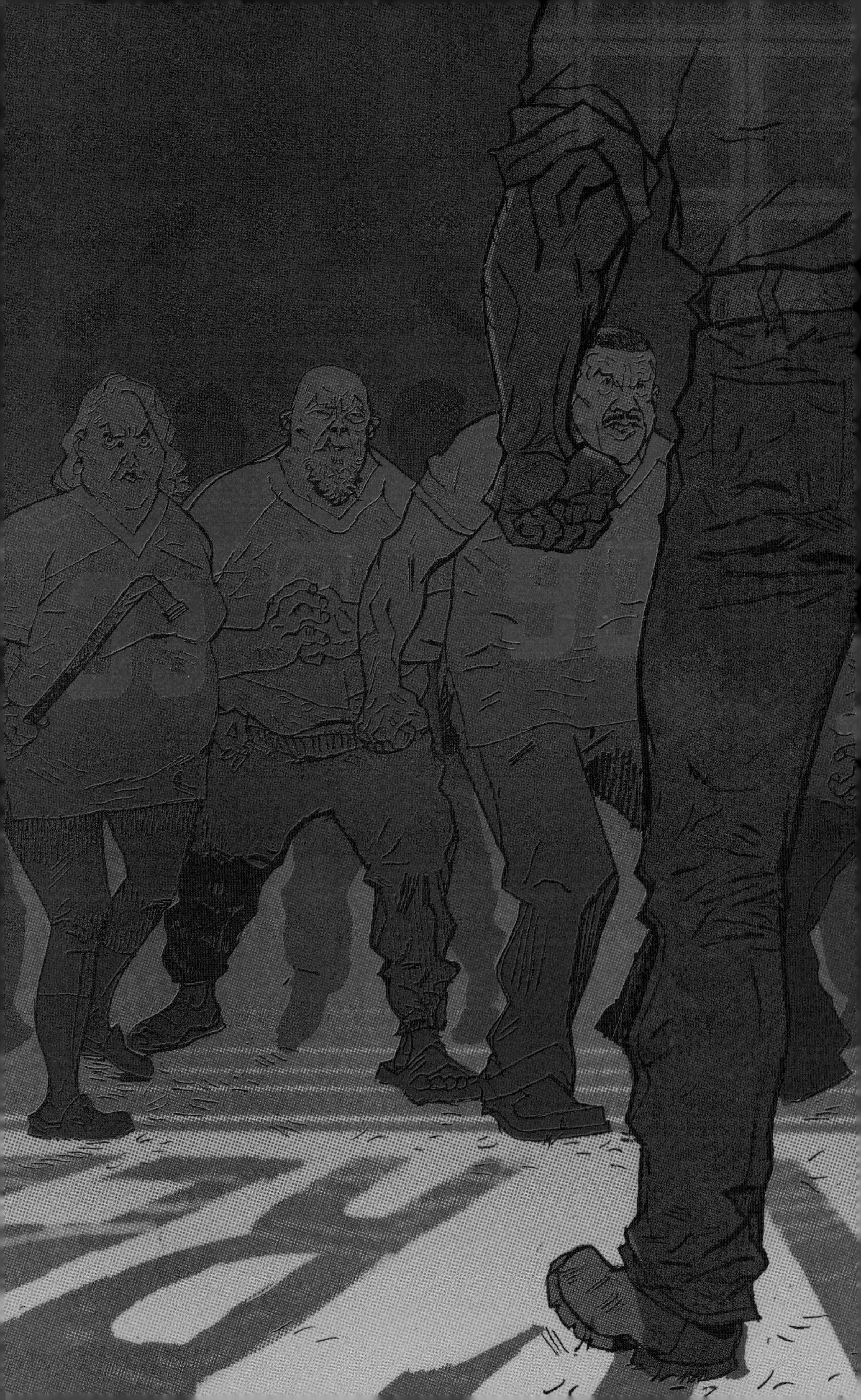

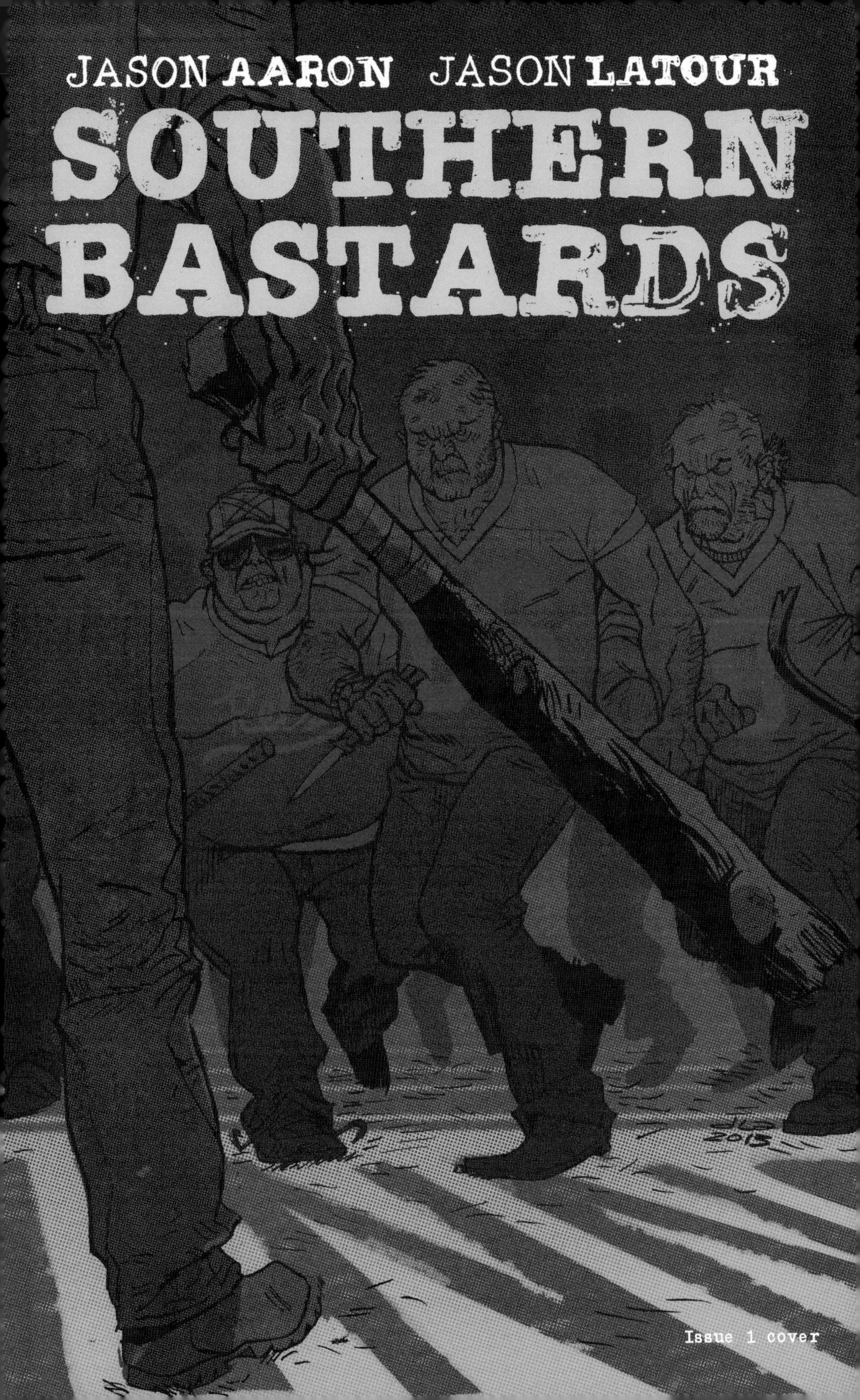
JASON AARON JASON LATOUR
SOUTHERN BASTARDS
Issue 1 cover

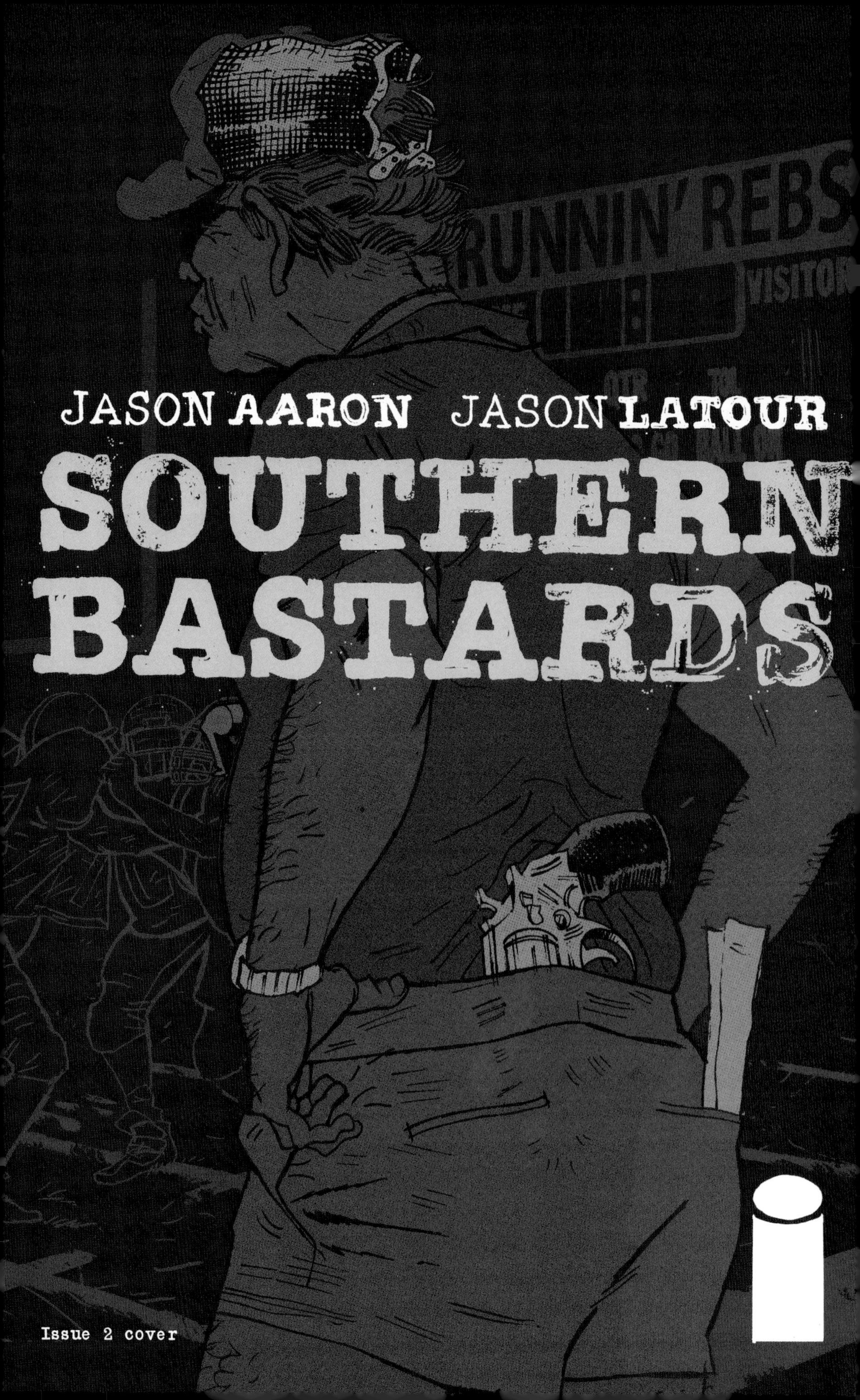
RUNNIN' REBS
JASON AARON JASON LATOUR
SOUTHERN
BASTARDS

Issue 2 cover

Issue 3 cover

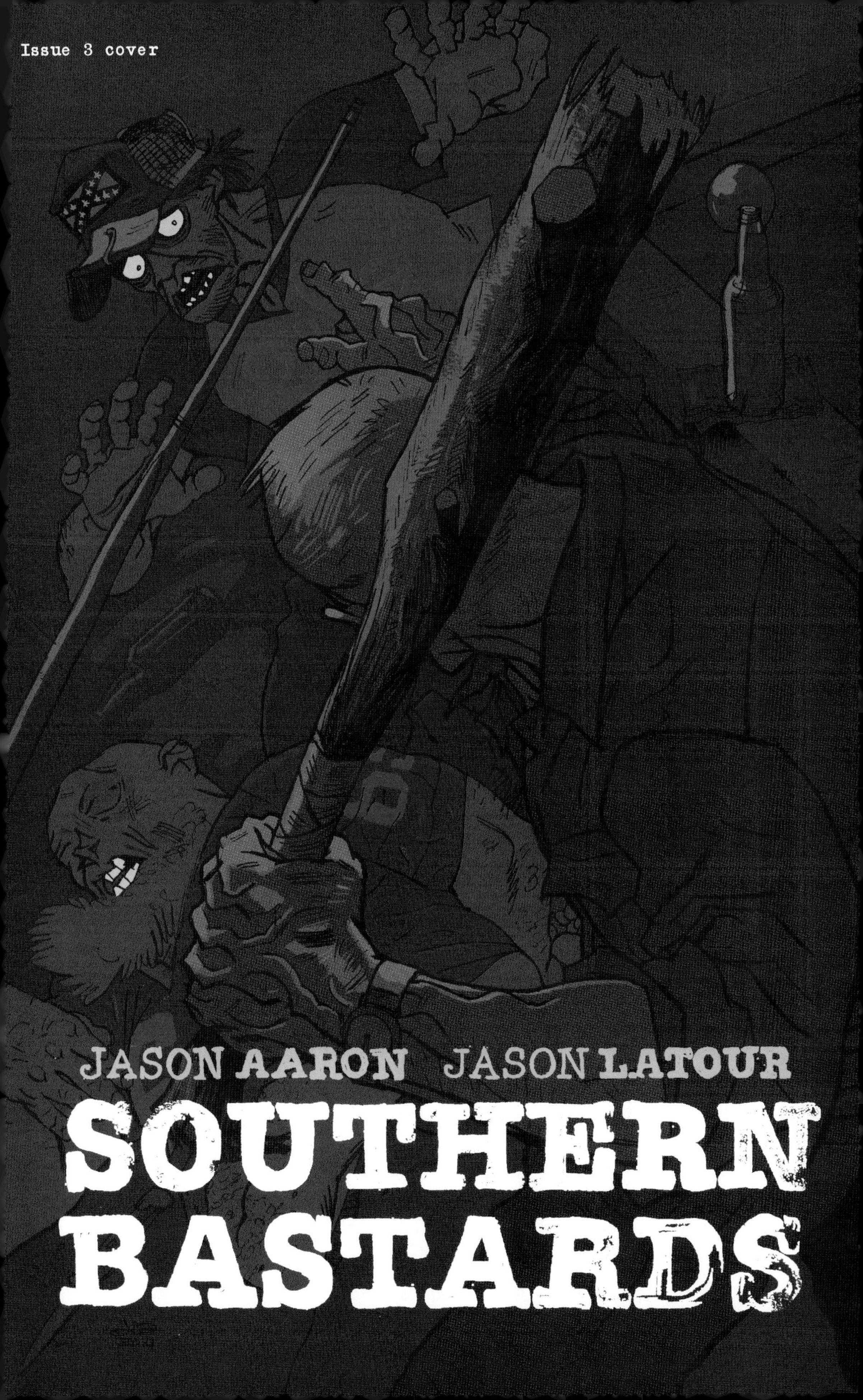
JASON AARON JASON LATOUR
SOUTHERN BASTARDS

Issue 4 cover

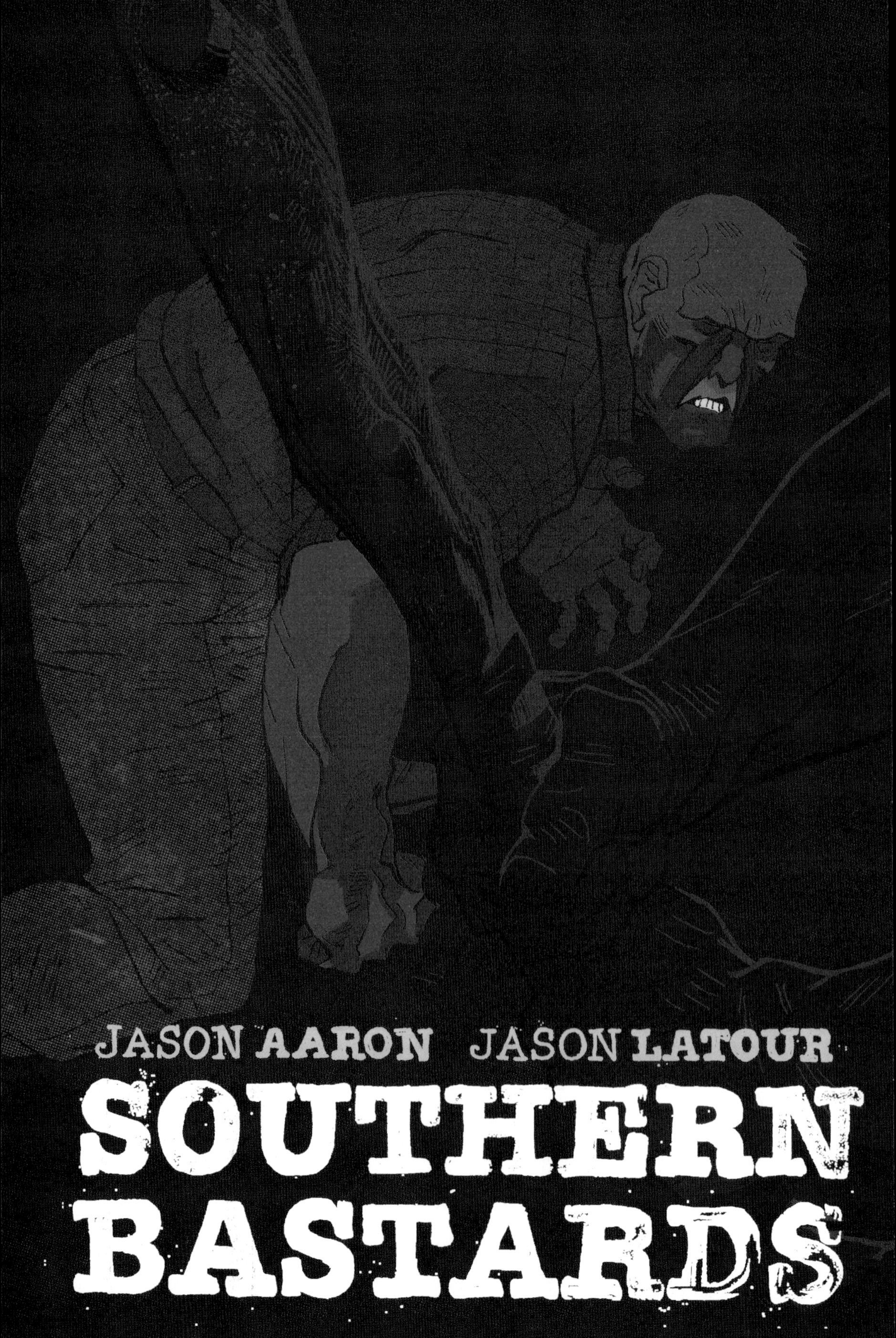
JASON AARON JASON LATOUR
SOUTHERN BASTARDS

Issue 5 cover

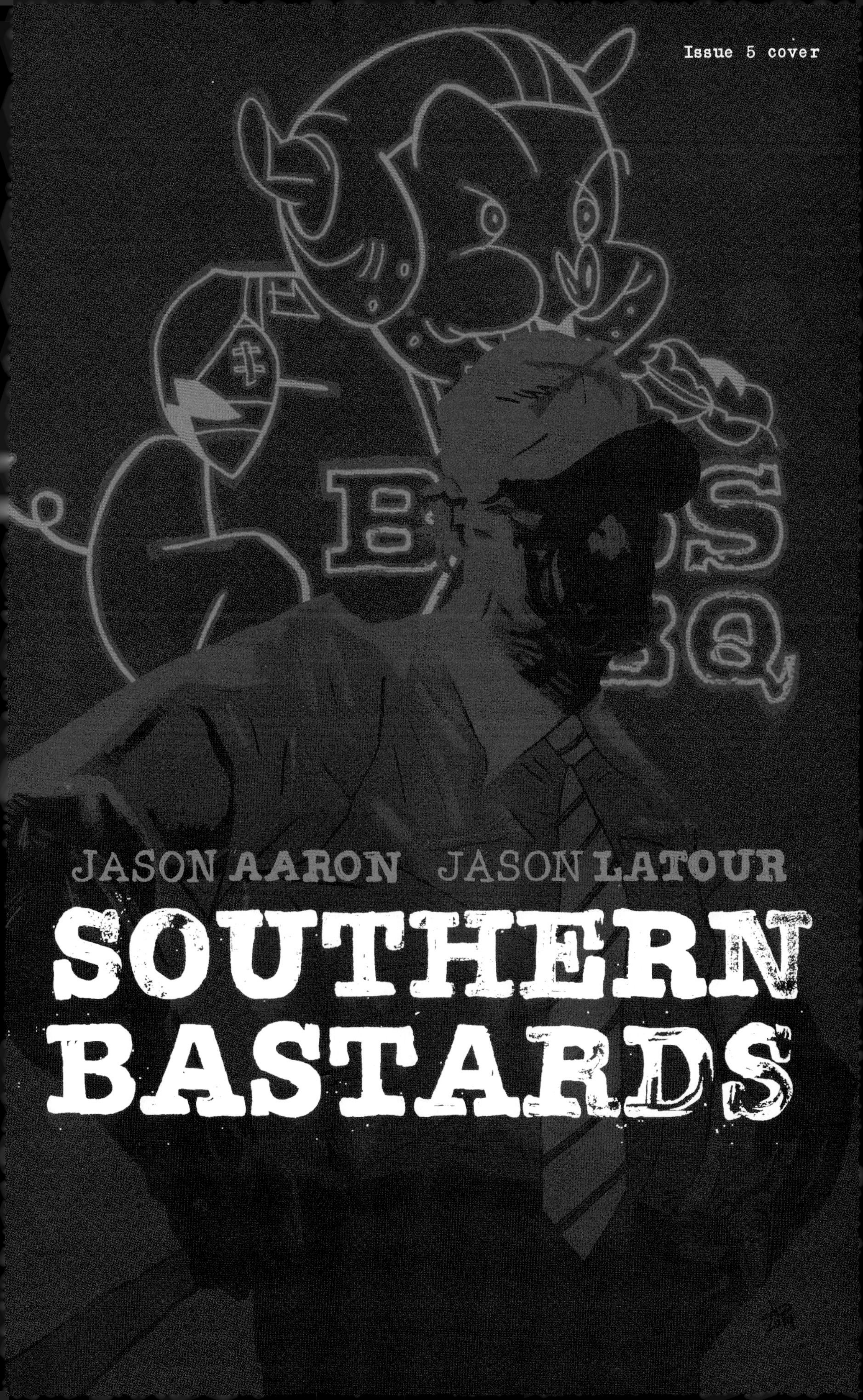
JASON AARON JASON LATOUR
SOUTHERN
BASTARDS

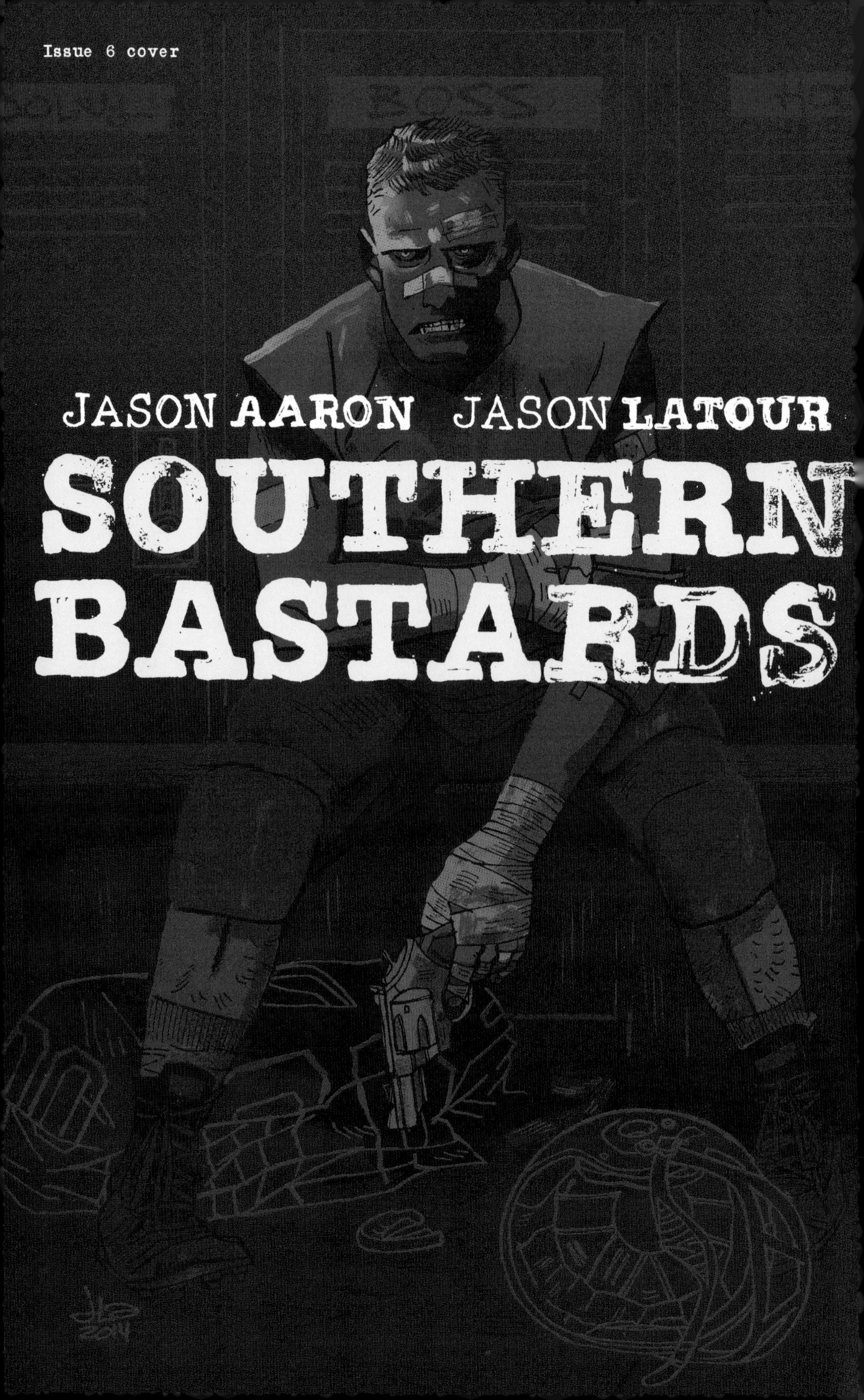

Issue 6 cover

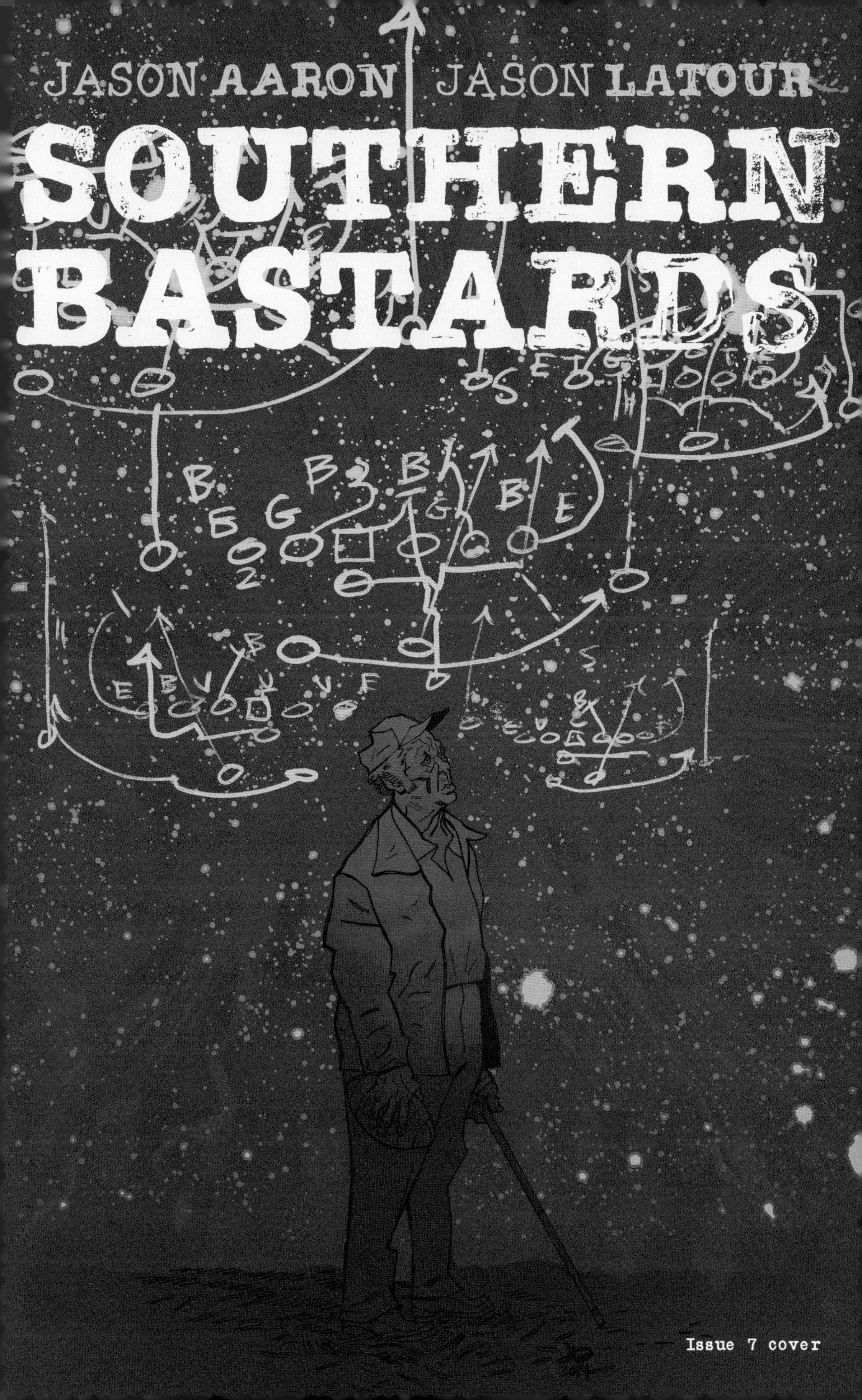

Issue 7 cover

Issue 8 cover

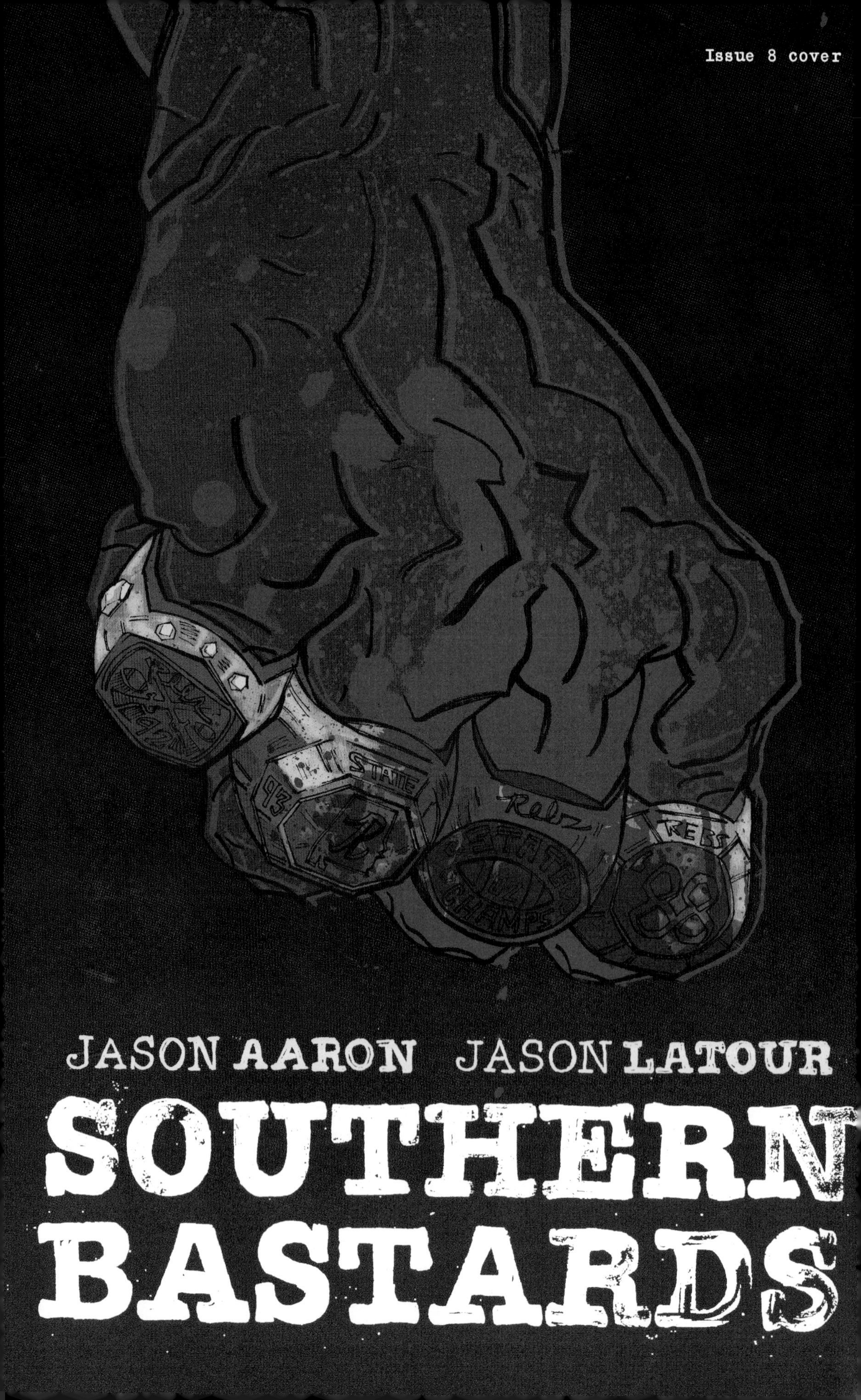
STATE
93
STATE
CHAMPS
REBS
JASON AARON JASON LATOUR
SOUTHERN
BASTARDS

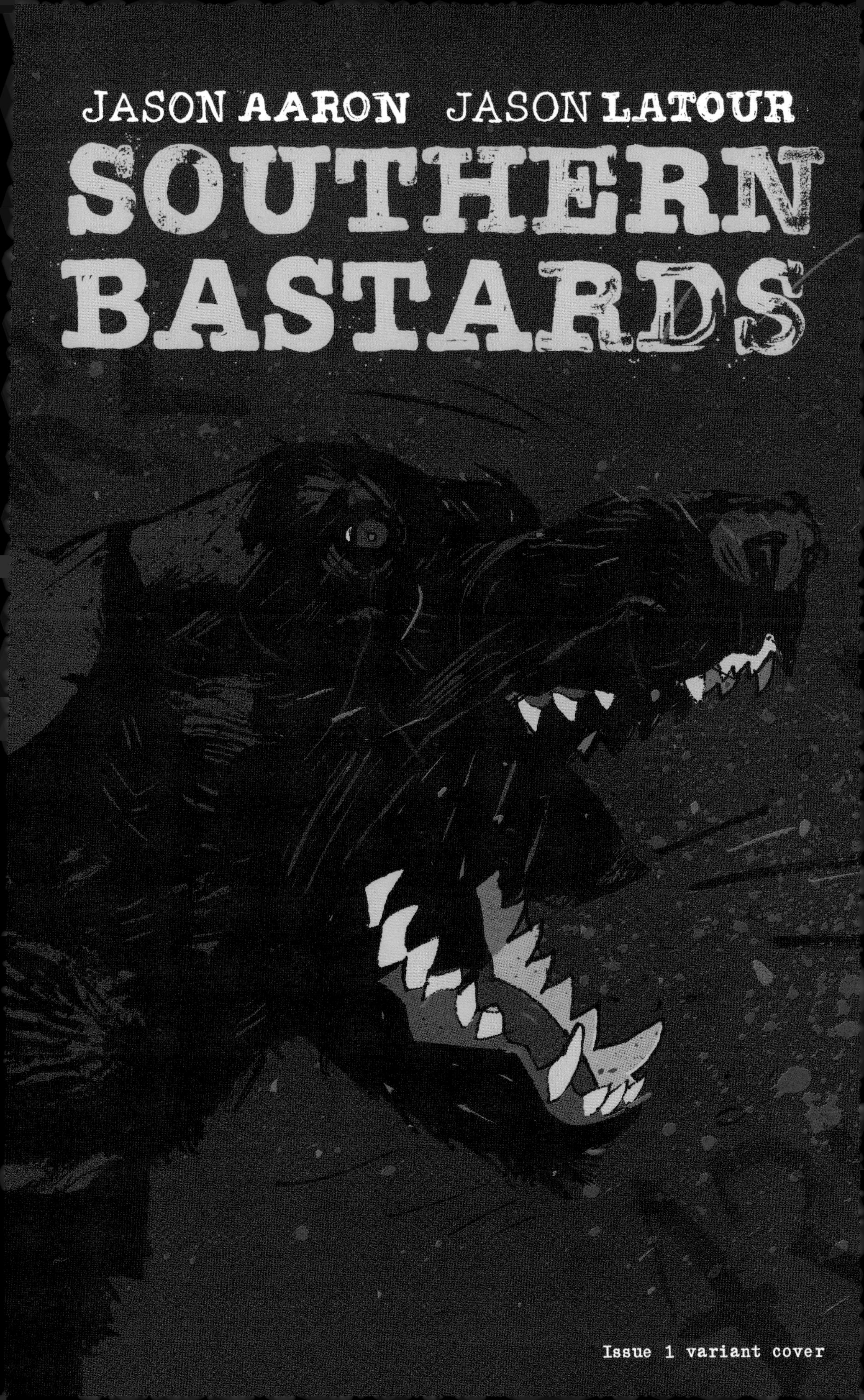
JASON AARON JASON LATOUR
SOUTHERN BASTARDS
Issue 1 variant cover

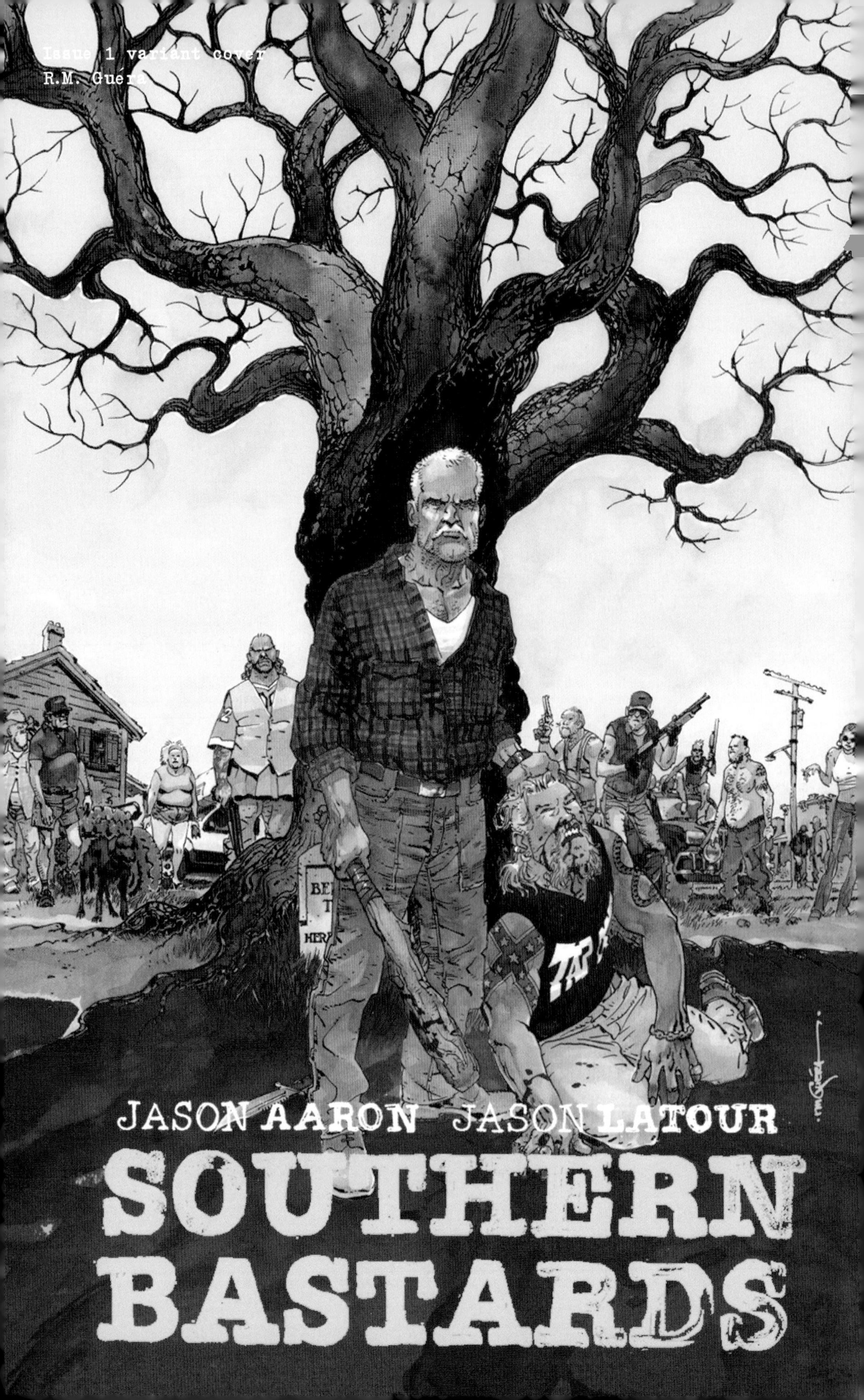
JASON AARON JASON LATOUR
SOUTHERN
BASTARDS

Issue 1 variant cover
R.M. Guéra

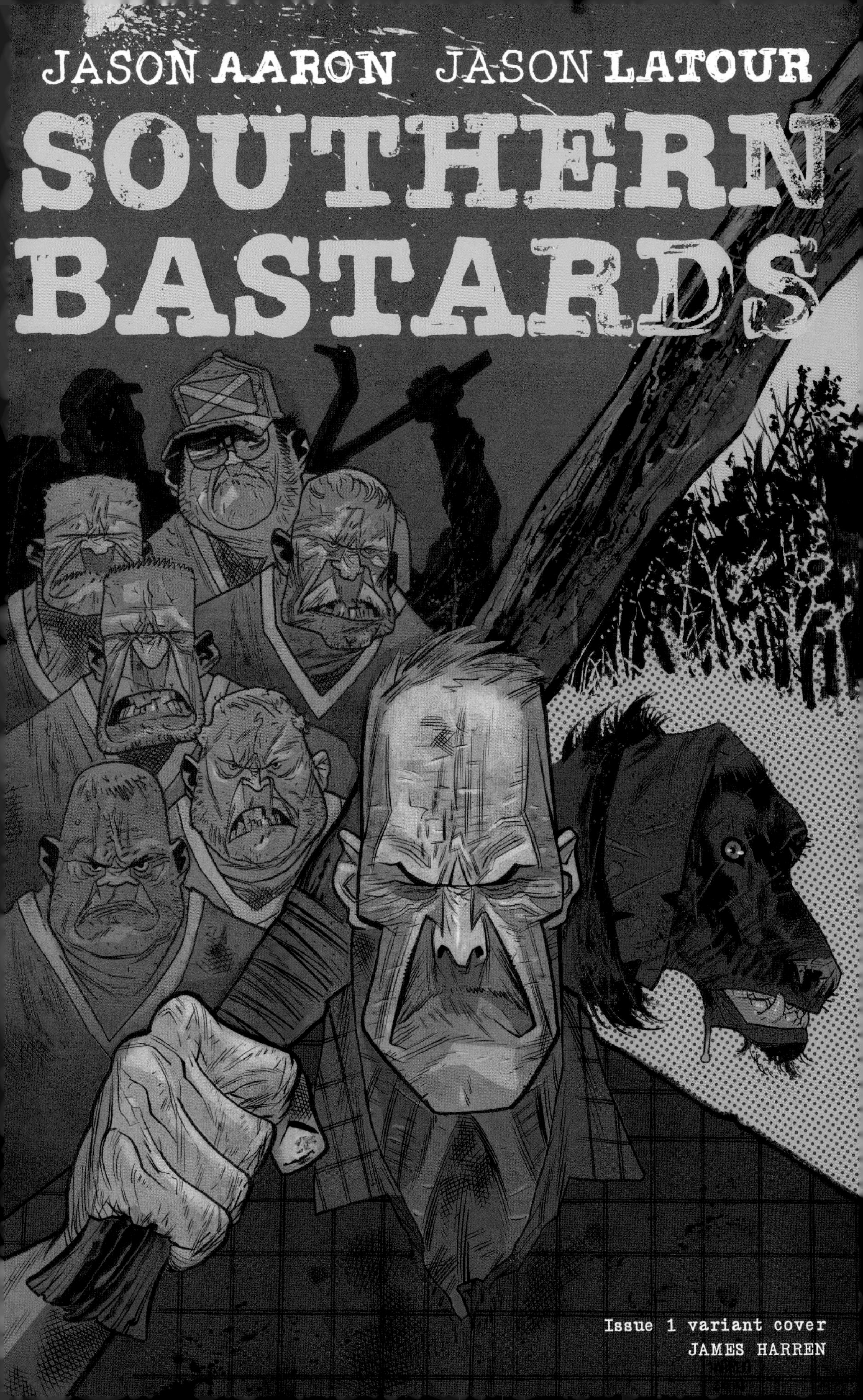
JASON AARON JASON LATOUR
SOUTHERN BASTARDS
Issue 1 variant cover
JAMES HARREN

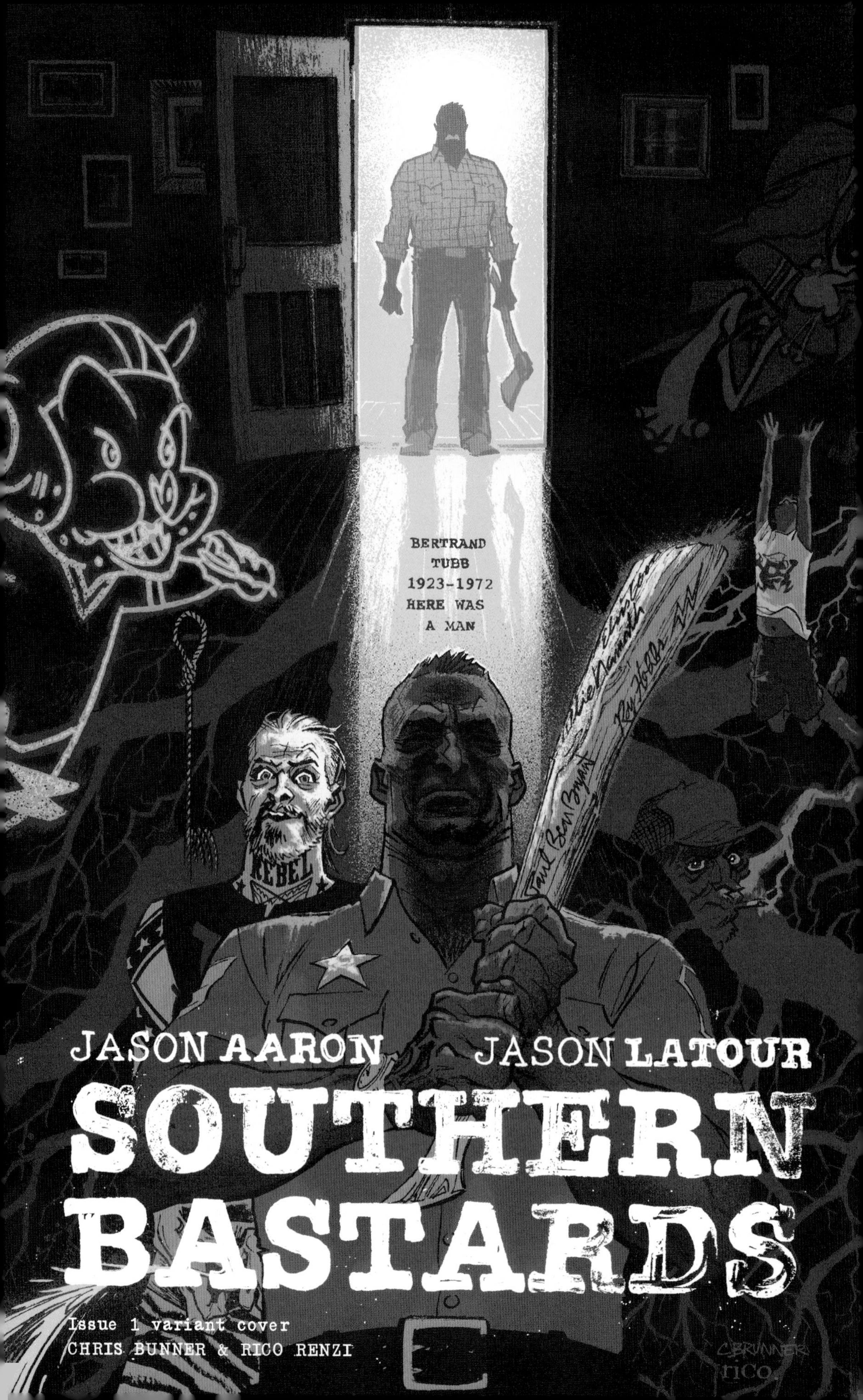
BERTRAND
TUBB
1923-1972
HERE WAS
A MAN
REBEL
JASON AARON
JASON LATOUR
SOUTHERN
BASTARDS
Issue 1 variant cover
CHRIS BUNNER & RICO RENZI

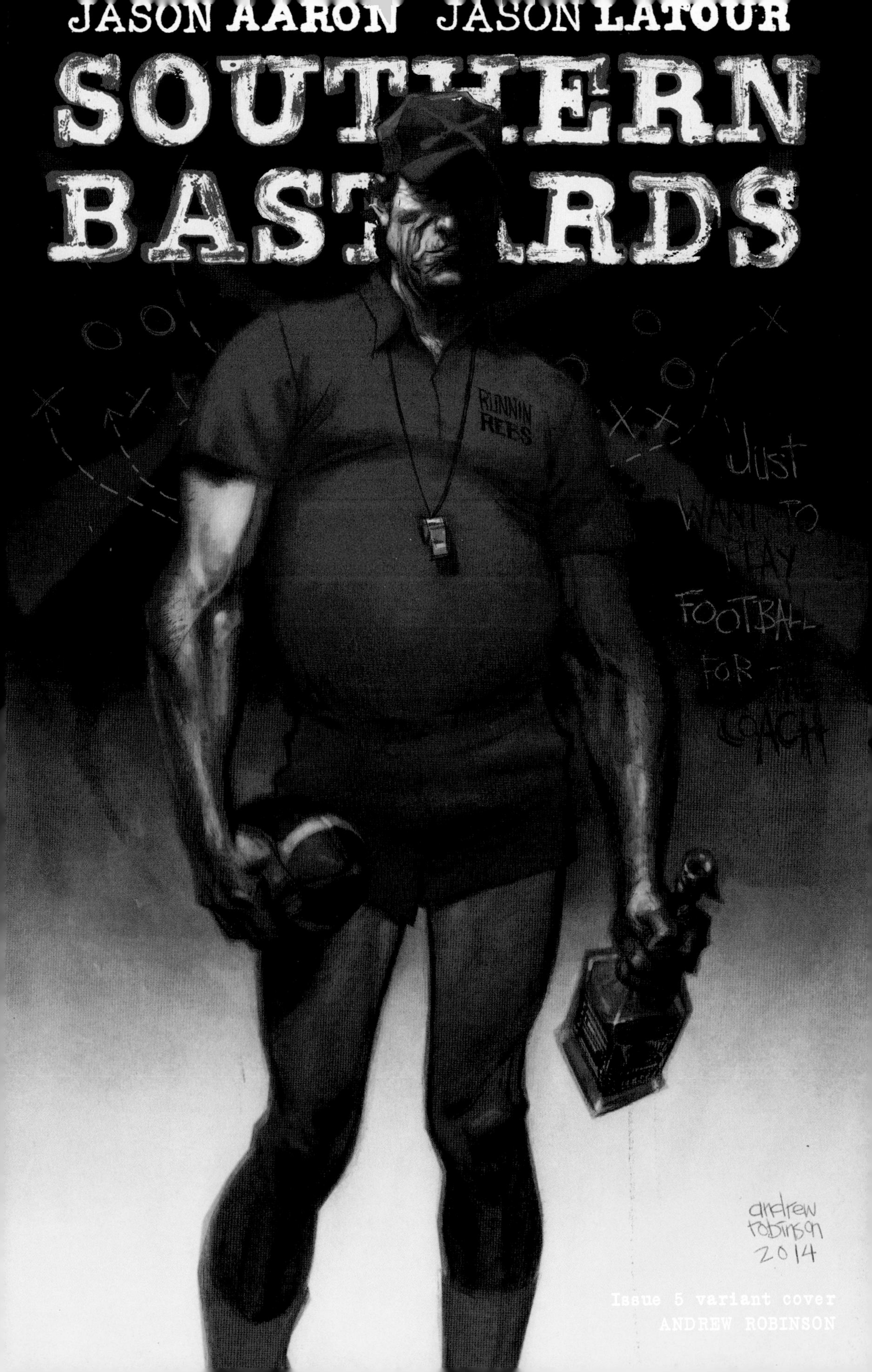
JASON AARON JASON LATOUR
SOUTHERN BASTARDS
RUNNIN REBS
JUST
WANT TO
FOOTBALL
FOR
COACH
andrew robinson 2014

Issue 5 variant cover
ANDREW ROBINSON

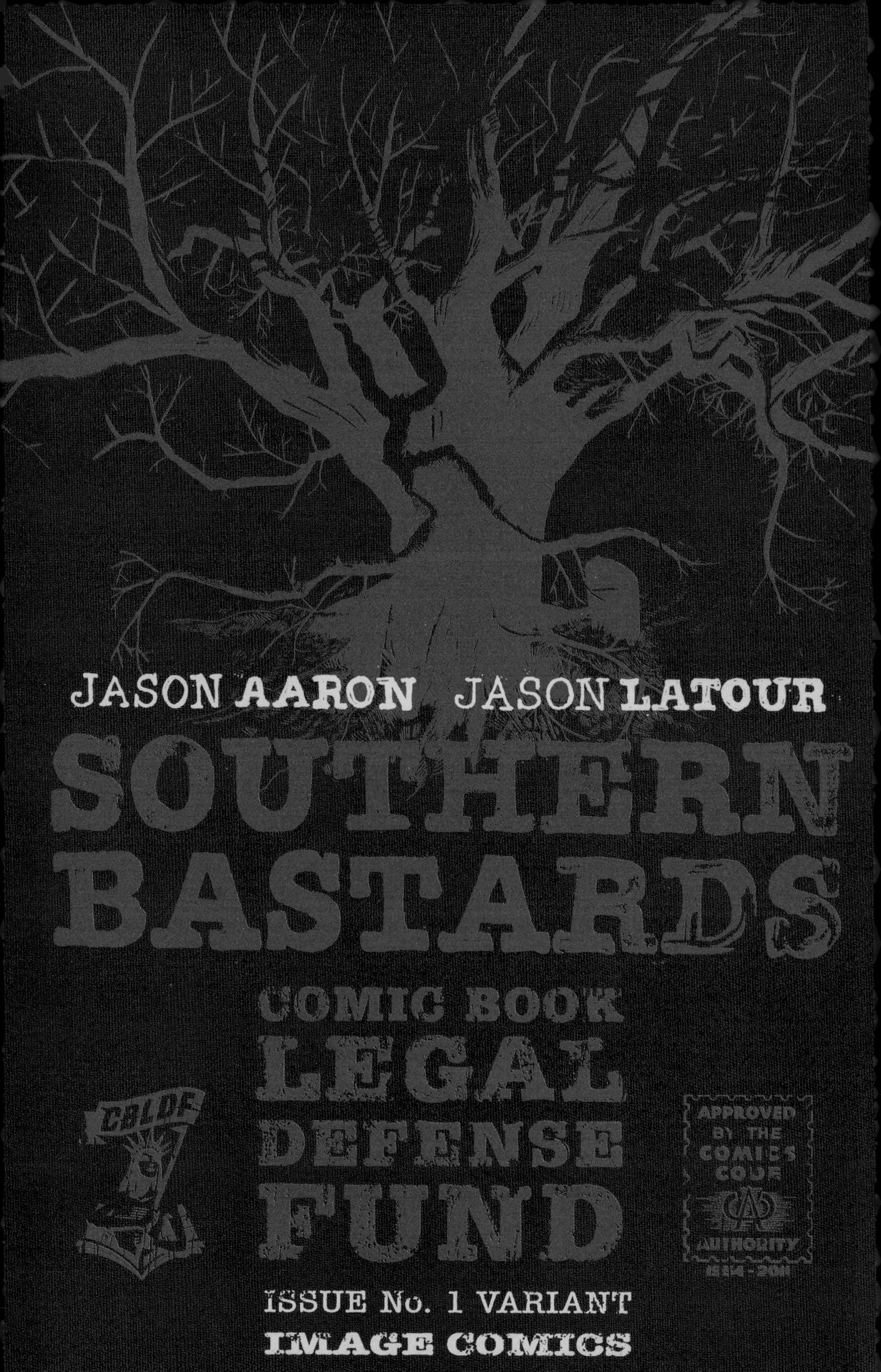
JASON AARON JASON LATOUR
SOUTHERN BASTARDS
CBLDF
COMIC BOOK LEGAL DEFENSE FUND
APPROVED BY THE COMICS CODE AUTHORITY
ISSUE No. 1 VARIANT
IMAGE COMICS

Issue 1 variant cover

SOUTHERN BASTARDS

Sketchbook

instagram/
jasonlatour

Desk shots
of art as it
was produced.

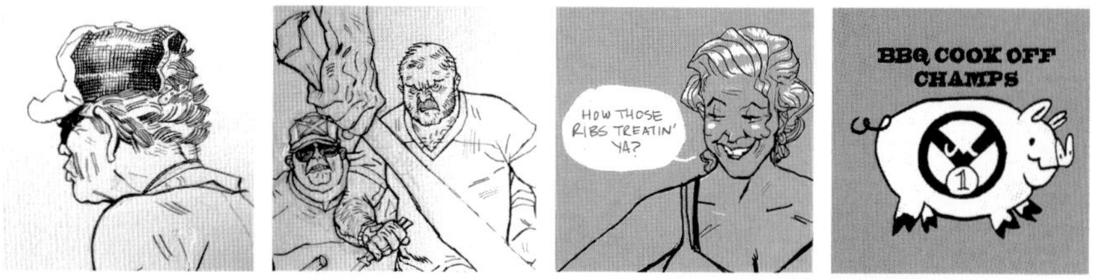
HOW THOSE RIBS TREATIN' YA?
BBQ COOK OFF CHAMPS

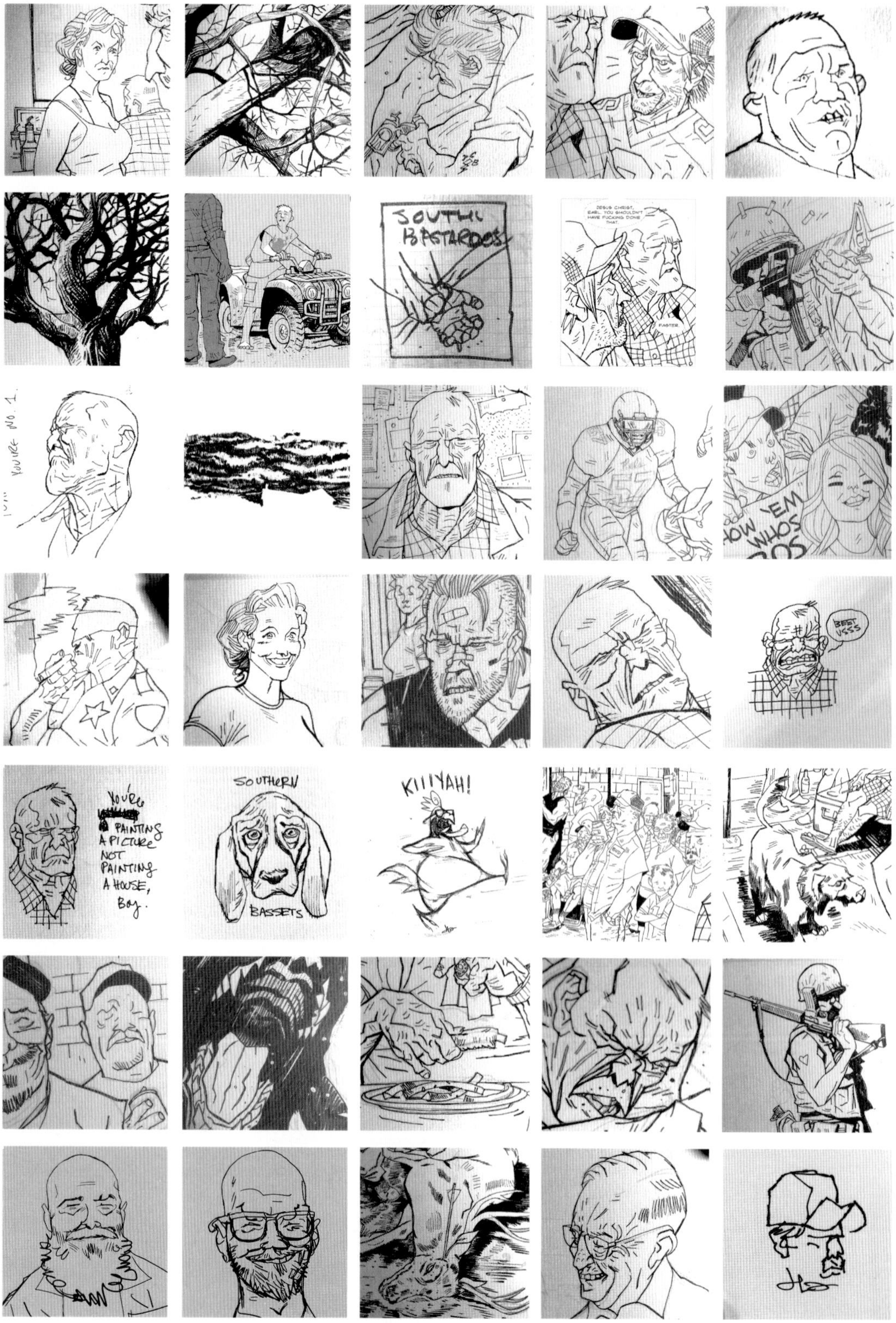
SOUTHERN BASTARDS
JESUS CHRIST, EARL. YOU SHOULDN'T HAVE FUCKING DONE THAT.
FASTER.
YOU'RE NO. 1.
You're PAINTING A PICTURE NOT PAINTING A HOUSE, Boy.
SOUTHERN
BASSETS
KIIYAH!

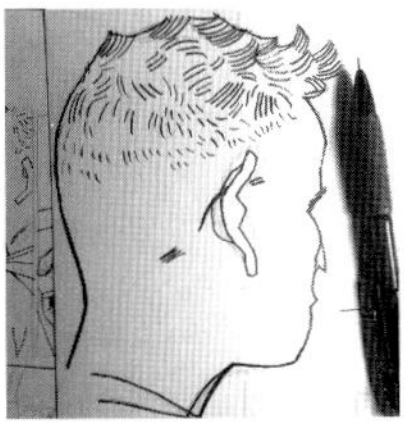
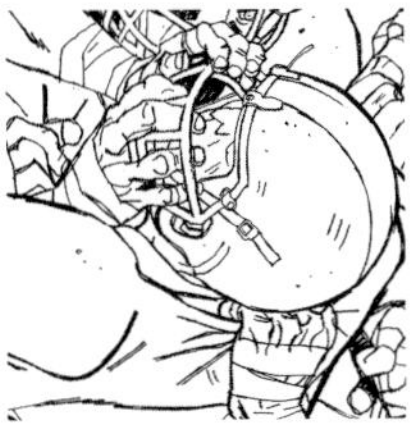
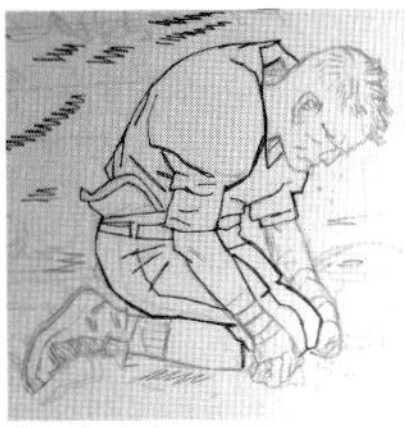
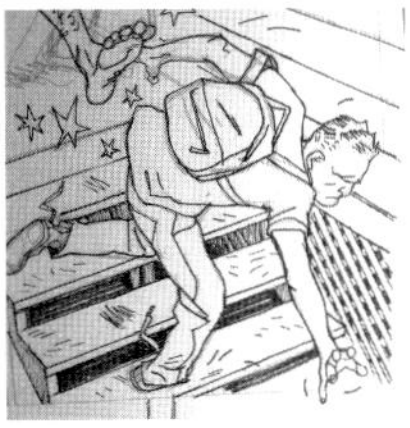
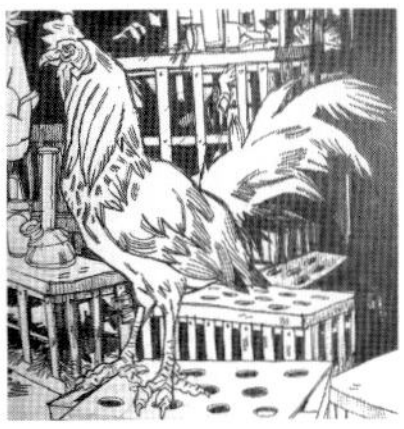
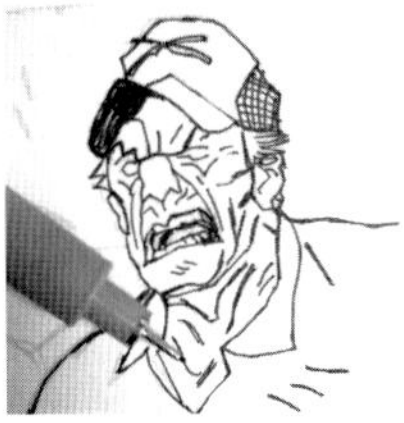
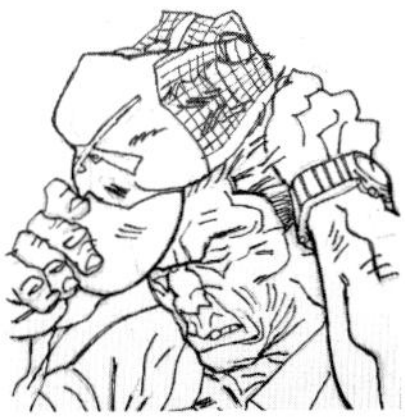
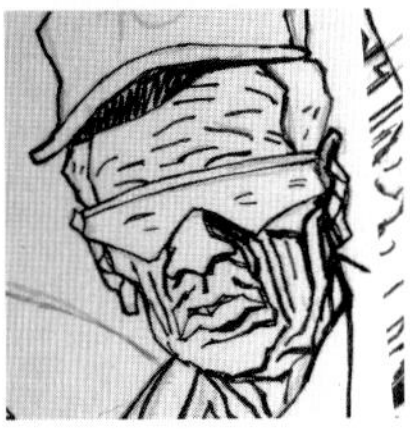
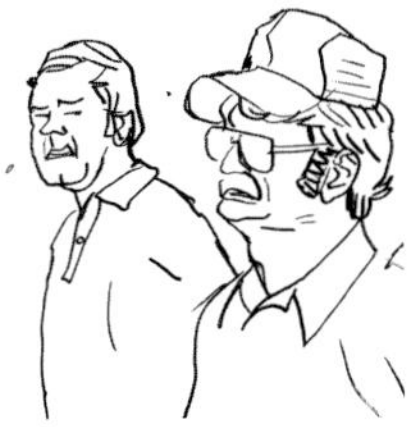
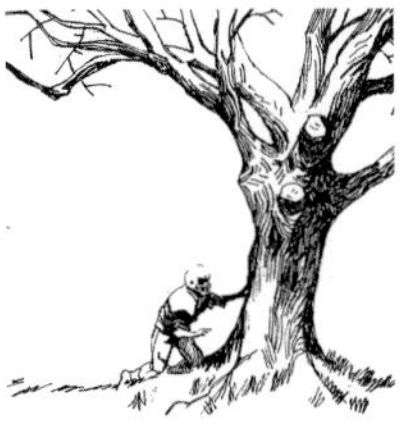
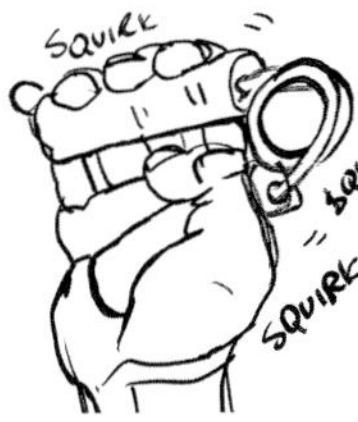
SQUIRK
SQUIRK
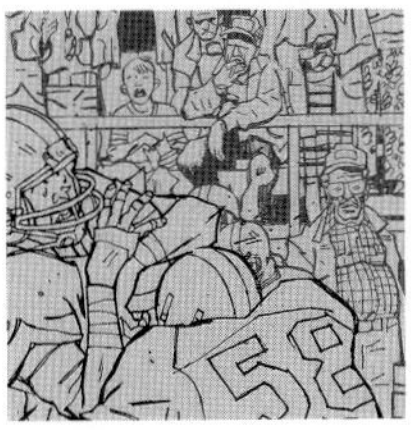
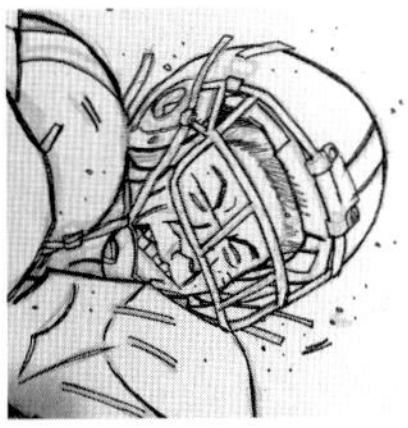
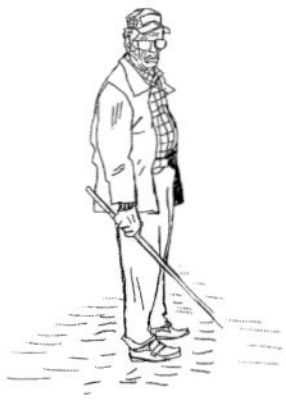
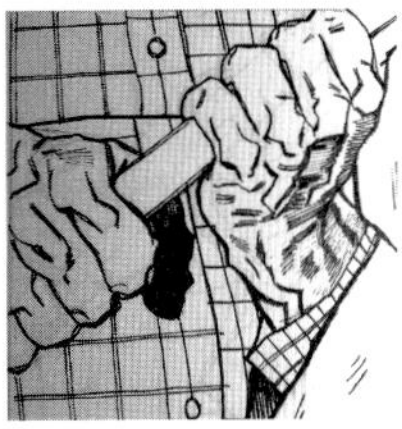
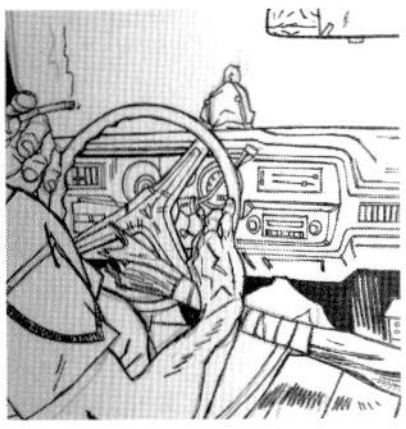
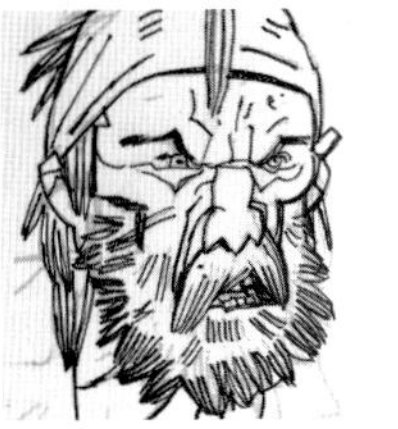
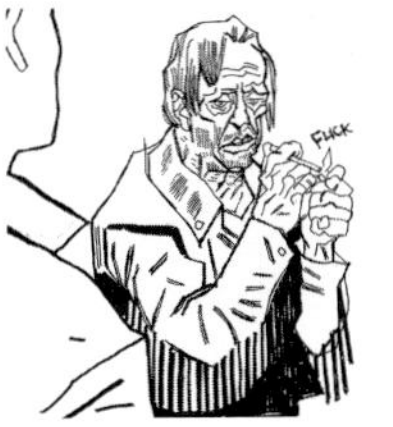
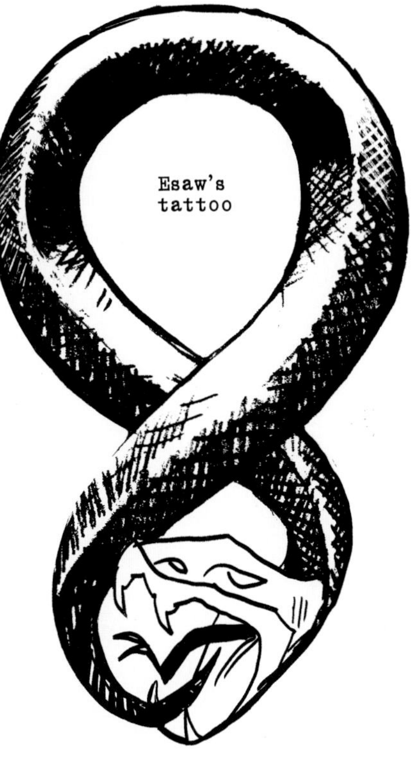

Esaw's tattoo

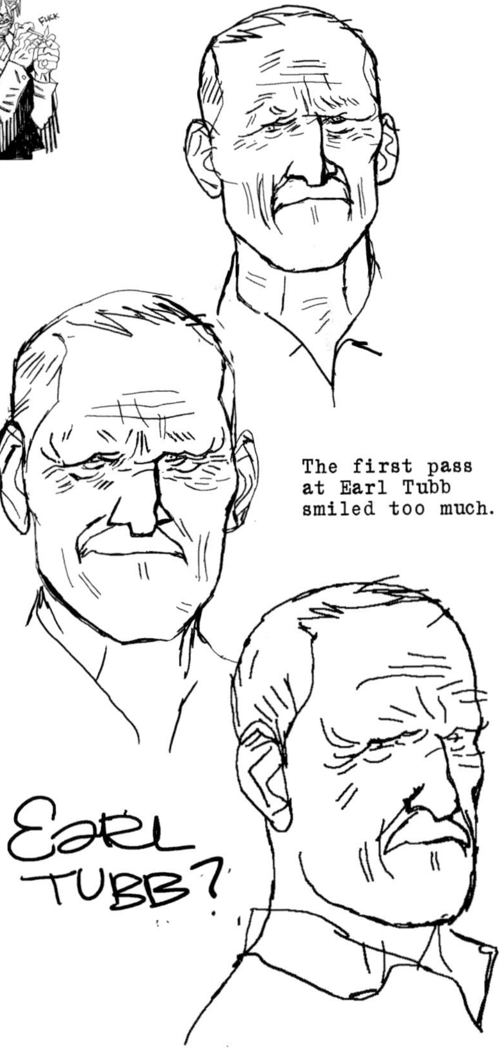
EARL
TUBB?

The first pass at Earl Tubb smiled too much.

Quick sketches from URBAN COMICS
Southern Bastards French release
at Salon Du Livre de Paris

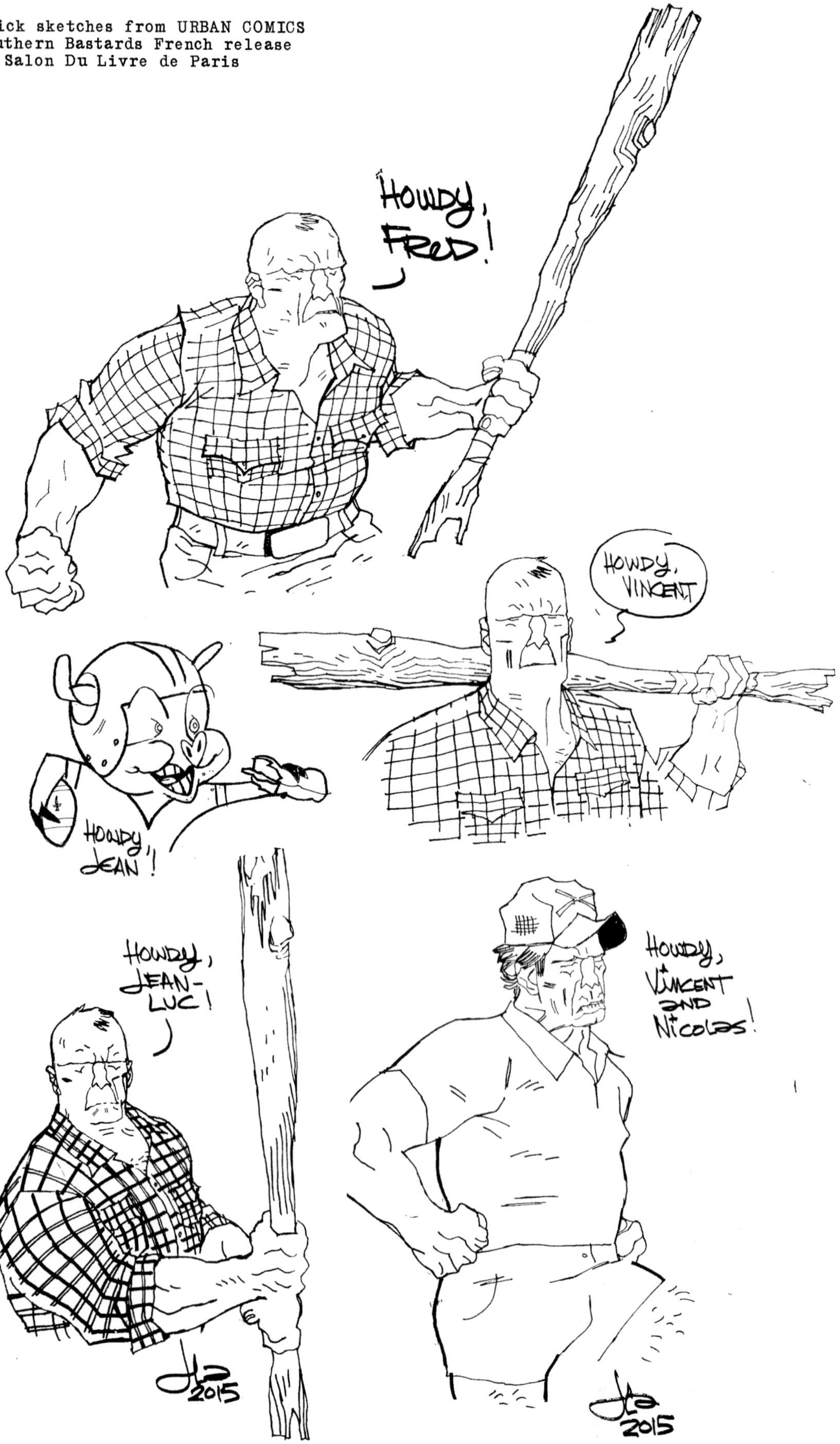
HOWDY, FRED!
HOWDY, VINCENT
HOWDY JEAN!
HOWDY, JEAN-LUC!
HOWDY, VINCENT AND NICOLAS!
2015
2015

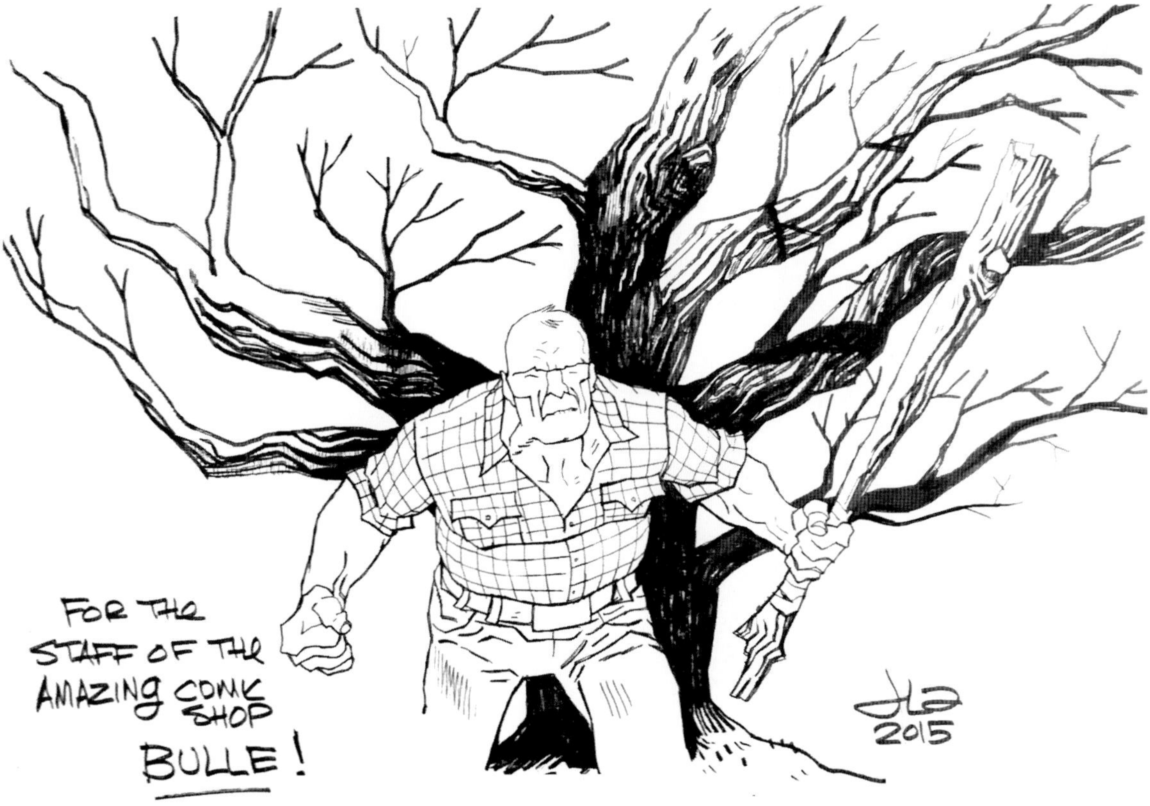
FOR THE
STAFF OF THE
AMAZING COMIC
SHOP
BULLE!
2015

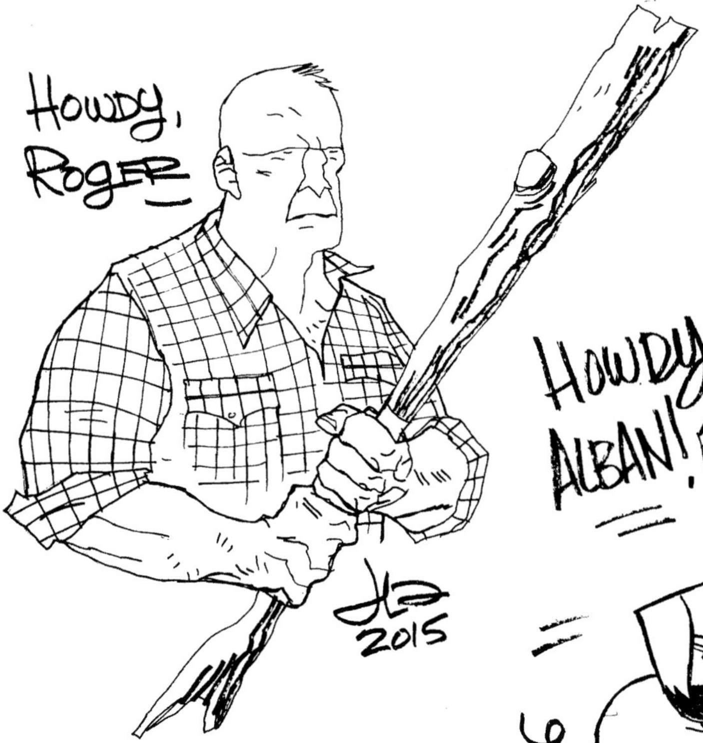
HOWDY,
ROGER
2015

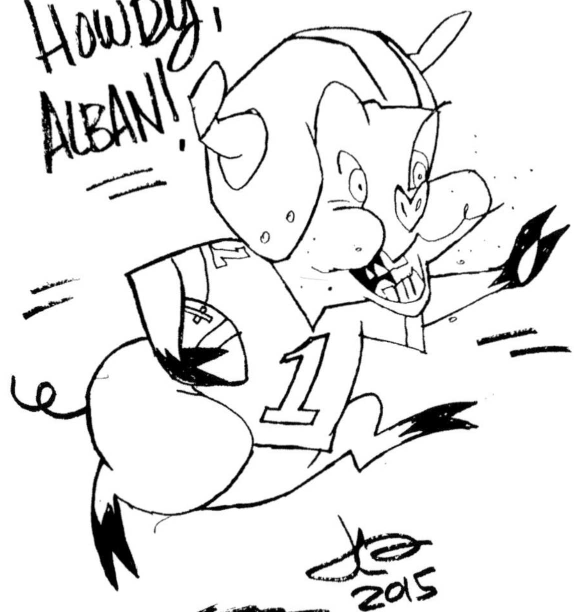
HOWDY,
ALBAN!
1
2015

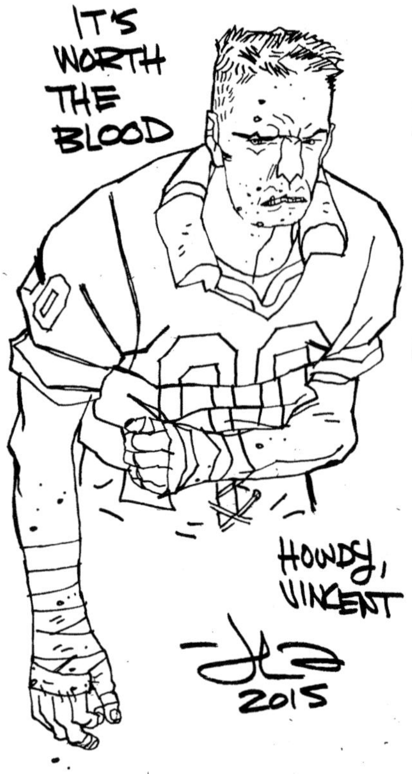
IT'S WORTH THE BLOOD
HOWDY, VINCENT
2015

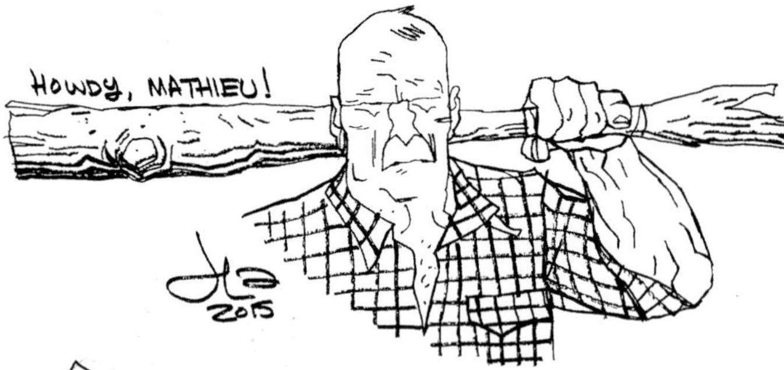
HOWDY, MATHIEU!
2015

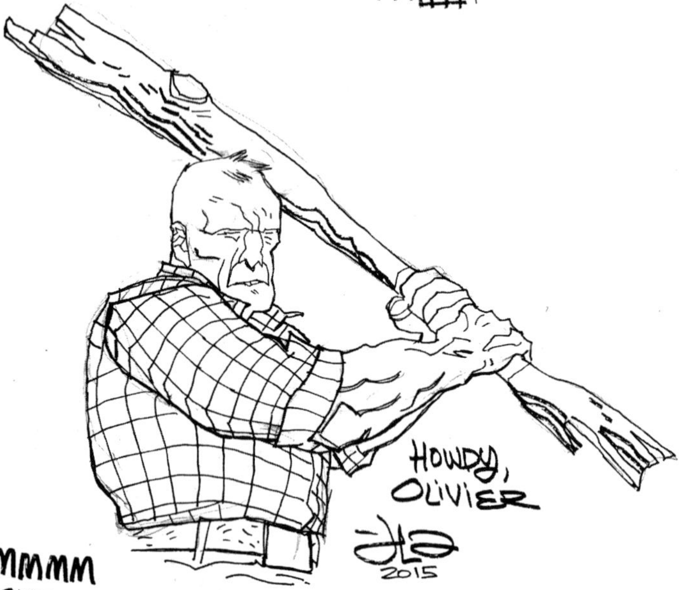
HOWDY, OLIVIER
2015

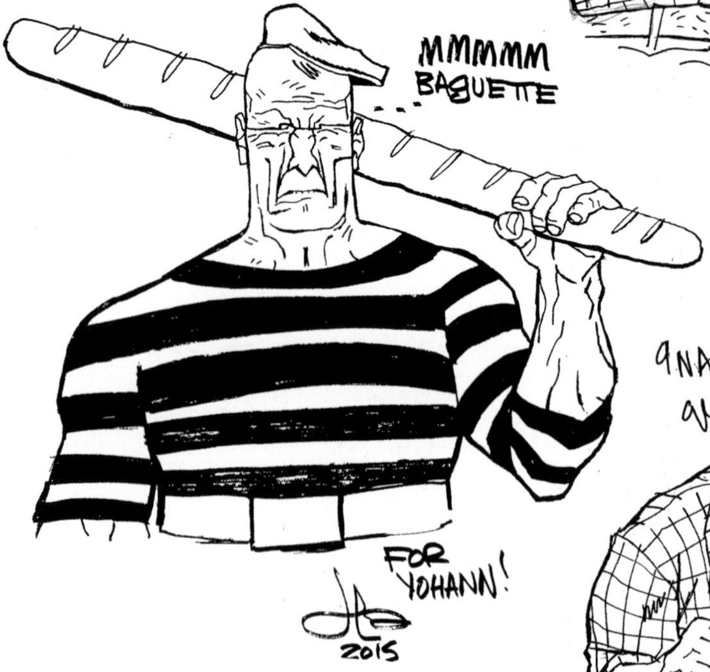
MMMMM BAGUETTE
FOR YOHANN!
2015

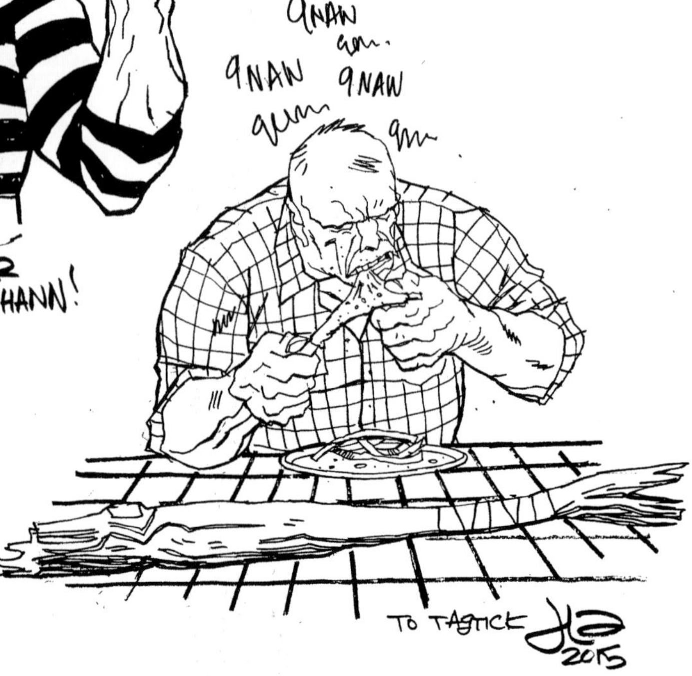
GNAW
GNAW
GNAW
TO TASTICK
2015

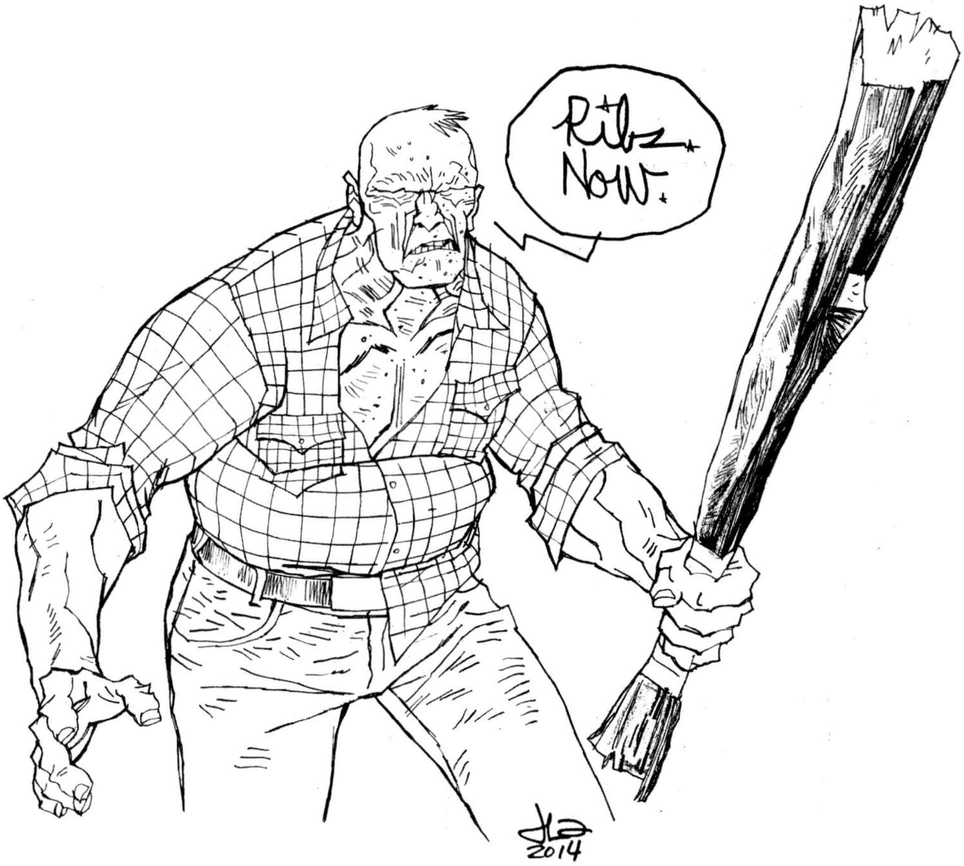
Ribz Now.
2014

"FRIENDLY FARMS" prelims from issue 8

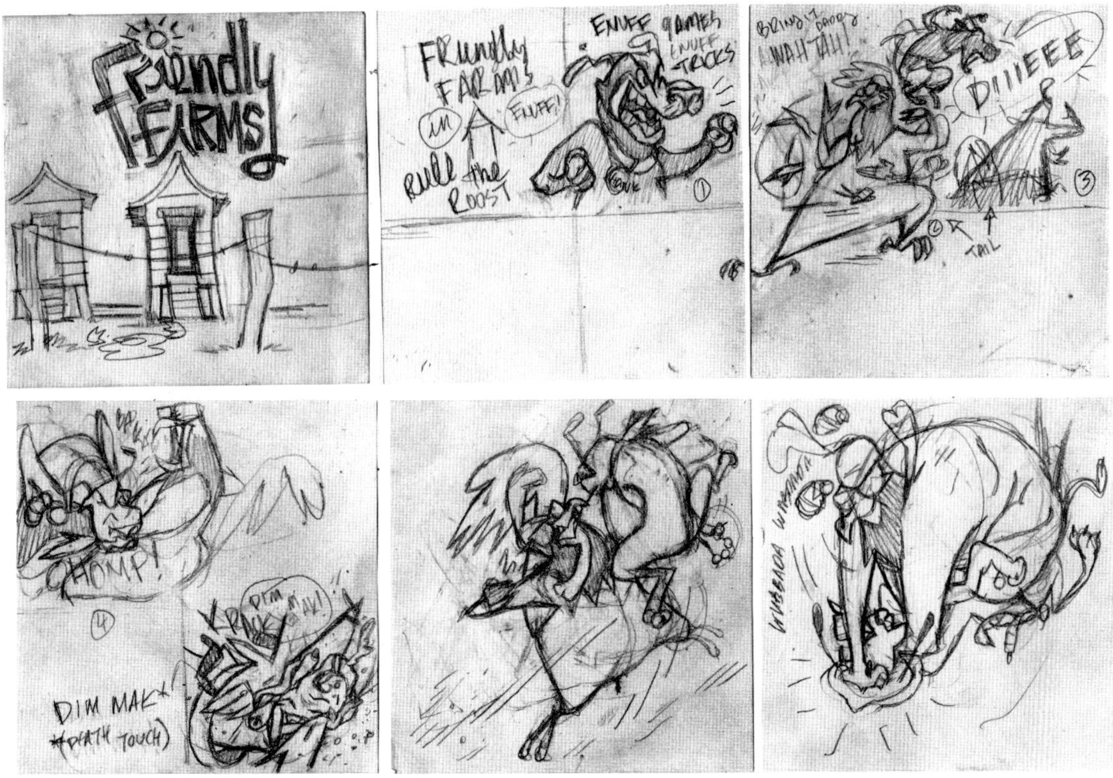
Friendly FARMS!
FRIENDLY FARMS in
RULE the ROOST
ENUFF GAMES ENUFF TRICKS
ENUFF!
DIIIEEE
TAIL
CHOMP!
DIM MAK*
*DEATH TOUCH)

T-shirt designs

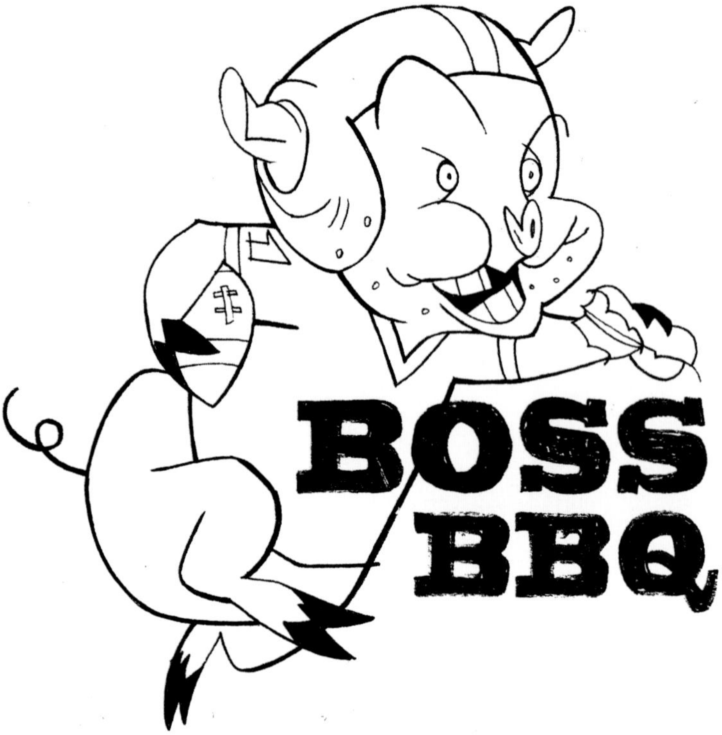
BOSS
BBQ

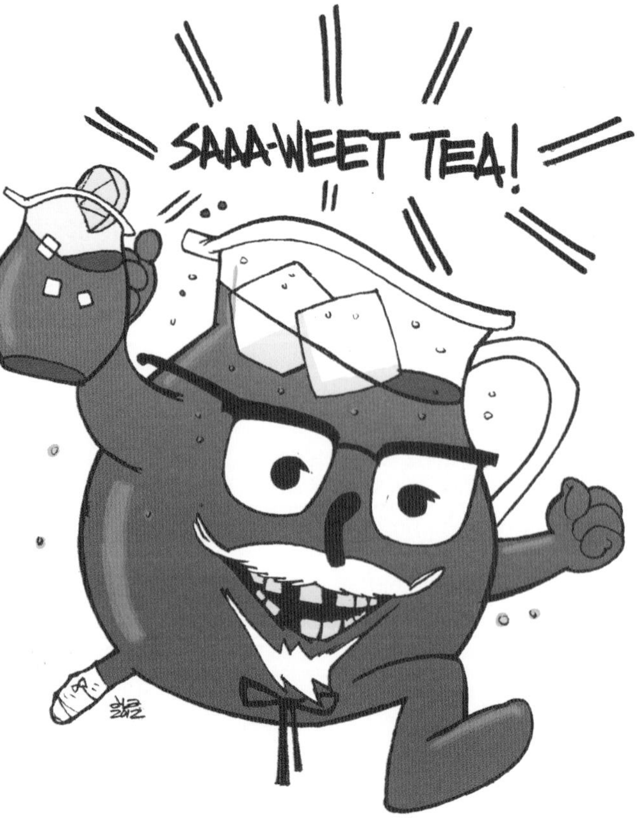
SAAA-WEET TEA!
NUTHIN' DIE-A-BEATS ME!

Runnin Rebs football
uniform designs

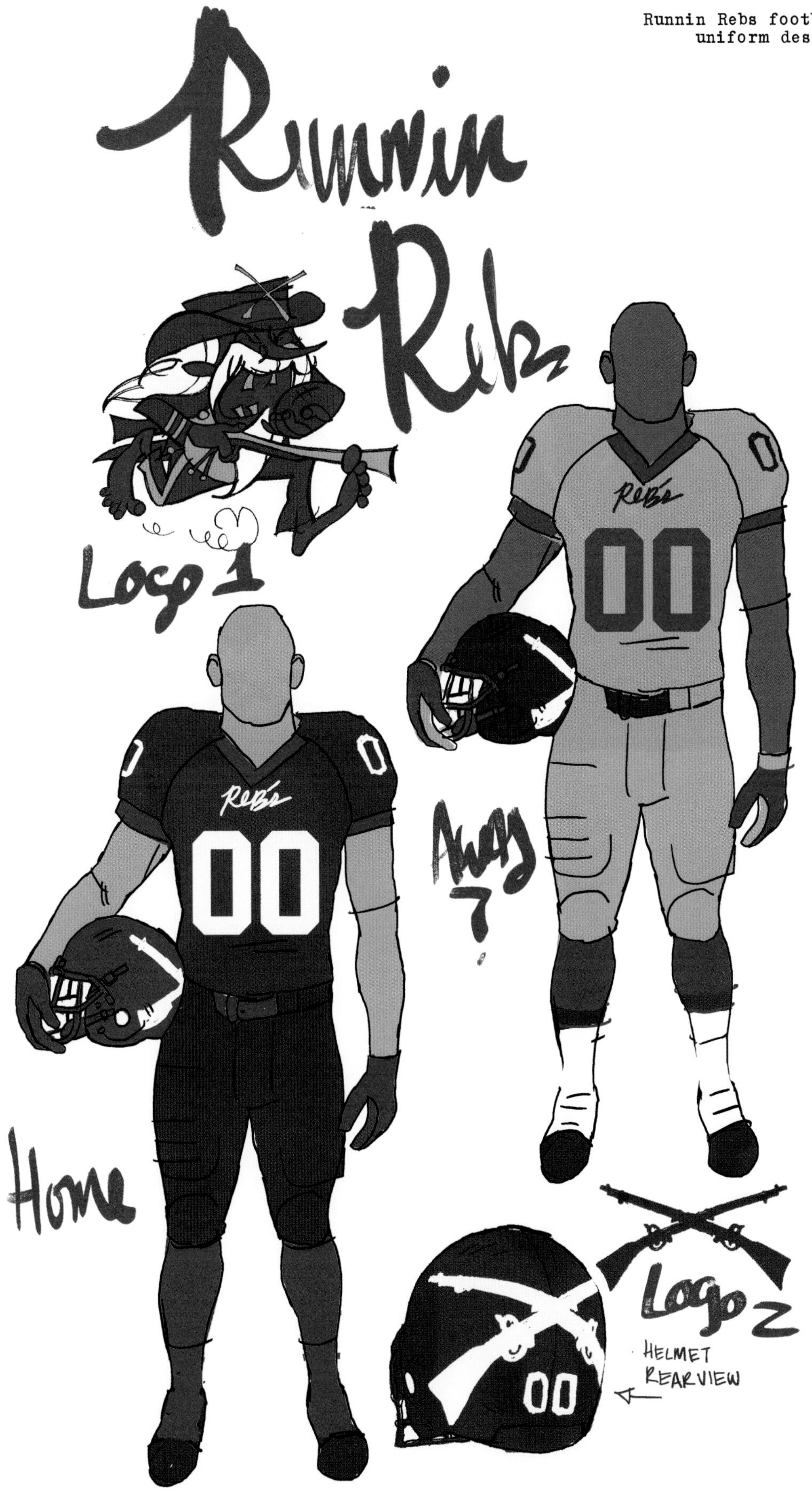
Runnin
Rebs
Logo 1
Rebs
00
Away
?
Rebs
00
0
Home
00
Logo 2
HELMET
REARVIEW

Prelim work for as of
yet unused cover designs

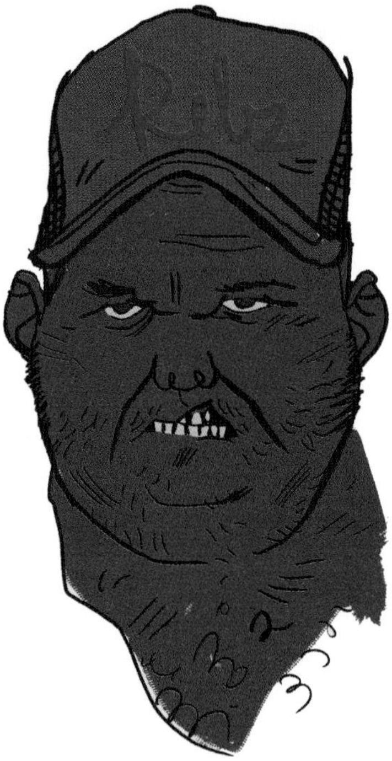

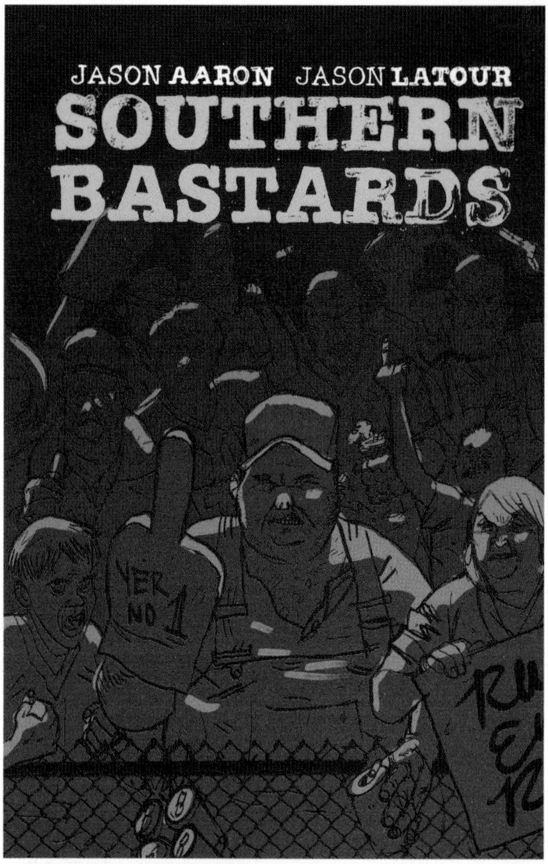
JASON AARON JASON LATOUR
SOUTHERN
BASTARDS
YER NO 1

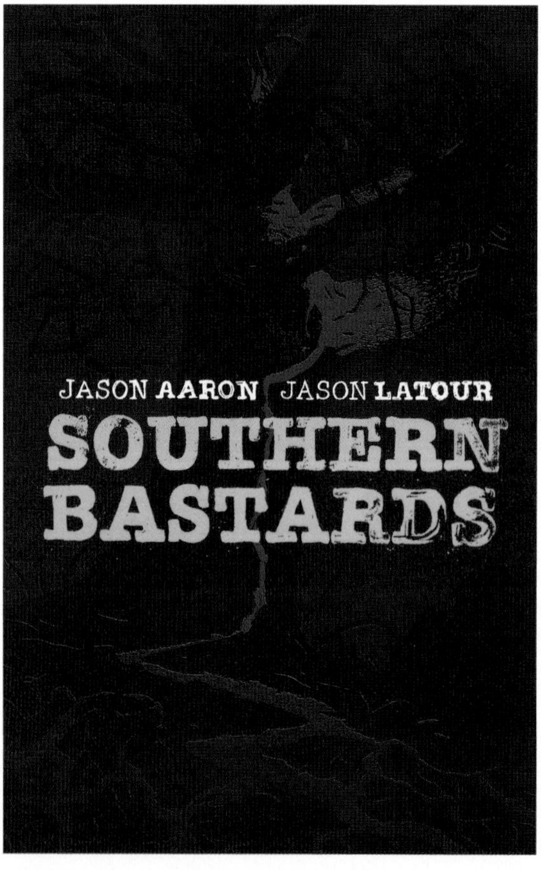
JASON AARON JASON LATOUR
SOUTHERN
BASTARDS

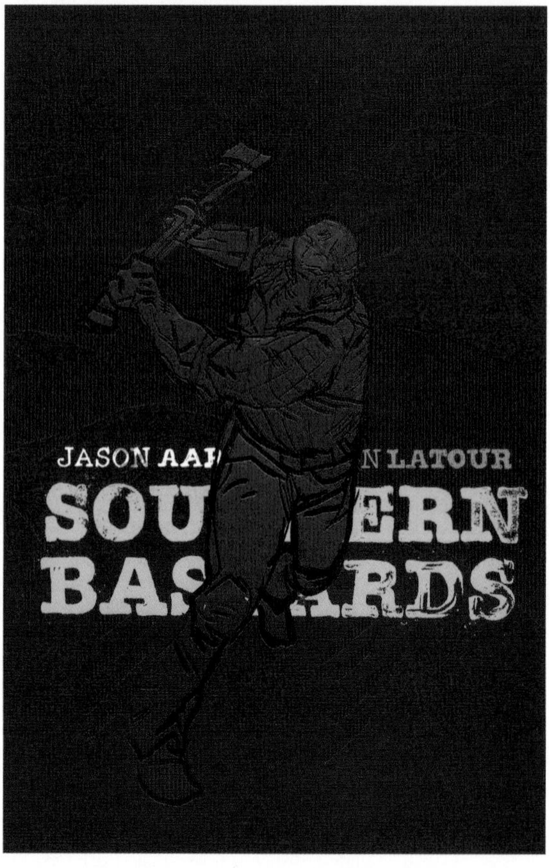
JASON AAR N LATOUR
SOU ERN
BAS ARDS

Promotional Poster

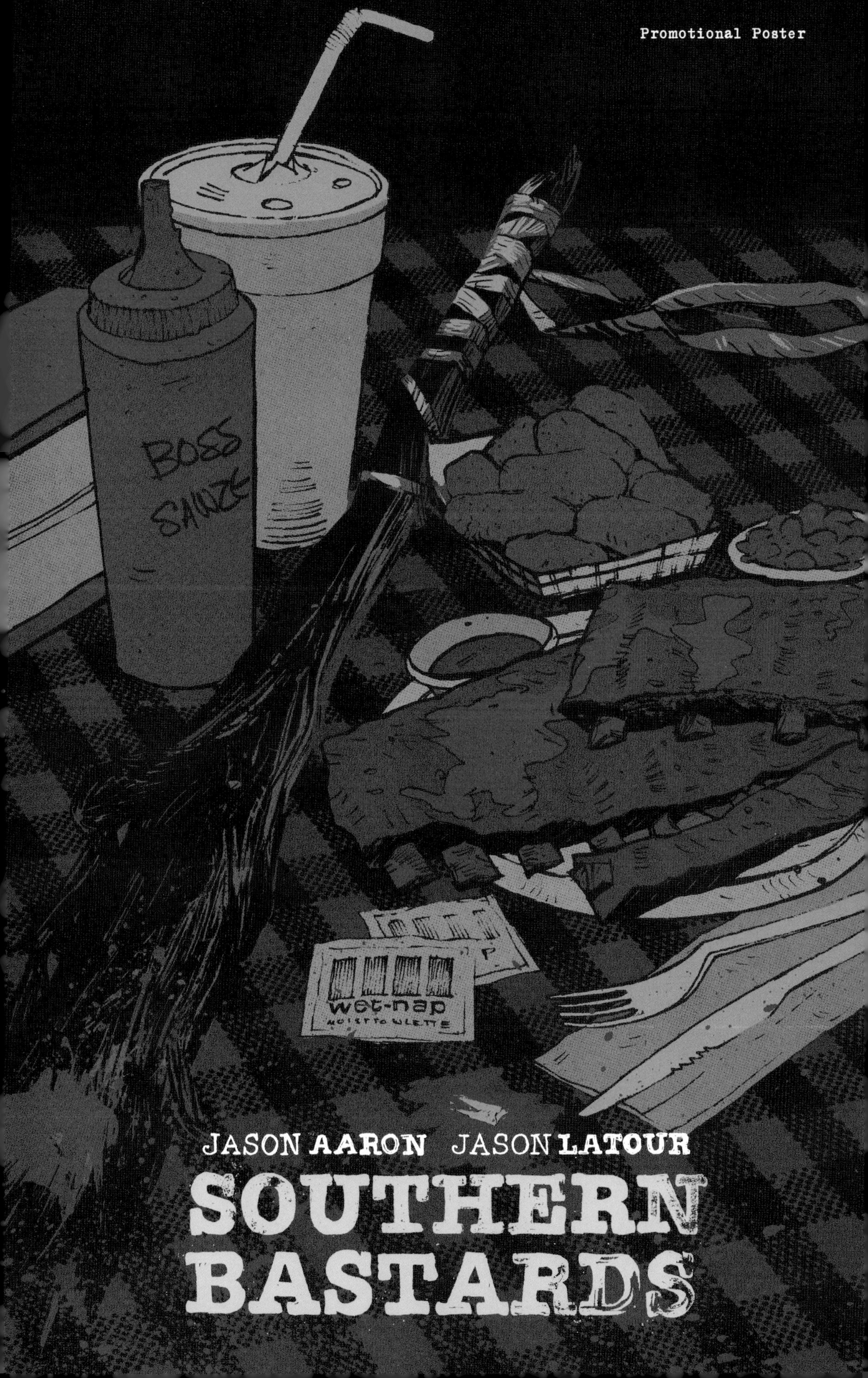

BOSS
wet-nap
JASON AARON JASON LATOUR
SOUTHERN BASTARDS

Sketches

TONY MOORE

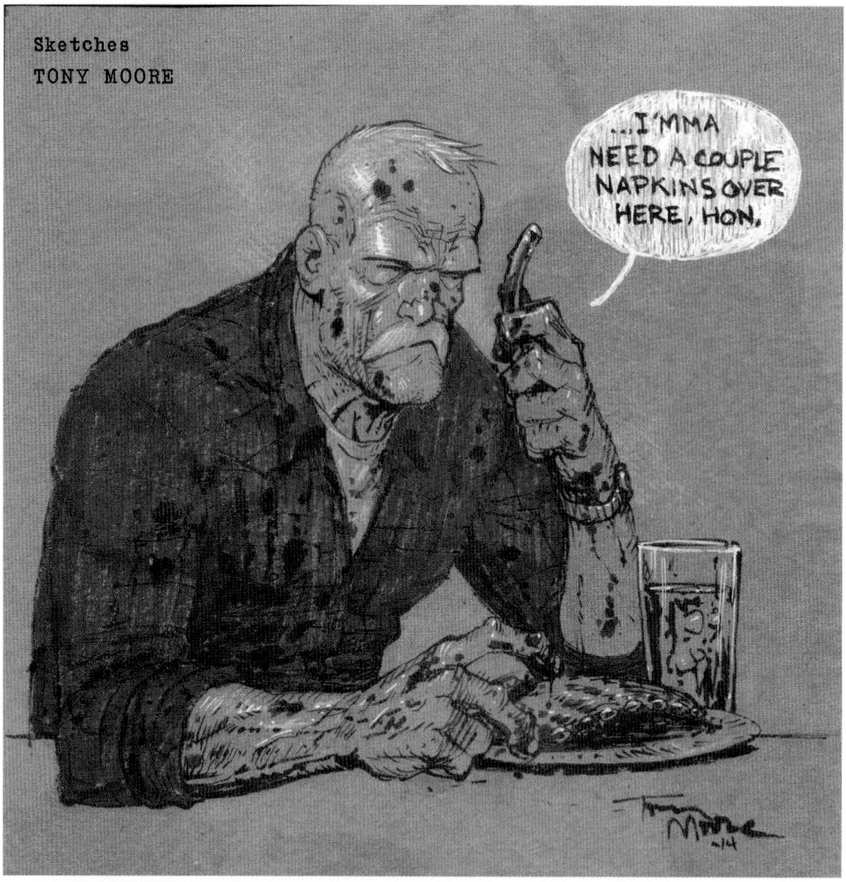
...I'MMA NEED A COUPLE NAPKINS OVER HERE, HON.

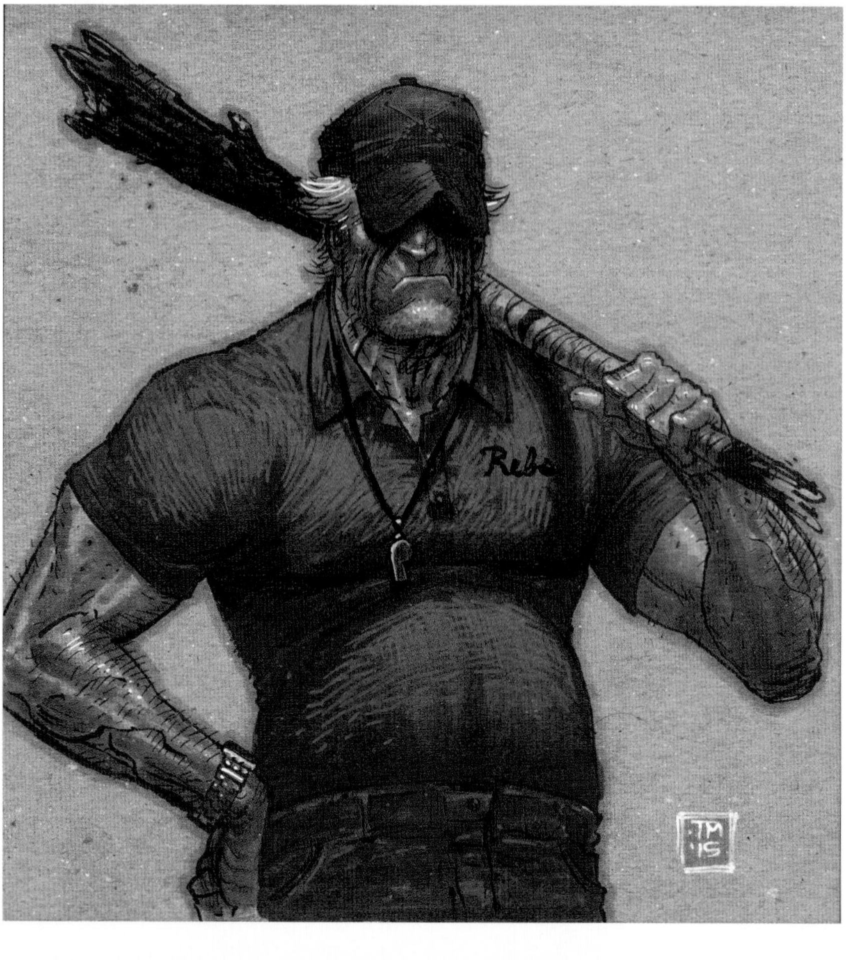

Earl Tubb sketches

1. CHRIS SAMNEE
2. PAUL AZACETA
3. BABS TARR

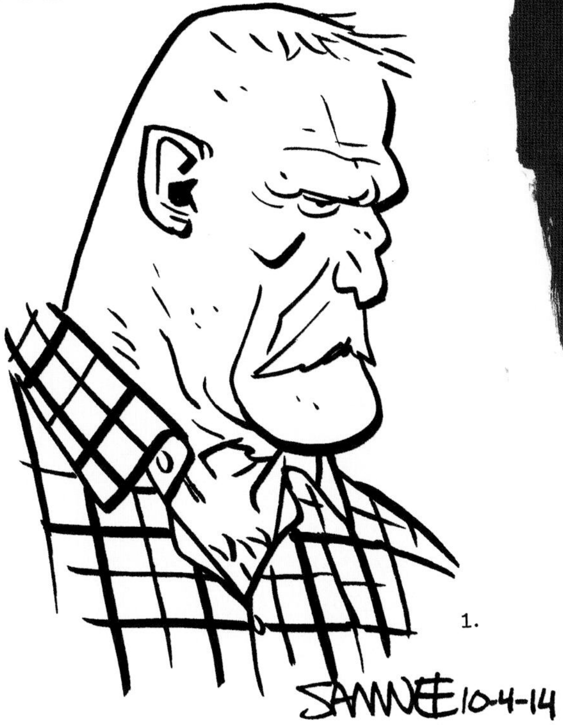
SAMNEE 10-4-14

1.

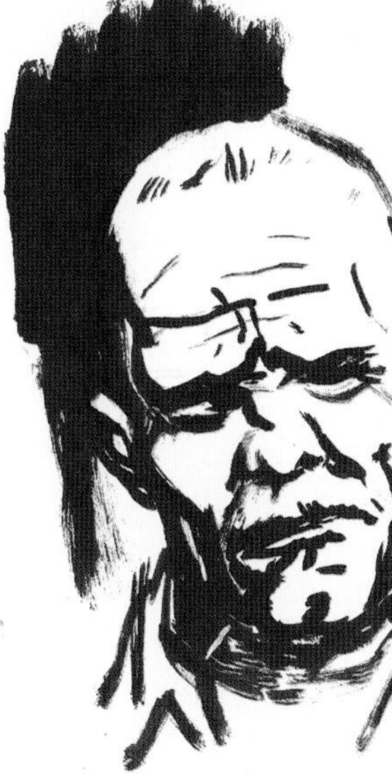

2.

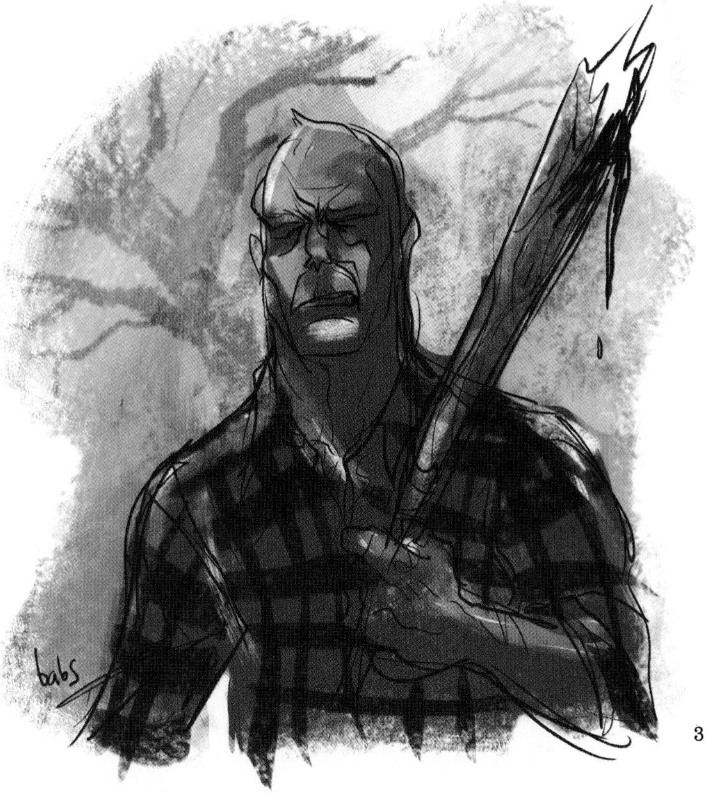
babs

3.

SOUTHERN BASTARDS

Readers' Recipes

FRIED APPLE PIES

By Betty Aaron, Jason's mom

APPLE MIXTURE

4 medium sized apples, peeled and sliced (I like Granny Smith)

1/2 cup sugar

1/4 teaspoon ground allspice

Cook apples in small amount of water over medium heat until tender, 15 minutes or so. Stir occasionally. Drain well and mash lightly.

Add sugar and allspice. Let cool.

PASTRY

1/3 cup shortening

2 cups self-rising flour

2/3 cup cold water

Mix shortening into flour until mixture resembles coarse meal. Add water small amount at a time until all ingredients are moistened. On a floured surface, roll pastry to about 1/8 inch thickness. Cut into 6 inch or so circles (a small saucer works well for a pattern). Spoon about ¼ cup apple mixture onto half of a circle. Fold other half over and seal edge with fork dipped in flour.

Heat at least 2 inches of oil in a heavy pan. Fry pies 2 or 3 at a time until golden brown. Drain on paper towels.

BANANA PUDDING

By Jerri Latour, Jason's mom

1/3 cup of flour	2 cups of whole milk
3/4 cup of sugar	A bunch of bananas
1/8 tsp salt	(six bananas)
2 egg yolks	1 box of vanilla wafers

1 teaspoon of vanilla flavoring

Mix together the flour, sugar, and salt.

Mix in the egg yolks and slowly stir in the milk.

Cook over medium heat (bring heat up slowly to medium), stirring constantly (stirring is a must as not to scorch mixture).

Cook until mixture thickens.

Remove from heat and add Vanilla flavoring.

Using a 9x13 glass pan line bottom and sides of pan with wafers. Cut bananas into thin slices and layer over the wafers. Next add the pudding mixture. Repeat the layering process ending with the pudding.

Making the Meringue

2 egg whites

(I have used up to four egg whites.

This makes for a prettier topping.)

1/4 cup of sugar

1/2 teaspoon of vanilla favoring

Beat until still peaks form. Add sugar and vanilla and mix a little longer. Top pudding with Meringue making peaks. Put in 400 degree oven for 10 mins., or until meringue is a little brown. Keep close watch, it can brown quickly.

Chill and enjoy! That how we do it in the South!

1-2-3-4 BISCUITS

By Ruth Abraham

1 cup milk

2 cups flour

3 tablespoons shortening

4 tsps baking powder

Mix everything together, roll it out. Use a glass or cup to press out circles. Throw it in a greased pan into the oven at 375 degrees for about 10-12 mins (until the tops are golden brown).

This is a great recipe for newlyweds because when you're just starting out, a pan of biscuits can really stretch out a meal.

7-UP BISCUITS

By Jeff Carver

2 cups Bisquick

1/2 cup sour cream

1/2 cup 7-Up

1/2 stick butter

Preheat oven to 450, put butter in an 8x8 glass pan & place in oven while warming up. Cut sour cream in to Bisquick, add 7-Up and stir, pour out on wax paper and shape in a square the size of your pan, cut in to 9 biscuits then drop them in to your preheated pan. Cook for 13 minutes.

MUSSELS IN GUINNESS BEER

By Diego Sieiro

1 kilo of mussels

olive oil

salt

1 litre (or two) of Guinness beer

Boil the mussels in salted water, add a little olive oil. Let it boil for six to ten minutes, until most of the water is gone. Add then plenty of Guinness beer, letting it all simmer for two to four minutes. Add rice, pasta or have a glass of Irish Whiskey and enjoy.

Cheers from Dublin, Ireland.

FRUIT SALAD

By Jerri Latour, Jason's mom

1 can pineapple tidbits

1 can mandarin oranges

1 cup of miniature marshmallows

1 cup of coconut flakes

1 cup of sour cream

1 cup of cool whip

Drain the can fruit.

Mix fruit with cool whip and sour cream. (Only a Southerner would mix these two things)

Then mix in the marshmallows and coconut.

I always double the recipe because one recipe is never enough for our family. My sons usually fight over the leftovers.

SOUTHERN BASTARDS

2015 Eisner Nominee for Best Continuing Series

2015 Harvey Award Nominee for Best Continuing or Limited Series

2015 Harvey Award Nominee for Best New Series

JASON AARON

2015 Eisner Nominee for Best Writer

2015 Harvey Award Nominee for Best Writer

JASON LATOUR

2015 National Cartoonists Society Reuben Award Winner for Comics Art

JASON **AARON**   JASON **LATOUR**

SOUTHERN BASTARDS

coming next...

Volume 3: HOMECOMING